Praise for Nick Ha

ANGELMA

"It's hard to put a finger on exactly why *Angelmaker* is one of the year's best books. Know this, though: it is." —Tor.com

"*Angelmaker* strenuously avoids falling into any usual category of fiction. Part science fiction, part philosophical exploration, part steampunk fantasy and part lovingly realistic description of contemporary London, it pays tribute to Charles Dickens in its quirky names and frequent coincidences, and to pulp fiction in its semi-clad damsels and grisly scenes of torture. It is also mordantly funny."
—*The Columbus Dispatch*

"[Harkaway] manages to write surrealist adventure novels that feel both urgent and relevant. His novels are fun to read without seeming particularly frivolous, and beneath all the derring-do and shenanigans, there's a low thrum of anxiety: everything and everyone you love could disappear at any moment. . . . *Angelmaker* is a truly impressive achievement." —*The Millions*

"A lot of books are fun to read for the plot; a smaller percentage display this artful mastery of the language. And precious few manage to do both. *Angelmaker* falls into that last category." —Wired.com

"An ambitious, crowded, restless caper, cleverly told. . . . A solid work of modern fantasy fiction." —*The Observer* (London)

"A genuine tale of fantastika. . . . And the truth of what we have done, and where we live now, shines through." —*Strange Horizons*

"A magnificent, literary, post-pulp triumph. . . . *Angelmaker* is an entertaining tour de force that demands to be adored."
—*The Independent* (London)

"Endlessly inventive. . . . An absurdist send-up of pulp story tropes and end-of-the-world scenarios." —*Publishers Weekly* (starred review)

NICK HARKAWAY

ANGELMAKER

Nick Harkaway is the author of two novels, *The Gone-Away World* and *Angelmaker*, the nonfiction book *The Blind Giant*, and he is a regular blogger for the Bookseller's *FutureBook* website. From 1999 to 2008, he was a jobbing scriptwriter. During that time he also wrote brochure copy for a company selling bottle-capping machinery, and the website text for an exclusive lingerie boutique. He lives in London with his wife, Clare, a human rights lawyer, and his daughter, Clemency, an infant.

www.nickharkaway.com

ANGELMAKER

NICK HARKAWAY

ANGELMAKER

VINTAGE CONTEMPORARIES
VINTAGE BOOKS
A DIVISION OF RANDOM HOUSE, INC.
NEW YORK

FIRST VINTAGE CONTEMPORARIES EDITION, OCTOBER 2012

The Library of Congress has cataloged the Knopf edition as follows:
Harkaway, Nick.
Angelmaker / by Nick Harkaway.—1st American ed.
p. cm.
1. Clocks and watches—Repairing—Fiction.
2. Children of gangsters—England—London—Fiction. 3. Fathers and sons—Fiction.
4. Older women—Fiction. 5. End of the world—Fiction.
6. London (England)—Fiction. I. Title.
PR6108.A737A54 2012
823'.92—dc23   2011028261

Vintage ISBN: 978-0-307-74362-6

Book design by Iris Weinstein

www.vintagebooks.com

Printed in the United States of America
10 9 8 7 6 5 4

For Clare,
like everything else

The gangster is the man of the city,
with the city's language and knowledge,
with its queer and dishonest skills
and its terrible daring,
carrying his life in his hands like a placard,
like a club.

—ROBERT WARSHOW

ANGELMAKER

I

The socks of the fathers;
mammalian supremacy;
visiting an old lady.

At seven fifteen a.m., his bedroom slightly colder than the vacuum of space, Joshua Joseph Spork wears a longish leather coat and a pair of his father's golfing socks. Papa Spork was not a natural golfer. Among other differences, natural golfers do not acquire their socks by hijacking a lorryload destined for St. Andrews. It isn't done. Golf is a religion of patience. Socks come and socks go, and the wise golfer waits, sees the pair he wants, and buys it without fuss. The notion that he might put a Thompson sub-machine gun in the face of the burly Glaswegian driver, and tell him to quit the cab or adorn it . . . well. A man who does that is never going to get his handicap down below the teens.

The upside is that Joe doesn't think of these socks as belonging to Papa Spork. They're just one of two thousand pairs he inherited when his father passed on to the great bunker in the sky, contents of a lock-up off Brick Lane. He returned as much of the swag as he could—it was a weird, motley collection, very appropriate to Papa Spork's somewhat eccentric life of crime—and found himself left with several suitcases of personal effects, family Bibles and albums, some bits and bobs his father apparently stole from *his* father, and a few pairs of socks the chairman of St. Andrews suggested he keep as a memento.

"I appreciate it can't have been easy, doing this," the chairman said over the phone. "Old wounds and so on."

"Really, I'm just embarrassed."

"Good Lord, don't be. Bad enough that the sins of the fathers shall descend and all that, without feeling embarrassed about it. *My* father was in Bomber Command. Helped plan the firebombing of Dresden. Can you imagine? Pinching socks is rather benign, eh?"

"I suppose so."

"Dresden was during the war, of course, so I suppose they thought it had to be done. Jolly heroic, no doubt. But I've seen photographs. Have you?"

"No."

"Try not to, I should. They'll stay with you. But if ever you do, for some godforsaken reason, it might make you feel better to be wearing a pair of lurid Argyles. I'm putting a few in a parcel. If it will salve your guilt, I shall choose the absolute nastiest ones."

"Oh, yes, all right. Thank you."

"I fly myself, you know. Civilian. I used to love it, but recently I can't help but see firebombs falling. So I've sort of given up. Rather a shame, really."

"Yes, it is."

There's a pause while the chairman considers the possibility that he may have revealed rather more of himself than he had intended.

"Right then. It'll be the chartreuse. I quite fancy a pair of those myself, to wear next time I visit the old bugger up at Hawley Churchyard. 'Look here, you frightful old sod,' I shall tell him, 'where you persuaded yourself it was absolutely vital that we immolate a city full of civilians, other men's fathers restricted themselves to stealing ugly socks.' That ought to show him, eh?"

"I suppose so."

So on his feet now are the fruits of this curious exchange, and very welcome between his unpedicured soles and the icy floor.

The leather coat, meanwhile, is a precaution against attack. He does own a dressing gown, or rather, a towelling bathrobe, but while it's more cosy to get into, it's also more vulnerable. Joe Spork inhabits a warehouse space above his workshop—his late grandfather's workshop—in a dingy, silent bit of London down by the river. The march of progress has passed it by because the views are grey and angular and the place smells strongly of riverbank, so the whole enormous building notionally belongs to him, though it is, alas, somewhat entailed to banks and lenders. Mathew—this being the name of his lamentable dad—had a relaxed attitude to paper debt; money was something you could always steal more of.

Speaking of debts, he wonders sometimes—when he contemplates the high days and the dark days of his time as the heir of crime—whether Mathew ever killed anyone. Or, indeed, whether he killed a multitude. Mobsters, after all, are given to arguing with one another in rather bloody ways, and the outcomes of these discussions are often bodies draped like wet cloth over bar stools and behind the wheels of cars. Is there a secret graveyard somewhere, or a pig farm, where the consequences of his father's breezy amorality are left to their final rest? And if there is, what liability does his son inherit on that score?

In reality, the ground floor is entirely given over to Joe's workshop and saleroom. It's high and mysterious, with things under dust sheets and—best of all—wrapped in thick black plastic and taped up in the far corner "to treat the woodworm." Of recent days these objects are mostly nothing more than a couple of trestles or benches arranged to look significant when buyers come by, but some are the copper-bottomed real thing–timepieces, music boxes, and best of all: hand-made mechanical automata, painted and carved and cast when a computer was a fellow who could count without reference to his fingers.

It's impossible, from within, not to know where the warehouse is. The smell of old London whispers up through the damp boards of the saleroom, carrying with it traces of river, silt and mulch, but by some fillip of design and ageing wood it never becomes obnoxious. The light from the window slots, high above ground level and glazed with that cross-wired glass for security, falls at the moment on no fewer than five Edinburgh long-case clocks, two pianolas, and one remarkable object which is either a mechanised rocking horse or something more outré for which Joe will have to find a rather racy sort of buyer. These grand prizes are surrounded by lesser ephemera and common-or-garden stock: crank-handle telephones, gramophones and curiosities. And there, on a plinth, is the Death Clock.

It's just a piece of Victorian tat, really. A looming skeleton in a cowl drives a chariot from right to left, so that—to the Western European observer, used to reading from left to right—he is coming to meet us. He has his scythe slung conveniently across his back for easy reaping, and a scrawny steed with an evil expression pulls the thing onward, ever onward. The facing wheel is a black clock with very slender bone hands. It has no chime; the message is perhaps that time passes without punctuation, but passes all the same. Joe's grandfather, in his will, commended it to his heir for "special consideration"—the mechanism is very clever, motivated by atmospheric fluctuation—but the infant Joe was petrified of it, and the adolescent resented its immutable, morbid promise. Even now—particularly now, when thirty years of age is visible in his rear-view mirror and forty glowers at him from down the road ahead, now that his skin heals a little more slowly than it used to from solder burns and nicks and pinks, and his stomach is less a washboard and more a comfy if solid bench—Joe avoids looking at it.

The Death Clock also guards his only shameful secret, a minor, practical concession to the past and the financial necessities. In the deepest shadows of the warehouse, next to the leaky part of the wall and covered in a grimy dust sheet, are six old slot machines—genuine one-armed bandits—which he is refurbishing for an old acquaintance named Jorge. Jorge ("Yooorrr-geh! With passion like Pasternak!" he tells new acquaintances) runs a number of low dives which feature gambling and other vices as their main attractions, and Joe's job is to maintain these traditional machines—which now dispense tokens for high-value amounts and intimate services rather than mere pennies—and to bugger them systematically so that they pay out only on rare occasions or according to Jorge's personal instruction. The price of continuity in the clockworking business is minor compromise.

The floor above—the living area, where Joe has a bed and some old wooden wardrobes big enough to conceal a battleship—is a beautiful space. It has broad, arched windows and mellowed red-brick walls which look out onto the river on one side, and on the other an urban landscape of stores and markets, depots and back offices, lock-ups, car dealerships, Customs pounds, and one vile square of green-grey grass which is protected by some indelible ordinance and thus must be allowed to fester where it lies.

All very fine, but the warehouse has recently acquired one serious irritant: a cat. At sometime, one mooring two hundred yards up was allowed to go to a houseboat, on which lives a very sweet, very poor family called Watson. Griff and Abbie are a brace of mildly paranoid anarchists, deeply allergic to paperwork and employment on conscientious grounds. There's a curious courage to them both: they believe in a political reality which is utterly terrifying, and they're fighting it. Joe is never sure whether they're mad or just alarmingly and uncompromisingly incapable of self-delusion.

In any case, he gives any spare clockwork toys he has to the Watsons, and eats dinner with them once in a while to make sure they're still alive. They in their turn share with him vegetables from their allotment and keep an eye on the warehouse if he goes away for the weekend. The cat (Joe thinks of it as "the Parasite") adopted them some months ago and now rules the houseboat by a combination of adept political and emotional pressure brought to bear through the delighted Watson children and a psychotic approach to the rodent population, which earns the approval of Mr. and Mrs. W. Sadly, the Parasite has identified the warehouse as its next home, if once it can destroy or evict the present owner, of whom it does not approve.

Joe peers into the piece of burnished brass he uses as a shaving mirror. He found it here when he took possession, a riveted panel from something bigger, and he likes the warmth of it. Glass mirrors are green, and make your image look sick and sad. He doesn't want to be the person he sees reflected in a glass mirror. Instead, here's this warm, genial bloke, a little unkempt, but—if not wealthy—at least healthy and fairly wise.

Joe is a big man, with wide shoulders and hips. His bones are heavy. He has a strong face, and his skull is proud beneath the skin. Passably handsome, perhaps, but not delicate. Unlike Papa Spork, who had *his* father's genes, and looked like a flamenco dancer, Joe is most unfairly designed by nature to resemble a guy who works the door at the rougher kind of bar. He gets it from his mother's side: Harriet Spork is a narrow creature, but that owes more to religion and meals high in fibre than it does to genetics. Her bones are the bones of a Cumbrian meat-packer and his Dorset yeoman wife. Nature intended in her design a hearty life of toil, open fires and plump old age attended by a brood of sun-touched brats. That she chose instead to be a singer and more latterly a nun is evidence of a certain submerged cussedness, or possibly a consequence of the strange upheavals of the twentieth century, which made rural motherhood look, at least for a while, like an admission of defeat.

From somewhere in the warehouse, there's a curiously suffused silence. A hunting silence: the Parasite, having declared war almost immediately upon making his acquaintance, enters each morning via the window that Joe props open to stop the place getting stuffy when the central heating comes on, and ascends to balance on the white moulded frame around the kitchen door. When Joe passes underneath, it drops onto his shoulders, extends its claws, and slides down his back in an attempt to peel him like an apple. The leather coat and, alas, the skin beneath—because the first time this happened he was wearing only a pyjama shirt—carry the scars.

Today, tiring of a.m. guerrilla war—and sensitive to the possibility that while he is presently single, he may one day bring an actual woman to this place, and she may wish not to be scalped by an irate feline when she sashays off to make tea, perhaps with one of his shirts thrown around her shoulders and the hem brushing the tops of her elegant legs and revealing the narrowest sliver of buttock—Joe has chosen to escalate the situation. Late last night, he applied a thin layer of Vaseline to the coping. He tries not to reflect on the nature of a life whose high point is an adversarial relationship with an entity possessing the same approximate reasoning and emotional alertness as a milk bottle.

Ah. That whisper is a silken tail brushing the mug tree with its friendly, mismatched china. That creak means the floorboard by the wall, that pitter-patter is the animal jumping from the dresser . . . and that remarkable, outraged sound must be the noise it makes bouncing off the far wall after sliding all along the coping, followed by . . . yes. An undignified thump as it hits the floor. Joe wanders into his kitchen. The Parasite stares at him from the corner, eyes spilling over with mutiny and hate.

"Primate," Joe tells it, waggling his hands. "Tool user. Opposable thumbs."

The Parasite glowers, and stalks out.

Having thus inaugurated Victory Over The Cat Day, it is in the nature of his world that he should immediately be overtaken on the ladder of mammalian supremacy by a dog.

To get to his first appointment, Joe Spork elects to take a shortcut through the Tosher's Beat. This is in general very much against his personal policy. He resolutely travels by bus or train, or even occasionally drives, because taking the Tosher's Beat is an admission of parts of his life for which he no longer has any use. However, the discovery of another garden full of Vaughn Parry's victims has brought a great deal of discussion in broadsheets and free papers regarding the nature of human criminality, and this is a conversation he devoutly wishes to ignore.

At the same time, certain recent events have given Joe a mild but undeniable case of the willies, and the Tosher's Beat has a feeling of security and familiarity which the streets above never really achieve. Blame his childhood, but shady alleys and smoke-filled rooms are more reassuring than shopping centres and sunlit streets. Although, even if Joe himself were not determined to be someone new, those days are over. Most of the Old Campaigners died early. The roly-poly court of crooks he grew up with is just a memory. There are a few still around, retired or changed and hardened, but the genial knees of crime on which the young Joe Spork sat, and from whose vantage he was initiated into the secrets of a hundred scandalous deeds, are all withered and gone.

Meanwhile, Vaughn Parry is England's present nightmare. Above and beyond Islamic extremists with rucksacks and policemen who shoot plumbers nine times in the head for being diffusely non-white, the great fear of every right-thinking person these days is that Parry was not unique, that there lurk amid the wide wheat fields and bowling greens of the Home Counties yet more bloody-handed killers who can unlock your window catches and sneak into your room at night, the better to tear you apart. Parry is in custody for the moment, held in some high-security hospital under the scrutiny of doctors, but something in him has cut the nation deep.

The upshot of this has been a scurrying of the middle classes for shelter, and a less-than-learned discussion of historical villains and in particular of Joe Spork's safe-cracking, train-robbing, art-thieving father, the Dandy of the Hoosegow, Mathew "Tommy Gun" Spork. Joe has a greater horror of this chatter than he does of the Tosher's Beat. Under normal circumstances he shies away from the idea that he is what a certain class of crime novel calls an *habitué of the demi-monde*, by which it is implied that he knows gamblers and crooks and the men and women who love them. For the moment, he is prepared to acknowledge that he still lives somewhat on the fringes of the *demi-monde* in exchange for not having to talk about it.

Inevitably, in crafting a thumbnail sketch of himself, he finds that it has turned into an obituary, to be held in readiness. *Joshua Joseph Spork, son of Harriet Peters and Mathew "Tommy Gun" Spork the noted gangster, died childless before the age of 40. He is survived by his mother, now a nun, and by a small number of respectable ex-girlfriends. It must be acknowledged that his greatest achievement in life lay in avoiding becoming his father, though some might assert that in doing so he went too far towards his grandfather's more sedentary mode of being. There will be a memorial service on Friday; guests are requested to bring no firearms or stolen goods.*

He shakes his head to clear it, and hurries over the railway bridge.

Between Clighton Street and Blackfriars there is a cul-de-sac which actually isn't a cul-de-sac. At the very end is a narrow gap and a pathway which leads to the railway line, and immediately on the left as you face the tracks there's a doorway into the underworld. Through this little door goes Joseph Spork like the White Rabbit, and down a spiral stair into the narrow red-brick tunnels of the Tosher's Beat. The corridor is absolutely black, and he scrabbles in his pocket for his working keyfob, from which depends a small selection of keys and passcards, and a torch roughly the shape and size of a pen lid.

The blue-white light shows him walls covered in grime, occasionally scarred with someone's only immortality: *Dave luvs Lisa* and always will, at least down here. Joe breathes a sort of blessing and passes by, stepping carefully around knots of slime. One more door, and for this he wraps a handkerchief around his mouth and smears some wintergreen ointment under his nose ("Addam's Traditional Warming Balsam!," and who knows why a balsam is exciting enough to merit that exclamation mark, but it is to Mr. Addam). This one requires a key; the toshers have installed a simple lock, not as a serious barrier to entry, but as a polite statement of territoriality. They're quite content that people should use the road, but want you to know you do so by their grace. The Tosher's Beat is a webwork, but you can't just go where you will. You need permissions and goodwills, and sometimes a subscription. Joe's keyfob will grant him passage through perhaps twenty per cent of the safe tunnels; the others are held aggressively by official and unofficial groupings with a desire for privacy—including the toshers themselves, who guard the heart of their strange kingdom with polite but effective sentries.

Ten minutes later he meets a group of them, bent double over the noxious ooze and combing through it in their rubberised suits.

Back in the day—when London was pocked with workhouses and smothered in a green smog which could choke you dead on a bad night, or before that, even, when open sewers ran down the middle of the streets—the toshers were the outcasts and opportunists who picked over the ghastly mix and retrieved the coins and jewels lost by chance. Even now, it's amazing what people throw away: grandma's diamonds, fallen down inside their box, and Auntie Brenda taken for a thief; rings of all descriptions, cast off in a passion or slipped from icy fingers on a cold day; money, of course; gold teeth; and on one occasion, Queen Tosh told the infant Joe at one of Mathew's parties, a bundle of bearer bonds with a combined value of nearly ten million pounds.

These days, toshers wear gear made for deep-sea divers—well, the filth itself is bad enough, but there's worse: hypodermics and other gruesomenesses, not to mention the chemicals which are changing the world's male fish into females and killing all the toads. The average corpse lasts a fortnight longer than it used to, pickled in supermarket preservatives. The work gang look like astronauts from another world, landed badly and picking through what they take to be primordial muck.

Joe waves to them as he hurries by on the raised pavement, and they wave back. Don't get many visitors, and still fewer give them a thumbs-up in the approved Night Market style, knuckles to the roof and thumb-up pointed at forty-five degrees. The leader returns the gesture, hesitantly.

"Hi," Joe Spork says loudly, because the helmets don't make for easy comprehension. "How's the Cathedral?"

"Clear," the man says. "Tide gate's shut. Hang on, I know you, don't I?"

Yes, he does: they played together as children in the velvet-hung torchlit corridors of the Night Market. The Tosher Family and the Market are cautious allies, tiny states existing within and beneath the greater one that is Britain. Gangster nations, however much diminished now from what they were when Joe was young. The Night Market, in particular, has suffered, its regents unable to inspire the kind of rambunctious, cheeky criminality which was the hallmark of Mathew Spork and his friends: a court without a king. *But let's don't talk about those days, I'm in disguise as someone with a real life.*

"I've just got one of those faces," Joe mutters, and hurries on.

He slips through a door into the old Post Office pneumatic railway (at one stage, Mathew Spork owned a string of Post Office concessions around the United Kingdom, and used them to distribute and conceal all manner of unconventional wares), then down a side tunnel and a flight of stairs and into Cathedral Cave. Dug as the foundation of a medieval palace which was never finished, subsided now into the mud of London's basin, it's wet and very dark. The arched stone has been washed in mineral rain over so many hundreds of years that it's covered now in a glutinous alabaster, as if this place were a natural cavern. When London's Victorian sewers overflow, as they do more and more in these climate-change days, the whole thing is under water. Joe suppresses a shudder of claustrophobia at the thought.

A rickety metal gantry leads through the room and through into the lower reaches of the railway, and then abruptly to an ancient goods lift which comes up near the riverbank: a highway for smugglers, ancient and modern.

The whole journey takes less than half an hour. You could barely do it faster in a car with an open road.

The dog's name is Bastion, and it is without shame or mercy. Any dog worth the name will sniff your crotch on arrival, but Bastion has buried his carbuncled nose in the angle of Joe's trousers and shows no inclination to retreat. Joe shifts slightly, and the dog rewards him with a warning mutter, deep in the chest: *I have my mouth in close proximity to your genitals, oh thou man who talks to my mistress over coffee. Do not irk or trifle with me! I possess but one tooth, oh, yes, for the rest were buried long ago in the flesh of sinners. Behold my jaws, upper and lower in righteous, symmetrical poverty. Move not, man of clocks, and heed my mistress, for she cherishes me, even in my foul old age.*

It's a tiny animal, the shrunken remains of a pug, and as if poor dentition is not enough, it has absolutely no natural eyeballs. Both have been replaced with substitutes made in pale pink glass which appear to refract and reflect the interior view of Bastion's empty sockets. This ghastly decision lends considerable sincerity to the growling, and Joe elects to allow the animal to continue drooling on his groin.

Bastion's owner is called Edie Banister, and she is very small, and very wiry, and apparently goes back slightly further than the British Museum. She has a tight cap of silver hair through which, in places, the freckled skin of her scalp is visible. Her face—proud eyes and strong mouth suggesting powerful good looks in her day—is so pale that Joe imagines he can actually see the bone through her cheeks, and the wrinkles on her arms are folded around one another like melted plastic, all scrunched up in unpredictable directions. Edie Banister is *old*.

And yet she is profoundly alive. Over the past few months, she has found reason to call upon the services of Spork & Co. on several occasions. Joe has come to know her a little, and in this respect she reminds him of his grandfather, Daniel: she is almost vibrating with rich, distilled energy, as if the process of living all those decades has made a reduction of her spirit which is thick and slow in her chest, but sweeter and stronger for it.

Bastion wears his age less well. He is uglier than anything Joe has seen outside a deep-sea aquarium. He seems an unlikely companion for a woman like Edie Banister, but the world, Daniel once observed, is a great honeycombed thing composed of separated mysteries.

Joe has cause to know this for the truth. When a child, he inhabited a variety of secret places, courtesy of his bad dad, and though he has very firmly left those places behind, with their daring characters and picturesque names—the Old Campaigners, the Sinkhole, Kings Forget—he has discovered that every aspect of life is a strange gravitational system of people-planets, all orbiting unlikely suns such as golf clubs, theatres, and basket-weaving classes, falling prey to black holes like infidelity and penury. Or just fading away into space, alone.

And now they come to him in their droves. Dotty, aged, and absent-minded, they file through his doors clutching little pieces of broken memory: music boxes, clocks, fob watches and mechanical toys they once played with or inherited from their mothers, uncles and spouses, now gone to dust and ash.

Edie Banister offers him some more coffee. Joe declines. They smile at one another, nervously. They're flirting; the elephant in the room—apart from Bastion's unremarked grip on Joe's nether parts—is a laburnum-wood box about the size of a portable record player, inlaid with paler wood around the edges. It is the reason for this latest visit to Edie Banister's home, the reason he has locked up early and come out to Hendon, with its endless rows of almost-pretty, boring houses decorated in little-old-lady chic. Coquettish, she has drawn him here repeatedly and disappointed him, with bits of spavined gramophone and an unlikely steampunkish Teasmade. They have played out a species of seduction, in which she has offered her secrets day by day and he has responded with quick, strong hands and elegant solutions to the intractable problems of broken machinery. All the while, he has known she was testing him for something, weighing him up. Somewhere in this tiny set of rooms there is something much more interesting, something which sweet, ancient Edie clearly believes is going to knock his socks off, but which she is not quite ready to reveal.

He trusts devoutly that what she has in mind is clockwork rather than flesh.

She wets her lips, not with her tongue, but by turning them briefly inward and rubbing them together. Edie Banister comes from a time when ladies were not really supposed to admit to having tongues at all; mouths and saliva and the oral cavity proposed the possibility of other damp, fleshy places which were absolutely not to be thought of, most particularly by anybody who had one.

Joe reaches down to the box. Touches the wood. Lifts it, weighs the burden in his hands. He can feel . . . *moment*. A thing of importance. This sweet, dotty old bird has something stupendous, and she knows it. She's been leading up to showing it to him. He wonders if today's the day.

He opens the box. A Golgotha of armatures and sprockets. In his mind, he assembles them quickly: that's the spine, yes, the main spring goes here, that's part of the housing and so is that . . . dearie me. Much of this is just so much dross, extra gears and the like. Very untidy. But all together, the useful parts . . . Oh! Yes, good: early twentieth century by the style and materials, but quite refined in its making. An artisan piece, a one-off, and they always get more, especially if you can link them to a known craftsman. All the same, it's not . . . well. Not what he was expecting, though he has no idea what that was.

Joe laughs, but quietly, so as not to waken the canine volcano burbling between his thighs.

"This is very fine. You realise it could be worth quite a bit of money?"

"Oh, dear," Edie Banister says. "Do I need to insure it?"

"Well, perhaps. These automata can go for a few thousand on a good day." He nods decisively. On a bad day, they can sit like a dead fish on the auctioneer's pallet, but never mind that for now.

"Can you fix it?" Edie Banister says, and Joe brushes aside his disappointment and tells her that of course, yes, he can.

"Now?" she asks, and yes, again, because he has his kit, never leaves home without it. Soft-arm clamp to hold the housing. Another as a third hand. Tensioners. There's no damage, actually, it looks as if someone took it apart on purpose. Quite carefully. *Snickersnack*, as it were, the thing is assembled, except . . . hmph. There's a bit missing—ain't it always so? It would crosslink the legs . . . hah! With a piece like that, this would have a veritable walking motion, almost human. Very impressive, very much ahead of its time. He's seen a robot on the television which works the same way, and is considered a brilliant advance. This could almost be a prototype. No doubt somewhere the ghost of a dead artisan is fuming.

He glances at Edie for permission, ignites a tiny blowtorch, heats a strip of metal and twists, crimps, folds. *Snickersnack* again. He blows on it. Crimps once more. Yes. Like that, around there, and . . . so. *Consumatum est*, as his mother would have it.

Joe looks up, and Edie Banister is watching him, or perhaps she is watching her own life from a great distance. Her face is still, and for one ghastly moment he imagines she has expired right there. Then she shudders and smiles a little fey smile, and says thank you, and he winds the toy and sets it marching, a wee soldier trump-trump-trumping around the table and rucking up the cloth with miniature hobnail boots.

The dog peers back at him: eerie blind hound, stubby ears alert, straining to look through glass eyes. *Not perfect, horologist. It drags one foot. But it will suffice. Behold: my mistress is much moved. This, for your pains. And now—begone.*

Joe Spork hurries away, suddenly quite certain she wanted something else from him; she has some other secret, a grander one which requires this endless testing of J.J. Spork before it can be unveiled. He wonders a bit wistfully how he failed, considers going back. But perhaps she's just lonely, and recognises in him a fellow isolate.

Not that he's alone the way she is.

And not that he's alone now, not entirely. In the corner of his eye something flickers, a dark shape reflected in the windows of a passing bus. A shadow in a doorway. He turns and looks both ways before crossing the road, very alert as he sweeps the street to his left. Almost, he misses it completely. It's so still, it's hard to make out; his eyes are seeking joints and movements where there are none. But there, in the shadowed porch of a boarded-up bakery, it seems that someone watches: a bundled figure in a dress or a heavy overcoat, with a veil like a mourner's. A beekeeper or a widow, or a tall, thin child playing at being a ghost. Or most likely an old burlap sack hanging on a rack, deceiving the eye.

A moment later a long green estate car nearly runs him over. The angry maternal face behind the wheel glowers at him resentfully for being in the world, and the watcher—if there really was one—goes right out of his head.

Moody and unsettled, Joe stops in at the corner shop to see whether Ari will sell him some cat poison.

When Ari arrived in London, he called the shop *Bhred nba'a*. He had come to the conclusion from watching English television that the people of London were fond of both puns and corner shops, and he reasoned that a combination must inevitably be a big success. Bread and butter became *Bhred nba'a*, and it emerged almost immediately that although Londoners do indeed admire both puns and convenience, they're not keen on shop owners who appear to be taking the piss out of them while looking foreign. Correct use of the apostrophe to denote a glottal stop was not a defence.

Ari learned fast, and shortly painted over the offending sign. It's not clear to Joe whether his name actually is anything like Ari, or whether he has just selected a comfortably foreign-yet-English noise which doesn't startle the natives with complexity or suggestions of undue education.

Perhaps unsurprisingly, Ari is reticent on the poison issue. Ari regards cats as lessons in the journey through life. Cats, he explains, are divine messengers of patience. Joe, one shoulder still sore from a near miss two weeks ago, says they are Satanic messengers of discord and pruritus. Ari says this is possible, but by the workings of the ineffable divinity, even if they are Satanic messengers of discord and pruritus, they are *also* tutors sent by the Cosmic All.

"They are of themselves," Ari says, clutching this morning's consignment of organic milk, some of which is leaking through the plastic, "an opportunity for self-education."

"In first aid and disease," mutters Joe Spork.

"And in more spiritual things. The universe teaches us about God, Joseph."

"Not cats. Or, not that cat."

"All things are lessons."

And this is so close to something Grandpa Spork once said that Joe Spork, even after a sleepless night and a bad cat morning, finds himself nodding.

"Thanks, Ari."

"You are welcome."

"I still want cat poison."

"Good! Then we have much to teach one another!"

"Goodbye, Ari."

"*Au revoir*, Joseph."

II

Two Gentlemen of Edinburgh;
the Book of the Hakote;
Friend in need.

He is nearly at his front door when he hears the shout. It is a breathy, asthmatic shout, more a gasp, but it is penetrating all the same in the stillness of Quoyle Street. Pigeons scuttle nervously in the alley round the side.

"Hello? Mr. Spork?"

Joe turns, and beholds a rare and curious thing: a fat man running.

"Mr. Spork?"

He really is running. He's not quick—although he's light on his feet, as so many fat men are—but he has considerable momentum and powerful thighs, and he is not trotting, cantering, or jogging, but actually running. He reminds Joe at this remove of his mother's father, the meat-packer, shaven-headed and layered with gammon and eggs. This specimen has his bulk, but not his heft, and is somewhere between thirty and fifty.

"Hello? I wonder if we could have a word?"

Yes, "we," for indeed there are two of them, one fat and the other thin, the little one concealed behind his enormous companion, walking fastidiously along in the wake of the whale.

It is the fat one who is calling him, between breaths, as he hurtles up Quoyle Street. Joe stops and waits, hoping to avoid any kind of cardiac drama or collision, and by some curious trick, the two men arrive at much the same time. The thin one takes over the talking. He's older, greyer, more measured and more unctuous.

"My dear Mr. Spork. I wonder if we might go inside? We represent—among other people, you understand—we represent the Loganfield Museum of Mechanical History in Edinburgh and Chicago." But he has no Scots lilt, just a pure English diction with a hint of apology. His sentences do not turn upward at the end, in the modern American style, but conclude on firm, downward full stops. "It's a matter of some delicacy, I'm afraid."

Delicacy. Joe does not like delicacy. Oh, he likes it fine in clocks and mechanisms, but in real life it means courts and money and complication. It sometimes also means that another of his father's debts or wickednesses has found its way home, and he will hear about how Mathew robbed a fellow of his life savings or stole a priceless jewel, and have to explain that no, the treasure of Mathew Spork is not his to disburse, that patrimony is nothing but an empty leather suitcase and a parcel of newspaper clippings detailing Mathew's mostly unconvicted outrages. Mathew's money is gone, and no one knows where to, not even his wife, not his son, and not his creditors. On this occasion, however, the matter appears to be related to Joe personally.

There is one person in Joe Spork's small circle of friends whose life is occasionally complicated by issues of law.

Billy, you bald git, what have you got me into? Soot and sorrow, I know it.

Soot and sorrow: the Night Market's invocation of desperate seriousness, of doom and disaster. He feels a powerful urge to run.

Instead he says "Please come in," because it is his conviction that England is a just place, and his experience that even where the law has been bent or broken, a little cooperation and courtesy can smooth over some remarkably large potholes.

The fat one goes first and the thin one second, with Joe bringing up the rear to emphasise that he is not running, that indeed, they are entering his lair at his urging. He offers them tea and comfortable chairs, which they regretfully decline. So he makes tea for himself, and the thin one says that perhaps he will, after all, and helps himself to a macaroon into the bargain. The fat one drinks water, a lot of it. And when everyone is refreshed and Joe has shown them around the more interesting bits of his workshop (the half-assembled chess-playing robot he is making on commission in the style of the notorious Turk, the wind-up racehorses, the Edinburgh case clocks) the thin gentleman steeples his hands, as if to say it is time to begin.

"I am Mr. Titwhistle," the thin gentleman says, "and this is Mr. Cummerbund. Those are our actual names, I'm afraid. Life is capricious. If you should feel the urge at any time to chuckle, we're both quite big enough to share the joke." He gives a demonstrative little smile, just to show he can. Mr. Cummerbund pats his stomach, as if to say that he, personally, is big enough for that one and a number of other jokes besides.

Joe Spork takes this for a species of test. He smiles politely, even contritely, a man who knows what it is to have an odd name and feels no need to laugh. Instead, he extends his hand to them both. Mr. Cummerbund takes it lightly. He has very soft skin, and he shakes gently but enthusiastically. After a moment, Joe unplugs himself, and turns to Mr. Titwhistle.

Mr. Titwhistle does not lean forward for the greeting. He keeps himself perfectly balanced, perfectly inside his own circle. He shakes hands as if mindful that Joe might at any moment slip and fall, that he might therefore need the solidity of his size eight feet on the carpet and the strength in his lawyerly thighs to lend support. He has very little hair; a mere haze embracing his head like the fuzz on a petrified peach. This makes his age impossible to judge. Forty-five? Sixty?

He looks directly into Joe's face, quite calmly and without embarrassment. In his eyes—which are grey, and kindly—there is no flicker of dislike or disapproval. Indeed, they are more like eyes that proffer condolences, or mediation. Mr. Titwhistle understands that these little disagreements come along, and that persons of intelligence and determination can always get around them in one way or another. If Joe did slip, Mr. Titwhistle would not hesitate to bear him up. Mr. Titwhistle sees no reason for unpleasantness between those who are presently on opposite sides of the legal tennis net. He is before everything a pleasant man.

Joe finds all his old, unused and unwelcome instincts rushing to the surface. *Alarm! Alert! Sound the dive klaxon and blow the tanks! Run silent, run deep!* He wonders why. He glances at the hand still gripping his own, and sees no watch. Gentlemen of this vintage rarely operate without watches, and watches communicate something of one's identity. Of course, if one wished to avoid such communication . . . His gaze flicks to Mr. Titwhistle's waistcoat, and finds what he's looking for: a fob watch on an unornamented chain. No charms, no Masonic badges, no club marks. No private signs or colophon. No military insignia. A blank, empty space on an item for display. He looks back at the wrist. Cufflinks. Plain studs. The tie is generic, too. This man is a cypher. He hides himself.

Joe glances back at Mr. Titwhistle's face. Gazing into those clear, benevolent eyes, he finds he is sure of exactly one thing: that Mr. Titwhistle, congenial sherry drinker and alderman of the city of Bath, would have precisely the same damp, avuncular expression on his face if he were strangling you with piano wire.

Unwillingly, he grants the Night Market self a brief leave to remain.

The formalities dispensed with, Mr. Cummerbund sits and lays out his notepad on his lap. From this angle, he is even more bizarre than when Joe first saw him galloping along Quoyle Street. He has a head shaped almost exactly like a pear. His brain must be squeezed into the narrow place at the top. His cheeks are wide and fatty, so that, if Mr. Cummerbund were a deer or a halibut, they would excite pleasurable anticipation in those fond of rich foods and delicacies. He smells strongly of a thin, high-scented cologne. It is a cologne advertised by young men who surf and then trip lightly into tropical casinos with curvy, dark-eyed women. It comes in a bottle made to look like a crystal glass pineapple. It is too young for him, and does not conceal the stinky *eau de Cummerbund* which is the natural product of his body.

"A matter of some delicacy?" Joe says.

"I'm afraid so," Mr. Titwhistle agrees.

"Regarding?"

"Regarding some of your late grandfather's effects."

"My grandfather?" It is an innocuous word, and Daniel Spork was not a firebrand or a red-toothed crook—unlike his son—but it puts Joe a little more on edge.

"Yes, indeed. Mr. Daniel, I believe."

"What about him?"

"Ah. Well . . . I am tasked to acquire your grandfather's journals, and any correspondence you might be willing to part with. Along with any examples of his work or his tools which you might still possess. And any curiosities."

"I see." He doesn't, or rather, he sees something, but cannot identify it.

"I'm authorised to negotiate the sale so that it can be done quickly, and to arrange for collection. The new exhibitions usually start in

January, and they take a while to prepare, so time is of the essence. Have you been to the Museum?"

"No, I'm not familiar with it."

"So few people are. A great shame. But the curators really do an amazing job. They build up the exhibits in a way which sets them off quite splendidly. You should visit."

"It sounds fascinating."

"Once I've seen the items, of course, I can give you a better idea of what we'd be willing to pay—but I have a considerable budget. American money, you see, not British. Additional zeroes, you understand."

"And are there any specific items you might be looking for? I have a small number of rather ordinary tools which belonged to him. Although I think I do have a table clamp he designed for engraving work. The best stuff I'm afraid my father disposed of rather informally, while my grandfather was still alive." Did he ever. Daniel Spork, measured and frail, shouting fit to raise the roof and shake the foundations. His son was a serpent, a buffoon, a deceiver. He was a crawling bug with no concept of honour, no understanding of humanity's better urges. He was vile. And Joe's mother, weeping and holding Mathew's arm, clutching at the old man. *Don't say that, Daniel, please! Please. He didn't know!*

But Daniel Spork was a pillar of flame. A great trust had been shattered. The world was poorer for it—and Mathew, flesh of his flesh, lying and unforgivable clot, was the weak link in a chain of such incredible importance that it could not be fully expressed. Daniel turned his back and shook and shuddered, and batted away their hands. And then he went down to his workroom to leaf through the remains of Mathew's "fire sale" and see what was still there and what could be reasonably brought back. It was only after a half-day spent leafing through his books and piling up bits and bobs upon his table, mouth still a bitter line of hurt and the Death Clock set appallingly in front of him ticking away these black moments of his life, that he looked over the remaining clutter and began to calm. His diary, yes, was here. His sketchbooks had gone to a friend in the trade, and could be had back, no doubt. His toolbox was gone—a magical thing of levers and cogs which extended and unfolded into a miniature bench—but the tools themselves remained.

Having lined up the survivors of the auction, Daniel paced and fluttered, opened ledgers and fussed with boxes, and finally gave a shout of satisfaction as he held up a collection of jazz records, old 78s, in a purpose-made satchel.

"Frankie," he murmured. And then, with a snarl to his son, "Your mother!"

Only the sight of Joe—knee-high and cowering amid all this splashy and appalling adult confusion—broke through his rage, and even then it merely unleashed his grief, which was infinitely worse.

"No," Mr. Titwhistle says, "nothing in particular. Unusual items always fetch a premium, of course. Anything idiosyncratic. Impractical, even. Or intricate."

But his hands—which he has raised, palms up, to convey his sincerity—have betrayed him. He is tracing the outline of something, absently sketching it in the air as he speaks. Something which Joe has recently seen. Something strange, of which gentlemen from Scottish museums might in theory be aware, but whose connection with Joe himself should be quite beyond their ken. In any case, what manner of museum sends two fellows with anonymous ties and empty eyes all the way to London on the off chance? Do they not have the electric telephone in Edinburgh?

Mr. Cummerbund has been silent so far, listening and watching with great acuity, and every so often he has made notes in an impenetrable shorthand. The top leaves of the pad he is using have wrinkled, because his hands are moist and because he presses very hard with his cheap supermarket-brand ballpoint—a thin plastic thing which has already cracked along one edge, and which he occasionally puts between his lips to chew. Now, he removes it, and the smell of Mr. Cummerbund's mouth is briefly added to the smell of tropical-fruit cologne, a tantalisingly disgusting flavour of old mint, tooth decay, and kidneys.

"Rodney," he says tightly, and Mr. Titwhistle glances at him, then follows the line of Mr. Cummerbund's gaze back to his own fingers. Joe sees the sequence of events unfolding, and realises a moment too late what will happen next: Mr. Titwhistle and Mr. Cummerbund look guiltily from the shape in the air to Joe to see whether he has made anything of it, and catch him staring guiltily at them. Between the three men, there is a moment of comprehension. *Oh, yes. All out in the open, now, isn't it?* Or, not all, but enough. The rusty machinery of his father's world wakes within him again, unfolding from an old corner of his mind that he barely knew was there; the forgotten instinct which prompts him to lie, promise, misdirect, all in one.

"I'm sorry, gentlemen," Joe says confidingly, "you place me in a rather awkward position. I had a similar offer not two days ago from another interested party, and this morning my phone has barely stopped ringing. I've made some enquiries and not all my suitors are in fact entirely reputable"—you two, in particular, but we don't say that because we want everyone to feel nice and safe and not disposed to rash action—"so I'd rather prefer to deal with you. If the price is right, of course."

He cringes a bit, inwardly. Joe Spork—new and improved and all grown-up—doesn't think that way. Not any more. There was a boy once, who did—a kid who picked pockets and stood lookout; who tumbled through the tunnels of the Tosher's Beat in search of pirate treasure, in the certain knowledge that there actually was some; whose nefarious uncles nipped up a drainpipe in the blinding dusk to relieve a duchess of her jewels, while Mathew Spork charmed and smiled and kept her on the hook and his one begotten son leaned against a wall and yoyo'd and kept an eye out for the Lily, as in Lily Law, as in Her Majesty's Metropolitan Police—but Joe had imagined that person no longer existed. He had no idea he could summon the pattern so easily.

Mr. Cummerbund closes his book, and glances at his partner.

"I'm quite sure," Mr. Titwhistle murmurs, "that some accommodation could be reached for the full collection."

"I'm so glad. Your good fortune, of course, is that I've begun to assemble it all. Mine is that now I have someone suitable to sell it to."

"We should greatly prefer to avoid anything like an auction."

You don't care in the slightest. This is another test. Why is everyone testing me? I don't have anything you want. Except, somehow, I clearly do.

Mathew is bubbling in Joe's brain, commenting and advising:

Don't sell. Not yet. If you make it easy, they'll see through you.

To what?

To whatever you're actually going to do.

Am I not selling, then?

Apparently not.

Cover. Conceal. Hide. Deceive.

A day of ghosts, most unwelcome and unawaited.

"Then I shall expect your pre-emptive offer to be quite striking. I'm sure it would have been anyway! And if you'll be so kind as to excuse me, gentlemen, I have another client appointment—on an unrelated matter, I assure you—at ten-thirty, and I really need to go. Shall we say, same time on Monday?"

There is a long pause. Jesus, Joe thinks, are they actually going to jump me? And then:

"Ideal," Mr. Titwhistle says. He reaches into his jacket and produces, between two meagre fingers, a crisp white business card. "Do call if you have any trouble—the Museum has a good many friends. We can help in all sorts of ways."

Yes. I'm sure you can.

Joe watches them walk away down the road. Neither one looks back. No car stops to pick them up. They seem entirely rapt in conversation, and yet somehow he feels observed, spied upon.

Fine. Then I'm very boring, aren't I? I do boring things. I live a boring life and no one can say I don't. I deal in antiques and curiosities, and I don't do surprises. I'm recently single and I'm about to leave the 25–34 demographic for evermore. I like Chelsea buns the way they don't make them these days and I fall in love with waifish, angry women who don't think I'm funny.

I wind clocks like Daniel.

And I won't turn into Mathew.

"Billy, it's Joe. Call me, please. We've got something to discuss."

He sighs, feeling the need for some consolation and knowing that he has no one from whom he can easily require a hug, and goes back to work.

Joe winds the clocks every day after lunch. He does not, as is the practice of many in his trade, set them all to different times so that there is always one about to chime. He gets his clients by appointment, by referral. Spork & Co. is what is known in these days when everything is studied and taxonomised as a "destination business." His customers, for the most part, already know what they want when they come, and they are unlikely to be soothed or cozened into buying something else just because it goes *bong* while they're having a quiet cup of tea and a jam tart with the owner. What they want is splendour and authenticity and a sense of craft. They are buying perhaps most of all a handshake with the past.

And the past is here, caught by the crook of the Thames and the endless whispering of ratchets and pendulums, the busy susurrus of oiled mechanical technology. If he is lucky, or when he can schedule an appointment with reference to the tide chart and the radio set he keeps against the waterside wall, the fog will come in and waves will lap against the brick, and some mournful barge will creak down the river or even hoot into the mist, and as the whole place slips loose in time, his client will tumble nose-first into the magic of it and buy that item they came for even though, inevitably, they came expecting to get it at half the asking price. He sometimes has to turn down considerable offers on the building itself. He jokes on such occasions that if one of them owns the other, it is almost certainly the warehouse, with his grandfather's patient ghost and his father's restless, relentless magnanimity, which holds the freehold to the man.

Joe winds the clocks. The winders are on a small trolley—a keychain would rattle and scratch against the casements, a bag would mean rummaging through each time for the right key. He pushes it around and tries not to feel like the nurse who wheels the gurney of the dead. *Clink, clank, I'm so sorry, it was his time.*

In the last year or so he has taken to playing BBC Radio 4 while he winds. The gentle burble of news and artistic wrangling makes a pleasant backdrop, and every so often there's the forecast for shipping, with its soothing litany of places he need never go. Flemish Cap, seven, gusting nine. Recently, Radio 4 has betrayed him somewhat, because current affairs are a bit tense. Alongside assorted climatic woes, the world is even now passing what is apparently called "peak oil"—the moment after which oil will only ever be harder to get hold of and hence more expensive and ultimately unavailable—and in consequence the latest meeting of the G-whatever-it-is has become tense. Joe hopes this does not mean the sort of tense which prefigures bombing someone. He does not find angry South American diplomats, resentful Irish aviation bosses and fatuously confident Canadian oilmen very restful, so today the radio is silent on its shelf.

And really, that's the most important thing he does with his days. It's a small, measurable success, in the face of diminishing sales and an empty double bed and a set of skills which were marketable one hundred years ago, but now look quaint and even sad. Every afternoon for the last six months he has been fighting an uneven battle with himself not to overturn the trolley with its many keys, and scatter them across the room. His better nature has won only because the image of himself on his knees, remorsefully gathering them again, repairing scratched case clocks and whispering apologies to the ghost of his grandfather—and for strange and different reasons also his father—is more than he can bear.

The chimes clink over the door, and he glances up.

The figure in the doorway is tall. It must be, because the top of its head is not so far short of the frame. It is silhouetted by the day outside, but even allowing for that, it must be wearing black. It has long arms and long legs, and wears a strange, cumbersome garment like a dress or robe. *Miss Havisham*. He wonders if the wearer is unpleasantly scarred. He cannot tell. Over its head, the visitor wears a piece of black gauze or linen, so that the face is quite invisible. The cloth is not cinched; it hangs down over the wearer's head, so that the top is a smooth curve. There's just the barest bulge of a nose. Other than that, the head is as blank and featureless as an egg. *Vampire. Alien*. And then, more shamefully, *suicide bomber*.

The last makes him feel guilty, and ridiculous, and the feeling propels him to his feet. Clearly, if suicide bomber is unlikely, it has to be conceded that the others are more so.

"Hello," Joe says. "What can I do for you?"

"Nothing for the moment, thank you." The voice is deep and scratched, but muffled. It sounds like a recording played through one of the old wood-horn gramophones Joe has in the back. The metal-horns are powerful, they make everything sound like old-time radio. The wood-horns are rounder, but lack belt. Joe automatically leans in to hear, and then away again when the blank linen face follows him, ducks down as if to kiss his cheek, coming too close too quickly. "May I look around?"

"Oh, well, please. Browse away. Let me know if you want anything in particular. I have some very fine gramophones with quite special horns. And a really good fob watch. I'm quite proud of the clean-up. It's a lovely thing." Joe lets his tone suggest that anyone who is just browsing should almost certainly conclude their visit with a tour of the smaller items which might have failed to attract attention.

The shrouded head dips in assent, once, and then deeper a second time, like a swan's.

"Forgive me for asking," Joe says, when his visitor does not move away, "but I've never seen anyone dressed like that before."

"I am on a journey of the soul," the other replies, without rancour.

"My clothing reminds me that the face of God is turned away from us. From the world. It is worn by members of the Order of John the Maker, who are called Ruskinites." He waits, to see if this elicits a reaction. Since Joe doesn't know what reaction would be considered appropriate, he allows himself none.

"Thank you," he says instead, by way of concluding the conversation. The man moves away with a curious, boneless lurching.

Glancing warily after the eerie, absent face, Joe goes back to work.

The visitor wanders towards a row of music boxes. One of them plays something light and perky, and the man looks down at it like a bird wondering whether it is something to eat. A moment later, he speaks again.

"Mr. Spork?"

"Yes, what can I do for you?"

"I am looking for something. I hope you can help me."

"I'll do my best."

"I believe you have recently dealt with a book I have an interest in. A very unusual book."

Oh, crap.

"Oh, dear. I can't help you there, I'm afraid. Music, yes. Books, no." Joe can feel a sort of prickling on his back. He turns, and sees the figure straighten and turn smoothly away.

"I believe you can. The Book of the Hakote, Mr. Spork." Laden with significance.

Joe hesitates. On the one hand, he has never specifically heard of the Book of the Hakote (huh-KOH-tay). Like the shroud the visitor is wearing, the word has the flavour of religion, and he takes especial care not to deal in religious items, be they church timepieces or sneaky weeping icons with internal reservoirs and clockwork pumps. They have almost always been pillaged at some time, and in consequence come with aggravation attached. On the other hand, he has recently been in contact with an object of various unusual qualities which might conceivably answer to such an outré name, an object which was brought to him by a moderately nefarious individual by the name of William "Billy" Friend.

Chief among the unusual qualities aforementioned: a fat man and a thin man turned up in his shop and lied, quaintly and unpersuasively, about how they wanted to buy the Grandpa Spork collection entire, when what they really wanted (see Mr. Titwhistle's betraying fingers) was anything associated with this same "very unusual book."

"I'm terribly sorry, you've lost me," Joe replies cheerfully. "I sell and maintain items of clockwork. Curiosities, mostly, things that go *bong* and so on. Pianolas and automata. But in general not books."

"There are some texts whose importance is not immediately apparent to the uninitiated. Dangerous books."

"I'm sure there are."

"There is no need to condescend." The Ruskinite's head turns on his neck, the shroud bunching at the shoulders. Joe wonders if it will turn all the way around, like an owl's. "I mean that the escape of knowledge into the realm of wider society irretrievably alters the nature of our lives. More mundanely, Mr. Spork, the Book and all its paraphernalia are of great value to me personally. I should very much like them back."

Back. Not: *I should very much like to locate a copy,* nor even: *I have been having some trouble finding the ISBN.* This person is seeking an item which at some stage they owned. A singular item. Yes, this has all the hallmarks of a Billy Friend situation, right enough.

"It is not yours, Mr. Spork," the Ruskinite says with soft finality. "It is mine."

Joe puts on his most accommodating expression. "Might I take your name? I have, in fact, dealt with a very unusual book recently, but I'm afraid I don't know the title. It passed through my hands as part of a repair job. I do hope there was no funny business involved." *Oh, I bloody do. But I'm quite sure there was if you say so.*

The Ruskinite circles the room in silence as if considering. Joe Spork affects an air of polite, shopkeeper's dismay, and does not watch. He fusses with his papers and listens, trying to track the other's progress in the room. Scritch scritch. Is the other man rubbing his chin? Mopping his brow? Clawing at the desk with an iron hook in place of his right hand?

When the man speaks again, his muffled voice is almost a whisper, and alarmingly close. "Very well, Mr. Spork."

Joe glances around and finds the shrouded face less than a metre away. He jumps slightly, and the head withdraws.

"I am sorry I startled you. If you do not have anything for me, I will leave."

"Do take a card and give me a call if there's anything else I can do. Or any other items I have which might be of interest."

"I shall consider that, and return."

Joe clamps down on his subconscious before it can make him say

"From the grave?" which would be rude. The shrouded man snakes out of the door and disappears into the street.

Billy. You are in so much trouble right now.

Before going to find Billy Friend wherever he is and shout at him in person, Joe makes a phone call.

Harticle's—more properly the Boyd Harticle Foundation for Artisanal and Scientific Practice—is an endless lumber room, one hundred and fifty years old and more; a winding mass of shelved corridors and display cases punctuated with reading rooms and collections, inadequately labelled and appallingly dusty, so that to go into the Archives is to risk coughing for days. It is stuffed to bursting with odds and ends, acquired and maintained and stored away, against the day when something may be required for a restoration or a recreation. There are pieces of Charles Babbage's unfinished machines here, and of Brunel's steam engines. Instruments designed by Robert Hooke rub shoulders with wooden models produced to drawings by da Vinci. Everything has a story, usually more than one. Boyd Harticle's ugly red-brick house with its unlikely turreted roof and neo-Gothic arched windows is a refuge for the disregarded children of man's study and conquest of the natural world.

The call is answered on the second ring.

"In this house, only art," proclaims a woman's voice, deep and rather forceful.

"Cecily? It's Joe."

"Joe? Joe? *Joe?* What Joe? I know no Joe. The phenomenon known as Joe is an illusion created by my conscious mind to account for the discrepancy between the number of scones I buy and the number I eventually consume. His putative reality has been demonstrated false by empirical testing. In any case, extant or not, he no longer cares. Gone off with some harlot, no doubt, and left me to my lonesome."

"I'm sorry."

"And well you might be. How are you, you heartless wretch?"

"I'm fine. How's Harticle's?"

"Big and draughty and full of old things no one gives a fig for. Me, among them."

"I said I was sorry."

"And you imagine once will get you off the hook, do you? Ask Foalbury how many times he had to apologise for the fiasco with the eggnog. Then try again." But Cecily's voice is grudgingly mollified, and a few buttered scones will see her right. The gates of Harticle's—as Joe well knows, and so does she—are not closed to him.

Part museum, part archive, and part club, Harticle's occupies one of those weird niches in London's life, both physical and social, which makes it almost invisible to the wider world and almost inevitable to those in the know. Cecily Foalbury is its librarian and in a way its library. Granted, with a following wind one might find a book or an object via the card-index system. It's a perfectly respectable arrangement, albeit outdated and—this being Harticle's—staunchly analogue. It's also true that Cecily is the codex, the concordance. If you want to find anything within any reasonable time-frame, it's best to ask her—but very, very politely, and if possible with blandishments. Cecily's nickname—the Man-eater—is not entirely in jest, and her husband Bob freely confesses himself a serf.

"Cecily, do you know anything about the Loganfield Museum in Edinburgh?"

"Not since it closed. Why?"

Joe Spork nods to himself without surprise. "Just checking. What about dangerous books?"

"Oh! Yes, of course. There are dozens. The churches got in such an uproar after Gutenberg, Joe, because now anyone could print anything and spread it about. Popes got in a bate about all manner of things. Local barons became irate about scurrilous gossip printed in pamphlets—much of it true and I must say almost all of it good reading!" A thunderous laugh down the phone. "There's even a couple of Bibles with printing errors which make them a bit odd. Thou Shalt Commit Adultery, and all that sort of thing. People collect them, bishops burn them. Silly sods. As if God gives a monkey's what's written in botched type."

"This isn't one of those. It's more modern."

"Come on, then, Joe. What sort of *tome*," she hits the word hard, enjoying its kookiness, "what sort of *libram* are we talking about?"

"He called it the Book of the Hakote."

There's a brief cough from the other end of the phone, a muffled bark.

"Cecily?"

"I'm here."

"What's wrong?"

"Hakote, is what's wrong."

"You've heard of it?"

"Of course I bloody have. Drop this, Joe. Run away from it. It's poison."

"I can't. I think it's stuck to me."

"Wash. Fast."

"How? I don't know what it is!"

"It's the ghost in the darkness, Joe. From the tip of Spain to the Black Forest and all the way to bloody Minsk. The Witch Queen at the Crossroads. Bloody Mary. Baba Yaga. It's a curse."

"Cecily! Come on!"

She doesn't. The line is silent. Then she asks sharply: "Who's 'he'?"

"What?"

"You said 'he called it'. Who is this 'he'? Not the nefarious little lecher, please?"

"No. Someone else. He seems to think I've got it."

"And have you?"

"I . . . no. I may have had it. Or something which could have been it."

He hears her sigh, or maybe just breathe out hard, letting it go.

"Hakote, Joe. It's . . . it's a bogeyman. All right? It's a leper or a . . . a banshee. Like Grendel's mother. You can die of it. She's supposed to have built a castle in a village, and one night the sea came up and swallowed the whole thing."

Joe Spork is trying to laugh. It is, after all, rather silly. Ghost stories are absurd, here and now, under the faint but reassuring sun—but Cecily Foalbury is a tough old bird and not given to fantasy or superstition. On the other hand: this morning, the strange, birdlike man in a linen wrap—a hood? A cowl? A bandage?—which hid his face.

"Leprosy is curable," he says firmly. Revolting, but curable and natural and not easily caught.

"Joe, they're not just sick. It's more than that. The lepers and the Hakote were both outcast groups, all right? So they got lumped together. People started to think of them as the same thing, but they weren't. And the lepers, Joe, they were more scared of the Hakote than the other way around. This is modern people, not medieval peasants. And . . . well, I don't know. It's like the tomb of the Pharaohs, isn't it? There's a long record of people dying from being too close."

"To what?"

"I think knowing that is what you're supposed to die of."

"Cecily . . ."

"Oh, don't be so bloody dense, Joe! Of course it's all hogwash, but it's hogwash with dead people attached and I don't want you to be one of them!"

"Nor do I. Well, fine. They're bad. Pirates, murderers, whatever. I don't have the book, but someone thinks I do, and that could be a problem." He can hear her pursing her lips to argue, pushes on. "I need to know more. If it's dangerous, that makes it more important. I'm in this somewhere. I think it might have something to do with Daniel. Can you check that, too?" He wants to get off the phone. He's irrationally angry with Cecily for turning his day into an emergency.

"Daniel Spork? Your grandfather Daniel? Why would you think that? Who have you been talking to?"

But Joe doesn't want to answer that one, not yet, so he mumbles something and repeats his request. Cecily, after a moment to make it clear she has noticed that she's being fobbed off, doesn't press.

"I'll check the file. You've got most of his things there, though. What there is."

"Just some old clothes and his jazz collection."

There's a brief silence, then: "His what?"

"Jazz. Music."

"I am aware, you young pup, that jazz is music—and one of the highest forms thereof. All right, then, start with that."

"Why?"

"Because unless I've gone completely mad, Joe, your grandfather hated jazz. Loathed it. Apparently there was a jazz band playing in the ship he came over from France in during the war. They came down into the hold and played for the refugees when the convoy was under attack. Bombs falling, the whole iron tub clanging and banging, and they danced their way to Blighty. Daniel couldn't listen to it afterwards. He said all he could hear was shells falling and men screaming."

"Oh. I didn't know that."

"Well, no. It's not a story for children, I dare say."

No. Apparently his day is going to be rather dark.

"I need anything you can find out."

"Be careful, Joe. Please."

"I will. I am."

"Yes. You are. All right. Give me a day or so, and bring me a pork pie."

Joe laughs for the first time, brief respite. Cecily is strictly forbidden pork pies by her doctor, but the Rippon Pie, which she regards as the Platonic form, is her absolute favourite and she will brook no denay. For a Rippon Pie, Cecily Foalbury, at twelve stone, five foot two and seventy-one years old, would gladly walk naked through Piccadilly in winter.

He puts down the phone and leans back, staring at the warehouse ceiling and listening to the Thames.

Beware of Greeks bearing gifts.

Oh, sure. It's easy to say that now.

"Tell you what," Billy Friend says, three days ago and cab-driver confidential, "I've got something which might be useful to you in your professional capacity, not to say your artisanal practice. And a bit of actual paid work, a commission, so to speak, for a reputable client, all above board and squared away. Right? So, what say you do something for me in exchange and call it a finder's fee? Mutual courtesy, no paperwork, no VAT, everyone's a winner." He waggles his eyebrows over the rim of his teacup.

Billy Friend's eyebrows receive considerable prominence on his face because they are thick and black, and he has no other hair of any kind upon his head. Around about the time that Joe's father was called to account by Her Majesty for being *in loco parentis* to a large quantity of imported cocaine (rather than being *in loco parentis* to, to take a random example, his son) Billy Friend acknowledged that his personal battle with male-pattern hair loss was at an end. On the day of the trial—quite coincidentally, there was no very strong connection between Joe Spork and William Friend back then—he ditched his fiancée, bought a shiny new suit, and had the last of his mortal youth removed by a Knightsbridge barber. Since which time, beyond varying the ridiculous waxes he uses to produce a manly gleam on his alarmingly sexual pate, he has changed not at all. Billy Friend, riding the coat-tails of Patrick Stewart's supersexed telegenic baldness—though Billy would tell you he was there first.

Joe generally avoids Billy in his professional context. They go out on the town every so often, share a meal, maybe some drinks. Billy is brash and embarrassing, and therefore exactly the kind of person who can force a moody Joe Spork to have a good time, even talk to women he finds attractive. It's the kind of friendship which endures, despite minimal tending and no apparent central plank. Billy in mufti, ordering another bottle from a cheerily scandalised waitress, is a part of the landscape, awkward and familiar and finally indispensable.

Billy the dealer is a trickier proposition, fraught with complex questions of murky legal ownership and tax-free cash jobs—but on this occasion Joe was so unwise as to pick up the phone without checking to see who it was, got blindsided, and as a consequence is here in this greasy spoon drinking thick, orange tea. An object lesson in paranoia, but not in the end a bad result, because Joe has to confess he is having minor money issues at present, and Billy Friend, when not attempting to sell him a pup or persuade him to take part in some dubious scheme involving Latvian modelling agencies, is a good source of gainful employment as well as a genuine if barmy long-time pal.

"What sort of commission?" Joe says carefully.

"Well, Joseph," because Billy likes to be formal when he's conning you, "it is—and at the same time, you understand, it is *not*—for it's an equivocal and quirky sort of object, hard to get to know and spiky about the edges, which is what made me think of you . . . It is a what you might call without fear of immediate contradiction though at the same time without expressing the fullest truth . . . a doodah. From an estate sale."

"Estate sale" meaning, most probably, nicked. Although Billy Friend, when he is not dealing in knocked-off antiquities and seducing the daughters of provincial publicans, is a member in good standing of the Honoured & Enduring Brotherhood of Waiting Men, which is to say he is an undertaker. He is therefore well-positioned to come across estate sales before the actual sale has begun, but Joe does not automatically accept that Billy actually buys from the bereaved, because in one of his many other professional hats, Billy is a freelance spotter of thievable items for burglars in London and the Home Counties.

"I've got a lot of doodahs, Billy," Joe says. "My life is in some measure awash in doodahs. How is your doodah different from everyone else's doodah?" And he realises too late that Billy has set him up.

"Well, Joseph, one doesn't like to brag . . ." Followed by a huge laugh which turns heads all around, and most particularly the head of the young, flirtatious waitress, whose personal attention Billy Friend has been working to secure since they sat down.

"Billy . . ."

"It's a book, Joseph."

"A book."

"Of sorts, yes."

"Then you're wasting your time. I don't do books. I mean, I like books. Books are good and we should have more of them. But I'm not a bookbinder, a paper specialist, or a restorer. I can't help you with a damaged book."

"You can help with this one."

"Is it a clockwork book?"

"It is."

"Because if it's not a clockwork book, there's not very much I can do, is there?" Joe pauses. Some part of the last exchange did not play out as he imagined when he ran it through in his mind.

"What do you mean, 'it is'?"

Billy waves his arms to indicate the magnificence of what he has to offer. "The item is a combination book and device. The textual part is in acceptable if foxed condition, nice leather cover, looks like a diary. The peculiarity is that the outer edges are punched in a grid, so that the book as a whole functions or appears to function as a set of punchcards. One might think of it as equivalent to the drum on one of your music boxes. Yes?"

Joe Spork nods assent. Billy goes on, waving his hands for emphasis, which he is pleased to call "emf-*arse*-is," because it generally gets a rise out of the ladies.

"And in, as it were, the same sack, the same rattling old box, the same shabby loft where the book was located, there is a collection of mucky, disassembled bits and bobs which could, under the right circumstances and through the intervention of a skilled craftsperson such as yourself, form some sort of mechanism which appears, on close and expert examination by me, to attach to the written volume along the spine. Further, there is what I can only describe as a large gold ball forming part of the mechanical apparatus, whose function I have not at this time been able to discern. Thus, a conundrum. A book which is more than a book, and the implication of a machine which does something with it. Hence, to avoid the practice of neologism, Joseph, which as you know I despise, I call it a doodah."

Joe Spork gazes at Billy through narrow eyes. It does not please him to be so easily led about by the nose. He knows that Billy knows this kind of thing is his particular delight. He anticipates some species of hustle, or possibly just a task of mind-numbing boredom by way of compensation for his pleasure.

"And what do I have to do in exchange for this doodah job?"

"Nothing dreadful, Joseph, just a bit of repair on something, nothing base nor wicked nor criminal—" Billy falters. He must see something in Joe's face which tells him the Sporkish forbearance is at an end. He holds up a hand in acknowledgement. "Let me show you the patient, all right? It's a bit special." And he already has the parcel on the table, so it's only a second before it stands revealed. It's quite a sight in a quiet café. "Spicy, eh? Those Victorians, they liked their toys. Their *erotomata*, to coin a phrase. Their *'ow's yer father*, though this looks more like *'ow's yer father, madame, and can I get you something to drink after, and maybe for your sister, too?* I knew some sisters like this once, mind. Frightful handful."

The object is indeed an automaton, a clockwork tableau in tin and lead paint, with fabric to flesh out the figures and a brass-and-steel movement visible through the glass floor. A lusty gamekeeper sort of fellow with red cheeks stands on one side, and two ladies in riding dresses stand on the other, and when Billy Friend flicks a switch the figures move around one another in a decreasing spiral until the gamekeeper's trousers come down and the ladies' dresses come up, and a somewhat improbable object emerges from the gamekeeper's burlap undergarments and goes smoothly into a matching aperture on Sister 1, while Sister 2 reclines on a wall and satisfies herself quite frantically, and then the whole thing starts to shake and Sister 1's head goes all the way around and the gamekeeper suddenly gets what appears to be a hernia and cannot continue, and the whole assemblage grinds and stutters to a halt.

Joe is furious to find that he is blushing. Billy Friend smirks at the waitress, who is staring with wide eyes at the contraption and looking not entirely unlike a sort of Sister 3. She collects herself and smirks back, then wanders off to the kitchen.

"For God's sake, Billy . . ." Joe says.

"Ahh, dear. Handsome fella like you, Joseph, you're a bit young to be so old. Tell you, why don't we go out together one night?"

"No, thank you. Tell me about the clockwork book."

"You used to be a lot more fun, Joe. You've got sensible, is what it is.

Terrible thing to happen to anyone, puts years on you. I know a place in Soho. No, not that kind of place, though if you've a mind . . . no, thought not. No, just a bar, matey, with convivial clients. Australians, mostly. Bored and up for it."

"Billy, I'm only going to say this once more, and then I'm going to assume you are pulling my pisser. And then we're going back to formal payments, cash on delivery. Right? Because I've got to open the shop. So, God help me: tell me about your doodah."

Billy Friend measures Joe and sees, if not resolve then boredom, and knuckles down.

"Party wants it cleaned up and repaired, made ready for use, and delivered to a gentleman in Wistithiel. That's Cornwall, by the way. Cash in advance, naturally, this being a hard and dishonest world." Billy Friend, in his time both hard and dishonest, sighs the sigh of a disappointed philanthropist. "Party has also supplied a tool to go with. I have taken to referring to this object as the whojimmy. It resembles no tool the like of which I have ever seen, and I am to inform you that you are permitted to keep it as a souvenir or part-payment. The whojimmy is apparently necessary to gain access to certain of the moving parts of the doodah. Thus not, in fact, merely a twofer, as our American cousins would have it, meaning two-for-one, but a threefer, which I believe is heretofore unknown in the world but which I am proud to bring before you now in the spirit of commerce and collegial respect." Billy smiles his winning smile.

"Who's the party?"

"A gentleman never tells."

"A lady."

"I think we may say without fear of breaching the seal of professional confidence that she is of the female persuasion."

"And there's no question that she owns these items?"

"None at all. Very respectable old duck, I thought."

"She acquired them in this estate sale you mentioned."

"Ah. There, Joseph, you have me. It is my unfortunate habit to refer to any object whose origin I am not at liberty to divulge as coming from an estate sale. It defers questions and creates a proper sense of *gravitas*."

He lifts his brows so that Joe can admire the clear, unquestionable honesty in his gaze. He waits. And waits. And waits, looking just a little hurt. Finally—

"Drop them round to me this afternoon," Joe says. Billy Friend grins and sticks out his hand to seal the deal. He pays the bill and collects a phone number from the waitress. Joe wraps the erotomaton in its tissue paper again, for transport.

"They miss you at the Night Market," Billy informs him from the door to the street, "ask after you. It's not the same without . . . well. You should come by."

"No," Joe Spork says. "I shouldn't."

And even Billy Friend doesn't quarrel with that one.

A tugboat hoots out on the river. Joe Spork puts Billy to one side—bad news always finds you in the end—and picks a key from the trolley and walks moodily across the road and down a narrow, mean little alley to a padlocked gate, and through a gap between two buildings, and finally to a row of rusted and barnacled doors facing the river. Traitor's gates, perhaps, or boathouses for very small boats. Or maybe, when the river was lower, nuclear-hardened bathing cabins. He has no idea. Ghost architecture, hanging on when the reason for it is past. Now, though, one of them stores the remaining bits of his past he doesn't wish to think too much about. He opens the door once every few months to make sure the water hasn't risen above the level of the little red splot of paint he marks on the wall each autumn, but aside from that he lets the place keep its secrets.

And secrets, undoubtedly, it has. One of the other doors, he happens to know, is not for storage at all, but dips down into an old ammunition dump, itself connected by a bit of Victorian sewer tunnel to a medieval crypt, which in turn gives on to a brewery. A man with an accurate map might walk from here to Blackheath, and never see the sun.

And somewhere down there, though he has never seen it, is the hallowed den where Mathew Spork prepared his first assaults on London's banking community. In a vaulted room of red brick and York stone, Mathew first fired his Tommy gun and learned to ride its kick. The young Joe, raised on a steady diet of comic books and tall tales, imagined that his father held off a Russian army in the sewers, killed aliens and monsters, and kept London safe for small boys. Every day was the day Dutch Schultz and Murder Inc. fought it out at the Palace Chophouse, and every day Joe's father came away unscathed. Through blazing, worshipful dreams, Mathew walked like a titan, wreathed in cordite smoke and glory.

Joe wonders, from time to time, where the gun is now. It sat for years in its case in Mathew's study, and the son of the House of Spork was not permitted to touch it. He would stare, wide-eyed, as Mathew cleaned it, and sometimes made bullets for it. But the gun was not a thing to be played with, not ever, not even on high days or birthdays.

One day, son, I'll teach you the proper way. But not today.

And never, as it turned out. Perhaps the gun is waiting down there, somewhere.

London is old, and each generation has added to its mysteries.

The door sticks, and he has to kick at it. Muck and more barnacles, and a splash as something alive makes itself scarce. A sign the river is getting cleaner. Mind you, that also means the door will rust faster. Oxygen, a bit of salt, and plenty of bacteria. He'll have to come down here and replace it. Or he could let the Thames have its way, and see Daniel's last bits and bobs go sailing away to Holland, and maybe walk a little lighter. Emptier, but lighter.

There's a wind-up torch hanging from a peg at shoulder height. It amuses him that crank-handle torches are all the rage now. He made this one under Daniel's supervision when he was nine. They even blew a bulb together, a glass balloon with a filament, pumped full of inert gas. This almost immediately exploded and had to be replaced with a commercial one.

The white lamplight picks out a mess of odds and ends: a china cow; a red and black molasses tin which Joe knows is full of decaying rubber bands; a terrifying marionette with all the strings cut. And there, on the far shelf, a stern, upright leather case in a clear plastic sack to protect it from the damp: Daniel's record collection.

He takes it down and then, for reasons he does not fully understand, draws out one record at random and puts the rest of the collection back on the shelf. After a moment he extracts from his pockets two further items—recent acquisitions, both—and rests them next to the record bag.

This is absolute paranoia. Like checking under your car for bombs because there's a bit of wiring on the tarmac.

He carries the record back to the warehouse under his coat.

The gramophone is a classic: horn in rich brown mahogany and body in inlaid oak, turntable covered in felt and chased in silver. Even the crank is beautiful. It took him months to repair it. The previous owner had had it stored in a loft full of bats.

He winds it slowly, because even in extremis and excitement you don't hurry a lady. The needle is old, so he puts in a new one. Then he makes a cup of tea, and reads the sleeve notes. Slim Gaillard. Joe has heard of Slim Gaillard. Tall, arachnodactyl Slim, who drank a bottle of whisky with every show and smoked all night, and could play the piano with his hands upside down. Not, please note, with his hands crossed while he himself lay on the piano stool, but actually inverted, with his knuckles.

He puts the record on the felt, and brings down the needle.

Well, that's not Slim Gaillard. That much I do know.

A woman's voice, soft and old and filled with emotion. She is not English. French? Or something more exotic? He isn't sure.

"I'm so sorry, Daniel."

A bucket of ice water over his head and down his neck. Hairs on his arms like guilty nightwatchmen, all awake. Impossible, impossible. A dead woman's voice. *The* dead woman. House of Spork's very own family ghost, speaking to him. It has to be. Who else would apologise to Daniel Spork by phonograph recording, made in some tiny booth in Selfridges for a few Imperial pennies? Who else would Daniel conceal in this bizarre way, discarding brother Slim and moving the label to this record so that no one would ever know what he had?

Frankie.

"I'm so, so sorry. I could not stay. I have work. It is the greatest thing I have ever done. The most important. It will change the world. The truth, Daniel. I swear it: the truth shall set us free!" Rich, splendid, throaty. An Edith Piaf voice. An Eartha Kitt voice. A voice filled with all the passion and regret of a refugee, and all the certainty of a prophet.

"You must never tell. They will stop me. The thing I must do now . . . it will uproot so many old and rotted trees, and there are men who have made their houses in them. There are men cut from their wood. All the bows and arrows in the world are made of this, and I will bring it down. I will make us better than we are. We must be better than this!"

Joe waits for her to say "I love you," but she doesn't, and the other side of the record is blank, an endless white noise spatter, like rain on old cast-iron guttering.

III

**Going postal;
amid the frills and bunting;
not your average music box.**

Edie Banister is feeling like a cow. More, she is conscious of sin. Not in any fleshy way, alas, but in her heart. She has transgressed against Joshua Joseph Spork. She has, in fact, stitched him up like a kipper, albeit for the good of mankind and the betterment of the human race. She persuaded herself that it was not personal. That this was the best way. Now, gazing at the little toy soldier he repaired so deftly, and recalling the stifled disappointment on his face when he saw that that was all she proposed to show him, she feels wicked. She is increasingly certain that some part of her has borne a grudge for longer than J. Joseph Spork has been alive, and has chosen this method to revenge itself. Duty, love, idealism and spite all discharged at once. She contemplates her soul, and finds it wanting.

"Bugger," she tells Bastion. He looks back at her with rosy-coloured marbles, and snuffles. She believes she detects approbation, even reinforcement in his suffering face, but it could be wind. No doubt she will know shortly if it is.

"Buggery bugger," she says. She picks up the toy soldier and puts it back in the box without a glance. It's too late to change horses. The deed is done. The wheels are in motion. Edie Banister, ninety years of age and a stalwart of the established order, has pushed the button on the revolution. She sighs again. It's so odd to be a supervillain, and at her age, too.

She has to admit privately that she may be mad. Although if so, it is a merciless, clear-sighted sort of madness and not at all what a lady might hope for. She has not lost her marbles or popped her garters, or any of the cosier sorts of madness she has observed in her contemporaries. She has, if anything, gone postal. She tries the expression on for size; it carries a sense of outrage, and fatigue.

Yes. Edie Banister has gone postal. A very British sort of postal which does not involve shouting, but rather a sudden and total reverse of a lifetime's perceptions. Although in truth, "sudden" is not entirely accurate. It happened by degrees, and actually by choice. She took a correspondence course in postality. She postalled herself up.

"I trusted you all to do the right thing," she tells fifty years of governments, lined up and sheepish in her mind, "I believed you'd get it right. And you!" she adds, to the electorate, "You lazy, venal, self-deluding . . . ooh, if you were my children, I'd . . ." But this brings her up short. None of them is her child. No sons or daughters for Edie Banister. Just Bastion, and the faded love of the one whose trust she has betrayed for half a human life. Betrayed in the name of stability and security. A few decades of calm, she reasoned at the time, and the world would set itself straight.

But somehow it all went wrong instead. The onward march of progress has wandered off down a dark alley and been mugged. The Berlin Wall and Vietnam; the Rwandan Genocide, the Twin Towers, Camp Delta; suicide bombings and global warming; even Vaughn bloody Parry, the little suburban nightmare who lived just around the corner, who killed and killed and no one knew because no one bothered to find out. Edie Banister had given her loyalty to an empty throne. There was no progress. No stability. There was just the question of whether things happened far enough away.

The Parry thing had been the end of her comfortable certainty. It began, according to the broadsheets, in a new allotment patch in some midway town called Redbury. The council had at last untrousered the cash and purchased a stretch of green once part of a railway siding, sold in Thatcher's time to make apartments and studios for wealthy buyers who never showed up. A vegetable competition was mooted, and organic food for the locality, and a sense of community and all the other things Britain no longer did because finance was cheaper and faster and the housing market made money out of nothing. And then they turned the first spadeful and it was over before it began. A grinning corpse, wrapped in a tartan blanket, and then another and another, and the burg of Redbury had a serial killer to call its own.

Edie could not help but notice that when Vaughn Parry tortured a prisoner and buried the corpse seven inches down in sandy soil, he was a monster, but when the same thing was done at the behest of her own government in a cellar overseas, that was an unfortunate necessity.

Well, perhaps it was. But if so, the world which made it necessary could go hang.

She had taken for a while to going out every night with Bastion, walking the streets and staring up at the houses and offices of a city she wasn't sure she knew any longer. *Mad Old Edie and her eyeless dog, side by side in the London fog.* Yes. Mad, in the American sense. And, alone in the vast encyclopedia of "furious of Derbyshire," Edie Banister had the power to make a difference to everything which was infuriating her. A mysterious difference, whose precise nature she did not understand, but whose originator swore would rock the world and unravel the darkness of a thousand years. A gift of science to a world of horrors.

On a Tuesday evening, with the sound of the BBC World Service (soon to be discontinued) in the background, she got a pen and a piece of paper and wrote down a flow chart of her personal revolution. An item to be acquired, and a man to put it where it must go. These in turn would entail disguises, forgeries . . . but not so many as that. More a confidence trick, really, than a covert operation. All at arm's length, of course, because there could be consequences, and because her name might still trigger alarms in places which must remain oblivious just a little longer.

And now, looking at Joe Spork's business card and stroking her eyeless dog, she thinks about those consequences and feels like a cow. She has webbed the young Spork into a muddle of almighty proportions. It was necessary, if distasteful, and ultimately he will be fine. Once they look at things seriously, they will see he was a patsy.

If they look at things seriously. If they take the time. If they don't need a scapegoat for the redtops. If they feel generous. And there's that word again: "necessary." A magic word to excuse a multitude of sins, and all it really means is "easier this way than the other."

The only thing she need do now is sit back and watch, and know that she has discharged her debt and made a difference. There's no danger of anything really bad happening to him. All the old ghosts are surely laid to rest.

So why, having ascertained weeks back that he would do for item two, has she been dragging him here ever since to work on junk? Getting to know him. Discovering that he's sweet and a bit lost?

No reason at all.

Except that she is feeling, as already noted, like a cow. Cow, cow, cow.

And to be honest . . . *was* it necessary? It may have been. It's quite possible that he's the only person around with the skills to do the job right. If he learned from his grandfather. If he paid attention. If there are complications any halfway competent clockworker couldn't deal with. If, if, if. She is conscious that she has heard these arguments before, in the pusillanimous mouths of modern politicians.

She peers at her reflection in the tabletop, wondering. Joshua Joseph Spork, grandson of the great love of her life, but not, obviously, her own. Evidence of her insufficiency.

Is it possible that she has put him in the line of fire out of spite?

Her reflection won't look at her.

"Mooo," says Edie Banister.

So now, having been the bad fairy, she will have to be the good one, too, and keep an eye on him.

And with that decision, she finds herself delighted. *Hah. Hah! Hold onto your hats, gents, and avert your eyes, you rose-petalled ladies in your mopsy, mumsy woollens. Banister is back! And this time she's leading the charge!*

Bastion looks up at her, and slowly staggers to his feet. A moment later, he turns his back on her and growls ferociously, then cranes his head round for her approval.

"Yes, darling," she says, "you and me against the world."

Which is when she hears a hiss of indrawn breath, and moves abruptly from jubilant to very, very serious.

She is not alone in her flat.

Edie Banister opens her bedroom door to find three men, the middle one very large, standing in her living room in attitudes suggesting that her arrival has come at an unexpected time. They wear solid shoes and drab, ho-hum clothes. The large one is carrying a hammer, held loosely in his left hand, and his zip-up tracksuit top is bulgy under the left arm. He has a small, ski-jump nose, the product of reconstructive surgery, fatuous on his slab of a face. His wingers are younger. Trainee bastards. Edie switches over to automatic. *Action stations, old cow*, she thinks, *these lads have your end in view. Too late to stop it all from starting.* The deed is done. This last meeting with Joe Spork was for the sake of her conscience, not her devious plan. That was set in motion some days back, oh, yes, and indirectly. This is consequence, not prevention. *But in time to take you out of the picture, sure enough. So.*

She smiles, a dotty old lady smile.

"Oh, goodness," she says, "but you made me jump. You must be Mr. Big—"—*oh, yes, bloody brilliant, Edie: Mr. Big, because he is big, and so many people have adjectives for family names. Dig yourself out, or fall at the first*—"—landry, from the Council. I'm glad Miss Hampton let you in, I'm terribly sorry to be so late!" *There. Someone else is due here at any moment, and I think you're them. Best come back later, eh? Finish me off in the quiet time.*

The newly-christened Mr. Biglandry hesitates. Edie steps brightly towards him, hand out, and he moves his body to suggest he may take it. Edie has no intention of touching him, oh, no, *not and get a hug from a lad with shoulders so broad. Though in our younger days, we might have enjoyed climbing a mountain like that, mightn't we? Oh, yes, indeed.* "Oh, where are my manners?" She takes her hand away. The junior bastards are spreading out to block her escape. *I must just get some milk, darlings, to make you tea, all right? Hah! They'd snap me in two. Softly, softly, old cow. You've a long way to go and a short time to get there. Objective: escape. Nothing else. So.* "I'll put the kettle on, shall I, and would you mind moving the furniture? I'm too old, I'm afraid, I did try, but the flesh is weak. Not like yours, Mr. Biglandry. And who are these?"

Junior Bastard A sticks out his hand when her gaze falls upon him and mutters "James." It clearly isn't his name, but Junior Bastard B and Mr. Biglandry stare at him as if he has taken his trousers off. *Hah! I fancy that's an instant fail on your test, young Jimmy, and quite right too. Mr. Biglandry will want a word later, I imagine, about talking to the mark.* "Hello!" Edie waves daftly. "And you must be Biglandry the younger, I can see the family resemblance! Was it George?" *You're both stone killers, there is that, but he's a red-faced old git and you've something pale and Hungarian about you, Georgie-boy, I wouldn't wonder your Dad was AVH, no, I would not, and likely a goon just like you.* She smiles even wider. "Would you mind pushing the bolt across? Sometimes the door rattles in the wind and it gives me a start." George Biglandry looks at Dad, and Dad nods. Edie slips into the kitchen: knives, rolling pins, the microwave oven (she pictures herself jamming the door open and threatening to cook them, the thing plugged in behind her and beeping, a little picture of a chicken in blue neon on the dash), *no, no, and no.* Edie Banister knows where she is going. *Flick the switch on the kettle. Now they have to separate you from that, indeedy they do.* No gentleman wants a lap full of the hot stuff when he's killing old ladies. *Permanent damage can occur.* Edie summons her first secret weapon.

"Bastion! Dar-ling? Bast-ion? Mummy's got a bit of pie, yes, she has, hasn't she, yessywessy, she has!" *And may the good Lord have mercy on your souls.*

It is not the hour for pie. Bastion knows it. He knows that Edie knows it, too. They have long ago settled between them that he is to be disturbed between three and nine only in the direst of emergencies or if there is steak. The steak should be meltingly soft and warmed over in the pan. The emergencies are more exigent: fire, earthquake, rains of frogs, the arrival of a cat in the building. Certainly, pie does not figure. Bastion's afternoon nap is sacrosanct.

"Bastion?" She looks around. He is in her bedroom, of course, at the foot of the bed: does not stir from it except at two-ish to go out onto the balcony and pee on passing truants. Edie smiles at Mr. Biglandry, who is busy preparing to insert himself between her and the kettle. James and George are still in the living room. Edie feints for the kettle, and Biglandry jumps a bit. His eyes narrow. She grins at him, a little wolfish, pro-on-pro. He looks back, hard-faced. Edie rests her hand on the Russell Hobbs. "Would you mind?" *You think this is endgame. It is barely begun. You want this? This kettle? Shall I throw it at you? But then there are the boys, no doubt eager to help out in doing me in. You may have this round.* Except Edie knows fine well, and Mr. Biglandry almost realises, she never intended to use the kettle for anything other than this. She brushes past as he takes possession of the boiling water. She opens the door to the bedroom, and Bastion barges out, bristling. He sees George first, and immediately charges over, yowling, and starts nipping at his ankles. *Who is this man, that comes to disturb my time of slumber? Woe unto you, that are rash enough to let your ankles within my scope. Behold! You shall not leave but that you are shorter by one foot, this much I promise you . . .*

"Oh, Bastion, darling, no!" Edie Banister says with manifest insincerity. She smiles broadly at George, who scowls at her and glances at his boss. But Edie is in motion. *Too slow, boys, far and away.* Bastion, unwelcome playmate, apparently decides that James has better legs. He lunges for them, and his single solid tooth makes an ugly hole in James's calf. *I should think that's jolly painful*, Edie reflects, as James swears. He lashes out with his foot, but Bastion knows this game well, and has latched onto the other leg. James would have to kick himself, and few people . . . no. No, James actually is that stupid. There's a thud, and James goes a bit white. It's amazing how much you can hurt yourself with your own toecap. Bastion, sensing victory, spins around several times and scents Mr. Biglandry. *No, darling. He's out of your league.* But Bastion is game, and more than game. His performance so far has made Biglandry Père nervous enough that he backs up, glancing at Edie with the outrage of non-dog owners: *'Ere, lady, control this dog or I'll 'ave the law on you!*

Like Hell you will.

Edie ducks into the bedroom, and lunges for her knicker drawer and Secret Weapon No. 2, amid the frills and bunting. *Yes, knickers! That's what I shall need. And it bloody would have been, too, in fifty-nine. I could have changed into something more comfortable and they'd have carried me to the nick and handed themselves in . . .* but honesty compels her to admit that even in fifty-nine it might not have been so. *Corset. Bloomers. Tights. Popsocks, how I loathe you. Woollen leggings—the shame. Edie Banister, toast of the Fighting 16th, swathed in bloody sheep's fur and with all the allure of a toast rack. Hard times. Suspender belt, that's more like it; garters, and stockings, and lace, oh my! And now I've thrown my memories on the floor, where the bloody hell is the item we came for? Because if I've put it in another drawer then we may assume I am about to die.* But the other belt is in her hands, cool and thick, brown leather and a strange, ancient smell. She cleans it once a month, checks it, the way most people do their accounts. And once—Edie Banister grins—once, she did actually wear this outfit as lingerie, to the absolute abandonment and lust of her lover and, she is forced to admit, herself.

Mr. Biglandry shoves the door to Edie's boudoir open with a very impatient hand. He has his hammer raised to crack her skull into as many pieces as he can. *Why a hammer?* Edie wonders. *Maybe because it's so unprofessional, so thuggish. Everyone will look for a lunatic—and you can always find one, if you try hard enough.* "It's fucking time, you crazy old bag," Mr. Biglandry says, angry now at the delay. Perhaps he has somewhere to be. "It is fucking time."

"Yes," Edie Banister says. "I believe it is." And she turns around, holding the gun in the Weaver stance.

Mr. Biglandry says "Fuck" again, but in a more impressed, appalled way. He drops the hammer and goes for his own gun (Edie guesses it will prove to be an automatic, unlike her own, which is a revolver). Edie shoots him in the head. The revolver makes an absolutely huge noise. To her relief, the back of Mr. Biglandry's head stays on, although it's clearly a close-run thing. She hears, in the other room, the sound of George saying "Fuck" as well, percussively, and trying to pull something from his waistband. *Idiot.* If George does not shoot himself in the penis in the next two seconds, he will get the gun out and start firing it, but anyone who sticks a gun in his jeans is probably not someone with surgical weapon skills. He will fire randomly. Edie's neighbours might get hurt. Or Bastion. She turns, and fires three times directly through the plasterboard wall, angling so that any misses will hit the bricks of the fireplace in the room beyond. The third shot makes a *splunch* noise, and George goes down. Edie moves, in case James is about to try the same thing, and sees him exactly where he was, next to the door, a look of absolute confusion on his young, sallow face. She points the gun near him rather than at him. Bastion, emerging from the kitchen in pursuit of Mr. Biglandry, finds his foe already fallen and clambers up on top of him to indicate his conquest. *Died of fright. I am mighty. You may now applaud.*

Edie looks sharply at James. "Get rid of it."

James has a gun, but it's in his pocket and, when it comes to it, not loaded. Sheepish, he puts the ammunition down on the floor next to the weapon. Edie shakes her head. He shrugs at her, surrendered.

"Who sent you?"

"Don't know. Honestly!"

"Ever see them?"

"No! They had hats on. Or sheets. Like in Iran!"

Like in Iran. Yes, she might know someone matching that description. She sighs.

"Have you got a mum?"

"Yes. In Doncaster."

"Best piss off back there, ey?"

"Yes, ma'am."

She nods, then peers at him.

"This your first?"

"Oh, God, yeah. Christ."

"Don't hang about. Don't go and tell anyone what happened. Best to vanish, all right? Go stay with your mum. No one cares if you didn't die, so long as you aren't seen again."

"Right."

"Ever. And James? Get a proper job," Edie says.

"Yes, ma'am."

"Now, I'm going to pick up two bags and I'm going to walk out of here and we won't see one another ever again. You're going to sit in that chair, facing the window, and you're going to ignore me for the five minutes I'll still be here, and then you're going to contemplate your soul in silence for another ten minutes in the company of these dead men you once called friends. And then . . . ?"

"Doncaster."

"Good boy."

Edie Banister waits until he sits in the chair and turns it round, and then she goes back into her bedroom and collects her flight bag (like the gun, maintained once a month to be sure it's all ready to go at any time) and Bastion's travel kit. She collects the dog, steps over Mr. Biglandry and George, and closes the door on James. In the hallway she wrestles briefly with her collapsible umbrella. Edie considers the name to be strictly truthful: the umbrella collapses well, but has issues with opening. Normally she wouldn't bother, but today it looks like rain, and having sent two men to their graves to preserve her own life, she has no intention of dying of pneumonia before seeing this business through. Death is a reality for Edie Banister, and has been since she was young. All the same, no reason to invite it. Bastion would be devastated.

The umbrella conquered, she glowers up at the grumbling sky, and leaves Rallhurst Court for ever.

The same London sky, grey with a touch of orange from the street lights, unburdens itself of sheets of blinding rain as Joe Spork hurries through the streets of Soho. He has given up on the telephone and decided to make his representations to Billy Friend in person. Since he is here, and since he is very quickly getting soaked through, he is also visiting a stringy, irritating man called Fisher, a former burglar, present fence, and a full-time member of the Mathew Spork nostalgia club. Fisher, not even a member of Mathew's outer circle, is one of the few people he can turn to on the subject of the unlawful and strange without incurring painful social obligations. Even so, Joe is troubled by a powerful sense of self-inflicted injury, and his grandfather's voice, now doleful, is telling him *I told you so.* He hunches his shoulders and buries his chin in the collar of his coat: a big man trying to become a turtle.

A bus—last of the much-despised bendy variety, as doomed as the clockwork business and equally clever and impractical—sprays him with road water and he yells and waves furiously, then catches his reflection in a shop window and wonders, not for the first time of recent days, who this person is who has taken up residence in what ought to be his life.

Fisher's shop is a merry little place with wind chimes and an aura of shabby hippy mercantilism, squeezed between a tailor and a mysterious bead-curtained place which conducts business entirely in Hungarian. Fisher has a lot of space because his family have lived here since before it was expensive. Customers can sit in an enclosed courtyard for a hookah and a cup of Turkish coffee. Fisher makes it himself, boiling the coffee and the sugar with his secret ingredient, which he allows particularly favoured customers—which is all of them—to learn, and which varies depending on what he's got in the fridge. Joe has known it to be lemon peel, cocoa powder, pepper, paprika, and on one occasion even a half-spoonful of fish soup. Fisher claims that each of these represents a different member of his Turkish family on his mother's side, but since his mother was and is from Billingsgate it probably doesn't matter that this is a lie: no wrathful Stambul cousin is going to show up and demand to know what the Hell crap he is putting in that perfectly good coffee, to the ruination of their shared good name.

"W-hoo is a-that?" Fisher cries out as the chimes go, all Turkic gravitas, but when he pokes his weasel head around the door frame from the back, his face breaks into a wide smile. "It's Joe! Big Joe! King of the Clockmen! The man in person and himself! 'Ullo, Maestro, what can I do you for?"

"I'm out of the loop, Fisher—" And then, holding up a forestalling finger, because Fisher's mouth opens to issue an enthusiast's reproach, "Yes, I know, that's what I wanted. But now I've got a question and there's only one place I can go, isn't there? Because you know everything."

"I do. It's true," Fisher preens. And in terms of the life of London's post-legals, he really does.

"I had a visit," Joe says, "from two men from a museum which doesn't exist. One fat, the other thin. Cultured. My heart said police. Titwhistle and Cummerbund."

Fisher shakes his head. "Nowt."

"Nothing?"

"Never heard of 'em, never bribed 'em, never even forgotten 'em. Sorry."

"What about witches?"

"Married one."

"Monks, then. All in black and—" But Fisher is on his feet and locking the door, closing the shop, and in his eyes is a feverish alarm Joe has never seen before, didn't think existed in Fisher, who is always chirpy or pompous by turns, and never, ever ruffled.

"Jesus!" Fisher says. "Those fuckers! Brother Sheamus and his bloody ghosts! Christ on a bike, boy! They're not *here*, are they?"

"No, of course not."

"But you've seen them? They came to you?"

"Yes, they—"

"Fuck, Joe, but you put a strain on friendship, you do—what do they want?"

"A book."

"A book? A *book*? Fucking give it to them, you daft streak of piss! Give it to them and thank them for being so kind as to take it off your hands rather than their preferred option which would be *taking your fucking hands off*, and then fucking run away and get a proper job in a far-off land. All right? Fuck! And fuck off, as well!"

"Who are they?"

"The sodding Recorded Man, is who they are," Fisher snarls.

Joe stares. "The what?"

"You don't remember? I told you when you were a nipper, your mother was so angry she nearly popped."

Indeed he does remember; it had given him nightmares for weeks. A London ghost story, whispered by the children of the Night Market.

Picture a man, the tale went, in a bed of silk sheets. And picture all around him wires and cameras and men taking notes. Everything about him is written down. They are making a record of him: his breaths, his words, his pulse, his diet, his scent, his chemistry—even the fluctuations of electricity in his skin. As he grows weaker—for he is very old now, and injured, and sick—they press filaments of metal through holes in his skull and into the fabric of the brain itself, and record the chasing flashes of thoughts running from fold to fold of the grey stuff inside his head.

And through all this, he is conscious, and aware. Is he a prisoner? A millionaire? Does he feel pain or horror at his own predicament? Does he have any idea why this is happening? It's so bizarre. And yet somewhere, somewhere, it is real, and he is lying there. Perhaps, when he is gone, they will need someone else. Perhaps they will need you.

Joe left the lights on for nine days the first time he heard it, and when he finally slept each night, he saw only the eyes of the Recorded Man, glaring at him from his prison of wires. *Perhaps they will need you.*

Fisher nods jerkily, still angry and afraid. "Right, so Sheamus's lot are the original. They're all about machinery and they sit and watch recordings of the bloke who founded their outfit. It's what they have instead of church. Revered relics of every thought he ever had, or something. I don't know because I don't ask because I don't want to end up in a fucking jar! It's all a bit Dear Leader, but one way and another it makes them scary as typhus, all right? They're a power in the world."

"Since when?"

"Since for ever. Your dad had a run-in with them way back. He got everyone together and showed them the exit. Even then it was touch and go."

"I don't remember that."

"Well, you were little. I was a tiddler, too, but, you know . . ." Fisher contrives to make it sound as if this means that Mathew considered him Joe's elder brother, the crook he never had.

"And now?"

"Now it's different, isn't it? There's no one like Mathew, but there's a lot more coppers."

"So they're careful."

Fisher shrugs yes. "But they don't ask nicely and they don't ask twice. Cold and surgical, and not like an aspirin and a lie down, like ice in the bathtub and selling your kidneys for cash. They've got a hospital somewhere, or a hospice. It's a bloody pit. People go in, they don't come out."

"Who are they? Where do they come from?"

"For all I know they're God's own thugs, straight from the Holy City. I met one once, he come in a place I was thinking of renting, told me to piss off. And do you know what else he said? He said: *If I have the mind of Napoleon and the body of Wellington, who am I?* Mad as a fucking box of frogs."

"Fisher—"

"All right! All right. Thirty seconds of wisdom. Then you go. Okay?"

"Okay."

"Fine. The way I hear, once upon a time, they were into good works. I mean, they're monks, yes? Elevate the soul, cherish the meek. Then the world got less amenable to the consolations of the Mother Church and they went a bit funny. Out with the old, in with the new, and the new is some silver-tongued bastard and his own personal heavy mob. Orphans, is the way I hear it, schooled by him for him at some old private house, so that's all they know and they don't care to learn more. Now it's conversion by fire and sword and let God sort it out."

"What do they want?"

"Whatever they feel like. And antiques. They've got a thing for antiques."

"Why? Fisher, this is important, they—"

Fisher cuts him off, one hand coming down sideways like a blade. "I don't want to know! All right? You've got something they want, give it to them. You're not Mathew, and that's your choice, but Honest Joe can't take them on. It's that simple. They're bloody scary. And that's all I'm saying and, old friend or not, you can piss off!"

Fisher throws open the back door and bundles Joe out into the yard, then slams the door and brings down the shutter.

Outside and now truly unsettled, Joe Spork ducks his head down and shoves his hands into his pockets like a man who has been given the Spanish Archer by his girl. He walks purposefully but not hurriedly, and very shortly slips back down into the Tosher's Beat.

At lunchtime on the day after the conversation at the greasy spoon, a bored courier rings on Joe Spork's doorbell and hands over a box containing a familiar piece of kinetic smut and a brown-paper parcel which promises to be Billy Friend's notorious doodah. The alternative being the quarterly VAT accounts, Joe hastens to open the parcel.

Item: all right, yes, it's a diary or a journal, no question about that. He sniffs at it; old books have a pleasing smell to them. This one is unusual. There's a sharp tang of brine and a whiff of chemicals, and beneath it a rich resiny note of old, old leather. Has it been under water? Wrapped in oilcloth? Hm. The cover is flexible, almost rubbery, and the leather is cross-hatched with wandering lines. Stamped into what he takes to be the front—the technical term is "debossed," like "embossed," but in reverse—is a curious figure like an inside-out umbrella or a funny sort of key.

Joe opens the book cautiously, and yes, again, it's an odd duck: along each page at the edge opposite the spine there is a half inch of perforated paper. The whole thing has been bound from individual sheets of stiff paper, and each edge—so far as he can tell—is different. The matrix is a four-by-four square or—if each page is taken as a single block of information—a four-by-sixteen column separated into groups of letters four holes deep. A hundred or more pages; not an insignificant amount of information, then, but hardly a vast trove, either. A longish piece of music for a pianolo, perhaps.

The spine itself has a dowel—no, it's metal—a rod running through it, protruding slightly at either end. Not a spine, then: an axle? The endpapers are marbled in rose and turquoise, and sketched over the pattern in pen is a brisk, clear diagram or schematic—electrical, and beyond his ken, but apparently for some sort of brewing or distilling apparatus which is oddly familiar. Where has he seen that?

A certain kind of mind—his grandfather was like this to an extent—is always trying in a spiritual sense to make the perfect mousetrap. Joe has the impression that it is an impromptu sketch, that this volume was not originally intended to have anything written in it at all, but at some point its owner was trapped without an alternative source of paper and defaced it. A long train journey, perhaps—there are periods of comparatively clear text and sudden jolts which could be points. Something which might be a teapot segues into a design for a fishtank sort of item and then dissolves into what he takes to be rather highfalutin mathematics. Quote: "Do something for the elephant." Quote: "I have written it all in my book." Quote: "The coffee is ghastly." Fine. So what's this then, if not a book? Well, a notepad, obviously; a jotter. A doodah.

Item: or rather, *items*, plural. A mixed bag of gears and sprockets, ratchets and cogs, bevelled and conventional, large to (very, very) small. The part of Joe which solves puzzles twitches and rolls its shoulders. That piece would go with that one, and that one would . . .

Jumping the gun, boy. Sure, put it together all higgledy-piggledy, and what will you have? Junk! A pile of nothing. I taught you better.

His grandfather's voice, husky with time and distance.

"I miss you, you know."

Don't be daft, boy. I was old before you were young.

"Still."

And another thing: don't talk to the dead. People will get the wrong idea.

"How about if I claim you're my imaginary friend?"

. . . You need a girl.

"Probably."

A helpmeet.

"A what?"

"A help meet for him." As in a person suitable to share his life.

"I really do."

He's lost the thread of the conversation. Daniel Spork never gave him advice about girls. Perhaps his own disastrous love life prevented it. Joe's imagination baulks at putting words in his mouth on that score.

Move on.

Item: a clamp or fitting, with armature, of a size to embrace the doodah and turn the pages. He touches the end of the armature curiously, and finds it briefly sticky with static. Curious, he taps it lightly against a page from the book. Yes, the page turns, and yes, the static is gone when he goes to lift the armature away again. He taps the next page, and it clings. Moves it, puts it down, and the charge is gone. Clever. He has no idea how it works. Something in the arm, perhaps, rubbing along the metal interior. Smart: clockwork doesn't take harm from static the way electronics does. A little clean occasionally and it barely notices. It's almost a credo: the right tool in the right place.

Item: a strange little ovoid box or ball, engraved rather splendidly on the outside, and by hand, no less. A spiral pattern, like a galaxy or a conch shell. The Golden Ratio, but don't believe all that muck you read about it. Very heavy for its size. Unless the ball is made of gold, there must be a weight or flywheel within. No indication of how it opens, though there is a seam. He turns it in his hand. Something inside goes *clish-tink*, which his trained ear recognises as a bad noise. Not a disastrous noise, but definitely a broken noise.

He puts the ball in a smooth hollow on the bench. Any number of things in his world are spherical or nearly so, and many of those should not be allowed to roll around. For a while, the company which supplied him with a particularly ferocious acid for cleaning and etching supplied it in round-bottomed containers so that you would have to use their rather expensive clamps and retorts along with the acid. Poison, *1d*; cure, a guinea. Well, anyway—the ball settles snugly into the hollow. Joe stretches, hearing things pop in his back and arms, then leans back over the bench. Must get a proper chair. Must get a proper chair. Yes, and half a dozen other things I can't afford.

Item: the whojimmy, precise function unknown. A tool, for the unscrewing of magic bolts and the opening of locks whose existence we do not presently apprehend. A thing made for a specific purpose. An object of destiny. A funny-looking gadget with a handle at one end and a strange twisting loop which winds around it, almost like the basket hilt on an old duelling sword. Joe waves the whojimmy dramatically, then stops. Like the ball, it's surprisingly dense.

And finally, a square of white card with words written on it in felt tip: a reminder from Billy that the said object is to be treated with respect and could he please have the bawdy gamekeeper in a hurry because his lady client is getting pressing.

So then: to the Batcave! Or at least, to work. He closes the door and puts the sign in the window saying "please ring."

The erotomaton (he glances at it guiltily, the fruit and milk he is ignoring in favour of cake) shouldn't be too hard to fix. It probably won't be all that interesting, either. It can wait until tomorrow.

He ponders the figures slumped in their first positions—the most orderly *ménage à trois* Joe Spork has ever heard of. He knows a few experimenters in polyamory, has observed from the outside the curious triangular relationships and sexual flat-shares, and come to the conclusion that in most cases there's rather more *poly* than *amory*, for all the protestations to the contrary. It's not that it can't be done, just that the odds of finding one person to share your days are bad enough, without looking for two who can also share their lives with each other and remain content with the situation whatever perturbations may arise along life's curious road.

Hard to find just one person, indeed. The big warehouse is very empty today, and the sloosh of the Thames is sorrowful. He makes tea, temporarily replacing the missing foot of his kettle with a pink reminder notice from the gas company, folded three times. He is reasonably certain he has paid it. Sort that out tomorrow.

At the workbench, tea in hand (the approved commencement of a difficult task, the stricture of patience to be borne strongly in mind, lest one be hasty and make an irretrievable error early in the proceedings) he contemplates the fragments before him. All right, well, simple enough: copy and photograph it all. Easy, in these digital days. Joshua Joseph has no great hatred of modern technology—he just mistrusts the effortless, textureless surfaces and the ease with which it trains you to do things in the way most convenient to the machine. Above all, he mistrusts duplication. A rare thing becomes a commonplace thing. A skill becomes a feature. The end is more important than the means. The child of the soul gives place to a product of the system.

By contrast, here is his grandfather's workdesk, with the tools Daniel Spork constructed for himself. It is polished by time, unvarnished but smooth, and on the left is a slight imprint: the pressure of the old man's elbow. On the right, a vise and a new rubber hose feeding an ancient Bunsen burner. Greying scars from heat, pale ones from tools. The grain of the wood is silvery, and in those lines is the literal DNA of the House of Spork, Daniel's own co-mingled with his grandson's—blood drawn by a moment's inattention, tears choked out in times of sorrow, each drop carrying the blueprint of Daniel's body, and Joe's. Even Mathew is represented, probably, because Papa Spork was no stranger to this bench, for all that in his hands it became an armoury, a pouring place of molten lead and sharp-scented powders: a den of alchemy.

For anything really important, Joe prefers something with a history, an item which can name the hand which assembled it and will warm to the one who deploys it. A thing of life, rather than one of the many consumer items which use humans to make more clutter; strange parasitic devices with their own weird little ecosystems. For reference and archive, though, he's glad to have his baby Canon with its lens by Zeiss.

So. Three pictures from each angle, close and distant. Each fragment documented. He feels Grandpa Spork's measuring gaze upon his back: Daniel Spork, dead these seven years and some, eyes bright in anticipation of a puzzle—and better, a puzzle shared with his best-beloved student, the son of his wastrel son.

Joe smiles to himself, a little sadly, in acknowledgement of the beloved, irascible dead. He doesn't look over his shoulder, doesn't want to see the empty room. Instead, he asks a question of the air, and lets his mind throw back Daniel's responses.

"What next, old man?"

Use your eyes, boy. What are you looking at?

"It's a doodah."

Joseph, no. No, no, and no. In the first place, tell me you have not been dealing with that William Friend?

"Once in a while."

Pfft.

"What's the second place?"

Idiot child of my criminal son, you know what I am going to say. You do. Of course you do.

Of course, he does. He knows the speech by heart. *Seek the stricture. Find the lesson, the purpose, the essence. The rest is window dressing, and will give itself to you entirely, if you first understand the thing and the nature of the thing.*

Joe Spork's grandfather believed—or sometimes believed, and always maintained—that every object on Earth was created by God with the capacity to impart to the attentive student some virtue or grace.

Consider glass. What is the nature of glass?

It is a curious material used for windows and drinking vessels. It must be created in a crucible, purified and smelted until its nature becomes clear—and during this period it can be ruined by a moment's inattention, which might also prove lethal to the unwatchful glazier; it is beautiful, friable, explosive and transparent.

Go on. What else?

At every stage in its existence—when it is molten, and must be poured from its cup at the end of a long pole; when it is glowing, and can be blown, but remains so vigorously hot that any organic thing placed in proximity to it will instantly take fire; when it is cooling and clear, and has acquired some definition, but will still shatter if it is not cooled with painful slowness in a series of incubating ovens; and when it is cold, and brittle, and the merest impact from a metal point causes it to become a collection of lethal knives which cut so finely that the nerves are sliced clean and a man may miss the fact that he is injured until he smells the blood or sees it upon his shirt—glass is a lesson.

Yes, Joe. Precisely. And so the lesson, the stricture of glass?

"Caution." He says it aloud, and jumps a little at the sound of his own voice.

Well and good. A salutary inquisition. Very spiritual.

Joe Spork, with his grandfather's waspish ghost at his elbow, considers the object before him.

So, question: what do we have here?

Answer: a mess. A book which is also a set of punchcards. A tool which doesn't fit anything. Fragments. A ball which may be an egg, but which, if so, is locked. There's something inside, but that need not mean it's intended to open. Like those Chinese concentric spheres. It's heavy. Gold, maybe. There's a design—a clue? Or just an embellishment?

He sets it aside for the moment, and continues his inventory: here's the whojimmy, right enough. One end carved mahogany wood with a pommel or stud, the other a funny, tangled thing with a circular mouth and a roller-coaster track of polished metal which doubles back on itself. Some ornamentation on one side of the track, the other side very smooth. Some mistake, perhaps, in the connecting of one with the other? This could be a child's game, a wild, weird variant of ball-and-cup. Cut steel, by the look of it, and quite pretty in a way. The Victorians rather liked steel for ornamentation, though this isn't that old. Still . . . hard to see what possible use it could be. Heavy, too. Oh, blast, and how has that happened?

He peers, vexed, at the whojimmy, and scolds himself. The tool is covered in a thin layer of grime and grease. A culpable error, to allow that to happen.

Or, no: not grease. He runs a finger over the strange stuff. Eyes are overrated. Touch. Touch is important. It feels dry and feathery. Cold. *Iron filings.*

The whojimmy is magnetic.

He sits back again, considering. The tool and the ball must interact, if any of them do. The whojimmy is the key. The ball is the keyhole. The book and the fragments fit together with the ball to make . . . what?

Question, then: what is the defining characteristic of this thing? He grins. "This thing." Not "these things." He has decided they are one object. Good. Follow the instinct. So: it is baroque, even Byzantine. It is complex. And yet, above all, it is elegant. His grandfather's voice comes back, excited.

I once saw a very elegant design from Shanghai. A sealed box in ivory. Traced on the outside, a pattern. Move a magnet over the pattern outside, and on the inside a metal rod slides through a maze and touches all the pins in the right order to open the box. Voilà! The original magnet was set in a ring, of course, so that the whole thing was like magic. A child's toy, for a princess. Like casting a spell, yes?

I showed it to your grandmother. She made love to me. Then we opened it together. The magnet was hers.

He remembers the conversation, an evening spent in this very room with a bottle of Ardanza and a plate of Italian sausage. Joe the apprentice, Daniel the mentor, sharing confidences and romances over glass after glass of Spanish red. Tricks of the trade and reminiscences, rolled together, and so convivial that Joe had eventually been so emboldened as to ask the unaskable question.

"Who was she, Grandfather?"

But Grandpa Spork did not answer questions about the woman he loved. It was known that he met her in France in the thirties, and together they had a child. It was all very Bohemian, very modern, and they never married. When the Germans invaded, Daniel and the boy escaped, but his lover was elsewhere and had to be left behind. She found him again after the war, but by then everything was different for reasons which could not be spoken aloud.

Mathew's mother, Frankie.

Frankie was the almost-glimpsed dream of the House of Spork, invoked with caution lest the use of her name summon her—or rather, fail to do so, to the jagged sorrow of her husband and the startling fury of her son. Swamp gas. An atmospheric phenomenon. A myth.

So, then. A magnet and a box. He waves the magnetic whojimmy in the general direction of the doodah. Something clunks, but beyond that it has no effect. Not surprising: you wouldn't make something like this and then set it up so that a single movement near a magnet would do the job. He grips the whojimmy. It's awkward. What's this wild tangle good for? Except, it can't be awkward. This thing is elegant. It is the shape it should be. More, the holding of it suggests the employment. With the handle against his palm, he is abruptly certain: it invites you to do the right thing. *What I want to do is what I am supposed to want to do.*

So . . . what does he want to do? Flourish it. But not wildly. Slowly. In a measured way. He wants to roll it.

To roll it.

He peers . . . Roller-coaster track . . . track. Now that he looks closely, part of the tangle is ratcheted . . . oh.

He hefts the ball in one hand, weighs the whojimmy in the other. Fiendish yet obvious. Hidden in plain sight. Perfect for preventing casual scrutiny, not hellishly hard to use in real life . . . very much in keeping with the mind behind this puzzle. A mind, he is increasingly sure, which was as bonkers as it was brilliant.

He slots the ball through the mouth of the whojimmy. It fits. It rolls along the tracks, the spiral engraving on the surface meshing nicely with the ratchet on the whojimmy, turning and turning. A complex pathway created by a simple structure. Very nice. *Puh-clink!* That's a new noise. Very good. *Clinkclunkscrrrr . . . glack.* The ball emerges from the pattern. Joe tests it gently with his hands.

It opens.

He looks at it for a while.

" . . . Bloody hell . . ." says Joshua Joseph Spork.

When he can breathe again, he reaches for the phone.

"Billy, I don't care. No, I don't. I don't care how limber she is or if she has three sisters. No. Billy, shut up. Shut up! I need to meet the client. I need to know where it comes from!"

Resolve is in his voice, and the novelty of this alone is almost enough to exact a moment of obedience from Billy Friend. All the same, Billy dislikes making introductions. It is against his middle-mannish creed. He objects that the client might be unhappy.

"Well, if they needed me for this they're going to need me again.

Whatever it does, it's not going to do it without me and you can say I said so. It will need maintenance and it may need work doing *in situ*. It's a bloody treasure and I want to know—What? Yes. Yes, I am shouting! Because it's important!"

Joe Spork draws a breath. He is aware that this is not his normal way of interacting with the world. One, two, three. All right. "You have to see it to understand, Billy. Or actually, I'm not sure you would. It's a clockwork thing. The point is, it's unique. All right? I mean, absolutely unique. What? No. No. Still no. Well, you could call it priceless. It depends on your perspective."

Just a little bit unfair, that. It might be more accurate to say that you couldn't put a value on it. From a scholarly perspective, it's a diamond unlooked for. In sheer monetary terms, it's probably not all that exciting, unless the machine of which it is a part does something really interesting or is as ridiculously beautiful as the item in front of him, which would be . . . well, epic. And not impossible. Billy Friend, however, has senses beyond the merely human, and words like "priceless" are a sort of dog whistle to him.

"Yes, Billy, I did say that. Yes. This is six o'clock news stuff. No, before the swimming bunny. Before the sports. Yes. Exactly. So we'll deliver it together, won't we? In person. Very good. Yes. Yes, 'priceless'. I'll see you at the station, then."

Joe puts down the phone.

On the work bench in front of him, the ball lies revealed in all its glory. He has photographed it already, so that he can prove it exists.

Metal like soft cotton, not linked but threaded; warming in his hand: Woven Gold.

The trick is whispered from time to time in kasbahs and jeweller's shops and at conventions and gatherings and markets, almost revealing itself and then vanishing so thoroughly that many consider it a fiction.

Joshua Joseph's grandfather came upon it this way:

"Good morning, madame. How may we be of service?"

"My husband's watch. Or rather, it is my watch, but it was a gift from him. He had it from a man in Cambodia, you see, and now it is broken. I think it may also be wise to see to the strap. It becomes loose. Although that may be because I am shrinking." And from this you might deduce that the lady client was elderly, and that English was her second language, learned in haste and never entirely polished.

From her bag, she withdrew a small parcel of bunched tissue paper, and this she placed in front of him, with some considerable misgiving.

"It is Asian," he said, "and I think it is beautiful, but there is no hallmarking, so I do not really know that it is gold."

Daniel Spork made haste to assure her that the craftsmen of Asia were capable of splendid things, though he worried that he would be forced, when the thing was revealed, to tell her that her husband's impulsive purchase had been an error. Many travelling gentlemen, lulled perhaps by a sense of north-western superiority, are gently gulled of large sums by enterprising persons in the streets and shops of Asian cities, and deserved in Daniel Spork's opinion no less for their hubris. He did not extend this judgement to their families, however, and did not relish telling little old ladies with treasured gifts that they were not gold and emeralds but leaf and glass.

He glanced at her, and when she nodded, picked it open with long, unsteady fingers.

The timepiece itself was unexceptional; well made and simple, the face a thin wafer of polished ebony in a gold oval, with a flat glass cover. It was the bracelet which arrested Daniel's attention, which clenched about his heart and stopped his breath in his throat. He had, until now, never seen its like. Rumours had reached him, and he had dismissed them. Now he held the thing in his hands, and knew it to be almost as far beyond him as it was beyond this nice, unknowing old dame who had brought it in. The difference was that after a lifetime of gears and movements, of gold and lamé and carats and weights, he knew when he was surpassed, when he was in the presence of a master's work. He passed it back to her, very gently.

"Your husband is—is?"

"Was."

"I'm sorry."

"It was long ago."

"He was a very wise man, madame. And this thing you have brought me, which he found for you, it is a thing for which a lesser man might search a lifetime. You must treasure it."

"I do."

"So, good. And if ever you should meet anyone who can repair such a thing—who understands how this is done—please say to them that you know a man in Quoyle Street in London who dares not ask if they will tell him the secret, but would count it more than a privilege to drink a cup of tea with them and know that someone, somewhere, retains the trick of this, and will make sure it is never lost." He sniffed.

"I have made you sad."

"No, madame. You have made me more than happy. I can fix the mechanism for you, but I will not touch the strap. I would not know where to begin. Come back when I am old. Perhaps I will learn."

Woven Gold. And that is not the most remarkable thing about the doodah. Joe Spork saw what was inside it for the first time twenty minutes ago. He has no idea what it does.

First, there is the matter of the lock. It is, in fact, five locks, each one tiny and rotated by a different section of the whojimmy, each one unlocking the next one, until the last twist releases a clasp and allows the whole to open. These locks are distributed around the interior of the ball in a strange cage-like architecture which reminds Joe distantly of the aviary at London Zoo. Disconnected from one another, they flip back like the wing-cases of a glorious beetle, clasped loosely around the ball's clockwork heart. That, by itself, is enough to attract his most alert scrutiny. It is good work, and that modest assessment is in the trade tongue, the dour speech of craftsmen looking at their own: *Not bad, your Taj Mahal, old son. Bit bald about the edges, mind.* And, *Oh aye,* replies the master builder, *it's all right. You don't think the water feature's a bit loud? Wish I'd had time to build t'other one in black, that would have been something . . . Still, it's nothing to be ashamed of, I suppose. You can't get everything right.*

That kind of good work.

Rare work.

Brilliant work.

White-gloved and with a pair of softwood tweezers (better they should break than this object should be scratched) he examines it again, unfolds the locking mechanism—not without a slightly filthy feeling that he's undressing a sleeping princess—and examines the mechanism within under his thick, jeweller's lens.

The largest cog is perhaps two-eighths of an inch across. The smallest is so tiny that Joe has no idea how it could have been made, except that he knows exactly: someone made a special tool, a thing which mimics the gestures of a normal-size tool on a far smaller scale. Write your name normally on the left, and it is scratched into the panel on the right small enough to fit on a grain of rice. Half a grain. And then—this is the part which boggles his mind—each individual piece, each spring and cog and counter, was made by hand and fitted together. It is a rippling, shifting landscape of interlocking gets and pins, tracks and catches.

The envisioning of this apparatus, the planning, without a computer or even a photocopier, must have taken a year in itself. If a normal piece of clockwork is a person, this thing is a great city. It is folded on itself, each section fulfilling several roles, turning in one axis, then another, then another. There is, just here, a yet smaller case which performs some outré function he cannot fathom, but which itself is also the weight driving some manner of self-winding system. The cog which is the output stream, which pokes through the ball at the north pole and meets whatever remarkable thing is driven by this tiny engine (although it's not an engine, of course, it's something far more strange and powerful: a storage medium, a computer's hard disk made of brass), is actually just a dust cover. When the thing is active it slides to one side to reveal a plug of gears so complex that Joe Spork has come to call it in his mind by a modern name. He calls it an *interface*.

Enigma, he wonders. Colossus? Is this a wartime thing? A code-breaker or a code-maker? He has no idea. He knows only that it is unrecorded, magical, genius. Hence: priceless.

And yes, there is a small flaw, but hardly a surprising one after decades in a sack somewhere. He reaches in—and stops. A tiny sparkle beneath his tweezers.

Impossible.

Joe peers, leaning down, adjusts the lamp. Then he brings two more lights closer, and a hand lens which in combination with the main one gives him a truly ludicrous magnification.

Absolutely impossible.

Beside the smallest cog, driven by a secondary ratchet on the face of the tiny thing, there is a glimmer of metal. Through the double lens he peers, and yes, there it is, appearing to hang in space: another layer of clockwork so small that it's barely visible even now, a tracery of gossamer meshed and geared and fading away into the interior of the ball.

He stares at it, awestruck and even a little upset. He can do nothing with this. He would need other tools, a cleanroom, practice in micro-gauge engineering . . . he is utterly outclassed.

Except . . .

Except.

If there's damage to the microscopic part, he's out of his depth.

There's probably no one on Earth who has experience with this. It is unique—and mad, because if you can make this, why wouldn't you use printed circuitry? Unless, of course, there was no such thing when you made it.

That aside: the macro part is familiar enough. And yes, the central section lifts out as a single piece. This problem was foreseen (of course).

He goes to the kitchen and cleans a glass casserole dish, dries it thoroughly, and lifts the impossible heart of the ball into the dish, then covers it with the lid. Then he turns his attention to the rest of the mechanism.

Yes. This he can fix. A weak pin has sheared away, leaving a small arm flapping. It's a matter of . . . well . . . it might take a little longer, actually . . .

At some point he finishes, and closes his eyes for a quarter of an hour to rest them. Catnapping is a skill everyone should have.

He checks his work and finds it good. The rest of the mechanism is perfect. There isn't even any dust.

He cleans and oils it anyway, out of respect.

You, who made this: I wish we could have met.

One thing is plain to a hedgehog, as his unlamented father would have had it: this is not your average music box. He should call a newspaper. He should call Harticle's. He should call his mother—not because of this but just in general.

He doesn't.

Slowly, he begins to assemble the other pieces of the doodah. They're splendidly done, but they look brutish and plain now. The puzzle comes together under his hands without effort. After a second, he realises he's mimicking the patterns of the ball. As above, so below. More elegance.

He'll have to give the whojimmy back. It wouldn't be right to separate it from the machine itself. Although if they were to give him a long-term maintenance contract, he could always . . .

He looks at his task and his tools, and allows his body to work without interference. Now that the puzzle is solved and the tasks are set, he knows how to do this at such a low level it's important not to think too much. This is the part he loves, the vanishing of self.

When he finishes, he realises how long he has been working, and has to rush.

IV

The True Origin of Vaughn Parry;
the hive;
the flat at Carefor Mews.

ourse of irritating stimulation in line with overall strategy," Billy Friend says, as the train to Wistithiel rolls out of Paddington station only a little tardy, "eight letters."

Joe Spork is tempted to think that this is not a bad description of his journey with Billy Friend. He shakes his head.

"Billy, where did it come from?"

"Blank, blank, C, et cetera. A gentleman never tells."

"Billy, this is serious."

"So am I, Joseph. Client confidences are sacred." Billy gives a pompous little sniff, as if to say they're particularly sacred among those people who habitually lie and steal. "If eleven down is 'London,' then it ends in 'l'."

"I have no idea. I'm terrible with crosswords."

"Well, so am I, Joseph, but this is how we learn."

"Billy, just tell me it's not stolen."

"It's not stolen, Joseph."

"Really?"

"Cross my heart."

"It's stolen."

"Who can ever be entirely sure, Joseph? None of us."

"Jesus . . ."

"Keep working on the clue, if you please. Hm. It could be 'lactose,' which I believe is a form of sugar found in milk. Well, no, it couldn't, but it had points of congruence."

"For God's sake," says the woman in the opposite seat, "it's 'tactical.' 'Tack' like on a boat, then 'tickle.'"

"All right, all right," Billy Friend murmurs, and then, rather waspish, "I notice you haven't done yours, missus."

"I set it," she replies icily. "It's the easy one today."

Billy's eyebrows climb involuntarily up his face, and his mouth turns down at the corners. He goes a bit pink on the top of his head.

"They're putting Vaughn Parry up for parole next month," Joe says quickly, because Billy doesn't stay civil long when he thinks someone's laughing at him. "Or whatever you call it when it's medical. They say he's cured."

"What, seriously?" Billy looks taken aback. For nearly a year now—since the appalling security-camera footage was obtained by a red-topped newspaper, and Vaughn Parry's effortless dance of death, liquid and horrible, was shown to a voyeuristically appalled public—he has been hinting that he knew the Fiend of Finsbury as a boy, and can offer unique insights or possibly salacious and horrid gossip about Vaughn Parry, if only someone would ask him. No one has.

"Seriously."

"Bloody hell. I wouldn't be on that parole board, I will say."

"He's hardly going to come at them across the courtroom, is he?"

"Oh, no. No, not like that. But what they're going to see, Joseph, I mean, I've no idea. Except I can sort of guess, I can imagine, and I'd rather not. I think you could go mad yourself, sitting on that bench. I wonder if that ever happens."

"Perhaps they get counselling and so on."

"Fat lot of use that would be. Some things, once you know them, Joe, nothing's quite the same again. Things you see and do, they make you what you are. Seeing inside Vaughn, well."

"Did you really know him?"

"Met him, yes. Know him . . . no. Thank God, Joe, and I don't believe, as you are aware, but when I think of Vaughn I thank God in the most genuine terms, that I did not know him in any real way."

"What happened? I mean, how did you meet?"

"It's a bit . . . well. It's unpleasant, is what it is. It's not nice stuff, Joseph." Billy looks down at his hands. He brushes something off the palm of the left one, and fiddles with his fingernails.

"If you don't want to, Billy, that's fine. We can talk about something else."

"No, it's all right. It's just more of a chat for the pub, you know. Cosy corner, after a couple of glasses, not in front of strangers." He glances around, and the other occupants of the carriage studiously do whatever they are doing a bit more obviously. Joe shrugs.

"Let's walk, then. Get a packet of crisps or something."

The huffy woman tosses the sports section of her paper onto Billy's chair as they leave.

Billy Friend lights a cigarette and leans out of the window, next to the sign forbidding smoking and above the one which cautions against putting your hands or head outside the train while it's in motion. He draws hard, sucking against the wind, and turns back to Joe. It's surprisingly dark here, at the junction between their carriage and the next, and the gloomy overhead light makes him look ancient and craggy, with deep black pouches under his eyes and lines like scars running from the corners of his mouth. He waves his hand, up and down, to get himself started.

"There's families, Joseph, right? In the Waiting game, I mean. There's the Ascots, been doing it since King James, and the Godrics since the Norman conquest and before. My lot started out when Victoria was new. The Alleyns reckon they've been at it since Caesar, and most likely they have. And each of them has his own daft way of doing it, embalming and making up and laying out, right? Secrets of the trade, and that. And the thing you have to understand is the differences are mostly crap. It all comes to the same thing. But part of the service is giving a sense that maybe it's not too late to show some kindness or some heart, right, even if you never did give a fig for the dead while they was still alive, or if they never gave a fig for you, because let's face it, as great a proportion of the dead are arseholes as the living. It stands to reason, although you won't find many funerals begin with 'he was a total pain in the neck and only half as clever as he thought, so let's put him in the ground and have a pint, and good riddance.' I've always thought that would have a certain charm, myself.

"So then there's the new sort, all Richard Branson shiny, right? They're different from us. Someone like Vince Alleyn, you ask him what he charges and he'll tell you he charges what his client can afford. So Lady Farquar Froofroo Lah-Dee-Dah Fudge Follicle, right, putting her husband in the ground costs a sodding fortune. But her butler, when he buries his wife as used to turn down her ladyship's sheets of an evening and sort out her ladyship's wig collection, that's dirt cheap. What you might like to think of as organic pricing, or *fairness*, if you're a traditionalist like me. But then along comes some bugger in a white dinner jacket like Barry Manilow and he says he's for transparent fees and it's more democratic and all that. So, as my friend Daniel Levin would say—because your Jewish families have a whole different set of things they do for the dead, Joseph, and rather better in my view—so, *nu*. Now we do price lists and not everyone can afford the trimmings they want, and some pay in advance on the never-never, which is as macabre as you like, but here we are.

"Now the other thing about the new sort, they're not families, right? They are companies, and they have logos and what all you like. They hire consultants. It's bloody hilarious, I'll tell you, watching a bunch of advertising berks try to find new ways to sell coffins. It's just great. *Buy one, get one free!* and all that. These are the people who thought it would be better if the Post Office was called Consignia, so you can imagine what they do to the Waiting game. One of them tried to tell me we should rebrand as 'AfterCare.' I'm not making this up.

"Now, to join the Brotherhood, and set up shop in the Waiting trade, you need what we call an *acquaintanceship*. You want to have seen a bit of death, maybe as a nurse or a soldier or a doctor. It can be anything really, but you need to know. You can't have your undertaker turn pale and chuck up when he sees the dearly departed, right? So Donovan Parry wants to set up shop and he's a man in the old style. He gets onto Vince Alleyn and the others, my dad and their lot, and says he wants in. And there's all hemming and hawing, because they don't know him from Adam, but they call him over to the Bucket & Spade at Canonbury and they put to him the question. Why in all the world does he want to be a Waiting Man?

" 'It's a living,' says Donovan.

" 'There's plenty of ways to make a living,' says Vince, 'and not many can do this one right.'

" 'Reckon I'd be one of them as can,' Donovan tells him.

" 'Lot of fellows ain't comfortable sitting up with the dead,' Roy Godric says.

" 'Makes no never mind to me if a man's living or he's dead, so long as he don't chatter on when I'm smoking a pipe or reading the *Post*,' comes back Donovan Parry.

"And that's how it goes on, and one by one they come to the conclusion that old Donovan might just have what it takes. He's got what they call the Quiet on him, don't fret much and don't give out at all if he does. It's a powerful thing on a Waiting Man, does half the job before the rabbit's off the mark, like the Blacksmith's Word for widows. But all the same it's making them half mad, because he don't talk like no doctor nor soldier, he's more like a schoolmaster. Vince Alleyn asks him point blank if he's a vicar lost his cassock, and if so what for, and Donovan Parry laughs and says no, he isn't a religious sort and never has been. He believes in the laws of man, he says, and that should be enough for anybody—but the way he says it, it's like a Bible verse, and steely cold.

"So finally Roy Godric says:

" 'All right, Mr. Parry, you've the Quiet on you right enough and the way about you to be a Waiting Man. So it's just if you've got your acquaintanceship. If not, you work with me a year and then we'll set you up.'

"And Donovan Parry laughs and says yes, he's got an acquaintanceship all right.

" 'Well, what is it?' Jack Ascot asks him.

" 'Well,' says Donovan Parry, 'back in the day, I sent a few the way of their final rest. More'n a few, I suppose. And spent the night before with each man, too.' He grins at them, clear and pale and cold. 'I was Crown's hangman at Raftsey Jail, y'see.'

" 'How many was it?' Jack Ascot says.

" 'I reckon nigh on fifty,' says Donovan Parry, 'but we don't call it right to keep a tally. A good hangman does one at a time, and don't dwell nor come prideful on the count. He meets his man the night before, and looks him in the eye and measures him for the drop, then on the day he hoods him if the man wants it—and tells 'em they should, there's no shame in fear and no dignity in looking it in the eye for most, just a wet seat and the horrors—and gets him from the execution cell to the noose as fast as he can so there's no time to think on what's to come. Fastest we ever done was a minute twenty-two, and we were well pleased with that. The lad hardly knew it was happening, and he fell like a rock. Never once,' says Donovan Parry, 'did we have one fall and not die right off. I never had to swing on a man's legs nor take a second pass. And that's something a hangman can be proud of, for it's craft and wit and mercy, all in one. Still,' he says, 'the hanging's done now, years back. There'll be no more in England and I've no desire to get myself to Jamaica or one of those places. So it's the Waiting trade for me, if you'll have it.'

"And they surely would. Well, of course they would. It's different now, because we don't execute felons, and I'm sure that's the right choice. But back then, Joseph, a Crown's hangman was like David Beckham crossed with the Archbishop of Canterbury. He was death's own coachman.

"Well, time went by and Donovan Parry himself passed on to his reward, and they say at the last he had a few qualms about the lads he might find on the other side, and what his ultimate destination might be. And his son Richard carried on the family trade, which he learned with his own dad, and in time he brought in young Vaughn, which was his son. And I'll tell you something, Joseph, which many would consider indiscreet. I'd always had half a notion that the Honoured & Enduring Brotherhood was somewhat of a swizz. A closed shop, right? Seemed to me that any fool could do right by a corpse and pat the bereaved and say 'He's gone to a better place' or 'They look so peaceful, don't they?' and suchlike rubbish. I thought, it's a Masonry, right, a dining club and a way of looking out for ourselves, and I've got no quarrel with that, but there's no call for all this pendulous mystical crap about acquaintanceships and so on, that's for the mugs, and one thing a Waiting Man doesn't like to be considered, it's a mug.

"Now, a fellow like Donovan Parry, they recognise his acquaintanceship and there's an end to it, right? No test for him. But if you come up in the trade there's a test, like a final exam, before they call you a Waiting Man proper. Lads who haven't done it they call the *twices*, because they're waiting to be Waiting. (Yes, I know, it's weak, but doing what we do you find the laughs where you can.)

"Now each test is different, each one's just for you. They don't tell you it's coming, they just do it, though of course once it starts you've a fair inkling this'll be it. Richard Parry had to lay out a leper, which is actually no great horror. Mine, they locked me in a room with a whole load of corpses and told me to lay them out over one night, and of course the wicked buggers had got some lads from the building site and made them up, so I was halfway through the first one (he was the only real dead 'un, right, sodding great hole in his gut from a car crash) when number two starts to twitch and moan and then up they all get and ghastly gashed they wander around going 'Wooooo' and so on. For about five seconds I near peed myself, and then I nearly called out for the others to tell them I'd seen through it, and finally I just got on with the dead fellow, because while they might want me to do something else, this lad still needed his laying-out, and buggered if I was going to mess that up, even if it meant another year as a *twice*. Took me two hours to get the thing done, and saying never a word nor looking around, even when these ghastly bastards all crowded about me and showed me their injuries and scabs and what have you. They'd done a good job with the make-up, of course, because it's part of the trade, only this time rather in reverse. Now I was ninety-nine per cent sure they were fake, but damn me if that lingering one per cent weren't a real possibility when midnight came along. No joke, Joseph, it was hard.

"So I finished him off, and then I gets my saw out and turns to the nearest moaning ghost and I says 'All right, my poor dead matey, I've to cut you open now, and I mean to do it, so you may as well hop up on this table and spare your grieving relatives an ugly mess!' Hah! *He* near peed himself then, and of course the Waiting Men come in and gave me the nod. Said I'd shown the Quiet, you see, which of course I had, and I never knew.

"Well, that was all good fun and actually I was a fair bit proud, after, of how I carried it off, and Jack Ascot said—he was nearly a hundred by then—he said when they had Vince Alleyn's test back in the day, they done a thing much the same called the Bloody Bride, and a woman from the local butcher's shop wore a set of cow's intestines around her neck and a slashed-open wedding dress. Vince damn near fainted, and then after, blow me if he didn't walk right over and kiss her on the mouth. He passed right away, and married the girl, to boot. Anyway, Jack said he hadn't seen much better since.

"So come the day, we had young Vaughn's test, and Richard said we'd best find something particularly dark, because his son had a steady nerve.

"Now, in the book—there's an actual book, can you believe, and I imagine it's worth a ton of money now, there's likely only the one—there's about a dozen really awful things they used to do. About the worst is to get the corpse of a condemned blasphemer and sew it up with cats inside, then tell the lad doing the test it's your dear old mum or someone close. As ghoulish as it comes. Modern times, of course, there's no way you'd get away with something like that, even if you were of a mind. But they found a way for Vaughn Parry, and this is what it was: they got a dead ape, and they shaved it all over and drew on a sailor's tattoo, and then they put it in a suit and smashed the head up some so you couldn't immediately say it wasn't a man, just a really ugly one. And then—well, they couldn't use a cat, that wouldn't be right—so they caught a fox from the rubbish tip, knocked him out with a bit of doped luncheon meat, and stitched the poor dead ape up around him. And then they put Vaughn Parry up to bat.

"So they did it in the Alleyn place, because there's a two-way mirror so old Vince could keep an eye on his lads while they were working and be sure the thing was done respectful. And we all crowded in to see what would happen. There's Vaughn, working away, and the belly of the ape wriggles and heaves, and Vaughn glances over at it, but it's stopped, so he goes back to work. And then a moment later it happens again, and then there's this appalling noise, I swear you never heard such a thing, a scream fit to make you think someone's being crucified, right there beside you, and the nails going in through bone and gristle. I swear, Joseph, I never heard such a noise. And we all thought it must be Vaughn, seeing what was happening, but it wasn't. It was the fox, screaming for his life. Vaughn . . . he reaches over like he's passing the gravy on a Sunday, and cuts the ape open, then goes inside for the fox and lifts it out, and without barely looking he snaps its neck and goes on with the job. And my dad, who never speaks in these things, never says a word, because he's a shy old bugger, he says 'Ah, well,' like that's decided something. And everyone leaves. They don't bother to go and get Vaughn and tell him the gag. They up and leave. And the next day, when he comes looking, they won't none of them talk to him, or even look him in the eye, and finally he goes to Roy Godric and asks what's the matter.

" 'Sorry, Vaughn,' Roy says quietly, 'but you're out. You failed your *acquaintanceship*. You're done.'

"Now, I've never heard of no one *failing* before. Not passing, yes, but you just try again. But *failing*, so the Brotherhood won't ever take you, I didn't even know that was possible.

" 'What? What do you mean?' Vaughn wants to know.

" 'Just what I say, Vaughn, boy,' Roy says. 'You won't be one of us. Not ever.'

"'But I passed! Look what you did, and I passed. I showed *Quiet*. I know I did!'

"'No, boy. You ain't got the Quiet. And you ain't now, nor never will be, a Waiting Man. Now, off you go.' And he points at the door, and Vaughn Parry just goes, because he doesn't know what else to do.

"'I'm sorry, Richard,' Roy Godric says to Vaughn's dad, and Richard, instead of getting angry, he hangs his head and he says he's sorry too.

"'But you knew, Richard, didn't you?'

"'Aye,' says Richard Parry. And then he goes off after his boy.

"Well, God, I sat there and I drank my drink and wondered if I came close to having that happen to me. And finally, after I've nursed that same pint for an hour or so, and more stared at it than drunk it, my dad comes and sits himself down opposite me.

"'All right, Billy?' he says.

"'All right,' I tells him, but I'm not.

"'Poor bastard,' he says.

"'I suppose he'll find another job, then, and Richard will train up one of the other lads or something.' And my dad looks at me as if I've gone funny in the head, and I realise he's not talking about the son at all. He's talking about the father.

"'Dad,' I say, because I need to know, Joseph, my world's upside down and I'm confused because there's rules I don't know about and penalties I hadn't imagined for breaking them, 'what did Vaughn do wrong?'

"'It's the oath,' he says, 'the Waiting Man's Promise. Remember?' Well, of course I do, but there's nothing in it says you kick a lad out on his arse for doing well on his test. 'Say it to me,' Dad says, 'and think it through.' So this, Joseph, is the oath we all take, and I'll thank you not to noise it about.

"'*To wait up with the dead; to take what they have no use for and set it aside, that the corpse looks lively on the day; to see the dead from bed to dirt, and no indignity more than what fate inflicts; to serve the wailing widow and the lonely man with grace, and carry the Waiting Man's Quiet like a comforter, that is lent at need; to hear the Screaming, and let it have no voice; to preserve the silence of the dead, and keep their secrets; to take fair payment and seek no favours; and to move on, without regret.*'

"'Aye,' Dad says. 'And there's the rub. Young Vaughn, he ain't got the Quiet, he's got the other thing. He thinks he's got the Quiet, Billy, and that's as well. Because the truth is, he's got the Screaming, and

Richard knew it. He opened that poor monkey like it weren't even a clutch purse, and he snapped that fox without a thought, and the whole thing as if he was making porridge.

" 'When you took *your* test, Billy,' he says, 'you smeared the pink on that lad's cheeks, and gave him too much dark around the eyes. In the morning I had to redo him, he looked like a Chelsea trollop. But one thing you done perfect, and I was never so proud. In your heart, you cared about the dead man, more than you wanted to get out of that room or show you knew it was your test or anything else. You cared about a dead, gone bugger you never knew, and you laid him out, because you're a Waiting Man. But Vaughn, he didn't flinch because he doesn't care one bit. And he doesn't care about the living neither, not even a little. Vaughn Parry looks at us, and he sees corpses walking. He didn't flinch in there because he's always seeing dead men shudder. It's how he lives. He was born dead himself, and that's what the Screaming is. It's a body walking without a heart to feel for anyone else. And if ever he realises that, Billy, you best not trust him, for the Waiting Man's oath ain't there for a laugh or our convenience. Them as have the Screaming, Billy, they're empty inside, and the things they can do when they start to understand what they are, they're black and cold and not for good fellows to dwell on. Time was the Brotherhood didn't just test the *twices*, but every lad in a village, and they'd have marked a lad failed the test, and maybe a month later there'd be a coffin weighed double going in the ground and some young fellow with rot in him instead of life would be never more seen. That's how it was.

" 'Truth, Billy,' my dad goes on, 'I suppose we're better off this way. But from now on, you see Vaughn Parry, you step to the other side of the street. You don't have him in the house, you don't have no truck with him at all. He's got the Screaming, and he'll show it soon enough.' "

Billy Friend grinds his cigarette against the sole of his shoe. It's a leather sole, grubby and stained with water, and the ball of the foot is thin and black with old burns. He tosses the butt out of the window.

"Well, he did, didn't he?"

The Wistithiel station is made of grey stone and old, black iron. Billy Friend wonders aloud whether Wistithiel sprang up around a prison, the way towns sprout to serve whatever industry is nearby. "Or a lunatic asylum, Joseph, that would do nicely. Friends of Brother Vaughn all around. Cousins and aunts, red of tooth and long of nail, sitting in a hundred rocking chairs and making jumpers out of hair!"

In fact, the Parry family came from a town miles away up the coast, just across the county line into Devon, but Billy, unsettled, is prone to flights of trenchant fantasy.

On a hardwood bench with green paint flaking leprously from it, a sullen, beery man growls in his throat. It might be words. It could just be phlegm. Billy flinches.

"I says 'No, it bloody wasn't,'" the drinker bites out. "It was baskets and fishing, and now there's no bloody fish because of the bloody Spanish and the Russians and their bloody giant factory ships, and who wants bloody straw baskets when you can have nylon or polyester or that rubbish? Eh? So it's tourism and piss all else, and London buggers like you come in, buy the place up, don't like the mist and fog and show up two weeks in the year. And then they act like they're doing us a favour. So the council puts bloody plastic slides and plastic cows and plastic bloody everything to bring 'em more and they come less, and who can blame 'em? So laugh all you bloody like."

"Good evening," Joe says, politely.

"Is it? Where?"

"Here, I hope."

"Well, you hope in vain, don't you? We bloody all do."

"I was hoping you could tell us where to find Wistithiel Rental."

The man nods once in the direction of the car park, and when Joe thanks him, he shrugs into life.

"I'll walk you. You're all right. Your chum's got a clever mouth."

"Yes. He has."

"I like that in a pretty girl." Joe doesn't know quite how to respond to that, and behind him, Billy Friend is frantically miming a banjo and rolling his eyes. "Going on far, are you?"

"Hinde's Reach House. But we're staying in the Gryffin overnight."

"Gryffin's a decent place. The House . . . well. I wouldn't go up there."

"Why not?"

"Bloody long way."

"Oh."

"And they were always funny round that way. Webbed feet and that."

"Webbed feet?"

"Aye. What farmers always say about them on the coast, and city folk say about countrymen. They eat missionaries, too." There's a glimmer of laughter in the man's eyes. "But the Gryffin's all right. Decent enough. And the barmaids wear those little T-shirts."

Billy Friend perks up, and they pass into the chilly, grey day outside.

"When I get my hands on the old trout gave me this job," Billy Friend murmurs in the saloon of the Gryffin, "there will be an accounting, not to say that harsh words will be spoken by me into her pious little ear. 'Lady,' I shall say, 'you are a troublesome old baggage, and you owe me extra,' and she, being a clean-living old bird and of a nervous disposition, will yield up the cash and introduce me to her lissom granddaughter by way of additional compensation. Bloody hell."

"You said I needed an adventure," Joe reminds him.

"You do. You need to relax and be yourself, not whoever it is you're trying to be in your mad little head. I bloody don't, though. I'm me and I'm good at it, and I hate the country. It's full of bumpkins and pies and godawful bloody warm beer." Tess the barmaid snorts, and Billy recollects himself. "Though it does have some compensations, I will say." She turns her back on him and walks away with great emphasis, but the effect is muted by the handkerchief top and low jeans she is wearing, which together afford Billy a revitalising view of her spine and sacrum. He makes an approving, canine sort of noise, and she scowls.

"I think she likes you," Joe says. Billy eyes him over his pint.

"Yes, you actually do, don't you?"

"She sort of wriggles when she comes over here, and so on."

"Indeed, she does, Joseph. She sashays, is the technical term. And do you know what all that proves?"

"She likes you."

"No, Joseph, alas. It proves that you are a prat."

Tess reappears a moment later with the food, smiles at Joe, and pauses on her heels as she turns back to the bar. "Got everything you need?" Billy nearly swallows his tongue.

"Yes, thank you," Joe replies. "And I don't suppose you've got a map, have you? We need to get out to Hinde's Reach House."

She gives him a funny look, as if he has made the kind of proposition Billy frequently does make and she weren't the kind of girl who usually hears that sort of thing.

"I'm superstitious," she says. "So I don't go up there."

"Don't want to get webbed feet, I 'spect," Billy suggests.

She scowls. "You've been talking to Lenny," she says, indicating the man from the station, now sitting at a table by the fire. "He thinks he's a laugh. Did he tell you they burn travellers as witches, too?"

"Something like, yeah."

"He thinks he's funny," Tess repeats.

"We've got a parcel for the house."

"There's no one there. And it's not safe."

"Not safe how?"

She shrugs. "Crumbling cliffs and holes in the ground. Tin mine back when we had tin, then a government place in the war. And if you believe in ghosts, it's haunted, too." She smiles, embarrassed.

"Whose ghost?"

"Hundreds of them. It used to be where Wistithiel was, but it went into the sea in nineteen fifty-nine. Most of the village. Or burned down. Or there was an epidemic. To hear my grandmother tell it, you'd think it was all three. Or Galveston. They wanted to make it a tourist attraction, but there's still people alive who remember and lost friends, husbands and so on. So we said, bollocks to that."

"The ghost of a whole town, then."

"Yes. Actually, if you put your hand on your chest and your foot on the right stones, you can feel the heartbeat of the dead. Hang on—" She peers around, then reaches over to a window ledge and hefts a small, solid piece of grey granite. "This is from the bay underneath. A lad from Bristol brought it back from the fields out there, then got scared in the night and left it in his bedroom when he went home. Silly bugger." She puts the stone on the ground. "Here. Put your foot on it."

Feeling silly, Joe puts his foot on the stone.

"Now, you put your hand . . . here." She puts his hand dead centre of his chest. Billy Friend watches, bemused. "Can you feel anything?"

"No."

"Well, it's been here in the Gryffin a long time, and you're not local. Here." She replaces his foot with her own. "That's better. Now, give me your hand a moment."

Joe gives her his hand, and she places his hand, palm down, on her chest and leans firmly towards him. Her skin is warm, with just a trace of perspiration.

"There," Tess says. "Can you feel that?"

"Yes, I think so."

"Sometimes it takes a while to find the right spot. It might be more to the left. Or down." She tugs gently on his wrist, pushes her shoulders back a bit.

"No, I've got it." He nods. "Definitely a heartbeat." He nods again.

"Oh," she says, a bit nonplussed, "good."

The moment lengthens.

"Yes." With the heel of his hand Joe can feel the curve of one breast. He has absolutely no idea whether this is deliberate. It's lovely. He tries to be polite and not notice.

And suddenly the stone is back on the shelf and Tess is busily serving someone else.

Billy Friend puts his head in his hands.

The car is a grotty old banger, the best in a very small selection. Joe tentatively believes it is younger than he is, but would not put actual money on the assessment. On his left, Billy Friend holds Tess's map. It is drawn in frustrated ballpoint, the road following the curve of the railway line, and there's a grudging kiss at the bottom as if to point out what might have been.

"What you did to that girl ought to be illegal," Billy Friend grumbles.

"I didn't do anything."

"Of that we are all painfully aware. Lovely Tess is even now weeping in some kitchen corner, lamenting the waste of her heart. Not to mention her other salient attributes."

"All right, I missed the point."

"Yes, I would say you did."

"We can't all be you, Billy."

"We can all be ourselves, though, Joseph, and who the hell can't tell when a woman is putting his hand down her top that she's doing more than discussing local folk tales? Are you in residence, Joseph, at all, inside your head?"

"Of course I am."

"I should coco."

"I just . . ."

"You try too hard to be a gent, Joe. It's all going on inside you but it never gets out. You're all buttoned up."

"I am not!"

"All right, then: what action could young Tess have taken which you would have regarded as an unequivocal invitation?"

"Read the map."

"I'm just saying."

"Make an instruction out of the following three words: the, read, map."

Billy does.

There's no sign of witch-burning as they drive through the narrow lanes towards Hinde's Reach. As they turn a corner, Billy Friend points out a large, rusted, black barrel which he asserts might be a cauldron used for missionaries, but the silent gloom of the sky swallows the joke. Neither of them mentions webbed feet. They've passed two men walking and a woman on a bicycle, and Joe found himself looking instinctively at their shoes to see whether they were larger than they should be.

They come over a hill, and there's a small cluster of houses. It's marked on Tess's map as Old Town, but in truth it's not even large enough to be a village, and made of concrete and corrugated iron. There's a farmhouse and a single lonely petrol pump with a battered credit card box on top.

Joe slows the car and winds down the window so that he can speak to the woman sitting on a bench watching the road. She has messy hair, dyed a shocking red, but when he speaks and she turns to him, he realises she is very old. Her cheeks are purple with broken blood vessels.

"Hello," he says, trying to be gentle and clear at the same time in case she's deaf. "We're looking for Hinde's Reach House?"

She peers at him. "What was that?"

"Hinde's Reach?"

"Ah." She sighs. "Gone back to the grass, hasn't it, and quite right, too."

"We have a parcel for the house up there."

"Do you, though?" She shrugs. "Well, I call that too late."

A man emerges from the bungalow behind her, wearing socks and slippers. He has a mismatched face, as if one half has been shattered and reconstructed, long ago.

"Wossallthisabout, then?" He tries to smile, or perhaps he's just twitching.

"Post office," she tells him. "Parcel for Hinde's Reach."

"Parcel for the dead, then." He spits. "Bastards, anyway." He wanders back inside.

She sighs. "I should have said not to tell 'im. He's still angry about all that as happened back then."

"The town going into the sea?"

"No, no. That was natural. Awful, but natural. He's cross about the other. His parents were taken off."

"Killed?"

"Not exactly. Brain damage. Jerry thinks it was a plague. Thinks they were making germ bombs up there for to use against the Russians, and one of 'em went off. Maybe he's right. Folks wrong in the head over one night, that's not normal. And Jerry never entirely the same. Well, you see his face, don't you? And no bugger gives a damn, either. These days everyone gets a handout. Stub a toe and you get one. But not for Jerry. Local trust says he's faking it. Government won't hear. The Church wanted him, ten years back. Wanted all the plague orphans and survivors and such. Said they could do wonderful things to help. But we're chapel round here, so Jerry told them to stick it up their cassocks." The woman sighs again. "Best you go over there, then. Close the gate after you, or the geese get out. Don't take no nonsense from them! Have you got a stick?"

"No."

"Kick 'em, then. Kick 'em hard, mind, you won't harm 'em and they need to know you mean it. Otherwise they'll have your arm."

"If you're sure," Joe says.

"Not my geese," she replies. "You want the second turning. Five minutes more."

She goes back to staring at the road, and Joe guides the car through Old Town and along to the second turning. A huge, fanged thing made of iron looms over the road from one corner, and Billy Friend swears sharply before realising it's a hay fork.

"I hate the fucking countryside, Joseph."

Joe nods in acknowledgement of this truth. And then, without warning, the wind picks up and he can hear a deep, thrashing roar like a huge crowd, and they're looking out over the sea, and Hinde's Reach.

They go through the gate carefully, watching out for enemy geese, but the birds are clumped miserably in the far corner of the field, keeping one another warm. And there, sprawled against a grim, ugly sunset, is the place they have come to find; a shattered frame and some foundations, and a sign which reads: Hinde's Reach House, Home Secretariat: S2.

The house is a pile of rubble perched on the edge of the cliff. A little further on there's a rusted railway line ending in a stark iron buffer. Stiff, springy grass bends in the wind, and clumps of gorse bow and twitch. Below, the sea makes a noise so deep he can feel it in his gut.

It's the emptiest place he has ever seen.

Joe Spork shoves his hands into his pockets and stares at the ruin, and out into the grim, blue-grey smear of sea and sky beyond the cliff edge. Spray spatters on his face. Reluctantly, he lets them extinguish this brief excitement in his life. Too late. Of course, much too late. The machine itself—the device which reads this magical book—is gone. This parcel, mysterious and beautiful and idiotic, is all that remains.

"Sod it, then," Billy Friend says at last. He turns and huddles into his scarf, pulls his woolly hat lower on his head. "I'm sorry, Joe, it's someone's idea of a funny, I suppose. I was took. Or she's mad, the old biddy. Doubtless wants to pay in fairy dust and cake as well. I got you all revved up over nothing. Still, maybe you can find young Tess and buy her a drink. No sense this being a total waste, is there?" and then again, with one last shake of the head, as he walks away: "Sod it."

Joe looks after him, then turns back to the sea. There are white horses on the waves, hard shapes cresting blue-grey water. Back by the road, he hears Billy get into the car.

This day is the pattern of his life. He is the man who arrives too late. Too late for clockwork in its prime, too late to know his grandmother. Too late to be admitted to the secret places, too late to be a gentleman crook, too late really to enjoy his mother's affection before it slid away into a God-ridden gloom. And too late for whatever odd revelation was waiting here. He had allowed himself to believe that there might, at last, be a wonder in the world which was intended just for him. Foolishness.

He considers himself, the wrong side of thirty-five and no closer to being who he wanted to be, if he ever knew who that was.

The stricture of Joe Spork is indecision, a departing girlfriend once told him. He fears she was wrong. There is no stricture to him, no core. No substance. Just a dozen conflicting drives which average out, producing nothing. Be a gangster. Be an honest man. Be Daniel, be Mathew, be Joe. Make something of yourself, but don't stand out too much. Find a girl, but avoid the wrong girl. Mend the clocks, keep the old firm going. Sell up and run, leave London and head to a beach somewhere. Be someone. Be no one. Be yourself. Be happy—but how?

He has no idea.

He is a nowhere man, caught in between.

Down in the caves, beneath the cliffs, the water surges and ebbs. A curious circle of white foam and crested water sits in the midst of the bight, where the sea swirls around a pattern of rocks. Up above him, indifferent clouds are gathering, and the rain is starting to fall. It's not yet four, but already it feels like the onset of night. He realises there's water running from his eyes, and is not sure if the wind is causing it.

"Damn," he says, a bit plaintively, and then with mounting anger, "Damn, damn, damn." The sea wind takes the words away, so that his voice sounds hollow and small, even inside his own head.

Well. To be honest, it always does.

He turns, and finds himself staring full into a fierce, angry face, inches from his own. He yells and stumbles back.

"Who the hell're you?" The man has white stubble and opium fiend's eyes which glare out of a sou'wester's grimy hood. "What're you doing here? This is my land! Private land! It's not some bloody tourist attraction! It's private, for me, and them! It's a grave!" The voice is northern underneath, but the pattern of words is coloured by decades spent down here, and the vowels have acquired a rounded burr.

"A grave?"

The man pushes him, sharply, on the shoulders; a stabbing of fingers to propel him back, but there's very little weight behind it because Joe Spork is a big man and the other may be tall, but he is not heavy.

"Full fathom, aye, grave and serious, cut in the rock, dead like winter, dead like silence, and what do you think of that, ey? The soil is bones and the sky is skin, and everything is rotting and so am I and so are you. Now go away. It's a shame, you coming here. You ought to be sorry, but you ain't."

"I am. I didn't know. I didn't mean to trespass. I have a package for the people at the house. This is the address. I didn't realise it was gone."

"The old house went into the sea. Ground went an' collapsed underneath it. Gawpers come in summer, looking for a little thrill. Time to kill. The dead went out to sea, down and down and down into the dark, and isn't that just the way it is? Ghosts like starlings, pitter-patter on my greenhouse roof. Ghosts in the ivy and the gorse. Choking the greenhouse, choking the hope, little fingers around your neck. Ivy drags you down like water . . . Have you ever cut ivy?" This last in a curious, conversational tone.

"No," Joe says carefully, "I haven't."

"You see the hands then, little fingers clasping. Ivy's a slow death, years in the making. Gorse is quicker, but it's not so cruel. I burn the gorse sometimes, but you can't burn ivy or you lose everything. Ivy's a metaphor. Dust you are, and to dust you shall return, and down to dust your house will come with you, down with ivy. I knew a girl called Ivy once. God knows what happened to her, down in the dark beneath the sea. Choked, I shouldn't wonder, leaves and hands and creeping through your window. Can't say as I hold much with God any more, though. Bugger 'im. Rigged the game and left the place to rot, hasn't he?"

"I never thought about it."

"She came here."

"God?"

"She came every day, for a while, and looked down into the sea. There's a standing wave." He points out at the ring of water.

"What is it? The rocks?"

"More complicated. It's a wave that never ends. Never moves, never dies. Just changes. Water hits rock, washes back, meets water . . . always a wave, always in a ring. It rises and falls and changes, but it never goes away. Not just a wave. The soul of an ocean. The physics is quite interesting."

Joe looks at him again. When he isn't furious, he seems . . . teacher-ish. A heart of books with the skin of a tramp.

The man nods to himself once, sharply. "Who are you, then?"

"Joe Spork." He smiles uncertainly, and sees or imagines a distant flicker in the hooded eyes.

"I'm Ted Sholt," the man says.

"Hello, Mr. Sholt."

"Oh, call me Ted. Or Keeper." He nods. "Ted's better. No one calls me the other any more." As if reassuring himself.

"Hello, Ted."

"Joe Spork. Joe Spork. Spork, Joe. You're out of season for a hippy and too poor for a developer. Might be a scout, though. Smuggler? Lovelorn suicide? Poet? Police?" It is unclear which of these he holds in lowest regard.

"Clockworker."

"Spork the Clock! Yes, of course you are! Spork the Clock and Frankie, in a tree. Gone now, of course. Spork the ticktock Clock . . . Wait for the day, she told me. Wait for the day. The machine changes everything. The Book is the secrets, all in a row. Death has the secrets, she said. Death bangs the drum, and his carriage never stops."

Joe stares at him. "What did you say?"

"Ticktock?" Glazed eyes wander across Joe's face, on their way to somewhere else he can't see.

"No, after that. 'Wait for the day'?"

"Breakers in a cauldron, the ocean in a box. Bees make angels. Book of changes." Sholt smiles benignly. "You know all that, don't you, Spork the Clock?"

"No," Joe Spork says carefully, "I don't."

"Oh, yes. Time is ivy and death is gorse and the turning sets us free. You look younger than you did, Spork the Clock. You were older when we met."

"Ted?"

"Yes?"

"What does it all look like?"

"Candle, book, and bell. For the exorcism of ghosts. No Heaven, no judgement. Just the Book, and pages like for a music box."

Joe Spork stares at him. *Yes. That's the job. This old loony is the client. The endgame. Not too late, at all. Just lost upon the road.*

God, I sound like him.

"Ted, I have a package for you."

"I don't get packages. I live in the greenhouse with the bees, and I cut the gorse and chop the ivy and that's all. When they say 'postal' these days they mean 'mad.' It's cruel, I think."

"Yes, it is. But look, here's the destination address, see? I wrote it down."

Ted Sholt's eyes fix very sharply, a moment of focus in the fog. " 'Destiny' is the state of perfect mechanical causation in which everything is the consequence of everything else. If choice is an illusion, what's life? Consciousness without volition. We'd all be passengers, no more real than model trains." He shrugs, and the sudden acuity is gone. "The enemy was transcribed, not transmigrated. Left himself lying around like an unexploded bomb. Don't let the Khan take you! Never!" He seems ready to flee, and then relaxes. "But he's dead, long ago. Safe enough. Did you say you had a cake?"

"No. A book."

Ted Sholt waves his hands. "I like cake. Chocolate, with butter cocoa icing. Golden syrup. It takes time to set, of course, but a man once told me time's a figment."

"Ted? I have the book. The book and everything."

Sholt peers at him, scratches his stomach. Under the sou'wester, he seems to be wearing a skirt made of sackcloth.

"Well, that would be lovely." And then the focus comes again, so quick and so strong as to be alarming. His hand shoots out, locks around Joe's arm. "You have it? Here? Now? How long do we have? Come on, man, they won't be far behind!"

"Who won't?" But Joe Spork is already moving, old instinct demands it: when someone says "they're coming" you go out the back first and get details later.

"All of them! Sheamus, for sure. Jasmine, maybe. Others, so many others, even if you haven't seen them! And I'm mad and useless. Not to mention bloody old. God, how did it take this long? Come on, come on!" He grabs Joe by the hand. "Did you say Joe *Spork*? Spork like Daniel? Spork the Clock? Yes? Where is it? Please! We have to be quick!"

"You knew Daniel? He was my grandfather—"

"No time! Reminisce later. Family stories by the fire, yes, and cake. You're buying! But not now, not now, now is the time, before it passes! This was supposed to happen decades ago . . . So late. Come on!" Wiry hands grasping and clutching, hauling Joe into motion. "No time!"

Ted Sholt does not, thankfully, smell the way he looks. He gives off an odour of wax, sap, and soil. He stops a yard from the car, pointing.

"Who's that?"

"Billy. He found me the job."

"Billy as in William. Don't know any Williams."

"He's a friend." Unintentional, and an old joke, that one. Sholt doesn't know, hops into the back of the car. Billy starts from a doze and shouts "Jesus!" and Ted lunges forward and shouts back that "Jesus was the mother of Mary, and Mary met Gabriel at the cross-roads, and the crossroads is where the ivy meets the gorse, where we fall down into the dark, where Frankie made angels in a tree," which does not calm the situation down at all. Billy twists around in his seat to see his enemy better and Ted lurches away from him, trapping himself in the corner of the rear windscreen and shouting at the top of his voice, "Angelmaker, angelmaker!"

Joe, for the first time in several years, is forced to shout. "Billy! Billy! Billy, it's okay, this is Ted, he's a bit mad but he's our client, or our client's representative, all right?"

"Joseph, he is mad as a coot. And he's wearing a dress."

"It's a robe," Ted Sholt replies with wounded dignity. "I'm a man of the cloth." Which is so surprising and so weirdly plausible that none of them says anything at all for a moment. Then Ted gestures. "Further down. It was back aways from the cliff, you see. So it didn't fall in." He raises his arm, and for a moment his face contorts in agony, so that Joe finds himself asking whether it's physical pain, rather than ordinary madness, which makes him wander.

Ted Sholt's home really is a greenhouse, but it's a greenhouse in the Victorian style, a great sprawling thing with two floors and transparent walls. There's a light on somewhere on the upper level, and Joe can see a makeshift bed and what might be a desk. The panes are cracked and taped, and yes, the whole place is wrapped in strands of invading ivy. As they get closer, Joe leans down to look at it, and yes, now that he sees it close to, it is somehow sinister, hungry tendrils slithering over a great wounded beast to reach the innards. He steps back rather quickly, and finds Ted next to him, bright eyes quick and head nodding.

Inside, it's warm. The glass and the ivy between them make the place airtight, or near enough, and hot-water pipes run around and about in a gasworks bundle. Ted removes his sou'wester, but not his green boots. His feet make a soft flapping noise against the wood floor.

Blittblattblittblatt. Joe stares at the boots. It must be his imagination, but they do seem awfully large. He wonders why Ted doesn't take them off now that he's inside. Perhaps he doesn't have other shoes. It would be ludicrous to imagine he might have webbed feet.

"Do you ever swim?" he hears himself ask as he follows Ted up the stairs. "In the sea, I mean. In the summer. I hear people do. On Boxing Day, even." Oh, bloody Hell, if the old place did actually go into the sea, could that have been a bit more tactless? He glances at Billy: *Help me, I'm drowning.* Billy stares back, mouth open: *You did this one to yourself, mate.*

Ted doesn't answer. Perhaps he didn't hear or perhaps he has decided to ignore the question, as a privilege of being mad. Instead he grasps Joe by the arm. "Come! Come!"

Joe and Billy follow him to the back of the house.

The back room is improbably enormous. It gives onto a set of open ironwrought doors over the sea, and Joe finds himself wondering again how this entire place doesn't simply shatter in the winter gales. It surely ought to. Even now he can see the glass panes bowing to the wind, hear the whole structure creak and moan. An alarming image fills his mind's eye, of all these glass walls bursting inward at once, a windstorm of razors.

Obviously, it hasn't happened yet. Perhaps the ivy protects the glass. Perhaps it's the gorse bushes or the short, stumpy trees in along the ridge. Perhaps the glass is some sort of legacy of the Second World War, a laminate, a pilot's cockpit glass. Perhaps he's never been safer in his life.

"This way," Sholt cries, "this way, this way, yes, we must go up! Up and over!" And up they go, out of the doors and onto a spiral stair which belongs inside a stone keep rather than outside a glass house on the edge of a cliff. The wind is treacherous, plucking and pushing. Joe finds himself regretting his big overcoat: it flaps and fills like a giant batwing.

Sholt draws him up the last of the steps, and they're on a sort of sheltered roof terrace on top of the main building, scattered with the odd detritus of decades: a handmower, two tyres, rolls of wire and fence posts. Billy Friend scowls into the biting chill, then yips as he treads on what appears to be a pile of human limbs. He stares down, and heaves a sigh as closer examination shows it to be a stack of mannequin's arms. "What's all this?" he demands.

"Waste not, want not," Sholt says piously, and leads them across the roof to a sort of tower.

There's a cool draught blowing through the room, and a strange smell of dry leaves, sugar, and turpentine, and now, above the sounds of the house and the wind, and the roar and rush of the waves, he can hear another sound, a deep orchestral twang which comes from all around. Or, actually, from tall, narrow boxes in neat rows.

"My bees," Ted Sholt says. "Live ones," as if this were in doubt. "I rather like them. They're simple. Uncomplex. They require care, of course. Although ironically what they mostly require is leaving alone. And the honey is good. They make heather honey, round here, and gorse. Sometimes other things in the mix. I trade it with Mrs. Tregensa. For eggs and such. I had three hives die last summer. Two the year before. The bees are not well. The Americans are having a terrible time. Some keepers have lost all of them. The bees are dying, Mr. Spork. All over the world. Do you know what percentage of the world's food production is based on bees?" he asks.

"No."

"About one third. If they die, the human effects will be appalling. Migration. Famine. War. Perhaps more than that." He shakes his head. "Appalling. But we don't see it, do we? We never see it." He's veering off again, into his own world, and his gaze slides from Joe's. "Another sign, I suppose. It's time, and past time. So . . ." He threads between the hives to a lump in the middle of the room, covered by a cloth. "Camouflage, you see? Where would you hide a tree? In a forest, of course. So . . . where to hide this? Amid a forest of bees!"

He throws back the cover, and underneath is a brassy object, three foot high and chased in silver. Sort of Art Deco. Sort of Modern. Sort of Arts and Crafts, and almost certainly handmade to order. Joe Spork stares at it.

It's a model beehive.

The body of the hive is in the classic style, like a tower of doughnuts, each one smaller than the one below. Etched into the metal, a fine tracery of curlicues and lines, and at the top, a curious basin which speaks of an absence. There's something missing, like a Rolls-Royce without a hood ornament. He wonders what it could be, then realises the answer is obvious.

"The Book," Sholt says fraughtly.

Joe starts guiltily, and takes the doodah from his bag.

"Yes," Sholt murmurs. "Read the Book, muffle the drum. Muffle the drum. Marching soldiers, someone comes." Then, with sudden suspicion, "Will it work?"

"I think so. I did my best with it. It's . . . special."

"Yes," Sholt murmurs. "Yes, of course. That was very good of you. Appropriate. I'm never sure whether Ruskin would approve of this. Truth and deception. Light and shadow. They used to say that Gothic architecture was about creating spaces for shadows. All that ornamentation was about what you couldn't see. Concealment. The divine in the darkness. I'm not sure he'd approve. But we're not Ruskin, are we?"

"No," Joe says, after a moment. "We're not."

Sholt gestures to the hive, and suddenly it can't happen soon enough, his hands are shunting Joe forward, little knobbly fingertips poking, faster, faster. Joe moves forward, and arranges the doodah and sets its various parts in place. So, and so. The armature immediately opens the cover, and starts to flick through. *Flickflickflick.* And back to the start. Teeth lock in the punched section of each page, rapid brass flickers like lizard tongues. Well enough.

He's delighted, actually. A clockwork item dormant this long (and unwound? Or, is this thing powered by something more baroque?). He closes the panel, noticing on the inside the familiar weird little symbol, like an umbrella blown inside out by a storm. From within the hive, he hears a sudden quickening, *flickaflackflack*, and thinks "It is alive!" He manages to refrain from throwing back his hands and saying this, Frankenstein-style, to Sholt. He suspects it would be inappropriate.

Sholt embraces Joe in mute delight, and then, because Billy Friend is too slow to get his guard up, him as well. Then the roof of the hive opens.

From within, bees emerge. In single file, each on a little platform, they come into the scant daylight and bask. They flutter their wings as if stretching or drying out. Ten, twenty, thirty of them, in a gorgeous geometrical spiral around the hive. More. Joe peers at them. They must be real. They cannot possibly be what they appear to be. Mechanical bees?

He looks closer. Black iron, yes. And gold. Tiny legs jointed with hinges. He's suddenly conscious that he doesn't know, really, how real bees are assembled. It is possible—plausible—likely, even—that he would not be able to tell the difference between the rare *Apis mechanistica*, with its deceptive metallic-seeming wing-cases and chitinous body which gives the appearance of etching (assuming such an animal exists), and a bee made of actual gold. In his mind, David Attenborough discusses the rare bee in breathy, pedagogic phrases husked out as he lies on his tummy and tries to get a closer look: *Dormant until the conditions are right, this is England's rarest insect. It's so unusual that it has no natural predators at all . . . Of all the inhabitants of the Earth, only man is a danger to this extraordinary bee . . . and it is splendid.*

Joe reaches out, then hesitates. He doesn't particularly like bugs. They are buggy, and alien. The nearest bee stops, and wriggles. He hears a whirr and imagines there might also have been a tiny *clank*. Breathless, he touches the bee on its back with his index finger. Ambient temperature. Dry. It does not apparently object. A machine would not. An insect . . . he has no idea. Probably. But bees are phlegmatic, and this one is sleepy. Perhaps *Apis mechanistica* likes to be stroked. He removes his hand. The bee rolls off the sculpture onto the floor, makes a very clear metallic *tink* and lies still.

He glances guiltily at Ted Sholt, but Sholt does not appear to be enraged. Joe reaches down to pick up the bee. Looking closely at the legs, he can see bolts, pins.

Amazing.

He puts it back onto the hive, and it pauses, then hums to life again. The others move into a new pattern. The little plates or platforms which brought them retreat into the hive to fetch more, but the original bees remain where they are, still fluttering. More magnets, Joe surmises, moving under the skin of the hive. Or—he's not clear on physics, but it must be possible—perhaps an electrical current running through the skin itself. If this object dates from the fifties, it's plausible.

Sholt watches, entranced.

"Breathtaking," Joe says after a moment. It is. It's a combination of craftsmanship and engineering beyond anything he has ever seen. And yet, it seems a bit disappointing. How much more could you do with all that effort?

But perhaps it does do more. Perhaps he's mistaken the timescale. Victorian automata are short-lived performances, like Billy's rutting nobility. Sholt's hive is more recent, and at least as much a thing of science as glamour. Someone took great pains with this, and set it out here on the edge of Britain, in the wind and rain. Wind powered? Waves? Perhaps it's a fanciful way of measuring weather: a barometer of bees. Or it could owe allegiance to an altogether different perception of art, a motile sculpture—the full cycle could last a year. With the right equations, it could be almost infinitely varied, a thing of beauty in constant flux. A mathematical proof, writ in precious stones. Cornwall is filled with the insane, brilliant products of men and women washed down from London to the farthest reach of the south-west: Fermat's theorems sculpted in *papier mâché*, Heisenberg rendered as music, Beethoven as blown glass. Perhaps this is some such piece, lost for half a century and now awoken. He smiles to himself. He's part of something.

A fragment of his mind tells him he needs to be part of things more often.

"Yes," Sholt breathes. "It is. It still works! All this time! Oh, the world's going to change now! Everything will change! Hah! Everything."

Joe peers at it. Perhaps the world will change for Sholt, he concedes. Ted Sholt, owner of one of the most prestigious mechanical mobile sculptures in the world, precious metals and jewels alone worth a hundred grand, value as an artefact almost incalculable. One of Joe's Middle Eastern clients would pay almost anything for this.

So, yes. For Sholt, the world will change. That sackcloth robe will be relegated to the greenhouse. There will be women, or men. He will have traction in the world, if he wants it. At least in a small way. Perhaps he will be on the news.

"What is it?" Joe asks. "What does it do?"

Sholt smiles. "Oh," he says. "It makes angels out of men." And when Joe does not immediately look as if he understands, Sholt continues. "It is an arrow, fired at the temples of Moloch and Mammon. It makes the world better, just by being. Isn't that wonderful?"

Yes, thinks Joe Spork. *That is indeed wonderful. However, it is also somewhat insane and a bit on the weird side.*

The bees are still sitting on the outside of the hive, soaking up the last rays of the weakling sun. They look like tiny holidaymakers on their towels. Joe experiences a jolt of alarm when one of them flies up and circles him curiously, bumping into his forehead, before realising that it must be a real bee which alighted on the hive while he was talking to Sholt. There are real bees all around, of course, in the real hives.

And what did you make of these things? he asks the departing insect. *Did you find them beautiful? Or did they frighten you? Will you declare war on the metal monsters? Or try to make love to them?*

"Do you mind if I take pictures?" Joe asks.

"Go ahead," Sholt says, almost limply. "It's started now. The only thing to do is wait and see. But have a care, Spork the Clock. There are men who will come. Shadows and ghosts." Sholt stoops, and grasps up the fallen bee from the hive, passes it to Joe. "For luck."

Joe is about to object, though he very much wants to accept, when Billy Friend stands heavily on his foot.

"Well, that's marvellous," Billy says cheerfully, to cover Joe's muted cry of agony. "Top notch. This is quite some place you have here, Ted. Do give us a call." He presents his card with both hands, Japanese style, and Ted takes it the same way and bows over it. "If you should need any more work done, Friend & Company will be pleased to advise you and assist, subject to the normal fees and suchlike, of course. And there we are, all good." Billy backs away a little nervously, as if Sholt may leap on him again.

"Yes," Sholt says. "It is good. Perhaps we can save the real bees. We really should. The truth will be known." And then the fog comes down over his face again, abruptly, as if he has been holding it at bay all this time and suddenly it has slipped past him. "You should go," he says. "It's not safe here. Not now. Not any more. They'll come. They will. This will be the first place. Go quickly. Use the back stairs." He hustles them over to the far door by the open windows, and Billy Friend makes a noise like a dog swallowing a whole squirrel as Sholt throws open the door and the sound of the sea comes not inward but upward.

"Oh, for fuck's sake," Billy says, going very pale, and when Joe looks down, he understands immediately why.

The greenhouse is perched on the very edge of the cliff, the land beneath eaten away by the waves. The entire back half of the room protrudes over the abyss. This gallery, with its weathered planks and rusted rail, is more than twenty feet out above a thrashing, white-capped sea.

"Go!" Sholt yells. "It's not safe!" And Billy tells him no, it fucking isn't, and bolts for the rear stairs and down to the car.

As they drive away, Billy's lead foot firmly on the pedal and a stream of furious invective pouring from him, Joe glances back, and sees Ted Sholt outlined against the sky, arms flung wide in a gesture to part the waters. Answering his prayer, a great cloud of bees rises up from the greenhouse and into the air, a swarming, gyrating fog which wraps him and wheels around him, then arrows up and out over the sea. Joe has a brief, mad notion that the tiny clockwork robots have taken flight, and wonders if this means he has committed some sort of robbery or been an artificial midwife.

"I have no idea, Joseph," Billy Friend says, and Joe realises he must have spoken aloud, "but one point on which I am very clear is that we should retire to the bloody pub and never speak of this day again."

Sholt is still watching the bees—perhaps fearing that they will never come back, insulted by their metal siblings—when Billy grinds the gears and takes the car down into a dip, and the greenhouse is lost from view.

Tess has gone home when they return to the Gryffin, but the landlord gives Joe a pitying look which says the story of his ineptitude has not been kept entirely out of the public domain.

"Would you give her my best?"

"Could do. Better idea might be if you came back at the weekend. Gave it to her yourself. There's a place in town does a decent bite."

"You think she'd like that?"

"I think you'll never find out if you don't come back and see."

Joe Spork sulks at himself. Of all the things he cannot do, the one he perhaps most despises in himself is his inability to flirt, and to move from flirting to more serious things. It is one reason he always ends up with impatient women, which is, in turn, why he is rarely in a relationship for very long and why the ones which last are usually rather sterile.

He shrugs off his gloom and reviews the day, flicking through pictures on his camera and contemplating in his mind his small treasures: the bee and the whojimmy. Amazing.

"Where did you come from?" he asks the collection, a little surprised by the loudness of his own voice. "Who made that thing back there?"

As if in answer, his fingers find an irregularity on the pommel, a dimple. He pokes at it with a thumbnail. A piece of silvered wax falls away—a jeweller's trick, metalled wax to conceal a flaw. He picks off another and then another, and another, until a shiny metal crest is revealed: the same sketchy angular symbol like an inside-out umbrella or a trident.

"Billy?"

Billy Friend, who immediately upon arriving back at the pub began the process of seducing a bubbly, bounteous American woman who is on a walking tour of the British Isles, is being taught how to say "You are very attractive" the way they do it in Idaho.

"Billy, come and look at this."

"I'm looking at something else here, Joseph. Two somethings, in fact."

"Billy . . ."

"My darling, would you excuse me? My boring friend over there needs the benefit of my enormous brain."

His *inamorata* makes some sort of off-colour comment of which Billy greatly approves, but releases him. Billy ambles over.

"Billy, do you know what this is?"

Billy Friend produces a jeweller's glass and pops it majestically into his right eye. This evidence of his prowess and wisdom does not go unnoticed.

"Hello, hello . . . yes, all right, yes, very good . . . fine. Didn't expect to see that here."

"You know what it is?"

"No need to sound so surprised, Joseph."

"It's on the book as well. I'm right? I have seen it around some-where?"

"As to that, I've no idea. But I do know what it means."

"Well?"

"Hah! Don't let young Tess see you with it. She'll never look at you the same way. It's a webbed foot, isn't it? It means someone unclean."

"Unclean?"

"In a nutshell. Look, my lot have been in the Waiting game only so long, right? Matter of economic necessity with us, and then it turned out we was good at it. But others, like I told you, they've been around a while. And back in the old, old days, right, some people were consid-ered unclean by birth. They weren't allowed to be around proper folks and they had to wear a goose leg when they were in public so people'd know not to touch 'em. Lepers, maybe. Or redheads. Maybe they really did have webbed feet. Who knows? So they ended up gravediggers and coffin-makers and all that. And now, if you'll excuse me, I'm going to take that young lady over there to Heaven and back, and I don't want any discussion of sewers. All right?"

"All right. Have fun."

"One of us has to. Be a shame to die grumpy, wouldn't it?"

And now, as Joe emerges from the Tosher's Beat and turns sharp left through a narrow gateway and into a maze of little streets, he is biting his lip and trying not to run. The logic of his worry is very simple and very clear. There are three ways in which Mr. Rodney Titwhistle and Mr. Arvin Cummerbund, *not* of the Loganfield Museum because it is entirely defunct, could have knowledge of the object Mr. Titwhistle so absently sketched in the air. They might know of it already. They might know of it from a third party. Or they might know of it from Billy.

That putative third party, of course, might be the irritated former owner of the Book, who paid a visit to the saleroom and whose merest mention gave Fisher the screaming heebie-jeebies. By inference, Brother Sheamus, or his successor.

There is, however, a limited number of ways in which any of them could know of Joe Spork's own connection with the item, and top of that list is Billy Friend.

Carefor Mews is a curious mix of old and new which the developer has in defiance of reason painted white, and which is now predictably grey-yellow with grime. Billy loves Soho. The ready availability of smut, late-night drinking, and intoxicated female tourists is part of the appeal, of course, but Billy confessed to Joe long ago that the place is his heart. Visiting Soho when it's thronging and celebrating is one thing, but if you live there you see the morning after, the grimy, mournful streets and plastered revellers staggering home after five, the irritable shop-owners starting work and the exhausted tarts knocking off. Soho is a perpetual carnival celebrating how beautiful it is even as the wrinkles set in and the make-up runs. It's always a last gasp, a last drink, one more fling before you die.

Billy Friend, the hardened realist, sees Soho as one long, sad poem or dirge, and he lives in the middle of it. Joe is unsure whether that makes him deeper than he appears, or just a little bit pathetic.

The street smells of urine and beer. The last of someone's chicken dinner sits in an open box. How it has survived the night, Joe cannot imagine. Carefor Mews has rats and urban foxes and human denizens who'd be more than glad to take a bite of such an obvious gift. Well. Perhaps it's recent.

The front door of the building has a combination lock, a new, electronic one. Joe knows the code—Billy gives it out quite freely, because anything which is stolen from him he can almost certainly steal back again, and he has no enemies. His neighbours find this habit infuriating, but Billy has a way of smoothing things over with people. It's hard to stay angry with him.

First flight of stairs—no carpet. That strange, silver-specked blue linoleum, with a sandpaper texture so you don't slip. His shoes make a noise like someone stepping on grit. *Scritch*. Why is that sound so familiar? Well, he's been here before. But that's not why. Hm.

Second flight—wood boards, the edges painted white, still no carpet. Mr. Bradley the building manager intends to put some down, but never quite has. There are drizzles of white paint across the boards, and dents and scratches in the bare wood from stiletto heels and heavy boots. Once, when Joe came here, the whole staircase was one enormous party, a weird stew of low-end toughs, party girls and party boys, and not a few film types with mournful faces complaining about tax equity over pisco sours in plastic cups. Each step goes *donk*, and some of them creak, too.

Third flight—hard plastic. The whole third floor is owned by one person, a cheerful Romanian named Basil who made some kind of once-in-a-lifetime deal and retired at the age of thirty-two. He bought this place to live in, installed some friends and family, then realised they were exploiting him and threw them all out. Now he lives alone, and paints very, very bad landscapes from his balcony. Basil is under no illusions about the quality of his work, but he likes to paint. Billy finds him infuriating. Joe can talk to Basil for hours about not very much, because Basil feels no need to control, prove, or even examine anything. He just floats, and paints, and occasionally gets very drunk and dances in clogs on the ultramodern floor of his enormous home. His bit of the staircase is a curious translucent block which looks as if it comes from an aquarium.

Fourth flight—rich, luxuriant carpet. "Deep shag," Billy always says knowingly. The top floor of the building is quite small, because much of Basil's place is double-height. Still, there's that strong feeling of James Bond about a Soho penthouse, and Billy plays it all the way to the hilt. The door has another combination lock, this one more serious and more closely guarded.

"Billy!" Joe says, banging on the door. "What the fuck is going on? Are you okay?"

Billy Friend doesn't answer. Not unusual. He's a heavy sleeper, and not often alone up here. He's probably putting on his silk dressing gown.

"Hoy! William Friend! This is Joshua Joseph Spork here, and before you bugger off to warmer climes I need a word in your earhole! Billy! Open up!" Joe bangs again on the door, and his heart gives a single, sickening lurch as the latch clicks, and the door opens just a crack.

Oh, shit.

On the one hand, Joe has never been in this situation before. On the other, he has been to the movies, and he knows that doors which swing open when you touch them are a bad sign. And somewhere in the back of his mind, Night Market voices are speaking in his head: old second-hand instincts are telling him to run.

Melodrama. Most likely is that Billy is downstairs trying to persuade Basil to lend him a Mercedes for his escape from his annoyed clients. And anyway, Joe Spork is a paragon of lawful behaviour, made his old dad an unlikely promise and stuck to it evermore. The world he lives in does not include gunfire or dirty deeds done dirt cheap. And this is London, after all.

He opens the door.

Billy Friend is a fastidious person. He likes to appear louche, but for all that the knot of his tie is forever resting against the second or even third button of his shirt, he is a very tidy man. Joe suspects this very tidiness is partly responsible for his decision to shave his head. The asymmetry, the unpredictability, the messiness of his half-covered head offended him at least as much as it decreased his chances with the ladies. Billy's only real girlfriend of the last ten years—a bubbly forty-something called Joyce, whose considerable cleavage was matched by a splendidly unpredictable wit—was eventually rejected not because she wanted to marry him or because nature's depredations on her body became too marked, but because she genuinely did not care where she left her socks. Joyce would roll in from a night at the Lab or Fioridita and throw underwear, overwear, and shoes into separate corners of the room. She'd drag Billy to bed and hurl his cherished Italian brogues into the sink, or blindfold herself with his best silk tie.

"I love that woman, Joe," Billy moaned shortly before the separation, "but she's death to a man's wardrobe and hell on his sense of place." For Billy, above the hubbub of Soho, his penthouse is a chapel of calm.

Which is why Joe's sense of alarm is growing. The penthouse is a mess. Is this a sign of Billy's urgent need to be elsewhere? Did he pack, unpack, discard and start again, leaving a trail of silk boxers and lycra briefs? (And oh, *my* God, the image that evokes!) Or has he been burgled? And if so, was it done, perhaps, by person or persons in the employ of a fat man with kidneyed sweat and a thin one with a surgeon's placid face? Or by shadowmen draped in black?

Or is it unrelated? Billy has plenty of irons in the fire. Perhaps he slept with a Russian mobster's daughter or a boxer's wife. Perhaps he sold to the wrong person (for the second time this year) a painting "possibly by van Gogh" which quite definitely is not.

Two of Billy's suits are laid out over the back of the leather sofa. There's a bottle of milk, half empty (and where does he get bottles any more?) resting on the bar. But still no cheerful bald erotomane, no glad halloo of greeting.

The floor is done up in more of the thick carpet so that Billy can have sex on it without grazing his knees or back. Joe's shoes make no noise as he walks. He is acutely conscious that a housebreaker, discovered in his profession and armed, might likewise make no sound as he prepared to strike. On the other hand . . . Joe Spork is a big man. His profile does not invite casual assault. It suggests rather that discretion is the better part of valour. He scoops up the poker from the fireplace.

Billy's penthouse is in three parts. The outer ring—you might almost think of it as the moat—is where he does his entertaining. It is furnished with glitzy scatter cushions and fertility idols from non-existent indigenous peoples, and a collection of somewhat risqué paintings by an eighties artist whose name no one now remembers.

The middle ring is made up of Billy's bedroom, in which resides his pride and joy, a great bed with four stone columns looted from a defunct museum in Croatia. The canopy is a driftwood panel carved by a girl in the Maldives whom Billy espoused as the greatest natural talent he had ever met. He brought this thing back as proof of concept and secured her a deal with a gallery in Holborn, only to find, on his return, that she had died in a road accident.

He wasn't even sleeping with her. He just saw beauty and loved it. On the frequent occasions when Joe asks himself why he remains in touch with Billy, this sad little story is one of the things which persuades him that Billy is more than he appears to be.

Joe stares at the bed. Clean sheets. Billy had time to change them after his most recent lover departed. But unravelled and hauled about the place. So. Billy packed, and then he was burgled.

Something crunches underfoot. Joe looks down. Corn? Wheat? Something like, anyway. Not a sexual fetish he can identify. Packing material? He's seen, recently, objects packed in popcorn as an environmentally friendly alternative to those pernicious foam nuggets which cling to everything and, if they once escape their box, take refuge all over his workspace. But popcorn is soft and fluffy, and this stuff is notably unpuffed. Gravel, probably, from whichever grand home Billy is presently selling to.

He peers into the bathroom. The same unkind hand has tossed all the shampoo bottles and colognes into the tub. The shower curtain is pulled halfway across, and Joe experiences another frisson of unease. He reaches out with the poker.

The most horrible thing behind the curtain is a bar of soap in the shape of a naked female torso. It's a fair likeness, but it's green, and smells of artificial apple.

On, then, to the innermost ring: Billy's study. It's a small, cosy little room at the back, with a view of the rooftops. There's just room beside the desk for a single bed and a bookshelf. After saying goodbye to Joyce, Billy took to sleeping in here so that the size of the double bed wouldn't remind him she was gone. Joe has a sad, never-uttered conviction that Billy, when alone, sleeps in here a great deal, that this room and this room alone is the truth about his life. Like Soho, the truth about Billy Friend is seen in the quiet times as much as in the loud. In this study, the lonely, almost scholastic little man takes stock, and looks into his mirror, and wonders who is looking back. He reads first editions (the only thing Billy will not chop and recondition, steal, or counterfeit is books) and eats cheese sandwiches made with granary bread from a local baker. He drinks tea. He wears jeans and a jumper and very occasionally calls his distant, disapproving family in Wiltshire to check on the progress of his nephew and two nieces through the horrors of school. University, by now—for the older ones, at least.

Joe pushes open the door. His breath catches a bit. There's a picture of Joyce in a frame on the desk; she's smiling a broad, hearty smile, the one she reserved for Billy and shared with him whenever she could. Billy, you're an idiot. You loved her. You still do. Call her up, get her back. She'll come. Tidy is a habit, to make or break. Love is more than tidy.

Perhaps he has. Perhaps, *in extremis*, he's fled to Joyce. Maybe that's what this is all about; not Mr. Titwhistle and Mr. Cummerbund and their facile deceptions, but Billy having a minor nervous collapse and junking his old life for a new one with Joyce, puppies, and a messy place in the country. That would be strange, but very nice. Joe could go and visit. He could bring a girlfriend, a serious one, and not worry that Billy would offend her by making a pass (or *not offend her* by making a pass).

Maybe this isn't burglary, but commitment. Make a mess. Let go the little streak of mean precision. Let it all hang out.

There's something on the picture frame. Jam, apparently. That almost settles it. Billy has been sitting here, eating jam (on granary, with too much butter) and realised the futility of his urban party lifestyle. He has tossed back the last mouthful of Mrs. Harrington's Finest Strawberry Preserve, snuffled up the crusts, and thrown his life into disarray in the name of love. Bravo!

The jam is odourless. Joe sniffs at it again. No. Very strange. It smells of nothing at all. Underfoot, another crunch. More gravel? Yes, but also . . . something white and bulgy. Popcorn. He prods it with his foot. Not popcorn. Hard. A plastic rawlplug, a picture hook, a binder. He leans down.

A tooth.

He picks it up. Wet. Cold. A tooth. He holds it in his hand. Nicotine-stained, just a little. Polished. Billy takes good care of his dentition. Joe stares at it. How does a perfectly healthy man lose a tooth all of a sudden?

The smell hits him all at once, as if it's been lurking around the edges of the room and now sweeps down and rushes into his nose and mouth. Flat, metallic, raw and vile, it makes him gag. *The tooth.* Oh, shit. Shit, oh, shit. The room is going round and up and down, and now there's an enormous amount of noise in his ears, a rushing static like a radio between channels. He leans on the desk, goes to sit on the bed, and realises just before he does so that it is the source of everything, the ghastly, misshapen lump beneath the sheet which he has been ignoring, somehow, since he came in: a huge, dead, butchered hog's carcass, except that it is not a hog at all, but a lonely, bald lecher with a monkish heart, and someone has done bad things to him, bloody things which have dripped and stained the carpet, and sprayed the walls in the dark, private corner above the bed.

Beneath the sheet, Billy Friend has been murdered, most awfully, most deliberately, most pointedly, and that is the world now, newborn and hard.

He must have died looking at Joyce's picture, and Joe cannot decide if that was mercy or a most appalling cruelty.

He shudders.

Billy Friend is dead.

V

**The trouble with shooting people;
girls wishing to serve their country;
S2:A.**

The trouble with shooting people, Edie Banister now remembers, is that it's so hard to do just one. Having shot her would-be assassin, and now being, as it were, on the lam, she has to return to her former quite abstemious attitude and not just shoot anyone who impedes her passage. She has already had to speak to herself quite firmly about nearly shooting two irritating pedestrians and a slow driver. She is positively proud not to have ventilated Mr. Hanley, the street-sweeper, who popped up behind her as she was leaving and wished her good morning, and she is really astonished at her own good behaviour in not shooting Mrs. Crabbe, who was merely walking by on the other side of the street, but whom she has never liked.

Focus, old cow.

The gun is extremely heavy in her bag. She has reloaded, out of habit; she does not honestly expect to be assailed in the street, and all that mystical jabber about expecting the unexpected is just so much toffee. Expect the unexpected, Edie was told by a sour veteran sergeant in Burma, and the expected will walk up to you and blow your expectations out through the back of your head. Expect the expected, just don't forget the rest.

The expected, then, is for her enemy to imagine that Mr. Biglandry has squished her like a bug. The assassin won't be missed for at least another half-hour, perhaps as much as a day, depending on how long his leash was. Edie has exactly that long to disappear. First step: a change of clothes.

She takes a taxi to a nondescript street in Camden Town, and tells the driver a story about her great-grandchildren so asinine that even she feels slightly sick. After a couple of minutes, he cannot actually look at her in the mirror, and Edie can feel her face sliding in his memory until it is generic: little old lady, average height, average dress. Lawdamercy, but the old baggage can talk.

Still twittering banalities, Edie pays the man, then fishes in her purse for an old-style penny, dated 1959. A proper tip back then, worth nothing at all today. She has a small trove for convincing people she's dotty.

"Here you are, driver, and God bless!"

He takes it hurriedly, eyes everywhere but on her. He just wants to forget that she was ever in his cab. The feel of round, cold metal, the wrong size and the wrong weight, makes him freeze for a moment. Then he looks down.

"Oh," he says automatically, "thanks very much." *You poor lamb.* She almost feels guilty, but hasn't the time.

She leaves him staring at the coin. He will recall the sense of aggravation she has engendered, but not much else. In an hour, he will remember her if at all as an amalgam of every fare he has ever disliked.

And then she goes shopping.

Four hours later, in the snug of the Pig & Poet: Edie has tied her hair up in not one but three separate knots, and she is wearing a T-shirt purchased from a barrow trader, a black skirt, and heavy leggings and boots. Camden Town has been good to her. She begged some safety pins from the respectable peeping Tom who runs a dry-cleaner's at the end of the road, and put the whole thing together to make a formidable new identity: mad old lady punk.

The Pig & Poet isn't much of a pub. It's a couple of tables and a miserable jukebox which didn't work even before Edie took one of her safety pins and shoved it across the two bottom bars of the plug and stuck it back in the wall, thereby causing a short circuit and a strong smell of melted plastic. The snug is now in partial darkness, which just about conceals how mournful it is, and how cheap.

The Irishman who used to run this place managed to get some joy into it just by being who he was, a kind of punchy, endlessly profane little man with a liking for large women. He went off to Exeter, apparently, and has nevermore been seen. Since his departure, the poetry has ebbed from the saloon bar, and the remainder is decidedly piggy. In consequence, it wasn't hard to get the attic room on cash deposit, no questions asked.

Edie is doing her accounts. By rule of long-ago decision, she does not allow herself unconsidered killings. For all that her recent shooting spree was in the heat, no death should go unnoticed, least of all if she had a hand in it. The power of knowing how to extinguish life in so many ways—and the power which stems from having done it—must be balanced with a respect for what it means to bring someone else's narrative to a close.

Edie, as she sips on her rum and Coke, takes a moment to wonder if she might have done things differently, and to appreciate the significance of *Biglandry et fils*, and the appallingness of having snuffed them out. For all that they were grotty, wicked, venal men, they were extraordinary things, both of them ravishing, complex creatures. Perhaps they were loving, too, in their own way. Soldiers for hire, certainly, and rough-hewn. That doesn't mean they weren't also dads or sons. Will Mrs. Biglandry curse and wail? Of course she will. Her horror at this circumstance will not be diminished by her husband's profession—if she ever finds it out. Her son will not be less orphaned, nor her daughter less broken, if she tries to explain that Biglandry's end was just.

If I were younger, Edie thinks. *Or if I had allies. Or if I'd thought a bit longer and planned a bit better.* She goes through it in her head, one more time. Killed two, spared one. Bad mathematics, but better than it might have been. *Less good than it could have been, too, old cow.*

So here's to the bungled dead, expired of their own incompetence and my experience. Here's to the long habit of survival. I'm sorry, Mrs. B and all the little Bs. I truly am. If I could bring them back—at a safe distance and possibly with a summary kick in the testes for justice's sake—I would do it. No one is so wicked as to deserve extinction.

Long ago and far away, Edie Banister was told that a human soul infallibly knew its own value when it was reflected in the eye of an elephant. She wonders what she would see if she went to London Zoo and somehow got close enough to check. The question of value has been very much on her mind of recent months. She can feel a cold-ness reaching for her, a chill she knows all too well, though these days it possesses a terrible finality. Mrs. Crabbe (whom she does not like) recently suggested on this basis that Edie must be a little bit psychic. Edie privately thought that anyone who didn't feel death approaching after nine decades on Earth was probably some sort of idiot.

Last dance. Best make it a good one.

She raises her glass in recognition of the recent dead, and, to everyone's vast embarrassment, not least her own, collapses into tears in the corner of the Pig & Poet. And then, little by little and aided above all by the damp, halitotic nose which settles on her chest as Bas-tion emerges from her shopping bag to give succour, she pulls herself together again, and very soon she is the woman she was, has always been—just a little older, and reddish about the eyes.

All those years. *Bloody hell.*

"Girls wishing to serve their country will need flat shoes and modest underwear."

It is the word "underwear" which wakes Edie Banister from the contented slumber into which she has fallen during Miss Thomas's morning notices. The teachers at Lady Gravely School very rarely speak of underwear, and the reference to flat shoes is astonishing, because all other kinds are most strictly forbidden. As for the implied existence of *immodest* underwear—Edie can barely believe her tender young ears. This much is clear: Miss Thomas did not write the notice she is reading, and the matter is considered very serious—sufficiently so that this informational contraband is all the same being given a place here, between duty roster and closing prayers.

"Underwear," she murmurs, as everyone else says "Amen," and duly presents herself at the appointed time in the headmistress's study, wearing her most unimpeachable shoes.

Three other girls have been bitten by the patriotic bug; presumably either the other sixty or so are not as mind-numbingly bored as Edie, or they fear they may be asked by their government to do something unladylike, a suspicion which was raised in Edie's mind by the men-tion of underwear and to which she clings like a drowning woman to a spar. Prostitutes were sent to assassinate Napoleon, she recalls, and in a racy novel of which she read two-thirds before being betrayed by a prim little cow called Clemency Brown (and consequently slapped thrice with a ruler across the palm), the heroine had given herself regretfully but unswervingly into the lustful embraces of Skullcap Roy the pirate in order to deflect his wrath from her younger brother. Not, Edie suspected, without a certain measure of anticipation. In time of war, she reasons, one must be prepared to sacrifice oneself. She imagines herself lying back and thinking of England in the arms of a brutishly delicious enemy. The horror is very nearly too much for her.

"Plant, good. Dixon, good. Clements, no, I don't think so, girl, you're in the Christmas play. Where shall we find another Magdalene who can sing? No, no. And . . . hmph." Which is all the approbation Edie is likely to see, but no denay, and that will do.

"I'm so sorry, Miss Thomas, I didn't catch that last?"

The little man is long-faced and pomaded. A pimp, Edie decides, like Quick Jack Duggan or Herb the Knife. On the other hand, he wears a blue suit of the most conservative kind, with a longish waistcoat and a fob watch. The fob has a small gold flower on the far end. Not worth pinching, or not yet, but a chunk of stuff all the same and very fine. Not Masonic, which is disappointing. The Masons, she has heard, perform depraved rites.

"Banister," Miss Thomas mutters. "A lost child."

"My, my. How so, lost?"

"In every sense, I'm afraid. Lost, because orphaned. Lost, because she must ask every question in her head and then another and another, and lost because she is stepped in spiritual grime and even in my most blessed and hopeful dreams I cannot see her ever casting out sin and admitting the Lord of Hosts."

"Oh, dear."

"Indeed."

"Well, I shall certainly pray for her."

"Oh, indeed."

"Is there a particular prayer one offers up for young girls adrift on a sea of dreadful temptation? Something in the line of 'Oh hear us, when we cry to thee'?"

"No," Miss Thomas says, displaying some exhaustion with the topic. "Just whatever you can manage."

"I shall manage what I can, then."

Miss Thomas nods, and proceeds to vaunt the other two girls and ignore Edie entirely. No surprise, and in any case Edie is not concerned. She has seen the spark in the gentleman's eye, and knows that he has seen her seeing it. And she knows, too, by the flat-faced sincerity of his mien and his bland, unamused expression, that this man is a most unmitigated crook. Crooks do not go looking in distant corners for virtue. They can find that anywhere. Kindred wickedness, on the other hand, is a thing which must be sought out, and the seeking is the more difficult because it naturally masquerades, where virtue is drably ostentatious.

"My name," the little gentleman says, "is Abel Jasmine. I am in the employ of the Treasury of His Majesty George VI, who is, of course, our king. At least, I assume he is. Is there anyone here who isn't a subject of His Majesty?"

Tittering. Even Miss Thomas titters. Edie does not. It's a perfectly valid question. There might be an Irish person, or an American, or even a French citizen in the room. Mr. Jasmine smiles and leans forward, hands clasped.

"Excellent. All Brits together, eh? So, ladies. I'm afraid we come to a most difficult question. Which of you has recently told an absolutely egregious lie? Miss Thomas?"

"No," Miss Thomas says sniffily. More tittering. Never, Jessica Plant says, has she even embroidered the truth. (Which is, of course, an egregious lie, but a very stupid one.) Holly Dixon admits to having lied about having a stomach upset to avoid kitchen duty. Miss Thomas makes a note. Edie smiles and says nothing, and sees Mr. Jasmine's eye settle immediately on her face.

"No deceptions in your life, Miss Banister?" Mr. Jasmine asks at last.

"It's frightfully embarrassing," Edie says breathlessly. "There must have been some, I'm sure. But for the life of me," she offers him a broad, empty-headed smile, "I can't think what they might have been, sir. Is that terribly bad?" She cancels the smile and the fluttery panic, and meets his gaze as hard as she can. "Is that what you had in mind, sir? Or more in the way of outrage at the very notion?"

Miss Thomas makes an outraged little noise in preparation for a scolding, but the little man holds up his hand and smiles.

"I believe you hit it on the head, Miss Banister," Abel Jasmine says. He shrugs. "Well. Welcome to Science 2. You best go and pack. Thank you, Miss Thomas."

Edie keeps her face absolutely even, as if she had expected nothing less, and sees Abel Jasmine notice that, too.

Tally-ho, Edie Banister thinks, with considerable pleasure.

Abel Jasmine's word is backed by most elevated persons, and while the laws of England cannot casually be broken, their action can be most miraculously expedited. Edie Banister finds herself in transit that very day, and her guardianship—never her most serious concern—is transferred from Miss Thomas to a stout woman named Amanda Baines who is Mr. Jasmine's Second Director.

Not "secretary," Edie notes, as they drive away in an official-looking car, and her old life—such as it was—vanishes behind her. Not "mistress" or the more cowardly "companion," nor "housekeeper" nor "cook." Second Director, meaning deputy and fully empowered, which if it is not an entirely new thing is all the same a notable and important thing. Amanda Baines is a force in her own right. When Edie calls her "Miss Baines," the woman responds with a deep, earthy chuckle, heavy hands on the steering wheel, and says that it is in fact "Captain Baines," but that Edie should in any case call her Amanda.

Captain as in—of—a ship?

Yes. The good ship *Cuparah*.

Is it a big ship?

It is a research ship.

What kind of research? What kind of ship?

Amanda Baines produces a narrow pipe in white clay, and allows Abel Jasmine to light it.

"A Ruskinite ship," she replies, and her grey eyes peer at Edie through the smoke.

Edie has not heard the word, but has no intention of admitting it. She has studied, in the cool classrooms of Lady Gravely, the work of an art critic named John Ruskin, who elected to refer to himself in Greek as *Kata Phusin* ("According to Nature") and whose distaste for the processes of industrial construction had once led him to describe the Lady Gravely school itself as "impoverished of heart, devoid of soul, and unsuited to its function; a carbuncle of a building festering upon the fundament of Shropshire." It is an assessment with which Edie can only agree. She pictures Ruskin leaning sadly on an oak at the far end of the drive and jotting in his notebook: *Lady G, Shrop. Bloody ghastly. Write to The Times. Spare no spleen.*

Ho hum. Ruskin was against standardisation. He liked each aspect of a building to be the product of a unique human soul, an expression of the relationship with (inevitably) God. So, and so.

"A unique ship."

"Yes."

"A special ship."

"We like to think so."

"A . . . a Victorian Gothic ship?"

Amanda Baines makes a snorting noise which could be either affirmation or disdain, and that is all Edie learns, because they have arrived at Paddington station and, through the gloom and smoke, she sees the train.

In this year of Our Lord 1939, of course, many people of means have private carriages which can be shackled to a train to provide the discerning—*id est* the wealthy and empowered, whose discernment need only reach so far as to know that they're more important than anyone else—with a railway voyage at some remove from the common rabble. The wagons of the Rothschilds, the Kennedys, the Spencers and the Astors are spoken of in hushed tones at Lady Gravely as the symbol of *grande luxe* life and the thing to which every gal of character, charm and class might aspire. But no one Edie has ever heard of had his own train entire, complete with an engine, twice the height of a man, scrolled and chased in brass and trimmed in black iron. Certainly no one has anything so absolutely warlike, so defensible, armour-plated and fitted with a ram at the front, the engineer's compartment sheltered from incoming fire. And . . .

"Steam?" Edie murmurs.

"Hah!" Abel Jasmine says. "Thought you'd like that. It goes over a hundred miles an hour, and barely makes a sound. And of course, it burns whatever you shove in the furnace, so it doesn't deplete our resources as badly as a petroleum engine would."

"But it's vulnerable," Edie argues in spite of herself. "A shot to the pressure tank . . ." She trails off. This sort of interjection is the kind of thing which caused Miss Thomas to call her a lost child.

"Quite right, Miss Banister!" Abel Jasmine cries, delighted, "quite right, indeed, which is why the steam is contained in the very heart of the vehicle and the cylinder is most heavily shielded. But you have spotted our vulnerability, all the same. Well done. The *Ada Lovelace* is a compromise between stealth, strength, versatility, and security. It is perfect in no respect save that it functions excellently in all."

Amanda Baines—the woman who has a ship of her own—looks at Edie as if to say "boys and their toys," but Edie is smiling at the improbable thing, not for what it is, but for the world it promises. Having your own engine means no timetables, no delays. It implies that Abel Jasmine, indeed, can command delay, can re-arrange the structure of the nation's rapid-transit system for his own convenience.

"It's amazing," she says, and Abel Jasmine allows that it's not bad at all. Edie stops, considering. "It's Ruskinite, isn't it?"

He looks at her very sharply, then at Amanda Baines, who grins like a big dog around her pipe.

"Yes," Abel Jasmine says. "It is. Mind you, it's behind the curve now. Out of date by the time we finished it. That's the pace of change . . . Well," he adds to the driver, a dour moustachioed fellow in blue, "carry on, Mr. Crispin. Let's be about it!"

The train is not less wondrous inside. Edie stares at rippling surfaces of wood and brass, trimmed with a rich azure and gold like a cathedral, and windows of resin-ish stuff which is like Bakelite, only tougher. She walks up an open spiral stair to the upper deck and peers out at the night as it hurtles by. For the first time in her life, she feels free. She presses her head against the not-glass and smiles a wide smile.

"Blue colour is everlastingly appointed by the deity to be a source of delight."

She turns. A broad, grey-haired man in overalls stands at the far end of the carriage. Edie judges him to be nearly sixty, but very strong.

"The train," he says. Edie scrutinises him for signs of condescension, finds none. As he turns, she sees a monk's tonsure at the back of his head.

"It's amazing," she says.

"It's called the *Ada Lovelace*. Do you know who she was?"

"Lord Byron's daughter."

"Much more. A genius. A visionary. We named this engine for her."

"I'm sure she would have approved."

"Perhaps. It's enough that we remember her a little. I'm the Keeper," he adds, and then, because Edie's mouth must be open as she tries to think of a polite way of asking, "Of the Order of John the Maker." When she doesn't immediately nod, he adds, "The Ruskinites."

It had not occurred to Edie until this moment that "Ruskinite" might be a noun. She ponders. The adjective, she has no problem with. A Ruskinite item is going to be crafted, considered, inspired. It will have respect for the human scale of things. It will strive to exemplify the divine in the everyday. It's an admirable set of qualities for, say, a tea service, or even a giant secret locomotive.

A Ruskinite person, however, is something other, and she's not entirely comfortable with it. A strange sort of Christian with strong feelings about the working man and the essence of the world.

The Keeper smiles.

"What?" Edie Banister demands.

"You're trying to work out if I'm an engineer or a cultist," he replies.

"I suppose I am."

"Excellent, Miss Banister. Very good, indeed. Come. Let me show you the *Lovelace*. You can interrogate me on the way." And to her amazement, he offers her his arm, like a baron to a duchess.

The *Lovelace* is eleven carriages long. There is accommodation, a kitchen, bathrooms, and two carriages of strange machinery in glass and metal which the Keeper will not explain, but which looks to Edie like a mixture of a franking machine, a music box, and an abacus. She deduces it has to do with numbers and therefore with logistics, and possibly also with ciphering.

There is a radio set, an engineering room, and a pair of administrative offices, a private stateroom occupied by Abel Jasmine himself, and a doorway leading to the engine beyond. From the cowcatcher at the front (first designed by a friend of the original Lovelace herself, a man named Babbage, remade by the Ruskinites and manufactured to specification by a foundry in Padua) to the scrolled ironwork at the back of the last carriage, there is not one inch of it which is not made and maintained by hand.

"This train is our blood," the Keeper says. "It is the product of our work. We know every part of it. The designs were perfect, but the materials are not. They cannot be. So we compensated. Does it look sheer? Does it look absolutely true? It's not. Here we shaved an eighth. There we padded. The rivets are not exactly the same. They are positioned to avoid splitting the wood. They are loosened here and there to allow for expansion. The machine doesn't know when it is vulnerable. The mechanical drill has no idea when it is destroying the substance it cuts. But we know. We feel and hear. We touch. Touch is a truer sense than sight."

"And all this . . . it makes your machines better?"

The Keeper shrugs. "It makes us better," he says. "Or at least, it means we do not become casual about effort and art. We appreciate the weakness of the world and come to understand the glories and stresses of our selves. But yes. The product is better, by perhaps a single percentage point, than it would be if it were made by machines to perfect tolerances. It doesn't matter until you stress it. Stress this train, and it will hold. It will hold beyond what the specifications say; beyond what any of us believes. It will hold beyond reason, beyond expectation, beyond hope. Derail it, drive it across sand, twist and heat it. It will do what it can for you. It will hold as if it was alive, and filled with love. And when it fails, it will fail hugely, heroically, and take your enemies with it. Because it has been made that way. But we trust it will not need to, in this case. The *Lovelace* is not a ship of the line."

"*Cuparah* is."

The Keeper smiles. "*Cuparah* will hold, too."

Which is reassuring, but does not tell her any more about Amanda Baines's vessel. Drat.

Edie Banister, six months later, in sensible shoes and modest underwear—although not entirely modest, because she has long legs and just a hint of womanliness about her now—sweats and toils amid strange machines. *Ada Lovelace* is narrow and sways with a strange, eerie motion, as if she were dangling off the edge of a precipice. For the first few weeks, this made Edie extremely nauseous, but now she hardly notices, except when something sticks briefly in its gimbal and falls out of sync with the rest of the room. The sound of metal against metal rings beneath her feet, and then is replaced by a sudden whooshing of waves and wind. Edie feels, around her ankles, a blessed gust of cool air. The machine room sheds a great deal of heat when it goes over a bridge.

The ciphering machinery—if that is what it is—burps frenziedly.

Edie's hair stands up and she feels dust and grime rush to settle on her. She scowls and taps the earthing rod on her left before reaching out to adjust the pegs and feed a new set of numbers into the machine.

The *Ada Lovelace* is where Edie works and lives and—to her amazement—learns. Before her shift begins in Hothouse 6 (this being the secret designation of the machine room on board the *Ada Lovelace*), she has four hours each morning spent studying any number of things girls are not generally encouraged to know, while the train rips across the British countryside, occupying empty sidings and blank slots in the timetable, rolling and slipping around the edges of the map.

The *Ada Lovelace*, she has begun to understand, is but one part of a curious pattern, a cross-hatched web of connections. Not all of them are trains, but each surely houses a machine room used for this kind of numerical unravelling. The work is not limited to code-breaking, but includes more generalised number problems and mathematical assessments of probability and chance. In the course of carrying answers from the machine to Abel Jasmine's office at the head of the train, Edie has glimpsed enough to understand what the numbers signify: maps, armies, and fleets. She cannot begin to guess which numbers relate to which problem, but she knows now what is being asked in Hothouse 6: the rate of the enemy's resupply; the depth of water in a harbour revealed by wave heights and frequencies; the presence of a secret installation by the early thawing of a snow-capped mountain. Properties of the real world, she realises, may be predicted by numbers on a slate. She has a sense that learning these things without ever being told them is a species of test, a continual assessment. Secrets, here, are prizes to be winkled out.

The train ducks into a tunnel, and Edie sighs as the heat immediately becomes stifling. She suggested a few weeks ago that they could probably go with a considerably less modest set of garments, and even the most reserved of the girls readily agreed until the Keeper respectfully submitted that a) it was hard enough to keep a group of monks and soldiers focused on running the engine and the galvanic system without surrounding them with sweating, naked girls and b) a lady should certainly not care, however patriotic she might be, to sustain a burn in a sensitive place such as might result from (here he hesitates, casting around for respectful terminology) an *uncorseted bosom* brushing against a hot pipe or valve.

Edie Banister: code-wife, secret engineer, plucking strange truths from the white-hot iron of progress to fight the advance of terror across Europe's fields. Learning poetry and history and languages and marksmanship. And doing much of it all but nude, too, surrounded by other girls in similar undress.

Edie has read some Greek drama, and is feverishly aware of the possibilities. Such understanding is one of the benefits of a classical education.

Edie Banister glimpses her reflection in a smooth brass plate, and tries to see resolve in her own face. This is the day on which she has determined to find out more about where she is working. She understands that Abel Jasmine is practising a thing called information sequestration—which is a clever way of saying that no one is allowed to know much about Science 2 beyond what is required for them to perform their function within the network—but three things occur to her about this: the first, that Abel Jasmine knows and presumably also Captain Amanda Baines, and also whatever minister has governance of their efforts and any number of that person's assistants and clerks, and that the addition of one junior employee to the list, while irregular, will not greatly compromise security; the second, that it is—while vanishingly unlikely—at least conceivable that Science 2 is in fact not a British operation at all, but a German one, and she has a duty to be sure she has not inadvertently been duped into betraying her country; and third, that she really, really wants to know about what's going on. If she is caught—and assuming that, being caught, she has not also been shot by German spies for uncovering their evil plan—she will lean heavily on items [1] and [2] as justification and skate over item [3].

Thus Edie Banister, now eighteen years of age and slender as the rails she rides, prepares for her first covert mission.

Over the last weeks, she has surveyed the parts of Hothouse 6 to which she has ready access. The dormitories are at the rear; the monks' last, with a small contingent of soldiers—it's a barracks, really, and defensible—then the women's, then the baths and communal mess, then the work area and the classrooms and finally a locked door leading to Abel Jasmine's study and the output room, snuggled up against the engine and, like the barracks, armed to repel invasion. It seems to

Edie—in her new guise as a student of strategy and war—that there is a tacit prioritisation here, a tactical triage. Edie has already ascertained that there is a remote decoupling system threaded through the train, operable only with a special key. There are access points along the main corridor, which zigzags around the rooms, making them more private but also obviating the possibility of an enfilade. A great deal of thought has gone into the construction of the *Lovelace*, above and beyond the strange, tactile prayers of the Ruskinites.

Which implies, of course, that measures have been taken to guard against infiltration as well as assault, but she's fairly sure none of the security systems she is likely to encounter will kill her unless Abel Jasmine specifically orders them to.

Seventy per cent sure, at least.

Edie racks a new valve and glances at the girl next to her—Clarissa Foxglove—with some wistfulness. Clarissa Foxglove has smooth skin and short hair, and Edie, working beside her, has become acutely aware of her proximity and her energy, and the strong, purposeful way in which she does things. Clarissa Foxglove's voice is husky, as if she has a throat cold all the time, and she smokes cheap cigarettes which her Free French uncle sends her in a monthly package which also contains admonishments to greater efforts in the cause of His Britannic Majesty's United Kingdom. Edie, observing Clarissa purse her lips and wet each cigarette before they go in, suffers from pangs of envy. Not that she wants a cigarette. Just that she wishes, sometimes, with a belly-curdling lurch of desire, that Clarissa Foxglove would treat her in the same way. Two days ago, Edie had to pass a pair of pliers to Alice Hoyte, Clarissa's neighbour on her other side, and at full stretch found herself pressed *corps à corps* with Clarissa, their hips rubbing gently and Clarissa's shoulders moving under her chemise as she worked on replacing a blown fuse. *Upon a soft cushion I dispose my limbs*, oh, indeed.

Edie Banister pushes this thought firmly down—not because of its content, which she files away for extensive later consideration—but because it is liable to distract her from the task at hand. Before she can move her eyes away from Clarissa Foxglove, the girl catches her looking and smiles a conspiratorial smile, then quite deliberately leans forward to borrow Edie's screwdriver, her lace-clad left breast drawing a line across Edie's arm and shoulder which she can feel long after the contact has finished.

Focus.

The interior corridor of the *Lovelace* is patrolled and likely impassable. Thus, Edie has ruled it out. But in a few moments, the bell will sound for end-of-shift and another opportunity will present itself. Edie's workmates (including Clarissa Foxglove, oh, my) will head for the showers. And isn't that an opportunity worth savouring? Mm.

Focus.

A slim girl—a girl with strong arms and no chest to speak of—might lift herself out of the carriage onto the roof, if she had a screwdriver to open the filter on one of the ventilation hatches. So long as the train was not going through any tunnels and so long as it was travelling relatively slowly, she might then make her way along the roof to the engine, and slip back in via the roof maintenance hatch, then rejoin the train proper in Abel Jasmine's study via the connecting door.

The bell rings. Time to go.

"Just got to fnafflebrump caddwallame, all right?" Edie says, and no one pays attention. She learned at Lady Gravely's that nonsense which can be misheard is a very good way to lie without getting caught. People just insert whatever they think you must be doing, and—having lied to themselves on your behalf—are disinclined to check up on you. She turns.

Clarissa Foxglove bends down, quite unselfconsciously, to pick up a spool of copper wire. Edie Banister, caught in amber, slides past her gingerly, trying extremely hard not to feel the rasp of cotton on cotton or the contours of Clarissa's buttocks against her hips. Edie hears a faint, earthy chuckle, or it might be a pleased yelp, and shakes her head to clear it.

Really need to corner her later and discuss this. It's very distracting. The whole thing needs discussion. Resolution. Needs to be laid out. We should bare our thoughts.

Um. Mm-hm. *Upon a soft cushion . . .*

Fortunately, Clarissa Foxglove's backside is now twenty foot away and the door to the companionway and the hatch is ahead of her. The other girls are heading in the opposite direction.

That's good, Edie tells herself sternly. That is not a pity. It is the whole point of the plan. I do not want to be wedged in here with Clarissa Foxglove.

God, I want to be wedged in here with Clarissa Foxglove.

But not now.

She levers open the hatch, and air roars in. Her ears pop. The rest of the train won't notice, though, because Edie has already closed the hermetically sealed doors between carriages.

This stretch of the line—which she has selected carefully—is somewhere in Cambridgeshire. There are no hills to pass through, and the winding track restrains the speed of the train somewhat. It's a gloomy, desolate stretch of fenland, though, with very little topographically between it and Siberia except shivering reindeer and mournful bears—so it's bitterly cold. Well, nothing for it. She had considered wearing two sets of underclothes for today's shift, but that would have made her sweat more, and thus increased the chill. She thought about concealing at least a jumper here, but reasoned that it would be discovered. The distance is comparatively short. She will be cold, yes. She will not be frozen.

She grasps the sides of the hatchway and lifts herself up.

Edie's first impression is of having accidentally coincided with a bucket of cold water hurled upward from the carriage in front. The air is a liquid, clinging and chilly, filled with moisture. It takes away her sense of smell, flattens her skin against her bones. She nearly lets go and falls back into the train.

No.

She heaves again, and flies up into the airstream, catches the breeze, and blows over backwards, rolling towards the edge of the train. She flails, and catches the hatch cover, then draws herself to a crouch. Her hand is cut across the fingers, not deeply, but jaggedly. She's covered in soot. And the alarming numbness in her fingers tells her that she has underestimated the chill.

She moves into the wind. *Bloody-minded, much?* Yes, she replies to herself. Yes, I am.

Half a minute later, she is standing on the next carriage, bare feet padding on the slick surface, toes gripping rivets and bolt-heads, hands reaching for ladder rails and corners, ventilation chimneys and antennae. Twenty seconds more, the next, and then the engine is in sight, long, sinister, strange, and dark. And what the bloody hell is that huge black thing blotting out the sky? Edie drops flat, and a scourging devil's hand slams over her head, spiny fingers and thorns, then another and another, one catching her back and scratching, tearing at her.

Ow, ow, ow. And blast, I like this chemise. Buggery bugger. A chunk of her hair is gone, too, pulled out in a handful, but she has at least identified the enemy: a copse, hawthorn and oak, gnarled branches clasping.

And now she can't undo the hatch. Her fingers are too cold, and she has no lever. She left the screwdriver she used to open the one in the companionway behind. Careless.

So. The way back is painful, the way forward, hard. Choose.

Edie's fingers clamp around the handle, and she heaves. Slowly, stiffly, it comes up. Mercifully this one has no filter, just a shutter which lifts up, so . . . and then it gives way entirely and almost throws her on her back again.

She lets herself down into the shadows. The chamber is lit in red, covered in lights and buttons: the generator room, turning steam power into electricity for the code machines. She touches nothing, sees herself reflected in the door panel and almost screams: red light behind her, hair mussed up and flyaway, blood on her face and eyes like holes in a mask. She looks like her own ghost, if ghosts can be mussed.

Out through the door, ten steps to the back of Abel Jasmine's office. Is there an alarm? Edie doesn't know. Certainly, there is one on the other door. But did he consider the possibility of infiltration from this end? Perhaps not. How would they get here? Parachute onto a moving train? Drop from a bridge, perhaps—but to do so without being seen and awaited? Academic, anyway—she's come this far. She checks it once with her eyes and—thinking of the Keeper—with her fingertips, too. No wires. No bulges. No secret switches. Surely there should be something?

She wonders whether there's just a bomb on the other side, then reasons that Abel Jasmine or the Keeper or someone must come through here all the time to check on the generator, and it is therefore unlikely to explode without warning. And then, too, that would run counter to her perceptions about the strategic construction of the train: everything runs to preserve this room, not destroy it . . . though no doubt there is a mechanism for that, *in extremis* . . .

Enough. She opens the door.

Nothing happens. No klaxons, no furious shouts. So. She gropes along the wall, finds the desk, switches on the lamp.

"You owe me five shillings, Abel," Amanda Baines says cheerfully. "She made it all the way."

They are sitting in the shadows on a leather couch, Abel Jasmine in his dressing gown, and Amanda Baines with a jaunty sailor's outfit complete with captain's hat. It is not the kind of outfit you would go to sea in. It brings new meaning to the description "saucy tar."

"Bloody hell, girl," Amanda Baines says, "we need to get you cleaned up."

"Good work, all the same, Miss Banister," Mr. Jasmine says. "Very good, indeed." He smiles.

"I'm not in trouble?" Edie asks.

"Oh, God, yes, of the most frightful kind. But no, you are not being disciplined. You are being promoted and transferred. You may shortly regard that as very big trouble indeed. But you passed what you may wish to think of as an informal test. You formulated a plan, acquired information, timetabled the whole thing, and refused to be distracted by . . . shall we say, physical blandishments?"

Edie blushes from the roots downwards.

"So now, my dear, you are moving up in the world. However, that's tomorrow. Today, we need to get that cut seen to and—good Lord, whatever happened to your hair?"

"A tree," says a husky voice from the doorway. "The Bracknell Woods." And there is Clarissa Foxglove, in her dressing gown. "I waited until they were gone," she tells Edie, "and the Ely bridge nearly took my head off altogether."

Abel Jasmine smiles paternally.

"Off you go, both of you. Things are going to change for you, Edie. We'll talk about it in the morning. But from all of us: well done. Well done, indeed. Now, Clarissa will sort out that hand for you."

Edie allows herself to be led away.

Clarissa Foxglove cleans her hand quite ruthlessly, and Edie yelps a couple of times as she goes after an embedded bit of dirt. Then she escorts Edie to the baths and hands her warm towels with a very professional air, and finally walks her back to her stateroom.

"You knew all along?"

"Oh, yes. Someone goes for it about once a year. It's who we all are. Fools for love of country, and so on." Clarissa smiles. "Come on. Time to put you to bed." She shunts Edie gently forward, pressing against her back, and Edie remembers the question of whether they should bare their souls. She can feel the other girl very clearly behind her. She turns around, smells mint and cigarettes, and knows it is the scent of Clarissa's mouth.

Clarissa Foxglove stretches. She throws her arms out to the side and lifts them very deliberately up above her head. Edie watches.

"I expect you're very tired," Clarissa says. "I know I am. It's been a long day. But on the other hand, you might—just might . . ." she shifts her weight against the door and lets it close, her back arched just a little, revealing a deep, broad V of skin " . . . want to stay awake a bit longer."

Edie makes a noise which is almost a groan and lunges forward. Clarissa Foxglove is already half out of her gown.

Edie Banister, girl superspy, lands on her back and makes a noise like someone dropping a set of bagpipes. She can see blithering yellow sparkles, playing on her eyeballs. *Ooh. Pretty . . .*

She tries to breathe. It's extremely uncomfortable. She can feel the train rolling under her, the rails in her chest. *Zigadashunk tchakak.* Points. *Shaddadtakak.*

Little yellow sparkles. Bit spangly and brown. Mrs. Sekuni appears next to her and pokes her sharply. It provokes a cough, and suddenly she can breathe again, clear and deep.

"That was not very good," Mrs. Sekuni says. "It was *very* not very good."

"Bad," says Edie hoarsely, now that normal services have been restored to her lungs.

"No," Mrs. Sekuni replies. "It was not bad. It was very not very good."

For Mrs. Sekuni, who is small and South-East Asian and very pretty, precision is important. If English does not possess the necessary nuances, the language will be modified until she can convey what she wishes to say. Thus a sequence of not-goodnesses ranging from "quite not very good" which is better than "not very good" but not actually acceptable, downwards to "very not very good" and "really very not very good" and "very very not very good." Mrs. Sekuni is entirely capable of using a selection of English words to fill these positions in her measure, but English words mean subtly different things to each individual English person, and Mrs. Sekuni some months ago got tired of demonstrating her version of those words and having soldiers and spies and policemen argue with her. So now she just uses English in her own way, and one of the first things her students have to learn is where on the slide rule of catastrophe their latest effort comes.

"Very not very good," Mrs. Sekuni says sorrowfully, and Edie feels a pang of remorse. Reading a dusty book from a great stack on his table, Mr. Sekuni clears his throat and glances at his wife reproachfully.

"It was better," Mrs. Sekuni allows. "Better."

So Edie, revitalised by the knowledge that although she is still useless she is at least improving, scampers to her feet and takes her position on the *tatami*. This is a Japanese word meaning "practice matting," except that it doesn't quite mean that, so now there is a new Sekuni-English word to mean exactly what the original means, and by happy coincidence this word sounds like an English person trying to say the word "tatami" in Japanese.

Edie has recently learned a number of interesting concepts from Mrs. Sekuni as part of her study of *budo*. "Not just bujutsu!" Mrs. Sekuni says sharply. "*Budo!* You will learn more than my skin and flesh." At which Edie blushed enormously and looked the other way.

Mr. Sekuni shouts "Hajime!" and Edie attacks, then finds herself flying through the air again, though this time she manages her landing well and rolls to her feet, once more on guard. Mrs. Sekuni nods judiciously.

"Better?" Edie asks hopefully.

"Very better," Mrs. Sekuni says.

"I don't understand," Edie says later, while Mrs. Sekuni watches a company of special soldiers work through their training in orderly pairs against the backdrop of the *Lovelace*'s dojo. "I thought Japan was our enemy." Because Japan and Britain have not been cordial since Tientsin.

"No," Mr. Sekuni says. "Japan is no one's enemy. It is an island composed of rock and earth, washed by the sea and the rain and shadowed by a great volcano. Japan itself has no political or even imperial opinions of any kind. Even the people of Japan—and there are many different kinds of people in Japan—even they are not your enemy. The Emperor, perhaps. The state, most definitely. But not us—which is why we are here."

"Do many people in Japan feel this way?"

"Yes," says Mr. Sekuni.

"No," says Mrs. Sekuni.

"Many," Mr. Sekuni asserts firmly.

"But not a large fraction of the overall population," Mrs. Sekuni says with great precision, and this Mr. Sekuni has to acknowledge is quite true.

"We are communists," Mrs. Sekuni says matter-of-factly. "We do not believe in emperors or queens or free markets or even the dictatorship of the proletariat. We believe in a world where people are equal in dignity, not contempt, and where resources—which under Capital are distributed through the quasi-randomness of a market operating blindly with respect to things which cannot easily be measured—are allocated in a sane fashion by the State.

"But that is all I have to say about that because I am not allowed to promulgate my disgusting Nippo-Marxian propaganda to operatives of S2:A, by special order of Mr. Churchill, who by the way is a fat, smoke-filled reactionary warthog and a very nice man."

She sighs. For a moment, her face relaxes and Edie can see the signs of early age in her: lines of gentle care and creeping sorrow. Then she rolls her head briskly, and there's a gristly popping sound.

"Come," Mrs. Sekuni says, drawing Edie back onto the mat. "Yama Arashi. The mountain storm." A wide space forms around them; Mrs. Sekuni has stern views about people who stray into her personal training area.

"Take this and strike." She hands Edie a long wooden stick, notionally a sword. "No hesitating! Strike!"

Edie does, as she has been taught. Mrs. Sekuni does not roll away or retreat. Instead, she moves forward, arms open as if she intends to embrace the blade. Edie has a horrible image of her doing just that, some furious soldier of the Emperor delightedly cutting her in half, and Mrs. Sekuni's beautiful, tiny figure parting company along a diagonal line, and Mr. Sekuni's genial, clever face moving from grief to rage as he tears the soldier apart and runs howling at his nation's lines and is in turn shredded by more modern weapons.

Edie has stopped dead. The wooden practice blade is hovering halfway down. Mrs. Sekuni meets her eyes.

"Yes," she says. "What we do here is very serious indeed. Again."

This time, Edie does not stop. Mrs. Sekuni does not stop either, and her arms embrace, not the sword, but Edie's own, and squeeze and turn, and Edie finds herself rotating and flying and landing on the ground, and now by some strange process Mrs. Sekuni controls the weapon, and Edie lies flat on her back, vulnerable in a way which is so total as to be very erotic. Mrs. Sekuni is locked along her, one knee on her chest and one hand on her face, the other on the hilt of the practice sword, which lies across Edie's neck. Her eyes stare into Edie's, brown and deep and very grave. They wear the traditional *gi*, a training suit, and Edie can smell sweat, wartime detergent, and something spiced and lingering which makes her mouth pucker. With a great effort of will, she does not glance down at the v-line of Mrs. Sekuni's jacket. She can feel the pressure of one small, muscular breast against her.

Mrs. Sekuni grins wickedly, then releases Edie and rolls smoothly upright. The Sekunis have an unconventional approach to issues of marital fidelity owed to their conviction that more familiar understandings of love are the province of patriarchal totalitarianism. They also, to Edie's considerable frustration, have a firm rule against sleeping with students.

Mrs. Sekuni's tongue appears briefly as she taps her front teeth with it. Edie looks away.

"Why is it called 'Yama Arashi'?"

"Possibly because *uke* hits the ground with a very loud bang," Mrs. Sekuni suggests. "Learn it, Edie. Yama Arashi is very good *budo*. Difficult, because it contains many things within it. But very very good." And then, looking over Edie's shoulder, she claps her hand to her forehead in horror.

"Mr. Pritchard! What are you doing? Is that *O-soto-gari*? No! It is not! It is a yak mating with a tractor! That is *really* very very not very good! My grandfather is weeping in Heaven, or he would be if there were such a place, which there is not because religion is a mystification contrived by monarchists! Again! Again, and this time do it properly!"

When Mrs. Sekuni is content with Edie's combat skills, Mr. Sekuni begins teaching her about guns and explosives.

Edie knew that her training was at an end as soon as she saw the message ordering her "station side"—this being slang in Abel Jasmine's organisation for the railway equivalent of dry land. She has a strange feeling in her legs, like a kind of inverted motion sickness; for the first time in weeks, she is standing on solid ground. She can smell bracken and earth, and on the wind, the unmistakable scent of heavy construction: hot metal and burned stone-dust.

In front of her is a rather grim Victorian manor or farm—if your idea of farming is waking at ten and walking along the hedges saying things like "I say, Jock, the wheat looks very fine this year, well done!"—made over into what she can only think of as a secret hideout. There is apparently also a secret greenhouse presumably filled with highly classified tomatoes.

On the other side of the manor, though, something else is taking shape; something the size of an aircraft hangar or a concert hall, with an earthen roof which resembles a hill or a burial mound and a great gawping maw of a doorway. Soon enough, Edie supposes, when the gorse grows back and the grass covers the works, the whole thing will look natural. Into the maw runs a row of railway sleepers without rails—yet—and this giveaway is being carefully painted green and brown, and broken with clever *trompe l'oeil* so that from the air it will look like nothing very much.

Some things, self-evidently, are either too big or too dangerous or too delicate to be done aboard a moving train, even a Ruskinite train with gas-baffle suspension and Brunel-Zeiss-Bauersfeld geodesic architecture, both of which the *Ada Lovelace* possesses and neither of which Edie even vaguely understands.

Edie ponders. The more aggressive aspect of Science 2 is called, prosaically, S2:Active, and is tasked with investigating and very occasionally implementing genuine scientific ideas which are probably completely impossible, but which, if confirmed, will reshape the world. If someone is going to invent a Gatling gun which can fire through solid steel, or an earthquake generator, or a heat-ray, or a devastating sonic cannon which causes tanks to shake themselves apart, Abel Jasmine is the man to ensure that fellow is working for the Crown and not the Axis.

Which brings up a question. "Is anyone doing anything like that?"

Abel Jasmine smiles. He did not announce himself, but Edie always knows when someone is behind her. This time she has also identified him, personally, and continued their conversation from the day before.

"Like what?"

"Superguns in space. Energy beams and lightning weapons."

"Oh, yes. And not just that. This is a strange time, Miss Banister. The invisible world, it turns out, is considerably larger than the one we know. Men and women wrestle with intangibles and produce . . . well. Wonders and horrors. Such as the X-ray. A medical triumph. A miraculous thing. Except that direct exposure for too long rots the body like fire and plague. What's the range? What's the most powerful effect? Imagine a battlefield of invisible light, scorching from a mile away."

Edie does, and doesn't like it.

"Is that what all this is for?"

"No, Miss Banister. This is much more important. Come." He gestures towards the manor house. A man is waiting for them on the step, an odd, elongated person in artificer's black.

"Ruskinites," Edie says, not without a measure of resignation.

It's not that Edie has a problem with the Ruskinites, exactly. The Keeper—who turns out to be not only the designer of the *Lovelace* but also the top of the Ruskinite tree—is a nice enough person to be around, because his passion is so obvious and so entirely unthreatening. And, yes, she has some sympathy for the notion that all these perfectly reproduced, same same same objects which are gradually replacing the more awkward handmade things she grew up with may be in some way damaging her country's relationship with itself, causing some kind of ghastly exile of the soul.

She just doesn't trust people who take things on faith, and suspects that a uniform group which purports to celebrate uniqueness is leaving itself open to going what Miss Thomas would have called "a bit funny."

She smiles as she reaches the manor.

"Hello," the Ruskinite says. "I'm Mockley."

"And what do you do?" Edie responds politely, because to a Ruskinite this is the most important question that can be asked.

"Welding, mostly. I've got a sort of gift for asymmetric joints which will experience extreme irregular shear. You have to get to know them a bit." He waves his hand vaguely.

"Oh," she says. "How wonderful."

Mockley beams.

"Take us in, please, Mockley," Abel Jasmine says.

Inside, the whole room is ringing. Edie can feel it in her chest, a wild, exultant creel of power. They're cutting solid rock away, digging and burrowing down towards the sea caves below. There's a glass oven (i.e. an oven for the preparation and blowing of glass, not an oven made of glass, although nothing would surprise her) and a furnace, a crucible, and several giant tubes or tanks whose function Edie cannot begin to guess. There are chemistry retorts and demijohns and vats and condensers and odd-looking gear which somehow resembles the code gear on the *Lovelace* but also looks a bit like a Jacquard loom. A wild hodgepodge, a scientific playground. Or, as Edie walks closer to the central pit, she realises she is wrong. Not a playground at all. A god's forge, for the making of magic swords and talking sculptures and all the stuff of fairy tales.

Down in the depths, the great, blue-green Atlantic is black and cold and seething, and something is being lowered down and down into the cauldron: a bomb-shaped thing with cables snaking back up the cliff. Below even that, in the probing glare of the giant search-lights which are pointed not up but down, Edie can see something else, a whale-shaped, whale-sized monster lurking on the edge of the light, a hundred foot underwater and more.

She looks back and around, and sees what's missing from this titanic mosaic.

"Who's the lucky girl?" she asks, because sure as chips and vinegar this lot is not for her.

"A scientist. It is a woman, actually."

"Well, where is she?" Edie glances around, looking for a bespec-tacled schoolmarm with chalk on her fingers. Abel Jasmine sighs.

"Ah. We were hoping you might be able to help us with that, Miss Banister. There's a slight problem."

"What sort of problem?"

"His name is Shem Shem Tsien."

The face in the photograph is in monochrome, tinged with a deep cel-luloid blue. It is no brighter than the faces around it, no older, no closer to the camera. And yet, it is indisputably *the* face, unique and apart.

Granted, it belongs to the man to whom everyone else is appar-ently deferring. He is richly dressed, and surrounded by dependants, concubines, and offspring. And yet, Edie has seen other pictures in the past where one child, caught by chance in an attitude of casual joy, has completely outshone such a parent; where one unthinking scullery maid has glanced at the camera and displayed for a moment her natural beauty, and the social order has been quite overturned. Photography is without mercy—though it's nonsense to say it does not lie. Rather, it lies in a particular, capricious way which makes beggars of ministers and gods of cat's meat men.

There's no such revolution here. The camera has fallen in love. It has given itself entire to Shem Shem Tsien, thrown itself at his feet and worshipped at his altar. He absolutely gleams, matinée-idol splendid, with broad white teeth and a hero's moustache in two delicate bars, as if drawn on with charcoal, emphasising the masculinity of his curving upper lip.

Shem Shem Tsien: graduate of St. John's College, Cambridge; debater, gambler, and rake; born the second son of the second son of the Khaygul Khan of Addeh Sikkim, a tiny tinpot nation on the edge of the British Raj. Industrialist and moderniser, favourite dinner guest of presidents and commissars alike, hunter of big game and bronze medallist at the Olympics in the foil event—would have done more, no doubt, but he'd spent the preceding six days drunk in the arms of a Hollywood starlet of pneumatic and renowned athleticism. His smile shatters marriages, unfrocks nuns. As a youth, he ravished Europe and the Americas, was the darling of the society pages—and then, disaster: his father, brother, and his royal master were taken all in one night by a sickness which swelled the brain, leaving Shem to look out for his beloved nephew (seen, indeed, in Abel Jasmine's photograph, carrying a butterfly net and clinging shyly to his uncle's knee) which he did by burning the corpses with due ceremony and installing the boy on the Khaygul's throne. Alas, all unforeseen and unimaginable, a fishbone lodged in the new sovereign's throat and could not be got out, leaving the wise, educated, clubbable Shem Shem Tsien the last (officially recognised) son of his line.

Or perhaps: Shem Shem Tsien, unfavoured and suspect child, his birth nine months after the visit of a noted British libertine, his face a little too beautiful, his hair too thick to be his father's boy. Not exiled so much as encouraged elsewhere, he served in the British Army and the Russian, carved out a kingdom in opium country before he ever came back to Addeh Sikkim, knows the Camorra of Naples and the

Yakuza of Kyoto, the Boxer Triads of Beijing and the Kindly Men of London. Red-handed enemy of the Barqooq Beys of neighbouring Addeh Katir, he is a trader, a producer, and a supplier of laudanum to kings and potentates, of anaesthetics and pain relief to armies; a Svengali, a Mesmerist, a blackmailer, an extortionist, and a kidnapper (all things one might expect, notes sniffy Abel Jasmine, in a Cambridge man). He is also a poisoner, a sponsor of thugs and an assassin, a bringer of plagues. Were his brother, father, uncle all dead when he locked them in an iron room and set them on fire? Not known. His inconvenient nephew, Abel Jasmine's agents report, was quite unquestionably held face down in a plate of Giant Mekong Catfish (and what idiot would eat such a magnificent, doomed thing? It's like tucking into the last mammoth, a dish for the dissolute and the small) until he choked.

Shem Shem Tsien owns the largest collection of preserved lepidoptera in the world.

He keeps nearly one hundred thumbs in a display case.

He is received in embassies from Brunei to Moscow, owns property in Mayfair.

Fifteen thousand infantry, nine thousand cavalry, and three thousand artillerymen, sappers, and murderers take their orders from his lips alone.

His word is law from Kalimpong to the southern reaches of the Katirs.

Shem Shem Tsien is the Opium Khan.

It occurs to Edie, powerfully, that Shem Shem Tsien is entirely Britain's fault. For whatever pressing reasons, the mother of democracies has given suck to this man. The Empire's great educational institutions have shaped him, her military has trained him, and her drawing rooms and salons have completed his development. Oh, all of Europe has played a part. In Shem Shem Tsien, Marx rubs shoulders with Wellington and Paine with Napoleon, each jostling for the unwelcome title of Kingmaker—but it is in Britain's melting pot that he has been composited. A British fiend, all manners and poisonous politesse, in every sense a home-made International Bastard of Mystery.

Of his whole family, saving himself, only one other member now remains: his revered and gentle mother, Dowager-Khatun Dalan, still known in Bloomsbury as Dotty Catty—quite the girl in 1887, got herself ejected from a music hall with a peer of the realm, and that was no easy task back then—the only one of the whole brood he trusts enough to leave alive.

The one who has now betrayed him.

Edie Banister, orphan child, born of some poor knocked-up wench in a poor town west of Bristol, adopted ward of schoolmistresses, charities, and latterly the British Government, occasionally has trouble understanding what other people see in families.

She glances at Shem Shem Tsien's photograph again, then flicks to the beginning of the file. The name on the frontispiece unsettles her: *Angelmaker.* It sounds altogether too churchy, too much like a funeral hymn. She shivers, and turns the page.

The Ruskinites are artisans for hire. They do not discuss the projects they work on. They evidence the spark of the divine in the detail of human labour; they do not engage in espionage.

But nine days ago, according to the file, the Keeper requested Abel Jasmine's presence at Sharrow House, the converted stately home over the Hammersmith Bridge, which serves the Ruskinites as their home.

The Keeper had a message. He was uncomfortable. He was betraying a confidence. This one time, with considerable misgivings, the Keeper wished Abel Jasmine to be aware of something. The Ruskinites felt what was taking place was more important than their general mission.

"More important than the human soul?" Abel Jasmine asked, with a smile on his lips. It was his pleasure to tease the Keeper, very kindly, just as it was the Keeper's pleasure to suggest by his bland expression and benevolent eyes that he had not noticed. This time, he frowned.

"Than the excellence we might achieve and the benefit to a finite number of souls. Yes. Possibly."

Abel Jasmine put away his sense of humour.

"In a far-off place," the Keeper said, "we are assisting a French-woman with the construction of . . . things."

"What things?"

"We are not sure. She changes her mind a great deal. At first it was Mechanical Turks."

"I beg your pardon?"

"Automata. Like the von Kempelen chess player, although that eventually turned out to be a fake. These . . . are not. You see the notion. Soldiers made of metal."

Abel Jasmine nodded. He did, indeed, see the notion. It had been a staple of popular fiction since at least the Great War. Artists had pondered it, thinkers had written on it. The horror of all those limbless heroes returning from Verdun and Ypres had made a forcible impression on Europe's ideas of war. It pleased many to look for a surgical solution to conflict, a clean, bloodless version of the thing. It did not please Abel Jasmine. A war fought by empty suits of armour did not strike him as a particularly merciful one; it did not even occur to him to imagine that they would do battle only with other machines. The world as he had seen it was not so fastidious.

The Keeper was still talking.

"Then the automata were discarded—somewhat; her sponsor remains rather enamoured of them—and she needed a great hydroelectric station. And mosquito traps. I don't know why. Then for a month it was vital that we construct a cinema for elephants, although . . . we are reasonably certain that represented a digression. Brother Scheduler tells me she is prone to enthusiasms. But now she is building something new. Something extraordinary."

"And this extraordinary thing . . ."

"Is what is—or may be—more important for the moment than our chosen task on Earth. Yes."

"Why?"

"The Frenchwoman—she is from the south somewhere—has stopped making soldiers. I think . . . when she was summoned, you see, she was one part refugee. It was the beginning of the war. I have the impression that she lost someone, and she was running from it all. She was asked by the client to create a device to end war, for ever. Well. That's usually a shorthand, isn't it? For a bigger gun.

"She now proposes to take her client at his word. She believes the device she is constructing will achieve that. She calls it an Apprehension Engine."

"I do not immediately see what that might be."

"Nor do we."

"The intention is very noble, of course, but . . ."

"But it has in the last generation given us the machine gun, poison gas, and germ warfare, and may shortly yield the atomic explosive."

"Yes." The Keeper drew his hand across his mouth, and then went on. "So. The mother of the original client has asked us to make contact with you. She proposed an indirect contact with the Crown through a friend from her time here. However, under the circumstances, we wished to alert you directly."

"What circumstances?"

"The client is Shem Shem Tsien."

Abel Jasmine sucked lightly through his teeth.

"That is not ideal."

"No." The Keeper bowed his head for a moment. "It is not, however, what ultimately caused us to take this step. By God's grace, even the works of a monster may inspire salvation—and indeed, by fostering our work, a man such as Shem Shem Tsien may learn to appreciate the miracle that is humanity, and become . . . better. That is our purpose. Temporal tyrants are of limited concern to us. The issue which causes us concern is the Frenchwoman. We have come to believe that she is Hakote."

Abel Jasmine listened to the sound of the wind rushing around his carriage, and the noise of the rails. *Hakote. Outcast. Unclean.* But so much more than that; Abel Jasmine, like the Keeper, knew the origin of the word, and what it entailed.

"Oh," he said unsteadily. "Well, yes. That does change things."

Attached to the file is the letter itself, and an assessment of the curious and circuitous route it took to arrive here. The handwriting is a spidery copperplate, very well-tutored but uneven, and there are faint traces of the blade of the writing hand, as if the author had to rest it in the wet ink to retain her grip.

To:
His Britannic Majesty King George VI,
c/o Tweel,
Chalbury House,
Chalbury,
Tweel

From:
Dowager-Khatun Dalan,
(Formerly Dotty Catty of 2 Limerick Street, St. James's, London,

and previously of Coddisford School for Young Ladies, Toxbury, where I took the second prize for Anglo-Saxon, Norse, and Celtic languages in my final year, and don't you pretend you don't remember me, Georgie, because I know better)
c/o Brother Scheduler,
The Order of John the Maker,
15 Barleycorn Street,
Dhaka

Dear George,
(or, I suppose I should say some such thing as "Dear Brother Sovereign" or "Dear Britannic," but I am extremely old, and foreign, so you will just have to make do.)

I was so sorry to hear about all your troubles. It really is too bad: this Mr. Hitler seems quite the wrong sort, although I understand he is vegetarian and so not getting his protein. One must make some allowances for a weakness of the brain. Also, I have heard it said he contracted a rotting disease early on and has curious spells. Be that as it may: he is <u>hateful</u> when he shouts and screams. We had a newsreel here in the palace, and it made me quite ill to see. Was it not enough that half Europe's manhood must die in the 'teens, that we must have another Great War about the world again?

Well, now my son has a Grand Idea and I am most afraid that it will be a horror. You know how it is between us, I think. I am quite amazed, to wake each day alive and not murdered. I would leave, but he holds over me the lives of my other children—no, George, not really my children: I mean the elephants, the great grey cavalry mounts of my fathers' fathers. They are most proper and most straightforward, and I must take care for them one how or another. Promise me you will help with that, too, if only you can?

Yes, yes, I know, I wander. Old women do that, George, so don't be unkind. Here it is, laid out the way he laid it out for me, most rational:

Addeh Sikkim is a small nation among stronger powers, and not always convenient to them.

In time of war, a nation may be contested by one power, defended by another, and in the confusion cease to exist altogether, so that even when the storm subsides, the small island that was has been quite inundated and cannot be got back.

Thus: the only weapon of use in the modern world is the vast and terrible one which cannot be understood or defended against, whose shadow will be a block on the dreams of madmen; a weapon so awful that the world cannot survive its use, so that no one would use it save in the moment of their own inevitable destruction, and no one seek or allow the destruction of the one whose hand is on the hilt, lest they find the blade cuts every throat on Earth.

Do you see, George, why I am afraid? This is a new talk, not like the good old days at all. It is entirely the wrong kind of Modern, and not Enlightened at all.

And so he has found a scientist—a woman, if you will credit it—to execute this construction for him. Find me a tool, he has told her, a thing which will end all wars. He has brought her here and she is prisoned, but I am not sure, but that she does not see things after his own fashion. She is an odd fish. Her family name is Fossoyeur, and she has letters after her name from a university in France. Because she is French and I cannot say her proper name—I lisp now, after my sickness last year—I call her "Frankie."

George, you must spirit her away, as you could not do for those poor Russians, while she still wants to go, for my son is a compelling man in all senses, and if she is persuaded, she will make this thing and then where shall we all be?

Send me someone fast and clever, George, and make it well again.

Please give my regards to your family and tell them I continue healthy.

Yours in haste,
Dotty

[Post script: Dear Tweel, I'm sorry to bring up the Anglo-Saxon prize, but you did promise if I helped you pass the exam, you would one day help me, and that day is today, Coddis girls together! Do please bring this to G. as swiftly as can be, keep it away from those frightful little Civil Service fellows or they'll want Frankie's wotnot for themselves. And "wot not" is the word, Tweel, I promise you: things we are not meant to wot of, and do not dare tell me that's a hanging preposition, because I know. Would you have me write "things of which we are not meant to wot"? It's sheerest drivel, Tweel, and I shall have no part of it. In any case I'm old and foreign. See above.]

Dotty Catty, in the fine tradition of Addeh Sikkim and Merry England, will not receive a man in private. Thus, Edie is the perfect agent. However, the Opium Khan regards women in general as chattel. No female admitted to the palace would have any freedom of movement nor security of person. Thus, an invitation has been secured for one Commander James Edward Banister, of His Majesty's Royal Navy, to come on a goodwill visit and discuss the disposition of the Khan's forces in any invasion of India by the Empire of Japan. Lodged in the palace, James Edward will hide away at night and transform once again into Edie, who will then present herself to the Dowager-Khatun in respectable style, albeit by climbing in through her window at dead of night.

The Opium Khan, in the finest modern fashion, desires that Frankie Fossoyeur create for him an Ultimate Weapon. Abel Jasmine would prefer that such a thing—if exist it must—exist in Cornwall, instead.

And all this is now the sole responsibility of one Edie Banister, the girl who wished to serve her country.

In the Pig & Poet, Edie drains the last of her brandy and shifts her backside on the ragged, uncomfortable stool. Since her eighty-ninth birthday, she's had a bad relationship with backless chairs. She stares at the darts board as a young tough with bad skin lands a trio in the treble twenty. Not bad at all. She sees Biglandry's face in the pattern of holes in the board, a martyred, hapless murderer, sent to do a job he was never fitted for. Not that he lacked talent in the direction of death. Just intelligence. She wonders if he'll be the last, and concludes that, if he is, she will almost certainly have failed—so she must assume at least one more session like this, with corpseguilt glaring at her from an empty chair.

She sighs, and begins to gather her belongings, not without a measure of bitterness. Here she is, a million years later, and not an older brother in all the world. No family to speak of at all, save for a foul-smelling dog clinging to life with grim determination in her handbag. And at that, he's liable to outlast her.

Edie Banister stands—a process which takes a distressingly long, awkward time—and goes upstairs to the relative tranquillity of her rented room. She stares around her. Oscar Wilde, she recalls, acknowledged the close of his mortal existence by remarking: "It's me or the wallpaper. One of us has got to go."

Looking up at the brown floral print, she feels a fleeting kinship. All the same, there's work to be done. Her shopping expedition was not just for clothes. A kitchen shop, two supermarkets, and a garden centre have yielded ingredients for some small advantages in what she suspects will turn out to be a very unfair fight. Tupperware boxes, thermos flasks, and liquid fertiliser, a kettle for a witch's cauldron: Edie lays it all out, and then jots down proportions from memory.

In the brown room, amid the cheap, well-intended furniture, Edie Banister makes saboteur magics, alchemies of resistance. And then she lowers herself gratefully into bed, and finds that Bastion has so far bestirred himself as to claim a space by her feet. She sleeps, and dreams of old work, unfinished.

VI

If ever;
not arrested;
the Bold Receptionist.

oe Spork holds his telephone in his left hand and pokes at it with his right. He has lost an indeterminate amount of time and is shivering, symptoms he identifies as shock. Fortunately, he knows the number by heart. He has never used it before, but it is the rule of the House of Spork, and always was, since he was old enough to count: if in doubt; if you ever; if you are accused; if you are nearby; if you are taken hostage; if you are arrested; if you hear a rumour that someone; if you wake up and she's dead; if, if, if, you call the magic number and you bare your soul.

At nine-twenty at night, it takes two rings for someone to pick up the phone.

"Noblewhite Cradle, Bethany speaking." A woman's voice, not a girl's. This number is not answered by receptionists or temps. It rings on the desk of Noblewhite Cradle's formidable office manager. When the actual Bethany is not in residence, there are three surrogate Bethanys who will take the call. At no time, ever, will it take more than two rings for one of them to lift the receiver. The extra Bethanys, in private life, go by the names Gwen, Rose, and Indira. It's not important. When they answer this phone, they are Bethany.

"Good evening, Bethany, it's Joshua Joseph Spork." Bethany (all of her) knows the name and history of every single client with access to this number. There aren't many—but even if there were, the name "Spork" is an absolute passport at Noblewhite Cradle.

"Good evening, Mr. Spork, how may I help you?"

"I need Mercer, please."

"Mr. Mercer?" Even Bethany hesitates for a second. "Really, Mr. Spork? Are you sure?"

"Yes, Bethany. I'm afraid so."

There is a brief stutter on the line. Bethany has just switched over from a standard phone to a headset, leaving both of her hands free to work. She's ambidextrous and she has two computers in front of her, each set up for use with one hand and patched into the communications system at Noblewhite Cradle. In other words, Bethany is now able to perform three distinct actions at once. One hand is tapping out an extension number in response to Joe's request. The other is discreetly alerting the senior partners to the fact that Mercer Cradle is now in play, and they should therefore expect the usual degree of insane fallout. In the meantime, she continues the conversation with Joe.

"I have the List here, Mr. Spork. Are there any matters arising from the last few days of which I should be aware?"

The Cradle's List is a celebrated joke in the legal journals, the Loch Ness Monster of documents. Jonah Noblewhite in his day was occasionally cartooned as a sort of black-lettered Santa, with his List displaying the peccadilloes of the mighty and the notorious, the better to conceal them from the world. If the matter being lampooned featured the Scottish courts, Nessie herself was often the client. Joe tells Bethany that his entry is as accurate as he knows how to make it.

"Putting you through now. Will you require any subsidiary services?" Meaning, will you be needing us to bail you out, or get hold of the negatives, or arrange a poker game for you to have attended last night?

"For the present, no, thank you," Joe says politely.

"Very well," Bethany says, not without a measure of congratulation. Joe has never availed himself of Noblewhite Cradle's more outré services, at least, not directly, though he suspects his father may have deployed them on his behalf when he was a child. Bethany is always glad when her charges are bystanders rather than arrestees.

"I am in the lobby of Wilton's," Mercer Cradle's voice says pleasantly, "where my rack of lamb has just arrived and is even now cooling next to a glass of unimpeachable Sassicaia. Since my dinner companion threw her gin and tonic at me shortly after the fish course, you have my full attention as long as someone is dead. Is someone dead? Because otherwise—"

"It's me, Mercer," Joe says.

"Oh," Mercer says. And then, "Joe, for God's sake, you've got my cellphone number." And then meditatively, "Oh, crap. What's happened? Don't say anything to anyone except me."

"Billy's dead, Mercer. I've just found him."

"Billy Friend?"

"Yes."

"Dead like slipped on a bar of soap or like Colonel Mustard in the library with the lead piping?"

"Very much the latter."

"And you, you poor rube, are standing there at the crime scene up to your neck in shit."

"Yes."

"Bethany? Police?"

"On their way, Mr. Cradle. Someone called them five minutes ago."

"Joe, you are a pillock. Was that you?"

Joe doesn't know. It may have been.

"Never mind, then. First question: are you Colonel Mustard?"

"No."

"You are not the Colonel in any way, shape or form?"

"No."

"Could anyone unkindly imagine that you have the look of a military man? Have you been seen entering the library carrying plumbing supplies?"

"I came to look for Billy. I needed to talk to him. I've been into all the rooms but I haven't touched much. I've got a poker."

"Not one you brought with you, I trust."

"Billy's."

"Fine. Quite shortly, the place will be swarming with unhappy coppers. Their first instinct will be to clap you in irons and give you the impression that you're going to prison for ever. Stay silent until I get there. Do not speak, even to say 'Good evening officer, the corpse is through here.' Just point. Do not make a voluntary statement. Do not be helpful. Stay in the corridor—are you in the corridor?"

"I am. I was in the flat, before. He's on his bed."

"And you no doubt touched him as little as possible? You did not, in a mistaken rush of affection for the little prick, embrace the deceased and smear yourself in blood and him in fibres of your clothing?"

"He's under a sheet. I didn't lift it."

"Good. Fine. What was my first instruction?"

"Say nothing. Wait for you."

"And did I say you could in any way do anything else? Did I, for example, give you permission to reminisce about your old friend William and his little ways? About your shared history as dealers in entirely legitimate antiques?"

"No. You said to say nothing and wait."

"Excellent. Then I shall ask the maître to stick the lamb in a bit of foil and cork the bottle for me, and we shall picnic."

"I'm not hungry."

"You will be by the time we're done, Joseph. This is apt to become a long and tedious soirée. Under what circumstances may you offer help and assistance to Lily Law?"

"None, until you get here."

"So that I may translate what you say into words which will be understood by Lily and her chums Bob Magistrate and Charlie DPP as 'I am not some tiny tit you can fit up for this heinous crime, I am a bystander and thus I shall remain.'"

"Understood."

"I am on the way, Joseph. Bethany?"

"We're making an incident room, Mr. Cradle. Keep us up to date."

"I will."

Joe Spork leans on the wall and waits.

Christ, the smell.

He breathes through his mouth, and feels he has betrayed a debt. When your friend is decomposing, surely you owe it to them to inhale their death. To do otherwise seems impossibly prim.

Billy, you're an idiot. Were an idiot.

In exasperation, not judgement. Then ungrudging acknowledgement:

You were my idiot. My friend.

In his mind's eye, he buries Billy, cries for him, misses him every time he sees a bit of dodgy Victorian smut, then slowly forgets him and misses him more seldom as life goes on, more lonely, and ultimately Billy really is gone, abandoned twice over to his end.

And at the same time, another part of him eschews all this love and poesy, and looks for edges, escapes, and angles. Joe reluctantly encourages it. This is bad trouble, and unless there's more coincidence in the world today than there was yesterday, it pursues him. Here, with Billy's repulsive mortal remains, he can feel its breath. So while he waits for Mercer, and for the predicted horde of arresting officers, Joe Spork unwillingly combs his mind for old habits and ways of thinking, and this inevitably begins, as all discussions of wrongdoing must, with Mathew "Tommy Gun" Spork.

He has been so successful in discarding his father that he cannot, for a moment, recall Mathew's face, or his voice, until he reaches for memories too old to be useful and hears it, mock-severe, coming from up above him, because he's a child and getting ready for his day.

"Hurry it up, Joshua Joseph, please! A man is always busy, a man has affairs of state to attend to! *This* man must also make breakfast for his offspring before delivering him into the vile jaws of school. *Booooo!* to school!" Joe's father wears a coat with a sheepskin collar and a fat-knotted, striped tie. Wide shoulders and narrow hips make him look like an isosceles triangle balanced on its point (his Italian brogues in two colours). The child Joshua Joseph pauses to consider his father as if he were, for the sake of argument, a scalene or an equilateral triangle. Both images are very odd.

On this day, Mathew Spork is playing the man of commerce rather than the gangster prince, and so he has left almost all of his guns in the box under the bed. Almost all, because a man in his profession does not generally walk abroad without something to give people pause.

He's waiting for an answer. The boy Joshua Joseph—who has been planning in his mind the theft of the Crown Jewels by a series of tunnels and hang-gliding escapades—responds: "Boo!"

In fact, Joshua Joseph quite likes school. It's controllable and therefore restful, and things which start out inexplicable become clear. It is in this way utterly unlike his life, which remains mysterious despite years of intense study. Also, he is by popular acclaim the hooligan-in-chief of a small band of under-tens. On the other hand, it keeps him away from his father, whom he adores for his magnificence and resents for his loudness in equal measure. He sets out two blue breakfast bowls.

"Quite right," Mathew says. "*Boo!* to school and hooray for Mum and Dad and Grandad and all the rest. However, Josh, school is a necessary evil. You hungry?"

"Yes. Dad, what are affairs of state?"

"Kings and Prime Ministers; Kings and Prime Ministers. Ruling the mighty nations of the Earth, taking weighty decisions—and among those mighty nations, which one has the brightest future? The finest soldiers and the greatest leaders? And which one, Josh, has the wisest and most brilliant heir to the throne?"

"England!"

"Close, Josh. Very close. But no! The nation I speak of is the House of Spork, with its fine and splendid Prince Joshua Joseph, and blessings be upon him and all he surveys. Yes?"

"Yes, Dad."

"All right, then. Eggs or cornflakes?"

And Joshua Joseph gives whichever answer he adjudges will satisfy his incessant parent. Papa Spork is completely unaware of how his banter sometimes compresses and confines his son. He thinks himself great fun, a Dad to end all Dads, but the sheer volume of him—the relentless effervescence, the way in which everything relates to the great, manifest destiny of the Spork family, the bone-deep conviction that success is just around the corner of his son's young life—is, on in-between days, just too much. The Crown Jewels temporarily forgotten, Joe considers instead a recent school visit to the British Museum, during which he saw any number of interesting and enlightening things, including—when she leaned to indicate a neolithic ritual object—his form mistress's startlingly erotic undergarments. The object he presently recalls most strongly, however, is the yoke in the farming exhibit, laid over a pair of mighty stuffed oxen.

Joshua Joseph, between bouts of hero worship and merciless inadequacy, occasionally feels that his father is laid across his shoulders in much the same manner, and that he must pull him everywhere he goes, whether his father is there or not.

Papa Spork burns the eggs, which in his curious vision of the world is just further cause to believe in the inestimable genius of the House of Spork, so they have cornflakes instead. On some level or other, however, Joshua Joseph's father must realise that this morning has gone astray from the usual perfect march to dynastic hegemony, because he makes a concession for which Joshua Joseph has been striving for weeks:

"D'you want to come to the Night Market tomorrow?"

"Yes, Dad, please!"

"I'll ask your mother if she's all right with it. And you look out some smart clothes."

"I will."

The Night Market is a dream. It is the magic heart of the city Mathew asserts confidently is the greatest and most magical on Earth. Joshua Joseph knows with an instinctual passion that it is the most secret, most remarkable, most improbable place in the entire world; the more wondrous because it moves around. It is a clearing house for everything and anything. It is beyond the reach of tax and tariffs; a shadowed, lamplit holdfast which bustles with forbidden trades and pirate's treasure. Mathew claims it was born of the wrecker's trade, that the Kindly Men came up the Thames from the inshore water, from Cornwall and the Channel Coast, with booty looted from sunken ships. He says it was Britain's first landside democracy (the pirate ships themselves being the first constituted parliaments). Perhaps it was. Mathew's occasional, unlikely erudition is startling even to his father, Daniel, who knows all things. And then, too, this Market, which Mathew has revived and of which he is anointed king (or elected president for life, if you prefer to retain your grip upon that great democratic heritage) is the one aspect of his profession to which Daniel Spork does not object, the one part of Mathew's life, aside from Joshua Joseph and his mother, Harriet, for which Daniel will smile.

Perhaps it's the hearthfire glimmer of the stalls. As reported, the Market is like a hanging garden of antiques and jewels, tiered and terraced or sprawling across some great space, or piled higgledy-upon-piggledy above one another in an old brewery or giant crypt. Each pitch is designed according to the owner's likes and lights, but must run from a single three-pin plug, for power is at a premium, and therefore most often the Market is lit by gas and heated by small coal fires in Swedish stoves or Victorian grates, and chimneyed out by whatever contrivance Mathew has arranged for the occasion. Food smells, too, Harriet said once, like a huge spiced kitchen: cake and meat and fish and herbs and condiments unknown in Merry England, but common in France and Italy. There's garlic and basil and turmeric and curry, and a kind of black fungus which smells of—but here, Harriet changed course rather abruptly. Of something exotic, anyway.

And amid all this, the trades and deals, marked by a flicker of torchlight as the buyer takes a moment to illuminate his—or her—prize, inspect it, assess or assay it, weigh it, measure it, accept or reject it. Money changing hands in purses, billfolds and bill rolls, occasionally in cases, and of that, each deal kicking back just a little to Mathew Spork himself.

But so far, all Joshua Joseph himself has witnessed—has been required to learn by rote, by heart, as one of the many curious rules of the House of Spork—is the trick with the newspapers.

Every Market culminates in the announcement of where the next one will be. The majority are small gatherings, but every month there is a grand one, the true Night Market, and that one is heralded by strange, encrypted messages in unlikely places. The clew—the thread by which the maze may be unravelled—is a lonely-hearts advertisement in a local paper: "Come home, Fred, all is forgiven!" The ad immediately beneath—by arrangement with the setters—gives a veiled time and date. A second paper yields a street or locality, and a third, a specific name or number. It is a jigsaw. From within, it's entirely simple. From without, impenetrable.

"Can you tell me where it is, then?" Mathew Spork demands, ferocious.

"Of course, Dad."

And indeed, that evening, with his mother's nail scissors and a half-hour of cutting and pasting, Joe has the address.

"We have a winner! A true son of the House of Spork!" Mathew cries proudly, and Joshua Joseph repeats it happily as his father whirls him through the air.

"You like to win, don't you?"

"Yes, Dad. I do."

"All right, then, we'll call this your exam: three-card monte!"

The traditional three-card monte is also known as "Find the Lady." It is played with three cards, one of which is the queen, and the dealer moves them around face down in an effort to confuse the player. The player then picks which one he thinks it will be—which it is, the first and maybe the second time he plays, but the third time inevitably pays for all, and the dealer comes away richer. It is the first con Mathew ever learned—from his father, of all things, for which the old man daily curses himself.

The simplest trick of the monte is the knuckle cast. In the language of the sharper, the dealer has a light hand and a heavy one, the latter so-called because it carries two cards, one above the other. The dealer moves the heavy hand and deals once. The mark tends to assume that the card dealt is the bottom one, and in the early rounds it will be. In the pay round, however, the upper card is released by a slight flex of the knuckles, so that the player is reversed. It's a magician's force.

Mathew is not asking Joe to perform this trick with his small fingers. There's time enough for that as he grows older. On this day it is the Gangster King's concern only that his son know a fiddle when he sees one, and the monte is a perfect metaphor for any game or trick you can name. See the world through the monte, and you won't be taken for a sucker. At least, not often.

Mathew rolls his wrists and flashes the cards, showing the heavy, the light, the heavy. He lays them out, exposes them face up. It is all so much distraction, hands not quicker than the eye but cleverer than the watcher. Joe grins as his father fakes a fumble, trying to get him to focus on the wrong thing, and Mathew nods appreciatively. Then abruptly Joe's father stops, alarmingly sincere.

"Your grandfather's told you about strictures, I suppose?"

"Yes, Dad."

"He's a good man, son. He tries his hardest. He believes in the game. He thinks if you play by the rules long enough, the right sort of fellow will win out. He may be right. Thing is, in my experience, the right sort run out of money or the wrong sort leave the table. The game is fixed. Always has been, always will be, and the only way out for a man is the gangster's road. Take what you can, do what you must, and know that being a right sort never saved anyone from anything."

Joe nods, taken aback by his father's sudden need to explain himself.

"I did listen your grandfather when I was little, Son, just the way you listen to me. Truth is I still do, but don't tell him I said so. So here's a stricture of the monte—of the Market, I suppose: if you can see what's going on around you, when other fellows walk through life blindly, then you're a better man. And like to turn a profit, which is life's way of letting you know your quality. All right?"

"Yes!"

Mathew's hands move again, fast and faster, and he lays the cards down on the table. "Then find the lady."

Joshua Joseph grins. His father has tried very, very hard to beat him. He has played a trick so stinkingly dishonest while he was talking that Joe can only read into it the deepest possible respect. He looks his father in the eye.

"It isn't this one," he says, and turns over the right-hand card. Mathew smiles. "And it isn't this one." He turns over the middle card. His father's smile twitches up at the side. "And that means it must be this one." He leaves the last card where it is. The queen, he well knows, is in Mathew's coat pocket, which is why he has played the monte this way around, revealing losers rather than picking the winner. Turning the con.

Mathew wraps him in a massive hug. "We have a winner," he says once more, into the top of Joe's hair. "My son. A real winner."

And that's it. It's really happening.

It is the best day of Joshua Joseph's young life, ever, at all.

Going to the Night Market!

Harriet Spork fusses with his lapels and the mustard polo-neck jumper one more time, and Mathew watches with a broad grin.

"It's scratchy," the infant Spork objects. Mathew Spork nods. He is wearing exactly the same outfit.

"It is, Josh, at first, but after a bit you get used to it and then you miss it when it isn't there. You want to look a fine figure of a man, don't you? For the Market?"

"Yes, Dad."

"Well, then."

Joshua Joseph waits patiently while his mother finishes with his hair—again—and sits quiet in the back of his father's car, very straight, with his eyes set in what he imagines is an expression of extreme adulthood. Through the streets of London they go, first fast, then slow, then fast again, and the big car leans and rolls as Mathew

Spork plays the accelerator and checks that there is no one in his rear-view mirror.

Joshua Joseph manfully feels nauseous and does not say so. Harriet leans against her husband as he takes a right-angle corner at fifty, and the tyres hold the road as if they were clamped to it. Mathew grins at her fiercely, at her flushed skin and ever so slightly open mouth.

After twenty minutes, prim residential houses give way to tall tower blocks. After another ten, the blocks dwindle into business parks and lock-ups, and then they're driving along next to a wide pastureland. In the moonlight, Joshua Joseph catches a glimpse of an urban fox on a fence.

"All right, Josh, we're here."

They get out of the car. Joshua Joseph can smell January frost and the sharp scent of burning wood. All around there are high, empty buildings and the sound of creaking hulks on the river nearby. His shoes squelch in mud, find gravel. His father tells them both to hurry, and they do. Across a courtyard covered in black ice and car tyres, past the brittle corpse of a misplaced winter duck. Mathew Spork opens a strange, oval door and draws them with him.

They step through, and he closes it behind them. They walk down some steps and on along a narrow, arched tunnel. Harriet's heels clip and tap on polished concrete.

"Where are we?"

"You know where we are, laddie. You found the way!"

"But I mean, what is it?"

"Well, at certain times and in certain seasons, those worthy persons governing great nations may disagree with one another. And in an effort to avoid any physical harm, all the lords and owners of banks and presidents construct underground places in which to take refuge." He leads the way down a short flight of stairs. "And then there are utilities. You know what that is? Sewers and trains and water and such. This part, now, this part has belonged to Her Majesty's Post Office since good Queen Victoria's time. I dare say they've no idea they own it, profligate spenders of the public purse that they are. The Post back then was a marvel, Josh, a genuine marvel, and in the capital it must be doubly so, so they made a little railway all their own, and pneumatic pipes of brass, and vacuum pumps driven by steam. Genius. Of course, there are man-size tunnels to care for it all. All closed up now, caved in and vanished, built over, filled in, as far as

Lily Law and her friends are concerned, but known to us, Josh, to men of the Market like me and you. Those fellows in Paris, Josh, they think they've catacombs, but that's nothing to what treasure is under London!"

And even as his father says the word, Joshua Joseph can hear music, and there's a yellow electric gleam on the edge of the tunnel, and a flat smell of smoked sausage and nutmeg, of perfume and the flowers his mother grows on the window ledge in the kitchen.

They turn the corner, and the Night Market spreads out in front of them like the main street of a medieval town, festooned with lanterns and crank-handle generators with meagre bulbs glowing, stalls and handcarts and even shopfronts laid in rows, and up the walls on wooden walkways, so that the whole effect is of being in a great oblong bowl or the hull of a ship, the hundreds of traders and vendors bellowing their prices and offerings and clamouring for attention. And into this sea, his father leads them both, and is greeted and admired by all around.

Red velvet walls and corduroy armchairs; oil paintings, gold coins, Cornish pasties, and tea; pipe smoke and mint jellies and Turkish coffee, yellowed playing cards and chess. The Night Market is all these things, but most of all it is his father and the Uncles, sitting amid cushions and eating baklava and crumpets in the small hours of the night, telling tales and answering the questions of a small, bewildered boy, while his mother smiles and gossips with a dozen Aunts. Everyone here is "Uncle" or "Aunt," or more unusually a cousin, like the boy and the girl seated on the next cushion along, the wards of Uncle Jonah, who is the only one wearing a suit, but whose crooked smile is like a lighthouse when it falls on the children.

Joshua Joseph asks very politely why no one has a second name. Mathew glances over at the broad-shouldered, very thin man whose barrow this is. He calls himself Tam, and in the daylight world he runs a smart shop where men of the upper classes purchase clothing and equipment for shooting and fishing. These goods, of course, he is happy to deliver by hand to the homes of his customers, so Tam is often very well informed as to the disposition of valuables in expensive houses.

"Men of the Market, Joshua," Uncle Tam says, his big head nodding over his whisky glass. "Men like you and me, we're bad with names. Bad with all kinds of recollections, really. We remember what's important, oh surely, but those other things we sort of forget, so they don't slip out when they shouldn't. The Night Market, it's not called that just because we hold it when the sun goes down. It's because the whole thing takes place under cover of darkness. Shadows and fog in the mind, so we don't see what we don't feel like remembering, if you get my drift."

Joshua Joseph doesn't.

"Well, my folk are from Cornwall, right? Wreckers, in days gone by. You know what a wrecker is?"

"A kind of pirate."

"Hm, well, yes and no. A pirate does a mighty job of work to get his booty, Joshua. He boards a ship and carries the day in battle, and he risks hanging and death in battle and all such. A wrecker is a quieter sort of fellow with an eye to business. He lets the coastline do his work, tricks the taxman—you *do* know what a taxman is?"

Insofar as the taxman is cursed by everyone he has ever met, a bad fairy who takes from the deserving to stuff the rich coffers of Socialists and Bankers, Joshua Joseph does indeed know, so he nods.

"So he tricks the taxman into crashing his ship full of gold and rum onto the rocks, and then all that's good is washed up on the beach by the waves. And sometimes the taxman with it, and more than a few of those revenue fellows—that's another word for a taxman—more than a few ended their days married to a wrecker wench and drinking rum on the beaches, for a taxman is a man like any other, ey?

"The point being that a wrecker does his work in darkness, so if the sheriff comes, no one saw his mates' faces, not for certain, and he can swear an oath on the Holy Bible if that's required that he has no sure knowledge of who else was there that brought the taxes onto the beach or took them away. So . . . what's my name?"

Joshua Joseph thinks about it. "I don't believe I ever heard it for definite."

"Very good. So, then, you sit by me and learn a bit more while your dad does his business over the way."

And learn he does, the strange skills of the Market: burglary and locks from Tam and Caro, and a dash of fisticuffs from Lars the Swede, the ways of the Tosher's Beat from everyone. And from their boys and girls and wives and brothers and mothers: how to spot a counterfeit bill, a fake painting, a recent Louis XIV chaise; how to tell if someone is taking drugs or shorting the count or talking out of turn, and what to do about it; how to climb an old drainpipe without pulling it out of the wall; how to make a plausible disguise; how to disappear in a crowded room. The Night Market is filled with people who know these things and will explain them to Mathew Spork's son over a fresh doughnut from the steel vat on Uncle Douggie's counter—Uncle Douggie the boxer, strong as a Liverpool Hercules and very partial to fried foods.

To Joshua Joseph, lounging like a sultan on silk cushions with fingers covered in cinnamon and sugar, chocolate and jam, the Night Market is a place of excellent cuisine and spellbinding secrets, and all his own. He runs free through a hundred barrows, discovers that he is a terrible painter and a passable restorer of art; that he has no knack for complex locks but could comfortably earn a Boy Scout badge in helping people back into their cars; that his skills in mathematics will never lend themselves to making book (so don't even try). He becomes a prince among the under-tens, dispenses fair justice and learns the rewards of getting caught with sugar on your hands when doughnuts are banned (and is promptly taught methods for concealing sticky paws and by inference also fingerprints). Mathew Spork is delighted, and in his jubilation, Harriet finds her happiness as well. Only Mathew's father, Daniel, is displeased. Grandpa Spork thinks school will suffer, and does not in any case approve of the Night Market, though he will not say why.

School does not suffer. Indeed, school profits. As the practical applications of his courses become more apparent, Joshua Joseph becomes more diligent. What fraction of one hundred and twenty is two? Who cares? But: what is one point five per cent of one hundred and twenty English pounds (rounded up for ease)? And is that a suitable courier's fee? Now that's a far more interesting calculation.

Joshua Joseph Spork, Crown Prince of Thieves, lies that night on his back and looks up at a vaulted brick ceiling, and finally falls asleep to the soft whisper of Tam's counting machine as it tallies stolen money.

With the lesson of the monte uppermost in his mind, Joe Spork slides his back down the wall outside Billy's flat until he is resting on his haunches, and considers what he knows about the Book of the

Hakote, and why someone might murder a man because of it. *If you can see what's going on around you . . .*

He can't. He has no idea. And that's the other rule of the monte: if you can't spot the sucker in the room, it's you.

A woman called Bryce, dressed in a paper suit and a blue cloth mask, insists that Joe give her his shoes. She does this, not in a suspicious, inquirish sort of way, but rather with almost overwhelming boredom. Ruth Bryce spends her days hoovering up the traces of untidy murderers, and the image of the galumphing Boot of Spork clumping over her crime scene and obscuring the tiny yet vital traces clearly looms large in her mind.

Joe, not wishing to be rude or obstructive, removes his shoes and hands them over, knowing that Mercer, when he gets here, will immediately call him an idiot, and ten seconds later turn this unforgivable lapse into a huge legal advantage. As he passes over his shoes (from a shop around the corner and much scuffed despite the yellow Eva-Nu label) he realises that he is also surrendering, as a matter of practicality, any possibility of slipping away. A man might quietly wander off after half an hour or so—"Oh, I had no idea you still needed me, so sorry"—but without his shoes, he must remain and see the thing through. Some part of him, perhaps, wishes to be enmeshed. Joe Spork has few friends, and he will not disavow a dead one merely because an unkind person could construe his presence at the last as guilt. Least of all will he forsake this particular corpse, member in good standing of the Honoured & Enduring Brotherhood of Waiting Men. In time, no doubt, Billy's fraternal order will turn up and sit vigil for him, but until that happens, Joe is all he has. Alone and—as Joe now realises—painfully lonely, that's no reason he should be uncared-for in death.

"Spork, did you say, sir? Like ess-pee-oh-arr-kay?"

Detective Sergeant Patchkind is an elf; an affable, chirpy little man with a high voice who has already shown Joe a picture of his nieces. Just the thing, according to DS Patchkind, to settle the stomach and soothe the heart after the unpleasant experience of discovering a corpse. While Joe was considering the girls and thinking that they looked a lot like weasels and a bit like storks, DS Patchkind asked him a couple of unimportant questions for the sake of his paperwork. Joe gave a brief estimation of what it was like to come upon the dead body of an old mate, and Detective Sergeant Patchkind tutted and sucked air through his teeth and was about to go and talk to Bryce of the blue mask when something occurred to him.

"And what time was that, Mr. . . . sorry, what was the name again?"

At which point, briefly unmindful of Mercer's stern injunction to reserve, he said "Spork" and immediately realised he was an idiot.

Now, with Patchkind looking up at him with an expectant face, he can do nothing but nod.

He doesn't actually nod. He's about to—has already sent a sort of "go" signal to his nodding muscles—when a subtle quiet ripples through the chamber. The forensics people stop chatting to one another, the coppers stop shuffling their feet. Joe, who has never been on a hunting expedition, imagines this is the silence which you hear in a large wood after the first stag has been downed. Into this silence speaks a most unctuous, most unpleasantly familiar voice, and Joe Spork recognises it for serious trouble.

"Dear me, dear me. Mr. Spork, what are you doing in such an unpleasant place? No, no, don't answer that without a lawyer. Goodness gracious. We mustn't infringe upon your ancient rights, that would be quite improper. Magna Carta and so on, I'm sure. Hello, Detective Sergeant Patchkind, a pleasure to see you once more, though regrettable of course that it should be in a house of death. Mind you, the exigencies of our professions, of course: we almost always meet in dark places, don't we?"

"Yes, sir," DS Patchkind says neutrally, "we rather do."

"Just once, Detective Sergeant, as I was saying to my esteemed colleague Mr. Cummerbund just this morning, just once it would be nice to meet the charming Basil Patchkind in a pub and share a jar of ale. Was I not, Arvin?"

And there they are, and Joe realises in this curious moment how very *binary* they are: an upright, narrow one and a rotund zero, side by side.

Arvin Cummerbund nods. "You were, Mr. Titwhistle. Just this morning."

"And alas, Basil—you don't mind if I call you Basil? I don't mean to be rude . . . thank you, my dear fellow—yes, friend Basil, I'm afraid we must take Mr. Spork from you at this time. He has a pressing appointment. It absolutely will not wait, and if he should miss it the consequences would be . . . well, all manner of chaos and confusion to the nation as a whole. Lest your duty to the mundane conventions of the law supravene, Basil, I did bring the necessary . . ."

And with this salvo, he removes from his inner pocket a long, pale document folded upon itself, and passes it to Patchkind. Patchkind unfolds it and peers, then snorts, then peers some more.

"It's not signed," he says, at last.

"No," Mr. Titwhistle says blandly, "these ones never are."

Patchkind sighs.

"I don't suppose you'd care to confess, Mr. Spork? To the murder, I mean?" He seems to be offering it as an escape.

"No. I'm afraid I wouldn't."

"Well, you know best, I suppose." Patchkind sighs and folds the paper up again. "He's all yours."

"Indeed, he is," Mr. Titwhistle replies. "I would say we were never here, but alas, that's not a fiction I imagine we can maintain. So never mind. See you soon, Detective Sergeant Patchkind."

At which, to Joe's outrage and amazement, Arvin Cummerbund steps lightly behind him and fastens his wrists together in the small of his back with a pale nylon strip. Joe gives a startled shout of "Hey!" and turns his head to Patchkind in mute appeal. *Do something!*

Patchkind looks very grey, and quite deliberately turns to face the scene of the crime.

"DC Topper," he says, as if through a mouthful of dust, "tell me about our corpse."

"You're not under arrest," Arvin Cummerbund murmurs into Joe Spork's ear, "because we don't do that."

The fat man drives, and Rodney Titwhistle sits next to Joe in the back. His earlier chattiness has evaporated, and Joe's bewildered affront has lost its edge, so that a sad, nostalgic quiet settles on the car as Cummerbund guides it through London's complex tangle, each man thinking his own thoughts in a curious kind of fellowship.

The traffic light turns red again in front of them, and Mr. Cummerbund tuts. Rodney Titwhistle sighs.

"Arvin, my apologies, I'm going to start the conversation. You'll just have to join in from the front. You can multitask, can't you?"

"Certainly, Rodney."

"Thank you, Arvin."

"Thank you, Rodney."

"In that case, let us proceed. I wonder, Mr. Spork, if you could tell me just one thing?"

"You could tell me who the hell you are. Not the bloody Loganfield Museum, I know that."

"Oh, dear me. No. Let us say, we are the embodiment of an unpleasant necessity of the global reality, specifically concerned with the well-being of the United Kingdom of Great Britain and Northern Ireland. And let us further say, in accordance with convention, that I will be asking the questions.

"I should also remind you that you are not in the custody of the police. The usual rules, as so often referenced in popular television programmes, do not apply. Our mandate is not justice. It is survival. In that context, you will understand when I say you should not attempt to 'take the fifth.' The U.K. no longer recognises a right to remain silent, you know. We protect the nation's future, rather than its conscience. I find this noble." Mr. Titwhistle smiles apologetically, then, as the car stops at a set of traffic lights, gazes out of the window to a small horde of teenaged girls in fishnet who are whooping and bouncing up and down. After a moment, he goes on.

"Suppose I were to ask you 'What is the Apprehension Engine?' What would you say?"

" 'I don't know.' "

"And if you were to speculate?"

"A device which makes people afraid."

Rodney Titwhistle gives a soft cough. "Which you conclude from the use of the term 'Apprehension'. Indeed. Well, Mr. Spork, in a way you are quite right. It is indeed a device, and it certainly scares the bejeezus out of me. Tell me, instead, about the Magic Beehive of Wistithiel."

"How do you know about that?"

Rodney Titwhistle sighs. "Very shortly, Mr. Spork, everyone will know about that."

"Why? It's just an automaton. What's any of this got to do with Billy, anyway?" Joe sees Billy's corpse beneath the blanket, smells the room, and swallows bile.

"Everyone will know because everyone will see. In the beginning, the bees will fly around the world. They will awaken further hives. The device is intended to encompass the globe. There will be—shall we call them 'outbreaks'?—during which the machine will function at its lowest level where the swarms are concentrated. Then, when they are all in position, it will activate. I would conservatively estimate that three or four million people will die shortly thereafter by ordinary human action. Murders and so forth. If the machine moves on to the second and third stages, as I understand them—and I will grant you that this certainly is not the notional purpose of the device—the fatality rate rises dramatically. In the worst case, it approaches one hundred per cent of the world's population. So you understand why I feel a little unwilling to let this slide?

"In retrospect, it should have been dismantled years ago, but governments do so hate to throw things away, especially dangerous things. Did you know, incidentally, that 'retrospect' can be an adjective? One might say 'Joshua Joseph Spork is retrospect; he's a man who learns from his mistakes.' In any case, Mr. Spork, the beehive is not just some clockwork toy. It is a scientific advance of ludicrous complexity, so secret that no one who knew about it could understand it and no one who would understand it could be allowed to know about it. A game-changer. And consequently in many ways we might also call it a time bomb. It is the Apprehension Engine to which I referred earlier. We are, as you see, somewhat nervous about what will happen now that it's active. So I must ask you: how do we switch it off again?"

An opportunity to come clean—perhaps without prejudice. Very attractive. Except that, on diverse occasions, unscrupulous persons have been known to use this line of argument to lure a suspect into unwise confessions.

Deny. Hedge. Evade. Play stupid. Which, in any case, is what you are.

"Oh. I'm sorry. I just . . . I have no idea."

"No, I am almost sure that you don't." Mr. Titwhistle sighs. "Ted Sholt's the fellow I need to talk to, isn't he?"

"I suppose he may be." A pleasant vision: urbane Rodney Titwhistle in his clean car, struggling with Ted of the foul-smelling sandalled feet, the burlap smock and the sou'wester pressed against the window and the weird battle cry sounding: *Angelmaker!* Although . . . no. Ted Sholt might not fare so well in that engagement.

And that word: angelmaker. That's much less funny, here and now.

One way of making angels, in cartoons and so on, is to kill people. He should mention it. But if he does, will they keep him for ever? And will "mention" equal "confess" in the watery eyes of Rodney Titwhistle?

The moment passes. Rodney Titwhistle claps his hands, very lightly, as punctuation.

"Taking myself as the example, Mr. Spork, the problem—and it's a common problem in this debased age—" the faintest nod of the head towards the horde, still audible over the hiss of the tyres "—is that while I am known to be mostly infallible, I have also been known, very occasionally, to be quite wrong. Do you see?"

"We're all wrong from time to time," Joe says nervously.

"Even on matters about which we have absolute confidence, alas."

"Even then."

"This is the basis of René Descartes' famous doctrine, you know."

"No, I didn't."

Rodney Titwhistle gives vent to a polite sigh of reproach.

"Debased, as I said. Well, Descartes realised that in his lifetime there had been any number of occasions on which he was absolutely certain and yet absolutely mistaken. He had dreamed himself in front of a fire attending dinner with friends when he was in fact at home in bed. He had seen what he took to be an eagle and discovered later that it was a buzzard, much closer than it appeared. Well, silly man, he was a mathematician rather than a naturalist."

Mr. Titwhistle's expression does not entirely conceal his personal feelings regarding this lack of ornithological *nous*.

"He therefore asked himself: 'If I were held captive by a malign fiend which deceived my senses, of what if anything could I be certain?' He inaugurated a method of doubting everything, and was finally reduced to the simple statement that because he was conscious, and aware of his own thoughts, he could not plausibly doubt his own existence. That's the famous 'I think, therefore I am.' You see? It sounds so trivial, until you see it in context. Here is René, half-convinced that his soul is a toy of demons. His sanity hanging by a thread, he finds this one, simple nugget of truth, and he stands with it in his clenched fist and he says: 'I'm real! I exist! And upon that rock, I shall build an edifice of reason!' It's magnificent, really."

"And does he?"

"What? Oh, no. No, he was worried about being burned alive by the Catholic Church. He said actually God would never allow such a terrible ruse to be perpetrated upon a human soul. I don't know where he found evidence for that. Seems to me . . . well. The point is that insofar as we are anything, we are things which think. Not *Homo sapiens* but *Res cogitans*."

This seems to warrant a confirmation, so Joe ventures a non-committal "I see."

"In this case, my point is that truth is a slippery item. Hm?"

"Yes, it is." Because he can think of nothing else to say, even though there are alarm bells ringing in his head.

"And although that slipperiness is a disadvantage in some situations, it is also vital to the way we live. The wrong truth at the wrong moment causes housing markets to plummet and nations to growl at one another. We can't have too much of it running about loose. We'd have wars all over the place. Economic crisis, certainly—well, we've seen that, haven't we?"

They share a little eye-rolling. The madness of bankers.

"And to make matters more troublesome, it has even been suggested that we human beings are incapable of knowing anything at all, in the absolute sense. We believe. We theorise. But we have no direct perception of whether our belief is matched by the objective universe."

Mr. Titwhistle sighs deeply. Epistemology is cruel.

"But . . . what if an engine might be constructed which functioned as a species of prosthesis? Which extended our senses into the realm of knowledge? An engine which allowed us after all to *apprehend truth*."

He nods as Joe's eyes flicker at the words. "We would behold wonders. But then . . . Old atrocities would come to light, old promises would be revealed as lies . . . And if one were of a scientific bent, one might worry ever so slightly about such a power of observation accidentally destroying life on Earth for the rest of time, or possibly changing the nature of this universe to make it inhospitable to conscious thought in perpetuity. Scientists will go on so about the precautionary principle, won't they?" He smiles benignly: boffins and their little ways.

"I'm sorry," Joe Spork says, his thoughts rather focused by this addendum, "what was that last part?"

Mr. Titwhistle shrugs in his seat. "Arvin, you will help me out if I go astray, won't you?"

"Of course, Rodney."

"I get lost among the quanta."

"Leave 'em out."

"This won't compromise our strict scientific integrity at all?"

"Needs must, Rodney," Arvin Cummerbund says, and philosophically puts his fat hand on the horn for quite a long time. A late drinker bangs on the bonnet of the car, raises two fingers, and staggers on.

"You see," Rodney Titwhistle resumes, "it seems that if all that extraordinary Heisenberg stuff is literally true, we as conscious beings have a sort of role in the ongoing creation of the universe. We cause tiny indecisions to go one way or another, just by looking at them. So one has to ask, if one's a responsible person: if we learned to appreciate the universe directly and without the possibility of error, would we inaugurate a sort of cascade? What if our way of existing is contingent on these little uncertainties in the fabric of our world? And what if knowing this entails knowing that, which implies that, and so on and so on until there are no open questions any more, and every choice is made as a consequence of every other, and finally we become little . . . well, to employ a metaphor, little clockwork people. Pianolos, Mr. Spork, rather than pianists. And wouldn't that rather mean the extinction of intelligence? Don't you think?"

"I'm not sure I follow."

"I grant," Mr. Titwhistle says, "that it's a little tricky. Arvin?"

Arvin Cummerbund glances in his rear-view mirror. "Let's say what we are now is like water, Joe," he says gently. "Our minds. All right? And this machine might—just might—be like a freezer. It's possible that it might freeze everything, anywhere, ever. And then we wouldn't be liquid any more, we'd be solid, and we might never notice, but we'd be following a pattern laid out in advance, feeling we were making our own decisions. Right now we have choice, you see, Joe. A man might decide one thing or another in a moment of stress. It's not random and it's not fixed. It's conscious. But after the freeze . . . There'd be no escape, ever, from a path set from before we were born to the day we die, which takes no notice of what we do along the way, except in that we are part of the mechanism creating more inescapable paths. We'd be no different from any other chemical reaction. Salt has no choice about dissolving in water, does it? We wouldn't be special, or conscious, we'd be so much rust. Clockwork men. See?"

"Oh," Joe says.

"Indeed," says Rodney Titwhistle gently. " 'Oh.' I quite agree. And now you are wondering how such a thing was ever built, and the answer ultimately is desperation. Or a species of carelessness—something which is, I'm afraid, rather a feature of the history of weapons of mass destruction. Suffice to say it is an old project. It doesn't really matter now.

"The Apprehension Engine is a device which would allow one to know the truth of a situation, without fear of error. You can see how that would appeal—to deceive the enemy and know that the deceit was successful; to recognise his lies infallibly. A massive strategic advantage.

"That wasn't its creator's interest, of course. She was an idealist. That's a term which has come to mean someone who is foggy and naive, but back then big ideas were still very much in fashion. Better living through science, knowledge will make us gods . . . and here she was, with her truth machine. Deception would be a thing of the past. The Apprehension Engine would usher in a new age of prosperity, economic stability, scientific understanding, social justice . . . But used unwisely, as it transpired, it could do other things less wholesome. And, well, as I say—do we really want to know the truth of everything? Of everyone? All our loves, our desires, our fears uncovered at a glance? Our weaknesses and petty gripes? Our sins?

"History is a well, Mr. Spork, a deep well driven into the strata of the past, through the bones of madness and murders. When it floods, we do well to run for the high ground. This machine, this Apprehension Engine which you so cavalierly reactivated . . . it is a hundred days of rain. A thousand. It is a flood and I am not Noah. I am Canute."

Rodney Titwhistle has turned in his seat and now his face is urgent and beseeching. At any moment, he will point his finger like a recruiting poster. *Join up! Your country needs YOU! To save the world.*

And Joe Spork is not unmoved. Of course he isn't. But he has no answers, and knows that he is, if not in the belly of the beast, surely in its maw and rolling towards its throat. He does not wish to encourage it to swallow.

Mr. Titwhistle lowers his voice to convey gravitas, and issues his most earnest plea. "So let me ask you again, with all my heart: how do I switch it off? How do I control it? How did you switch it on? And what did you hope to achieve by it all?"

Joe, looking at him, knows that Mr. Titwhistle believes everything he has just said. Yet at the same time, the whisper of the Night Market within him notes bleakly that all that truth could be assembled artfully to produce a most elegant, most deceptive lie.

"Supposing," Joe says, to Mercer's imagined strenuous objections, "hypothetically supposing all this is as you say: can you not just unplug it?"

Rodney Titwhistle nods. "We might try. But how would we recall the bees? And how should we know that we had succeeded absolutely? In my uninformed tampering with the machine, might I increase the power and wreak havoc, destroy my nation and my self? Or activate a dead man's switch and bring about Armageddon? No. Better, by far, to have your help. This must be got right."

"I'm sorry," Joe says again, "I just don't know anything."

"No, Mr. Spork. You need not be sorry," Rodney Titwhistle says. "I am. I am."

They don't speak again until Arvin Cummerbund turns the car into a narrow street and through a set of modern steel gates, into the front court of an anonymous, sandy-bricked block with wide swing doors.

"Well. Here we are," Rodney Titwhistle says, in his "unpleasant necessity" voice, as he helps Joe out of the back seat. "I'm sure it will all work out for the best."

The phrase is familiar and *pro forma*, but on his lips, here, now, it is a funeral oration. It is a prayer for the dying. As they walk towards that bleak, ugly little door and the lino'd official rooms beyond, Joe can feel his life coming to some kind of watershed. He steels himself for the kind of testing Rodney Titwhistle might unleash upon him, and wonders what he will say or do, and whether he will come out of here with all his fingers and teeth. He whimpers, deep in his chest. He wants to say "Don't do this," but is embarrassed, and knows, anyway, that while Mr. Titwhistle doesn't want to do this, he will absolutely not relent, and even if he did, the time-serving Arvin Cummerbund would be there to see it through. Arvin Cummerbund the bureaucrat, who knows the value of everything, the better to take it away.

Joe glances to his left, and sees a long grey-black Mercedes bus, windows tinted very dark, and beside it three tall figures all shrouded and veiled, waiting in silence. More vampires, and that thought isn't half so funny or so easy to get rid of as it was in his shop, during the day. Three faceless heads turn slowly to watch him as he walks. Rodney Titwhistle does not look at them, and from this Joe realises with a nauseating jolt that it is to them that he will be given.

"Who are they?" he asks quietly.

"Ghosts, perhaps," Rodney Titwhistle answers, uncharacteristically whimsical, or perhaps a little unnerved. Joe glances at him, and he waves the moment away. "Technically they are contractors. The interrogation techniques they deploy are a matter of commercial confidentiality, of course, and in any case beyond our competence to assess. They assure us that everything that happens to you will be compatible with the law. It is not our job to pry. In fact, we would be breaching your rights under the Data Protection Act to do so. Do you understand? No one will ask. If they did ask, no one would answer. I have the option of rendering you to them under a piece of recent legislation. Do you wish to know its name? I have it written down somewhere. Alas, much of the detail is redacted."

Joe looks at the ghosts again, and sees that they are not alone. Behind the bus, a strange, armoured Popemobile is sitting, and in it is one more, familiar, figure: a man, sitting stooped, somehow recognisable as the first Ruskinite he ever saw, the one who came to the shop.

The man's face is in shadow, but he has slipped the spiderweb veil back onto broad shoulders so that he can see clearly in the dark, and from him emanates a stark, rigid malice and a terrible anticipation.

"They're called Ruskinites," Rodney Titwhistle adds, "a benevolent order of monks. They're just around the corner, as it happens, nice old manse. They have a vested interest in the Apprehension Engine. When we have switched it off, they will study it. They are concerned with encountering the divine. Unfashionably sincere, of course, but they have considerable expertise. Inspired by John Ruskin. Although I understand they've changed a lot in the last few years—so much so that the term 'benevolent' may no longer be entirely accurate. Still, they look after the orphans of a particular accident. That must count for something."

Joe Spork, looking at the shadowed, alien trio waiting to take him away into the dark, can well believe it. He recalls the strange, heron steps and the featureless cotton face, and feels like a small boy being left on the steps of a very frightening school. He will tell them everything. Even though everything is not very much, and when he is dry, they will continue to wring him out. He will be crippled by their benevolence. May die of it. He breathes the wet night air and determines he will treasure every second of his life. He promises himself that he will not cry.

And then, as he mounts the moulded concrete steps, the door opens and a yellow shaft of light from the reception hall picks them out. Three figures step through the breach, in perfect counterpoint to the trio coming up. On the right, a gnarled, angry youth in a tracksuit, and in the middle a dapper outline with a Savile Row suit. On the left is a security guard or a soldier in civvies, looking vexed and hurried. Some manner of apology is already emerging from his lips, but his protestations of innocence are utterly overwhelmed by a glad yodel which echoes off the surrounding buildings, and Mr. Titwhistle hunches as if struck with a plank.

"Joshua Joseph Spork, by all that's holy! Good gracious, you've been bound, what appalling brutality! A client of mine . . . I'm shocked. And you've been so cooperative in the face of such gross provocation. In this age of chat-show rage, Joseph, I believe that makes you a paragon of virtue. Isn't he a paragon of virtue, Mr. Titwhistle? How do we spell that, by the way, for the writ? 'Titwhistle,' not 'paragon.' Joe, congratulations, you're rich. Rodney here is going to give you all his money, or at least, all of his organisation's money. What organisation is that again? I suppose, ultimately, the Treasury? Well, then there'll be plenty, won't there? How very fortunate, although if you wouldn't mind having a word with the Chancellor, Mr. Titwhistle, and letting him know not to buy any nuclear missiles or bail out any banks until we've settled, I'd be grateful, one wouldn't want there to be a shortfall. Yes, Mr. Titwhistle, I am aware that you believe you are beyond such mundane considerations but allow me to assure you that, if we marked lawyers the way we do military aircraft, I would have painted on my fuselage the outlines of a number of untouchable government departments now defunct. I am Mercer Cradle of the old established firm of Noblewhite Cradle, and I can sue *anything*. And is this your henchman? Do you know, I've always wondered what that means. How exactly does one hench? Is there a degree in henching, or is it more of an apprenticeship? Good evening, Mr. Cummerbund, I declare I never saw a finer figure of a man; Mr. Spork is my client and a very respectable one at that, please desist from giving him what our forebears would have called the fishy eye. Which of you would like to be the happy recipient of this paper ordering him released immediately into my care? But where are my professional manners? You must think less of me: do you consider Mr. Spork a suspect and how does it come about that you're interrogating him when he specifically requested that I be present, and before you have clarified his rights and status in the investigation?"

Rodney Titwhistle looks reproachfully at Joe as if to say "This person is your friend?" and "You didn't have to do this to me, I was only asking."

"Good Lord," Mercer says, with rising glee, "I happen to have my client's shoes here. Joe, you lemon, put these back on, you'll get muscle cramps in your toes and then where will the compensation end? Joseph! With me, please . . . He is often absent-minded under pressure," Mercer Cradle avers as he helps Joe into his shoes. "Suppressed guilt relating to his father's heinous acts, I shouldn't wonder. Why, he once went on a date with a lady officer of the police service and proposed to her over dessert, quite extraordinary, of course she said 'no,' well, who wouldn't when there was still coffee and *petits fours* to come? Tell me, Mr. Cummerbund, how long has it been since you saw your ankles . . . ?" Mercer keeps up his barrage until they're out of earshot and in the street, and Mercer and his mute companion are hustling Joe into the car.

The Ruskinites watch from behind their veils, silent and motionless as lizards on a wall. One of them takes two bobbing, birdish steps, then draws back. They make no sound.

"Joe, you did fine," Mercer says. "You were great. But there is no question that we are in the shit. We are in the savage jungle. For some reason, which I do not yet apprehend, there are titans stirring in the deeps and shadows on the stairwell. As my youngest cousin Lawrence would say, we are up to our necks in *podu*. This, incidentally, is Reggie, who is one of my occasional thugs," indicating the gnarled youth on his left. "Now retiring to become a vet, would you believe, but for the next ten minutes you can trust him with your life, only don't, trust me instead. Anyway . . . good evening, and what the fuck is going on, and try the lamb, it's excellent."

Because Mercer, good as his word, has brought a picnic.

Below the thunders of the upper mezzanine, behind the first of three vast tungsten-alloy security doors, Noblewhite Cradle maintains a suite too elegantly attired and well-plumbed to be called a panic room, but too well-fortified and paranoid to be anything else. Joe is a little disappointed, but also massively relieved, to find that he is not actually lodged in the fortress itself. It is on the sofa in the Raspberry Lounge—which may be thought of as the barbican of Noblewhite Cradle—amid the deep pink cushions and highlights of damask, that he falls asleep for a full hour before Mercer rouses him by placing under his nose a mug of thick coffee made in the approved Noblewhite fashion, so that it tastes the way fresh coffee actually smells. Mathew Spork, in the olden, golden days, used to say that he only ever got caught in the act when he really needed some of Jonah Noblewhite's home-brew. *Nach dem Grossmütterart,* Jonah Noblewhite would respond in gentle remonstrance. *Not mine, Mathew. My grandmother's,* and Joe's father would say *Yes, Jonah, we know. In all our Earthly strivings for perfection, we shall none of us reach the greatness of the foremothers.* And whether the conversation took place in this bolt-hole or in the great mustard-yellow living room in the Mathew Spork mansion in moderately unfashionable Primrose Hill, there was Joe listening and absorbing it all, and thinking his father was a leader of men and a ruler of thousands.

"Hail, the conquering hero! All hail!" Mathew Spork cries, five foot eight and lean as a river trout, his arms thrown up as if to display the trophy, then snapping down to receive, not a great silver chalice, but Harriet Spork in a great fluster.

Mathew wraps himself around her and lifts her up and murmurs horsewhispers in her ear, and kisses her soundly on the mouth until she stops speaking (which is quite some time) and strokes her like a much-unsettled cat. She soothes, and slows the stream of questions and remonstrance, and remembers to include in their embrace the boy they made.

Joshua Joseph scrambles up his father's suit and perches between his parents, much delighted by this position, and presses their heads together with infant muscle, so that their noses squash, and this causes a great volcano of laughter from all three.

The source of Harriet's alarm is never precisely stated, but earlier this same day some enterprising scoundrel concealed himself in a pur-loined armoured truck and managed to gain access to the Bridlington Fisheries & Farming Mutual Lending Society, from whence—with the aid of three further gangsters, identities unknown—he secured some two and a quarter million pounds and diverse objects of value totalling yet more.

The tommy gun was not in its box this morning when Joshua Joseph sneaked into his father's study, and there was a smell of oil on the workbench. Imagining what great works must be afoot, Joshua Joseph laid his hand across the velvet dips and forms of the case and tried to imagine the heft of the thing, the coolness of it, before his mother found him and chased him out. Now, though, he understands that another blow has been struck by the grand House of Spork against the iniquitous forces of the financial community.

So tonight is the victory bash, in the shag-pile carpeted, chromed and bear-skinned lower floors of the Primrose Hill house, there on the corner of Chalcot Square. Everyone who is anyone is here. Over by the bar with an oyster in each fist is Umberto Andreotti the tenor, talking dog-racing with Big Douggie who is out on bail and thinking he may need to spend some time abroad. Eyeing them both with speculation is Alice Rebeck, until recently a geisha and still dressed like one. But something in her face says to be careful; Alice has given up the oldest profession. She has business in hand with clients around the world. "Retrievals," she tells Mathew politely, and "people, darling, not objects" when he asks if there's anything he might have run across that she's needing returned (ho ho, huge wink: the gentleman thief returning his stolen goods as a gesture to a lady). Smoothly stepping in to occupy her time is Rolf McCain of the Glasgow McCains, the best family of housebreakers in the business, the cleanest, the fastest, and the most loyal. Rolf was party to one of Mathew's more splendid crimes, that business with the brontosaurus. He was nearly sent down for it and never breathed a word. The McCains never turn on a friend, not ever, not in two hundred years and more of solid crookery, but that doesn't mean Rolf will let Mathew monopolise Alice. Even a generous Scotsman must draw the line at that.

On a sofa of his own for obvious reasons is the Honourable Donald (known as Hon Don), unfavoured son of the grand banking house of Lyon & Quintock, indentured into the civil service and utterly desperate to get his rocks off as many times as possible before the inevitable blue-blood bride. Swaddled in Savile Row and primped by experts, noted habitué of brothels from Bangor to Bangalore, the Hon Don is a redhead in the vein of Peter the Great, a wet-eyed sex maniac with thin arms and enormous hands, each of which is presently occupied with the exploration of a different doxy of the day: the curvaceous Anna and the sagacious—if lewd—Dizzy.

"'Lo, Hon Don!" bellows Mathew, and "'Lo, Dizzy, 'lo Anna!"

"Hullo, Mathew, hullo indeed," carols back the amorous octopus, and then there is a shriek of outrage, because Anna has goosed him. They fall *en groupe* over the back of the sofa into the mess of cushions, and it is revealed that all three are wearing suspenders, although (for which relief, much thanks) the Hon Don's are of the respectable sock variety. For sheer devilment, Mathew snaps off a picture, and there's another cry of outrage from Donald, "Spork, you bastard, you'll ruin me! Wait! Wait! Wait! Did you get Anna's calves? Well, did you get Dizzy's? Bloody hell, I want that picture! Can you get me a copy? Wey-hey, Spork's the lad, he bloody is! Ho ho, me young lovelies, now I can take you with me wheresoe'er I go!" And more, but it's muffled in lace and laughter.

All around, lounging aristocrats and whipcord sportsmen, singers and entertainers including—to Joe's vast retrospective embarrassment—a noted cabaret act in which a white man from Torquay paints his face and sings Louis Armstrong numbers. But this is the seventies, remember, and no one bats an eye, least of all the three West Indian Cricketers or the Sudanese princeling who turn up at midnight to demand a dance with the great Harriet after she's sung her set. If Mathew has one redeeming feature, it is an absolute lack of prejudice.

Joshua Joseph loves them all. In miniature flares and a cowhide double-breasted jacket from Tickton's, he dogs his father's footsteps as Mathew congratulates a new MP on his win and steals a kiss from the man's overspilling wife, then dives behind the bar at the urging of Dave Tregale—the casino boss who's making his way in the world with a few favours from the House of Spork. To the delight of the multitude, Dave pours absinthe and sugar into a shot glass and sets it on fire, and Mathew drops the lot into his mouth and closes his lips on the flames. Joe waits for steam to come out of his father's ears, and so, it seems, does everyone else. Mathew tosses the glass in the air with a flourish, rolls it down his arm onto the table and grins. "That's a man's drink, David, and not a word of a lie!"

After which nothing will answer but that Dave do the trick for a Soviet Cultural Attaché, third class, lately arrived after the opera and gasping for a snifter. Very shortly the bespectacled Russian is singing and dancing and the whole crowd is thumping on the floor, faster and faster, and beside Tovarich Boris (whose name is not Boris) is Mathew Spork, matching him kick for kick and spin for spin. *Hoy hoy HOY!*

Yet all these are just appetisers for the young Joe. His favourite thing comes later, when the guests are mostly gone, and he is admitted to an even more select company of adults. When everyone has shimmied and twisted and the conga line is played out; when the Funkin' Walrus and Lady Goodvibe have gone home, and the respectable, florid faces have departed, Mathew is left with his close court—and the real party begins.

The great treat of robbing a bank—really robbing it, not just grabbing the cash from the registers like a piker and running headlong into twenty coppers when you get home—is looking in the safety deposit boxes and seeing who had what squirrelled away, then arguing over whether to hang on to it or sell it on, and very occasionally uncovering something truly special or bizarre. Mathew once found, in a box from a bank on the Essex coast, a human jawbone wrapped in crumbling cloth, together with a card identifying it as a holy relic of Saint Jerome. In the same box was a collection of erotic icons detailing a very unconventional version of the impregnation of Mary by the Holy Spirit which a second card asserted had been painted by Michelangelo. Even as forgeries, they were unique. If real . . .

Mathew donated them anonymously to the British Museum, and by coincidence was invited to a string of glamorous parties by the directors. The icons were not widely seen, though the Museum retains them for very special visitors.

Scotch and hot coffee have replaced absinthe. Harriet is smoking a cigarette in a long holder, others have cigars and pipes. The cash money is being counted elsewhere, there's nothing so dull as watching two accountants tally and cross-check one another, licking their thumbs and getting paper cuts on their fingers, riffling and complaining and trying to enlarge, without appearing to, their one per cent cut, rising on the far side of the table in proportion to the main stack. All the same, Mathew's working bag is at his feet, clanking when he puts his foot on it, and Joshua Joseph knows the tommy gun is within; it is his father's iron rule that he does not put it back into the case until the count is done and the tally split.

So here are the safety deposit boxes, all in rows, and warming up to a box each are the best and most dishonest locksmiths in the country: Aunt Caro with a pipe in her yellow buck teeth and a low gown which reveals, as she leans forward, remarkably conical white breasts; Uncle Bellamy in his sheepskin, even here, indoors and hot as a greenhouse, and sweat coming down his red face from his comb-over; and Uncle Freemont, born in Bermuda and possessed of spiderlong hands, with his half-moon specs on the end of his nose and a hat in Haile Selassie's colours to remind everyone to show some respect.

"Are you ready?" Mathew Spork demands from the sofa, where Harriet has her stockinged legs across his lap and is shuffling closer to snuggle against him.

They nod. Of course they are. Tensioners and picks in little glimmering lines, rakes in different sizes. Each pouch also contains a few bump keys, not for the competition, but for later, when it's just about getting through the haul.

"Three, two, one . . . get 'em open!" Because this is a race, of great seriousness and intensity. How many boxes can each locksmith open in ten minutes? The outer locks are all the same, of course, but the boxes have a second, inner layer to which each customer must affix a lock of his own. And while they struggle and work the tough inner locks, the neophytes and apprentices whisper to one another about what's being done. The young Joe learns the secrets of the vise and pin, the shunt and the bump key, the tension and the torsion, all wrapped up in laughter and delight, so that another curious skill is added to his repertoire and to his inner list of tasks whose execution is a joy and a matter for laughter and celebration.

Aunt Caro was the fastest, Joe remembers, muzzy and partway asleep on the Raspberry Room sofa. One might argue that she cheated. On the third round she complained that she was hot, and stripped off her top half altogether, letting everything hang out. Broad, muscular shoulders beaded with sweat, strong hands twisting, she carried on. The two men just watched and then Uncle Freemont asked her outright to marry him, to which she replied she'd never marry a man without credentials. She made the word sound so dirty even the infant Joe understood vaguely that this was about sex. Aunt Caro, with a mouth full of bad dentition and roomy about the bust and flank, was all the same a woman with a direct line to the male libido. They left together to pursue the formalities in private.

That merry evening marked the beginning of the end for Mathew Spork. Mathew had come to believe he should shift his game, build a power base and join—at least to some degree—the legitimate economy. The mob had Frank Sinatra, Mathew said. They had movie stars and casinos. Why couldn't Mathew Spork do the same?

He bought into a chain of newsagents, Post Office concessions, car dealerships, and a pier by the seaside, joined a club called Hawkley's, and tried without great enthusiasm to restrict himself to low-risk jobs and show thefts. He stole underwear from the bedrooms of visiting starlets and worked very hard to get caught in his domino mask going out of the door. He replaced a set of paste diamonds used in a stage detective story with real ones lifted from the owner's wife. He lounged and sprawled and took meetings with American businessmen who wanted to touch a genuine English gangster.

And then the eighties came; just-for-fun heisting and games of tag with the coppers were out, and shoulder pads and cocaine were in. Mathew Spork was on a list of people that Lily Law proposed to take down, one way or another.

"I'm sorry, mucker," Mercer says, "but there's no help for it."

"What time is it?"

"It's five, Joe."

"I slept the whole day? Fuck! What's happening?"

"No. It's five in the morning. You've slept an hour. We need to talk about all this. There's no time, Joe, I'm sorry."

"Fuck," says Joshua Joseph Spork again, through the haze, and drinks his coffee. The f-word has become devalued. It doesn't remotely express how he feels. He remembers his mother, very upset the first time she heard it from his lips, despite the fact she used it on a regular basis to Mathew. These days he can say what he likes unless it's blasphemy. If he says "Christ" she prays, then weeps. And *(Christ) what am I going to tell her?*

Mercer lays a small digital recorder on the table.

"From the beginning, Joseph, please."

"Mercer, I'm tired—"

"You can sleep later. I'm sorry, Joe. Splash some water on your face. If you need more coffee, or some other stimulant, it can be had for you, but we cannot wait for you to nap. It is not nap time. It is talk-with-your-lawyer time, because at this moment I do not know enough to keep you safe."

Joe scowls. "Just make it go away. Don't get into it. I'm nothing. I didn't do anything. I never do. It's a bad rap."

"Joseph, I have done several things since you went to sleep. I have initiated all manner of false-arrest proceedings and discovery petitions which will create a paper trail and cause dismay and gnashing of teeth in the House of Titwhistle. I have started researches into the dealings of Billy Friend and his acquaintances unto many generations so that shortly I shall no doubt know more about cadavers and the theft of antiques than I ever dreamed I should. However, these are sideshows, and you know it, and I very much suspect that this is about to get political. If that is the case—if this is national-level statecraft—then the efficacy of Cradle's to get between you and the villains of the piece will be vastly reduced, because they have recently acquired a nasty habit of ignoring the law. So please, for your own good and the sake of my sanity, tell me what has passed and what is going on. Because, not to put too fine a point on it, I have stepped in the path of Behemoth on your behalf and I must know more if we are to avoid being squished by his horny-toed feet!"

Joe Spork shrugs yes, and Mercer tuts.

"Billy called you. You went to meet him."

"Yes."

"Go on."

"He had a job. Clean up and install. I cleaned it, I looked at it, and it was . . . different."

"Define 'different,' please. For those of us who weren't there."

"Unique. Special. Skilled. Complex. Unfathomable."

"All right."

"We went down to Cornwall. The book—Billy called it a doodah—was part of a big mobile sculpture thing. There was a mad bloke who looked after it. I plugged it in. Bees came out."

"Does the mad bloke have a name?"

"Ted. Ted Sholt. Or he called himself Keeper, like a title."

Mercer nods. "And bees came out of the sculpture?"

"Mechanical simulacra of bees. There were actual bees as well. Ted keeps them. For company, I think."

"Did they strike you as in any way remarkable?"

"They existed, that was pretty remarkable. They were expensive. I mean Cartier-bespoke expensive, all right? You remember the Woven Gold?"

"Your grandfather's thing."

"They were like that. Stunning. But they didn't speak in tongues or turn water into wine or fly off into the sunset. They just . . ." Joe stops talking.

"What?"

"There was a moment when I thought they had. Obviously, they hadn't."

"Turned water into wine?"

"Flown away. They're too heavy. It was the real ones."

"You're sure?"

"Yes."

"How?"

" . . . They were clockwork. Made of gold!"

"So, in fact, you assume."

"Mercer . . ."

"Joe, much as I am loath to believe anything I hear through men like Rodney Titwhistle, there is some very significant *ordure* hitting the fan here. If this really is an old government science project, we have to acknowledge your bees may be more than they appear. Maybe they are nuclear bees or plague bees or some other bloody thing. Certainly, they could be magnetic or rocket-propelled bees. We don't know."

Joe shudders. He will have nightmares about French philosophers and Ruskinites—whatever they are, with their alarming birdlike walk—but most of all about not knowing, about not ever knowing anything for sure. And to be honest, he supposes it could have been the metal bees, after all. He would just prefer very much that it wasn't.

Mercer nods. "Yes. I refer you to the usual pithy folk wisdom regarding assuming anything. So what do we know about your machine?"

"Titwhistle said it was a sort of evil lie-detector." Joe tries to make this sound risible, but Mercer isn't in a laughing mood.

"Don't parse, Joe, please. Don't paraphrase. His words, as far as you can remember them."

"He said that it might be a way for the human mind to recognise truth, perfectly. That someone built a machine to make it possible."

Mercer makes an uncertain gesture with his hand, this way, that way. "Hm."

"What 'hm'? What does 'hm' mean?"

"Well, I can see why he's worried. I'm amazed they let you go, after telling you that."

Joe Spork smiles a feral smile, out of nowhere; a savage, biting grin. For a moment, he looks dangerous. "You mean the nice man lied to me?"

Mercer stares at him. "Maybe," he says watchfully, "or maybe he told you something because he didn't expect you to see the light of day again. It was touch and go, there, when we came to pick you." He studies his friend's face for signs of . . . something. But the unnerving smile has vanished as swiftly as it came. Joe continues.

"Sholt said—"

"Sholt? Oh, this 'Keeper.'"

"A sort of a hermit. I liked him."

"You would."

"He said the world would change. He said it was . . ."

"He said it was what? Come on, Joe!"

"He called it 'Angelmaker'. I nearly told them everything, when I realised what that could mean."

Mercer Cradle stares at him, then picks up the phone and speaks very clearly and rapidly. "Bethany? Would you please be so kind as to add the following to your researches: 'Ted Sholt'—I don't know whether that's Edward or Theodore or what, so do them all, and try 'Keeper' as well, could be a name or a title; Wistithiel; and the word 'angelmaker' and all related terms. And cross-reference with Daniel, Mathew, and J. Joseph Spork and everything we have on whatever Rodney Titwhistle does when he isn't incubating a brood of vipers or eating his own young. Thank you."

"Mercer, he was crazy."

"Which makes it all the more imperative to recall things he said which might imply that this item you have resurrected for him is some kind of weapon of mass destruction."

"For God's sake, it's a clockwork toy in a greenhouse!"

"Joe. You are neck-deep in denial. All right? Here is the news. You switched on a machine, and you have no real notion of what it is. You are now pursued by the earthbound fiend who goes in the mortal realm by the name of Rodney Titwhistle, and the homunculus Cummerbund, men who are most probably employed—and let us be very clear about this, because hilarious though they are to look upon they are less funny than Typhoid Mary and more serious than the whole of Her Majesty's Revenue & Customs—at the shadiest end of the non-deniable civil service. By the looks of things, they are the interface between the world which draws a pay cheque openly and the one which holds the key to the barn in Suffolk where they hide the corpses of people murdered by members of the royal family. These men do not have any notion at all of gadding about. They do not grab people for a lark. They have absolutely no sense of fun. So when I find that they are involved, and you tell me it's all a ghastly mistake but you have no real notion of what's going on, what I take away from that is that we are in even more trouble than it might at first appear. So please, go on."

"They came to my shop this morning. They said they were from a museum. They wanted to buy everything. And then later, one of those monks was in my shop. A Ruskinite. He wanted . . . I don't know. Whatever they wanted."

"Which would be?"

"He said he wanted the Book of the Hakote. And everything which went with it."

"Presumably the book brought to you by Billy."

Joe nods his head. "And the tools, I suppose."

Mercer picks up the phone again, and adds "Ruskinite" and "Hakote" to Bethany's list. Then he turns back to Joe.

"Small mercies. Your uncharming callers wanted this Book *et alii*. Which you don't have, though you were briefly in possession of a book which might have been it. I don't like the capital letter, do you? Well. It's not too much to assume that he wanted it because of what was happening in Cornwall. In which case—" The phone buzzes sharply. Mercer scoops it up and sighs. "Thank you. I'm afraid I anticipated . . . yes. Well, only just, to be honest. Thank you, Bethany." He puts down the handset. "There's been a massive police deployment in the West Country. I imagine when the smoke clears we'll find someone's paid a visit to your friend Ted. They're very fast, Joe. They worried about the machine first and you second. I did the opposite, which is why you're here. I suspect an hour later I wouldn't have found you."

"I know."

"But if they had the book already, they didn't really need your tools."

"It would make things easier."

"But not more than that."

"No."

"Is there anything else? More parts? An instruction manual?"

"No. I don't know. Not that I ever saw."

Mercer paces. "All right, go on."

"I asked Fisher about the Ruskinites."

"Fisher? Not the Fisher I'm thinking of who is a Night Market irregular?"

"Yes. I was worried."

"I should think so, talking to a twerp like Fisher. What did he say?"

"That they're a heavy mob. They scare the crap out of him. And something weird. He said one of them asked him something once about Napoleon. Some sort of riddle."

" 'If I have the memories of Napoleon, but the body of Wellington, who am I?' "

"Yes! What does it mean?"

"It's a philosophical puzzle. An unsolved one. The question is what constitutes identity. Is it the memory, the body, or some combination of the two? Very donnish. You seem to have fallen into a well-educated personal crisis."

"How reassuring."

Mercer bares his teeth. "Quite so. To finish . . . you found yourself in Billy Friend's flat in Soho, where you discovered the body of your dear chum of many years, childhood mentor and fornicator, in a state of extremely dead. You are uncertain, at this point, whether you called for the myrmidons of the law in the person of the wheedler Patchkind—who is, by the way, a liar of the first class and has no nieces of any stripe. You gathered your resources, however, and summoned the font of wisdom which is Cradle's to take charge of the emergency."

"Yes."

"Always assuming that one can be said to summon a font, which, on sober consideration, I find unlikely."

At this attempt to lift the mood, Joe Spork has somehow had enough. He loves Mercer like a brother, but sometimes the plummy, playful verbiage is obnoxious. It conceals emotion. Actually, it mocks emotion, the better to pretend to be above it. Joe Spork jackknifes to his feet and grabs his coat. He has no clear idea of where he will go, but he wants out, out of this ludicrous mayhem and back to his old cosy life. Perhaps he will take a ship to India and open a shop in Mumbai. Perhaps he will shave his head and make clocks in a monastery, or marry a Muslim girl and move to Dubai, where they have a decent respect for clockwork and automata and the men who produce them. Perhaps he will just run through the wet, uncaring streets of London until this furious confusion abates. He doesn't know what he will do, but being locked up in this cellar is no answer to what rides him, that much he is certain of. He wants Ari to sell him cat poison. He needs to call Joyce and tell her Billy Friend is dead. He needs to see his mother. He needs to sleep.

It would be very nice if someone would hug him, just for a minute.

He piles through the door into the front offices, with every intention of letting himself out and continuing in an approximate straight line until he can come to some arrangement with himself about what to do next. He is prevented from doing this by a toe.

The toe catches him in the upper-thigh region, quite hard, so that he jolts to a stop. In other circumstances, the presence of a toe in this area might well be erotic, even sexual, and indeed, it's a very sexual toe. It is pale, and round; of perfect size—if one were so inclined—to slip into one's mouth and suck. It is smooth and buffed, with the nail polished in a bright, glossy red, except for a slender strip of tiny black fishnet which has been set into the polish at the tip. It is a toe which knows the world, which has done the wicked, secret things other toes only fantasise about.

The toe is accompanied by four others in a bright patent-leather mule. The whole segment is then attached to a muscular but quite slender calf. Around the ankle is an item which briefly arrests his attention: a stylish women's watch threaded on a narrow gold chain. It is pricey but not extortionate, with a single glinting crystal set at the top. He doubts that the designer ever intended it to be worn around the leg, but is reasonably certain that he or she would approve mightily of the effect. He also considers, briefly, that this woman either does not need to know the time or is able and willing to read the watch where it is, which implies a supple and frankly sexual movement of her body.

Above the calf is a strong but not offensive knee, and an upper leg which vanishes almost immediately into a grey pencil skirt. Joe adjudges this is technically a knee-length item, but the act of sitting has raised it to a more intriguing status. The leg has, as is customary, a mirror image on the other side, making a total of two, the matched pair belonging to a bold-eyed woman resting in the receptionist's chair. She speaks.

"Sit, please."

She smiles up at him, then, when he does not smile back, she scowls, and repeats the instruction. Joe, not really knowing why, perches himself on the edge of a modern red cloth stool, and wobbles. The woman in front of him gives an encouraging smile.

"Mercer asked me to wait around in case I was needed. This almost certainly isn't what he had in mind, but that's the thing with Mercer. His genius is extremely obscure, even to himself. Perhaps particularly."

"Bethany?"

Her mouth quirks for a moment, whether in annoyance or approbation he cannot tell. "Not me. Bethany is still in the control room arranging a night of intense confusion at the London traffic-management centre, which will alas preclude the charming Mr. Titwhistle from locating you by speed-enforcement camera. Tomorrow will not be a good day to drive in London. No, I do some investigative work. However, at present I am here for menial tasks. I have, for example, more coffee. And sandwiches. Would you like a sandwich?"

It's a perfectly innocent question. It must be the faint sound of her stocking as she removes her toe from his thigh and puts her feet neatly together which makes the word "sandwich" sound rude. Joe has never found it so before. He tries it now, in his mouth.

"Sandwich." No. Nothing rude about that. He tries again. "Saaan-d-*witt*-cha." Yes, that's more like it. He gives it a couple more goes.

"Yes," the bold receptionist says, "a sandwich. In this case, avocado and bacon between two slices of granary bread. I can also arrange for other," she smiles at him, "sandwiches."

"Anything goes," Joe says, and watches the words spiral out of his mouth and settle. *I am a berk.*

"Yes," she says brightly, "it often does, with sandwiches. I, however, hold very clear beliefs on this subject. I do not believe in allowing tomato to soak into the bread, for example. Tomato, in a sandwich, should be applied latest of all ingredients and sealed between pieces of lettuce or salami, to prevent," and here she purses her lips, "*leakage.*"

There it is again. A perfectly ordinary word, but she's done something to it. A shiver passes down Joe's spine. *Leakage.*

It ought to be a disgusting expression, but actually, as it passes her front teeth, which are briefly exposed as she enunciates the second syllable, it becomes a vibrant, enticing notion. This is not slurry from a rusted pipe, this is the beads of honey emerging languorously from a slice of baklava. Joe shuts his eyes for a second to stop himself from staring at her mouth. Red lips. Pale, sharp teeth. Very precise diction. The tip of her tongue. What a woman. For the second time tonight, he is rescued by Mercer.

"I see you've found Polly."

"Oh, um, yes."

"Polly, were you listening in?"

Polly nods at a notepad on her desk, covered in scribbles and question marks. "Of course."

"Any thoughts?"

"What's a book?"

"I had hoped for something a bit more—"

"Mercer. Seriously. What is a book? Is it a collection of papers bound like something by Dickens? Or is it a gathering of information, an archive? In this context, particularly, it seems to me it's the latter. Joe's book wasn't just paper, it was an ignition key. The book gives control of the machine—except, somehow, it doesn't. There's a missing page or a cog or another volume. I don't know. The point is, they thought they'd have it all by now and they don't. So they need Joe."

Joe finds himself thinking of the Recorded Man again. The book of someone's life, of their every waking sense. He shivers.

Mercer nods, conceding Polly's point. "Well, they need Joe for something. By the way, did I hear you mention more coffee?"

"Indeed you did."

"Is it the particularly aggressive kind?"

"It has potential in that direction."

"You could coach it?"

"I believe so."

"And then we can get to the business of seriously examining what's going on while Joe catches another forty winks."

"Ideal."

"Then by all means, Polly, please do."

"I shall."

And off she goes, leaving Joe to wonder whether she is Mercer's girlfriend, and when his tongue will cease to adhere to the roof of his mouth, and whether it is obvious that he finds this woman frantically attractive, albeit for no doubt complex and inappropriate reasons owed in part to his state of fight-flight agitation.

"You still want to leave?" Mercer demands.

"No."

"Good. Then come back in here and let's go through it in detail, please." He pauses. "Joe? I can almost certainly get you out of this. It's going to be okay. But it's going to get harder from here and you have to do what I say and live very, very small for a while. Maybe even take a holiday. All right?"

Holiday. He has an image of Polly in the shade of a beach umbrella. "All right."

It is all right. Mercer always gets him out of it. Mercer always can. And with the bold receptionist somewhere around, Joe Spork feels suddenly very content in the Raspberry Room of Noblewhite Cradle.

VII

Cuparah;

dinner with the Opium Khan;

close encounters with insects and bananas.

n the fitful dreams of Edie Banister, crazy old punk lady and dog-bearing fugitive, the broad black deck of *Cuparah* is slick with brine, and she reels as another wave strikes the bow. The ship yaws hugely, lurching in the swell. Edie swallows bile, but even the sense of imminent vomiting can't dampen her delight.

Cuparah is a submarine.

More than that, it is a Ruskinite submarine, a nacred, seaswell ghost which cuts through one wave and plays on the next. The shape is functional—a whale-ish blunt-headed shape, swirled with weird water patterns for camouflage, asymmetrical and misleading—but every detail is splendid. The conning tower is swept back dramatically, not bolted on but seemingly grown from the body, and inside, a stair unfolds from the main body to the hatchway which makes the tower look like the entrance to a ballroom. The hatch itself is trimmed on the underneath with oiled brown leather, tooled with the names of the men who built it, and despite years of use the principal odour wafting from below is leather and varnish: warm, living smells.

"For Christ's sake, get up here and in," Amanda Baines says. Corporal Albert Pritchard—known mostly as Songbird, and last seen gasping in Mrs. Sekuni's Number 4 wristlock—gamely grips Edie by the shoulder and buttock and boosts her over the guard rail to the hatch. Songbird is one of Edie's lads, a team of veteran uglies who will support her by breaking heads and blowing things up should she require it. The others are already on board and no doubt arguing over bunks.

Edie peers down into the depths of *Cuparah*. There's red light in the depths, and a cool scent of unwashed male rises out of the dark. Curiously, her nausea ebbs. She climbs down inside the hatch, and Songbird follows.

"Welcome aboard," Amanda Baines says, passing Edie a waxed canvas grip filled with something heavy and soft. Behind her, the rest of Songbird's squad nod greetings and grin shyly. Edie's command. Her boys. Lethal and wicked and noble as the day.

Edie nods, stares at the narrow gang and breathes in the air. A Ruskinite, draped in black, hurries past with a strange brass tool in one hand and a concentrated expression on his face. As he passes through a hatch, she sees in the cabin beyond a familiar bank of valves and vacuum tubes. Of course. What could be more mobile, or more difficult to destroy, than a submarine code-breaking station?

The dead man's hatches between compartments are fitted out in brass, and the cut steel is scrolled with elegant spirals and curlicues, a maker's mark stamped into the upper left quadrant. *Mockley fecit.* "Mockley made me." Edie grins. Nice to know who created the machine on which your life depends. She trusts Mockley, and hence also *Cuparah*. When she looks up, she finds a wide sky above her, a beautiful illusion of clouds and air. *Cuparah* is a thing to lift the heart, even down here in the dark beneath the waves.

"Best get used to the uniform," Amanda (Captain) Baines adds, gesturing to the case. "Try it on before you sleep, and wear it in the morning."

"Yes," Edie says. "Of course."

In her cabin—*Cuparah*, of necessity, is big; in fact, it is huge for a submarine, like a Gothic destroyer sunk and overturned, with an Art Deco cruise ship inside, so cabins are like rooms in very expensive boutique hotels—Edie Banister stares at the photograph, and the face in it stares back at her in the light of her cabin's curlicued reading lamp. All around her, there's a whisper of water and air: the submarine has two hulls, one within the other. The inner walls are a honeycomb—for strength, flexibility, and lightness, the Ruskinites on board have told her, and to permit cabling and pipes. As the ship moves, it sighs and chuckles to itself, so that Edie fancies herself surrounded by a giant, generous, asthmatic dog.

The white shirt has trim sleeves and a severe cut which vanishes her already minimal bust. Over the top goes a jacket with broad shoulders, making a very male, very triangular torso dropping to her hips. Rummaging in her bags she finds her rank pins, and twists them through the thick collar. She also has a false moustache not entirely unlike Shem Shem Tsien's, a brace of neat sparrow's wings. Careful, she fixes them very firmly to her upper lip (in absolutely no sense does she wish to have a conversation with the Opium Khan which begins: "Commander Banister, your moustache has fallen in the gazpacho") and turns to look in the mirror.

The effect is rather more than she had anticipated. A pale, severe face stares back at her, a young man's only just out of boyhood—perhaps trying a little too hard—but definitely not a woman's. How curious. She puts her cap on and looks again. Actually, that young man in the glass is quite attractive—not in a rugged way, but in the manner of a refined creature, inexperienced yet supple, in need of Edie's skilled, frank schooling. An entirely different set of fantasies winds across her inner vision. *My oh my . . .* her hands trace the outline of his—her—uniform. *Ho hum.* It's rather a shame she can't go to bed with herself. She turns sideways . . . *Delicious.*

And distracting. Edie sneers at her reflection, hoping to produce a dangerous expression. *Hm.* That's not a look which will stop an advancing foe. She tries again, going for confident disdain. It doesn't work, but produces a strange, fey look of murderous intent instead.

Cuparah shudders and barks; it's something called the thermocline. Edie doesn't know what that may be, but hitting it and bouncing off it is like running the rapids, and every time it happens she abruptly remembers how far beneath the waves she is, and how very far from home. If only she could get some warmth into her bones. A hundred feet down in an iron cigar filled with working men, why the Hell is it so cold? She wonders if she can ask Amanda Baines for a heater.

Actually, she knows why it's cold. Excess heat is a major problem in submarines, and *Cuparah* is worse than the average because she is bigger and contains all manner of clever doohickeys, including the coding machine, which gets so hot that in England it would be operated by girls wearing only their most sensible underwear. Because this is a Ruskinite submarine, it has an incredibly clever solution involving water being pumped around the vessel between the inner and outer hulls. This water is also—even more cunningly—used to assist in manoeuvring, and because it is not compressible, actually adds to the strength of the hull. *Cuparah*'s cooling system is the Keeper's best work. Amanda Baines calls it Poseidon's Net, and smiles a little when she does because she is the only submarine captain who has one. It is brilliant.

It also makes all the cabins in Edie's section really cold.

Conscious of the weight above her, Edie slips out of her uniform. She steps carefully, feeling a ridiculous nervousness about leaning on the walls in case she punctures the armoured skin and drowns the boat. Ridiculous. Impossible. But she can't shake the aching horror of the idea, shed the imagined feeling of an eggshell cracking.

She draws her blanket around her and falls asleep, wishing very devoutly for a friend in need, or actually, just the warm embrace of a friend in bed.

James Edward (Edie) Banister, sword on hip, walks along the gang of *Cuparah*. His boots are very black and very shiny, and his steps are the clipped, certain steps of a son of Empire. The playing fields of Eton have birthed him, and if they have not also been successful in teaching him classical Greek or mathematics, nor made any attempt to instil a sense of compassion, they have at least prepared him for his likely tasks with a sense of monstrous entitlement. Wherever he goes, in whatever ridiculous foreign court he walks, he walks in the warm shadow of Henry V and Queen Victoria, in the palm of the hand of Shakespeare, and let the heathen take heed.

"The gig is waiting, Commander Banister," Amanda Baines says, without a shadow of humour. "I believe you already know these men?" And yes, he does—four of Mrs. Sekuni's really very very not very good students, now grudgingly approved, in full rig and quite respectful.

"Yes, Captain," Edie replies quietly.

"Carry on, then, James. Good luck."

The long, maroon Rolls-Royce has grey leather seats and is driven by a respectful man called Tah. Tah assures his passenger that the journey will pass without incident. From behind James Banister's whiskers, Edie wonders what sort of incident he is thinking of. She peers back along the road, comforted by her escort in their own car. A small squad of hard cases from the fighting parts of England, and very welcome, too.

The road is very straight and very flat, and lined with cherry trees. It is a perfect road through a barren place. Once, along the way, Commander Banister sees a grandmother plucking a stone from the track. Looking back as the car whooshes past, Edie sees the woman stoop again, and again, and realises that this is her task.

"The Khaygul-Khan is very progressive," Tah says proudly. "He believes in full employment."

"So I see."

"And in civic works. This avenue is the work of the Khaygul-Khan's modernising project. The cherry trees are brought from Japan. They are the most beautiful cherry trees in the world. Matched pairs."

"The Khaygul-Khan believes his country should have the best," James Banister agrees.

"Also, in engineering for the future. Our nation will not survive in the new world without infrastructure. We use modern construction techniques. No elephants."

"What, none?"

"None at all. It is not modern."

"That seems a shame."

"The Khaygul-Khan does not greatly admire elephants. He says they are lazy by nature and prone to outbursts of temper. He was forced to have several of them impaled, because they would not serve in his army of peace. Elephants are of the past. In the future, there will be none in Addeh Sikkim." Tah chokes a little on this last. James Banister makes haste to move the conversation along.

"I'm sure that's very wise," he says.

"Naturally, all our people wish to be part of the Khaygul-Khan's great project," Tah asserts stoutly.

"Naturally."

"It is only the brigands from over the border who are against this. They foment rebellion and unrest. And the pirates from the Addeh."

"I'm sure pirates are very wicked."

"Yes. Pirates are wicked. Exactly."

Tah nods emphatically.

In the gaps between the proud, imported trees, squalid houses and hopeless faces.

Edie hears Abel Jasmine, in her head: *This is not the fight, Edie. No crusades. The fight is survival. We'll do the good things, the right things, later. For now, the fight is the thing.*

She doesn't like it, but she knows it's true. She settles herself, twirls her false moustache with one hand, and tries to think like a bold scion of Empire.

From the Door of Humility—where appellants enter the throne room of the Opium Khan—to the dais where Shem Shem Tsien sits, fanned by houris and waited on by eunuchs, is a distance of forty paces. The whole chamber is lit by row upon row of gas lamps, tiny globes burning very bright and hot, but interspersed between them are strange coils of actinic blue. Every so often they crackle and spit as a moth or fly blunders into them. A lavender silk carpet runs the length of the room and culminates in a shin-high bar of gold and rubies at which one is required to kneel. The Englishman, Banister, removes his cap and places it under his arm. He has already politely given up his sword and pistol to the flunkey on his left. He turns, leaving his personal guard of four at the back of the room, and walks the long carpet slowly but without ceremony. The Opium Khan watches him every step of the way, past the sturdy marble columns sheathed in mosaic to give the impression of being quarried whole, and the great gold sculptures depicting the achievements of the Khan (suitably edited) and the organist playing the Khan's personal anthem, and finally— this is where most petitioners are finally overawed—over the small bridge which crosses a jagged chasm, the bottom of which cannot be detected, so deep it is, but from which emerges in strange, sudden flashes yet more blue light and a sound of seething geology, like a dragon turning in its sleep. Behind the Opium Khan is a huge spiderweb of blue coils, the radial arms like the limbs of a many-limbed god. Approaching the throne is like walking into a storm cloud; one's hair stands slightly on end.

Commander Banister reaches the bar, and bows his head respectfully.

"From Her Britannic Majesty, greetings," he says briefly. His voice is light, even high, but then the English nobility are often said to be an effeminate race.

The flunkey coughs.

"It is customary that visitors kneel before the Khaygul-Khan," he says.

"I ain't a customary visitor," the young man replies smartly, with a condescending smile. "I'm an ambassador o' the British Crown. Don't kneel in Beijing, don't kneel in Moscow. Never been done. Never will be. Might kneel for Don Bradman, mind you. Decent batter. Whaddaya say, Khan? Bradman any good?"

"Bradman is excellent, Commander Banister. Although I always feel that Larwood's better nature precludes a proper confrontation."

"How so?"

"Larwood declines to risk hurting him severely, Commander Banister. Even with the new bodyline. He holds back."

"Nature of the game, Khan. In the end, victory ain't the point."

"A very English game, Commander. Which is why I do not play."

"Dear me. But however do you spend the summer, athletic fellow like you?"

"Fencing, Commander Banister. Hunting. War, sometimes. And of course, I must tend to my flock."

"Sheep? Curious notions you fellas have. Sheep, eh? No pastime for an aristocrat, I'd say, but you know your nation, I s'pose, Khan."

The Khan's eyes are very sharp upon Banister's face.

"My people, Commander."

"Oh, indeed. Metaphor. Well, to each his own. Need a lot of looking after, do they?"

"Constant."

"Int'restin' how that happens in warmer climates. Your Frenchman requires very little maintenance, your yeoman Wessexer none at all. The Scots and the Dutch are positively against it. But come down into the heat and everyone needs schooling and regulation. Inconvenient, I call it."

"It is a solemn duty which affords me the chance to be closer to God. Do you feel close to God?"

"Course I do. *Dieu et mon droit*, you see. Bein' an ambassador's very nearly like bein' a bishop."

Shem Shem Tsien smiles. "Bishops cannot make love."

"Ambassadors should avoid makin' war and nuns ain't supposed to drink; fishermen are silent, not to mention ministers are selfless and judges are incorruptible. Surprisin' how often all of us slip up, though." Commander Banister smiles a broad, idiotic smile, his eyes very sharp in his pale, girlish face. Shem Shem Tsien nods in appreciation. Yes, indeed. Here is a man worthy of his attention. A buffoonish mask offered without pretence of truthfulness, and just a hint of a dare: Shem Shem Tsien has been challenged to find the truth of James Banister and just perhaps his price as well.

"Nice decorations," Banister says, indicating the great disc behind his host.

"You like them? The aesthetic aspect is secondary, of course. Still, a throne decked in storms is something of a statement, I feel."

"Secondary, eh? So what's primary?"

The Opium Khan's smile thins a little. "I have a morbid fear of insects, Commander Banister."

"Insects? Big fella like you?"

"Mm. I once caught a Japanese merchant wandering through my kingdom, Commander, with a selection of wine glasses. Amid some truly excellent English crystal and some lost wax pieces by Lalique, he had a small number of cylinders containing mosquitoes which had been fed upon dying men. The diseases they carried were extraordinarily virulent. Do you see? I believe the idea came from an American author—a man who had no love for Asia, as it happens. Of course, the Americans by which I mean, I suppose, the white Americans—have some history with spreading disease among those who are in their way."

"Charmin'."

"Indeed. As a ruse of war, it is efficacious. As an act of man, despicable." *See me, Commander Banister. I say the word, but I do not feel it. Understand: I have no limits.*

James Banister's bland expression does not falter, and the Opium Khan snorts lightly through his nose. Is the man dense? Or brave? The Englishman goes on.

"I understand you've been havin' a wee war of your own?"

"Rabble from the forests. Woodcutters and charcoal burners. There is a real conflict abroad in the world, and it is at my gates. What you refer to is but a local issue of authority, nothing more."

"Unruly peasants?"

"Misled by the last remnants of an old conflict."

"Dear me. Best to finish that sort of thing at the time."

"Indeed. It's rare that I have occasion to regret my mercy."

Commander Banister nods. Yes, he has grasped the implication there. "I imagine that it is," he says coolly, and snaps his heels together by way of punctuation. "If I may?"

Shem Shem Tsien nods magnanimously. "We will eat in an hour, Commander. My chef has been instructed to prepare some traditional dishes for your amusement."

"Not goat, I hope."

"Addeh swan with a pearl and vinegar sauce, gold-leafed potatoes and a confit of Sikkim Red Tiger."

"Never had tiger. What's it like?"

"I understand that depends very much on what the animal has been eating."

"And this one?"

"I have been feeding it personally. I can assure you the flavour will be entirely appropriate."

"Taste of steak, then?"

The Opium Khan smiles, and raises one thin eyebrow.

"Steak. Yes. And perhaps just a little of the woods, Commander Banister. One never knows what will come through."

" 'E's a cauld bastid, an' noo error," Flagpole says in Edie Banister's chamber, when Songbird has given the all-clear. "A total, un-miti-gayt-ud bastid. World'ud be bettah off wi'oot 'un. Noo chance, I s'pose, Countess?"

" 'Commander,' " Songbird says, reprovingly, glancing at the hum-ming coil in the corner of the room. Edie isn't sure whether a coil like that might be made to work as a microphone as well as a bug-zapper, and has no desire to find out by being discovered as a spy. Well, all right, as a girl spy with an inimical mission: it's pretty clear that Com-mander James is a spook of the first circle, but people in this world seem to take that sort of thing as natural. It's like not minding that the other fellow has a gun so long as he points it at the floor.

"Aye, weel. Commander, then. Noo chance?" Flagpole looks down at her, rough countryman's face hopeful, like a boy asking for a new bicycle.

Edie glances around the room; bordello chic, very much in the

Soho style of accommodation for louche gentlemen wishing to try out the harem style. A subtle insult to the British soldier, or an assumption about his ignorance? Or . . . a warning that her disguise has been penetrated already, and here is a false room for a false fellow, as fake and obvious as her fake moustache. No way to tell. She fingers a length of orange satin, draws it across her face. Delicious. *Focus.*

"Not unless something goes very wrong," she replies. Flagpole brightens.

"Whul, it usually does, ey?"

"'Ope not," Songbird mutters. "Some other bugger can go aftah that 'un. 'E looked at me on the way oot a' the room. Fair 'n' I widdled meself. Go op agin that wi'oot orders? Buggeroff!"

A large number of Songbird's pronouncements end in this one word, which is how he gets his name. Shortarse (who is predictably enough around six foot nine and scrawny) christened him after the first few days on *Cuparah.* "Fookin' Nora, 'e's too sophisticated fer the likes o' me, Cap'n, I can't sail wi' no flutt'rin' songbird!"

Shortarse was also the first to call Edie "Countess," after Flagpole tried his luck getting her to share his bunk back before they made landfall. "Now then, wee lass, best we get it oot tha way, like. You'll be wantin' to hoist the colours fer Flagpole, sure enough, I says let's do it reet off the bat, and mayhapp'n ye'll be cured o' yer infatcherashun 'fore we leave . . ." And so saying, he planted a wet smacker on her lips. Edie bethought herself of Mrs. Sekuni's Second Method For Repelling Improper Advances From Bourgeois Intellectual Sex Maniacs (of which Mrs. Sekuni assured Edie there were an infinite number and they were not, absolutely not to be despised, because many of them were quite as interesting as they wished a lady to believe). She let the kiss linger and then she helped herself to a chunk of his meaty backside in each dainty hand, and locked herself against him. She drew the kiss out as the rest of the section whooped and growled, pressed her tongue between his amazed lips and squirmed in the most lewd way she knew. She roved her hands all over him, down, up, down, up . . . up. And as the roar subsided, she pressed her thumbs lightly against his neck at the sides, slowly and imperceptibly closing his carotid arteries. *One, two, three . . . four.*

Flagpole dropped through the circle of her arms in a dead faint. The section stared at her.

Edie Banister grinned a wide, well-fed grin, and walked out.

"Fook me," Shortarse said, "she socked tha fookin' life oot o' 'im!" And then, because the British Tommy is nothing if not adaptable, "Hah! Look oot, Tojo, we're bringing a witch, is whut it is, tae draw doon the Evil Eye on ya! Magic o' the Islands, lads! Our varrah oon Bloody Countess!"

In the castle of the Opium Khan, Flagpole considers the ways in which this operation could go wrong. "Aye," he says, firmly. "Let's 'ope."

James Banister, Cmdr., RN, holds a foreign fruit in one hand and a spoon made of ivory in the other, delving deeply in the first with the second, and reflects that a real secret agent would solve the whole thing by using the spoon on Shem Shem Tsien's domed forehead. Sadly, spoon mayhem is harder than *Boy's Own* comics would have you believe, and the Opium Khan somewhat notoriously knows how to take care of himself. Then, too, there's the matter of unseen but no doubt well-situated archers who would almost certainly conclude any attempt before it caused their master any serious grief.

The fruit has the texture of cooked fish and tastes of mango, ginger and salt. The Opium Khan calls it a fire pear. It apparently grows only on the shores of the great Addeh River as it winds down towards the Dhaka delta.

"In unenlightened times, it was said to be the egg of a giant catfish," Shem Shem Tsien says. "A special preparation of the plant was believed to contain the Elixir of Divine Immortality. And the dried flowers were prized . . . as an aphrodisiac."

James Banister looks at him for a moment, worried on cue. *You do love your theatre, don't you?*

"The fruit is quite safe, Commander, I promise you. I have many, many tasters between the river and the table. Their instructions are specific."

Yes, Edie thinks grimly from behind James Banister's moustache, *I'm sure that they are.* There's a pleasant, itchy warmth in her gut. She suspects the fruit is part-fermented or soaked in hooch—at the very least. Abel Jasmine's lessons included a brief but memorable week of sampling amphetamines and minor poisons. Edie remembers her molars buzzing and an overwhelming desire to shout her name out loud and be worshipped. *So.*

James Banister makes a show of swallowing the last mouthful before letting the empty carcass of his fire pear rest on the plate.

"A very vigorous flavour," he murmurs, without enthusiasm. "Is it the gas lamps make it so warm in here?"

The Opium Khan gestures, and more flunkeys emerge to remove the detritus of the fruit course. "Just the climate, Commander, I'm afraid. The gas we keep for lighting, and possibly for export to . . . friendly nations. It is not known whether Addeh Sikkim has any great reserves of petroleum, but it seems likely. Of course—" But whatever follows as a matter of course will have to wait. A great rustling erupts at the far end of the dining hall, where a double chair, like a throne or a day bed, stands in place of a carver. Something resembling a trumpet is blown repeatedly, and more flunkeys rush around laying out utensils and cushions. In the distance, a gong sounds.

"You are greatly honoured," Shem Shem Tsien says, in the voice of a man who is himself feeling somewhat less than thrilled. "The great beauty, the rose of Addeh Sikkim and beloved of us all, my mother, graces us with her presence. Good evening, Mother." He rises abruptly, and walks towards a litter borne by two wide-shouldered men. He stoops perfunctorily to kiss the tiny bundle of finery they carry, and it moves, revealing itself to be a grey-faced, frosty old woman who must be the letter-writing dowager, Dotty Catty. She raises one hand to her son in prohibition and turns away.

"We are at odds," the Opium Khan explains calmly. "A family matter. Of little consequence save to historians."

"Murderer," the old woman replies without much energy.

"Nonsense, Mother," Shem Shem Tsien says blandly. "Don't be unkind."

Dotty Catty is very small, and her chair swallows her entirely, so that when she drops without grace onto the cushions she almost entirely disappears.

"My mother's hostility is what the alienists refer to as transferred aggression," Shem Shem Tsien murmurs as he resumes his seat. "She feels I have failed in my duty to provide myself with an heir, and transfers this unhappiness to a false memory of the past, where it assuages her own survivor's guilt. The mind is so very agile."

"Don't hold with all that stuff myself," James Banister replies. "Freud and wotnot. Not very British, to my mind."

Shem Shem Tsien snorts. "Quite so."

The dowager settles a little, and beckons to one of her bearers to move the table furniture so that a floral arrangement almost entirely conceals her from her son. The Opium Khan continues.

"Heirs provoke notions of succession. Replacement. You see? One must time such things appropriately."

"Wait until you're older, eh?"

The Opium Khan smiles.

"You mean, until the child's majority will approximately coincide with my incapacity?"

"Somethin' like that. Why, didn't you?"

"In truth, I meant that the population must grow again before I can massacre enough to demonstrate the fate of those who might seek to replace me, once the idea of an eventual succession is acknowledged."

James Banister stares back at him.

"Bit steep," he murmurs, after a moment.

"I cannot agree," Shem Shem Tsien replies. "I accept that it is hard. And yet, it is godly, or god-like, do you not think?"

"Pretty heathen sort of god, Khan."

"I wonder. Indeed, I have wondered since I was a boy. The Bible says that we are like gods, because we possess knowledge of good and evil. That is part of our sin. But it seems to me that the most salient feature of God, the most commonly experienced aspect of His existence, is His silence. His great, divine indifference to our doings and affairs. Christians will tell you that God gave us free will, Commander Banister, and in the same breath they will say that they know He exists because He speaks to them constantly in their hearts, and by means of signs.

"Well, I am not content with signs, and my heart is good for pumping fluid around my body and nothing else. The day someone *speaks into it*, I shall have died from loss of blood. So I propose a great project, Commander Banister. I propose to find out. I seek to be close to God."

"That's a noble ambition."

"It is a unique one. I alone in the world seek to be close to God by becoming more like Him. There are a thousand holy books, and ten thousand holy men and priestesses and prophets for each word of each one of them. Nothing is revealed which can be assured. Sophistries abound and circularities pervade. Mendacity is ubiquitous. Corruption is rife. I have . . . cut it out . . . of many I have met. I have made them honest, at the end. But the only thing I have discovered, in all this time, is that we know nothing of God."

"How do we even know there is one?"

"Indeed. And yet, I believe that there is. My only article of faith." Shem Shem Tsien smiles a self-mocking smile, a wry quirk of the lips. "My sense of the universe, the way it interacts, the coincidences and accidents, the very neatness of evolution, persuades me of this. I behold a watch and I seek knowledge and conversation of the watchmaker. It persuades some scientists, some philosophers, some theologians. It does not persuade others. I am not concerned. It is enough for me that I believe it follows. However . . . the nature of this God, Commander Banister, remains opaque to me. God is obscure. Absent."

"I know a nun says he isn't."

Shem Shem Tsien scowls, and claps his hands again, then gestures. The lights dim, and along one wall a drape draws back to reveal a secondary chamber. It is filled with medical paraphernalia and tiled white, and in the middle of the room hangs a man, crucified.

The Opium Khan stands, and perforce also James Banister. It appears there will be a tour.

"His body is supported," the Opium Khan says, conversationally, as they draw closer. "I will not allow him to suffocate. And as you see, he is draped to keep him warm." Solicitously, he lifts a soft wool blanket away to reveal the victim's body. "The impalations were done under anaesthetic. By me, personally, Commander. I require no amanuenses. No angels."

The crucified man moans softly as they draw near. Indeed, the rods through his hands and feet are very neat. They are also apparently made of copper. Behind his moustache, James Banister quails a little in understanding: there are scorch marks around the wounds.

Shem Shem Tsien moves around behind the man and, with a conjuror's flourish, removes a last drape from the frame on which he hangs. A huge actinic coil sits behind the cross, dull and dark. "God, surely, should not permit this. My citadel should ring with His voice in thunder. This man was a bishop once; his church sent him here as an emissary and he chose to side with the marshy underclass against me. He raised them in a rabble and brought them to my gates. Truly, Commander, it was a remarkable day. And now here he is." Shem Shem Tsien flicks a switch with one long finger. The coil does not light immediately. There is a buzz and a hum, during which time the man seems to wake or return from whatever refuge he has found inside his mind and realise what is about to happen. He turns imploring eyes on James Banister, and opens his mouth to speak. The coil lights, and the man arches and screams. From his hands and feet comes a smell like pork crackling. James Banister swallows bile and concentrates on the details. He suspects that if he throws up or even looks queasy, he will be murdered.

The victim is middle-aged, and was once moderately fat. Now his skin hangs like wet, grey pastry from his bones. The screaming starts long and high, then drops into an awful repetitive yapping.

"For the first month he prayed," Shem Shem Tsien says. "Then he cursed. Now he barks. I have reduced him to the level of a beast. I strongly suspect that he worships me. In time, I will make him into clay. I will grow roses in him. Perhaps I will wait until he is dead, perhaps not. Yet God remains silent; endlessly, tediously silent. I find that frustrating."

Shem Shem Tsien waves again, and the screaming bishop is covered again, the coil hissing and spitting as the victim's convulsions scatter sweat across it. The sound is muffled, but not blocked, by the cloth. The Opium Khan looks briefly concerned, caught in a gaffe.

"My apologies, Commander. That was rude. Please sit. Eat. What I wished to express to you was that . . . many people have opinions. None have knowledge. I have no interest in more of the former, only in a full and unquestionable experience of the latter."

"I see."

"No. But you shall. I seek to know God by becoming more like Him. Thus I have replicated the many paths of God as recorded in our many holy books. Fratricide? Yes. I have committed fratricide, patricide . . . I have slain generations. I have been merciful—terribly merciful. Capriciously so. My mercy has driven men insane. I have done things so dark, countenanced monstrosities so appalling, that my cruelty has inspired fear in nations great and powerful. Even your own.

"I have drowned men in their thousands. I have extinguished species, decimated populations with disease. On that frame I stopped milord bishop's heart. It ceased to beat—for our entire history on this Earth, Commander, the very measure of death. And I reached down and clawed him back. I returned him to his body. Because I wished it. Because it was godly.

"And never, Commander, never do I explain myself—save to you, tonight, so that you can be my prophet in the court of the English King. Do you see? God is indifferent and God is silent and God is alien. And thus I shall become. I shall rise through horror and disaster, and in doing so I shall be more and more like Him. I shall be His mirror.

"I shall have words with the Silent God, Commander. I alone, of all men, shall know God as an equal. And then, we shall see."

Behind the drape, the former bishop barks loudly. Shem Shem Tsien frowns, and flicks his glass. The drone of the actinic coil abruptly stops. There is a gulp, and then sobbing, which rapidly fades away.

Bloody hell.

The Englishman raises his glass to his lips in acknowledgement, and wonders what to say next.

"How do you find London, Commander Banister?"

The question is abrupt and harsh. It echoes down the table from the far end, the pile of cushions where Dotty Catty is sucking some species of soup through a gold straw. Shem Shem Tsien closes his eyes for a moment. Diplomatic banter with the agent of a foreign power is like seduction, especially in that it is not greatly aided by the presence of an elderly female relative with a grand disdain for everyone else's conversations.

"There is a war on, of course," James Banister replies apologetically, "so I'm afraid the city you remember is much altered, at least for the moment."

"What?" The bundle of rags cups an ear. "What did you say?"

"I say there is a war on, Madame."

"I'm sure there are! There were always whores in my day, too. And young bucks who'd make efforts on a respectable girl. Disgraceful!" She titters.

"The Dowager-Khatun does not hear well," Shem Shem Tsien mutters. The movie-star burnish is coming off a little in the face of this maternal assault.

"Here in Addeh Sikkim, we have elephants. They are known for their moral fibre."

"I hadn't heard that about them," Commander Banister says carefully.

"Oh, yes. Moral suasion is to be found in the eye of an elephant. You should have them in London. For education!" She nods firmly.

"And the Germans, too, now," Dotty Catty adds. "If they had elephants, Europe would not be in such a mess. Yes. I shall write to George and propose it. Or is that why you're here? For the elephants? Eh?"

"No, Ma'am. My King wishes to discuss affairs of state."

"Affairs! Hah! Moral fibre, as I say. I never heard such rot and impertinence. Although, one fellow in particular I do recall," Dotty Catty continues, "used to wear flowers in his hair. Can you imagine? An Englishman. Now, what was it? Lavender? Geranium?" She scowls. "Are you even listening, man? I say 'geranium'! What about it, eh?"

James Banister glides smoothly to his feet, glancing at his host, and walks neatly up the table to greet the dowager.

"From His Britannic Majesty, greetings," he says.

"From gorgeous George? How splendid. There was a proper man, not like some." She gestures angrily down the table at her son.

"Forgive me, Your Highness, if I may: is it possible the flower you're thinking of was jasmine?"

Dotty Catty glowers up at him through rheumy, suspicious eyes. "No."

"I said: 'Was it *jasmine*'?"

"Don't raise your voice to me, young man!"

Commander Banister stares at her.

"No," Dotty Catty says, "quite the contrary. I believe it may have been daisies. Yes. Very plain and dull. I do not like you. You are as pretty as he is, and quite the wrong sort. Tell George to pick his men with greater care. Tell him from me." She gets to her feet and slaps at him. "Out of the way. Out! Out! Must I be assailed in my own house? Will my son do nothing for me? Murderer and weakling is a grim combination. The highest rooms of this palace I have, to keep me from my loves, and guards and girls to wash my feet and the mad foreigner for a guest, with her worrisome machines, and far, far from my treasures and my pretties I must dwell, oh, yes. And now you! You frightful man from London, telling me it's all changed. Of course it has! Nothing good can last. All beauty turns to dust, and into ashes all our lust. Do you see? Pah! Out of the way, boy! I was made this way before you were born!"

Dotty Catty grabs for James Banister's coat and misses, her ancient hand plunging instead for his crotch. And for the first time, a broad, wicked grin lights up her face. She stares at the figure in uniform and nods to herself in confirmation.

"Dearie me," she says clearly, mad old eyes darting towards Shem Shem Tsien, "you'll need more than that in life."

Edie Banister removes her hand with a delicate flourish, projects her James voice ever so slightly. "I have always found what I possess quite sufficient to the task in hand, Your Highness."

She grins again, delighted. "No doubt you have. And now he'll offer you 'entertainment' to persuade you you're a real man." *A warning there. So.* And with one final "Good luck, boy," and a rustle of paper, nearly inaudible as she thumps her other hand into a metal bowl of fruit and sends it scattering all across the table, Dotty Catty pops a missive into the British emissary's inside pocket in fine secret agent style, and humphs out. "Not like some," she says again, glaring at the Opium Khan.

And there is a very profound, nervous silence.

"Good Lord," James Banister murmurs to the Opium Khan, "I thought she was going to pull the damn thing off. Narrow escape, what?"

The Opium Khan stares at him, then finds a diplomatic laugh from somewhere, and nods acknowledgement.

"Indeed, Commander Banister. Indeed, so."

"Still, I will say, must have been quite a girl in her day, your old Ma, what?"

Shem Shem Tsien claps his hands.

"Commander Banister, you are a rare fellow. You have quite lightened my mood . . . Honour to our guest! Have my cygnets bring out the swan," he says. And a moment later, the room fills with women in very small outfits made of feathers. Somewhere, amid a great deal of bare flesh, there's an evening meal on a golden plate.

Edie Banister has one foot in the cleft of a tree and the other in a narrow noose of rope suspended from her window sill. She is still wearing James Banister's moustache, and in addition a stiff underjerkin made of a material she has never seen before which will, in an extreme situation, offer her a moderate amount of protection from light weapons. Abel Jasmine emphasised the words "moderate" and "light." It will make it harder for someone to slash her with a straight razor. It will not protect her from, for example, a crossbow bolt or a shot fired from the weapons carried by the Opium Khan's guards, patrolling below. Not even a little. She tries to concentrate on what she is doing, which is climbing up the outside of Shem Shem Tsien's palace, over the heads of three of his patrolling soldiers, to visit his mother in her chambers without getting caught. They are taking an indecently long time to patrol what seems to her to be a rather unimportant bit of garden . . . oh. She can smell tobacco.

Lovely. They have stopped to have a gasper some thirty foot below Edie's exact hiding place.

It seemed like such a good plan on paper.

For additional difficulty, a large, remarkably ugly centipede is now strolling insouciantly along the trunk towards her leg. In fact, it is hunting. The disgusting creature has no concept of relative scales; it apparently proposes to take her leg by surprise, paralyse it with a single venomous bite, and feast on it at leisure. In its tiny, skittering mind, it is perfectly concealed from Edie Banister's leg.

Edie wonders briefly what Mrs. Sekuni would make of this single-minded ambition. It is open to question whether a Marxian analysis of *Chilopoda* economics would reveal pre-proletarian profiteering or proto-socialist communalism, and whether the insights gleaned would be transferable to human society. Suppose for a moment that the centipede successfully killed her leg (it hasn't actually realised yet that its prey is part of a larger animal which is patiently waiting for it to make a move so that she can nail it silently with a *kukri* and continue her climb without being bitten); would it in fact share with the wider group of centipedes to which it is presumably related, and without whom it cannot fulfil the reproductive imperative, but also with whom it is in savage competition in a battle to secure territory, mates, and food? Or would it declare a temporary mini-state and try to patrol the border of her leg while consuming it?

The centipede—she has christened it Richard—is fifteen whole inches long and thick like a blood sausage. Revoltingly, it is also the approximate colour of blood sausage (pre-cooking). *Bleugh*. Everyone in Addeh Sikkim kills these things on sight because, revoltingly, they bite. Edie would very much like to smash Richard flat, but she can't take the risk that the corpse might fall on a patrol, alert them to her presence, and cause what Songbird would call a "total goat-fucking."

Thus her *bleugh* is internal, and she observes Richard with watchful loathing. *Bonk bonk bonk bonk BONK . . . BONKBONKBONKyoulittlebastard.*

Richard is the second thing to have designs on her inside leg tonight, the first having been a mostly naked waitress with a plateful of baked cat. The Opium Khan likes to mix his pleasures; the feather-clad bimbos of his personal brothel went into rhapsodies and paroxysms of joy when he removed his jacket and revealed arms bare to the shoulder and beautifully tanned. Edie wasn't entirely unmoved herself, the fire pears bubbling away in her gut like an erotic combustion engine, and when he began to dance a tango with one of the girls—a slow, lingering statement of absolute sexual abandon, ya ta TA TA TA, ya ta-ta taaaaah TA!—she began to sweat a little. Part of that was a concern that she might be required likewise to disrobe; by this time Shem Shem Tsien was entirely bare-chested (hence her concern; her own chest would have been cause for non-trivial comment and discussion) and giving off a scent like a mating fox. Then the whole thing became rather more immediate, as a young woman who refused to be known by any name other than "At Your Service" sat in Edie's lap and insisted on feeding James Banister slices of swan and bits of veg doused liberally in precious metals.

Between mouthfuls, At Your Service allowed her hands to stray sharply downwards (and thank God, Edie thinks, that the Opium Khan's houri has no interest in foreplay) and stroke at what she imagined was the Commander's suitably heroic male organ through his uniform trousers. Indeed, on discovering the impressive proportions of the object in her grip, she became vehement and just a little demanding, pressing and cajoling and revealing by way of encouragement parts of herself not normally seen during the middle stages of a meal.

At Your Service would likely have been somewhat piqued to discover that she was practising her seductive arts on a large green banana which Edie had taken the precaution of stowing in the relevant area after Dotty Catty's timely warning. But Edie was unable to be smug about this because the dratted thing was pressing directly against her skin in a most lewd way, fitted tight to the curve of her body and pressing with a pliant, rubbery accuracy against her most sensitive parts. While At Your Service's ministrations were not directly effective, therefore, simple mechanics and the relative stiffness of the banana entailed a degree of . . . there was no other word for it . . . stimulation.

When At Your Service sat down on top of her and wriggled a slow, eager figure of eight, Edie bit down on a piece of Red Sikkim Tiger and managed not to make a noise like a woman being driven to the brink of sexual ecstasy by an intimately concealed Asian plantain. She was only marginally successful. Fortunately, the Opium Khan was otherwise engaged.

In the warm darkness, she peers at Richard the centipede. There is a distinct resemblance to a young Guards officer she met in Pimlico about the mouthparts. *Right, that's it. You're definitely for it, laddie-buck.* And *bleugh* again . . . The original Richard was clean-shaven, and proud of his monumental chin. This one has fine hairs on the lower half of its mouth. Possibly a sort of Puritan beard. *Son-of-Richard.* Edie shifts her weight slightly, and unsheaths the *kukri*. Son-of-Richard edges closer, as if finding something terribly interesting off to Edie's immediate left. From the clock tower above, there comes a loud, convenient bonging. Edie brings her arm down hard in time with the next bell, and Son-of-Richard is pinned to the branch with a soft *slee-utch*.

Hah.

A moment later, the patrol has gone and Edie continues her climb. One foot up, and here's a convenient ledge . . . she reels in the rope. *Off to meet a fair lady, tra la la.* Yes, indeed: Dotty Catty, not dotty at all but sharp as a tack. In Edie's pocket, the note telling her where to go and how to get there, and when. Other foot, up. She stops, listening for the sound of a karabiner tinkling against a stone wall, giving her away. No. It's fine. Someone moving glassware on the second floor. Up, up.

Sweat rolls down her back, between her shoulder blades, and her legs tremble. It's a long way down. She grins to herself, and starts the traverse. Girls wishing to serve their country, indeed.

Ten minutes later, she hauls herself up through a narrow window, and finds herself looking into the saddest, most beautiful, most aged face she has ever seen.

Dotty Catty is waiting for her.

VIII

Unwanted;
the type to give a girl trouble;
on the river.

Mercer puts down the phone and glances at Polly, the Bold Receptionist, who shrugs. Mercer frowns.

"No arrest warrants," he says moodily.

Joe Spork contemplates the changes in his life over the last twenty-four hours which make not being under warrant of arrest a piece of active good news, and tries to imagine a further twist in the world where it is for some reason worse rather than better.

"Does that mean I can go home?"

"It does not. Bees have been seen in the sky over Paris. And Berlin. An unseasonal swarm which baffles apiarists. There's a quirky story about a mechanical hive in Florence, too. 'An ornamental sculpture at Palazzo Lucrezia near Fiesole, believed to be a timepiece, has resumed its function after nearly thirty years . . .' And a rumour from Mumbai. Apparently there's been a distressing lapse in normal diplomatic practice. A deniable operation through Jammu into Gilgit-Baltistan to stir up trouble—which is normal, only this time everyone seems to know about it. Karachi isn't taking it well at all. And remember, Joe, please, these are nuclear states. All right?"

"This is still going on. In fact, it's getting bigger." Mercer shakes his head plaintively. "Who makes mechanical bees, for God's sake? Who creates a superweapon or a superwhatever-it-is and makes it so bloody whimsical?"

When Joe makes no answer, Mercer picks up his cup and starts to wander. It is his habit, when he is thinking very hard, to pace and talk and sip at something which ought to be hot and is now cold. Occasionally he complains about it, as if someone should have done something. Then he fights off any attempt to remove it, and carries on. At least two of his assistants have quit after being growled at for cup theft when they were under orders to bring fresh beverages.

Joe waits for Mercer to explain. He doesn't. He just wanders jaggedly, eyes fixed now on the middle distance, now on the surface of his gelid coffee.

"I need to go and see Joyce," Joe says finally. "She needs to hear it from someone she knows. They won't call her because she's not officially family."

Mercer sighs. "I will talk to Joyce."

"She doesn't know you."

"Even so. No, Joe," Mercer adds sharply. "I said there were no arrest warrants. That does not mean that there is nothing fishy going on. It means only that the fishiness is fishier than that."

"What fishiness?"

Mercer sighs. "I can't find Tess."

Joe stares at him. "What?"

"It's perfectly simple. The barmaid who by your own admission had the hots for you is not available for comment. I cannot find her."

"I don't see—"

"I sent a man down to Wistithiel to retrace your steps. It seemed like a good idea. No one can find her, Joe. She's missing."

"What do you mean, 'missing'?" Joe demands, but Mercer considers this question too ridiculous to deserve an answer. Joe shakes his head. "She's probably gone off on a trip or something. Visiting an old boyfriend."

"Almost certainly. Her credit card was used at the railway station. All perfectly normal. But then, as well, there has apparently been a fire at Hinde's Reach House. An old wartime agricultural facility, you'll be pleased to know, and presently mothballed. The place seems to have been completely immolated. Brother Theodore Sholt, a hermetic monk, was rescued by firemen and taken to a medical facility for the treatment of mild smoke-inhalation. Which medical installation is a matter of some confusion. The paperwork has been misfiled. Do you not smell the fish, Joe? Honestly? Because they seem pretty ripe to me."

"All right, I smell them."

Mercer hesitates. "In your own right, Joe, there are people you could call on regarding the extra-legal aspects of all this. People with their ears to the ground who have connections in shady places."

"No."

"I realise you're not fond of being Mathew's son, and that you might incur liabilities as a result, but at the same time—"

"No. I'm not going down that road. I'm me, not him. Not his shadow or his remnant. Not their bloody crown prince, to bring back the glory days. Me."

Mercer raises his hands, palms up. "Well. If you will not exert yourself to your own advantage, can I at least take it that you will not work to your detriment?"

Joe shrugs. Mercer apparently takes this as a yes. "So as I say, if you will forgive the repetition, I will talk to Joyce."

"I can do it."

"Of course you can. But no one is looking for me with a view to arrest and interrogation."

"Well, no one's looking for me, either."

"Yes, they are."

"But—"

"It is a ruse."

"But—"

"Joe, listen. Please. The fact that there is no paperwork means one of two things. It could theoretically mean that you are home free. It could mean that Rodney Titwhistle has looked more closely into the matter and realised that you are a cog in someone else's machine, and not a very interesting one. Or it could mean that he has ascertained that you are absolutely dead centre of his bullseye, and he has vanished you from the official files so as to facilitate his next officially unofficial but unofficially official move."

"And you think it's the latter."

"Did he give you any reason to think he was likely to go away? Do you honestly, cross your heart, look back on last night and think it could possibly all be okay this morning?"

". . . No," Joe Spork mutters at last.

"Then I will call Joyce." Mercer pauses, as if reviewing the conversation. "When did you get so gung-ho?"

"I'm not. I don't want this. I want to be left alone."

"Then keep your head down."

Joe scowls mulishly. "What about my VAT?"

Mercer stares at him. "What?"

"My VAT. I've got to get my papers in order for the shop. Otherwise it all comes down. I could lose the warehouse."

"Joe, please—"

Joe Spork hunkers down upon himself. For all the world, he looks like a human tortoise, and might remain in his shell for another fifty years, until Mercer's arguments have dried up and blown away. "It's my home, Mercer."

"I will send someone for your papers. We'll get them done and delivered through the firm. But this is not the time to worry about VAT. All right?"

"I have obligations, Mercer."

Mercer contemplates him for a moment with an odd expression. "Obligations."

"Yes."

"To yourself? To Joyce? I need to know about these obligations."

"Why?"

"Because your obligations are germane. I need to take them into account. I thought I was only protecting you. If there's more to it than that, I need to know."

"He was my friend!" Joe yells abruptly. "That's all I mean. I suppose that doesn't really matter very much now, does it? He was annoying and loud and he got me into trouble. But I never had to be alone if I didn't want to. There was always Billy and he's dead. All right?" He has risen to his feet, fingers curled and palms up, legs about a shoulder width apart. A pugilist, rooting himself for a fight. He stops, glances down, sees his hands and puts them away. "Sorry."

"Don't be. I liked him, too. Infuriating little berk." Mercer blows air through his teeth. "But that is all, isn't it? You haven't got some other stake in all this?"

"That's all."

The Bold Receptionist shifts in her chair. Something hosiery-related makes a shuddering sound which draws the eye. "What would you do if you were free to act, Mr. Spork?"

"I am free."

"Well. Assume there is no threat. What would you do?"

"I'd get some sleep. And a shower. Go to Harticle's and find out about my grandfather. Get his jazz recordings from the lock-up, and the bloody golden bee! I want to know what's going on!"

Oh.

"All right," Mercer says. "Thank you, Polly. Joe . . . There are rules to your situation. All right? And these are they: do not look for new faces in your life. Be paranoid. You have been shown the stick. At some point they will show you the carrot. It is a lie. There is no carrot. Polly and I are your only friends. We are all the carrot you have. Is that understood?"

"Yes."

"For twelve hours or so, we are quite possibly in hiatus. Something big is going on and you are touched by it, but unless you are actively deceiving me, which would be very bad . . ."—Joe shakes his head vigorously—"then you have a chance of dealing yourself out. If you can be demonstrably dense and unexciting—if after your recent brush with the very wide and alarming world of power, you dive like a mole into your hill and do not emerge—then there is a vanishingly small but pleasing possibility that you may be bothered no further. I suspect that is greatly to be desired . . . But for it to happen . . . you need to be a small person."

Joe ponders. Then, with a reluctance he himself finds very curious, he nods. He understands the argument, understands it in fact far better than meteoric Mercer, whose own life is strewn with moments of significance, public showmanship, and occasional catastrophe. It is the chosen path of Mathew's son: be quiet, be compliant, let the world slip over you and around you unnoticed. Bend with the wind. Because the tall tree gets hit by lightning and the high corn breaks in a gale. A child's promise: I will have a life, not a legend.

And yet here, today, it feels like cowardice instead of prudence. Billy is dead and Joe has been assailed by myrmidons from a sort of shadow Britain where the rules do not apply. Some unacknowledged part of him is angry and combative, wants answers and confrontations, wants to be judged and found rightful, and doesn't want to look like a small person in front of the Bold Receptionist.

"You need a shower," Polly says. "Mercer, he's just lost a friend and he wants to do something about it. He needs to wash and have a cup of tea and he needs to sit there and let it settle a bit."

"That's right," Joe says, because Polly says it, and then realises that it may also be true. His skin is twinging at the thought of hot water.

"Actually," Polly puts in, "a bath would be better. With a duck. And possibly toast."

"There's a bathroom here," Mercer says a bit doubtfully.

"What's it like?"

"Eerie, to be honest."

"Then I'd prefer a hotel," Joe says firmly. Eerie, on top of everything else, he can do without.

Polly tuts. "He can stay with me." She glances at Joe politely. "If you'd like. You shouldn't have to be by yourself in some hotel. I've got plenty of space and Mercer will know where to get me if anything happens. It's discreet and it has Cradle's panic buttons for emergencies. There's a nice bed in the spare room and lots of hot water. And a rubber duck you can borrow."

Rubber duck has somehow become the most erotic expression in the English language. Joe Spork stares at her. He looks at her mouth and wonders whether she will say it again. She doesn't.

"You really have a rubber duck?" he says hopefully.

"Actually I have two rubber ducks," she confirms, "but one of them is no longer seaworthy and is, as you might say, retired. I like ducks." He sees a flash of her tongue on the D.

I like ducks. She cannot possibly have meant that to sound the way it did. Did it sound that way? Or was that only him? Mercer looks quite unaffected. Fevered imaginings. Restraint. Joe finds himself wishing he could be a duck, see the things that duck has seen, though of course he would then be unable to do anything about them. Polly smiles at him encouragingly.

"See?" she says to Mercer. "He looks less like a dead mouse just thinking about it."

This ought to dampen Joe's sense of acceptance, but somehow it doesn't. Being called a dead mouse by Polly is better than being called handsome by anyone else—or so it seems to him at the moment. A shower or—amazing idea—a bubble bath might just be the beginning of life. He still has his arms crossed, but he loosens them a little to say thank you. He wonders whether he really does want to have sex with this woman as much as he thinks he does, or whether it's just deprival and crisis. And then he wonders what it means to wonder whether you want to have sex with someone. Surely it's a thing where you want or you don't want. He concludes that he thinks too much. He wonders how many times in a day he thinks that, and then stops himself, because the Bold Receptionist is looking at him as if she can hear every word.

"My car's parked at the back," she says.

"Good, then." Mercer puts down the cup. "We'll all be in touch."

Polly drives a very well-loved and stylish old Volvo, from the time before their cars were made with the intention of conveying boxy solidity, back when Volvo was a gorgeously curvaceous Continental designer with an eye to quality. The car itself is silver-grey, with chrome trim. The brown seats are extremely soft and smell of beeswax. She turns the key and the engine fuddfudds into life, then growls a little, like a sleepy cat smelling tuna. The seat belt is an actual old-fashioned racing harness, and Joe struggles to get into it, the more so because part of him is absolutely determined to watch the Bold Receptionist as she twists her upper body lithely around and about, then reaches back with both hands to catch the clips and fasten them across her breast. Muscles move under her skin, and for a moment he can actually taste her scent in his mouth. He blinks hard.

She smiles. "This car," she says proudly, "won a road race in Monaco in 1978. Of course, I wasn't driving. But I was alive. Just."

So now he knows her age—a little older than he would have said, a little younger than he is. Did she mean to tell him that? To let him know they are of comparable generations?

"Have you smelled the leather?" Polly asks.

He nods. The car smells richly of old leather, cracked and polished and in one or two places stitched. It's like a members' club in St. James's, or somewhere his father might have played cards with the Old Campaigners.

"Sometimes I just put my nose into it and breathe in. Mm-mm. Lovely!" Her eyes are very bright. She loves the senses, loves the world. He finds that . . . admirable, and a bit daunting. I am a mole. I am hiding, in the company of a woman who adores the sunlight and the rain.

Seeing that his harness is fastened, Polly puts her foot on the pedal.

The car moves as if smacked on the arse, and his head bounces slightly against the seat back. There actually is a head restraint, which must be a later modification, although not much later, because it seems to be made of clay. She snorts slightly, then looks guilty, and changes gear, which nearly does it to him again. For a machine this age, Polly's car has some notable grunt.

The house is, in some way, very much the same. It's elegant and a bit ramshackle and surprisingly large, tucked away at the end of a cul-de-sac. A railway embankment rises up behind.

"The trains are a bit loud," she murmurs, "which makes it afford-able. But I'm used to it."

"You just sleep through?"

She smiles again, and this time it starts at the very middle of her mouth and spreads like ripples in a pool all the way to the corners and across her face, until she has dimples on both cheeks and a glint in her eye which is unmistakably mischievious. "Something like that, yes. If you want to know, I'll tell you later."

Later, as in, *when it's dark and secret and we know each other better.* She opens the door and beckons him inside.

The bathroom is bitterly cold and very blue. Cracked powder-blue tiles line the walls and the blue wooden window frame is moulting flakes of paint. The floor is silvered wood, warped by years of wet feet and splashes, at some time or other carpeted and now bare once more. Joshua Joseph lies in the chipped blue ceramic tub and lets the hum of the single bulb and the coils of steam rising from any limb he allows to surface from the water lull him into a trance.

He drowses, and for once there are no ghosts, no relevant memo-ries clamouring for his attention. A drop of very hot water scalds the top of his foot, and he barely flinches. The foam is slowly dissipat-ing into a silver marbling on the surface of the water, and he can see the action of plate tectonics playing out on the meniscus. He waves his hand an inch below the surface, pictures tiny marsupials suddenly separated from the rest developing into sapient kangaroos, then—when their wildly rotating island rejoins the world—finding themselves at war with angry evolved lizards from beneath the great mountain of Knee.

Joe sighs. Why at war? Why not coming together for a great cel-ebration of lost kin, two sentient species sharing the world of Soap?

"I blame you entirely," he tells Mathew Spork, seeing his face for a moment in the steam.

"Very wise," Polly replies from the doorway. He jumps a bit, man-ages to keep the water mostly in the bath. She smiles encouragingly, then goes on. "How do you feel?"

"Fine. Great, actually. Just . . . talking to my father. I do that, sometimes. Talk to dead people in my head." *Oh, marvellous. I also have a collection of ears and eat puppies. Oh, by the way, would you like to have dinner sometime?*

But Polly is nodding.

"Yes. I do it, too. Do you find they're helpful?"

"Sometimes."

"And sometimes just as infuriating as they were when they were alive."

"God, yes." He grins. He's extremely nude, but even this is insufficient to alarm him. The bubbles will do as a fig leaf, and he's in perfectly acceptable shape. She's a grown-up. If she's happy, so is he.

"Good bath?"

"Wonderful." He swirls his hand again. The United Nations of Soap is convened in a mountain fastness, for the betterment of the inhabitants of the world. Good.

The Bold Receptionist walks lightly into the room. He watches her wonderful, worldly toes work their way across the wood, and idly traces the name "Polly" on the bottom of the bath. Polly polly polly. Pollyanna. Pauline. Polikwaptiwa. Appolonia. Polly.

"I brought you a towel in case you were getting wrinkly." And she has, a giant bath-sheet in dignified brown. "It's warm."

Joe expects her to put it down and walk out again, but she doesn't. Instead, she faces away from him and extends her arms so that the towel spreads behind her like a superhero's cape. John Wayne does this for someone, he's pretty sure, probably Katharine Hepburn, to spare her blushes. He gets out of the bath, noticing with pleasure that from his vantage point he can see the V of her robe reflected in the mirror, and that—as with the business of putting on the safety harness in the car—this awkward position shows off her arms and shoulders beautifully, and just a whisper of her chest. He leans forward to take the towel, wondering what she can see in turn in the mirror. When she turns around, though, her eyes are screwed tight shut. He could reach down and kiss her. She's easily close enough.

He doesn't. She opens her eyes and looks at him for a moment.

"Come with me," she says, taking his hand, and leads him, not to the guest bedroom with its sofa bed, where he has carefully laid out his clothes, but through the door to the back, and to her own room.

The Bold Receptionist's bedroom is almost a cave. The back of the house is dug out of the embankment, and the rear wall is bare stone— not brick, but something coarser and thicker, quarried and cut and set in place here. The carpet is deep and wine-red. There's a small television and a nightstand piled high with books, a small Victorian railway clock, and against one wall, the most remarkable double bed Joe has ever seen.

It has an iron frame and a thick, iron bedhead, and it appears to rest on two vast metal tines or prongs driven deep into the stone wall. A cantilevered bed: heavy engineering in the bedroom. Something deep down in him grabs onto it, devours the sight. *Wonderful.*

Polly pokes him sharply in the flank. "Sit," she says. "I want to talk to you eye to eye and I don't want to stand on a chair."

He sits on the cantilevered bed. It's quite high. She nudges at his knees until she can stand in between them, and yes, they are on a level. This appears to please her.

"You, Joe Spork, are the sort of man to give a girl trouble. I see it in your eyes. And do you know what sort of trouble?"

"I'm not—"

"Exactly that sort of trouble. Wilfulness. Constant backchat." She rests a finger on his nose. "Hush. Pay attention."

He nods: yes, ma'am.

"I shall now explain my plan. You may then speak, but only to amend the detail. The broad outline is not subject to negotiation. Are you ready? Good . . . I propose to have sex with you. I believe it will be excellent sex. Your obedience on one particular issue of timing will be required to make it unforgettable sex. I will explain that issue as we go. At the moment, I wish to hear your inevitable objection to the general sex part of this plan."

"I . . . you're very . . . you don't think we should know each other better?"

"Ah. Yes, I'm familiar with that question. Tell me, you feel we might do better to wait until we know each other so that we can ascertain whether we do, in fact, want to have sex?"

"Er . . . yes."

"And if we don't, then we won't?"

"No."

"And if we do, we will?"

"Yes."

"I find your logic extremely strange. I want to have sex with you now. You—I'm reasonably certain of this, and I can . . ." Her finger traces down the towel. "Yes, I can, in fact, say it with some confidence owing to certain evidences now in my possession—you want to have sex with me. Yes?"

Hard to deny. So to speak. "Yes."

"So if we follow my plan and discover tomorrow that we do not like each other, we will still have had exceptional sex. On the other hand, on your pattern, we will have rejected sex when we want it in favour of no sex now and no sex later. Alternatively, we will have missed an opportunity for sex when we could have had it if we later decide we do, in fact, want to have sex."

"That's true, but—"

"Your plan is a very bad plan. What is more, you know it is a very bad plan, in the first place because you want me very much and you know that I know this, and in the second because I want you very much and you now know that, too, and in the third because you do not in fact believe that we should not have sex right now, you simply believe that some people believe that you ought to believe it and although they are not here you do not wish to offend them. I say they can find their own damn entertainment."

She kisses him, firmly, on the mouth. He does not resist, so she does it again, and makes a happy little squeak when he grabs her head and returns the kiss, then wraps one arm around her back and half lifts her against him.

"Back!" she cries, as soon as she can struggle free. "Back! We now come . . . hmm, mm-mmm . . . stop it! We now come to the issue of timing of which I spoke. Ah! Mmm. Oh, God, you awful man. You have roving hands. Mm-mmm-mmh." She gives a lewd, throaty chuckle. "Stop! Now. The timing is to be my department. So. Up on the bed."

Polly's bathrobe is now in a state of considerable dishevelment, and Joe's towel is mostly around his left thigh. He scoots up the bed to the position she indicates, then pulls her firmly to him. The bathrobe remains where it is, so that by the time she is in his arms he can feel every bit of her. She wriggles deliciously and draws back for a moment.

"Ah! Ah ah ah! Do as you're told! (Typical man.) There. Now . . . Oh, it's like that, is it? Very well, Mr. Spork. I can fight dirty too." He's too late to trap her or baulk her intention. Her head vanishes beneath the towel. He reaches for her, and her left hand slaps his away. *Stop it. Busy now.*

And indeed, she is.

Thirty minutes later, the 12:14 Chemical Waste Train from Chichester Paints goes past Polly's house at ninety-one miles per hour. The vibrations from the train's passage shudder through the embankment and into the cantilevers which hold up Polly's bed. Polly, lying on her back, grabs hold of Joe in desperation and says "Now." The instruction is quite redundant, and the two of them, pummelled by the energy of hundreds of tonnes of evil liquid freight passing by them and juddering them against one another, do indeed experience unforgettable sex.

Initially, Polly explains a few moments later when she can speak again, it was just a matter of opportunity. Her iron-framed bed rested on bare wooden boards, and the five-fifty-one train (it's actually the three-eleven from the Fitzgibbon Chemical & Organics plant in Clyst Martington) sent strong, enjoyable vibrations through the whole house. Her internal erotic clock began to set its alarm for five fifty-one a.m., and she woke, ecstatic and bleary-eyed, every day at five fifty-three. (Chemical-waste trains are more regular than commuter trains. If a few people arrive half an hour late at work, it's a normal day, but governments and safety executives get tetchy if a boatload of lethal swill goes off the map for twenty minutes.)

By the end of the first year she had arranged to be in the house for all four trains whenever possible at weekends. She obtained long-term timetabling information so as to be present on those special days when eight trains ran, at which times she would loll, exhausted, in her iron-frame bed, and eat pizza between gut-wrenching orgasms. From time to time, she would acquire a boyfriend and have actual chemical-waste sex, which was even better. But as with all addictions, she began to want more. The vibrations through the mattress were strong, but not vigorous. She looked with envy at the plates on the dresser in the kitchen, clattering and screaming in china bliss. So.

Polly moved her bed into the basement. The earth conducted the vibrations more strongly there. She removed the carpet. She bought a stiffer mattress. Eventually, she drove stout iron rods into the earthen bank behind the house, and welded the bed frame directly to these to cut out the intermediary. She fitted springs to the bed feet to cut down on destructive interference from road traffic on the other side of the house. Finally, she put more rods into the bank and suspended the bed three foot from the ground, held only by the conductor arms, and she could lie in the embrace of the shuddering rails. She knew, not being stupid, that this was unusual behaviour, but she simply did not care. As time went by, she knew more and more about the network, the trains, the engines, and the men who rode them. By degrees and in her own mind, the Bold Receptionist became the bride of the iron road.

"Again," she says, and indeed, twenty-five minutes thereafter, a passenger express thunders by, and Joe actually growls like an animal, something he has absolutely never done before in his life.

"Mmmm . . ." the Bold Receptionist murmurs into his neck, and stretches her shoulders, then looks up at him through tousled hair. It changes her face, or perhaps it just frames it correctly, because he experiences a curious lurch, a sudden, powerful déjà vu. *I have seen you before.* But where? She's not an enemy or an antiques dealer or a policewoman, of that much he is sure. The memory is more comfortable, and much, much older . . . *oh.*

"Oh, bloody Hell," he says. "Not Pollyanna. Polly, like Molly. Molly like Mary. Mary like Mary Angelica . . ."

"See?" Polly Cradle murmurs happily. "My plan was much better than yours. Imagine all the trouble I'd have had to go to if you'd known that before we went to bed."

"Your brother is going to kill me."

"He's really not."

"But—"

"He won't. He'll be very pleased. Or he will hear about it from me." She kisses him earthily and falls asleep, just like that, on his shoulder.

Mercer Cradle is not exactly an orphan, but more a reject. That is to say, his parents subcontracted his upbringing and management to the London firm of Noblewhite's, the same firm which handled Mathew Spork's more egregious business and went to great lengths to keep him out of prison—an effort in which they were ultimately unsuccessful.

Mercer's parents chose this unconventional approach to the business of education and nurture so that their personal involvement in the conception of a child should not become a matter of public knowledge, the liaison being both secret and dazzlingly inappropriate for a variety of reasons. Mercer was thus afforded all the care and fiscal security a boy could want, save for any information as to his biological antecedents. His filial affection he vested in the senior partners, and in a series of nurses, tutors, fee-earners and chauffeurs. On the day of his majority, Mr. Noblewhite—very tentatively and not without regret—took his charge to Claridge's. After an excellent venison pie, and while the waiter laboured over crêpes Suzette, Jonah Noblewhite laid upon the table a slender white envelope which, he said, contained a cheque for a very considerable amount of money, and the true and accurate history of Mercer's parentage and the very good and sound reasons for his progenitors' reluctance to acknowledge him.

Mr. Noblewhite was a shy person. He had a pouchy face and a prominent nose, and he secretly believed that the secretarial pool thought him sweaty. His dignity was his professional blood, and he spared no pains in his dress, and researched exhaustively, so that he would never, ever be shown to be gauche or wrong about anything. And yet, he had consented on numerous occasions, when Mercer Cradle was very small, to play horsey through the file room. Later, he had broken a lifelong abstinence and taken Mercer to a football game, where a woman from Teesside had poured tomato ketchup into his lap and called him an ugly old toff. Jonah Noblewhite *was* ugly, and he was not young, but he was in no sense a toff. Toffs know one another. They keep the club secure. *Noblewhite*, any genuine toff would have told her, was an anglicisation of *Edelweiss*. It was a made-up name, plucked out of the air at Dover, and anyone who has to make up a new name when he travels is no toff. But rather than say any of this, or even object to this lady from Teesside that he had done her no wrong and was only here at this match to make the birthday weekend of an unwanted child that much less awful, he concealed the mess from Mercer and cheered (albeit without comprehension or enjoyment) and parroted with such precision the cries of the men around him and the tactical theories he had committed to memory regarding the game, that Mercer Cradle thought himself the companion of the most football-savvy man in London, and bathed in glory.

Mercer looked at Jonah Noblewhite, and thanked him very much. He picked up the envelope, and, taking care not to look at the text of the missive within, he removed the cheque. He considered the amount, which was prodigious, and the cold, blank pages of the exercise book in which one of his schools had demanded he make a family tree, and came to a decision. He returned the cheque to its place, waited until the crêpes Suzette ignited, and thrust the envelope firmly into the flames. When it was burning he withdrew it, and held it calmly until his plate was filled with steaming pancakes and his nose was filled with the heady scent of orange and brandy. Then he dropped the letter and its secrets into the empty copper pan, and asked the waiter to take it away.

Part of the reason for this *froideur* was that Mercer Cradle had not been alone when he was abandoned. When the son of Mathew Spork ran riot in the Night Market with Mercer, and roughhoused with giant guard dogs and skipped stones on the river Thames, the two were followed dutifully by a stringy, mouse-haired infant named Mary Angelica, whose birth certificate bore the same false flag as her brother's.

The Bold Receptionist is Mercer's beloved sister, rather different now from when last seen at the age of eleven, but—Joe Spork has no doubt—still the apple of her brother's eye. And that eye is apt to look with a jaundiced glower upon this latest sequence of events. Joe just hopes that this outrage which he has inadvertently perpetrated upon the innocence of the Cradle family will not offset the Service, the ancient deed of valour which bound the firm of Jonah Noblewhite—and his adopted son—to the House of Spork unto the nth generation and for ever and ever, amen.

Mathew Spork was a-courtin', and the world was bright. This was the dawn of all good things, when Mathew for all his bluster still stepped a little cautious around the law, and when he still felt the need to impress a girl instead of just overwhelming her, and here was Harriet Gaye, the finest singer in London, with deep brown eyes and strong forearms made to grab a fellow about the neck and draw his head to her lips.

Mathew took a table at Leonardo's, because it was expensive and they knew him, would kowtow and make a fuss of him, would tell him he had the best table in the house because he was opposite this beauty, would actually give him the best table into the bargain. And Leonardo's was the place, the in spot. If you knew London's miserable food and iffy wine cellars, you knew that the one place where they really could cook halibut or slice a truffle, or would give you lamb which hadn't been cooked unto its utter destruction, was Leonardo's. It was swish and smooth and Continental, it whispered of Monte Carlo and Rome, of champagne and casinos and sharp suits. The kitchen at Leo's (and there was no Leo, he was an opium dream of all the best cooking in the world, a fat hallucination whose white hat was occupied by seven unemployed Shakespearean actors between '62 and '79) used garlic and plenty of it, traded in spices that the rest of England hadn't heard of and wouldn't dream of using in a Christian dish if they had.

They were five minutes from Leonardo's when Mathew stopped the car abruptly and reversed so that he could look down a particular alleyway, then swore in terms that even Harriet, making time with musicians from the far corners of the world, had rarely heard.

"You stay here a bit," Mathew told his future wife. "I just need to straighten my tie."

And then he got out of the car and walked into the night.

Jonah Noblewhite—at this point, Mathew only thought of him as "the tubby bloke"—had his back to the wall and a short length of wood clutched in his hands. He looked like a cornered guinea pig. In front of him stood three men with shaven heads. One of them had a swastika tattooed on the back of his neck, which Mathew considered very thoughtful, as it gave him something to aim for with his billy club. The blackshirt went down on one knee, which was impressive, as most people just fell over unconscious. Mathew reckoned he still had the initiative, so he hit him again, with interest. The remaining two stared at him, and Jonah Noblewhite took the opportunity presented to cudgel the man closest to him with his chunk of wood.

The third man was fast. He stepped in and smashed Jonah twice with his elbow, once up, and once down. Jonah collapsed.

Mathew looked at the third man. He looked at his heavy, ugly boots and his studded denim jacket. He looked at his narrow face and almost invisible eyebrows.

He obviously didn't see much to write home about.

The man dipped one hand into his pocket and produced a knife. Mathew looked at the knife. That didn't seem to interest him very much, either. The man set himself in a crouch, the blade weaving. Mathew stayed exactly where he was, knees not locked, dancing shoes steady in the alley's grime. Then he spoke.

"Mucker," he said, "at this moment, you and I are having a little local disagreement. Your friends will shortly wake up and you can all go to the pub, although you'll want to find one which isn't in my manor. But if you have a go at me with that pig-sticker, I will take exception."

He did not specify the consequences of his taking exception. He waited, with his hands at his sides. At some point, he shifted just slightly, giving the other a view of his pale silk shirt and of the snub-nosed revolver in its holster at his hip.

Twenty minutes later, Jonah Noblewhite joined Harriet and Mathew for dinner, and it emerged that he collected American base-ball cards and was a fan of Joan Greenwood. Harriet had declared him the sweetest man in the world, and had fastened her grip upon Mathew's hand and clearly did not intend ever to let him go. He was a hero and a warrior and he protected the good from the wicked. A week later, Mathew proposed, and Jonah was the first person they told. When Joshua Joseph was born, Jonah pronounced him a great scion of the British people, and shortly thereafter, finding himself by coincidence charged with the care of a newborn boy and girl, sug-gested that the Heir of the House of Spork might relish the com-pany of his two castaways. The three grew up together as a matter of inevitability, though Mary Angelica was somehow aloof from the two boys, and life whisked her away to a foreign school just as she began her transformation from gosling to swan.

And now, it seems, Joshua Joseph Spork has just had steamy, ath-letic, back-arching, chemical-waste-train sex with Mercer's sister.

The blissful doze recedes from him. Joe Spork lies looking at Polly Cradle's ceiling, then gazes at her. Her face in repose is beautiful, with just a quirk of mischief around the wide mouth. She snuffles, and Joe has a profound urge to bury his nose in her neck, wake her with his lips. He contents himself with inhaling her scent, and closes his eyes for a moment.

He wakes again a little later, and finds that she has rolled over on her side. The cello sweep of her back is exposed. He pulls the blankets up over her, and she makes a small, happy squeak. Content, but now very much awake, he slips out of bed and wanders. On her book-shelves: a generous selection of crime novels, a spread of P.G. Wode-house, and a selection of erotica notable for its breadth and gusto.

He turns on the kettle, thinking he will make her tea, and absently glances at the Nokia handset he carries reluctantly for business. A picture of an envelope is sitting in the grey corner of the display: voicemail. He nudges the retrieve button with his thumbnail, and winces as it presses back. The phone seems to have been made—actually, they all do—for an elf or a pixie. For a Polly Cradle, perhaps. He feels like a troll. Big bad troll, in a cave. He has kidnapped a maiden and wrought his wicked will upon her. Grr. Arg. Soon the villagers will come, with pitchforks, and all will be well again.

He thinks about the figures who came to visit and the ones who were waiting for him. Shadows. Inquisitors.

Ruskinites.

He listens to the message.

"Joseph? Joseph, it's Ari, from the corner shop. You're being burgled! Or you have been late with your rent. There are men here with a truck. They're taking everything. Or are you moving house? You did not tell me. I don't know whether to call the police. What should I do? My daughter is frightened. She says she saw a witch in the back of their truck, a spider witch all in black. It is very unpleasant here, I think you should come. Or call me, Joseph, please."

"Oh, dear," Polly Cradle says a few moments later, "I had thought we could avoid this part."

Joshua Joseph Spork, caught red-handed—or rather red-footed—fully dressed at three p.m. and about to go out of the door of her house, blushes from crown to chin.

"The whole point of that conversation we had was to assure you that—" She peers at him. Her hair hangs a little over her face, but he can see genuine alarm in the portion of it which is visible. Whatever irritation she feels on finding him sneaking out is failing to bite, finding no purchase in her heart. It is already too full with something which is almost worse—a kind of confusion which comes from the contemplation of things which are very strange and very new. Polly Cradle, at this moment, is struggling to understand a world she had thought she knew. Joe Spork, by comparison, is an open book. A moment later, she snaps her fingers and glowers at him.

"Oh, bloody Hell!" she says. "I'm an idiot! You weren't sneaking out on me, at all. You were sneaking out on Mercer. You were going to do all the things he told you not to." And to his amazement, the look on her face now is relief. Then she frowns again.

It had not, in fact, occurred to Joe Spork that his vanishing might be attributed to moral cowardice regarding sex. Only five heartbeats ago—and his heart is beating very fast—when he saw Polly Cradle's lower lip between her (delicious) teeth, did he suddenly consider what hurt she might take from his clandestine departure, and on the heels of this realisation came an urge to repentance and explanation which was still in fullest flood when she short-circuited that part of the argument—he is fairly sure this is about to be an argument—by divining in a flash his true purpose.

"You are a putz," Polly says. "You are a lemon. Also a blockhead, a dimwit, a dunce, a ninny, a nitwit, and a nincompoop." She pauses. "Nin-com-poop! You have one of the best lawyers in London looking after you and you propose to ignore him. You have a safe place to be and you want to go into danger. And you propose to do all this and leave me behind?" She punches him, not gently, on the shoulder. "You . . ." she can't find the right word ". . . fool!" It's considered a mild description, these days, but it comes out of her mouth with real weight, and Joe hangs his head. "Well, never mind. Let's go."

"What?"

"You think you need to go there. We shall go. We shall do so wisely, and by that I mean that we shall do it my way."

"What?"

"Please stop saying 'what.' It makes me doubt your intelligence. I am taking you to do whatever it is you think is important. You can explain on the way. When we do it, however, we will do it according to the Polly rules, not the Joe rules, because my rules are sophisticated and practical and yours are very strange and confused. I will make this happen for you, but not at the expense of your freedom or mine. Are we clear?"

"Yes."

"You are going to sit very low in the back of my car and wear a very large, disgusting hat I bought for a wedding, which has fruit on it, and you are going to wrap yourself in a lace blanket and hunker down so that anyone looking will see a short, fat old besom being driven around by an attractive daughter-in-law."

"Oh. Right."

"This is where you say, for the sake of your own interior peace, 'But why are you helping me?'"

"Why are you?"

"Because I am considering investing heavily in J. Joseph Spork stock, and I do not care to have the opportunity taken away. Also, this fidelity to the right thing over the clever thing speaks well of you as a romantic lead. It seems unlikely I will have to detach you from an Estonian fashion student or some similar harpy at any point down our mutual road together, if there should be one. This is a quality which a girl should value over and above common sense, although in doing so she must take on the burden of keeping you alive in the face of your own considerable nincompoopery. Thus. My way, or the highway."

"Oh. Oh! Your way. Absolutely."

"Yes. Now wait here. Because I swear if you run away on me, I will hunt you down and do terrible things to you."

"Oh."

"And later, Joe, be advised, you are going to do terrible things to me by way of compensation for missing the four fifty-one from Finch Chemicals."

"Oh, right, yes! Of course."

Polly Cradle favours him with a brain-melting smile.

"Then we can go."

From the back of Polly Cradle's car and disguised like Mr. Toad escaping from the clink, Joe Spork stares at his home.

Quoyle Street is a foreign land, overrun with blue lights and bailiffs' vans and private security. A lone plain-clothes officer is there to see fair play and supervise the ruckus, and in case the homeowner (known to have shady connections and presently a person of interest in an ongoing murder inquiry) should return and kick up a fuss. Three large fellows are lifting a long-case clock, Alexander of Edinburgh, 1810, and they have left the workings loose, so even as Joe watches the weights roll up inside the case and smash the face through the glass front. He wonders if they have been instructed to be as brutal as possible with his stock. That bit there, in the light: that's the pendulum, and those are the pieces of a very fine hand-painted dial. Now it's kindling, and the pendulum could as well be a divining rod. He watches another man carry the Death Clock in a bear hug, more gentle. Typical. The one thing he really wouldn't mind seeing smashed.

"They're fitting you up," Polly Cradle says.

"What?"

"This is a frame. All this mess and confusion. They're leaving room in the thing for planting evidence later. When they want the truth, they're tidy." She glances at him. "Don't look surprised. I am a Cradle."

"That clock," he murmurs, "is two hundred and fifty-nine years old. It has never done anyone any harm."

"I'm sorry, Joe," Polly says. A sharp-eyed policeman peers at the car. Polly Cradle ignores him.

"It's not mine, really. I mean, I own it, but I never meant to keep it." He shrugs. "I got it to sell on. But it's . . . It's a real thing. You could spend a lifetime just understanding what's happened in front of it, how it got all those little nicks. I think it went to America and India. I've got provenances. That clock saw the rise and fall of the Empire. It outlasted Queen Victoria. My grand-father would have said the stricture of that clock was endurance. Or craftsmanship, maybe."

"I don't think they care."

"No. I suppose they don't."

Joe stares through the car window into the broken doorway of his home. He can see things, scattered and strewn on the ground, which are his. He makes a noise he can't classify, and hopes it sounds like an old lady if anyone's listening. He fears they may think she's dying and come to help. One of the bailiffs glances over and snorts. *The old dear's having a blub. Probably coming in to buy back Daddy's watch.*

The car glides on. Ari's shop is just around the bend.

"Stop here, please," Joe says.

"Not a good idea." Polly glances over her shoulder. The policeman is looking away. She wonders if he is talking to someone. He seems very relaxed.

"Please, Polly."

Ari stands outside his shop, hands clasped behind his head. Joe winds down the window and squeaks at him.

"Young man?"

Ari comes to the car in a series of half steps, then frowns. "Who's that?"

"Ari, it's me. Joe."

"Joseph? You should not be here."

"Yes. No, I shouldn't. I know."

"What is going on?"

"It's a fix, Ari. I'm being screwed. Feel free to deny me to all comers. Thrice, if necessary."

Ari sighs: a long-drawn-out noise of self-reproach and appreciation of tragedy. "Well. I should have seen it. I thought it was burglars and I rang you. Then there were the others, and then the police, so many of them. Are you a terrorist, Joseph?"

"No. I blame the cat for this. If you'd just let me kill it when I wanted to . . ."

"That would be a sin against the great ultimate, Joseph, for which I could never forgive myself."

"The great ultimate likes demon cats but not antiques dealers?"

"It is not known. The universe is ineffable. Ineluctable. Sometimes intolerable."

Ari smiles gently, forgiven, empathising. Then:

"I am so sorry, Joseph. Truly . . . I have something for you. They left a bag in the rubbish. My daughter went and fetched it. I tried to stop her, because I was afraid. But now I am glad . . ." He reaches into his shop and comes back with a pale plastic sack containing some fragments of wood, some cogs, and the broken remnants of two blue ceramic bowls. "It's not much, and I don't know what . . . well, there are pieces of springs and so on here . . ."

"Thanks, Ari."

Ari nods again, and turns to go. Then he stops and turns, hesitantly. Joe sees guilt in his eyes, and shame.

"Joseph, I'd consider it a favour, if you wouldn't speak to me for a while. Until all this is over. I don't want my shop to burn down. I'm not proud to ask you, but you offered."

Joe nods under his ridiculous hat. "Of course, Ari. I quite understand."

"It's not that we're not friends."

"Ari. I understand. I'd do the same."

"I wanted to see where you live," Polly says angrily.

"I'm sorry."

"God, it's not your fault."

This seems like such an astoundingly astute and important observation that he nearly starts to cry. Instead, he swallows bile. There is a sharp determination in him where he expected to be desolate. It's as if she turns him inside out, and things which should destroy him make him stronger instead.

The policeman is looking over again. Polly Cradle edges the car around the corner. "Where now?"

He can't get to the riverside store by his usual route. The image of an old lady, six foot tall and wearing a Carmen fruit hat, pegging it along an alleyway in the company of a dark-haired bombshell with erotic toes would almost certainly attract some attention.

"Down here, then right," he tells her, then guides her onward through the maze of almost-dead ends and derelict warehouses. Twice, he actually takes her through one of the buildings, cavernous spaces with the river wind blowing through them and rags hanging on the broken glass of the windows. He hopes nothing cuts up the tyres.

A few moments later, they're standing on a long wooden pier. A thick snake of electrical cable runs along the edge out over the water, and at the far end dives into the hatch of a top-heavy old riverboat. Aboard the riverboat, towards the prow, is a sandy-haired man with a pony tattooed on one arm. He holds a grubby life-jacketed toddler on a sort of lead, and over some manner of infant rebellion is trying to read aloud from a dog-eared copy of *Winnie The Pooh*. Griff Watson is an anarchist and the husband of an anarchist, not to mention the notional owner of that evil cat known only as the Parasite, but he looks more like the sort of person who would write a book on professional fly-fishing.

"Hullo, Joe!" cries Griff. "Where away?" Because it is his fantasy that the houseboat is a vessel under weigh, and not moored for ever on the muddy bank of the Thames.

"Hullo, Griff! This is Polly. Polly, this is Griff."

"Hullo, Polly! Come aboard. It's not too choppy today."

Polly Cradle looks at Joe, and he nods. "Yes, Cap'n," she says gamely, but Griff Watson corrects her gently. To an order from the captain, he explains, the only proper response is "aye aye."

Joe Spork has shed his hat disguise, but is still wearing a rather unbecoming floral wrap. If Griff Watson sees anything odd in this, he doesn't say. Before he can get too cosy, though, or start to discuss conditions in the German Bight, Joe raises a hand.

"Griff, I need a favour. But you have to think about it—you can't just say yes."

"Yes."

"It's not that simple."

"Is for me. You're one of the good 'uns."

"I need to borrow the dinghy and go up to the riverside store. You remember?" Griff once kept an ancient harpsichord there, found in pieces and reassambled in Joe's workshop, a present for his wife. It's in the top cabin even now. On summer nights, you can sometimes hear her picking out a tune, hesitant, arrhythmic plinking rattling over the water. The harpsichord needs tuning, but even if it didn't, Abbie Watson has a tin ear.

"'Course I remember. Shall we go now?"

"That's the easy part. The hard part is that I may be in some trouble. I haven't done anything wrong, but I'm mixed up in a mess, and you could get some stick for it."

"Will this help you get out of the trouble?"

"It might."

"So do you want to go now?"

"You don't want to ask Abbie?"

"She'd want to know why I hadn't done it already. You're a good neighbour, Joe. Decent man. One day the scales will fall from your eyes. There's not many like you round here. Or anywhere in the world, come to it." He glances at Polly. "He's awfully stubborn about taking help, isn't he?"

"He thinks everything that happens anywhere on Earth is in some way his fault," she replies. "My brother says it's some sort of inverted egotism."

"What sort of trouble is it, then?"

"I'm not sure."

"Government?"

"Yes. I think so."

Griff spits very precisely into the river. The gesture doesn't suit him, which makes it oddly powerful. This is not a spitting man. This is a mild fellow, but that's how strongly he feels.

"Got a name?" Griff has an encyclopaedic knowledge of conspiracy theories. He can summon information about everything from black helicopters and the arms trade to drug cartels to MJ-12 and the Freemasons and a curious body called the Ark Mariners.

Joe glances at Polly Cradle. "Titwhistle," she says.

Griff growls. "Bastard."

"You've heard of him?"

"'Course I have. He's on the Legacy Board. *Is* the bloody Legacy Board, most likely."

"What's that, when it's at home?"

"Tidies up the government's messes, doesn't it? All the odds and ends. All the secrets they kept so long they don't know what they mean any more. When one hand mustn't know what the other one's up to, the one doing the whatever-it-is is the Legacy Board. Started in Henry the Eighth's time, killing bastards. Illegitimates, not bastards like Titwhistle. You watch your back, Joe."

"If you'd rather not be involved . . ."

"Piss off. You're in the war now, mate. Brother in arms. Just don't know it yet." And with this alarming endorsement, Griff leans down into the boat. "Jen! Come up and look after your brother. I'm sorting out the whaler."

Polly glances at Joe.

"The correct term for Griff's dinghy," Joe Spork explains, because he doesn't wish to talk about whether the Legacy Board is a fantasy on fringe websites or a serious problem, "is technically a 'whaler'. These things are very important."

"Are they?"

"They are if you're Griff."

Griff hands the toddler on a leash to a smudged, whey-faced girl with coloured cotton wrapped into her hair and purple dungarees. In one hand, she clutches a cracked china doll on a wooden base.

"How's Rowena?" Joe asks her, indicating the doll. Jen smiles and touches the base. A pleasing musical tinkle strikes up, and the base rotates. If one were to stand the toy up, the doll would now be turning in a slow circle to the music. One of the small bits of bric-a-brac Joe Spork passed to the Watsons in calmer days. "Good," Joe says. Jen nods.

From the water side of the houseboat, a dull gurgle announces that the whaler has been woken from its slumber. The smell of cheap fuel burning in a mistimed engine washes over the boat. The toddler makes a face.

"Flow tide," Griff calls. "Time to go!" He hesitates. "Do you need me to come with you?"

"No, Griff," Joe says firmly. There are limits to the gifts of trust he will accept. "I can handle an outboard. You took me fishing, remember? We'll just be ten minutes." And nearly crashed us into a coastguard ship, insisting we had right of way. Which no doubt we did, but we were very tiny and those things have no brakes.

"All right, then! Godspeed." He casts them off.

The whaler whickers out across the oily Thames, and along the wood-buttressed banks. It's perhaps a mile to the warehouse, a little less to the store. Are they watching the river? Are there faces pressed against the glass? A thin man and a fat man, perhaps? But there's no direct access to the river unless you count the Victorian flood run-off pipe under the basement, which goes into the Thames itself, and he doesn't see them as desperate enough to swim in the Thames on the off chance. Besides, as far as they know, he's hiding in the Raspberry Room at Noblewhite Cradle, like a good, sensible boy. And why isn't he?

Joe cuts the engine and the whaler drifts in towards the shore. He hands the tiller to Polly Cradle. "You know how to do this?"

"Yes."

"Let the whaler run back with the tide. Give me about two minutes, then start the engine again—red button there, I know you know—and come and get me. If we keep it running, someone might hear."

Talking to his girl. His confederate. His co-conspirator. His accomplice. Jesus. I'm on the lam. I'm running from the Law.

A moment later, Joe steps onto the slimy lower step of the store, and opens the door. He scoops up the record bag, along with the golden bee and the mysterious tools, wishing he'd thought to add a portable gramophone to the trove, and turns to go. He sees something drop from above onto the narrow ledge. His first thought is a dead crow or a rubbish sack falling from the ledges above. Then it seems to expand out of itself, straighten and stiffen.

In the doorway stands a faceless figure swathed in black linen.

Witch. Vampire. Leper.

He opens his mouth to speak. The Ruskinite steps through the door and peers at him. At least, he assumes it is peering at him. It tilts its head slowly, one way, then the other. Then it ignores him, and goes around him to the shelves.

Jesus. It's blind.

But no, that's not true. It steps smoothly around him, around the clutter on the floor, seasick steps.

It's not interested in him.

He stands in the middle of the tiny storeroom, very still, wondering what to do. Then, very slowly, he moves towards the door.

The Ruskinite lunges forward, hands shooting out in a straight line towards him. The linen makes a sharp crack as it whips against itself. Joe jerks his face and neck out of danger, but the hands—gloved hands swaddled in cloth, bony hands, fleshless under the linen—are reaching for his arms to pin him, and they are ludicrously strong. Narrow fingers like handcuffs and immovable muscles lock him in place. The featureless face seeking his own, but under the cowl there must be a mask; the head pressed against his as they struggle is hard. He tries to punch: no give. He tries to separate his arms. The cloth-covered face snakes towards him again, very fast. He moves his head and hears a mouth snap shut like a beak. There's a solidity to the bite, like the door of an expensive car closing. *Sharp teeth. Jesus.* He hears a rasping sound he hopes is breathing. There is a fear growing in him, deep in the gut and powerfully strange, that this is not a man at all.

Flee. Fight. Survive.

His entire life has been about *flight* for so long that his instincts for *fight* are rusty, but here, in this tight little space with the river on one side and the dark passages of London's past on the other, there is nowhere to run to. The monster has come, and the retreat is closed off. Clumsily, he gathers his legs and surges upwards. It's . . . oddly easy. He's strong. Stronger than he usually thinks about. At the same time, he has a sense that the Ruskinite is trying to restrain him rather than kill him. Perhaps they have orders regarding Joe Spork.

Not reassuring, actually.

He lifts the Ruskinite into the air and slams him against a wall, using his enemy as a cushion. No response. Not even a gasp. He does it again, and feels the grip on his right hand loosen slightly. He lifts and surges again. And again. They grapple, winding around one another. Joe moves closer, forearm braced under the other's chin so it doesn't bite, his shoulder grinding into the enemy's armpit to take that hand out of the fight. All the time, the head is reaching for him, a constant, jerking, snake-strike motion which is somehow very wrong, and very frightening. Joe yells something wordless which means *get off*! and shoves his enemy back, hard. It's an explosion from the heels, through the hips, into the hands: the whole of his weight and muscle going into the other's chest.

The Ruskinite flies back into the old, metal-braced shelves, and hangs there, jerking sharply and rasping as if stuck on something. Joe edges around him, and peers.

One of the struts has come away from the wall and the shelf. The sharp, pointed metal end comes to a halt in the shoulder of Joe's enemy, and he hangs there, pinned like a butterfly. From his mouth emerges a low, rasping hiss. After a moment, he begins to inch his way forward off the spike.

Joe Spork turns and runs for the door, slamming it behind him. Polly Cradle is just bringing the whaler into the dock.

"Get us the fuck out of here!" he shouts, then, rather embarrassed, appends a more Joe-ish "please," but Polly has already spun the whaler in a tight arc and twisted the throttle, and the little boat is virtually standing on its end.

"Are you okay?" she yells back.

"Yes." And then on sober reflection, because it seems in retrospect that he has just impaled a man on a shelving unit, "No. I hurt someone. I don't know what that means."

"It means he didn't hurt you," she says firmly, and reaches out to poke him, making sure he's all still there.

They leave the whaler with Griff Watson and tell him to take his family to France for a long holiday. When Griff opens his mouth to explain that he can't, Polly Cradle assures him money will appear in his account to cover the cost. It's just to be on the safe side, she says, and she knows a hotel where they'll spoil them rotten. There will also be work for him and Abbie when they return, to whatever extent they want it. Positions will be found, educational bursaries made available for the children. Things will be arranged so that none of these blessings place the Watsons in the clutches of the system. The Cradle umbrella has opened over their heads as of this moment.

Joe Spork watches her tread the narrow line between charity and bribery without ruffling Griff's feathers. He says nothing, admiring her skill and fearful that his big, clumping feet in the conversation will ruin what she has done. Then they get back in the car and head off, away from the warehouse and into the wilds of Hackney, on a road running along the side of a bizarrely rural scene of cows and a purple sunset.

"I couldn't have done that," he tells her, watching the cows. "I couldn't have found the words."

But when Polly proposes that one adventure is enough, Joe becomes obstinate, and persuades her—she is afterwards absolutely unable to say how—to make one more stop before they go home.

IX

Women of Consequence;
the Treasure of Mansura;
Habakuk.

Edie Banister, wearing a false moustache which tastes of tiger flank and erotic dancer, sitting six storeys up on the windowsill of the aged mother of a renownedly murderous prince, takes a few seconds to contemplate the unusual direction of her life. She realises she had no idea what she was expecting, but if she had been expecting anything it wasn't this. Dotty Catty's bedroom is papered in a very fine rose and green vertical stripe. There's a picture rail, and a lot of tables with doilies. A china cow sits on the mantel, the base declaring it a present from Salisbury, and a red baize card table is covered in writing paper, all weighted down with a metal model of the Westminster Clock Tower.

And yet, this is not the Dotty Catty she saw at dinner, or even the author of the letter which brought her here; the affronted trout is gone, and the waffly old broad and former socialite is not in res. This is Dowager-Khatun Dalan, wearing a simple white robe and gown and with her aged hands trembling ever so slightly in her lap. There is a smear of soot on her left thumb—lighting her own lamps?—and she looks as if she's just run a marathon. Not surprising, in context. This is something of a big moment for her. Softly, softly, lest the old dear take fright and this mission be for naught.

"My son murdered my husband and his brother, Commander Banister."

"Yes," Edie says. "I know." Because what the Hell else do you say to a statement like that? She stays on the windowsill, her hands flat on the stone, legs dangling like a child's.

"He burned my grandson in an iron box."

"Yes."

"He is still my son," the Dowager-Khatun says. "What can I do? He is still my son. I should not love him any more. I hate him. But he is still my son. So I hate him, and when I hate him the most, I see him when he was very young and I remember the way he looked at me, and I wonder what it was that I did so very, very badly that he became this man. This perfect, awful man. This Opium Khan of Addeh Sikkim, that all the world knows is a monster. That makes me a monster's mother. *Grendels modor.* Wretched hag . . . But am I also *aglæc-wif*? That's the question . . ." And, seeing Edie's blank look, "Have you read *Beowulf*?"

"My headmistress at school called it a work of pagan darkness touched by the dawning of Christ."

"Then I suspect you only got the highlights. To be *aglæc* is to possess greatness, for good or ill. My son has it. He killed his family. I was drowning in the scale of him. I chose to float, to be carried on his tide. I did not know what else to do. Monster's mother.

"And then there was this. This new design, this plan: a thing to end war. The Frenchwoman has *aglæca*, no doubt. A divine smith, perhaps. Or a woman Prometheus, a thief of fire. She has no idea what my son will do with what she makes in her forge. Or perhaps she does. Perhaps she plots, too. The gifts of gods were always dangerous. A hero's sword may be the blade on which he dies. So. But I do not know. I do not think she sees the world like that. She is not . . . small . . . enough.

"But something in me said: no. No more. This far and no further. I will not let him make the world in his own image. Horror and war and selfishness. No." Dotty Catty sags. She waves her hands once, twice in front of her face, warding off flies and memories. Edie suspects she sees the young Shem Shem Tsien, looking for a lost ball or a favoured pet: Mother, can you help me? No, child. Not now. Not any more.

"So I betrayed him to your King. But I told them, I shall only meet a woman. They assumed it was customary. Bah! What do I care for custom, here, now? Do you imagine that I do? I plot against my son.

Of course I do not care who comes to my room. Send the first five regiments of the British Army in India! Send them all, naked as they were born! I shall not be afrighted in the slightest. But I knew, if they sent a woman, she must be a rare one. To do this work at all, to be accepted, to be trusted with such a thing. They would have to think carefully. Send the best." The Dowager-Khatun shakes her head, and Edie can smell rosehips and oil. From the lined, empty face, little dark eyes are measuring, probing. *She wants something.*

"I have a choice. I can float to my death, on the tide of a man's destiny, or I can make my own. I can decide I will be great in my own way. I can accept that I, too, have a little *aglæca* within me. So I asked for you."

Edie takes the line she has been given. "What for?"

"Those soldiers downstairs—they follow your orders?"

"Yes."

"*Aglæc-wif.* A woman of consequence. A devil hag or a goddess. Do you see?"

"No. Nearly."

"If I must do this thing—if I must betray my one remaining, murderous son—then it is an act of greatness. I do not mean that I am great. Just that this choice is the great kind of choice. So, then: let it be a matter between women of consequence. Between queens."

"I'm . . . I'm sorry they sent me, then. I'm not that important."

"Pfft. You have no rank, you mean. You are not Lady Edie or Duchess Edie."

"No. Plain old Edie."

"And yet here you are, on the far side of the world, with your King's commission and soldiers to do your bidding. You have achieved things."

"Small things, maybe."

"With grand results. You play on the great stage."

"I suppose."

"And you will carry this through. You will get it right, whatever the cost?"

"I will."

"Then you are a woman of consequence, *Commander* Banister. You will do very well. You will acquire secrets and treasure and weapons. And so that is the second thing: I have a treasure. All crones and witches do, do they not? A great treasure, that must not be held by one such as Shem Shem Tsien. You must take the Frenchwoman, and her impossible mind, and you must take my treasure, and you must spirit them away so they will be safe."

"I'm only supposed to concern myself with the scientist—"

"Of course. But to concern yourself with the scientist, you must do as I ask. Or I shall not help you at all."

Mad old hag, Edie Banister thinks, with considerable approval, and extends her hand. Dotty Catty smiles—terrible sight—and shakes it with vigour. *Consumatum est.*

"We're ready to go," says a shallow, nervous voice from the door, and Edie turns to see a pale young Ruskinite in a sort of warm-weather version of their usual kit, looking very unhappy and clandestine, but trying to be brave about it.

Dotty Catty leads the way.

Shem Shem Tsien is a man who likes, after taking his pleasure, to sleep with his hand upon his conquests. Amid the half-eaten carcass of the swan, row upon row of ewers and a heap of slumbering, exhausted trollops—Edie recognises At Your Service on top of the pile—the Opium Khan lies on his side, rapt in dreams of war and pillage. Edie wonders sickly whether he forced the crucified bishop to watch the whole debauch.

Dotty Catty's rescue party steps lithely past the doorway of the sleeping Khan and on through corridors of dressed stone and down staircases to rougher tunnels and mazy passages, until a strange, caustic smell floats in the air and a sound as of water falling on a bass drum the size of Kentish Town thrums around them. Dotty Catty holds up her hand, and her two attendants step to the side of the corridor and wait.

Ahead of them is a stout wooden door. Dotty Catty eyes it with a mixture of anticipation and uncertainty. Edie glances at her.

"Best get this rescue on the road, ey?" she says.

Dotty Catty nods. She steps forward and opens the door.

Edie has a sense of space even before her eyes adjust to the gloom beyond, and in that space, a great presence, as if she has come into the kennel of a titanic dog and can feel the hound snuffling around her. And then her brain lumbers up behind, assembling the pieces.

The room is *vast*.

It's so big, it isn't properly a room. It is a chamber, or a cavern. And yet there is a sense of the familiar, even the homely . . . oh. Of course. Abel Jasmine has been making a place just like this in Cornwall, to greet his transplanted genius when she arrives.

Above and to one side, Edie can see part of the depthless shaft which plunges from the Khan's throne room, and passes on through the floor of the cavern to a river down below. And all around, there are figures, man-high and higher, frozen in aspects of combat and carnage, and a battlefield littered with limbs, as if a chess game has come alive and then stopped in mid-course.

Edie's first thought is of the lair of the Gorgon Medusa, populated with the petrified corpses of defeated foes. Then she wonders whether at some point some primordial glacier has rolled through this cavern and deposited its frozen passengers here, and finally whether the Opium Khan has arranged a great graveyard of his enemies under his throne. Then she realises that all the warriors—lying atop one another, transfixed and hanging on spears, or slumped over on their knees— are made of metal. The ground is littered with cogs and springs, wires and belts, and the whole cavern smells of heated metal and construction. As Dotty Catty leads the way between them, Edie can pick out the stamps of individual Ruskinite craftsmen on the beautiful, broken arms and fanciful masks. Cogs jut through burnished skins of brass, and the black, grimy stains which run from their wounds are oil, not blood. A legion of homunculi.

She steps closer, and nearly loses her head as the nearest one swings its sword abruptly forward. She steps back and the blow swooshes past. She stares: the homunculus is pinned to the ground by another's weapon, but the eyeless face tracks her all the same. A moment later, its opponent turns to face her too. When she stays still, they go back to looking at one another. Behind her she can hear Songbird swearing continuously under his breath.

"Some respond to light," Dotty Catty says softly, "others to sound. They are clumsy and simple. But do not imagine they are harmless. They learn. Frankie says it is too much trouble to make them clever, so they start stupid and grow less so, writing their own punchcards. Although I understand they are not actual punchcards. It is all very modern. There is a limit to their understanding, of course, but Frankie has connected them. They appear to be individuals, but they are . . . like bees. A swarm. Albeit a swarm in which each member hates the others. Frankie says they are useless because their capacity is too small. They learn very little before they are full. But . . . they can surprise you."

Righty-ho.

Carefully, Edie picks a path which keeps them all out of range, and steps through the curtain of broken toy soldiers only to find that they are barely the beginning; the cavern is a battlefield of broken mechanical armies, generations of soldiers rolling back in time from the most humanlike to the more crude and finally to helpless, curious boxes with fragile arms, all of them locked to one another, half or completely shattered, reels of paper tape, punchcards and springs trailing from gaping wounds. There's a word . . . Yes. *Roboti.* Metal slaves, mindless clockwork trapped in their own for-ever war.

She can see her team looking at them, and hopes like Hell they aren't seeing some kind of ghastly reflection of themselves. One of the boxes claws at Flagpole's leg. He kicks it, then stands on the box and jumps up and down until the metal folds and concertinas and the grasping hand fails.

"Spunky wee bugger," Flagpole says, half admiring, and then, when the others look at him askance: "What? Am I noo allowed to touch the furniture, ey?"

Edie leads them on into the cavern.

The river must at one stage have thundered through unimpeded, surfacing here and there where the floor has caved in above it, but now it has been yoked by a succession of wheels and turbines, huge screws twisting inside scaffolds and tanks, armatures and driveshafts humming on greased bearings. Coils of copper in huge amount spark and hum behind glass shields which protect them from moisture, and loops of cable and wire like hawsers connect this endless city of capacitance with fizzing globes, crucibles, and other things more strange: wafers of silverish metal, nuggets and pills which hover spinning in the air, and towering black rods topped with shining arcs of electrical power.

Thick cables trail from one bench along the cavern wall to a small cleft, about five foot across at the widest. A strange, flickering light—not blue like the actinic gleam of the throne room but clearer, whiter—emerges in sporadic flashes. And then, a moment later, Edie hears gunfire. Worse yet, she can hear *Americans*.

She draws close to the wall and steps inside. The corridor widens abruptly, and she can smell jungle and something else: a rich, pungent stink of mammal, hot metal, and straw.

She rounds a corner, and sees a cave opening onto a lush night-time mountain, and—lined up and gleaming in the light of a cinema screen—row upon row of grey legs and towering flanks and wrinkled, trunked faces, staring with mute intensity at the image of a man firing a revolver desperately into a dark alley.

"Hell, no!" cries the fugitive. "You'll never take me alive, copper!"

She draws breath to call out, but Dotty Catty draws her back.

"They don't like it when you interrupt the film," she says, very quietly.

"They're elephants," Edie objects.

"Yes. In my father's time we put on plays for them, and music. Now they watch films." Since Dotty Catty thinks this is quite ordinary, Edie doesn't argue. The old woman sighs. "They're all I have," she murmurs, so quietly that the gunfire from the film almost drowns her out. "My fathers' fathers' faithful friends. Like children. They trust me. Not him. Only me. And so he will erase them.

"In armour, they cannot be stopped by anything. But the gift of them is that they will not be used wrongly. They are soldiers of the heart, not machines. And that is why he needs this other thing, this Apprehension Engine. Because he cannot command my elephants. Because he is evil."

Her voice remains quite calm and even, but her cheeks are wet. Edie does not embrace her, because she does not wish the woman of consequence to weep upon her shoulder.

"Frankie's through here," Dotty Catty says, a moment later.

Edie follows the Dowager-Khatun into another chamber, where someone is being very French.

A throng of Ruskinites is slaving over what appears to be a fish tank made of brass. It is suspended from a hoist or crane, and a broad-backed monk is hauling hard, in company with two others, while his brethren steady the tank as it comes out of the water. The liquid alone, Edie Banister guesses, must weigh a tonne, and then there's the metal. Those pulleys are very well calibrated indeed.

In the midst of all this is a small person with a shock of black hair sticking up from her head and an inexpensive ladies' blouse which has seen better days. She wears a leather apron and a pair of trousers which at some time or another have been either a blackout curtain or a counterpane. Even at this distance, Edie can hear that she is complaining; a sharp, rhythmic patter of what might generously be called "discussion." The object of her ire is a big Ruskinite wearing a harried expression and forge-master's gloves.

"Will it . . . You are an idiot! Yes, Denis, you are. Look! You have disturbed the wave, and now we have it all to do again . . . *Non! Non*, the apparatus is perfect. It will preserve . . . it will! It will because I say it will! The constructive and destructive interference patterns are cancelled by the . . . oh, *nom de Dieu!* It is not switched on! Why is it not . . . Look! Have you even bothered to engage the secondary coils? *Mais non*, you have not . . ."

"Oh, dear," Dotty Catty murmurs. "I hope we haven't come at a bad time."

The dark-haired woman—she cuts it herself, Edie guesses, from the strange, uneven fringe and the curious near-baldness on one side—throws her hands in the air.

"We must begin again!" she says. "Entirely! From the start. Immediately! Where is the compressor?" She turns around, and something makes a bonging noise, and then a soft gurgle as it falls into the river. "*Connerie de chien de merde!* Was that it? Pray to Heaven that was not my compressor?"

"It's all right," the burly monk says calmly. "It was the teapot."

This does not seem to be a huge comfort. The woman pulls a piece of chalk from behind her ear and begins writing on the ground. Then she gets another piece from her pocket and starts writing with her other hand to save time.

"She is ambidextrous," Dotty Catty whispers, "unless she is thinking very hard, she does different things at the same time. She says it is good for the brain. I tell her to eat fish, but apparently that is not sufficient."

"I can hear you," the woman calls, without looking round. "Please do not imagine it is any less distracting to have someone very conspicuously trying to be quiet while I work than it is to have a brass band come wandering through here playing 'Hope And Glory' while the Home Fleet fires all its guns at the Guggenheim Glass and China Collection, because that is in no sense the case."

Denis—the big monk is apparently Denis—sighs into his hands for a moment, then looks up. "You have visitors, Frankie," he says firmly.

"I cannot possibly have visitors because no one knows I am here and no one would care if they did know," Frankie replies firmly, and carries on writing. Over by the side of the torrent, two monks have managed to draw up the teapot by hooking it with a rod. It looks . . . odd.

"Are you sure that's a teapot?" Edie says.

"I have redesigned it," Frankie announces.

"That happens to rather a lot of things here," Denis says neutrally.

"The one we had was inoperable," Frankie continues, "because it was designed on the assumption that it would only ever be half full. At least, I trust that is why it only pours correctly when the upper volume of the pot is empty. Unless . . . hm . . . is it possible that there are benefits to the steeping process in having a gas convection environment directly above the leaf suspension? Well, be that as it may, the pouring issue is a serious one. I scalded myself. Also, the quality of the tea was uneven. The end product, you understand. I controlled the leaves very carefully." She appears to regard this as some species of deliberate action on the part of the old pot, which is now forming part of another apparatus over by one wall.

"My name is Banister," Edie begins.

"I'm Esther Françoise Fossoyeur. You may call me Frankie. Hello, Banister."

"Hello, Frankie."

"It was nice to meet you and I'm glad we had this little chat! You can see yourself out, can't you?"

She turns away. Edie stares at Dotty Catty, who gestures to keep things going, as fast as possible. The Dowager-Khatun looks a little twitchy, above and beyond what might be expected of a woman betraying her mass-murdering son.

"As for the Apprehension Engine," Frankie says sharply, over her shoulder, "you may tell the Khan that it is not yet functional. There are some difficulties I had not anticipated. Observation of certain aspects of matter produces glitches which . . . *eh, bien.* I have almost perfected a power source. In fact, it is possible . . . hm." She stares away to one side, and Edie can almost hear the sound of the universe splitting open as her gaze reaches into it, prods at it. "Yes. Interestingly, the tea experiments may provide the key. I . . . hm."

Dotty Catty intervenes. "Frankie, Commander Banister is from the British government. I asked them to send someone . . ."

Edie Banister nods. "I'm here to rescue you."

"Rescue me?"

"Yes," Dotty Catty says. "We did talk about this."

Frankie stares at her a moment longer. A single curl of black hair is tickling her cheek, and she brushes it away, leaving a smudge of char on her skin. Her face is very pale and pointed, and she has freckles. She must be all of five foot two inches tall, and proportionately tiny. The sleeves of her blouse are covered in mathematical notation written in ink. She frowns. "Oh. Did we? Yes, you're quite right, we did. Because Shem wants me to make him a weapon. Yes. Do you know, he is very charming? I had no idea that was what he meant. He seemed so philanthropic. 'An end to war.' I am an idiot. I should have seen. Well, I won't do it, of course. But now's not the best time for me to leave. I'm just in the middle of something rather important." She peers at Edie, flaps a hand. "Do you think you could come back in a few weeks, Banister?"

Edie stares at her. "For the teapot?"

"No, no. That will take a day, at most. No, for some testing of the compressor and the . . . *eh, bien,* your eyes are glazing over. For the machines, then. I have begun the process. I am isolating a standing wave. This wave, of course, is composed of water, but the dynamics are mathematically similar." She gestures at the suspended water tank.

"A what?"

"A wave. From the river. I am taking the wave from the river and maintaining it in the box. You see, obviously, what that would mean?"

"No."

"When I am very old I shall make a school for intelligent young persons to be educated in basic science."

"Frankie," Dotty Catty says firmly, "don't be rude."

Frankie gives a growl.

"All right! Very well, Banister, please listen closely and try not to say 'What?' too often or I shall scream . . .

"Truth may reasonably be understood as the consonance of our impression of the universe with the underlying reality. Yes? When what we believe matches the external truth about the world . . . You are staring at my trousers. What is wrong with them?"

Edie, who has been wondering whether to wallop this garrulous loony over the back of the noggin and carry her off, replies that there is nothing wrong with the trousers. In fact, this is true. They are odd, but shapely, and suggestive of decent legs beneath.

"*Boff.* So then: truth is the mind correctly understanding the world. So, like the water in the tank, the human mind is a wave. It is formed around the brain. A very complicated pattern generated by a moderately complicated thing according to fairly simple rules. Your brain is a special sort of stone. The stream runs over the stone, the surface ripples, yes? We call it a standing wave. So, your mind is the ripple. Life is the motion of water through the pattern. Death is the pattern disappearing when the stone is moved or ground away. You understand? For the mind to apprehend truth—to know, rather than simply to believe, the nature of the wave must change. The ripple must extend so that it is able to touch the bottom of the river, to know the reality directly, not via our eyes and our ears. The machine I make will extend the wave. It is like this new sonar: a new sense. A sense of knowing the truth. From this it follows that the world will change in positive ways. *Voilà. C'est simple.*"

"What's the water?"

Frankie Fossoyeur stops and looks at her sharply. "I beg your pardon?"

"In your example. What replaces the water, in the case of the mind?"

"That," Frankie Fossoyeur says, "is the first intelligent question I have been asked in twelve months. But you see, this is exactly the point. The water is the basic stuff of the universe. It is what matter and energy are made of. Hah! Tell the little Swiss I have overreached him!"

"Miss Fossoyeur . . ."

"Doctor."

"Doctor Fossoyeur. What does it do?"

"It doesn't do anything yet. It is a science, not a technology."

"But in theory?"

"In theory it allows us to see the truth of things. The absolute truth. And perhaps later . . . well. The absolute truth is good enough to begin with, no?" She looks at Edie.

Edie looks at her a bit blankly. "I don't understand."

"How many wars will be averted? How many lives spared, if the truth cannot be obscured? If any statement can be tested for verity? Imagine the advances in understanding. In science. To *know* . . . Suppose you could look at the world, Miss Banister, and recognise lies and deception when you heard them. Would that not improve the lot of mankind? The death of falsehood. A new age constructed on the foundation of truth, Banister."

"Commander Banister."

Frankie Fossoyeur smiles suddenly. It's like an English summer; a rare, rich blessing, warm on the skin. "Of course: Commander," she says impishly. Her eyes travel the length of Edie's body and she grins rather wickedly.

Edie Banister actually blushes. *Lions and tigers and bears . . . oh, my . . .*

"We really, really need to go," she says.

"*Non.* I cannot escape. I must finish my work. You must come back another day. Or perhaps after, it will not be necessary. *Hein?*"

Dotty Catty huffs. "Frankie, no. Absolutely no. She cannot come back, she cannot wait, the whole thing must be tonight. The timing is precise."

Frankie Fossoyeur waves this away. "Consider . . . by how much might the lot of man be improved, in a world where truth was ubiquitous? One per cent? Five? How much positive adjustment is necessary to pass the tipping point and enable the spontaneous formation of a utopia?" Frankie beams. Then her face falls. "Oh. Although too much truth could create problems on a physical level. And one most definitely would not wish to create a determining cascade . . ." She scribbles frantically.

Dotty Catty throws her bony hands into the air. "Frankie! Commander Banister! You must leave, now!"

"I cannot, I am working—"

"Now! It must be now!"

"We could possibly wait a few hours," Edie suggests, still looking at Frankie Fossoyeur's smudged cheek.

"No, you couldn't. It has started."

This is true, but Edie catches in Dotty Catty's voice some hint of more, and she wrenches her eyes away from the bemused Frankie Fossoyeur and looks at her guide.

"What's started?"

Dotty Catty shrugs, a fine, unapologetic old-lady shrug, and half-turns her back.

"My plan."

"Your plan."

"My diversion."

"What diversion?"

"I have created a diversion, in the finest military tradition, so that you may carry out your mission."

"What diversion?"

"The gas taps in the kitchens," Dotty Catty says. "I have arranged that they should catch fire." She beams. Somewhere to one side, one of the Ruskinites makes a horrified choking noise. Brother Denis the Ruskinite stares at her, aghast.

"But this palace is constructed over a natural-gas reservoir," he says in horror. "The entire citadel . . . You'll blow the whole place like a bomb!"

"Yes," Dotty Catty says. "It will be very distracting."

And just like that, Edie Banister is having a really bad day.

Still swearing in terms fit to curdle whisky, Edie Banister hurtles through the burning palace with a wooden crate on wheels.

"My treasure!" the dratted old woman said, after Edie had screamed at her and put Frankie Fossoyeur in a fireman's lift to short-circuit the escape discussion. "The last of all of them from Mansura, that is no more! In all the world, there is no greater virtue, no more splendid thing. The crate in the west chamber of my apartments—for God's sake, take it to George in London! There are others here, but they are old, they cannot go with you. This will be their grave, one way or another. But this one . . . promise me!"

Edie has never been one to turn down a friend—never mind the grey-haired old tub has blown this operation to six kinds of shit with one finely judged insanity (Rig a gas explosion, you potty old trout? You're out of your bloody head!) and never mind there may be utility in it, too, for good King George. This is a personal matter between Women of Consequence, and hell if whatever is in the crate will come to harm, even get a flake of ash on it.

She gave Dotty Catty a piece of her mind, though, while through the corridors she staggered, carrying that damned squealing scientist on her back and feeling the while a wash of sympathy for the abductors from the seraglio, and why in all the world was she running away with this bony genius without the sense God gave a hedgehog when she could be legging it out the back door with At Your Service and a couple of close friends for an entirely more agreeable adventure?

Girls wishing to serve their country . . . Aiee, what a mess. Although it was almost worth it to see a dozen monks hike up their habits and run for the hills with only what they could carry and Frankie's blessed compressor—whatever that may be—on a trolley.

At her room, Edie handed the outraged Frankie to Songbird and told him to *get her to the river, get help, get it now, signal* Cuparah, *get us the Hell out! Let's have the marines and never mind who knows it!*

Then she barged out into the corridor, demanding directions and bloody quick, smelling smoke and thinking about how many kilos of gas at how much pressure per square inch exploding with how much force? Which was about when the first explosion erupted and the whole place shook and seemed to heel over like a ship in a beam sea, and when she got to her feet again the fire was really under way and a lot of bits of palace were looking alarmingly diagonal where they should have been perpendicular.

Dotty Catty embraced her and wrapped a purple sash from her frocks around Edie's upper arm, which was for some reason terribly significant, and hugged her again and cried "Women of Consequence!" which was very nice except Edie had a strong desire to belt her.

So here she is now making the return trip, hauling the crate along—and bloody Nora, it's heavy, whatever it is, and something in it rattling around fair to capsize the box. No time to complain, though: get to the boat, and worry about it later. Though how she will explain herself to captain and crew in her present state, as far from covert as is easily imaginable, she has no idea.

Bugger it.

A carpet flops flaming off the wall, tries to snag her. Hah! Missed me . . . But oops, that was a near one for the fragile crate, oh, yes—the floating ash spreads spectral fingers. Edie wrenches the crate into motion, and this time the thing or things within are cooperating—they rebound off the inside back wall. The crate flexes, damnit, and creaks and wheezes. That's another concern: pull too hard and it will apparently break open, slew its contents across the steaming floor and then where will we be? *Fine reet'n' harsefuckered*, as Songbird would have it. Edie lets the crate surge ahead of her on its lanyard, finds herself, ludicrously, admiring her own forearm against the ruddy firelight.

Focus.

Another colossal boom shakes the palace. An arch collapses to one side, great chunks of solid stone crumbling and cracking in the heat, popping as air bubbles rip them open from the inside. Edie growls sulphurously—a spark has scored her shoulder through the jacket—and gets her mind on business. This isn't nearly the mother lode going up, this is just the appetiser, plus who knows what appalling muck lurks in Fossoyeur's cavern, or what will happen when it is burned or crushed or otherwise perturbed? Frankie seemed to think—between bounces on Edie's shoulder—that this was a thing to be viewed from a great distance or not at all . . . At this rate the place will explode long before she can get clear, and that is absolutely not on the menu for today. No immolation, so she needs inspiration . . . Oh ho! *Induction, Compression, Combustion, Exhaust.* Four stages of the internal combustion engine (which Edie learned for the purposes of sabotage) but here's the key: locomotion. The horseless carriage. And there it is, no motor but lots of momentum and didn't the boys back home all have one of these? A go-cart, a tray with wheels. Yes, they did, and no girls allowed to play. Hah!

Edie grabs the lanyard and braces her feet against the back of the crate, lets the thing's weight carry them both, kicks off the ground from time to time to steer and add velocity. Escape by go-cart, not bad at all. She sniffs. There's a strange smell, peppery and agricultural. The contents of the crate are apparently padded with river mud. *Focus.*

Aye, indeed, for there's a way to go yet, here's the bad part starting: dead men, burning, in heaps. *Cuparah*'s marines at work there, or Songbird and the lads. Edie's stomach lurches at the sweet, appetising smell, then revolts as her mind catches up with the notion, and she nearly brings up. Some friendly (if thank God not well-known to her) others not (well, mercifully neutral now) but all men and not kabob, no matter what the nose believes. She kicks hard to take the go-cart around the edge of the slaughter, don't slow down, don't stop, not for anything.

Ah! Good decision: there's a live one, armed, the bastard, and swirling his cleaver about the place and gnashing furious teeth. *Fine reet'n'harsefuckered* . . . Edie skates towards him, thinking fast. Speed and heft are their own advantage, and this unconventional conveyance has confused him slightly. The man is a brigand in the pay of the Opium Khan; it's not every day he is assailed by a willowy white lunatic in forest green, borne along on a wave of fire by a box on wheels.

Indeed, there probably aren't many people who have great familiarity with this situation.

He regains his composure and comes towards her. Edie grounds her heel abruptly, sends her carriage into a spin, then lets the heavy crate swing her around like a child at the village fete. Maypole *budo!* Her right foot catches him in the noggin, and down he goes like a sack of taters. Blast it, though, he has a friend in the corridor, a few paces away, and that's a really nasty-looking knife, so it is, more a sword. Under Mrs. Sekuni's tutelage, she has learned to identify weapons; this is a bastard crossbreed, of course, not a wakizashi or a cutlass or even a bowie knife, but the offspring of a machete and a cleaver. Damn, he's big. Hypersomnia big.

The man raises his weapon, and roars.

Bugger.

Edie scoots out of the way, abandoning the precious crate, and has to duck very fast as Hypersomnia Boy comes charging in much faster than she anticipated. Just her luck: he's got brains and skill to match his brawn. Surely that's not allowed?

First thing: don't die. Edie scoots left and he chops the other way, misses her.

Cla-boiiing! That sword's a decent piece of work, too, throwing up sparks and vibrating, but not a chip nor crack as he drives it solidly into the mosaic floor and hauls it out. Hauls it out very close to Edie's hips, and that would have cut her in half . . . she rolls away, regains her feet. *Yama Arashi* . . . a woman would have to be very skilled or very desperate, and in either case very brave . . . Edie wonders briefly whether the big lad would listen to a discussion on the relative merits of Asiatic Despotism versus planned economy and a dictatorship of the proletariat, culminating in a suggestion that he change sides, and concludes that *Yama Arashi* has the edge—but only just.

He comes again. She moves forward instead of back, and commits the cardinal sin of anticipating the attack, beginning the technique before he has given the opportunity. Fortunately, he misses the mistake, or doesn't know what her movement portends. Edie's arms slide between his, her hips come between him and the sword. *Merge the ki.* Or as Frankie Fossoyeur would no doubt say: let your centre of gravity and rotation displace your opponent's . . . The movement continues, and she feels a feather pressure on her back, hears him land and swirls on. In the dojo, you finish with the sword against *uke's* neck. In real life, the sword is heavier and *Yama Arashi* and mortal combat have their own logic . . . *tchuck*.

Scratch one giant.

Don't look too closely. Don't think about it too much. Collect the crate, and find the good guys.

Edie rattles away down the passageway, surfing the crate, scared out of her mind and appalled at what she has done and loving every primal second.

At the throne room, it all comes apart on her.

"Well, Commander Banister, goodness me. There seems to have been some tragic misunderstanding. Your men here are very eager to release you from some dungeon or other—I couldn't persuade them you were an honoured guest. And in the meantime, my soldiers here are most anxious to protect me from any violence, and some unhappy soul has set my great palace on fire. Why, Commander Banister, whatever is that remarkable box?"

"A gift from your mother, Khan," Edie says in James Banister's voice, pats her face to make sure of her moustache, though God knows what difference it makes now . . . yes. She's still a boy. "Wants me to take it to the King, apparently. Tell me, is this place full o' bandits or did one of your fellows just try to cut my head off?" She gives it an extra sting, says *awf* rather than *off*. "Dashed poor form, if so, Khan, me being an ambassador and all."

The palace guard of Shem Shem Tsien are not armed in the full modern style—the Opium Khan likes the feel of antiquity, or doesn't trust his lads with serious automatic weapons—but there are a few pistols, and a crossbow will kill you just as readily as a bullet—or more so, if you happen to have taken shelter behind something. In training, Edie saw a crossbow bolt pass through a metal plate. There are comfortably two hundred of the Khan's warriors in this room, all around their master. Standing opposite them are the thirty-odd marines from *Cuparah*, led by Songbird and Flagpole, looking very determined and very doomed. No sign of Frankie or Dotty Catty, which pray God means they're aboard already, and the mission is all but complete. Now . . . just a question of everyone not dying here. Stand-off, but not the good kind.

The Opium Khan surveys his situation, and seems about to speak. Then he looks at Edie, and for the first time she sees the truth of him. The hectoring matinée villain fades away, the cheery roguish smile vanishes, and in its place is the thing which locked a family in a room and incinerated them. It's like watching a snake emerge from the corpse of a wolf. Another explosion rattles the room, closer this time.

"This no longer interests me," Shem Shem Tsien says flatly. "Kill them all. Put out the fire. I will want their heads, of course."

The soldiers of the Opium Khan roll forward in a wave, and Edie's boys go to meet them. It is the time-honoured tradition of the sons of England's North: when all is lost, advance to give the enemy his scars. They are making a fight of it, too, impossible though that seems, and then Shem Shem Tsien unsheathes his sword and joins the fray, and Edie learns what butchery is.

Shem Shem Tsien is perfect. It comes from his feet, she's fairly sure. His feet take him where he wants to go and you least wish him to be. He comes at your bad side, your wounded leg, your blackened eye. He is lithe and strong, but it's not his arm and shoulder which power the narrow blade he carries, but his heels and hips. He moves through the battle like the shuttle on a loom, trailing threads of human extinction. Edie wonders, honestly, whether even the Sekunis were ever so graceful.

She moves towards him as he skewers a man whose name she has forgotten, one of Amanda Baines's marines, and even the weight of the corpse adds to his momentum and his rhythm. He steps to one side and brings his wrists together as another soldier surges at him, then rolls his blade in a gesture she has always assumed is pure swordsman's swank. The edge rolls around his opponent's neck in a perfect circle, the man twisting as if trying to follow the hilt with his lips, his blood pouring from a massive wound.

Edie watches Shem Shem Tsien and knows she cannot beat him or even survive him unless God provides a miracle. She goes forward anyway. Her vision narrows to Shem Shem Tsien and him alone, and he sees her, and—to her fury—barely notices her intent. He draws a pistol from his belt and fires left-handed as if to swat her away, and only the broad back of Flagpole saves her from death.

Flagpole stares at her, genially lascivious. "Ey, Countess," he says quietly. "Tha's a shame." And then he falls forward into her arms and she can see the hole in his spine.

Shem Shem Tsien smiles, and Edie can feel his satisfaction. She can hear him in her head. *Alas for the limitations of* budo, *Commander Banister. I find it is a particular pleasure, to the sophisticated mind, to force an officer to watch the death of the soldiers in his care. It has piquancy. Wouldn't you say?*

She realises that she has lost. Frankie will get away, it's true. Edie will have completed her mission. But she will have died a secret agent's death in a far land, and no one will ever know. She wonders if Abel Jasmine will cry, or Clarissa Foxglove. She wonders how many sweethearts of her soldiers will weep into ragged pillows, back home, and whether they will blame Commander James Banister personally, or just curse the fortunes of war. She raises her hands into the most cautious of guard positions, and gets ready to die.

To her surprise, Shem Shem Tsien raises his hand in salute. He looks almost human. And then, a moment later, she sees the pleasure in his eyes at her resignation. Not empathy. The sating of an appetite.

He comes towards her, boots barely brushing the tiled floor. She feels clumsy and small, adjusts her guard. He smiles again. *I am killing you piece by piece, Commander.*

Salvation comes, all undreamed of. With a sharp crack and a noise like a cornet call, Edie's burdensome crate flies open, and out charges a small, angry grey object decked in ornate metal plates. It fixes eyes on her purple sash, and places itself stoutly between her and her enemies. Then it raises up its head, and the cornet call sounds again: a shrill, high note, amazingly loud and penetrating. In the near distance, something gives answer: a deep hallooing hunter's horn, or a tuneless brass band with a tuba the size of a house.

Edie does not recognise the grey object for what it is until the Door of Humility explodes inwards, and through the breach come massive, muscular shapes in a mighty rush, bringing a scent of sweat and dung and spice, and Shem Shem Tsien hurtles backwards away from her, sword tumbling in the air, swatted end over end in one furious motion of denial. She stares, then gives vent to a delighted yawp of victory.

The greatest cavalry force ever raised up from one end of the great Addeh River to the other, from the topless Katir mountains to the wide blue Indian Ocean, stands ready to give answer to her need: in the vanguard, a wall of maternal indignation blotting out the light, ploughing into the soldiers of Shem Shem Tsien and sending them fleeing after their master. Behind this titan are other shapes even bigger, smashing walls and doors and charging onward, trumpeting unleashed fury. All are urged on by the armoured shape of Edie's newest guardian, shoulder high at best, but bristling with affront and duty.

Dotty Catty's gift: a baby war elephant.

The tide of the battle turns.

Relative calm; this means there are no guns. All the same, Amanda Baines is doing a great deal of shouting. The reason for this is that her upper turret has a number of holes in it (holes are considered a Bad Thing in the submariner trade) and Edie was supposed to run a covert intrusion and appears instead to have declared war on a minor principality and reduced it to rubble. Worse, she has failed to kill or capture the offended party, which is apparently very important when you launch a *de facto* surprise attack on a foreign nation. The *Cuparah* is presently going at one-third ahead towards the open ocean, and no one seriously expects there to be anything between her and that ocean, because the last attempt to block her way is still burning. More than that, it is burning in a somewhat emphatic way which is the product of Amanda Baines completely losing her temper. It is burning in such a manner as to suggest that other ships constructed in the same place or around the same time may also be burning out of sheer sympathy. Amanda Baines has achieved the nautical equivalent of punching the enemy very hard in the crotch and then kicking them repeatedly as they lie incapable on the ground, and the assembled pirates and seamen of the Addeh maritime have noted this action and responded in time-honoured fashion by finding very important things to do on dry land. Not even the Opium Khan's bounties are sufficient to tempt them into the path of *Cuparah*. This proactive indifference is not sufficient to quell the wrath of Amanda Baines, who is even now drawing breath to express her further lack of impressedness, but realises at the last minute that she has nothing else to say.

"And," yells Amanda Baines, as if trying to persuade herself that this is worse than unsponsored declarations of war, "there is a baby elephant in my stateroom!"

"Yes," Edie says, "there is."

"Well," says Amanda Baines, trying not to think about the limpid-eyed beast and how delighted she was when he passed her a woolly hat from the rack, "what are we going to feed him? Eh?"

And at this, Edie Banister is suddenly aware that she is not dead, and has survived, and even done well, and she starts to cry. Amanda Baines, hard-bitten woman of the open water, mutters something about highly strung people and how they should stick to making bad art, and trudges over to examine the wreckage of her periscope.

"This is fascinating," a new voice observes in Edie's ear. "But the construction is quite wrong."

Amanda Baines peers at Frankie Fossoyeur. Frankie peers at the dials on *Cuparah*'s highly classified bridge. Mockley the Ruskinite, who personally built quite a lot of *Cuparah*, raises one eyebrow ever so slightly.

"In what way?"

"You make inadequate use of resources. This vessel could be far more impressive than it is."

"Could it?" Amanda Baines asks levelly.

"Oh, yes," Frankie Fossoyeur replies.

"How very kind of you to notice."

"A matter of the greatest simplicity for someone of my capacity," Frankie continues, matter-of-fact.

"Is it?"

"It is. The construction of your vessel is innovative, but not complex."

"Oh, good."

"I could design a schematic for you."

Amanda Baines unkinks slightly, in spite of herself, then glances guiltily at Mockley.

"A schematic?"

"Of course. Do you have paper? The mathematics is quite interesting, but the practical application is not difficult."

"That would be very kind," Mockley interjects. "Have you studied this kind of system before?"

"*Non*. It is unique, is it not? But very clever. The individual who designed it possesses considerable flair. I shall enjoy improving on his work."

Mockley hunches a little, then sets his expression in a look of monkish placidity. The face of Amanda Baines takes on a sour expression.

"I suppose you know what to feed an elephant, too."

"*Hein*. Of course. A varied vegetable diet. Roots and leaves, bark . . . ah. I see the problem. We will improvise. Kelp, yes, some other weeds. I shall prepare a list. It would be best if he were not allowed to swim."

"They swim?"

"Extremely well. And of course, the trunk functions like your snorkel, yes? But it would be very hard to get him back on board."

"I shall bear that closely in mind."

From the captain's cabin, a noise like an accordion landing in a rice pudding. Frankie Fossoyeur shrugs, her narrow shoulders rising almost to her ears.

"Elephants are like people," she says, without great sympathy. "Not all of them are good sailors."

Six days later, *Cuparah* is five hundred foot down and diving, and Edie Banister can hear the riveted sections of the boat growl and yap. The faithful hound is struggling. Far from friendly waters, the *Kriegsmarine* and the *Nippon Kaigun* are too many, the cold and the pressure too harsh. Enemy ships have spotted *Cuparah*—tipped off by a spiteful Khan or merely put in her path by ill luck—and now they are searching the sea and listening for her quiet engine, pouring explosives down into the sheltering deep. Every few seconds the whole cabin shudders and the plates of the walls howl and shriek as *Cuparah* is kicked and harried, and the dull boom of another depth charge throws her one way and another. No dog should have to suffer this. Indeed, no dog can be expected to take it for long. *Cuparah* is in danger, here in the dark.

Beneath and beyond all of which, Edie is apparently going mad, because she seems to hear choral music. When the door opens, she realises that no, someone is actually singing, low and weird and deranged, deep in the hull.

"Commander Banister?"

Edie is wearing her uniform and moustache, since she may in theory be called upon to do something devious if they surface and surrender. And here is Frankie Fossoyeur, that same desirable, distracted expression on her face as she explains that she thinks the *Cuparah* may be overcooking it, may be about to implode.

Implode. A very, very bad word indeed. Edie had believed, until she heard it down here, that the worst bad words were Anglo-Saxon in origin and referred to parts of the body. Not so. Not one of the unspeakable sexual terms she has heard is anything like as bad as bleak, measured, Latinate *implode*.

"Do you think they will continue this . . ." Frankie waves her hands ". . . this dropping?" A wrenching impact causes the ship to heel over, and Edie is thrown upright. Frankie is holding onto the frame of the door, so they are suddenly very close. Edie nods.

"I'm sure they will, yes. If they have the charges."

"The boat is strong. Remarkable, even. But not like this. The repeated stresses accumulate. The hulls will not hold." Frankie stares into space as if she can actually see the fractures, the stresses.

Edie, ungifted mathematically, is nonetheless inclined to agree. *Cuparah*'s groaning has taken on a distinctly frantic edge, a shearing, fatigued sound which is far more ominous than the bell-like tone it emitted when the first charge went off a few moments ago.

"Well," Edie says, "then we will probably die."

Frankie Fossoyeur stares at her.

"That is not necessary," she says after a moment. "It is wasteful. There is much we have left to do. *Boff.*" She throws her hands up, as if all this drama is so typical of the silly people she has to deal with. "I will not permit it. Accompany me, please, Banister."

Since the alternative would appear to be waiting alone for the inevitable rush of icy water and ensuing death, Edie follows.

Frankie is slight and determined, and Edie's uniform counts for something on Amanda Baines's ship, so they pass smoothly through the mill of shouting, frightened men doing their best to be cool under pressure. Also, the place they appear to be going to is not anywhere any of the sailors needs or wants to be. It is the place the weird, disturbing singing is coming from: *Cuparah*'s decoding chamber. Frankie opens the door and steps inside.

The Ruskinites are praying. The coding machine is shut down— no need for it at the moment, obviously—so they are kneeling on the floor in front of it, facing one another to avoid the appearance of worshipping the machine, which is very much *not* what they're about, and chanting like Gregorians. It's monotone, and very sad. Now that she is inside the room with them, Edie recognises the chant as a prayer for the dying.

Hear us, O Lord, and issue not the decree for the completion of our days before Thou forgivest our sins. There is no room in death for amend-ment. Deliver us not unto the bitter grave. Lord, have mercy.

She shudders. There's nothing like religion to make you feel utterly doomed.

"*Eh, bien,*" Frankie Fossoyeur says, clapping her hands. "*Ça suffit.* That is enough. There is work." The Ruskinites stop chanting and stare at her, a bit annoyed. Frankie in turn finds their lack of compli-ance vexatious, and grabs the nearest one by the cheeks and shouts into his face. "Get up! We. Have. Work. To. Do!"

And whether it is because they take her sudden arrival as the answer to their morbid prayer, or because in all honesty they are just people looking for a way to divert their minds from the imminence of crush-depth and the endless drumming of the enemy above, they get to their feet, and Mockley asks what is to be done.

"This," Frankie says, waving her hand at the coding machine. "It gets hot?"

"Yes," Mockley says.

"And you cool it with?"

"We have ice-makers. Poseidon's Net."

"Excellent. And we have my compressor for additional cold. Good. And do you also have wood? No, wait. Kelp. We have kelp for the elephant."

The Ruskinites look a bit shifty. The issue of the elephant has not been a happy one. They have been required to vacate some research space for him in *Cuparah*'s forward hold, and one very rash person suggested *sotto voce* that perhaps elephant steak might make a nice change from cod. Songbird chanced to overhear, and nearly throttled him. Edie's team are a little irrational about the elephant, because so many of his relatives were injured or killed in the business of saving them from Shem Shem Tsien, and because without him there is every possibility that they would be hanging on hooks on the walls of the Opium Khan's palace.

"Yes," Mockley says, "we have kelp."

"*Bon.* Then we must . . . *hacher* . . . the kelp, into little pieces, and make pulp. Slime. Yes? And then add water, very cold. Supercold. Then squirt it in the pipes. There are pipes everywhere, yes? Squirt squirt. Then we must overload the pipes. They will burst outwards? Good. How good are the pumps? Never mind, they are not good enough, I must make them better. Make kelp, what is the word? It is

Scottish and disgusting, not haggis, the oats, yes: *porridge*! Make porridge, quickly! And you," she adds, with a keen eye for the would-be eater of elephants. "Hoses! I will need all the spare hoses."

"What are we doing?" Edie asks, as she throws her jacket onto the floor to sit on it, and Frankie rips the cover off the first of Mockley's refrigeration units.

"We are making a new submarine," Frankie Fossoyeur says, "before the old one is broken." A particularly loud roar sounds through the boat. "Which will be very soon. So." She gestures to the machine in front of her. "We work."

And they do. Edie's fingers get red and her nails chip, threading washers and nuts onto bolts by hand, grabbing pliers and spanners to finish the job, passing the tools to someone else and starting again. Splice, fix, rotate, tension, and all the while the boat is dying around them, screaming and shuddering.

Cuparah yaws and rolls all the way over. Edie clings to the compressor and Frankie clings to Edie, the two of them clinched together. Edie's arms do not have time to hurt. Then the boat slams back over and they fall to the deck. One of the Ruskinites has cut his own finger almost entirely off in the confusion. He holds it up for inspection. Frankie tells him to pull it off and keep working, because he can live with nine fingers, but not with multiple atmospheres of water shattering his body like an empty eggshell. He shrugs, and does as he's told. Shock. Or courage. Edie isn't sure there's a difference. Being dead is a sure remedy for pain . . . She suddenly remembers being very young, hearing an old woman say:

Tes a zertin cure, Mam, I 'zure 'ee, starps 'ey bagg'rin' wetchess f'om g'wen te zay in eggbote.

It took her years to work out what it means. She says it now, and Frankie stares at her.

"It is a certain cure, madam, I assure you; it stops those buggering witches from going to sea in an eggboat!" *Cuparah*, eggboat. Far below crush-depth, metal shell fit to fail. It's just right, somehow; meaningless, idiotic, and right.

One of the Ruskinites laughs, and repeats it. His voice is Cornish—the woman she heard, Edie reckons, must have been from Dorset—and Mockley says it, too, miming eggs and toasted soldiers, and it becomes the rhythm of their work, an antidote to the percussion all around. Frankie swears in French that they have all gone utterly mad, but they connect the compressor and the pumps to the pipes as she requires, and fire them up. Frankie peers at the switch, then starts to scribble in chalk on a bulkhead.

"Yes, yes, seawater, good, so far, so good, yes . . . cold, of course, very good, better! So. The pressure is a factor, and the salt . . . The units will have to work hard initially. The cold inside the vessel will be . . . it will be cold. Everyone must dress warm. We have no time for that. After it is done, we can warm the interior, yes. Then there will be . . . *bon*. Then . . ." and she's off, seconds ticking, bombs kicking, until Edie realises she's gone abstract, and nudges her hard. "Oh, *mordieux*, I am an idiot, there is an issue of trapped air," Frankie mutters, and begins drilling a hole in the bulkhead wall, which is when one of Amanda Baines's sailors comes in and screams at her to stop.

The visceral horror in his voice is enough to cut through the other sounds of fear and horror on the boat, and another man looks around the door. He screams as well.

"Idiot!" Frankie Fossoyeur is shouting. "I am a professional!"

Twenty seconds later, and it has all gone significantly to hell, as if the previous situation—depth charges, water pressure, deteriorating vessel, general doom—had not been bad enough. Now the bosun is holding a gun on Frankie and Frankie won't stop drilling, and sailors are starting to shout at the chief to shoot her down. Any second now the whole thing will become moot because, with the sailors here instead of where they should be, vital tasks are not getting done, and in any case *Cuparah* is responding only sluggishly, with one engine's bearings not doing their job and a shriek of dying metal ripping and buzzing through the air. Up above, the enemy knows they're on the edge of the kill. One of the Ruskinites starts to mutter: *Into Thine arms, O Lord, I commend my soul, that Thou hast made and nourished. Look kindly on me now, that am flawed*, and then Edie treads on his toe.

And then there comes a moment of perfect quiet. Edie can't understand how, at first, and then she realises that a charge has gone off right on top of the boat, and the pulse of pressure has burst her left eardrum and the other one is shrieking. The pain is so awful that she can only feel it in slivers, little bright fragments which punctuate everything. In between times the world is grey and purple as if she is in the dark and her agony is the only illumination. Everything happens in pieces.

She sees the water welling up, up, up from below them, far too fast.

The chief of the boat waves his hands, ordering everyone out of the compartment.

Frankie Fossoyeur ignores him.

The flood door swings shut, sealing them in.

The water rushes up, so cold Edie can actually feel it over the pain. But she can't move. She has nothing left.

Through the deck, she can feel bad things happening all around. *Cuparah* is wallowing, rebounding off one blast after another, reeling like a drunkard in a bar brawl. Another blast kicks her sideways, and she does not right. She begins to fall. Edie can feel it in the hairs on the back of her neck. *Cuparah* is going down, down in an anticlockwise spiral, not sinking but plummeting.

Soon, the water will cover the generators and then the game will be over.

Frankie Fossoyeur throws the switch, then grasps Edie's arm and drags her up on top of one of the benches.

"You must not be in the water," Frankie says. It seems like a rather silly thing to be worried about.

Crush-depth is somewhere around nine hundred feet. No one knows for certain. They are falling fast. They will reach it very soon now, if they haven't already.

Edie's good ear registers creaking.

And then, something changes. Something strange, but—Edie can tell this by the Frenchwoman's pleased expression—something expected, and good. The water stops rising. And then it goes white. Frozen in place.

Cuparah shudders, as if throwing off a great weight, rolls and heaves.

Down deep—too deep—*Cuparah* does not implode. She hangs in the dark. After a moment, the depth charges stop falling. Edie stares at the frozen block a few feet below her.

"They think we are dead," Frankie says.

"Why?"

"Because we lost a large piece of the hull, of course."

"Then why aren't we dead?"

"Because we have a new one."

"A new one?"

"Yes."

"How? Where did it come from?"

Frankie smiles brightly.

"Ice," she says, as if nothing could be more natural. "And kelp fibre, for flexibility, about fourteen per cent. In an irregular pearl formation. About ten foot of it, I think . . . yes. It's only slightly weaker than steel." She smiles. "And, of course, we have rather a lot of it. This vessel is excellent. I had not considered the idea; rather than seeking to rule out variations in quality, accept and adopt the reality of imperfection. A very powerful model indeed."

Cuparah, in the night of a thousand feet down—the ghost of a fly, caught in ice instead of amber.

X

Buggeration to the enemy;
Brother Sheamus;
Ahh-knuu-haha.

I must be out of my mind," Polly Cradle mutters, as the car turns into Guildholt Street. She sounds for a second so like her brother that Joe laughs, then stops sharply and looks to see if this has annoyed her.

"No," she says, grinning, "don't stop. You have a nice laugh. Although it sounds a bit rusty."

He grins back. "It probably does." He tries again, a variety of chuckles and cackles, then hears himself and wonders if he now sounds quite mad. But Polly is still smiling.

He points. "Over there. We have to walk the rest of the way."

"Yes, sir!" She makes a Girl Guide salute, and for some reason that makes him laugh, too.

The building Joe is heading for rears up on the far side, a weird, helter-skelter piece of old English stonework topped with some ghastly Victorian Gothic additions. The doors are vast: black oak weathered and stained by coal fires and then by petroleum fumes, the only bright part of them the great bronze knocker and handles worn shiny and pale with constant use.

Joe Spork has not been here for months. He has nightmares sometimes about turning a corner in the stacks and finding an empty case with a white card in front of it, waiting for his brain.

"Name?" says Bob Foalbury, Harticle's factotum and husband of Cecily the archivist, through the thick wood.

"Spork," Joe answers, though Mr. Foalbury has known him for twenty years and more.

"Enter and be welcome in the house of art. Abide by Harticle's rules and settle all debts amicably before leaving the building.

"Hawking, spitting, solicitation, speculation, gossip-mongering, usury, duelling, and gambling," Mr. Foalbury says severely, as he opens the door, "are not countenanced within these walls. Good morning, Joe."

"I need help with something," Joe says, and there's just enough tension in him that Bob Foalbury grows serious.

"Not the law, is it?"

"It's bailiffs, Bob, and all manner of government."

"Venal office-holders?"

"By the bucketload, I think."

"Buggeration! The worm shall eat them up like a garment, Joe, and the moth shall eat them up like wool, but your righteousness shall be from generation to generation. The Bible, that is, and I've always fancied the Lord was particularly thinking of revenuers and debt collectors."

"Thank you, Bob. And this is Polly," Joe says awkwardly, and Mr. Foalbury puffs out a sergeant major's chest and extends his hand.

"And very nice too, Miss Polly. Bob Foalbury, commissionaire of the house of art. Would you be maker, mischief, or muse?"

"A bit of everything."

Mr. Foalbury smiles. "Call it muse," he says. "Always my favourite." He leads the way down the main corridor, proudly showing off his domain. On wood-panelled walls, oil paintings of Brunel and Babbage rub shoulders with works by lesser-known (but excellent) watercolourists, early blueprints, and pages from ancient mathematical texts. Everything at Harticle's, Mr. Foalbury explains to Polly, is special, handmade, or orphaned—usually all three. Even the building is special, riven through with trial technologies: Victorian pneumatic message tubes, a Thomas Twyford sanitation system, a retractable roof on the third-floor annexe for observation of the moon. There's also an antique burglary-prevention device, including panic buttons in all the main rooms, though even Bob Foalbury is a little wary of actually using it.

"You'll be wanting the old Man-eater, then?" Bob says. "She's writing a monograph on her teeth." Cecily Foalbury has a personal collection of assorted sets of false teeth down through the years. The most remarkable is probably the clockwork set made for a sailor who had lost part of his brachial plexus to a cannonball and therefore could not chew. The somewhat grisly archive of gnashers is kept in its own room at Harticle's and has resulted in this alarming nickname, an insult Cecily resolutely courts—and this is where Joe Spork baulks somewhat—wearing items from her collection to suit her mood.

Bob Foalbury apparently finds this quirky and charming.

"I want both of you. And I need to borrow a record player."

"Well, we're here! I'll sort you out a portable, shall I? . . . Taxmen! Buggeration to the enemy!" Then, over his shoulder into the woody hallway and the dim, panelled rooms beyond, "Darling? It's the Spork boy!"

From within comes a noise like a trombonist being goosed during the overture, and then a mighty roar from a pair of elderly female lungs.

"Well, well, don't just stand in the bloody doorway, come on in. You're letting out the heat and that's a grave infraction of our environmental policy, and bloody chilly to boot!" Cecily, silver-capped and mountainous, is still invisible behind a half-closed door, but her writ runs through the house of art.

As they enter the room, a chair skitters back from a kidney desk, and sensible shoes slap on burnished boards. A short, muscular woman with hair like a steel bathcap bounds towards them from the gloom, a vast pair of clear-rimmed National Health glasses making her eyes enormous.

"The Spork boy? Joe Spork? Why didn't you say so sooner, you bloody fool! Joe? Joe! *Joseph!* Get in here and give me a kiss!"

The Man-eater spreads wide her arms and clasps him to her chest. Mr. Foalbury sighs.

"Shout out if she gets peckish, Joe, or even looks at you funny. We've got some raw meat in a biscuit tin for emergencies."

"Calumnies!" cries the Man-eater. "Lies, lies, lies! Who's this? What? What? How can you possibly be called Wally? Oh, *Polly*, yes, of course. How splendid. Got some meat on her, thank God, not like these modern pipe-cleaners . . . Foalbury, hush your mouth! I was not considering her for the pot. No. No! This nonsense about anthropophagy must cease! Make tea. Make it thick and orange. I sense the Sporklet is mired in shit and comes with a mission. And how do

I sense it? Because the ungrateful little sod is here at all." She scowls at him, goldfish eyes and Mona Lisa brows behind the lenses. Bob Foalbury departs, smiling.

And now, in the quiet, she surveys Joe Spork once more, with greater care. She takes in his lantern jaw all covered in stubble and his drawn, deep eyes. Then she glances at Polly Cradle and sees something between them of which she approves. X-ray vision with subtitles. *Old lady fu.* She embraces him tenderly.

"My dear boy," she murmurs. "My dear, dear boy. You must go and hug Foalbury when the chance presents itself, please, and tell him I've forced you to agree to dinner some day soon. He misses you when you don't come for a while."

"I will," Joe says.

"He gave me a scare," she says. "I mean, a real one. Woke up and couldn't breathe, and of course I thought it was his heart. Turns out he's allergic to our new pillows. But come, Joe, please?"

"I will."

"Because one day, you know, it *will* be his heart."

"I will," Joe says. She peers at him, weighs the promise.

"All right, then. Now, what can I do for you?"

"Ted Sholt. The Ruskinites. Brother Sheamus."

"Oh, Joe. Bad stories and old deaths. And half of it lies, I'm sure. You ignored me, didn't you? You went and pressed ahead with that wretched Hakote business!"

"Yes." He cannot lie to her.

"I told you and told you!"

"Yes. But it was too late by then."

"Yes, I suppose it was. You best give me the lot, then, and we'll go from there. I shall not interrupt."

She never does. Cecily Foalbury's unique brand of eidetic memory is cantankerous and wayward, making strange connections and seeing unlikely consonances, but it is absolute and requires no second chances. She sits in silence as Joe tells her, belatedly, about Wistithiel and the machine, about Ted Sholt, and about the thin man and the fat man running, and the robed strangers with their alarming heron's gait, and finally about Billy Friend and Mercer's rescue. More than once during the narrative, her eyes narrow, and Joe knows she is cross-referencing, walking the long alleys of her memory's maze and pulling out old business for new examination.

When Joe has finished, Cecily Foalbury sits in absolute silence for a long while with her eyes fixed on the tabletop, and her lips wriggle as she combs the front and sides of her false teeth. The soft sucking is the only sound in the room, and the only indication that she has not fallen asleep. Then, at last, she opens her eyes.

"Bees," she says. "As in, the golden swarm."

"I think so."

"They say there are more, now. Other hives in other cities. They must have been just sitting there, forgotten in corners, waiting for . . . whatever this is. People will be frightened. I was. I am, actually. There were riots in Moscow and Nanjing yesterday. And Caracas. They're all over the place, Joe. Put there. Hidden, maybe."

"I know. I'm sorry."

"Don't be ridiculous," she snaps. "You were set up." She glowers at him, then looks closer. "You do see that, don't you? Good Lord, boy, of course you were. Don't tell me," she says to Polly, "he's been moping about imagining this was all his own work?" And when Polly nods, "Tcha! You know better. If you cut yourself with a chisel, is it the chisel's fault? No. Don't blame the tool."

He really hadn't thought of it that way. He smiles at her in gratitude. She frowns at him thunderously, then goes on.

"All right: the Ruskinites, then . . . There's a lot to tell, and things you need to know. I'll get Foalbury to type it up. But for now, I think you need the quick version, right away."

"With notes as necessary," Polly Cradle says, and Cecily Foalbury shoots her an approving glance, and replies that she will condense, but that a breath of context would be just as well.

Harticle's, Cecily Foalbury says by way of caution, is like an old Victorian gas lamp in a dark street: a flickering light atop a wrought-iron post, surrounded by greenish smog. Close to the centre, everything is clear. The history of the wristwatch, the rise and fall of the clockwork toy, the enduring charm of the gramophone—all these are stories well known and simple. Further out, things become bizarre, like Mad Ludwig's clockwork carriage, complete with iron horses driven by a flyweight, which probably never existed save in the mind of an Austrian confidence man.

Finally there are stories which make no sense or cannot be quite right: rumours of half-truths and reports of whispers. The fall of the Order of John the Maker—also known as the Ruskinites—is one of them.

The Ruskinites were a society of craftsmen who believed in the power of art to raise the human soul, to enlighten and uplift. They were so good that, when the British government found itself short of resources and in desperate need, they drew as many of them as were in England to their cause and set them to work with a genius to create machines of war.

The genius was a woman, come to England for refuge. By all accounts she was temperamental and infuriating, as such people often are.

The nature of the collaboration being what it was, the products of this endeavour were unusual, even eccentric. And yet, they were effective for all that. They made machines and vehicles and uncovered scientific secrets which were of use, and they rivalled Bletchley Park for their ability to solve insoluble riddles and deceive the enemy. They were so effective that they continued long after the war was over, shoring up Britain's defences against the Soviets, and never discussed even with the Americans, who had by that time defaulted (Cecily Foalbury snorts) on the deal to share nuclear information with their wartime allies.

And then, sometime around the end of the sixties or the beginning of the seventies, there was a tragedy. Something went wrong with the greatest project of the collaboration, and a village on the coast was wiped out. It was rumoured the experiment itself was not to blame for the physical destruction, that that was done afterwards to conceal the consequences. The genius behind the thing fled, died, who knew? It was over, and the Ruskinites were cut loose to fend for themselves after thirty years in the warm breadbasket of government. They lost their way.

"Soot and sorrow," murmurs Joshua Joseph Spork.

"Exactly, darling," Cecily Foalbury replies. "Exactly." She draws a phlegmy breath—tears unshed or a winter cold, he isn't sure—and looks up at him with suffering eyes. "You'll want to know that bit, won't you? And there's no one better to tell you, because I was there the night it all began; the night they chose Brother Sheamus."

And then she settles to tell it, mouth turned down and damp eyes staring into history.

What the Ruskinites wanted—had always wanted—was to be part of any project in the secular world which might, by its presence and execution, reveal the divine in man. Indeed, the bravest of them whispered, was it not likely that the eye of God was drawn to the most profound, most perfect artefacts of human effort? And were these not in any case the ones which touched closely upon the divine within?

Cecily sighs. "But they were fighting a losing battle, weren't they, Joe?"

"I suppose."

"Oh, yes. Of course they were. That time was gone. After the war, there was no room for craft. If it couldn't be machine made, mass-produced, almost no one could afford it. So there was a new doctrine: uniqueness was elitist, mass-produced art was good. Perfection should be made available to all, just small enough to put in a cloth bag and carry home.

"They soldiered on, but by 1980 they couldn't pretend any more. All those shoulder pads and the beginnings of consumer gizmos. Walkmen instead of music boxes. VHS instead of charades. A nation plugged into the industrial machine. Everything had to be mega. Megabucks. Megastar. Megadeath. It means 'million,' you know. Well. If you're a Ruskinite, a million is too many. A million days is more than thirty human lifetimes. A million miles is four times the distance to the moon. But the eighties were all about millions.

"It tore them up. If God was in the detailing, then God was dead."

The Order of John the Maker began to wither, which would have been sad, but fitting. Artisanal movements do that; they go a certain distance, and then they stop. But then, as a new, inexperienced Keeper named Theodore Sholt cast around for a remedy for the secular world itself, he found himself beset by a rival. A false prophet.

"I was there," Cecily says dully, as if speaking of a public hanging. "A friend of Foalbury's called us and said there was a wonderful man. A strange, compelling man who was going to save the Ruskinites. ·Well, we went, of course. Wouldn't you? But when we got there it was something awful. He wasn't rescuing anything. He was taking it away and making it his own, and none of them could see."

Bob Foalbury puts an arm around her, and—when Cecily seems unable to continue the story—he takes it up.

"He called himself Brother Sheamus, and he was . . . he was perfect. He looked like Professor bloody Moriarty. You just wanted Basil

Rathbone to come in and stop him. Or I did. And he was no more Irish than a Scotch egg."

Sheamus went to the heart. He came as a prodigal son, a bird returning to the nest at dusk. He came to Sharrow House on foot, through wrought-iron gates and past the old rails of the artillery store from the war, down the yew alley and past the moat some Victorian fellow had felt the need for, and over the drawbridge. He stood with them on the grand balcony, looking at London's rooftops and hearing the traffic and the clock tower, lamented the housing blocks which obscured the view of the river. He let them know he loved it all, the garden, the view, the house which was the soul of the Order of John the Maker. He loved them. He understood their pain and their fear. He was a man of God.

His English was expensive, and foreign. Rumour had it that he'd trained in Jerusalem with the Armenian Orthodox Church. It was whispered he'd been to Eton and served in the SAS, that he had worked with Wilhelm Reich. He said he'd taken the cowl in Burma with a monk who'd died of malaria, then gone to Rome in the sixties to study with the Jesuits. Before he even arrived, he was a sort of myth.

The world was changing too fast, Sheamus said, and in the wrong way, so he had come to make a stand. In the grand hall at the heart of Sharrow House, beneath stone arches cut by hand, ceilings painted and sculpted so that each column and nook was a statement of identity and uniqueness, Brother Sheamus wove a trap in words.

"He was a matinée idol, Joe. He told them he loved them when everyone else thought they were hopelessly obsolete. He swept them off their feet. And he was surrounded by people, all the time, photographers and journalists writing everything down. Even a television camera. You have to remember how rare that was then, Joe. We only had three channels until eighty-two. But they watched everything he did, and we knew he was important. There's nothing so impressive as someone everyone wants to be with, who says he only wants to be with you.

"I sat at the back," Cecily Foalbury growls, "and I hated him. I hated him with everything I had because I knew he was a liar and he would leave them with nothing. He stood in the pulpit and looked down at them and he broke them, and they thought he was making it all better.

"'Artisanship,'" he said, "'is a means to an end for us. Is it not? Did we become artists because we love art, or because we love God?' And Joe, you have to understand, they hadn't been addressed like that in a sermon before. They weren't Charismatics, they didn't feel the Holy Spirit in them, and they didn't ask one another to testify. They were Ruskinites. They were makers, and very sensible. Very calm.

"Well, that just made them easy pickings. I saw, next to me, an old fellow stop breathing for a moment as if he was frightfully offended, and then he got this odd sort of smile, as if he'd always wanted to do this and suddenly he was being allowed.

"'We love God,' someone said, and then they were all nodding, and I heard a lot of people saying 'God.'

"'We seek revelation,' Brother Sheamus said. 'Is it not so?'

"'Yes,' they said.

"'Well, God has abandoned us. Perhaps it is a test. Perhaps He does not care. Who can say? He is God. He is ineffable. He has done many things in our shared history, but He has never explained Himself. But there is a keener revelation in this world than art and craft. There is a machine which could reveal God. An automated prayer wheel which will show us the truth. But it might . . . it *will* do more than that.'

"'What more?' they said.

"'If God has abandoned us—if our creator has left us to our own devices—then this device will draw His eye.'

"'Draw it?'

"'The Engine is most compelling. It is like a puzzle to the eye of God, a whirlpool. With it, we will end the silence of God. We will see Him. And He will see us. We will pass His test, and we will come of age. We will demand—demand, as Moses did—we will *demand* that he speak to us.'

"Well, that was blasphemy, clear and simple, but it didn't sound like it when he said it then and there, it sounded like a perfectly reasonable thing. They all sat there for a moment as if he'd hit them with a kipper, and then someone shouted 'Sheamus!' and then they were all on their feet and shouting and poor Sholt, the little fellow who was supposed to be Keeper, was bundled off the platform and they elevated Sheamus on the spot.

"He didn't hang about, Joe. He got right to it. That same night he told them to cover their faces as a symbol of God's disregard, and they did, and somehow there were bits of that horrible gauze ready and anyone who wouldn't wear it was out into the dark. They tried to take possession of all the other buildings and so on, but someone blocked it, I always assumed it was the government.

"And very soon after that, the Ruskinites became something else. The craftsmen were gone, people we'd known for years were either sent into seclusion or kicked out, and Sheamus brought in his own people, thugs and bullies as lay members, and a whole host of new monks who never spoke. He called them the Cornish Orphans."

Joe jolts a little in his chair.

"It was a hostile takeover," Cecily Foalbury says, brokenly. "Well, it was the eighties, wasn't it?"

Into the mournful quiet, Joe ventures a last question. "Cecily . . . the friend who took you along . . ."

"Yes," she mutters. "It was. It was your grandfather, Daniel."

They sit for a moment without speaking.

"Joe," Polly Cradle says at last, "we should go. We have to check in with Mercer."

"One minute, I just need to make a call," Joe says.

"Joe—"

"It's important, Polly, I promise. It might help."

She sighs a yes, and Joe gets permission from Cecily Foalbury to use the telephone. Cecily's gaze sweeps over Polly, resting for a moment on the bag of records on its strap over one shoulder. She raises her eyebrows just a little, and Polly nods. The Man-eater smiles, and pats Polly lightly on the back of the hand.

"Partner in crime," Cecily says happily. "The right sort of girl. At *last!*"

The phone is in a separate wooden booth, an elegantly carved enclosure with a special noise-reducing design. It was made, according to the handwritten label, for an Estonian noble in the late 1800s. Joe cannot remember the number, but he can remember dialling it on his father's grey desk phone, the purr of the tone and the endless clickety-clack as he went through the digits. Back then, it was an oh-one number. Now it's oh-two-oh-seven. He hopes the rest remains the same.

Someone answers on the second ring.

"Fucking intolerable *cow*!" cries an aggravated male voice.

"Don?"

"Oh, I'm terribly sorry. I thought you were Erika. My lover," the voice clarifies, in case Joe knows more than one Erika who might be an intolerable cow. "Who's that?"

"Don? It's Joe Spork."

"Joe? Joe Spork? Oh, for God's sake, little Josh?"

"Yes."

"Little Josh, who must now be almost as old as I am, you have the pleasure of addressing the Honourable Donald Beausabreur Lyon, master of a thousand bureaucrats and Prince of Quangos! That's Quasi-Autonomous Non-Governmental Organisation, for those in the audience who don't know, such as the intolerable cow who thinks she can boss me around like a puppy dog and make me go to bloody Sheffield when I don't bloody want to . . . Honestly, it's bloody Sheffield, not Saint-Tropez . . . How may I be of service?"

"I've got a spot of bother, Don, and I thought you might be able to help out. For old times' sake, as it were."

"Well, I don't know. I might. What sort of bother?"

"I'm involved in this bee thing. By accident."

"The bee thing?"

"The crazy bees from Cornwall? The police were called out."

"Oh, bloody hell. *That* bee thing. That's far beyond me, old lad. Go and see that weasel at the office and confess all, is my advice. Unless . . ."

"Unless what?"

"Unless you'd prefer not to?" This last in a strangely wheedling tone.

"I'd really prefer not to."

The Hon Don doesn't speak. Joe realises he's waiting for something. *There's a password, but I don't know what it is.*

Finally, "Well, I'll look into it, Josh—Joe, is it?—but I can't promise anything. Where are you?"

"I'll call you, Don. It's better that way."

"What? Oh, yes, of course. I see what you mean. But you can trust me. Mum's the word."

"Oh! Yes. Don, did Mathew ever mention anything to you about his mother?"

"God, no. Harriet was the only person he ever talked to about that sort of thing. Go and see her, is my advice. Tell her I said to sing 'Georgia Brown' one more time for the Hon Don! All right? Then I'll hear from you? Grand. Grand . . ."

And Donald Beausabreur Lyon is gone, in a flurry of false bonhomie.

Joe turns to find Cecily Foalbury watching him from the doorway. From the non-display collection in the basement her husband has retrieved a small portable gramophone known as a Piglet (Jacobs Bros. of Stroud, 1940) because of the noise it makes when you wind it. "We're always here, Joe," she says very seriously. "We'd go to the wall for you. Don't ever forget it. That's what Harticle's is for, and it's our trust. 'No craftsman stands alone, nor in his darkness lacks for light, nor has no shield against his patron's spite.' Frightful piece of doggerel, but it's real to me. And I love you like my own, all right?" She hugs him powerfully, then turns hurriedly away.

Subdued, Joe allows Polly to drive him back to her home. Mercer calls when they are still a few streets away with strict instructions that they remain in the house.

"I'm coming to you," he tells her. "Something's happening."

"What sort of something?"

"Turn on the television when you get home," Mercer says, "and then stay exactly where you are, which is what you're supposed to be doing right now. Where did you go?"

Polly tells him.

"Well," Mercer says after a moment, "that was insane. But apparently it was also a good idea. I find the combination unsettling. Please try not to have any more good ideas until I get there to measure them against the possibility that you have gone entirely off your rocker."

Polly Cradle sits close to her old television set and waits. She has crossed her legs in a position which Joe finds almost yogic. On her right is a yellow legal pad and in her hand she has a pen. One of two pieces of up-to-date technology she owns, a digital TV recorder, is running so that she can replay the news. The other—a chunky laptop with a thick cord snaking out of it to the wall—rests on a stack of thick foreign dictionaries so that she can follow the signals chatter of the internet.

"Do you speak all those languages?" Joe wonders aloud.

"No," Polly Cradle says. "That's why I have dictionaries." She wiggles and waves her arms, and by this strangely powerful method she conveys an image of herself, with a stack of documents, painstakingly working out the precise meaning of each, phrase by phrase.

"Watch!" she says abruptly, and turns up the sound. On the screen, a fishing fleet in mid-ocean, seen from a helicopter. The newsreader is playing for drama. His voice is filled with the special "keep calm" tone which suggests crisis. The shot cuts to a shot from on board one of the boats.

It is awash in perfect, golden bees.

There is no one on board.

And, as the camera pans, so it is across the entire fleet.

The news cuts away to a coastguard ship a few miles away. The sailors are here, in life jackets and blankets.

"We had to abandon ship," one of them says.

"Why? Why did you have to abandon ship?" the reporter demands.

"Too much," the man says obscurely.

"Too much what?"

The man doesn't answer immediately. He looks up and off to the side, remembering. "I understood things," he says at last.

"What sort of things?"

"Just things."

"I see—"

"No," the man says. "You don't. You think you do. But you don't."

"I don't think people will understand what you mean."

"No. They won't. Not until it happens to them."

"Is it going to, do you think?"

"Oh, yes. Definitely. And when it does, they'll know what I know."

"Which is?"

"Too much," he says again. "Questions I ask myself in my head, and don't really want the answers to. I knew them, I couldn't not know. I have to go home and apologise to my wife. I screamed at her before we left. And my kids. I was wrong and I need to be better. I need to eat right, too. And my uncle, he's a monster. I've told the police: he beats my aunt. I don't know why I never said it before. That's all right, I suppose, but it's hard feeling it all at once. But then there's more and more. There's too much of it. You do what you can and there's never an end, just more things wrong that don't have to be." He shudders, and starts to cry.

A moment later, the bees depart skyward in a great rush, and the show cuts back to the studio where people with no notion of what is going on speculate on what it all means. There is a note of panic, and fear.

Mercer comes through the door about ten seconds later.

He looks at his sister, and then at Joe. His eyes open very wide.

"Oh, God," he murmurs. "As if there wasn't enough trouble in the world, you two have had sex."

"We made speculative love," Polly replies airily.

"What?"

"Honestly, you sound just like him. Well, no. That sounds wrong . . . I mean that he also asks an enormous number of questions about perfectly obvious things. We made speculative love, Mercer. We had sex pre-emptively, in case we fall in love later. I think of it as an investment in satisfaction."

"And if you don't?"

"Then you're right. We had really great sex."

Mercer appears to consider this for a moment.

"Suddenly," he says, "I find that my present line of questioning has lost its appeal." He glances at Joe. "Well. Not before time. The rest of the picture, as you see, is not so bonny. So . . . Fasten your seat belts, my lad and lass. This could get rocky."

A moment later the doorbell rings, and one of the Bethanys is standing on the stoop with a concerned-looking man in his forties.

"Mr. Cradle? Mr. Long is here to see you."

"How does he even—" Mercer breaks off as Polly drums her fingers on the desk. "Fine. Mr. Long, who he?"

"A curator."

"Is he relevant?"

"No. He has a kind face and he keeps cats and I thought . . . yes, Mercer, of course he is. This is what I do."

Mercer waves his hands vaguely, as if already wanting his teacup. "Sorry."

Bethany—it's number two, Joe Spork is fairly sure—follows this exchange with a suffused expression of concealed but potent delight.

Mr. Long is a damp sort of specimen with a jowly neck and a large, square head. Joe thinks of him immediately as a nervous local darts champion.

"Mr. Long," Polly murmurs, bringing him inside, "would you like some coffee?"

"Oh!" Mr. Long says, his balloonish nose pointing briefly at the ceiling as he tosses his head to indicate enthusiasm. "Oh, yes, that would be marvellous. Only not too much." He makes an apnoeac clunking noise in his sinuses which is apparently indicative of humour. "Ahaha *knuu* haha, because it makes me extremely jumpy! Aha ha hnn."

Polly favours him with a devastating smile.

"Mr. Long," she murmurs as she lounges out, "is the director of the Alternative Paradigms Institute at Brae Hampton. I believe he may also be the victim of some sort of confidence trick."

"Oh, I am!" Mr. Long nods again. "I am. A rather wicked trick has been played upon us. At least, I trust it's a trick. I do hope it's nothing more serious."

Mercer looks at Joe. *This one's yours. I do coppers and spies and lairs and monsters. I don't do curators.*

"I'm afraid I'm not familiar with your organisation," Joe murmurs invitingly.

"Oh, no one is. We're very quiet. Although recently we've been getting some tourism for the tank exhibit."

"Tank? Like . . ." Joe mimes a vague armoured vehicle, machine gun firing.

"Oh, not like Panzers, oh no! *Knuu-knuu* haha! We have the largest freshwater tank in Great Britain, and the largest enclosed one in the world, for the exclusive use of model-boat enthusiasts, you see. Just a sideline, of course."

"A sideline?"

"Oh, yes. The purpose of the Institute is to preserve lines of research science and technology which are presently unfashionable. So, for example, we carry the translated notes of Akunin, the eighteenth-century Russian specialist in bacteriophage medicine." Mr. Long smiles as if this should make things perfectly clear; a wide, millennialist's grin filled with genial crazy. "Treasures which *one day*, when they are *retrieved from obscurity*, may greatly benefit mankind . . . although between you and me some of them should probably stay hidden, they're a bit daft. Ahah *knuu!* Ahahah."

"And you also have . . ."

"Oh, yes, a collection of . . . well. I say 'a collection' . . . in fact it's several collections, classified together by the Institute. They're all Second War, you see. There's the Pyke Papers. There's a very small set on

Tesla's work, donated by an American gentleman, and some Russian documents regarding psychical research which I personally regard as *disinformation*, like the SDI programme in reverse . . ."

"Perhaps you should ask Mr. Long about his present problem," Polly Cradle says, re-entering with a tray.

"Oh, indeed!" cries Mr. Long, "Indeed! The item we had was linked with a rather special woman, a scientist . . . Gave Pyke himself a run for his money, though if I'm honest he was more an innovator and an engineer than a pure scientist, of course . . ." It's as if he's telling a very dirty joke. All of us over the age of consent here, eh? Don't mind a bit of *engineering*, do we? Nudge, nudge.

Joe abruptly misses Billy Friend very much.

"I understand the Americans were working on some of her early research when they had that rather unfortunate accident with the USS *Eldridge* . . . That's another one most people think is a myth, but of course *we know better*, don't we? *Aknuu-knuuu!*" Mr. Long is nodding so hard now that it seems possible he will strain himself. Mercer stares fixedly at the ceiling.

Polly Cradle turns her smile on Mr. Long again, and he goes back to his theme. "And then there's the Abel Jasmine collection. That's the problem for today, I'm afraid. We allowed an exhibit to be taken away for cleaning by one of the original donors—though on examination it appears she did not donate this specific item—and I rather fear it's gone for good. It was supposed to come back days ago. A very pretty item, too—unique, so far as I know."

Joe looks at Polly, and she nods. "A mechanical book," he says.

"Yes! However . . . oh, well, of course you know, otherwise why would I be here? We did place an advertisement offering a reward for its safe return. I don't suppose you have it?"

"We may know where it is," Mercer says judiciously, then holds up a hand as Mr. Long hoots again through his restricted airway. "I need to make further inquiries. But out of curiosity, what is it? Where does it come from?"

"Well, we don't really know. Very hush-hush, we think. Mr. Jasmine, you know, was a very senior fellow. Deeply involved. Meetings with Mountbatten and even Churchill himself. Bath meetings. You are aware . . ."

"That Churchill took meetings in his bath. Yes."

"Well, these were often two- or even three-tub meetings!"

"Remarkable."

"Oh, it is, it is."

"But you have no idea what it might actually be?"

"Well . . . one doesn't wish to speculate . . ." He's dying to, actually, flirting with them, daring them to ask. Mercer makes a face of utmost interest.

"There are *rumours*," Long says. "Quite *unsubstantiated*, so one can hardly call it serious research . . . the book, now . . . we fancied that was quite special. All that code along the edges . . ." He looks at them hopefully: *Have you seen it?* Joe suppresses the urge to nod. "Well, in a way, it's the Crown jewels for some of us, because it harks to a time when Britain was at the pinnacle of science and everyone else was just . . . well." Mr. Long leans close, with the air of one imparting a tremendous secret.

"We think . . . it's a command set . . . for the British space effort!" He smiles triumphantly. There is a long, uncomfortable pause.

"British . . ." Mercer says faintly.

". . . Space effort!" Mr. Long repeats. "Von Braun was working for German dominance in space! We couldn't let that happen in the long run, could we? Of course, it was all covered up later." He puts a finger alongside his nose and shows them his septum a few times.

Mutinous glares flow in two directions while Mr. Long sips oblivious at his coffee and makes another weird little noise.

Polly rolls her eyes at her brother and perches on the arm of Joe's chair. He does not pay attention to the way her backside compresses firmly against his arm. He listens to Mr. Long.

Mostly.

The theft was deftly accomplished. It was probably done to order. It was particularly vexing because a gentleman representing a large company had recently inquired about taking the item on loan for a substantial sum. Joe describes Rodney Titwhistle and then Arvin Cummerbund, and even the Ruskinite who visited his shop, but Mr. Long does not recognise them. Nor is he familiar with the Apprehension Engine—though the mention of an engine intrigues him, of course—or the word "Angelmaker." Then Mercer shows him a picture of Billy Friend.

"Oh, yes, he was there, definitely. Oh, dear, is he a criminal?"

"Yes," Mercer says, at the same time that Joe Spork says "No."

"He's dead," Polly says gently.

"Oh, dear," Mr. Long says again. "His poor mother."

"His mother?" Mercer repeats.

"Very respectable lady! I hardly think she was involved. Rather too old to go shinning up a balcony, ahah *aknuu* hahaha. And who'd take care of the terrible dog?"

Joe Spork is abruptly paying very close attention. "What dog?"

"Right little monster, *aknuu*, yes, with pink glass eyes, if you can credit it."

"A pug," Joe suggests, "with only one tooth."

"Horrible! Mind you, *aknuu*, you have to admire the tenacity, don't you?"

"Oh, yes. I suppose you do."

Mercer asks a few questions and then bundles Mr. Long gently out of the door with a promise of vague assistance down the line. When he has gone, his expression speaking somewhat of disappointment at their reaction to his revelation, Joe Spork introduces Mercer to the name of Edie Banister, and Bethany adds her to the list.

"To recap," Polly Cradle says, in a tone Joe Spork finds both schoolmarmish and extremely sexy, "it would seem that at some time between 1945 and 1980, Joe's grandfather and grandmother built a bee-machine which is either a rocket ship, a mobile sculpture, or a brain-melting lie detector. They were assisted in this questionable enterprise by the Order of John the Maker, at that time under licence from the British Government to create objects of philosophically and militarily efficacious art. Sadly, during the testing phase, the item in question immolated the town of Wistithiel and the project was discontinued. Subsequently, the Ruskinites were co-opted by a sinister personage determined to attract God's attention—to wit, one Brother Sheamus—who ousted the Keeper at that time, Theodore Sholt, but was unable to lay his nasty mitts on the Apprehension Engine itself, being blocked by person or persons unknown. We shall hypothesise a combination of the aforementioned government entities and the good Keeper himself, who then removed to a greenhouse to look after the item personally until such time as Joe's grandmother should choose to resume its purpose, which as far as we know she never did.

"At some point in the recent past, it would seem that an old lady living in Hendon took it into her head to unleash the Apprehension Engine and in doing so save or possibly destroy the world. She deployed Billy Friend as a catspaw, roped Joe in to do the technical bit, and gulled poor Mr. Long out of his prize exhibit. Joe activated the machine, the bees flew, and both the Ruskinites and some shady bit of the Civil Service, possibly but probably not known as the Legacy Board, realised what was going on and pounced, acting for the moment in concert—though we should not take that to mean that they are united in their goals. They grabbed Sholt and the machine under the appearance of a fire in an old house, traced the whole thing to Billy and he got killed either under interrogation or because someone is very keen to keep this from getting out. From Billy they found Joe, and would have vanished him also without the intervention of Mercer Cradle of the old established et cetera, et cetera. And here we all are. Does anyone have anything to add?"

"Yes," her brother says. "It's getting a lot bigger very, very fast."

He thumbs on the television, without the sound, and they watch as bulletins interrupt regular programming. Parliaments debate and leaders demand explanations from one another. The UN is in session, and so is NATO. Britain is on high alert; the government's misdeeds in Congo have become painfully public. Israel and Egypt, once friendly, now nervous, are positively spitting. So are Germany, France, Italy, and Spain. A swarm of bees in Santiago has revealed secrets: excesses, debauches, and betrayals. The United States, China, India, and Pakistan have all announced their intention to destroy the bees, though what they will do—Shoot them? Nuke them?—is unclear. To the leaders of the world, though, they are bad bees. They are bees of aggression, not bees of honey and peace. They are evil bees, and cannot be tolerated.

Too much truth cannot be allowed.

In London—stung, perhaps, by the implication that all this originated here—a nasty red-topped anger is building. Bee-keepers are told they must register, must submit their hives for inspection. No, of course, these are no ordinary bees, but it pays to be safe. It helps to rule people out. Any bee-keeper, after all, might be a sympathiser, a fifth columnist. Meanwhile the people growl back at Westminster: Who is responsible? Who is answerable? Who must give back his pension? (Not that anyone ever is, or does.)

Who will be held to account?

Who did this?

Who must be thrown to the beast?

"It's getting much bigger," Mercer Cradle repeats.

XI

Ancient's history;
a personal matter;
Lovelace.

Edie wakes, still cold from *Cuparah*'s icy salvation of decades gone. It's earlier than she intended, and the effort of getting vertical is for the moment too much to contemplate. Her body is old, and the bones themselves have taken up a kind of muttering. Even Bastion, she sometimes thinks, is in better overall repair than she is.

She ruffles his ears gently, and he makes a sound in his belly like a lawnmower but does not wake. Almost, Edie lifts him up for a hug, but a dog must be allowed his dreamtime. She refrains, and curls around him instead, hoping his hot-water-bottle body will draw her down into her own sleep. She gets, instead, the strange, meandering kaleidoscope which has recently been her mind's recourse: the weird pageant of her life.

Alas, without many of the dirty bits.

Edie Banister could never decide if it was a dream or a nightmare, that long, strange fugue which carried her—and, incidentally, His (and then Her) Majesty's United Kingdom—from 1946 to the end of the century. The Cold War framed everything, the great Soviet steamroller looming to the East and the plucky Yanks to the West— but Edie fought an altogether different war of her own: a long, shadowy, personal one against an enemy who somehow never went away. It did not matter how many times she beat Shem Shem Tsien. He always came back, and each defeat served only to make him more cruel.

Sleep clearly isn't an option. With the assistance of the headboard and being careful not to disturb Bastion where he lies, Edie rises and stands naked in front of the mirror in the attic of the Pig & Poet. Not twenty any more, alas. Not even thirty or forty or fifty, or any of those comfortable landmarks which come before people call you "old." And yet there is muscle, still, in her narrow arms, and though her joints protest, they will move, will serve, will—in absolute necessity, and on the understanding that the following day will be a world of pain— glide through the steps and swirls of the featherlight *hiji waza* Mrs. Sekuni recommended for senior combatants.

She brushes out her hair and trims it, then puts on her next identity: a severe grey suit and flat shoes—Sunday School Edie, complete with ugly handbag big enough to conceal Bastion and some other items she has recently cooked up.

The arrival of Mr. Biglandry at Rallhurst Court implies, of course, that Billy Friend has been interrogated, and if he gave her up he has likely also yielded the name of Joshua Joseph Spork. Assassins, though . . . Edie did not anticipate that. An arrest warrant, for sure— but killers, no. If Shem Shem Tsien were still alive, that would be a different matter, but age and cumulative injury have by now surely achieved what she never could. The Opium Khan would be a hundred and twenty-five this year. No. Shem is dead, and good riddance. Which implies either someone new, or that her own country's secret service has just attempted to erase her.

She has seen the news, of course, knows that there are golden bees in the air over warships and cities and stock exchanges and homes, knows that governments are screaming blue murder. All the same, she had expected something more subtle. But perhaps she is simply sugar-coating the past. Maybe Abel Jasmine would have ordered her death: former agent launches one-woman revolution, engages doomsday device.

Edie stares back down the tunnel of the years, and feels the urge to shout advice to herself. Follow your heart, make the world you believe in. Governments promise everything, but change nothing. Beyond anything else, trust Frankie.

At last, she wakes the dog and ladles him gently into position, ignoring a burble of profound betrayal. Bastion does not approve of the handbag as a method of conveyance. Edie slips her hand between the leather straps and gentles him. Thinking about it, she realises it may not be the handbag *per se*, but the three or four Tupperware containers on which he sits, which smell of strange chemicals and plastic tape. Bastion most especially does not approve of Tupperware. He views it as a means to keep him from things rightfully his own, such as liver. The list of things of which he does not approve is long and complex, embracing such varied sinners as cats, thugs, wellington boots, brightly coloured umbrellas, cows, and unlicensed taxi cabs. But things which keep him from liver are near the top.

Edie catches the bus in Camden and lets it take her all the way west, then waits for the Catholic school in Goldmartin Street to disgorge its students and teachers, equally dressed in grey uniforms, so that she is suddenly just one of a great throng of severe women striding along the wide pavement. If anyone is following her, she has just made their lives almost impossibly difficult and annoying.

In the Underground she doubles back on herself and heads towards Harriet Spork's convent. Sooner or later, she's fairly sure, Joe will go there, and that is a calculation others will make, too.

Love causes people to do stupid things. That does not, she realises now, make them the wrong things.

The war came to an end and—as with the one before it—everyone was too exhausted to cheer. People smiled at one another not like victorious heroes but like punch-drunk prizefighters, eyes swollen shut and lips rippled and split, who do not understand why everyone is clapping. A numb silence settled over Europe from Snowdon to Ararat. Edie Banister—in the person of Commander James—was detailed to accompany Frankie from London to Calais and down to her family's home in rural France.

"Did you win the war for us?" Edie asked her in the grim little sleeper compartment of the southbound train.

"No," Frankie said seriously. "I would say I am responsible for no more than a few percentage points of variance in the outcome. The military men are incapable of asking a clear question. If they can only see one way of doing a thing, it follows that there is only that way. I spent six weeks working on an issue with sonar before I established that the use they proposed for the new technique was utterly . . ." She waved her hands in a gesture of aggravation and stared moodily out of the window. Then she looked back at Edie, and forced a smile. "I'm sorry. It was frustrating. More honestly . . . I do not believe this will be a pleasant journey for me. There will be pain of the soul. But . . . it is pleasant to see you, Commander Banister." She reached over and grasped Edie's hand, and smiled a wide, inviting smile. Then she drew a little closer. "More than pleasant, if I am honest."

"Frankie," Edie said after a long moment, "my name is Edith and I am a female person."

Frankie Fossoyeur nodded, puzzled. "Yes," she said, "I know. The ratio of your hips to your head is inconsistent with maleness. Also, the formation of your voice, while the note is quite deep, is not indicative of the presence of . . ." She waggled her fingers and then leaned closer, touching Edie's throat at the midpoint.

"Adam's apple," Edie Banister said, after a moment.

"Yes! Exactly. Also the skin, the eyes, the odour of the body, the hands . . . these are not mathematical observations, by the way. They are qualitative . . ." She had not removed her fingers. Edie could feel the second one, resting on her neck just to one side of the first. If she stepped forward, she would feel the third, then the little finger and eventually the palm and the thumb, then the forearm, and then all of Frankie at once.

"Just so that we're clear," Edie said. She shifted her weight. Frankie's nails grazed her skin.

"We are," Frankie said. "Quite clear."

How long they stood there Edie was never sure. At some point, they began to kiss, and the distance to Marseilles seemed very short. Undressing, Frankie announced sternly that she did not believe in exclusive love, which was a ludicrous construction of the Judeo-Christian Patriarchy. Edie agreed, never having thought about it, and wondered distantly whether the Judeo-Christian Patriarchy was a plot to which she should alert Abel Jasmine, or one he had perhaps created. Certainly, she wasn't going to argue about it now.

The journey was easy, but arriving was hard. Frankie's home was burned out. A pair of tweezers and a copper pot lay broken on her old hearth, beside a single, charred shoe. She asked about her family, her relatives, but once they knew who she was, the remaining local people would not talk to her. The young ones looked ashamed and the old ones turned away and muttered. A soldier said he thought it likely they'd been denounced as traitors to Vichy.

"They did a bit of that," he said, looking out at the town. "Pointed the finger at those they didn't like. People who were too rich or too pretty. All over occupied Europe, belike. Here for sure." He shied a pebble at a man pulling a handcart. "Half the world at war with the other half and good French lads fighting in the shadows to set 'em free, French soldiers in England readying for the day, and these buggers down here were just settling old scores. Bollocks to 'em, is what I say. Still . . . they had to live somehow, I suppose." He showed them a pile of belongings, dug up from the town dump, and Frankie moaned, clutched an ugly beaded necklace of her mother's from the pile.

Edie walked her away from town, followed a narrow track to a tree stump on the shore of a mucky lake.

"They hate us this much . . ." Frankie whispered, between gulps of horror. "My people. Because we are witches. Hakote. Children of the Sea. Webbed feet and shadow. Because we see the world, my mother said."

"I don't understand," Edie confessed into her lover's hair, because she knew already that when Frankie needed to talk about human things and life, you had to give her the cues or she became convinced you weren't listening.

Frankie swallowed. "Numbers," she said, after a moment. "Always numbers. We are born with numbers as you are born with sight. Do you see? So we are witches."

"Because you can count?"

"*Non*, not exactly. It is like that, but it is more than counting, and less. It is . . . *Alors* . . . Suppose I am a crude peasant girl—which I am, but suppose it is Louis XIV's time. I see a waterwheel. I see the rotation and the angle, and I know that in thirty to forty rotations, it will wear away and collapse. I do not know why I know. How can I express periodicity when I have never learned to write? When I have never needed a word for 'rotation'? But I run, anyway, to the miller and I say to him to stop the wheel. Now, the miller is a rich man and he did not get that way by listening to foolish girls. He does nothing. The wheel breaks and a man dies. Now I am a prophet! A witch! It is all my fault! Do you see?"

"Hakote."

"Sorceress. Yes. So they make up stories. Lies, embellishments. And my mother's house is a ruin and my . . . everyone I loved is gone. Because people are too stupid to know the simple truth when they hear it, and believe the most outrageous lies." And then something else which Edie could not quite hear, but which sounded like: *Please let them have escaped.* More family, more vulnerable witches. More targets.

Edie beside her, Frankie made inquiries from anyone who would speak to her. She discovered her mother and uncles had been put into one of the Vichy French camps quite early, and had died. Two more relatives—Edie wasn't sure who—had perhaps escaped over the hills to the coast, but been in a convoy which was sunk by U-boats.

The following day, they travelled on into Germany. It was not like seeing a fallen knight or the corpse of a monstrous wolf. It wasn't even the way Edie had imagined it, with burned-out tanks and beaten, thankful people.

It was like the aftermath of bad surgery, or a pit fight in Calcutta.

Lady Germany had taken a knife to her own face. In a strange, bewildered frenzy, she had cut off her proud, Semitic nose, and skewered her brown Romany eyes. And then came her violent rescuers, no more subtle than herself: they beat her, burned her, stabbed her, and then finally could not agree which of them should own the mess, so split her Solomonically (yet more bitter irony to which no one paid attention) and both parties were now having their way with the remains. A truly befitting European tragedy. *Fossoyeur*: it means *gravedigger.*

In the rain amid the mud and twisted metal: Frankie Fossoyeur was crying, water from her eyes as if they were the very Möhne and Eder dams themselves. Slick-cheeked and open-mouthed, she stared as if seeing the whole of Germany spread out below her on a table. The country had undone itself as much as it had been undone.

"More dead of lies. More millions."

Leaning on Edie Banister, Frankie choked out horrors and sucked in air which was half mud.

Back home at Edie's flat in Marylebone, Frankie bawled and wailed and stared into space. Germany had been her enemy, but France had betrayed her. France was dead to her. She would never visit the Louvre again. She would never take Edie to the Orangerie to see Monet's water lilies. Monet was a bastard, and his style was evidence of a myopic condition, not of genius at all. No genius ever came out of France. None. Not even Frankie. Frankie was not French. She was Hakote, and that was all. She would work.

She would work. The Apprehension Engine, yes. The truth would come out. Everyone would see. The world would become honest, mankind would be better off. No lies, ever again.

Edie took her to bed and kept her there for most of a week, and by the end she wept only occasionally. Edie bought her oil pastels and paper from an art shop in Reading, and Frankie sketched faces Edie did not recognise over and over again, and touched her hand and said "I love you," which she had never done before. Occasionally, she stopped sketching and wrote numbers on the wall, and other symbols Edie had never seen, symbols which expressed things for which spoken language had no name. Warmed and lit by the single bar of an electric fire, Frankie Fossoyeur drew the faces of the beloved dead, and surrounded them with wild, dangerous comprehensions no one else on Earth could have understood. It was the first time Edie heard her speak of her book, in the ghastly lethargy which took her between bouts of mania.

I shall write it all down, like Marie Curie! Not just numbers. I shall tell the truth. It does not have to be this way, Edie. It does not! We do not have to be small, and stupid, and weak. I shall make a book unlike any you have seen. A book of wonders . . . A book of the Hakote, and you shall read it and see it and still you shall not believe what I have done!

Frankie's handwriting was so bad that most of the words were single letters followed by long wiggly lines. Edie brought her tea and wrapped arms around her, and Frankie allowed herself to be held. A month later they were sharing the flat, Edie's small number of belongings swamped by Frankie's accumulated books and devices. In the evenings they huddled together under a quilt, and Edie did crosswords while Frankie wrote.

It was winter, and it stayed that way until 1948.

Shem Shem Tsien had not died in Addeh Sikkim.

Edie had known this, peripherally. She had been aware of him quitting the field, leaving his soldiers to burn where they fought. She had seen him take a moment to kill the crucified bishop, slicing across his gut so that the man would die painfully rather than quickly. She had known, too, that the subsequent explosion regrettably failed to claim the Khan—Abel Jasmine had shown her the reports, so that she would not be surprised into betraying herself if ever she met him again. Edie had assumed that Shem Shem Tsien would be occupied with rebuilding his citadel, licking his wounds and looking for another genius.

He did nothing of the kind. Before he had been Khaygul of Addeh Sikkim, she realised, he had been the Opium Khan, master of the heroin trade in Europe and Asia. The nation he had usurped had been little more than an amusement park for him; his own personal Brighton Pier. He had killed his family because they were in the way not of some great unfulfilled desire, but of a whim. He had no need to be ruler of an actual country. His power was in himself, and in the men who served him, and ultimately in the extremity of his vision. A prince of horrors is no less a prince if the land he holds lies in ruins.

All the same, it seemed his hate for James Banister was surpassed only by his rage against Dotty Catty. To hurt her, the report said, he had evolved a system for the torture of elephants, and the outlaw hills where he kept his fortresses howled and bellowed with their agony and the markets of Asia were filled with his bloody ivory and the contorted heads of his victims. Moreover, he had let it be known: Frankie Fossoyeur was his. The man who brought him his genius should be exalted above all others. He should be rewarded with wealth and concubines and whatever else he wished, so long as she was *compos mentis*, and could work.

Abel Jasmine supplied guards for Frankie, and Edie made her practise escape and evasion. She taught her how to do a flat bolt: how to drop everything and leave a country without stopping at your bank or getting a change of clothes; how to find someone who would supply you with a passport; how to vanish from view in a city and in the countryside. Frankie thought it all a nonsense. She barely listened, and yet by the end she was suggesting improvements and refinements and Edie was wondering how long it would take her to understand the tricks of invisibility better than Edie herself.

But if Frankie was learning to be a spy or some variation thereof, she was learning with the smallest necessary aspect of her mind, as if she sent Frankie-the-stenographer to pay attention so that some other, inner Frankie could do the real work. The Apprehension Engine was in her heart, and its defining numbers were scrawled in chalk on a blackboard in her study. She no longer found herself distracted by things. Brother Denis, visiting from the Ruskinite mother-house, worried that she was alarmingly focused.

"There's nothing wrong," Edie said discouragingly.

"Well, you don't have to tell me," Denis told her. "But you bloody better not kid yourself about it. She's not the same. She's got a look."

"What look?"

"Vision," Denis said. "Monomania. I don't know. But it's not her."

"Maybe it is," Edie said. "Maybe this is how she is when she cares about something." *Someone*, she was saying. *This is how she is when she loves someone. Me. And she only needs one big project and me to fill her attention.* Denis had the good, unmonkish sense to leave well enough alone.

The following day Frankie went out, and three thugs in a black sedan jumped on her in front of a shop called Cadwallader's which sold soap, but Songbird and a few others, now notionally part of a civilian service, sent the would-be kidnappers to Paddington Green for a sharp discussion about British law. A week later, Shem Shem Tsien sank a British warship in the North Sea and a Russian one in port at Helsinki and tried to start a war, and while the eyes of Whitehall were fixed on that little disaster, two more hoods tried to steal Frankie from a symposium in Cambridge where she was meeting Erdös and von Neumann.

Edie Banister glued on her moustache and flew to Tallinn, and found Shem Shem Tsien posing as a Russian prince. He even carried a purse full of Romanov gold and swore Romanov-style, in French. He was surrounded by secretaries, men writing in books. A photographer bustled around him. There was even a cameraman with a Bolex.

"So, Commander Banister. You look well," Shem Shem Tsien murmured across the card table at the Kolyvan Casino. "I myself do not. I am well aware." He was craggy and drawn, and there was a newly healed scar on his neck, but his film-star eyes were glittering and cold. He gestured at the secretaries. "Forgive my affectation—I am preserving my journey for posterity. My pathway to transcendence is noteworthy. I suppose that makes these good men my apostles. My gospellers. 'If I have the mind of Napoleon . . .'" He smiled at the nearest one, then leaned closer. "You stole my scientist, Commander Banister. I want her back."

"She's her own woman, old boy."

"No, she is not. Everything that is, is mine by divine right. It is used by others on sufferance, and by my leave."

"Well, I suppose I ain't a believer."

"No," Shem Shem Tsien said, without irony. "But you will be." Abruptly, he changed the subject. "I understand Frankie is writing a book. Fiction, no doubt."

Edie shrugged, but James Banister's face gave her away. Shem Shem Tsien smiled.

"Oh. Not fiction. Surely not mathematics? My mathematics?" He leaned across the table. "I will have it all back from her, Commander. Her brain is not yours to plunder. Oh, but I have a gift for you." He smiled, and slid a small wet thing across the table. "My mother's tongue. It's quite fresh, I assure you. I kept her alive for some time to watch the deaths of her elephants, but eventually I tired of her. I did keep her head, for a memento. I feel inclined to share."

Commander Banister stared at the tongue, and wondered whether it was better that it should be Dotty Catty's, or that Shem Shem Tsien should have ripped it out of someone else's mouth purely for effect.

Edie couldn't think of anything clever to say, so she just smiled James Banister's most irritating patrician smile, and saw Shem Shem Tsien stiffen in fury. Later, they tried to kill each other in a frigid dockyard among giant shipping crates. The gospellers did not intervene. They simply watched everything, and recorded it.

James Banister and the Opium Khan lost their guns in the first exchanges, emptying the magazines and discarding them as useless junk, and then it was hand-to-hand. Shem Shem Tsien moved with a weird, loping step, spine slightly bent, and Edie realised he had scars on his back and could not straighten it. The fire, she thought, or the elephant. It did not change his speed, or his lethality. Remembering him in Addeh Sikkim, she judged it likely she would lose, and therefore die.

On the other hand . . . Edie grinned tautly, recalling Mrs. Sekuni: *Cheat, Edie. Cheating is much better than skill. Great skill improves your chances. Great cheating guarantees victory, which is why it is called cheating. And some people are so horrified by it that it is an advantage in itself.*

"You've picked up a rummy habit," James Banister said cordially as they approached one another. "Sort of a crouch. You look a bit . . . well, I'm sorry, but you look a bit Victor Hugo, if you catch my drift. Would you like to adjourn to a cathedral or something?"

"By all means, Commander, do amuse yourself while you can. I owe these scars to you, after all. You should get some satisfaction from them. Although I am depressed to see such a dear enemy giggling like a girl at a soldier's wounds."

Gotcha, Edie thought. *Of course.*

"Shem Shem Tsien," she told the Opium Khan in her own voice, "I laugh because I am tired of you. I cannot imagine that you aren't bored with yourself. There's very little about this which is clever or funny. With all that's going on in the world, with all that is possible and wonderful, this is what you do. You're a sideshow. A hack. A waste of time." His eyes bulged in absolute, stunned fury. Edie unbuttoned her shirt and opened it, baring a proud—if slight and somewhat foxed—bosom to his view.

Shem Shem Tsien himself was silent with what Edie took to be actual amazement. When he spoke, it was with a genuine, unaffected truthfulness. *First real moment of communication we've ever had*, Edie thought.

"Oh," the Opium Khan said. "I honestly had no idea." Then he swung at her, not to kill but to erase, and they were back on familiar ground.

She taunted him, drew him out into the open, keeping the wind at her back. It cut through her jacket and made her shiver, but it was in his eyes, and the ice on the ground made the fight a matter of footwear as much as skill. Edie was wearing steel toe–capped boots with discreet metal studs, the better to emphasise her masculinity and conceal her relatively small feet, and also because she liked unfair advantages. The Opium Khan, fresh from the gambling tables, wore dinner shoes. She attacked, and he slid towards her with that familiar ghastly smoothness, then lost his grip, skittering and sliding on the frozen stones while he wrenched his upper body around to guard against her. She threw a rusted iron chain at him, then followed it to drive her forehead into his face and grapple with him as bluntly and brutally as she knew how. Shem Shem Tsien, with his nose squashed to one side and his fine moustache clogged with blood, looked quite amazed. Edie took advantage of his hesitation and applied Mrs. Sekuni's sixth wrist-lock, a working man's pugilism which lacked elegance but got the job done, and cut off one of his fingers with his own knife. He lost the fight, but she couldn't bring him down, and he fled. Even so, Edie had the sense that Shem Shem Tsien was having fun. To her this was work, and very hard. He was playing out his passage to godhood, and he enjoyed hurting people.

In April the North Atlantic Treaty was signed, and Moscow fumed. Abel Jasmine moved Frankie's laboratory to the *Lovelace* and kept it moving, effectively making her disappear. Shem Shem Tsien faded away into Europe's shadows, one more hateful little bastard in a forest of them. Edie could almost hear him shouting "You haven't heard the last of me!" in the darkness of the winter sea.

And that much, at least, was certain. Nine years later, Edie stood on the lip of a chasm and stared downwards. She had battled with Shem Shem Tsien across the world, and it never changed or got any better. He did something awful, she went and tidied up; in Rome, in Kiev, in Havana. They fought on boats and in caves, on the roofs of houses and in alleyways. Sometimes one or other of them had an army, sometimes they were alone. It went on and on and it never settled anything. Shem Shem Tsien didn't change, didn't learn, did not accept that the new age had no space for him. Her body was a dictionary of woundings now, courtesy of his impossible speed, and she had learned to distract him, harry him, cheat him of her own death by guile. Once or twice, on good days, she had even survived him by skill. She tried not to think about how their addiction to this private, predictable conflict mirrored the ridiculous proxy wars the East and West were fighting with one another.

The wind brought the smell of sulphur and decay to her nostrils, and she gagged.

She was in Addeh Sikkim at the palace of the Opium Khan, except that the citadel was gone, replaced by a giant pit. The water which had powered Frankie's machines roiled in a simmering lake heated by the Earth, and the whole place was walled and scaffolded in black iron. A pit of industry. A birthplace of monsters. Edie wrapped herself in a local shawl and coat and staggered down with the other women who went to work in the pit. The long circumference road was punctuated with heads on poles. Some were human. Others were elephants, the flesh long gone and the pikes bowed beneath the weight of bone.

At the bottom, Shem Shem Tsien had made a sort of factory and mine combined. Vast presses turned out metal sheets and slaves worked them into parts for mechanical soldiers like the ones Frankie had made. In the very centre, beneath his tents, there was a ring where they were pitted against one another. They were clumsy and hopeless, the same awkward chessmen Edie had seen before, and when he wanted blood, the Opium Khan was obliged to hobble a prisoner or blind him so that the machines could get close enough to strike. And yet, they were improving. Fractionally, painfully, whatever pattern Frankie had created to guide them was refining itself, and when an automaton fell, the animating mechanism was recovered so that it would learn from defeat. Already, they followed his minions around like dogs, lunged at whatever the minion indicated. One day they would work, Edie thought, and hoped she never had to see it.

She took photographs and went to the embassy in Dhaka to report. She was walking to her hotel when Shem Shem Tsien's car pulled up next to her and the Opium Khan shot her twice in the gut.

"So nice to see you, Commander Banister," he drawled at her as she bled into the gutter. "I do hope your visit was satisfactory? Are you dying, do you think, or shall we meet again? I should miss our little chats."

She honestly did not know, and when her vision went grey at the edges and she felt cold, she was terribly, terribly afraid and alone. Shem Shem Tsien got back into his car and drove away, apparently content to leave the decision to Edie. She had no recollection, later, of the long crawl to the ambassador's residence which stripped the skin from her hands and knees.

Edie woke in a hospital bed, and the first thing she saw was Frankie. She thought Frankie was so beautiful, so perfect, that she started to cry. Frankie stroked her face and told her it was all going to be all right, and Edie wanted to say "I love you." But she fell asleep.

"Please do not do that again," Frankie said sternly when Edie woke, "this getting hurt. I do not appreciate it at all. I would not like it at all if you went away and did not come back."

Edie dutifully promised to try her best. Frankie growled that "try" was synonymous with "fail" and then—when Edie looked crestfallen—immediately apologised and embraced her, very carefully. Later, the nurse came, with a look of deep disapproval, to change Edie's bandages.

"Children will be more difficult," the nurse warned, "if that is a consideration. But not impossible, I don't think."

There were two red, round intrusions above Edie's hip.

"Now we both have scars," Frankie Fossoyeur murmured.

Yes. Frankie had old scars, had them when Edie first met her, and Edie had never asked how they came to be there and now barely saw them any more. Except . . . now that Edie saw them anew, she recognised them for what they were. She stared. Frankie gave a little sigh.

"Oh, dear."

"Frankie . . ."

"I was very young, Edie. I was in love. I was foolish and we were not careful. And yes, I had a child. Matthieu. And then . . . the occupation, the war. They were on the ship. You recall, we learned of it when I went home." The refugee ship. The one which sank.

"Frankie, I'm so sorry I never asked."

"And I am sorry I never told you." There was something else she wasn't saying, but Edie did not push.

Frankie didn't come to the hospital again. Edie couldn't understand why not, wished that she could hold her hand. She assumed that Frankie was afraid Edie would die, that she could not bear to see her so weak. Edie worried that she might indeed die, and then Frankie would feel guilty. She worried that Frankie not coming might make the difference, but it didn't. It just made her cry, alone. And now there was something else in her mind, something deeply unworthy and unkind and inescapable: Frankie had found someone else.

Edie didn't care if Frankie was screwing the entire Coldstream Guard, so long as she loved Edie. So long as she was there, in the world, with her ridiculous refinements of the teapot and her upholstery trousers and the way her hair always fell into her cup when she drank.

Edie went home, and found the flat empty. No Frankie. No pastel mathematics. It was cold and dark. She went to the *Lovelace*, to the strange carriage filled with coils and tanks and bubbling jars. It was empty, too. She called Amanda Baines, and found she was in dock and *Cuparah* beached for repairs, and Frankie nowhere to be seen. Finally, she went to the elephant house at London Zoo, where the only pachyderm servant of the British Government had a very special enclosure and a personal bath. She fed him bits of fruit and leaves and an occasional morsel of kelp for Auld Lang Syne, and wondered how much of it all he understood, and whether elephants gossiped.

Frankie came back just as Edie was heading out again on another mission, silent and obscure. She kissed Edie as if the world was ending and wept on her, then fled to the bedroom and they made love over and over and Frankie said she was sorry, so sorry, so sorry she hadn't come to the hospital. She would not say why, or where she had been. In the middle of the night, Edie woke to see her standing at the window, looking south.

"Where have you been?" Edie said at last, in the awful silence. "I needed you."

"Elsewhere, I was needed more," Frankie said. "I promise, Edie. It won't happen again."

But, of course, it did.

Edie told Abel Jasmine she couldn't do it any more, she needed to be at home. Abel Jasmine said he quite understood. The world was changing, anyway, and perhaps it was time for the new guard to have their day.

The new guard struck Edie as very efficient.

Frankie came and went, and Edie didn't know where to. In the end, she did the thing she had always promised herself she would never do: she spied. She saw Frankie take a taxi to a clockworker's shop in Quoyle Street, saw her greeted chastely by the little artisan, with his sad-looking bird's face and his open adoration. She sat on a bench in her daft, obvious disguise, furious that it had worked and more furious with Frankie for being so loving, so faithful, so true. This was not an affair. It was another life. There was no sex. This was so much worse.

A moment later, a boy—no, a young man, well-dressed and brimming with frantic energy—arrived on foot. As he rapped on the door he turned slightly towards her and Edie almost screamed at the sudden likeness. The artisan ushered him inside.

Frankie's son.

Edie was appalled at herself for intruding. She was furious with Frankie for everything. She stormed home and was even more furious when her attempt to conceal her rage was successful. Finally she packed her life into two small bags and left. Frankie wailed and howled. Edie snapped at her. Bad things were said. Unkind things. More unkind, because they were all true.

Edie took refuge in work, because work was a thing where you could lie, sneak, and hit people in the nose and it was considered laudable. She demanded and received her old job back. Since she was in that sort of mood, Abel Jasmine sent her to Iran, and Edie spied on Iranians. Tehran was a melting pot of intrigue; almost everyone there was a spy. On one occasion, she went to a clandestine meeting and realised that not only was no one in the room actually who they claimed to be, but in fact everyone was notionally representing their enemy. She got reckless and told them all, which was either very rude or very funny. There was a short, huffy silence in which gentlemen and ladies from various secret organisations sneered at one another, and then everyone got very drunk and they had a party. Edie woke up between an agent of the Mossad and a ravishing Soviet girl with bad skin on one cheek and a sailor's mouth.

Over breakfast—the young man from Mossad was still in the shower—the Soviet girl told Edie that the KGB had killed the Sekunis in Cuba. The girl didn't know why.

Edie hoped it was misinformation, but knew it wasn't. The world was getting old and cruel. The great game she had played, the wild, primary-colour roller coaster, had become something harsher. It wasn't brother monarchs scoring points any more, or empires testing one another, or *Vell played, Commander, but vee vill get you next time, you may be sure . . .* What difference does it make if one crowned head replaces another? What matter if the Queen's nephew displaces the Queen? But now it was different. It was about ideas, and fed by science. An idea could never die. A city, though, could burn, and its people.

Abel Jasmine called her back to Europe. She knew from the lack of detail that something was wrong. Something had happened, and it was bad.

"Is it him?" she asked. "Is it Shem Shem Tsien? Because this time I'll kill him, Abel. I don't care what it costs."

Abel Jasmine sighed. "Come home, Edie. I need you here."

She took a plane to Istanbul and then on to London, and when she got there she found herself going to Cornwall, and she knew it was worse than she had imagined because no one would tell her, and she gradually realised this was not secrecy or oversight, but fear. They didn't understand what was going on, and they were afraid. Which was when she knew, absolutely knew, that it was Frankie.

"The Engine," Abel Jasmine said, and that was all Edie needed to know. Frankie had tested the Engine, and she had somehow got it wrong. Or, more likely, too right.

"Get me to the *Lovelace*," she told the Wren in the front seat of her staff car. "Do you know what that is?"

"Yes," the girl said, and Edie realised that she was getting old, because the Wren looked too young to drive.

Edie sat in the front passenger seat and listened to the road surface change beneath the wheels. She recognised the route, knew where she was going. She forced her mind not to speculate on what she would find when she got there. When they crossed the Tamar and left the main road, it was the in-between hour, too late to be properly twilight but not yet full dark. The other woman's nervous chatter slowed as she concentrated on the turns and dips, and then stopped altogether when they reached the outer perimeter and were waved through. Ambulances rushed silently in the other direction. Edie had heard somewhere that when they didn't use the siren, it meant the patient was already dead.

There were soldiers along the road and soldiers in vans and soldiers standing guard over farmhouses and cottages: regular men, veterans who had seen service. They were grim and tired, and as the car wound through a tiny group of buildings on a hilltop—too large to be a farm and too small for a village—Edie saw a private vomiting into a ditch, and his mates holding him up. She'd seen British infantrymen make fun of one another during field amputations. None of them were smiling now.

The car slowed and Edie thought for a moment they'd arrived, but there was an obstruction in the road, a big, green-canvased transport. It had clipped the stone hedge on a turn and brought down a big block of granite. Three soldiers were levering it out of the way.

Edie watched. Inside the car, sound was muffled. She could hear the Wren breathing.

A moment later, something slammed wetly into the windscreen.

Edie lurched back in her seat, recoiling from a wide, gawping mouth which smeared across the glass. She saw a circle of red lips and a line of saliva, and she had her gun pointed directly into it before she realised that it belonged not to an escaped lion or a giant leech, but a bearded man in a blue Sunday-best jacket. The Wren had turned in her seat and was ready to slam the car backwards and away. She glanced across for instructions, and Edie held up her gun hand, palm out: wait.

The man licked and snuffled at the glass, tried to get a grip on it, and slid hopelessly down onto the ground. Behind him were two more figures, slack-jawed and moaning, slopping bonelessly out of the back of the transport. One clutched a knife and fork. A dinner party, Edie realised. They were dressed for dinner. The one with the cutlery sawed aimlessly at the air. The other stepped from one foot to another, a strange, heron's waddle: quick quick slow.

A sergeant appeared, spun the bearded man smartly around and folded his arms across his chest, bundled him into a bear hug and back into the transport. Two burly privates did the same with the others.

Edie called the sergeant over.

"How many like this?" she asked.

"Near on a thousand, but we won't rescue all of them," he said, looking right at her to make sure she understood. "About half of them are dead before we get there. Best we can figure is that they're all still doing whatever they were doing when it happened. Stuck in a groove. Mostly that's fine. Bloody awful, but fine. But then some . . . well. There's a cattle farm over Tregurnow way. The farmer was butchering some steers. Killed all of them before we got there. Went back to the farmhouse and just kept going." He trailed off, waiting to see if she needed him to explain. She didn't. "Is this a Russian thing, do you reckon? Is it war?"

"No," Edie said firmly. "No, this is an accident. Chemical spill from a container ship."

The sergeant scowled. "Well, I hope they hang for it."

Frankie. What have you done?

The *Lovelace* creaked to and fro in the darkness of Frankie's cavern, a tiny incremental rocking like a shudder, on axles not powered but not restrained. Every so often, Edie could hear something which might have been footsteps, and beneath them and the sound of nervous soldiers standing guard in a circle around the train, came a steady, cockroach rustling she could not name. At one end of the passenger section, a single light flicked on and off, on and off.

Songbird swore softly and crossed himself. Edie had never seen him do that before. In S2:A, very few men prayed; they'd seen too many stupid chances, for good or ill. The same unfamiliar itch was tickling Edie's fingers, a sense that this was too big to be her problem, too strange and desperate. *There must be someone above me to deal with this.* But that was the other thing you got used to in S2:A—the person who came along and took over when things were bad was you.

"Radio?" she asked.

Songbird's radio man, Jesper, shook his head. "More crackle than a pigling roast."

Abel Jasmine had told Edie, in London, that Frankie might still be inside the train. Was she dead, then? Or at her desk with wide eyes, like the farmers and fishermen Edie had seen?

Edie gestured to Songbird and to the others: wait. Songbird frowned and shook his head. *Coming in with you, Countess*, his face said. *All for one, ey?*

"Give me five minutes," Edie said. "Then follow, but follow soft, you understand, because those are ours there, whatever's happened."

Songbird looked stubborn. Edie sighed.

"Please," she said. "If Frankie's dead in there, I just want to be the one to find her." Although, until this moment, she had not allowed the thought to form in her mind.

Songbird scowled, but acquiesced. Edie turned and walked towards the train.

Edie stepped up onto the rearmost carriage. *Lovelace* had changed a bit since her time—new carriages added and others gone—but it was fundamentally the same train she had known: defiantly ornate, with the stamps of Ruskinite artisans pressed into the iron. Entering, she let the door spring shut against her back and push her gently in, so that it would make no noise in closing. The solid pressure reassured her, and then an instant later she felt a wild claustrophobia, a deep desire to go no further.

No time for that now.

Inside, the carriage was only partly lit, the curtains closed and keeping out the light from the big siege lamps outside. Tiger stripes fell across one of the *Lovelace's* communal spaces, a smoking room. Edie was about to move forward when a faint breath stopped her, a tiny puff of moving air. It smelled of laundry. She folded herself into a low crouch and slid smoothly away, finding her own patch of darkness. She peered around, but her eyes were still adjusting. A crawling sensation whispered along her spine. *I am in a room with a dead man walking.*

Unfair thought. Irrational. If there was a man in here, he was not a monster, he was a victim. *Unless he was eating when it happened. Then perhaps he is both.* She was sure it was a man, without knowing why. Scent, perhaps. The length of a stride she couldn't hear, the weight of a person she could not feel. She just knew, as meat knows salt.

There was a game she used to play with the Sekunis, a training game in the dark. Feel your way. Know your body, your space. In the dark, she would take a guard, and in the dark, they would attack her. The key was not to expect anything, not to look for anything. You moved, you waited, you acted only when you knew.

She dropped her centre and relaxed her body, and waited.

He appeared in front of her as if stepping from behind a curtain. He must have been curled up on one of the seats. One hand reached out to embrace her, or to tear at her, or to take her gun from its holster at her side. She didn't know. She slipped beneath the hand and laid her arm across his chest, twisting around her own centre and sweeping his leg. *O soto gari*, firm but not murderous. She followed him down and barred the arm as he tried to continue the motion.

Was he shaking hands? Opening a door?

Abruptly, he bucked, and she heard the shoulder pop, felt the bone shift under the skin. He twisted against the joint, destroying it, and when she saw his face she was so shocked she nearly let go of him. The look of emptiness was gone, replaced by an appallingly focused fury. His head lunged at her like a striking heron, snarling and snapping. He bridged, more vital components snapping in the arm, and she relinquished her lock as she realised it was useless on a man who didn't care how badly he was hurt.

She backed away. She didn't want to use the gun, because she had no idea how the other people in here—there were more, she was sure—would respond to a sudden noise. They might ignore it. Or they might converge on it and stare at her. Or they might suddenly try to tear her apart. There was no evidence for that. There was no evidence of any kind, just Frankie inside, in the furthest carriage, the innermost keep of the *Lovelace*.

The man lurched upright and fell towards her, and she dodged. He lunged again, and this time she stepped in and wheeled him over her back, claiming a leg and twisting it hard as he went down. The knee dislocated. It might not knit properly, after this. He might walk with a limp. But she hadn't shot him, and that was worth something, although she doubted in her heart he would ever be anything more than he was now, a man reduced to the level of a shark.

She watched him try to get up and fail, then lose interest in her altogether. A moment later she heard a strange, wrenching noise, and turned to see that he was swallowing the fingers of his useless arm.

Edie retched, recovered, and then lost control of her stomach again, emptying it into a corner bin. Then she wiped her mouth on a hand-woven curtain and moved on.

In the connecting section between carriages was an alcove with a wind-up lantern. It would make light. It would also make her a target. She considered, then took it down and cranked the handle. Better to see what was going on than miss an ambush, whether intended as such or not.

She opened the door and shone the lantern into the next compartment. It was a dormitory, with berths on alternate sides of the carriage to make a sense of privacy and to block enfilading fire. She listened, and knew that it was full.

Edie rounded the first bend and found a Ruskinite and two soldiers, all vacant and still. She shone her lantern directly upon the face of the nearest, and watched his pupils contract. He showed no other sign of having noticed, just stood, loosely. She was walking past him, looking full into his face, when he spoke.

"I think you'll find—" He seemed to have more to say, but somehow he didn't. He just stopped.

"I think you'll find—"

She stepped back.

"I think you'll find—"

That same intonation, over and over. A recording. Or rather, all that was left of the man. A trace of him, the rest obliterated. She heard a sigh, and turned sharply, gun pointed at the next man, but it wasn't an expression of anything, just a noise made by air in his lungs when he moved.

Edie surveyed them all, and they watched her in return. They were not curious, but they watched all the same, endlessly. There was an African word she had heard from Songbird when she arrived: *zumbi*. A corpse which hasn't the decency to lie down. You have to tie his jaw shut so he doesn't speak. (Back down the corridor the man said: "I think you'll find—")

"Hello?"

Edie turned sharply and raised her gun. The man flinched. He was young, in his thirties, and stout. A hamsterish sort of fellow in a robe. A Ruskinite. She was so glad to see him, alive, in here, that she almost hugged him. Instead, she growled: "Who are you?"

Her gun was still pointed at his head.

"Sholt," he said. "Call me Ted. I came this morning."

He was holding a glass. She realised after a moment that it had milk in it, that his chest was covered in splatter and what might be milky vomit.

"Don't corner them," Ted Sholt said, "and don't put them in a position where they cannot possibly do whatever they seem to be doing. That makes them . . ." He glanced up, saw her face. "Oh. You know that."

"Yes."

"What . . . did you have to . . ." He was asking her if she had killed one of his friends.

"No," Edie said, and they shared a moment of stark understanding: *not that it will probably make a great deal of difference.*

One of the *zumbi* brushed past, very close, and she jerked away. He pursued, brushing against her. She turned. He turned, too, slack-jawed face following her own like a reflection. She bobbed. He bobbed. When she straightened, so did he, and when she stopped still, he did too. She turned, walked straight ahead, and he stopped, his path blocked by a chair. He stood still, hips resting against the chair's back, making no effort to sidestep, as if the concept was far beyond him.

"I've been trying to feed them," Sholt said, following her gaze. "They don't swallow. You can make them, but it just comes back up

again. I'm not sure why they're still breathing. I'd have thought . . ."
He stopped. She looked at him again, seeing him properly for the first
time. He must have come in here in spite of—no, because of—what
had happened. No gun, and no lantern. Just a bottle of milk and a lot
of faith, or maybe this counted as charity.

Plucky little hamster.

"I'm Edie."

He nodded. "Hello."

"Have you been in?" She gestured up the line of carriages towards
Abel Jasmine's office.

"No," Ted Sholt said. He raised the milk, lowered it again. Edie
saw him for a moment in her mind, patiently pouring the stuff into
the mouths of men he knew, even loved, and having them gargle at
him, or choke, or let the milk trickle out down their chins.

They moved on. Corridor. Living spaces. Galley kitchen.

And then the Code Room—where Edie worked before the night
of Clarissa Foxglove and the great train burglary.

Ted Sholt made a little noise of grief.

There were Ruskinites in the Code Room, or men and women
who had been Ruskinites. Edie recognised a boy named Paul, a glass-
blower. He had made a set of wine glasses for her and Frankie a year
ago, beautiful things. He was lying on the ground, staring at the ceiling. She waved her hand in front of his face.

"Glah," he said. When she did it again, he repeated the one word,
with exactly the same intonation, and she thought for a moment he
was alive, still in residence, still Paul, but it was the only response she
could get from him. *Glah, glah, glah, glah* . . . She had a moment of
horror when she thought he was never going to stop, that the eerie, sad
little noise would follow her through the train, but when he had said
it exactly as many times as she had moved her hand across his vision,
he stopped.

Edie moved on. *Frankie, I love you. Please don't say "glah."*

At the door to the room which was apparently Frankie's laboratory,
she found two Ruskinites and a crowd of soldiers, and a woman from
the support staff. They were moving forward, bouncing gently off the
wall, then moving forward again, as if the architecture of the train
might somehow be worn away by their repeated attempts. As they
walked, they rose and fell slightly, and Edie realised after a moment
that they were standing on another man, or his corpse, because he had

been slowly flattened and pulped by the footfalls. As she drew closer, she realised that he had not actually died yet. Nor was he trying to scream; whatever had happened had removed even his sense of his own shattering.

Problem: this was the only door.

Problem: these lost ones were in the way and would crush fellow humans who intervened between them and their objective.

Problem: Edie needed to be on the other side of this wall, and not admit the crowd to Frankie's laboratory.

And then someone grabbed her by the neck and hit her with something, and she saw stars and Ted Sholt rammed against the window, and then the same someone started choking her.

No time. Her assailant was killing her. Strangulation is fast. Her vision was brown already.

She moved.

Drop your weight. Never mind that it constricts your breathing. You can't breathe anyway. Find your base, your connection to the ground. Yes, there. Now: snuggle closer to your attacker. Lock his arm where it is. Grab him by the elbow and bicep and twist your whole body, pivot on your feet. Ninety degrees, more, away from that bicep. Project your hands forward, as if you were pushing a grand piano with the heels of your hands.

Tai Otoshi.

It was like *Yama Arashi*, but for stranglers.

A man flew over her hip into the desk. He reared up, bloody-faced. *There is no compromise in this fight. No pain, no retreat.* Edie twisted with his movement and out of the line of his attack, then scooped his neck in a fluid circle and dropped him on his back across the sharp edge of the mahogany veneer. She hoped it would paralyse him for a few seconds, but he was heavier than she had realised and she heard a sharp snap. *Iriminage*, but she hadn't meant to kill him. She peered down at the slack face, and recognised it.

Denis. Frankie's assistant in Addeh Sikkim. Big, friendly, patient Denis.

After a moment, Edie said "Shit." It came out croaky and loud. And then hated herself. And then hated herself more, because, as she started to say there was no other way, she realised that there was, had always been.

I knew the trick to this one when I was a wee slip of a girl.

She checked on Sholt and found he was conscious, but his collarbone was broken on the left side. She moved him gently back into the previous carriage and told him to stay put, then levered herself up and out, through the skylight, and onto the roof of the train.

It was warm up on the roof, and pleasantly calm. Abruptly, she didn't want to go back inside. Actually, she wanted desperately *not* to go back inside. But down at the rear of the train she could see her soldiers. Songbird looked up, hope in his face. Edie sighed.

Yes, of course. He—and the others—needed her to fix all this. Not to be afraid or confused or alarmed. *The Bloody Countess never wavers, ey.*

She moved forward, and lowered herself through the ventilation panel into the laboratory carriage, holding her breath and praying.

Frankie's laboratory was empty. In the middle of the room there was a plinth, and on it was a gutted shell of Frankie's strange making, a Ruskinite casing for a Hakote device. There was nothing inside. Coils of cable hung from the ceiling to the plinth, messy and typically Frankie. The room was calm, and clean.

Edie searched methodically, and tried not to rush. She looked under tables and in cupboards, opening each one with a horrid anticipation of finding Frankie standing inside. A stack of pencils fell on her and she screamed sharply, then threw them with considerable force across the room, her fear changing its face: what if Frankie was *not* here? If she was not in the lab, then where? Gone, wandering, mindless in the night? Eating the dead outside? Or taken? Was this a kidnapping, rather than an accident? Edie knew of someone who would consider a thousand murdered a good diversion.

She turned, and found her answer: a single word written in chalk on the blackboard: *Edie!* And underneath, a note, folded neatly. The handwriting was Frankie's.

Edie grabbed the note and ripped it open.

Edie. I know they will send you. I know that you will come and see what is here and I am sorry. No one should see this.

You will need to know that I have done this. It is not a trick or a trap. It is not Shem Shem Tsien or the Russians or anyone else. It is just me, and I am a prideful idiot. I am alive. In the heart of the storm, there was a safe place, where the field was not projected so strongly. I saw what was happening and I knew, my Hakote eyes could see, and I stood there to preserve myself. I tried to keep Denis with me, but the penumbra took him. I think he was angry with me.

It began with truth, which was splendid. It was a gentle thing. We asked one another questions and congratulated each other on the rightness of the answers. We played with lies, telling outrageous ones and then subtler ones and taking joy in seeing—though it was not actually like sight, more like touch—that those lies were not in accordance with the objective universe.

Sometimes it was sobering, inside one's head. I understand that I have treated you poorly. I know exactly how poorly. We cried, all of us, for a while, and then we confessed our sins. They were not so many, nor so exciting. We shared forgiveness, and knew that was real, too. I thought I had achieved everything I had set out to do.

And in the moment of thinking it, I knew that I was wrong. So wrong. The machine was too powerful. We had only to look at one another to see not only truths but outcomes of our future interactions. We had only to consider something in the wider world to know about it. Most of them, Edie, they lacked the background to understand, but I saw the mathematics rolling out in front of me and I knew, immediately, what was coming—my knowing and what was gifted to me by the machine ran together, each trying to outpace the other. I cried out, told them all to leave, but they were raptured by the Engine. The second stage, Edie. Knowledge.

I grabbed Denis and I ran for the place in front of the machine which was clear of its function, but he shrugged me off. He shouted that I was a fool, that I had killed them all, and when he said it there was one of those awful silences and they all heard and knew, knew it was true. In that moment, each and every one of them knew that death was inevitable. And worse, Edie. They knew what death was. I have never heard such screams. I did not see death, Edie. I was in the eye of the storm. I went to switch off the machine, but it was too late.

Too late. The third stage began. They began to know everything. The air was thick. Everything seemed to become solid around me, safe in my little cocoon of life. I watched the world around me become sterile. Devoid of life. And yet they did not fall. Their bodies continued.

Denis was right, Edie. I was careless. I must spread the load— but that is enough. I will not tell my secrets now. The government will want this, as a weapon, and they cannot have it. It is so much more awful than it seems.

Have my people taken care of, please. They deserve that much.

They have died for their country, or their God. But do not misunderstand: they will not recover. I have killed them.

I have taken the heart of the machine. I will carry on my work one way and another. And Edie, there is one other thing also which I realise now, as I picture you standing, reading this, shaking your head at my foolishness and still so glad that I am safe, even in the face of this horror that I have made. I have taken the heart of the machine, but I have left my own behind.

You are my heart, Edie. Always, you.

Edie stood in Frankie's lab for ten minutes and stared at the empty plinth. She looked up, and realised that Frankie must have gone out the same way she came in. How many hours? Ten? Twelve? Frankie was doing a flat drop. She would take what she had and run. She might have a bag somewhere, or she might not, but she was gone as best she knew how.

Edie gathered the papers, the victims, and hid them away. She hid the *Lovelace*. She mothballed her only real home. Because it was her job. Because she believed more than ever that the world didn't need Frankie's machine or Frankie's desperate conviction or anything of Frankie except her silence. Build a better mousetrap. Fix the mill wheel before it breaks. Leave the bloody secrets of the universe alone.

"Bring her home, Edie," Abel Jasmine said in Whitehall. "If someone else gets hold of her, they might force her to . . . well. Bring her home."

Edie went.

She traced Frankie to Salzburg, then Budapest, then Delhi and Beijing, then back again. Frankie was a genius. She had a way of distracting you. People saw curious machines and worried about them. They celebrated breakthroughs in mathematics made by obscure, hard-working local academics who had had a random conversation with a slender, bookish woman in a café or a bar. They got stock tips derived from some strange, inspired formula, made a fortune and went on holiday. Frankie herself, with a schoolmistress's bag in one hand and the secrets of the universe in her head, leaving a trail of brilliant, cometary solutions to impossible problems, was weirdly invisible. All the same, you could find her from time to time, if you knew how. Edie could. Shem Shem Tsien could.

They played cat and mouse—or cat and mouse and dog, perhaps—from one corner of the world to another. It got to be a bad joke among the intelligence services of thirty countries. Where one went, so also the other two, and mayhem and bombs and guns inevitably followed. They fought, they fled, they raged, and nothing changed. It was as if the world was elastic, and always returned to the same rotten, stupid shape.

To this day, Edie has no idea where or when Frankie died, only that she must have, because at last she truly wasn't there any longer.

On the bus, Edie cries dry tears and silently tells Frankie she is sorry for waiting so long to change everything. From the ugly handbag comes a consoling nose. She laughs. Yes. Whatever else, Bastion is for ever.

He arrived very small and badly injured, late on a September evening. He had marbles instead of eyes and a vague, confused expression of discontent. *A stray*, Edie thought, *of course*. Frankie could never resist such a thing. And with the dog, a last letter.

Edie tipped the waiting cabman and carried the whole package indoors. She knew she should call Abel Jasmine, or rather, whoever had taken over his job. But by then she had persuaded herself she no longer cared, and for sure she no longer trusted anything to do with governments.

Dearest Edie,
Please look after this one. He has a hero's heart, for he was raised among elephants from Addeh Sikkim, and all his brothers and sisters were casualties of Shem Shem Tsien's most recent monstrousness. I have done what I can for him. He reminds me a little of you. He does not know when to give up. He loves hugely and imprudently and his forgiveness inspires awe in me, as does your own.

When I saw Mathew in the street with Daniel the first time, I thought I had gone mad. I saw with my own eyes their deaths listed on the municipal noticeboard. Daniel told me they escaped and came to England, but he thought I was dead.

I do not love him. I do not know my son. But their existence has changed everything in me and now I understand what I must do. Do you remember Germany?

I should have understood then, but I had you, and I had no son. I should have understood when England ignored Hungary's pain in '56 or Prague's in '68. I should have seen it in Vietnam and in Hiroshima. We can land on the Moon, Edie. We cannot be good. We are wicked. This is a wicked world. There are islands of joy, but they are small and the tide is rising, and even on dry land there are those who would embrace the tide. It cannot be. Not any more.

It cannot stand. The world must change. We must change.

I will make us change. My book will be written in words which cannot be ignored. A veritable Hakote book, a book of mathematics and revolution against the nature of man. I mean to publish it very soon now.

And if I do not, there is another way. I have made a copy of the book and of the calibration drum, Edie. The book alone will only begin the process as I have arranged it. I have sent it to that funny little museum, with a bequest so that they will not discard it. If my copy is lost, that is where you must start. But Edie, this is vital: if ever there is a reason to change the settings of the Engine—I cannot think what it would be—you will need the calibration drum. I have given it to the only other person I trust. He will hide it, Edie, but if you ever need it he knows to give it to you. If I am prevented in my purpose, go to Wistithiel, put things in motion. Change the world for me.

I love you for ever. I am sorry I cannot love you now.

Frankie

With decades between her and Frankie's confessional letter, Edie alights from the single-decker bus and clutches her bag like a woman who fears the temporal world for its sin and iniquity. She wanders as if aimless or bewildered, and her long, roundabout route brings her by happy coincidence to a convent on a dull, dreary street, where Sister Harriet Spork keeps her vigil for a life lived in wickedness.

Edie sits on a public bench and feeds the pigeons. She sits for an hour, with a Bible propped against her hip in case anyone comes, and watches and waits. And finally, her patience is rewarded. Not Joe Spork, whose approach she suspects will be less direct, but a long black car with tinted windows. Edie peers myopically at a seagull, and gets up to shoo it away from her breadcrumbs. She waggles her hands vaguely at the bird, and it glowers murderously before taking wing. Her return path brings her into the orbit of the car, and she glances in to see a robed, shrouded figure at the wheel and another in the second seat, whose stooping, hesitant motions she finds nauseatingly familiar: quick quick slow. And then she looks into the back and sees the passenger as a car, passing in the other direction, illuminates his shrouded head from the side, and his profile is briefly visible beneath the veil.

Edie stares. Belatedly, she hides her face, panic and outrage rising inside her.

Impossible!

But Edie no longer uses that word, having long ago learned its worth.

XII

Nzzzzzeeeeyaoooooowwww;
not strictly a nun;
taken.

Mercer Cradle stands in his sister's living room with a vastly valuable and possibly insanely dangerous gold bee in one hand and makes zooming noises. It is the defective bee Joe was given by Ted Sholt, of course, the others being out and about causing consternation in the wider world. Mercer is holding the thing between thumb and forefinger and trying to persuade it, by means of demonstration and sound effects and occasional words of encouragement, to take wing.

Mercer did not begin this scientific experiment immediately upon viewing the small collection of trophies which Joe and his sister brought back from the riverside storeroom. His initial position was that the bee should be imprisoned and X-rayed, MRI'd and electron-microscoped, until it yielded whatever alarming secrets it possessed. Joe Spork observed that these options required equipment they did not have and Polly Cradle speculated that attacking the entity might provoke it, whereupon Mercer adopted a strategy of aloof watchfulness in which Joe was permitted to examine the patient while Mercer loomed nearby with a lump hammer—a sort of short sledge—which Polly had formerly used to drive the iron pilings into the walls of her house.

When the bee remained quiescent and indeed rather boringly inert, Mercer became less cautious. His first approach was a very tentative poke, administered with a pencil held at arm's length, in case the bee should turn into an evil machine of death before his eyes. When this elicited no reaction, he nudged it solidly with the blunt end, and it fell over. He blew on it. He shouted at it, coaxed it, wheedled it and scolded it. Finally, he touched it with his index finger, and when he remained unexploded and unzombified, he picked it up and shook it. Joe was moved to protest that it was delicate, and Mercer agreed not to stand on it or throw it at the wall, but refused to hand it over to Joe for closer inspection using his jeweller's loupe. It was at this point that Mercer began his attempt to educate the bee by example, and Polly Cradle, who had appeared on the brink of objecting that Joe was the expert in curious automata, was apparently stunned into silence by the image of her brother spinning in place with the bee on his outstretched palm and making buzzing noises.

"Nzzzzzeeeeyaoooooowwww!" Mercer concludes excitedly, and stares at the bee with the hopeful pride of a new father. There is a faint sound of someone sneezing from the street outside, and the skitter of leaves on the paving in the little courtyard garden beyond the patio door.

"It's broken," Mercer concludes. He glances at Joe Spork. "You broke it."

"I broke it?"

"Probably. Maybe it was the damp. Or it's bust a spring. Or you got fluff in the wind-y parts."

"Fluff."

"Yes. Lint. Pocket funk."

"In the . . ."

"Wind-y. The parts that wind."

"Those parts."

"Yes. Which I imagine are susceptible to lint."

Joe is about to explain that any item which can remain functional for forty years by the seaside, which is made furthermore of gold, and which is purportedly an engine of revolutionary change constructed on the principles of arcane mathematics, ought to be immune to lint. But, in fact, the use of gold in the production might be an attempt to avoid rust and oxidisation, and any machine can be gummed up with goo. So instead of saying "You're a pillock," which uncharitable assessment had been on his lips, he says instead "Give it to me," and sits in the lightest corner of the room with his loupe and his tool bag. A moment later, he opens the bag, and uses a set of padded measuring calipers usually reserved for the interior of watches costing more than the average flat in London to tug at the gemmed wing-cases of the bee.

The cases lift, revealing splendid, gossamer wings beneath. Gossamer, but very strong. The thin stuff gouges a tiny scratch in the edge of the calipers when his hand shakes.

Note to self: *Pointy. Do not cut your fingertip off.*

Although in fact the wings are made carefully. It's hard to expose the edge in a way which would let you do yourself an injury. A momentary vision of flying razorbees fades away.

The saddle of the bee comes away, wings and all, revealing an inner cavity. Even through the loupe, he can barely make out the parts. Cogs, yes. Springs. Everything spiralling downward, inward, smaller and smaller and smaller, each layer geared to take instruction from the one below in a repeating pattern. Cellular clockwork? *Fractal* clockwork?

One thing is certain: he can't fix this. It's absolutely beyond him, and beyond Daniel too, without question. And yet . . . oh. There is something. A change in style where the impossible meets the merely brilliant. Yes. The layer which is humanly imaginable was made by hand, and from the shape of the works and the way in which they are arranged, it could be Daniel's: it has his finicky preference, his bullish allegiance to the leaf spring and the conventional metals of his time. Below that layer, it's a different matter, a thing of physics. Mathematics made real. But there at the join, there is . . . something. The central driveshaft is too thick . . . oh. Mercer is actually right. There's a foreign object. Too thin to be an eyelash, and too supple . . . a single strand of silk. It could actually be a cobweb, wrapped around the spindle. But how to remove it?

He ponders, then laughs, and stands up.

"What?" Mercer asks.

Joe scuffs his feet back and forth vigorously across Polly's carpet. "It's clockwork," he explains. "It's not electrical. At least, I don't think it's electrical." He grins, and leans down with the loupe, extending his finger to a quarter-inch away from the bee. Through the lens, he can see the thread stand to attention, the static charge from his finger plucking at it. Fatal to electronics. Fine for clockwork.

He waves his finger one way, then the other, and it unravels a bit. He tries again, and then it flies to his fingertip and away. He catches his breath. The bee doesn't move.

Slowly, he puts everything back in place, layer after layer and then the wings and the cases, and finally sets the bee down on the table.

"Well," Mercer says after a moment, "I suppose we are no worse off than we were before."

After a moment, they leave the bee where it is, and turn to the record collection, and the small portable gramophone known as a Piglet.

The little machine does indeed make a soft whiffling noise when Joe Spork turns the crank, and then a sort of grating *roink* when he gets to the stop point of the spring. He puts the first record on the turntable and a fresh needle in the clamp, and lowers the arm.

The ghost voice speaks again, scratching down through decades, musing and melancholic. His grandmother. His blood. It's not even a letter, this one. Joe Spork wonders whether she had a recorder of her own. Perhaps Daniel made her one. He pictures her alone at her desk, and his imagination inserts, of all things, an inkwell in front of her and an actual quill in her hand, because all this was such a long time ago. She clears her throat, and speaks.

You said once I knew nothing of the real world, and I replied that you had it exactly backwards. Only mathematicians know the world for what it is. I can see you, waving your hands and shaking your head, Daniel, but it is true. I will prove it to you.

Suppose that you take two clocks, and you place one upon a pedestal in your house and put the other on board a rocket and fire it around the Earth. When the rocket lands, the two clocks will tell different times. Why? Because the clock in the rocket has been closer to the speed of light and less time has passed on the rocket than in your office. That is the least strange thing about the universe, Daniel: that time, which appears most absolute to human beings, is nothing of the kind. It is relative.

Do you still not see what I mean? Very well, then consider a cat in a box with a bottle of poison. At any moment, the bottle may open, or it may not. At any moment, the cat may die. Now: take two pictures, one after another, of what is in the box. Look at the second one first. At that moment, the observation determines what is in the first picture, and what happened to the cat. From our point of view, the information flows backwards through time. This is not a joke or a romance, Daniel. It is quite simply the way of things. The universe is undecided without us—and our minds are part of what exists at some level we do not yet begin to understand.

That is the true nature of the world we inhabit. Not the easy one we mostly encounter. Anyone who tells you otherwise is living in a dream.

The record comes to a stop, the needle looping around the inner ring in an uneven swirl.

Joe leans back as Frankie's record comes to an end, and looks around. Mercer Cradle is seated on the floor, Buddha-like and unexpectedly limber, a cross-legged legal statue cut from the stone with his eyes closed in thought. The Bethanys have taken up flanking positions on the sofa behind him, slightly fidgety because they were unable to force him into a comfortable chair and they feel strange about sitting above their boss. Polly sits next to Joe, and has a single sheet of paper on a glass clipboard, ready to take notes in soft pencil.

"Next one," Mercer says quietly, before Joe can wonder aloud whether there is anything here of value.

It is Polly who picks the next record, and this time, the voice is not dissociated or melancholic, but desperate with pain and horror.

They are all dead, and I killed them. I am a murderer now! Yes, I am. Don't say it is not my fault. I built the machine, oh, with such great intentions. I was saving us all! But I got something wrong, Daniel. Me. I got something wrong, the train stopped at Wistithiel and they are dead, and worse than dead, and I have no idea why I am alive, and I should not be, and Edie came to save me.

I want to believe it was him. Shem Shem Tsien, like an old, bad dream, breaking my machines and pushing buttons. But he was not here, Daniel. I did this all by myself. I killed a multitude, and now they will close me down and the engine will never exist unless I can find a way alone.

I do not want to be alone, Daniel. I am sending you something. You must seal it away. No one must see it, because it is death; death such as no one has ever died until I came along. Death by destiny, by crystallisation, by inevitability. I killed their souls and left their bodies alive. In the history of human life, there has never been anyone so dead as they are.

I am the greatest murderer there has ever been.

And then she cries until the message comes to an end.

Almost unwillingly, Mercer turns the record over. *Crackle, pop. Fizzle, splot. Crackle, pop.* After the savage horror of the confession, it is almost soothing. They listen for a while. Finally, Mercer scoops another from the bag and sets it on the turntable. The voice is older, and mercifully the horror is absent, though in its place is a soul-deep regret, a sorrow which has weathered in and will never leave.

I confess, I thought you were an idiot. Yes, Daniel, I know, you have never given me cause and I am an impatient old baggage. I am what I am, and what life has made me. I try to be better.

You were right. I made the machine strong so that it would cover a larger area and that made it too strong for the mind.

Pause.

I know the solution, now. How to make it work. I knew even while it was happening, but it was too late. The answer is to retransmit. To have a great network, so that the signal can be very gentle and yet reach around the world.

Do you remember that we made love in the field outside my mother's house? And you were stung on the rump by a bee and mourned for her because you said bees were creatures of creation, and having only one sting were loath to attack? That this was why almost every culture in the world venerates the bee and hates the wasp?

Make me a bee, Daniel. Just one. Make me a glorious bee which people will love, and I will make something wonderful. Bees will be the messengers of my truth. They will spread across the world and connect everyone.

Make it splendid, Daniel. Make it wild and pretty. The thing I do now must be so much more than a machine.

Polly Cradle is grinning, and so is Joe. Mercer frowns at them both. "What?" he says. "Don't tell me it's just that they were still in love. I shall be sick."

"No," Polly says. "I was just thinking: maybe this isn't a disaster. The bees. The machine. Maybe it's a good thing that's happening, and all we have to do is wait."

Joe nods. Mercer does not. He opens his mouth to make some objection, but then three things happen on top of one another and whatever it was he was going to say is put aside.

The first thing is that the absent Bethany returns and passes a slim folder to Polly Cradle, who frowns at it and then lays it out on the table.

Two photographs, freshly printed from old images, most likely magazines or newspapers: a gorgeous matinée idol with a high forehead, smiling lightly into the camera, and his older brother, grim-faced and silvered, scowling from the hood of a cloak.

"Shem Shem Tsien," Polly Cradle says, "also known as the Opium Khan. Think Idi Amin with a dash of Lex Luthor. And this Brother Sheamus of the Order of John the Maker. This is a picture of him from before they all started wearing veils all the time."

Yes. The same man. Although . . . it can't actually be the same Sheamus, now. A son, surely, taking up his father's vocation.

I thought I had it rough, father-wise.

And then:

Does that mean the Opium Khan has reformed, or that the British government has been corrupted?

But while that's a question which might have made sense a few years ago, no one seriously believes in the good conduct of their leaders any more.

Just as he is about to share this with the others, the second and third things happen, and the world changes.

One is silent and invisible; an intangible explosion which occurs entirely inside the head of Joshua Joseph Spork. The other is very public and very specific, and takes place three and one-half feet off the ground. They happen at approximately the same time, and so the strange, inaudible detonation which afflicts Joe is missed even by Polly Cradle, who otherwise would spot it clearly for what it is.

Between two records—one claiming mendaciously to be by Duke Ellington and the other labelled with equal falseness as being by Eddie Lockjaw Davis—is sandwiched a single sheet of shiny accounting paper, split down the middle into two columns with a single sure stroke of red pen. It has no timer, no spring, and no pineapple indentations which will fly off as shrapnel, and in fact looks almost exactly not like a hand grenade, and yet all the same it goes off under Joe Spork and vaporises him entirely.

Joe Spork, the exploded man, cannot understand why everyone is looking so calm, until he realises that none of them, not knowing Mathew and Daniel and their appalling confrontations, can understand the columns of figures for what they are.

Here, squeezed between the secrets of Daniel's non-jazz collection, is something the old man squirrelled away. Something he couldn't face? Or something he treasured and understood, which brought him some measure of peace?

If these numbers are to be believed, if Joe correctly interprets the figures in Mathew's own somewhat careless hand—and he surely does, having struggled himself for a decade against the same rip tide— Daniel Spork's great, stand-alone, splendid business of clocks, the bulwark he set against the surge of modernity and careless consumerist tat, lost money hand over fist. The shop was not, had never been, profitable. Only the ceaseless intravenous transfusions of money from Mathew, evidenced here on this hastily scribbled account, ever made it possible to balance the books. And these transfusions Mathew had managed as best he could in conditions of total secrecy, above all from his father, so that Daniel could continue to believe in his straight-arrow path and continue to deride his son's choices.

Mathew the gangster, Mathew the liar, Mathew the thief, had begun his life of crime to save his father's honest business. Had carried it, all along.

Joe is still staring at this earth-shaker, this profound and alien intrusion into his universe from another where everything is different, when he hears Mercer's voice calling to him through the fog and the final event changes the game once more.

"Hey, sleepyhead!" Joe turns, and Mercer tosses him the golden bee. "It's warm!"

Joe extends his hand, but—he has never been any good at catching, kicking was always his thing—fumbles the take. He drops instinctively to catch the bee before it hits the ground, and misses again.

Misses, because it is not falling.

Six inches from his cheek, the multifaceted rose-quartz eyes glint at him, and gold-veined wings hum in the air. It flitters towards him very slowly, and lands on his nose. Joe tries to look at it, winces as he inevitably crosses his eyes. He swears he can hear the whisper of golden legs as it moves onto his cheek. *Am I in danger?* And if he is, what can he possibly do about it?

The bee drops back into the air and lands on the tabletop again, where it wanders bee-ishly around in a random pattern.

Apis mechanica. Live and in person. He watches it without thinking about it, because all of his mind is burning with Mathew and Daniel, and the sense that he has misunderstood everything he has ever known to be true.

A moment later, the bee takes wing again and bumbles around the room. It bumps cheerfully into Polly Cradle's head, the lampshade, and finally the window.

Everyone starts talking at once, and in the confusion it's quite natural for Joe to slip out and wash his face.

When Joshua Joseph Spork steps out of the door of Polly Cradle's house, it is with a strange feeling of coming home and a powerful sense of betrayal. Moving down the street in the gathering dark, knowing that he is to some degree on the run, he feels a kinship with his father which surpasses anything he has ever before experienced. He flinches at shadows, ducks away from lamplight, and when he accidentally catches someone's eye, he rides the stare, throws such aggression into it that they immediately look away, and do not see him. Indeed, they actively seek to forget him. He steps onto a bus, and out of sheer perversity steps off at the next stop and takes another which goes the long way around to his destination. Or rather, not perversity, but a natural understanding that what he is doing now is rash, and stemming from that, the certain knowledge that it must be done well, or not at all. It must be done in the high style of the Night Market, with all due deference to misdirection and sleight of mind.

He feels alive.

On the other hand, he feels rotten. Mercer will be fine, will call Joe an idiot and then set about rescuing the situation. It's not quite so certain that Polly Cradle will be fine. Obviously, she will take no physical harm, but that Joe has sneaked out—successfully executing this time the plan he formulated when she caught him before—will wound her, and he knows it and she will know that he knows it and has done it anyway, and that will hurt her again. He has no regrets about his decision: this isn't a case of wanting to recant. Blood is not optional. At the same time, whatever is happening between them is also not to be underestimated. They have found in each other some kind of jigsaw-puzzle match, a mutual knowing which goes beyond the smell of her still on his skin, and which he is at pains not to define or recognise until it has time to settle into him.

That Polly could be family one day, that she might—and he might—unite Cradle and Spork in one great dynasty of unlikely rules and criminal histories, his present, practical mind puts firmly to one side. Before he can even reach for that future, or one like it, he has to climb up on top of the rubble of the past and see what the world actually looks like. The rubble of Mathew's past, which now appears to have been less a wrong turn than the heavy footsteps of a man carrying more than his fair share of other people's history—a description which Joshua Joseph Spork has always considered applied to himself, and which it now appears applies to almost everyone.

He changes buses again and peers through the window, seeing his own eyes as black gaps in his reflection, and looking through them. The building he needs will be an absence against the dark; a shadow in a shadow. It's not a tourist spot. The nuns do not light their façade with burning lamps as some churches these days do. The place is less than a hundred years old, and ugly beyond reasonable measure. It is the most woebegone religious building he has ever seen.

The gate is black, and so is the path leading up to it: black gravel, pieces of marble and basalt. It must have seemed like a good idea in '68 and now no one is allowed to change it; the design is protected by all manner of orders and by-laws.

The walls are yellow stone, stained by time and by London's population of motor vehicles. When Harriet Spork first came here, there was a pile of flowers left at the foot of a lamp-post in memory of a cyclist killed in a collision with a glazier's van—decapitated, apparently, by a sheet of reinforced safety glass destined for a local school. From sideways on, the safety turned out to be limited.

All of the bouquets were removed after a few weeks save one, a narrow vase the woman's brother glued to the lamp-post and the concrete slab in which it is set with some concoction not even the borough's street-sweepers have been able to undo. Joe came once a month in those days, until Harriet asked him to stop, and over half a year he watched the grim little flowers go from living, to dead, to dry, and finally to a kind of strange fossilisation.

And there it is. He lets it slip by, ignores it. There will be danger here, of that he's quite certain. The enemy—he doesn't name them because when you name something you believe you have understood something about it, and he has no idea, still, what his enemy really is—would have to be stone stupid to miss this one. They will anticipate disguises and diversions. They will be watching.

Mathew, in his head: *Watching is a mug's game. You watch for something, you think you know what it will look like. If it doesn't look like that, it can walk right past you. The human brain, son, is a miracle of rare device, but it dreams and fabulates and it can be induced to deceive the eye. Remember the Monte? Yes? Well, this is like that. You watch too hard for one thing, you miss the other. So when you're lookout, Joe, don't watch for coppers. Just wait and see who comes along. You'll know trouble when it turns up. That's science, that is.*

Joe skips off the bus and turns left down a small street with a crowd of kids. He walks with them as if he's their big brother, then carries on when they duck into a building site for cigarettes and chilly, frustrated foreplay.

Careful to look merely curious rather than like a man contemplating a spot of B&E, he glances up, feeling a long-suppressed and pleasurable thrill.

Here's to crime.

The far end of this alley is the back wall of a modern block built at a time when human aesthetic preferences were not considered a factor in local government architecture and all housing was to be neat, sheer, and above all cheap. Somewhat less attention was paid than should have been to London's clay soil and underground rivers, and inevitably the structure bowed and sagged, and had to be saved from collapse using metal struts which run through the entire frame. These struts, the housebreaker's friend, protrude from the end wall like rungs on a ladder, affording access to a neighbouring Victorian fire escape on a far more elegant building, which in turn—if you have long arms—offers a way onto the flat roof of the block.

Joe the clockworker never quite got out of the habit of pull-ups on the lintel, so Joe the burglar has lean, narrow muscles which play and crunch under his coat. One, two, three . . . and up.

Wish Polly could see this. Or Mathew, even. I'm good at this.

Joe skids as he lands; water has collected on the asphalt. He flaps his arms and yelps, half-joyful, then remembers that this is a deadly secret mission and he will almost certainly have terrible things happen to him if he is caught, and drops to his knees. He hisses a swear word as sharp grit in the mud grazes his leg through his trousers.

No alarms. No klaxons. No searchlights. He grins. Oh, yeah. Joe the kid cracksman. He scurries across the roof and climbs down a maintenance ladder to the gables of a red-brick schoolhouse. From there, he walks along the ridge to the far end and lowers himself out over the air. Strong hands, long, thick fingers. Bad for guitar, good for burglary . . . A downpipe, yes, as expected. Burglars have more than a passing knowledge of exterior plumbing. And sometimes, of course, plumbers have a knowledge of burglary, too . . . metal pipe. Not more than three years old. Good screws . . . fine.

He swings around the drainpipe. It creaks, but holds, and he drops to an external walkway of another housing block. Heavy landing on concrete. Faint smell of things best left unexamined. Chipboard doors and graffiti. A woman with her shopping comes round the corner and jumps on seeing him. (Well, indeed, how did he get here? It's a fair question.) He taps his forehead to indicate a tip of the hat, and she settles. He resists the urge to help her with her shopping, ducks into a grimy concrete corridor and along to the end to a utility staircase. Doesn't even have to unlock it—the door is rusted through around the bolt.

Inside, more smells: bleach; spray-paint; elderly pet; marijuana and incense. Caretaker's closet, lock permanently broken, emptied out and pushed shut. He looks out of the grubby window and sees, spread out below him, the glass skybridge joining the next floor down—which is a shopping centre—to the train station beyond.

And how does he know all this? He has mapped it from the ground, committed it to memory against a rainy day when, for whatever reason, he must make this trip without alerting whatever watchers there might be. His Night Market self, maligned and paranoid and never entirely abandoned, has scouted his entry. He has criss-crossed London, delivering packages and wandering gloomily, and he has catalogued possible escapes and entrances without ever admitting it to himself. Ready. For this.

He knocks the window catch with his elbow, a sharp tap, and it breaks. He worms his way through and lets himself down.

The glass roof sags beneath his feet. For a moment, he thinks it will break. He doesn't look right or left, and wishes he was wearing rubber soles. His leather ones are soaked and sheer on the muddy surface, and the ground is a long way down. Not that he's looking. He walks forward slowly, without running. That would be a mistake. He tries to make haste, all the same.

Joe steps onto the station roof and edges around the guttering, hand over hand. The station is two hundred paces long. He counts every single one of them. And then the parapet of the convent is below him, perhaps ten feet, but it looks further, and of course, there's the small matter of the four-foot horizontal gap. There's no way to turn around, not without risking a serious mishap. He's never jumped backwards before, not when it mattered. He wonders whether he should try to spin around, or just use his arms to give himself a little extra momentum, and then he's in the air, and thinking *oh, shit*, and he has just enough time to think this is a very strange way to visit your mother. Then he lands, tumbles backwards and knocks the wind out of himself, and lies on the parapet considering that perhaps he could just have telephoned.

Hell, no. Fifth-floor man, my friends. King o' the skybridge. Yes.

The door from the parapet into the convent is locked. Possibly nuns do experience a high incidence of cat burglary. More likely they're just punctilious. Or possibly the job of closing up still belongs to Sister Amelia, the kindly but stupendously old former disc jockey who, according to Joe's mother, likes a tot and a fag on the balcony before bed, and therefore takes pains to be sure the job is done right lest someone else take her pitch.

He lets himself in.

Joe has never seen this upper floor before, and so has no idea what to expect. One thing which occurs to him, briefly, is that it may be some extraordinarily secret bordello for bishops with the urge. Another possibility is that it is a casino or moonshinery for bored Anglicans. Then he peers along the sad, green-painted corridor and knows that it's nothing so bold; it's just a very quiet, very lonely place where people who have chosen this particular way to spend their lives contemplate the divine. He wonders whether they all believe. Faith has always struck him as either a tremendous gift or an appalling deception, depending on whether there's a God or not. His grandfather was scathing about "speculative faith," which is the kind you get from worrying about the possibility that God exists and may be cross with you. Daniel Spork observed that God, if there is one, is well aware of the interior dialogue, and most likely unimpressed by it. Much better, he said, to get on with being the man you are, and hope like buggery that God thinks you did as well as could be expected. Hence all the lessons and strictures concealed in everyday objects. *Learn the shape of the world, know the mind of God.*

The shape of the corridor suggests that God wants Joe to go down a flight, across the building, and catch his mother when she comes back from evening prayers. If he hurries, he should make it before the place is awash with wimples and he is sternly ejected for possession of external genitals and an unsanctified soul.

Halfway there, he nearly trips over a medical sort of nun who is snoozing on a chair outside what must be the infirmary, and has to sneak by her the way people do in cartoons, actually on tiptoe and for no good reason with his hands held up to his chest, palms out. In a battered brass plaque enumerating the virtues of Saint Edgar, he catches a glimpse of himself in this position, for all the world like a pantomime robber, and sheepishly lowers his hands.

Joe lets himself into his mother's room and sits on the bed, trying not to notice that the picture of Mathew is on the night table and the one of him is lying on its back by the single chair. He tries to believe that she hugs it, but the chair is not a chair for relaxing but rather one for being penitent, so he suspects she mourns his lack of ambition or his failures, or apologises to him for being a bad mother in her conversations with God. That last one makes him angry, because she was a great mother when she was around: loved him, sang to him, tended and ministered, helped with his homework and stood staunchly behind him in adversity. It was only after she exchanged a gangster for a deity that she began to slip away.

In his earlier life, there were times—perhaps they were even more common, in fact, than the other times—when spending time with his mother was a renewing experience for Joe Spork. They would walk around together, his small hand in her larger one, the cold strap of her watch rustling against his sleeve, and he would feel like a battery plugged into a giant recharging station, warmth and certainty filling him up. After half an hour spotting kites and dogs and ambling with Harriet, he could soak up days of his father's jittery, electric-fence presence. It worked in reverse, too; Harriet stood taller when she was with her son. She relaxed the muscles of her face, letting go the sultry, coquettish scowl and permitting herself to be domestic, homely, and happy.

Those times faded away in almost perfect synchrony with the change in relative scale of their palms. As Joe's first equalled and then exceeded his mother's, so both of them became unwilling to share the inverted contact which told them the years had moved on. The young man became prickly about being seen to be a mama's boy, and Harriet found it distressing to have such a grown-up son, and then later too full of unwanted memories to be touched by a powerful, wolfish young man so like her dead husband in his prime. By the time Harriet found God in a grimy chapel at Heathrow Airport, they found one another's company painful, not because it was unpleasant but because it drained what once it had animated. They spoke occasionally, met rarely, and touched little if at all. When Harriet became Sister Harriet, and announced that her retreat from the temporal world would mean she could only see Joe once every six months, it was hard to say whether the announcement implied a greater or lesser distance between them.

And then she's there, in the room with him. When he was a child, she towered over him and could have worn his pyjama bottoms as Bermuda shorts. Now he looks down at her in her flat shoes, and she'd fit into one leg of his trousers, and with her hair pulled straight back she is hardly as high as his chest.

Harriet Spork stares at her son, and he can see her wondering whether she should call the porters and have him thrown out. Well, no; there's no question that she *should*: she's a cloistered woman and his presence is absolutely against the rules. She's trying to untangle whether she *will*, because in the end—in the absolute, final analysis—he's her son. He hasn't actually considered what he might do under those circumstances, and wonders abruptly whether his indecision will be tested.

Apparently not.

"Joshua," she says.

"Hello, Mum."

"You're in trouble." Not a question. She knows, or she has correctly deduced. Or perhaps she has always expected. "I can't hide you, you know. The Church can't give sanctuary any more."

"I don't need sanctuary."

"Oh. Oh, dear." Because if he is not here to be concealed, he is here for some other kind of help. He considers telling her he has come to see her before he gives himself up. He wonders whether the lie would bring her joy or guilt, and what it would do to him. He wishes he could stop trying to play her, and just be her son, but he never knows any more whether he's talking to God's wife or the woman with the plasters and the warm neck who could make everything be all right.

He is briefly, irrationally furious that God should require of her the abandonment of her son, and almost tells her, but remembers that this approach triggers a lecture on the testing of Abraham.

Instead he says "I'm going to hug you," and does, and she, after a moment's appalled hesitation—because it is very much not what they do these days—hugs him back, fiercely, throws her arms around him and shudders massively and asks him what on Earth is going on, and is he all right, and then for the second time what it's all about and what it means, and he replies that he has no idea, does not understand, but Billy is dead and the world is upside down and it's not his fault, but please, please, please, she must be careful, she must, she must. This seems to unzip Harriet's emotions entirely, because she cries silently into her son's shoulder and he does the same, feeling all the while that he's being unfair offloading all this on her, because she's so small.

At last, she manages to peel him off, or perhaps the point is reached where the hug is finished, and the comfort it grants is offset by awkwardness and self-awareness. They part, and he looks at her.

Harriet Spork—Sister Harriet—is still attractive. The voice which sang "Ma, He's Making Eyes At Me" is now more commonly deployed for the Eucharist, and make-up has given way to a stern expression which mingles faith and devotion with compassion and—on the rare occasions when she is wrong-footed, as now—a confident anticipation of clarity. She is everyone's mother now, and Joe feels an absolutely dreadful hunger, and a jealousy, even alone with her in this room. *These blessings are mine*, his heart shouts, *mine and no one else's!* It seems so unfair to him that she should bestow her empathy on others and yet bar her door against him, who most rightfully deserves it.

She has grey hair now; the last black streaks are gone. Perhaps they were a final vanity, now dismissed. Her eyelashes are still spectacular, her hands still elegant.

"I don't want you to forgive me, Mum. I don't need that." Normally he calls her Harriet, because she has asked him to. Today is not normally.

"We all need that." And Harriet perhaps more than others, which is why she's so quick on the draw. He pushes the thought away.

"How long do we have?"

"How long do we have before what?"

"When do you next pray or eat or whatever?"

"Long enough." To achieve whatever God has in mind for this conversation. The fatalism terrifies and angers Joe in equal measure. The answer could mean five minutes or a week.

He takes the folded sheet of accounting paper from his pocket and lays it on the bed, as if it were the final piece in one of Agatha Christie's murder mysteries and he the detective explaining why he has called everyone here this evening. Except there are only two of them, and it seems far from the last piece, alas.

"Mathew paid for Daniel."

She looks at him, and then down at the paper, and nods. "Yes."

"He fiddled the books."

"Yes."

"And then later, when Daniel had them done in town—"

"Mathew got Mr. Presburn to fiddle them for him."

Presburn the honest dealer, accountant *pro bono* to craftsmen and persons of good character. Except that Presburn, apparently, had been Mathew's creature, the conduit for his completely illicit largesse to his angry father. All true, then. But what does it mean, here, now, to J. Joseph Spork, who tried as a child to be Mathew and then as an adult to be Daniel, and never, really, has focused on being Joe? And who is, in his various persons, now pursued by demons through this world of sin?

"Did you know?"

"Yes."

"But Daniel never did."

"No. I considered telling him." Because God loves truth. "But it would have been cruel."

Yes. It would. But you might have told me. It would have made my life easier, because if I'd known Daniel's trade didn't pay the way he ran it, I might not have spent ten years of my life doing exactly the bloody same and being so confused when it didn't add up.

Harriet sighs, and clasps her hands for a moment. May God grant both of them peace.

Again, Joe feels that peace could be granted more generally if people inside his family told each other fewer whopping lies, and left their children somewhat less complex and occult heritances.

At least she hasn't mentioned the ineffable nature of the Lord at all. When Harriet first came here, Joe assumed that this kind of answer was a sort of polite, convent version of "Fuck off." Later, he came to believe it was an assertion of faith.

"Daniel built something with Frankie, didn't he?"

Harriet's face undergoes a stark transformation, from beatific to furious.

"Oh, he would have done anything for her! He did do anything. She asked a lot, and he always did it. And what she didn't ask, what she just left him to do . . . that was worse. She was wicked, Joshua! So wicked. So blighted and dark. They all thought she shone, all those clever men, but she was rotted inside like a windfall apple. Maggots and death. She was a witch, from a witchy breed, and God save her, because I think she's in Hell. I won't talk about her. She was a bad one."

"I thought we were all bad, unless we tried."

"Oh, we're all sinful. But we're not evil, Josh. Not unless we really put our shoulders to the wheel. She was evil. She had such eyes. They saw everything, right down to the bottom of creation. She saw like Einstein, they say. And look what came of him: burning cities and charred shadows on the wall. A half-century of fear and loathing and now we're all waiting for the first suitcase which turns a city into glass. But Einstein was a godly man, wasn't he? Frankie was none of that. Oh, no."

"Why? What did she do?"

"Oh, Joe, these are old sins. Old shadows. It's better they stay buried."

"Well, they haven't. What did she build down there? What did Daniel help her build?"

"She lied to him. She said it was a great mechanism to heal the world. She thought the truth would make everything all right, that she'd usher in a new utopia. Salvation through science, that was the doctrine back then. Salvation comes from the soul, and is the gift of God. But Daniel . . . he said God helps those who help themselves, of course. He said that everything under Heaven is an opportunity to learn. He said God wanted us to strive to be more than we are, and this was part of that striving. It was all so noble. The Devil turning love into sin."

"What sin? What was so terrible about it?" Harriet is fumbling at her neck for the cross she wears, and her lips move between breaths in whispered prayer. Devotion. A fear of heresy. Obsessive compulsive disorder constructed around faith. Joe has no idea, never did. She takes his hand and grips it, suddenly fierce.

"It was like a praying wheel, like they have in Tibet. A worshipping machine, all made of gold, like the old heathen temples in the Bible. It prays to Hell."

"Mum . . ."

"No! No, Joe, you asked and I'm telling you. It's a vile thing. It calls to all the old monsters, from the back end of creation. And she knew! She knew. She opened it once and the Devil came and took a host of souls. Innocents, too. She told him, and still! Still he loved her! Oh, she was wicked, with those wide French eyes and the endless evasions and disappearances and then she'd be on the doorstep and 'I must speak with him.' And never a word for Mathew. Always about herself. She. Was. *Bad!* And, of course, no one would listen to me!"

She glares at her son, furious. She is willing him to believe, to understand at last. Her world now is four parts in five invisible, and the remainder is filled with shadows. Once, before she took the last step and swore herself through these gates, she came home early to the house and he wasn't there, and he returned to find her weeping in a corner, quite certain that the Rapture had come and gone and left her behind—that God had lifted up her bonny boy and cast her back on the heap for her dusty sins and inadequate contrition.

Joe Spork sits and waits for her to run down. It is no good—never was—objecting that this does not sound like the work of a benevolent, loving God; that the universe she believes in is more like something from a Hammer horror movie, vampires skittering like spiders up drainpipes.

A brief image coalesces in his mind—crumpled linen faces watching him from the windows of a black van. He glances at the window and sees himself reflected in the glass, and for a moment is afraid to look directly at his image in case there is a tall, heron-stooped figure close behind, black-shrouded hands reaching out to clasp him. He strains his ears for the sound of breathing, for that strange rasping. He can feel the presence of someone else in the room, the uneasy knowledge of someone standing in the dead space behind your spine. Spider hands trailing threads.

He turns.

And sees Harriet sitting loosely on the edge of her bed looking at him and, for the first time in a long while, actually seeing him as Joshua Joseph, with the fullest understanding of their shared life. Here, now, she is his mother, and nothing else.

"Have you called Cradle's?"

"Of course."

She nods, and rubs a hand across her mouth. She cocks her head pensively. "But you're here. You sneaked in. So you're not doing as you're told."

"I was." He wonders whether to tell her that he may possibly be about to fall in love with Mary Angelica Cradle; that Polly has invested in him and he in her.

"And it's Frankie's machine?"

"Yes."

"You need the Night Market, Joe."

"I don't have it. I never did. I'm a watchmaker."

She snorts. "You're my son. Mathew's son. The Market's yours, if you want it. If you decide to take it."

She levers herself down onto the floor, slipping her knees into the shiny indentation of her daily observances. He stares. Has she gone again, back inside her faith? If she prays now, she will pray until he leaves. She will not talk to him any more. He has seen it in the past, when they fought over her decisions, when he asked her to come out and be his mother again.

But this time she prostrates herself entirely, and reaches in a most unconventional way for a small metal box, wedged between the frame and the mattress. She hoicks it out and sits back on her heels, looking pleased.

"Here," she says. "This was Mathew's. Perhaps it's meant for you."

It is a locked green cash box, the kind you saw in every shop when Joe was a child, perhaps seven inches long and five across, with a little metal handle on it and a slot for the coins.

"What's in it?" he says.

"I don't know, Joshua," Harriet Spork says. "I never opened it. I don't have a key. But that won't stop you, will it?" She smiles grimly.

He shakes the box. It rattles, metal on metal, and something solid goes "fwfp," something thick and rough. A box within a box, perhaps.

"Thank you," he says, and goes to hug her again. Before he can, there's a noise like a car crash outside, or many car crashes all at once, and the clangour of alarms. A bright-eyed old woman in a severe grey suit puts her wimpled head around the door without knocking.

"I'm so sorry to disturb you," she says. "But I think you better come with me."

"Why?" Joe asks.

"Because your enemies have just broken down the front door and I suspect they propose to carry you off."

Harriet stares. The other woman makes a face. "Hurry up, please." And it is only when she steps fully into the room, carrying a small, vile-looking dog under one arm, that Joe Spork recognises her as his erstwhile client. It takes him a fraction of a second longer to observe the large, old-fashioned revolver in her other hand.

"You!" Joe growls at the author of his misfortunes.

"Yes," Edie Banister says. "I suppose I should acknowledge at this time that I am not, strictly speaking, a nun."

Edie Banister leads them off down the corridor and back the way Joe arrived. On the floors below, something bad is happening, loud and angry. Nuns are shouting—not screaming, but shouting, stern and outraged and very certain of their ground—but those fearsome voices are falling away into what sounds like one shared gasp or indrawn breath. Where indignation and affront should be growing, it is muffled, reduced to an appalled whisper of dismay.

At the head of a flight of twisting stairs, Joe glances down and sees a group of sisters standing in a huddle. The front nun has her hand flung out in a gesture of accusation, but she is faltering already, and the furious finger is being modified into one of warding. She is afraid.

A single figure lopes past her: a black-linen werewolf on the hunt, wide shoulder brushing her aside, feral head turning this way and that, seeking prey. Edie Banister grabs Joe unceremoniously by the collar and drags him back and away.

"Don't be a fucking tourist," she hisses angrily. "We need to be away, youngster. Or didn't your daddy teach you that? Piss off first, sightsee later?"

"He told me never back down," Joe Spork replies grouchily, following her down a small side corridor.

"Oh, aye, that I'm sure he did. But reading between the lines, did he say you have to stand when you will definitely lose? Or did he say regroup and retrench, then fight back?"

Polly and I are your only friends. But somehow, that advice does not seem intended for this eventuality. Joe growls. "I don't trust you."

"Good! Then you may not die. But for the moment, shut up and do as you're told by the nice old lady. Or take your chances."

He mutters something between a complaint and an acceptance, and Edie turns on him for a moment a dazzling smile of encouragement and fellow feeling. Then waves the whole conversation away.

"Down here," she says sharply, and they duck into an access staircase which is, if possible, even tinier than the corridor. Joshua Joseph feels that he is entering a wonderland constructed for the habitation of little old ladies, and hopes he will not have to shrink to survive. Then he grins, because he knows all about shrinking to survive, and is pleased—if disturbed—to find that it's not him any more.

"Where are we going?" Harriet demands.

"It's your convent," Edie replies.

"This goes to . . . the kitchen garden."

"That's what I thought, yes."

"There's no way out. The garden is walled off, and there's no gate."

"There will be shortly."

"What?"

Edie Banister doesn't answer—she just cocks her head in a way which states eloquently that answers are a luxury and time is pressing, and nuns are supposed to be a bit more placid and a bit less lippy.

Harriet nods. Joe has never seen her cave in so quickly, and suspects that in Edie Banister he is in the presence of a master. Mind you, the eyeless dog is an unfair advantage; the potty-old-bat equivalent of a nuclear bomb.

That his mother's acquiescence might have something to do with the danger he personally is in, or that this must be weirdly familiar to her from half a dozen heady escapes with his father back in the day, occurs to him only as they reach the foot of the stairs.

The garden door is a bit rotted and decrepit. A large selection of wellington boots, in various sizes for assorted nuns, stands arrayed along the wall. Bastion whiffles curiously at the enticing smell, and there is a noise behind them like a hydraulic press: a very soft, very powerful sound of escaping air.

There is a Ruskinite one flight up. He has jumped or fallen from the fourth floor and landed on his feet. His arms are spread as if ready to grasp something, and his head is rocking to and fro on his shoulders as if he is sniffing. A second later, Joe actually sees another one slump ungracefully through the air like an empty sack and land next to the first. It seems to hit the ground all at once, as if it is just a bundle of clothes with sticks inside, but seconds later it's upright, rolling its shoulders and briefly touching the first one in a strange, physical recognition. Not a human gesture at all; arachnoid, or lizardy. Then both of them spread their arms in that same wrestler's crouch, and their heads turn towards him. In unison, they lurch for the stairs.

Edie Banister grasps Joe by the hand and hauls him bodily out into the garden. Harriet is a few steps ahead, but going slowly even at full stretch. He lifts her as he catches up, and is nearly rewarded with a bony elbow in the eye for his trouble before she realises who he is. Edie nods approvingly and skitters past, spry as a sheepdog. Joe glances back and sees the Ruskinites coming out of the door, virtually on top of one another. They stop still, and a moment later are joined by a third. They touch again, that same strange spiderhug and bob, and then spring forward, fast, strong, and eerily silent. He jerks Harriet up onto his chest and runs like hell.

The garden at Samson At The Temple is a retreat within a retreat, a twisting, mazelike place of concealed meditation spots and beds of roses, dead ends and alcoves. It's a place where a girl can get away from all the noise of a dozen Trappists playing ping-pong and appreciate the wonder of the creation. Edie Banister ducks down into a sunken garden, through and out the other side, doubles back along an avenue of laurel and then through a narrow gap behind a greenhouse and in front of a potting shed. Always, always, she is heading for the outer wall. Always, she puts turns and forks between them and their pursuers, forces the enemy to guess, to hesitate. When Joe pauses to catch his breath and look over his shoulder, she grabs him again, draws him on up another laurel path, this one winding and wild, and suddenly they're hard against the back wall, high red brick topped with unchristian spikes, three-pointed stars on an axle, sharp-edged and aggressively private.

She hands the dog to Harriet and dips her hand into her bag, then slaps a small Tupperware box against the wall. It sticks.

"Come on," she says, ducking behind a small stone chapel, and when Joe hesitates, she slaps him on the back of his head to get his attention and takes advantage of his utter amazement to get him where she wants him. As he ducks, he sees with horror the Ruskinite hunters surge through the laurel bushes, huge black shapes swooping and lunging, appallingly boneless. They wheel around one another, then jointly focus their attention on the chapel. The nearest one takes a loping step forward. Edie pulls Joe down and sticks her fingers in her ears.

The world is a bass drum, and the conductor has just given the percussionist the biggest nod of his career.

The sky is white.

Joe's nose is bleeding. There's dust in his eyes.

When he looks around the corner, the outer wall is gone. So are the Ruskinites. In their place, a crater, black and charred, and the smell of phosphorus and saltpetre, Guy Fawkes Night come early.

"Home-made," Edie Banister says happily, a soon-to-be-novagenarian with a bad attitude and a fine knowledge of exothermic reactions. "I think I may have over-egged the nitro and gone a bit heavy on the toluene. However, nothing succeeds like excess, ey?"

The garden of Samson At The Temple is breached.

They make it as far as the car Edie Banister has stolen. Team Spork—Harriet and Joe and their new friend—are making the escape of the decade, a corker in the annals of derring-do with added points for age, infirmity and spontancity. Edie considers the thing something of a masterclass, and hopes someone, somewhere, will take note and teach it to the young. Classics in survival, evasion, resistance and escape: the Banister Exemplar.

And then, from nowhere, the street is filled with skittering, scuttling figures, ragged in their shrouding black, like a plague of spiders. They pour through the doors of surrounding houses and out of parked cars, five, ten, twenty, a myriad bobbing heads and grasping hands. Joe Spork stares at them, takes a step forward in front of Harriet and Edie, and sees them all, every last one, turn their eyes to him. He freezes under their gaze. He can feel the spotlights and the great salvo of bullets, the awful *splink* as his heart ruptures. He sways. The Ruskinites rush forward.

The first wave tries to grab Harriet, but Edie Banister menaces them with her trusty side arm and they fade away, parting in the line of fire. The second wave approaches from the north and seeks to cut them off from the car, a ghostly interdictory line. Joe recovers himself enough to raise his arms to a sort of fighting posture and forces them to reckon with him. They hesitate and draw back, but before he can be pleasantly surprised, wave three cuts across perpendicular to wave two and sweeps him up and away, iron-banded fingers and corded muscle clamping down on his limbs and lifting him into the back of a van. Behind him, he can see his mother's placid face turn rapidly to something like a figure from a nightmare, a sudden flash of fury such as he has never seen on her, and she hurtles forward and clutches at the van, screaming like a banshee and demanding him back, give him back, he's not yours, he's my son.

Joe Spork struggles, like Gulliver beset by tiny men. They have him in a grip at every corner, and all he can manage now is a sort of billowing. On the other hand, if he can get a hand free he can do some damage. He twists, and feels the grip on one wrist slacken. It hurts, but he does it again, and again, and the vise skids over his arteries, tearing away some skin, and that hand is free.

What's soft?

Eyes are soft. Throats. Noses and lips. Genitals, too, but many layers of linen make them hard to find, and men and women both learn early to move those parts fast.

He rips at someone's face, feels flesh and eyes under the cowl, hears a cry, feels them reel away, sees someone guided forward, wide-shouldered and heavy on his feet. A blind wrestler? He rips again at this new enemy, and the Ruskinite slaps at his hand, hard. It hurts, the way it hurts to bang your shin on a glass table. He doesn't care, reaches again. *Come on, then! Let's go! Let's do this. Come on, you bastard.* He is clinging to the man now, feeling huge, solid limbs, his fingers seeking soft parts, vulnerable flesh. A black linen mask tears free, and he shouts with fierce delight, then feels the war cry freeze in his mouth.

Joe Spork stares up into a face made of gold.

An eyeless face, with a snapping turtle's jaw and the merest suggestion of features on the burnished plate.

Not a mask.

A face.

An un-face. An un-man.

The Ruskinites close in. They have him, and they are taking him. He screams.

That's all he knows, because someone clamps something cold over his mouth and he inhales.

XIII

Panopticon days;

Coffin Man;

Escape.

The room is very small. In the centre of each wall, and in the centre of the floor and ceiling, there is a circle of transparent stuff with a light bulb behind it. The bulbs are always on. Behind or in the walls—Joe isn't sure—there are speakers. Sometimes they blare out instructions. Sometimes they play music, very loud. Sometimes they just shriek, electronic wails of protest.

He's not sure how long ago it was that he tried to go to sleep, or how long they have kept him awake. He thought he knew roughly, because there's only enough stubble on his chin to indicate a day or so, but when he finally did sleep—he realises he has slept many times since he arrived, but he doesn't know for how long—he woke to find a ghost face very close to his own and a razor moving very precisely over his cheek. He jerked away, or rather, he tried, but found he was restrained. When he kept trying, someone pressed a cold thing against his neck and his world was fizzy and bright and he screamed a lot. He assumes the cold thing was a taser. The linen face peered at him, as if wondering why he was upset. He wondered whether it was human or not, whether it was like the one he'd seen. He wondered whether he'd dreamed that part.

When he came back to himself after the taser, he was inexplicably and appallingly aroused. He wondered if they had drugged him, and then wondered why they would. Then he realised that this kind of dialogue about himself was probably what this was all intended to achieve. They are asserting ownership of him. They own his sense of time, his captivity, his sleep. They have his body entirely; it's not relevant whether they have drugged him. It is only relevant that they could. The one thing he can preserve from them is his mind—and that is what they want. They cannot approach it directly, so they are holding his body to ransom.

He remembers reading about a man who had been tortured. The man said the worst part was when they played the same music over and over and over until he thought he would go mad. He said even the razors were not as bad as the sense of losing himself. Joe is greatly concerned that he has very little self to lose, and so this will not take long.

He shouts out something, and regrets it instantly. He does not want their attention. Mr. Ordinary comes, anyway.

Mr. Ordinary has a face like a country vet's. He is not a Ruskinite. He is apparently a specialist, brought in for the occasion. When he speaks, he has a mellow baritone, suited to explaining that Rover has the canine pox or that Tiddles will do better on a more varied diet.

He asks questions. It doesn't seem to matter what Joe says in answer to these questions, so he begins to make up jokes. Mr. Ordinary is apparently of the opinion that funny jokes merit a reduction in discomfort. Silence is punished mightily. Mr. Ordinary is kind enough to explain this on the first occasion that Joe becomes mute.

"By all means, lie. Lying is fine. Or if you have no notion what I'm talking about, you should feel free to babble, make stuff up. That's fine, too. Mulishness, however . . . I take that as a sign of disrespect."

When Joe obstinately clamps his lips closed, Mr. Ordinary sighs, and directs operations with a sort of genial competence. They put Joe into strange positions and make him stay that way. The pain arrives quickly and he accepts that, was expecting it. It becomes blinding much later, when he has become used to the aches, and thinks he's doing quite well. Mr. Ordinary listens to him screaming, and does not appear to react at all. Joe starts to speak, randomly selecting the price list for repairs to self-winders, hoping that compliance, however belated, will yield mercy.

It does not.

He loses track of everything, but at some point the man with the hate-filled eyes sits in front of him and listens to him screaming.

Brother Sheamus moves with the same alarming fluidity he displayed that day in Joe's shop. It is as if his bones are articulated in more places than they should be. His head moves smoothly to follow Joe's eyes, to peer into his face. Blank, black-linen monster. Eggshell face. Mask. And yet, somehow, not expressionless. Whether his emotions are carried in his body, or whether they are so strong that Joe is catching the lines of the face through the shroud, the way he feels is quite apparent in the tiny room.

He hates Joe Spork. He hates him as you hate someone you have known your entire life and whom you cannot stand. Whose existence in the world offends you in your bones. Every line of his liquid body aches with it.

Joe has no idea what he can have done to inspire such wrath. He is not old enough to have hurt Brother Sheamus in that way, and would surely know if he had inflicted an injury of that kind on his fellow man. He has, after all, dedicated his life to being mild.

He tries to say so. Unfortunately, he can't speak, because when he tries his teeth chatter and his tongue won't behave.

"You have formed impressions of me, Joshua Joseph Spork," Sheamus says clinically. "It cannot be otherwise."

He is not asking a question, so by Mr. Ordinary's rules, Joe doesn't have to respond.

"You imagine I am a man in authority but under orders. You may know that I wear a variety of hats and crowns, and you may imagine that where these things contradict it is evidence of deception. But those impressions are shallow things. They are based on an understanding of the world which is impoverished by modern weakness, by this modern irony, which is so frightened of grand ideas that it must pick pick pick them apart. Britain's ultimate triumph, Mr. Spork: a world of shopkeepers." This last with contempt. Joe makes a mental note: modernity, shopkeepers: bad.

"I am so much more than you imagine. I am more, and yet I am a fraction of what I shall be in days to come. My victory is inevitable, child of my hate, because I shall become God. And being God, I shall be perfect, and being perfect, I shall always have been perfect. All of this apparent meandering is a straight line to my apotheosis, when viewed from the timeless and ineffable understanding of the divine."

Joe Spork receives all this and knows that a week ago he would have laughed at it. Not now, not here, in this room. The eyes are not funny at all. In them he sees himself vivisected—not for interest, but for enjoyment. He knows absolutely that that is what this man would like to do. His only hope is that the master of the Ruskinites is lying, that he is indeed held in check by someone. And then, with a sinking feeling, he joins the dots and realises that the man so tasked would be Rodney Titwhistle, and the good Rodney has already sacrificed conscience in this matter for some greater good which only he can see.

"A different question, then, for variety. But you must get this one right, no half-answers. Are you ready? Good.

"If I have the mind of Napoleon, but the body of Wellington, who am I?"

And at Joe's stricken look, he laughs, quite genuinely.

Joe Spork has no idea what the right answer may be, so he tries very hard to ask what it is that he has done to make his interlocutor so angry, and how he can make amends, but his mouth betrays him and he chokes, and spits slightly. The man takes this as a challenge, and a moment later Mr. Ordinary comes back and says he is very disappointed.

Joe tries to slip away and remember good things, but good things are far away and very pale, and there are sharks in his mind with him, memories he does not want and cannot avoid any longer.

On the occasion of Joshua Joseph's fifteenth birthday, the young man opened the door to find his father on the step in a splendid suit, with a present under his arm. This was a surpassingly impressive feat, because Mathew was serving time in one of Her Majesty's prisons for grand (even "grandiose," the wits had it) theft.

"Hello, Joe," Mathew Spork said genially, "thought I'd drop in, hope you don't mind."

"You're out?" Joshua Joseph demanded.

"As you see, Joe. As you see. I am a free man—for the day, at least."

"Just for a day?"

"Longer, if I can manage it." This very drily, and the quirk of wickedness which is his father's trademark alerts young Joe to an alarming possibility.

"You've broken out!"

"Yes, I have. Rather well, too, I must say. I had to see a man in Harley Street, you see, about my health. Prison food is terrible, my boy, it tastes of fat and is bad for the digestion. So I thought, well, why not? I'll drop in on my son and hug my loving wife, and then I shall leg it for the bosom of Argentina, and you can pop out and join me from time to time. How does that sound?"

"You're mad!" Joshua Joseph cries, delighted, "You can't stay here, they'll find you!"

"Your father, Joshua Joseph Spork, may be an old man and a decrepit one, but he is no fool and this is not his first fandango. There is even now a fine fellow by the name of Brigsdale, wearing a Mathew costume, waiting in the queue for the ferry to Ireland. Mr. Brigsdale has done no one any wrong in his life, Josh, but he greatly resembles your old man. He will go to the ferry and he will be apprehended, and Lily Law will falsely believe for several days that I have been caught, at which point Mr. Brigsdale will explain that there's been a terrible misunderstanding and sue them for false arrest, not that he'll need to because I've set him up somewhat . . . But by the time it's all sorted out I shall have buggered off to Buenos Aires and all will be well." Mathew Spork beams.

And to Joshua Joseph's amazement, the door does not come crunching down, the Flying Squad does not arrive. Father and son sit there on the sofa ("I'm a bit puffed, Josh, I had to climb a very high wall, you know. This prison breaking is best left to younger men—I shall put that in my memoirs!") and they drink tea, and wait for Harriet to come home. In honour of the old days, when Joshua Joseph used to slumber like a puppy, curled up on his father's lap, the gawky teen rests his head on Mathew's chest as they watch John Craven's *Newsround* to see if it will tell them about the escaped felon, Mathew "Tommy Gun" Spork, and list his many iniquitous acts, but fame is fleeting and there's a swimming rabbit instead.

"Will you teach me how to fire the gun in Argentina, Dad?" Because the day is coming, undeniably, when he will be old enough to learn.

Mathew sighs.

"Do me a favour, Joe, all right?"

"Of course."

"Don't be like me. Be a judge, be a rock star. Be a carpenter. Just . . . find a better way. Leave the gun to someone else if you can."

"I want to be like you."

"No, you don't. You think you do, but this is what it comes to. It's rubbish. Hiding in my own house. Promise me, you'll be better than this."

"I promise."

"Gangster's oath?"

"Gangster's oath!" And if the backwardness of that is apparent to either of them, they don't say.

"All right, then."

They fall asleep that way, and it is only when Harriet Spork comes through the door from her yoga class and shrieks that Joshua Joseph awakes, and realises that his father has died, very quietly, with a smile on his face.

In the aftermath, it turns out that Mr. Brigsdale was a figment of Mathew's outrageous imagination, and that there was no plan to get to Argentina. When Mathew Spork visited the prison doctor and learned that his life was coming to an end, he secured permission to visit his son on his birthday, and then he did, in fact, find a way to elude the clutches of the law for evermore.

Two shrouded faces watch Joe through a panel in the door. They jockey for position at the narrow hole, bobbing around one another. The room fills with a stink so vile he begins to vomit. When he reaches the point where his stomach is quite empty, and even the bile has stopped coming, they pipe more of the stink in, so that he arches convulsively, forehead and toes touching the ground and nothing else, as his body tries to get rid of things which are not there.

In his mind, he holds onto his father's hand, that last day. Mathew would have known what to do.

"Where is it?"

They have been asking him the same question, over and over.

When he objects that he does not know what "it" may be, they are particularly harsh. It is not their job to explain. It is his to offer possible locations of any object they might be looking for. He is to cultivate a habit of mind which opens to their inquisition.

"Where have you hidden it?"

He tells them he keeps it in the sugar jar. He wants to tell them that whatever it is they already have it. They have everything he owns. Or owned.

You've got it. You've got everything I had. You took it all from my house, from Ted's.

"Did Daniel hide it? Did he explain to you what it was? Who else is aware of it?"

Yes. Daniel hid it. He hid it so well you will never find it. And nor will I. In a library. In a bookshop. In a church. He burned it. He sold it.

"Where is it?"

It exists only in your mind. My mind. Our minds. We are all one.

Joe's own mind is wandering, and he knows it, and knows that the wandering is a relief from pain. He fights against it, all the same, because he is frightened he will never come back.

"You cannot continue to resist us. In the end, you will tell us everything. Everyone does. In the end, we will become bored listening to you share your secrets in tedious detail. Where is the calibration drum, Mr. Spork?"

I have absolutely no fucking idea.

This is true, but at the same time he realises that the question tells him something. The calibration drum is used to change the settings on Frankie's machine. Brother Sheamus wants to use the Apprehension Engine for something other than what Frankie had in mind.

He squashes this understanding, lest he blurt it out. He is sure that knowing too much is as bad as knowing too little.

"Where is the calibration drum?"

It occurs to him that they really do not know that he does not know. He is in the hands of incompetent torturers—and from this he conceives a new fear, that their physical skills are as limited as their analytical ones, and they will let him die by accident, by a moment's inattention.

He finds himself in the bizarre position of hoping they are better at this than they seem to be.

He dreams that Rodney Titwhistle comes to visit him. He wishes he could dream something less grey and equivocal.

"They're torturing me," Joe Spork says through numb lips. Rodney Titwhistle shakes his head.

"No," Mr. Titwhistle says, "they are not."

"They are. And you know it." He sounds like a child in his own ears, and something in him rages, but he wants to be rescued. He wants the Queen or the BBC to reach down and make it all stop. Rodney Titwhistle is neither, but he's as close as can be had.

"They are not. And it is very wrong to suggest that they are. It is counterproductive. Worse, it gives assistance to the enemy."

"What enemy?"

"Any enemy. All enemies."

"So they're torturing me to keep everyone safe."

"They are not torturing you, Mr. Spork. That is against the law. I could not use them if they were to subject you to any sort of degrading treatment. However, I do use them. I know them to be lawful. I have asked exacting questions. I have received assurances. Therefore you are either making this up, or you are deluded. If you are making this up, I should warn you that manipulative falsehood is now considered a technique of Lawfare. You understand what that means? Warfare using the legal code, thus Lawfare. There are penalties for illegitimate Lawfare."

"They won't even tell me what they want. I want to tell them, you see. Only I have no idea."

Rodney Titwhistle sighs. "They want the calibration drum for the Apprehension Engine, Mr. Spork. A small item. A thing no bigger than your hand. The Book, as it transpires, will turn the machine on but not off. We must have the drum. There is some suggestion that you possess it. Or that your grandfather did. You would do well to consider carefully before denying anything."

"I don't know. I want . . . I want my lawyer! Get me Mercer. I have rights. You know I do."

"No, you do not. Not here. Not in this room, or this building. Here you are a patient. You are suspected of an act of terrorism so gross, so destructive, that it is the definition of madness. Patients have no rights. And I told you before, sir: there are penalties for Lawfare."

Mr. Titwhistle leaves in a huff, and it turns out that there are, indeed, penalties. But Joe knows there are penalties for everything now, and they touch him less and less.

He lets himself go away for a while.

"This task. These words. Are against nature. They are against everything. Fathers should not bury their sons." Daniel Spork, pendulumstraight, choking like a gritty caseclock.

"Not in war, not in peace. I have seen both." He stops, and works his right shoulder, his neck. He contains a furnace of sorrow, and he is burning through. "My son was not a good man. By the measure of our country's law. He was a transgressor. He. Could not be made to see. I tried, but I was alone, and I cannot. I am not. Good with words. Or people, even. I understand machines. So. He was a bad man. He stole. He robbed. He broke things and fired guns and he encouraged others to do the same. He tried to sell drugs. He went to prison. My son was bad. I mourn my bad son." Defiance flares in him.

"But he was not. He was not bad. He was not. He loved. He loved his son. He loved his wife. He wanted above all to love his mother. My Frankie. His Frankie, that he barely knew. I believe he loved even me. Even though I failed him. Every day, I failed. I am so sorry that I could not. I could not." Daniel stops again. Whatever, exactly, he could not, Joshua Joseph will never learn, because his grandfather must gather himself and go around it, or he will not recapture himself, will fail this one last time, and that is something Daniel Spork will not permit. The spring must unwind all the way.

"He was not bad. He was not. He was intemperate. Angry. Lawless. Not dishonest. Although sometimes the truth could not—like many of us, could not—could not keep up with him.

"And in this last thing, he is revealed. That he knew he was. He knew. He was not long. That he was. Dying. He got out of prison. To see his son and say 'goodbye.' He did not tell me he was coming. I could kill him."

And this, impossibly, makes them laugh, not bitterly, but wholeheartedly. Yes. Mathew Spork, in going to his grave, is as infuriating as he ever was, and as stupidly, stubbornly heroic about it.

"So grieve. Please. Today, let it out. For me. Scream. Weep. Drink too much and be unwise. Be like him. Let go. Because I cannot. I do not know how.

"Fathers should not bury their sons."

Outside, they lower the coffin into the ground. For some reason, the hole is decked out in AstroTurf. Joshua Joseph had imagined the soil would be loamy and soft, and that he would be able to scatter it, but London is built on clay, and so instead he hefts a great mustard-coloured clod into the hole and it makes a muffled, hollow thudding as it lands. He worries he may have chipped the varnish, and then feels stupid, because no one will ever know, or reproach him if they did.

The burial goes on and on.

Until, nearly an hour later and the box buried safe and sound, Joshua Joseph stands with his grandfather looking out across a little road. For five minutes they have stood thus, the old man boiling with whatever self-reproaches he has not voiced, and the boy seeking by instinct the one person equally responsible for Mathew Spork in life and death. Together, they watch—but do not watch—a red double-decker bus, the first of two, draw up to the stop across the street. After a moment, it pulls away again, revealing a single figure in mourner's black, gaunt and straight against the newsagent's window.

Joshua Joseph has a brief impression of grey hair cut in a severe bob, a scrawny neck like a silver birch tree, and two knobbled, arthritic hands clutching at a pair of severe black trousers. Very slowly, very deliberately, she raises the left in a gesture of greeting, and Joshua Joseph can see, even at this distance, that she has been crying. By her shudders, he deduces that she is crying still. He wonders dimly whom she mourns, and if she comes here every day, or every week, or if there is another funeral following on the heels of this one, and then his dawning realisation finds voice in his grandfather's appalled, desperate shout, as the old man lurches forward, one hand outflung as if reaching from an icy sea for one last chance at the lifeboat's ladder.

"Frankie!" he shrieks, "Frankie, Frankie, please!" as he flings himself, heedless of his gammy knees and his spindly ankles, towards the East Gate. "Frankie! My Frankie!"

And she responds. She does. Her face lights up at this unlooked-for, unimagined blessing; that even now, even in this cruellest moment, his love remains. The waving hand extends towards him as if blown by a breeze. And then, sharply, the open door slams shut. She is not yet done. She is not ready. She snatches back her hand and begins to turn away, and the second bus draws a temporary curtain between them. Daniel struggles with the catch on the gate, his grandson torn along in his wake, as desperate—almost—as the old man himself. The gate swings open—but when the bus moves off again, Joshua Joseph knows already what he will see. Sure enough, the bus stop is empty.

Daniel stares without understanding, and then whips around to follow with his eyes the departing double-decker, and sees—they both see—that narrow figure clasping tight to the silver pole at the back. Her face is turned away from them even as her body and her heart refuse to complete entirely the abandonment, and she remains rooted to the running board, standing full square as if she will embrace them both even as the bus carries her away and turns a corner, and she is gone.

They find Joe's resistance—his unresistant resistance—curious and frustrating. They shut him in his little white room and a moment later the box seems to detach from the building and hurl him around, up, down, around. It occurs to him, as he hangs suspended, watching one side of the box retreat and knowing that the other must be rushing up behind him, that if he is moving at fifteen miles an hour—not unlikely—and the box at fifteen as well in an opposing direction, then he will strike with a total force of thirty miles an hour and quite possibly die.

He spreads his arms out and tries to slow himself. He does not die, or even suffer serious injury—although he suspects he may have dislocated a thumb and cracked some ribs, and wonders at the change in circumstances which causes him to see this as minor—and when they are finished, they let him out. He staggers and weaves and empties his stomach onto the white floor. They hold him, and he thanks them.

Mr. Ordinary smiles.

Instead of taking him back to his box (he struggles with himself to avoid identifying it as "home") they put him into another room just next to it. There is a man inside, smelling of rubber boots, mud and seaweed, and his body is a mass of burns and scabs.

"We're down in the ivy," Ted Sholt says.

Joe, looking down at this silvered head and the man he suspects is dying, feels a strong familiarity.

They have done something strange to Ted Sholt, something odd and clever and very terrible. He is shaking, but not like a man who is cold or tired or afraid. He is shaking as if his muscles are coming away from his bones, and his skin has a strange, stretched look, as if the fat of his body is pooling in places where it should not.

"Ivy inside," Sholt says hoarsely. His eyes are searching, but not finding, and Joe realises that he cannot see. "Ivy in the blood. Ted's head's full and Ted's a fool, God's a figment, devils rule."

"It's me, Ted," Joe says softly. There's no need to shout. They are pressed against one another like lovers. They can have something approaching privacy only if one of them stands. "It's Spork the Clock."

"You can't let him go through with it," Ted says vaguely. He tries to lift his body with his stomach muscles, and something makes a gristle noise. He moans.

"Ted . . . I don't think there's anything I can do. I don't know what's going on."

"Brother Sheamus. Frankie's machine."

"Yes, but I don't know what that means. I don't know what they want from me. I don't know anything. I'm just the idiot who turned the key. You were there, Ted."

Sholt tries to speak, and then screams again, and this time when he arches his back he crackles, as if his bones are breaking. "What cart will Frankie's engine pull? Science has many faces, each mouth whispers to the world in different ways. Frankie's gone, her blade will cut in all directions. Whose hand holds the knife? Sheamus, of course. Always Sheamus. Bastards." He shudders, and Joe feels something move inside the other man's body, something which a profound instinct tells him should stay in one place.

"Ted, please. Stay still."

"She said it was salvation. She said too much truth turns us to ice and we shatter, so she set it all perfectly. But Sheamus . . . he wants more than that. Wants a reckoning with God. Wants to reset the machine. See all the truths at once. He'll kill the world."

"But he can't do that without the calibration drum, and he doesn't have it, does he? Of course, he doesn't. Because Frankie wasn't an idiot. She gave it to someone she could trust."

Oh, shit. Daniel. She gave Daniel the keys to the apocalypse. Of course, she did. Who else do you give something which can destroy the world, which will be hunted by monsters and thugs, except the father of your child who still loves you even after you've played hide and seek with his heart for thirty years?

Daniel, and hence, Joe.

Shit, shit, shit.

If Joe has it, he does not know. If they took it when they raided the warehouse, they also do not know. Therefore it is concealed. It is hidden, of course, hidden by Daniel against this very day. Hidden too well. Perhaps it was in Daniel's lost effects. Perhaps Mathew, all unknowing, sold the ignition key to the most dangerous object in the world for the price of a meal at Cecconi's.

Shit.

Ted Sholt is rattling on. "But Sheamus just wants to know his score. Wants to know if he won or lost. Stupidity is a symptom of enormous power, they say." And then: "You must stop him. You must! Go to the *Lovelace*. Where I left her."

"Don't tell me, Ted. Not here. I can't keep it secret from them." *They will have it from me. What they did not get from you, I will give up. I cannot keep it inside.*

Sholt stares right at him, into him, madman's fox-eyes seen briefly in the dark. He lifts his head, and something gristles softly in his stomach, something broken. He snarls. "Yes, you can! You must!" and he is going to tell, without question.

Joe bends his neck, and Sholt whispers directly into his ear barely any sound at all: "She's under the hill at Station Y." He slumps back.

Joe shakes his head, relieved. "Ted, I don't know where that is."

"Matter of public record. Obscure, but simple. No: *listen!* I can tell you how . . . Stand on the box and see the hill, down the tunnel into the dark. Open the door with Lizzie's birthday. And you're in. Now! Garble it, in your head! Mix the letters and remember the jumble. Say it: Matron Fry. Nation's Eye. God loves sinners, patients cry. See? That way you can always choose whether to say it aloud or not. You can scream it, if you have to. Shout the answer at them and let them figure it out. Tell the truth, but keep it from them. You must, Joe! You must!" He wheezes and shuts his eyes tight. "It's all in there. Do anything. But stop him."

Ted gasps and squirms, and more things crackle inside him. Joe wonders whether, if he banged on the door and offered to talk, he could get Ted a doctor.

Probably not.

So he lies instead, mercifully:

"I will, Ted. I will."

Later, when they use the water, Joe dies for two minutes and eighteen seconds.

The water is cold and fresh against his face, but tastes of salt and chemicals. It is a special preparation, Mr. Ordinary explains, to reduce the risk of fatality. Joe thinks, objectively, as it worms into his lungs, that it does not work very well.

He starts to drown. One of the Ruskinites is next to him, very close, listening to the sound of his choking. It turns its head, listening for the sound of water in his lungs. It has experience. It is a craftsman. It can tell by the noise his body makes when it is time to stop.

He wonders when he stopped thinking of the Ruskinites as people. He wonders whether they ever thought of him that way.

Part of him cannot help but notice that they have not asked him any questions recently. Perhaps they do not intend to. Perhaps they are just going to kill him.

The idea is horrible, and he starts to struggle. He struggles until he cannot continue, and inhales a great deal of water, and the listener holds up his hand. A crash cart barrels in, orderlies and doctors shouting.

They have to resuscitate him, which they do with a machine, because—when one of them goes to give him mouth-to-mouth—Mr. Ordinary warns that he is dangerous and may bite their lips off, also that they have no idea whether he carries any diseases.

Joe wonders why on Earth they haven't checked for that. It seems so obvious. While they struggle to force him not to die, he debates whether to cooperate. He suspects he could just depart now, and be gone. But death does not seem much of an answer, and he has things to do. People are depending on him.

He has always avoided thinking too much about death. The whole idea appals him, and always has. Damn Daniel's Death Clock, commended to his special attention. He wonders why it seems important, here, now: a wretchedly gloomy bit of Victorian tat. And why would Daniel be so keen on it, when he loved life so much?

He decides to give Daniel the benefit of the doubt. He won't die just yet.

When his heart is beating again, Mr. Ordinary declares it's time he had a break.

In pale yellow scrubs and with his throat still sore from tubes and retching, Joe sits in a room with window boxes and wishes himself a thousand miles away, wishes himself someone else, wishes he had never met Billy Friend, never chosen to follow his grandfather into the dying world of clockwork. Wishes his father had forced him to be a lawyer, which at one stage was very much Mathew's intention, until Harriet's tears pried him away from it.

So now he's playing Snakes & Ladders with a woman inmate and watching the clock. In twenty minutes it will be eleven a.m. He wonders whether they will come for him then because it's a round number.

Not all of the staff here are Ruskinites. Many of them are, as far as he can tell, conventional medical personnel. He is in a Ruskinite hospital for the mentally ill. One of the nurses— a pretty, roundish sort of woman called Gemma—told him in confidential tones that he is receiving the best possible care and will be all better soon. He responded that he was sure that was true, and she dimpled.

All the same, she would not reveal to him the name of the hospital ("I'm not allowed") or get in touch with anyone for him ("You just think about getting better, all right?") or give him any news from outside—about golden bees, for example, or whether they have yet provoked a war.

He has christened the place Happy Acres. The other patients—not all of them, he's fairly sure, are prisoners—are mostly silent and bewildered. One man sings the first bars of a pop song over and over in the corner. A woman whimpers.

At five minutes to the hour, seven men walk into the room and clear a space for a sort of coffin. It is like the board which Joe was strapped to during the waterboarding ("saline disclosure therapy," Nurse Gemma said reprovingly), but it appears to be made to measure and is more absolute in its restraint. The man inside is almost entirely cased in nylon straps and rubber. He is older than Joe but younger than Mathew when he died, and he has wild hair and a full beard and tanned, working man's skin, pale beneath the restraints. Even when this man is outside, he is in his coffin.

At last. Someone they hate more than me.

They put the coffin man by the window so that the inmate can see the flowers, and he makes a rough, gargling noise, which Joe eventually realises is the man saying a polite "good morning."

After a moment, they take Joe to stand in front of the coffin. All he can see of the man inside is one brown eye and one blue, staring back at him unblinking. Joe realises the man probably never gets to see anyone's face for very long. He looks past the coffin and sees Mr. Ordinary watching him intently, reads the warning: *There are worse places than the one you are in, lad.*

"Hello," he says to the prisoner, "my name's Joe. What's yours?"

He wonders briefly why they all laugh at him, even the man in the coffin.

They do not take him back to his cell. He can feel the little room behind him, not much bigger than his body, waiting to embrace him again. He stares at the white light from the windows and commits it to memory.

He plays draughts with the coffin man. They have to use an electronic board. The coffin man has a remote control, like the ones used by paraplegics. One of his fingers is released to operate a little joystick, one click at a time. Forward. Sideways. Forward. Sideways. Apparently it doesn't do diagonal.

Joe wins. At the last minute, though, the coffin man gives him a scare with a rampaging king. It menaces, threatens, and bullies Joe out of position, captures a few pieces by sheer force of threat before he can corner it. In the midst of his pieces, the king is not at bay. Rather, it is surrounded by targets.

The coffin man says something around his bite plate. It's hard to decipher. He hawks and plays with the thing in his mouth, curls his lips. Spittle glistens. He says it again.

"That's how it's done."

And then he laughs.

When Joe asks why they don't just let the coffin man speak his instructions, everyone laughs again. A tall orderly rolls up his sleeve and shows a scar on his arm, a long pale strip of grafted flesh. He doesn't seem to resent the coffin man at all. The orderly seems to feel they're all in this together. The coffin man gargles cordially.

Later, Joe is given a meal. They feed him, because he is shaking too much to do it himself. While they do this, someone else gives the coffin man an intravenous feed. At some point they make a mistake, and the coffin man opens a long, rich cut across a man's face with his joystick hand. He snarls something. It is muffled, but somehow quite clear.

That's how it's done.

The coffin man howls, an incredibly loud, appalling noise. They taser him, which is utterly pointless because he is already restrained, and he starts to choke. A moment later he turns purple and slumps, and they call a crash team. When they try to resuscitate him, he casually claws across a woman's eyes. He glowers, bright and angry, and finds Joe.

It is a question of focus, Joe realises. Of intensity. It is the thing Mathew must have had but which he never allowed his son to see, because it was only for emergencies, and in Mathew's world—the version he allowed his son to know about—emergencies were forbidden: everything which happened happened to the advancement of the House of Spork. But when your back was to the wall and someone else had the knife, there was, in the end, a simple decision: *They are not the monster. I am.*

You can't care about consequences. Every second becomes an end in itself. *That's how it's done.*

They beat the coffin man down, and he laughs the entire time. Joe abruptly realises what has just happened.

Tuition.

He stares at the wild, angry eyes, and feels comradeship. Then the orderlies drag the coffin man away.

"State of the nation," Mr. Ordinary says regretfully from behind him. "I see you've made a new friend."

"Crazy man. I don't know his name."

"Really?"

"Really."

Mr. Ordinary ponders. "Huh," he says. And then break time is over.

"I wanted to show you this myself," Mr. Ordinary says, "because I'm very much responsible for it. I had to work hard to make this happen. No one is coming for you."

The letter is very plain, written on an expensive vellum. It is addressed to Joe, care of Rodney Titwhistle.

> *Dear Mr. Spork,*
> *We regret to inform you that in view of your involvement in activities against the interests of the United Kingdom, specifically the terrorist murders of various persons and associated crimes, we can no longer act on your behalf. The protection of Cradle Noblewhite is withdrawn from you as of this moment, and we would appreciate settlement of our outstanding bill for services rendered in the usual 28 days.*
> *Yours sincerely,*
> *Mercer Cradle*

There is a PS, in Mercer's execrable handwriting: *I'm sorry, Joe. It turns out they punch harder than we do.*

The letter is countersigned by all the partners.

Mr. Ordinary smiles. "There's one from your mother, too."

He seems to think that's a victory for his side, which shows a pleasing lack of information about Harriet.

They leave the door to Joe's cell open. He steps towards it, wondering. A shaft of light beckons him, and any moment he will hear Mercer's voice. It is all a stratagem. He is free.

When his foot touches the ground outside the cell, it is like stepping on nails, except that he feels the pain through his entire body. He leaps back into the cell, and the door slams.

It opens again, and he doesn't bother to step through. He realises, a moment later, that they have trained him to imprison himself.

They collect him and strap him on a trolley, then leave him in a different room. It is large and cold, and filled with people on gurneys, just like him, except that they are not restrained.

It takes him ages to realise that the others are not restrained because they are corpses, and even longer to recognise Ted Sholt, slack and waxy, alongside him. Sholt's head is turned all the way around on his neck.

In the moment after he finally understands, Joe pictures Ted on the chariot of Daniel's Death Clock, a wild rebel beating the Reaper with a sandal and demanding to be released back to his greenhouse. He smiles. Yes. That's how it should be.

Except it isn't. There's just Ted, and Ted is dead.

Mr. Ordinary has another letter to show him. He seems particularly pleased with himself.

Dear Joe,
I'm very sorry. It's been months now and I don't know where you are. I really like you, but I can't wait for ever. A man called Peter is taking me to dinner tonight. I'm moving on. Please don't hate me.
Polly x

Joe lies on his back and refuses to say anything, and they take him to his tiny white room and cram him in and shock him over and over until he is one solid convulsing muscle. He starts to laugh at them for being so predictable. The pain just makes him laugh more, even when the electrodes run too hot and burn him, but then abruptly he wants it to stop more than he can remember wanting anything, ever. He wants not to laugh at the smell of his own burning skin. He wants not to go mad. Not to join Ted Sholt on the wheel of Daniel's ridiculous, horrible clock.

Your special attention.
Daniel, who held the keys to the world.
Special.
Attention.
He knows where to find the calibration drum.
He feels something stretch in his chest and then suddenly release,

and hears the crash warning. A strange peace is in him, cold and odd, and he realises he cannot hear his heart.

And then, abruptly, he is not in the cell.

It is as if someone has turned on the lights, and all the shadows have disappeared. The white room is gone. He feels fine. Good, even. A bit bored.

He knows, objectively, that he is experiencing some kind of break. It does not seem a bad thing. He looks down, wondering if there will be grass. When you are held in a cell and your mind snaps, surely you should get grass, and trees, and birds.

"You're an idiot," Polly Cradle says.

He stares at her. She wears the clothes in which he first met her, right down to her fishnet-and-varnish toes.

"They showed me your letter."

"Poppycock. They showed you *a* letter. I certainly didn't write it."

"You might have."

"They lied to you. That is what they do. Joe, look at me. Look at me right now. Look at my face. My eyes." He does. "I will not leave you. You may try to send me away. But I will not leave, ever. I. Will. Not."

"Oh."

"So now you know."

And even when he goes back to the cell and everything hurts again, it doesn't matter.

He realises he has begun to say "I'll tell you." But things are different now.

You lie. You lie like a bald man in a fur hat. You lie like a rug. You lie, you lie, you lie. You went too far. I see you now. I see all of you.

You should have said she was dead. Or captive, like me. That she was here. You should have said anything but that.

You lie. It is what you are.

You lie.

Something inside him is burning.

When they come to take him away, he goes placidly, then thinks of the coffin man. The coffin man, who had been completely restrained and yet had somehow been able to hurt them. Who rode out the taser and whatever drugs they give him and was still so dangerous they had to keep him strapped down, and even then could not control him. The coffin man is captive, but he is not imprisoned. And he is an ally.

Joe reaches out sharply and breaks Mr. Ordinary's nose with his right hand. He hangs on, twists, feeling gristle between his fingers, and blood. Mr. Ordinary screams at him.

"That's how it's done," he tells Mr. Ordinary. "*That's* how! That's how it's done!"

It takes five orderlies to hold him down so that a sixth can sedate him.

As grey rushes in from the edges of the world, he sees that they are afraid.

He wakes, and the aches and bruises are like balm. Up is down and the torturers fear the victim, and that is exactly the world as he wants it. The world of misrule.

He grins to himself and, tasting blood on a split lip, grins wider. There's a curious beauty in the white walls of his cell: the textureless tiles are fascinating, the dry, tasteless air is a feast on his tongue. He flexes his legs and arms, feels himself, acutely aware of each muscle and its strength, its tolerances, its limits. He scents his own body, feels his ribs and knows that the layer of fat which has rested there for years has gone. He has not broken. He has actually, medically died here. Perhaps more than once, he isn't sure. And yet he lives. He is more himself than he has ever been. He is the refined essence of himself.

He looks at his life, and sighs at it. There's a pathos in seeing how foolish he has been, how he has fallen into an obvious trap of bad personal logic, but it's still a cause for regret. So much wasted time . . . He follows the track of his error, just to be sure.

Daniel Spork always said that Mathew was no good, that there was never a time when his son was not on the make. He said Mathew was unrestful as a child, and then again as a man. He made no space for the possibility that Mathew's badness was not a quality which inhered in him, but rather the outcome of a learning process which began when he was quite small.

Looking down from his new mountaintop, Joe can trace the path quite easily. Mathew was a refugee. Mathew came into a world which was immediately broken. He was without his mother from almost before he could say her name, and when she returned she did so in a strange, half-hearted way, and she—like him—knew that everything about the world he inhabited was wrong at the most basic level. Fundamentally, Mathew could not believe the pleasant fictions which make life within the law palatable to others. He saw a world in a constant state of war. His father was losing money and losing his shop, which was the external manifestation of his self, because he did exactly what society said he should and society was a cheat. Daniel spent much of his life creating more and more wonderful things, a cargo cultist desperately seeking to achieve something so beautiful that his goddess could not resist. Mathew knew better. He watched, and learned, and saw that she came only in response to things most horribly broken.

So he cheated back. He abandoned Daniel's world in order to preserve it, and from that lesson drew his entire life. He broke laws, cracked safes, smashed windows and shattered the public peace, and from destruction he drew consolation. The biggest lie was that the world worked the way it was supposed to, and having seen through it, Mathew Spork was free.

As his mother was free. And as his son, now, in this white cell which no longer frightens him, is free.

Outside in the corridor, Joe can hear footsteps. The Ruskinites are coming. Mr. Ordinary, perhaps. They will expect him to be cowed, as he has been before. They will expect him to wait and gather his strength. But his strength now is a thing made from opposition. If he backs down, he knows, it will ebb, and he will lose track of this spectacular certainty. That is not something he can afford. Beyond this, he has nothing left.

Which leaves open war. Each time the door opens, he will fight them with everything he has. He will no longer be restrained. He will drive himself against them until they shatter, or he does.

The door opens, and he moves.

He goes to meet them with a growl in his teeth which becomes a roar, and since his mouth is open he bites the hand which unwisely comes close to his face. He keeps going until he feels something crunch and hears a ghastly howling, but is too busy with his hands to worry very much about that. His left grips and his right hammers downwards, once, twice, like a copper pounding on a door. When the weight on his left hand increases, he lets it open, and instantly uses his left elbow on someone else, a scything downward spiral which opens the man's forehead to the bone. He bowls on, barging and lunging, and suddenly they are all on the ground and he stamps and kicks, wading through the tangle as through a garden full of leaves. He keeps going and going and going, and he gets stronger rather than weaker with each blow.

Abruptly, he stops, because there's nothing left to do. There are five men on the ground. Two are moaning softly. Three are quite unconscious.

It had not occurred to him that he might win this fight. Winning a fight, in his mind, is associated with some sort of skill. He had not realised that you could win by just doing the worst things you could possibly imagine, one after another, until your enemies fell over. There's even a sort of cycle to it, like a very dangerous, very angry clock: grab, rake, gouge; twist, pummel, drop. Repeat. Repeat. Repeat.

But now here he is, and—within certain limits—free. Not likely to remain so, perhaps. But he can wreak havoc while he's out. Do some damage to the machine which has hurt him. That has considerable appeal.

He kicks the nearest of his gaolers once more in the spine and gets no reaction. He searches the man and finds a keycard, repeats the process until he has several more. He considers pushing the men into his cell, but there are too many of them and it's too much like hard work. Instead, he takes a shroud from the biggest man and drapes it over himself. *On hemmed-in ground, use subterfuge.* Billy Friend had been a devotee of Sun Tzu, though mostly in relation to women.

He walks away down the corridor, trying the cards on anything he can see. Doors click. He doesn't bother to look inside. If there are inmates, they will either come out or they won't. Behind him, he hears strange voices and cries, so he assumes there are at least a few. He hopes they are as angry as he is. Or mad in some horrible way. That would be fine.

He reaches a different sort of door, a double door, and when it opens, he realises it's a lift. He goes in. Naturally, he will try to escape. They will know by now that he is out. Therefore they will expect him to go up. Up and out. They will be waiting.

So he goes down.

As soon as the lift doors open, he smells smoke.

There are red lights set into the walls on this floor, and they're shining brightly. Somewhere there's a klaxon going off. A crowd of Ruskinites slither past him, single-minded. He remembers at the last minute to bob his head in an approximation of their sinuous weave, but they don't pay any attention.

He can't assume it will last. There must be surveillance. They will in any case shortly realise he is wearing this rather minimal disguise, and they must have ways of knowing one another.

He walks on. A security door requires a different card, a blue one, from the deck in his hand. He steps through. The smell of smoke is much stronger.

In his head, he realises, he has a sort of ragged notion of how this place is laid out. It is a pyramid or ziggurat, of which the uppermost level is the garden and the common room. Below that is the standard accommodation for patients, and below that is his level: the holding cells for inconvenient people to be tortured, and a selection of actual torture chambers. This level, being below that one, must be more secret or more important in some way.

He rounds a corner, and finds himself in a cinema.

Or not. There is a screen, and there are chairs and speakers, yes. But there is also a species of stage or platform, and each seat has what appears to be a set of electrodes attached. The walls are covered in grey foam moulded in geometric patterns, like a sound studio.

"If an ordinary man were to wake with Napoleon's memories, men would call him mad." A vast face fills the screen, elegant, lean and cruel. A man in early middle years, his skin very clear and tanned, his features an indefinable blend of cultures. His mouth quirks. "But what if he woke with demonstrably accurate memories which were recorded nowhere else? What if he woke with the face of Napoleon as well? And finally, how, if this man arose from his bed with no mind of his own? What if John Smith ceased to be, and in his place was a perfect replica of the Emperor in body and memory? At what point would we acknowledge that he was identical with that first Napoleon? That he was not merely a copy, but an actual regenesis? What if the pattern of the mind itself could be measured and found to be identical?"

The camera draws back. The man lies on a plush, opulent bed, and his body is festooned with wires and sensors. Almost, he hangs in the bed, so many cables are affixed to his skin. More cameras are visible around him, recording him from every angle. He gestures off to one side, to a circular screen—Joe guesses it must be green—showing an oscillating pattern. A wave.

"This is my mind. This is my body. Make my history your own. Match it perfectly, and become part of me. Part of God."

Joe Spork stares for a moment at the lean, evil face of Brother Sheamus. There is an intensity to him, a power, which is both alien and familiar. It reminds him of someone. And then he hears the screaming.

The screaming is very hoarse, very desperate. It's a man, or a very big woman, because it's deep. It's not horror-movie screaming, designed to rattle the chandelier. It's something else entirely, a mammalian noise. *Alarm. Alert. There are tigers. I am taken. I am down.*

Joe has recently made the same sound himself.

Around a corner, through a door, another door, and then:

Two men. One of them is Mr. Ordinary.

Mr. Ordinary stares up from his chair at another person, an altogether different sort of person. A tiger.

The tiger is smiling. He has a thick beard and greying hair tied back with a piece of orange string. His skin is pale, but leathery. Good teeth, a little snaggled at each corner of the mouth; you can see it in the line of his face. Wide lips.

Joe does not recognise him; not his movements, nor his face, nor even his eyes, until a glance at Mr. Ordinary shows an appalling, absolute despair, and then—as the torturer glimpses Joe in his Ruskinite shroud—the desperate hope of rescue.

There's really only one person here who makes anyone that afraid. And now that he looks, he recognises the eyes, too.

The coffin man bends down in front of Mr. Ordinary, gets his head close to the other's face.

"Where's the way out, boy?" His voice is thick and he lisps. Those snaggles at the corner of his mouth: the bite plate has deformed his teeth, and he's not used to not wearing it yet, can't compensate. He'll need practice, and a good dentist. All the same, there's something about the voice: "buuwoy." A fisherman's voice.

"It's down!"

"Is it bollocks." Plymouth, with a taste of London, maybe. The coffin man shrugs, and lays his hand gently across Mr. Ordinary's face. When he withdraws it, he is mysteriously holding something wobbly, and Mr. Ordinary is screaming again, this time sharply, and Joe realises it is an ear. The coffin man tosses it aside. Then he speaks again.

"Seen you." He glances over at Joe. "You, I'm talking to." He shrugs. "You ain't what you look like, I know that."

Joe realises he is still wearing the shroud. He pulls it off.

"Thought so," the coffin man nods. "Trick of the walk, maybe."

"How did you get out?"

"Well, some bugger poked the anthill, didn't he? Set off all the alarum bells and what have you. Someone got careless. That don't pay with me. I got him, and his friends, and I set 'em on fire. Doesn't pay to show me disrespect. I keep trying to tell 'em. You look like you've come of age, though."

"I've what?"

The older man shrugs. "All that strength. You walk through everything as if you're afraid of breaking it. Keep it all down in the dark. Or you did, maybe."

"Keep what in the dark?"

"Don't be a tit. You know perfectly well what I'm talking about. Here," he adds reprovingly, as Mr. Ordinary tries to get up, "no call for that, is there? Don't be giving me force." Force is a bad thing. The coffin man reaches down and does something at the open mess which used to house an ear. Mr. Ordinary doubles over and vomits, drily. "So what's a Hakote, and what do they write about, that this bugger cares so much about it?"

Night Market instinct: *evade*. Joe shrugs. "Search me."

The coffin man stares, and then starts to laugh. He can barely keep upright, he is laughing so hard.

"What's funny?"

"You are! Bloody hell. Ohhh, bloody hell, that's too much . . . You've got no more real clue what's going on than I have, do you? And they knew it, too, but they were giving you the full works, and the more you didn't tell them the more they were scared you were a real hard case, the more they did, the more you didn't know . . . bloody marvellous!"

Joe stifles the urge to tell the other man that actually, yes, he does indeed know what's going on and now he knows the one thing these bastards don't. It's like being at school. Instead of boasting, he laughs, too.

The coffin man leans on the desk and knocks over a stack of reference books, which is even funnier, and it appears that Mr. Ordinary is the only person in the room who is not having a good time. When the coffin man notices this, he sobers a bit.

"Where's the way out? Come on, now."

"Down! Down to the basement!"

"I don't think so. That's where they had me."

"It's a fake! Everything's upside down! When you go to the basement the lift goes up! The mechanism's so smooth you can't tell. It makes everyone sick unless they know! The way out is down there!"

The coffin man grins at Joe.

"That's got the ring of truth in it, for sure. Off you go, then."

"Are you coming?"

The other man glances at him.

"You really don't want me to, matey. I'm unpopular out there. I'm not a bad man, as it happens, though I will confess I'm pretty aggravated right about now. I'm of a mind to share my displeasure." He leans down and does something quick and disgusting to Mr. Ordinary, who makes a dreadful little wheezing noise which suggests he may have torn something and now cannot scream any more. Joe steps back a pace. "Ah. You're getting it now, aren't you?"

"Who are you?"

"No one. Oh, sure, I was somebody, once. I liked Kenny Lonergan's plays and Eartha Kitt's music. I liked . . . orange juice. Fresh, from the sandwich place at the end of my road. Weekly treat, that was. I was that bloke. Who knows what I am now?"

"You're a patient."

"That, too. Mind you, that doesn't make me bad, now, does it?"

Mr. Ordinary plunges one hand abruptly into his pocket and jams something the size of a mobile telephone sharply against the coffin man's leg. There's a strange, sharp noise like a robot blowing a kiss. The coffin man jerks, and smiles.

"There now," he says, stuttering slightly, "that's the moment we've all been waiting for, isn't it?" He rolls his head on his neck and taps his teeth together. Even from this distance, Joe can feel static on his skin. Mr. Ordinary presses the taser again. The coffin man jolts a bit, then steadies.

"It's all about p-purpose," he says. "If you've got purpose and you just . . . nghh . . . you just hold onto it, these things are a b-b-blast. Like someone ss-s-scratching your back for you, from the inside . . . ggdah. Still, you can have too much of a good thing, ey?" He leans down and slaps the taser away. There's a burn on his leg, twin black marks of charred skin.

"You've bollocksed my sock," the coffin man says, and sticks his thumb sharply into Mr. Ordinary's eye. Joe can feel his lips coming back around the question, as if he's going to throw up.

"Who are you?" But he knows, now, or thinks he does.

"My name's Parry," the coffin man says. "You better call me Vaughn. My friends all do. I think it's better off we're friends, you and me."

Fuck, yes.

"Tell you what," Vaughn Parry says, "I think I was supposed to do for you. I think that was the idea. That other bloke, Ted . . . they gave him to me to scare him. 'One for you, Vaughn,' and all that crap. Ought to know better, I didn't want anything to do with him, so they had to do it themselves.

"I think I was going to be your last stop, too, before they put you in the ground. Your destiny, as it were. Think about that for a sec." Parry turns back to look at Mr. Ordinary again, and the man whimpers. "D'you believe in destiny? Seems to me there's a thing about destiny. If there's destiny, then choices don't mean anything, do they? So I do something bad—" He does, and there's a hard, flat scream, cut off in a fit of coughing. Mr. Ordinary is vomiting. "If I do something bad, I didn't choose it. Or rather, I was always going to choose it, never was any way I could be me and not choose it, which amounts to the same thing. So I'm a monster from the day I die all the way back to when I'm born. It's all one, isn't it? But the question is, where am I in all of it? If I can't choose anything, am I just watching? Am I there at all? That's destiny, for you." He shrugs. "Best you piss off now, young 'un," he says, without looking back. "I've got a reputation to maintain," he snarls at Mr. Ordinary sharply, as if this is all his fault, "and I'm going to extend myself a bit."

Joe hesitates. Part of him has a natural instinct to stay and assist Mr. Ordinary. Mr. Ordinary has done very horrible things and is clearly a total bastard, but no one deserves what is happening to him. Joe would under other circumstances cheerfully give him a clean kick in the crotch and, say, break his jaw. This seems an appropriate iteration of his personal feelings. But Vaughn Parry, according to popular rumour and the opinion of Billy Friend, is not really a human being. He is something entirely different wearing a sack made of skin and gloating. There is some commonality of human experience, however attenuated, between Joe and Mr. Ordinary. Joe does not wish to feel any such thing with Vaughn Parry, who hears the Screaming and plucks off ears by way of diverting himself.

And yet, he does. He feels a fierce kinship for him, for his élan, his acquaintanceship with horror. Parry inhabits this world—this new world of professional torture and dark secrets for which a man may be killed—far more elegantly than does Joe the Clockmaker. It makes sense to him. He's at home in it, in a way Joe absolutely is not. Vaughn Parry belongs here, and is unafraid. That is something Joe greatly envies. In one way or another, he has been afraid his entire life—until a few hours ago, when he found clarity and broke Mr. Ordinary's nose.

He is afraid again now. He is terribly afraid of Vaughn Parry. It's reasonable. Parry is the great bogeyman of the moment, a suburban killing machine with an apt sense of the appalling—and here he is, in living Technicolor, with a man's face between his tapered fingers and blood on his shoes. Even if Joe wanted to argue with him, he could not. Parry would kill him.

Or not.

Joe rolls his shoulders again, for a moment fascinated by the very idea. He could scream and leap. He is a big man and Parry is not. He finds he does not care what happens now. The world is wrong. In fact, it is Parry's world. Vaughn Parry makes sense, in a world where this can be done to Joe Spork. The gentle clockmaker, now: there's a fellow who does not understand the way of things. A law-abiding fellow, is Joe. He never considered that the law might not abide by him.

He could scream, and leap, and things would happen. Either he would destroy Parry and the world would be that much better, or he would die, and his problems would be rather finally resolved.

Vaughn Parry glances at him, and grins.

"Not going to, are you?" he says, shaking his head. "Where are you, boy? What does it take to get you out?"

"I don't know. I'm thinking maybe you make more sense than I do."

Parry's eyes open wide for a moment in surprise. "Ey, well, that's not something I hear often. I suppose you're right, anywise. I ought to leave this lad alone before I do him a serious harm and regret it. Lead on."

With this unexpected sentiment, he shunts Joe out of the room, leaving Mr. Ordinary gasping in relief and misery on the floor.

Joe hesitates, then extends his hand to Vaughn Parry.

After a similar pause, Parry takes it awkwardly and shakes. They move quickly back through the building towards the lift. In the cinema, Joe pauses to look at the screen. The Recorded Man is running now, moving, his body strangely clenched as if around an old injury, yet possessed of a familiar, unpleasant fluidity. Joe scowls.

Parry nods. "This is where they make them," he says, and goes to leave. Joe lingers.

"Make who?"

"Them. The monks. They run current through your head until it's empty and then they turn you into one of them. With this." He gestures around. "They tried it with me."

"What happened?"

"A lot of them were damaged beyond repair, is what fucking happened. After that they decided I wasn't monk material." Parry grins, eyes sharp and teeth bloody, and Joe hopes devoutly he has bitten his tongue and not eaten part of Mr. Ordinary. "So can we get the fuck out of the burning mental prison, please?"

"Yes. Of course."

Joe lets Vaughn Parry lead the way to the lift.

Parry pushes the button for the basement. Now that he knows, Joe can feel the lift rising. Up, up, and away. The doors open, and he sees actual daylight, grim and grey and very wet. English weather. The fire has not reached this floor yet, but the alarm is ringing. He listens to it, curious, and looks at the exit. Perhaps if he tries to cross the threshold, he will feel pain. Perhaps the entire Order of John the Maker is waiting for them. Perhaps there's a sniper, a crowd of armed police marksmen. Perhaps the bees have come home and everyone has gone mad. Perhaps Polly Cradle really did write that letter.

He walks forward anyway.

XIV

The Secret History of Vaughn Parry;
the Monte;
homeward bound.

His name's Dalton," Parry murmurs meditatively in the shady back seats of the night bus. Having paid their way with Mr. Ordinary's cash, he is examining the credit cards. "Oh. Driving licence. Home address. I wonder if he's married . . ." and then, seeing Joe's look, "Oh ey, for God's sake, no! I only meant if he's not we could break in and get some clothes, empty his fridge. No reason to . . ." He sighs, maligned. Joe stares out into the grey-green landscape of concrete and pathetic little trees in local-council industrial pots.

Neither of them is entirely sure where the bus is going, because they're not entirely clear on where they are. Vaughn Parry was all for ducking into the hedgerows, but Joe persuaded him that a city was a better place to hide than a field. They climbed aboard and said "into town."

"That business with the lift was clever, turning me upside down. Smart, that is. Your man Brother Sheamus, that'll be, no? Nasty mind he's got, I will say."

Joe Spork looks at Britain's most wanted serial killer and wonders if this is professional admiration. Vaughn Parry sees it, and sighs again.

"I ain't what you think, Joe. Granted, I'm a bit feral now, but I bin in there a long time and it wasn't any kind of fun. But I ain't what you think."

"I'm not sure what I think."

Parry looks at him, sceptical, then—apparently considering their situation—nods. "You want it from the beginning?"

"It's a long drive, evidently."

"An hour, he said. Well, then."

Parry talks.

The nursery in the Parry household was decorated in pictures of scarecrows. Vaughn Parry's first memories are of playing with wooden building blocks in the middle of the red rug, looking around at ten different ghoulish turnip faces and their withered arms, and—being an undertaker's boy—he deduced at the age of four that all men die, and all women, too. He grew up numb. He disliked the other children, who seemed to be unable to understand what this entailed. If death was coming with such pointed inevitability, of what possible value was the Earth and anything on it? He lived in a darkness he couldn't penetrate. It lurked at the edge of his vision. He slept with the lights on until his father made him turn them off, and each night they fought like dogs, snarling and snapping at one another. His mother had died already, of pneumonia. He went to the Waiting Game because it was as good a way as any to wait for his own burial.

"And then they bloody pranked me," Parry mutters. "Bloody ghastly, ey? Stitched up some fox in a corpse, I don't know. I passed out on my feet, like. Didn't remember a sodding thing after, and there's some old gaffer telling me I'm a monster. I said 'Bollocks' and stormed out."

He drifted. At some point he got into the make-up trade, an offshoot of what he already knew from undertaking. Dead faces are harder because they're dead, easier because you can use plaster and putty and actual paint. You can even cut bits off if you have to, but don't tell anyone.

And then he was living in a town upcountry, in some old house, when a thin man and a fat man came calling. He was using a false name because he didn't want anything to do with his family, but they knew who he was anyway, no notion how.

"This was years ago, mind. Five, six. Don't know what the bloody date is now."

Nor does Joe, in point of fact. How many weeks has he been imprisoned? Or is it months? He has no idea. He's exhausted, he knows that much.

"'Mr. Parry,' says the thin one, 'there's a certain task we'd like for you to do. It pays well, but it's quite secret.' Well, I did it, didn't I? Dress a corpse, they said. Make him look respectable. I knew how to do that. A few weeks later there was another, and another. Two thousand quid a time, thank you kindly, and the promise of more work to come. But I was getting a funny feeling, wasn't I? These lads—they were all lads, thank God, no lasses and no kids, or I couldn't have stuck it—they had the look of . . . well. We know now, don't we? They'd been in that place back there, or somewhere like it, and they hadn't made it out. Died on the operating table, most like, and here was I covering the tracks. They tried to make me patch up your friend Ted, you know, left me in there with him and some slap and so on. I told 'em to fuck off. Screamed it . . . God, you get like an animal, don't you, it doesn't take long, or much. You get like King Kong in a cage!" He laughs, a strange, unwholesome laugh, like a plague survivor.

"Ey, so. They noticed me noticing, didn't they? One day I turn up with my kit and there's the body, but he's . . . fresh. Still warm. I good as pissed myself, and then I heard sirens. Didn't occur to me until they come in through the front door what was going on. They'd set me up, hadn't they, to take the fall for the whole lot. For fifty or sixty poor dead bastards . . . and then there was the back room, wasn't there?"

The back room was famous—infamous. Parry had been escalating, according to the story. Serial killers apparently do this. Not content with one expression of their madness, they develop more and more outré, dreadful rituals and appetites until they are stopped.

In the back room was the latest victim's family. What was done there had caused one of the investigating detectives to take an overdose. Two more retired from the force.

"They said it was all me," Parry reports woodenly. "The mother, the kid. All me. I'm sorry if I can't cry any more," he adds, "but I've been in for over a year. First in the police nick and then some hospital and then there. I've been Vaughn the killer all that time. I've got false teeth now, after they kicked them in. I'm . . . someone I never was, now. It's what happens, isn't it? We lose who we are. Become someone else." He shudders.

"What about you?" Vaughn Parry says at last. "What's the deal with you? The way I hear it, they hate you even worse'n me."

Joe sighs, and gives an abbreviated version of recent events, and an even more curtailed description of life in the House of Spork. He doesn't want Parry inside his life, even if his confession is a true one. The man who was considering giving Mr. Ordinary a taste of his own medicine is not someone he wishes to share intimacies with, more than he must.

"Mechanical bees," Vaughn Parry mutters. "And you say it's big?"

"Huge, I think. Going-to-war sort of big."

"Bloody hell."

The road surface changes, the whine of the tyres giving way to a deep grumble.

"Well, for what it's worth," Parry goes on, "I've got more to tell you. I s'pose I owe it to you, or to bloody Dalton. Payback. And if it's that important, too . . ."

"What is it?"

"Your friend Ted . . . confessed to me, is the only word. Because I was an undertaker once. I didn't tell him I wasn't a Waiting Man proper. Didn't seem to matter much at that point. Not to him, anyway." Parry's face flickers with something like horror. "He was all messed up. They'd had at him, then they let him know who I was and brought him to me. They wanted him to be scared of Monstrous Vaughn, you see, but he was past caring. Something was broke in his chest. You could hear it flapping about . . . he wanted absolution." Parry sighs. "From me. Of all the people on God's Earth, he wanted absolution from the man supposed to be the worst bastard ever walked. And I couldn't give it to 'im because it's bin so long since anyone even looked at me with anything other than hate I didn't have the words. I just stared at him and he choked out the 'ole thing and then he died."

Vaughn Parry shudders. "You've got this thing they want, though?" Vaughn Parry says abruptly. "I mean, it's not all a complete bloody joke, right? Not a total waste of time?"

"Yes," Joe says absently. "I worked it out, in there."

"Sholt said you had. It was like a kind of revelation for 'im. Like an angel, he said. But I was—" He stops. "I'm rattling on like a pillock."

"No, it's fine."

"I haven't talked for a bit."

No. You haven't. But Parry's lisp is already better.

"It's fine," Joe assures him. "What were you saying?"

"When he said that, I was, well . . . I was afraid. For the first time in howeverlong I had something to hope for, that you'd find this blessed whatsis and stick it up their collective arse, ey?" Parry laughs. "Although, maybe you better just hang onto it. Keep it in a safe place."

It's a relief to be able to talk about this aloud. Joe has been screaming it, in rhyme, for—he doesn't know how many days. *Breath of the docks. Beneath the rocks. Frankie's drum has chicken pox.* He frowns and makes an uncertain gesture with his hand: this way, that way. "It's safe for the moment," he says. "It's in the Death Clock. She sent it to my grandfather and he kept it in the Death Clock, because it's so ugly no one looks at it twice. And he commended it to me for 'special study.' I thought he was just being annoying and educational. And now they've got it and they don't even know. All this," he waves at himself, his bruises and by extension the whole of Happy Acres, "and it was there, all the time. They've probably got it in a box."

Vaughn Parry peers at him. "Well, I'm sure you know what that means to the world at large," he says at last. "Buggered if I do, though. No, for God's sake, don't tell me! Bloody hell, I don't want your trouble as well as mine, do I?"

Joe Spork shakes his head. He feels an urge to get back to his natural habitat, even if he has to hide beneath the streets among the Tosher's Beat, in the rooms the toshers don't bother with.

The bus stops briefly, and a man climbs on board who must be a fruit picker. His hands are swaddled in elastoplast. He wears a T-shirt written in a European alphabet Joe doesn't recognise, and carries a white plastic bag full of unseasonal greenhouse plums.

Joe Spork considers his good fortune. He has escaped from a heavily guarded institution in the company of a monster who turns out to be quite nice. He has eluded what must be a major search—by speed? Stealth? Confusion? And he alone in all the world—apart from Vaughn Parry—knows the location of the calibration drum.

Just the two of them.

"This bus is now non-stopping all the way to London," the driver says. Joe feels a momentary claustrophobia, and then his mind jumps sideways and around a corner. Not claustrophobia. Vertigo, on the cliff of impossible convenience. A straight course, all the way home. Back to Mercer and Polly. Parry giving answers to questions desperately asked. Parry as Sholt's confidant, in that strange clarity before dying. Parry, the country's most wanted man, suddenly a kindred spirit.

Too easy.

All that time being tortured, and then this. So simple. A bit of pain and a bit of work, and the whole place gone. A prisoner's dream.

They have shown you the stick. Soon, they will show you the carrot.

A prisoner's fantasy.

There is no carrot. Polly and I are your only friends.

This game is fixed.

Not lucky at all. Three-Card Monte.

I thought I was choosing the card I wanted, but the bunco man was slipping me the one he wanted me to have. I haven't found the lady. I've drawn the Joker.

Vaughn Parry.

In which case, you work for someone, don't you? I'm wrong. You're not a loner at all. You're not what you say you are. You're a lie and a liar, and I'm taking you where you want to go. Telling you what you want to know.

In which case, you could well be a killer, after all.

Hell, hell, hell.

But this is a new, activated Joe Spork. His body has a plan before he does, is already moving when he gives the okay, flows into the shape he needs without thought—thank God, because if he thought about it he'd mess it up, no doubt.

He times it exactly right. The driver takes off the brakes and the bus jolts. Joe Spork grabs Vaughn Parry by the shoulders and slams his head sharply into the chrome steel pole in the aisle. Parry's face flashes through shock and pain, then for the briefest instant into a bottomless, appalling rage. Then the bus judders again and Joe repeats the manoeuvre, and Parry slumps. Joe rests him against the window, and rushes to the front.

"I'm so sorry," he says, "I'm on the wrong bus."

The driver sighs. "Anyone else?" he asks. The rest of the passengers shake their heads or stare in venomous accusation at the idiot Joe, and the driver lets him off.

He watches the red tail lights fade, and runs to a phone box to call Mercer.

Joe is expecting a large black car with tinted windows, or possibly several cars. He allows himself to wonder if there will be a helicopter. He is quite sure there will be people in dark suits, grave of mien and taciturn and fraught with black-lettered magic.

In the event, Mercer sends four ambulances, two fire engines, a climate-change protest, a Scottish travelling circus, and a fox hunt. These various distractions arrive separately but with immaculate coordination, so that one moment Joshua Joseph Spork is hiding in the shadows of a pub garden and hearing pursuit in every whisper of wind, and the next the whole suburb is lit with blue lights and resounding with sirens, and seventy-eight beagles and a gross of meteorologists are sharing road space with Darla the Bearded Lassie.

Through the midst of this paralysing confusion comes an unremarkable Volkswagen people-mover in green. It slips gracefully between the hunt master and a brace of urban foxes who are apparently admiring the view, Mercer himself at the wheel. The side door slides open.

"Get in," Polly Cradle says gently, and Joe's heart leaps to see that she is here. Then he stops abruptly: beside her sits Edie Banister, complete with odiferous pug and giant revolver.

"Come on, Joe," Polly says. "It's time." She glances over her shoulder at Edie, then extends her hand to him. "Get in. We'll explain on the way."

By a circuitous route and through lanes and towns and all around the London Orbital, they leave the circus behind.

Joe Spork gazes at the back of the passenger seat. The leather—or it may be leatherette—is torn around the headrest, revealing a sliver of foam. Part of him wants to explore it with his fingers, touch something real and simple and solid outside Happy Acres and know that this is not a dream. That he is not still on the operating table, dying. The world is oddly quiet and colourless, as if he has slipped sideways into a monochrome film or an underwater documentary. He assumes this is shock or post-traumatic stress, but does not particularly care.

He lifts his eyes from his study of the leather and looks around. Polly Cradle is like a log fire, a warm, comforting thing. She catches him looking and smiles, puts her hand on his leg, and a little patch of heat grows where her palm is. He looks the other way and finds Edie Banister.

Edie Banister looks back at him and waits. And so they pass a few miles: Polly, Joe, Edie. The front seat is another country.

"Did you do this to me?" Joe asks.

Edie sighs. "Yes. Well, yes and no. I put you in the line of fire." After a brief struggle, honesty compels her to add, "I thought it was necessary and then I realised it was rather out of spite. I'm sorry."

He looks at her some more, and wonders why he hasn't pulled her head from her shoulders and thrown it out of the window. Carefully, so as not to cause an accident. He wonders if she is really sorry, and if sorry helps in any way. Then he says, "Spite?"

"Your grandmother, not you."

It's always about his bloody family, somehow. "How's Harriet?" he asks belatedly.

"Your mother is fine, Joe," Mercer says firmly. "The C of E has hidden her away—I'm sure you can talk to her if you want."

Joe goes back to studying the seat, and finally does reach out to play with the loose edge. He flicks it one way and another until Polly very gently encloses his big hand in her two smaller ones and draws it away to kiss it as if he'd burned it on something. She does not ask if he is all right.

"I'm all right," he says, a bit fuzzily, only now realising that it may turn out to be true. If only the colours will spread out from her, into the world.

She manages not to burst into tears, but it's a close thing. Instead, she looks sternly at Edie and tells her to get going on the story. Edie nods, and then abruptly stalls, mouth open. "I don't know where to begin," she says. "I've lost it. Senility."

Joe nods. He is familiar with the sense of not being able to trust your own mind. "Who are you?"

Edie nods, grateful. "You know my name. I used to—well, I used to work with your grandmother. We were friends. I've been a lot of other things, too. A spy, mostly. Sort of a policeman. And now a revolutionary, I suppose. A terrorist." She sighs. "This changing-the-world business is harder than I imagined."

"I didn't know Frankie had any friends," Joe says.

"Joe, don't be dense," Polly murmurs, kissing his hair to take the sting out of it. "They were lovers."

Joe glances, automatically, at Edie, and sees her embarrassment become a wide grin.

"Well, yes," Edie says. "We were. And you, young miss, are a bucketload of trouble, aren't you?"

Polly shrugs. "I believe in getting these things out in the open. It saves misunderstandings later."

Edie finds that she agrees, and a moment later she begins the whole story from scratch—albeit in highly abbreviated form—telling it without restraint from the moment Abel Jasmine came to the Lady Gravely school, all the way to her recent abrupt decision that something had to be done.

Joe listens to the secret history of the House of Spork—or Fossoyeur, as it seems—and feels, beneath the monochrome, a sense of place. This is where Daniel's sorrow came from. Where Mathew's mania was born. This is how it was, and how it came to be.

That it is also the root of his recent pain is less important. Edie is a treasure house of his own self, his roots. He wants to put her under glass, wind her up and play her in the evenings. Her life is so bright. And he, Joe, is part of this story, and her story is part of his. Finally, he is not too late for something, after all.

"The world is in the hands of idiots," Edie cries, by way of exculpation, mistaking his quiet for doubt or disapprobation. "The Cold War is over and what do they do? Go looking for a new one. We're richer than we've ever been. What happens? We burn the forests and borrow so much money that suddenly we're poor. Everything's upside down and it's just because people don't pay attention. It ought to be a perfect world! That's what we wanted. That's what I worked for. For decades! I hid Frankie's machine for years and years. For nothing. For a bunch of charlatans to tell me I've never had it so good while they steal my neighbour's pension!"

She subsides, muttering. Mercer purses his lips.

"The bees are now distributed over most of the globe," he says. "From time to time there are outbreaks of truth, but I have to say I don't see a new age of love and understanding being ushered in. The West Bank is in flames, but I suppose it was going that way already. A lot of Africa is looking bad. The Special Relationship is effectively finished. The nuclear states, by the way, have reciprocally pledged to launch their weapons should it turn out that the Apprehension Engine—they're calling it a weapon of mass destruction—has been deliberately deployed against their citizens by another nation. All of which, I gather, is before the machine is properly effective. These are just tasters. If this is a global improvement of the lot of mankind, I don't want to know what a crisis looks like."

Edie ducks her head. "It'll get better. Frankie worked it out. She was never wrong. When the bees come back, the array will be complete and things will . . . get better." Her certainty is fading as she says it out loud. What made sense in the twentieth century sounds odd in the twenty-first. Blockish, even, and naive.

Mercer sighs. "Possibly. Although I was never very fond of perfect, sweeping solutions. I always feel sympathy with the people who get swept. But in any case . . . the machine is no longer going to do what it's supposed to, is it?"

"I don't see what he gets out of it," Polly Cradle interrupts. "How does all this make him godlike?" She looks over at Edie.

Edie scowls. "Chaos. Confusion. Wickedness. It's always like this with him. Becoming God is an excuse. He says God's alien and appalling, so that anything ghastly he does just makes him more transcendent. It's a fiddle. Not that it is him. It can't be."

"Only," Polly goes on, "from what you say, he doesn't strike me as chaotic at all. He strikes me as the opposite. You called him a spider. You said he loves elegance. Chess and bluffing and forked strategies. Heads I win, tails you lose."

"Well," Edie says, waving her hands vaguely to indicate, perhaps, that evil is as evil does, and you just can't fathom it, you have to shoot it when the opportunity arises. Mercer waits a moment, but that seems to be the extent of her response. He carries on.

"But in the meantime it would appear that the apparatus from Wistithiel is now in the hands of a monster who proposes to abuse it in some way so as to bring about the end of the world or his own elevation to godhood or possibly both. And my best friend has spent the last while in a government-sponsored torture farm being given the full works. So while I greatly sympathise with your perception, Miss Banister, I imagine you will understand when I say that I'm not sure your actions have greatly improved our lot."

Edie looks stricken. Joe finds himself confessing in turn the days of his captivity, and his brief, strange, un-friendship with Vaughn Parry.

"I should have killed him," he concludes. "That would have been the professional thing to do. I told him what they wanted to know all along. I just didn't think. I just wanted to get away. I should have finished it."

Edie Banister sighs. "The professional thing. Yes. The tactically wise thing. You might have bought us some time, at a cost. But I have come to believe, young Joe, that it's no bad thing to be a bit amateurish, in one's heart. The professionals have been in charge for a while now, and it hasn't done a blind bit of good."

She shrugs, including herself in this damnation. Joe realises he has not touched her, this strange leftover person from his family's life. He reaches out to shake her hand.

There is a noise like someone jointing a chicken, and the car fills with the sharp aroma of doggy regurgitate. The handshake never quite happens.

After a few minutes with the windows open, there is general agreement in the car that a brief stop for a cup of tea may be in order.

The café table is made of scratched red plastic with a metal surround. The chairs are uncomfortable, and the tea tastes mostly of sump. Joe Spork drinks his and then steals Mercer's, too. Edie, having washed out her bag, stares into the swirling circle of her cup as if it is showing her mysteries. Mercer leans on the wall next to the till, watching the car park. Joe worries that they're worrying about him, that he needs to say something which will make them all feel better. He can't imagine what it would be.

Only Polly seems to be exactly who she always is. She smiles charmingly at the lovestruck teenage boy who brings the tray, tips him too much and tells him she's a rock star and not to admit to anyone she was here, and then looks across at Edie.

"This isn't what you had in mind," she observes.

"No," Edie says.

Polly waits, but Edie doesn't continue, so she tries again. "What was supposed to happen?"

Edie waggles her hands in the air. "Good things. Frankie had the maths, you know. She actually calculated the consequences. If they'd just leave it alone, the machine would make the world better. Nine per cent better, she said. Enough to push us in the right direction over time. Make a perfect world." She stops. "A better one, anyway. But I didn't imagine all this would come out of the woodwork."

"'All this' meaning Sheamus. The Ruskinites."

"Sheamus is dead. The one I knew, the Opium Khan. He must be. He was years older than me."

"You're here."

Edie snorts. "Barely."

The roads are empty and the night is very dark. Inside the car, the only light is from the instrument panel and the street lights as they zip past. Joe knew a man once who made a career out of chopping them down and stealing them for the aluminium. It's an expensive material. He counts, in his head, reckoning weight and value, and London draws closer, green motorway signs displaying the distance to the statue of Charles I in Trafalgar Square. It occurs to him that he has no idea where the car is going.

"Can't go to the shop," Mercer replies, meaning Noblewhite Cradle rather than Joe's shattered warehouse. "It's being watched. Bethany's gone in a few different directions to lead them off. I told her it was dangerous, and she said—they all said—'Bring it on.' They're a doughty bunch, my Bethanys. And good lawyers in their own right, of course.

"But we don't have a lot of options. The firm is under a ton of pressure from the forces of illiberal and irresponsible government; writs and control orders and demands for our account numbers. We're fighting back, but it's hard to win anything when the other fellow changes the rules under you. I did persuade a local magistrate to grant me an Antisocial Behaviour Order in respect of Detective Sergeant Patchkind, which I must say was very satisfying . . ." He flashes a grin, then sobers.

"But we couldn't risk using any of our regular London places. We set it up as if we were heading for our out-of-town offices, which are frankly a sort of fortress. I suspect they'd be delighted with that: all the rats in one sack . . . We're going somewhere a little more out of the way. Blood over law. Or friendship will do, in the pinch."

Joe doesn't bother to point out that this is not an answer to his question. He's too tired to fret, and the aches in his body are burning everywhere except where he rests against Polly Cradle's shoulder. "Ted said we need to go to Station Y," he murmurs, but the sounds of the car smother the words and only Polly hears them. He lolls, and mercifully does not dream.

When he wakes, he finds himself on familiar ground. The car turns a final corner, through a private drive—the Cradle slush fund has been at work—and over someone's front garden and onto the road again, and there is Harticle's, its great fortress doors open to receive them.

Joe glances at Polly. She shrugs. "Mercer's better at this part than I am. I get very cross when he tells me how to investigate, so I do as he says for things like this. We can't get you out of the country tonight. And if we could, I'm not sure where you'd go. So you have to go where people care about you and hope for the best." She glances at Edie, who nods.

Joe Spork contemplates a world on the brink of chaos and disaster which still finds time to hunt for a bewildered clockworker.

He wonders whether they should call ahead, then thinks of all those movies where the fugitive briefly activates a cellphone and is immediately traced. He realises Mercer has been without his this entire time. It's practically like seeing him nude.

They get out into the damp of the small hours. The car flashes its lights twice, orange lamps illuminating the gutter and the curtained windows of Guildholt Street, and wait.

After a moment, Mercer growls. "There should be thugs. I asked for thugs."

"Stay or go?" Polly says.

When he hesitates, Edie intervenes. "We stay. If we're buggered, we're already buggered. If we're not, we run from a safe place. Maybe your thugs had to take care of a scout."

Mercer nods: possible. Joe the habitué leads the way up the steps, smelling the wet oak and iron. The door, unlatched, slides silently back at his touch. The corridor is discreetly dark, welcoming. He breathes in old carpet and lubricating oils. For a moment his nose tingles at a scent like pepper and he stops, but the flavour is gone and he cannot recapture it. Edie dawdles, peering at the pictures and the glass cases, and at an ornate waste basket (cut iron and laburnum wood, circa

1920). After a moment, she drops a lunch box into the bin, and carries on. It seems an odd moment to be cleaning out your handbag, but Joe supposes that when you're old, the time is always now.

"Bob?" he murmurs into the dark.

From within, the sound of voices, a sense of a presence, but no reply. Edie shuffles forward, Bastion snuffling alertly from her bag.

"Cecily?" Joe calls.

"In here," the gruff voice answers. Joe Spork smiles and half-runs to the reading room.

Cecily Foalbury sits in her usual chair at the long central table, surrounded by papers in a great pile of chaos and consilience. Two sets of false teeth lie discarded among the debris, along with the container for a third set and a plate of chewy caramels. Cecily looks tired and worn, and she smiles wanly at Joe and then looks away to the great, friendly log fire in the grate. The smell of woodsmoke wafts back, and the crackling flames give the hall a kind of medieval vitality. Joe grins at her, at the place, so far from the white room at Happy Acres.

The door is barely closed behind them before the dog Bastion starts to howl.

"I'm sorry, Sporklet," Cecily says brokenly, looking up. "He got here five minutes ago." Bob Foalbury takes her hand, but cannot raise his head at all, so great is his shame.

"Good evening," a voice murmurs softly from the armchair by the fire. "It's so nice to have you all here."

Joe Spork stares at the craggy face and the cavernous eyes, the wild beard now trimmed close to the chin in a severe, grand vizier's crop, the fresh purple bruise on one side of the head, and at the hooded, faceless figures bobbing on either side.

Vaughn Parry.

Edie Banister growls "You!"—and reaches for her gun.

XV

**The limitations of *Yama Arashi*;
the Recorded Man;
the most orange place in England.**

H ello, Joe," Vaughn Parry says conversationally. "Commander Banister." The Ruskinites beside him rustle at the name, and one steps softly forward. The others duck in behind it. Parry holds out his arm at chest height, and the Ruskinite stops.

"I'm so sorry to have been less than honest with you, Joseph," Parry murmurs gently. His voice is different, shorn of its friendly West Country tones. Now it is deeper, more elegant, more insinuating. A voice to speak blasphemies and reveal secrets. "My name—my real name, which most closely approaches an accurate summation of my history—is Khaygul-Khan Shem Shem Tsien Sikkim, of the nation of Addeh Sikkim. I was a soldier and a scholar and an emperor of thieves. More latterly a monarch, and then a fugitive, but always, always, I was on a path to something greater. Something which cannot be prevented. Because when I am done, it will always have been inevitable. I am a tautology."

Edie points the gun directly at him.

"You are dead," she says. "You are dead, and before you were dead you were old. You are not here, and you are not, not, not young, not . . . *you!* It is *not possible!*" This last, in what is almost a shriek, and as she says it, she pulls the trigger.

Shem Shem Tsien—Vaughn Parry—Brother Sheamus—moves from his chair with impossible grace, letting the bullet fly over his shoulder and on into the wall. If he is old, it is a strange, new kind of old, a serpentine kind where bones melt and become muscle and frailty becomes sinew. He whips his hand around and produces a narrow blade like a gymnast's ribbon, and forward he comes in the same appalling motion, the blade a flicker of light slashing this way and that towards Joe, Polly, Mercer, Edie, around and about and back, ever closer even as he weaves away from the line of Edie's aim as if the gun is nothing more than a long, heavy spear and he can duck the bladed point. From behind him, with him, come the Ruskinites, heron shadows bobbing in line with his own eerie, awkward, perfect steps.

Edie Banister, knobbled finger pressing the trigger with painful slowness, fires again, misses again, then uses the trigger guard of the gun to guide the blade past her shoulder, and barges her bony hip into her enemy's gut. He rocks back, ripples his shoulders like a juggler rolling a ball, and the pommel of the sword smacks sharply into her wrist. The revolver skids away across the floor. They draw back from one another, assessing. Edie moves her weight to her back foot, settles her hips. Somewhere inside, a joint goes pop, and Edie winces. Shem Shem Tsien shifts the line of his body by a fraction, and exhales.

After a moment in deadlock, the Opium Khan smiles contentedly. "Yes," he says. "Yes. It is finished between us."

"Run," Edie says over her shoulder, offering the dog in his bag to Polly Cradle, fiddling briefly with the contents and then seemingly changing her mind.

Polly keeps her eyes on the sword. "What about you?"

"I'm not leaving."

"We can—"

"No, we can't. Don't you recognise this? He's having fun. He's better than I am. He always was, and now he's younger and faster, too. Just run, girl. Take the boy. Do what you can."

"Edie—"

"You've got what you need. *Aglæca*." She grins. "Now, go."

"They won't let us—"

"Of course they will. This is a step on his path to godhood. It's not . . . legendary enough if he just mows you down. It has to be dramatic with him. Canonical." Edie points at them. "He's saving you up for later. But me . . . I'm old news. Old and tired. And . . . it's time. I can do this. The rest is up to you."

She thrusts the dog into Polly's arms, then turns and shakes her hands lightly and winces. She smiles a fey little smile and stands waiting. "Go," she says again, without looking back.

Shem Shem Tsien raises his sword behind his head.

Bastion sets up a feeble howl from Polly's arms, but it has little defiance in it, only an old, bone-deep sorrow too big for a small dog.

Edie's feet flicker across the floor, smooth and very definite. Small steps, perfectly chosen. Her back is straight, her hands out like a schoolteacher conducting an orchestra. She moves again, and the point of the sword slips past her as if her opponent has simply misunderstood what it is for. She sways towards him and her palm flicks out towards the weapon's hilt, catching nothing but air. They separate, regaining distance. Edie smiles, and waves her hand. A tiny circle of light glitters: a crescent of metal. Shem Shem Tsien glances at his hip and finds an empty sheath. Edie opens her other hand, palm down, letting a few hairs drift away. "Nearly had you."

He smiles. "No."

The Opium Khan moves forwards again with that same light-hearted fluidity, and Edie swirls to meet him, arms outstretched. Her feet brush the ground as she steps, and her face is a serene smile of certainty.

Her arms collect Shem Shem Tsien's, the little knife deflecting the sword's edge as he changes direction at the last minute, and she corkscrews down and around: *Yama Arashi*. They blend into one.

Shem Shem Tsien tumbles through the air and lands on his back. Edie follows him down, her hand on the sword to bring the blade close across his neck, but the Opium Khan changes his grip and does not release the blade. He holds her off, and smiles upward into her eyes.

"The limitations of *Yama Arashi*, Commander Banister," he murmurs almost fondly.

"Oh, yes?" Edie growls.

"Yes. It works with swords. Less well with a pistol."

And as realisation dawns Edie looks down, to see his other hand pressed to her chest, and the muzzle of a small modern gun against her ribs.

"Look after Bastion, please," she says calmly to the room. "He doesn't do well by himself. And I'm sure I told you all to get going. Young people today . . ." And then she glances back at her enemy.

"You think you've won, don't you? But you're in real trouble now, you silly sod."

Shem Shem Tsien arches one eyebrow, and pulls the trigger. Edie Banister's back erupts sharply, a narrow hole spraying bone and blood. She shudders once, and then she dies, collapsing to the ground as rags and bone.

For a moment, there is silence, like the end of a piece of music. Then the dog Bastion locks his pink, sightless eyes on the Opium Khan and makes a hard noise in his chest. *You are mine, old fiend. Mine.*

Shem Shem Tsien gets to his feet.

"Oh, Mr. Spork. How very uncouth of you to bring old business into all this. Old *baggage*. Really, it won't do. I shouldn't be surprised. You're a coarse sort of person, in the end." He indicates his bruised forehead, the faint yellow smudge of an impact.

Joe Spork just looks at him. Yes. The beard, the wild eyes, the straggly hair, all gone, and in their place, this smooth, appalling man.

"Vaughn Parry," he says.

The other man shakes his head.

"No. I am Shem Shem Tsien. The Recorded Man. Vaughn Parry is dead. A coat I wear. A vehicle of flesh that I inhabit. An avatar, if you prefer." He smiles.

"If you aren't going to run—and I'm afraid Commander Banister was entirely correct in saying that you should—let me tell you a story. Unlike the last one I told you, which was of course entirely fictional, this one is true. It is the true story, Joshua Spork, of the rebirth of a living god—so you may wish to consider it a new Bible story."

The Opium Khan gestures, and the Ruskinites move to surround the little group. As they go past the corpse of Edie Banister, they seem to stutter, even bow.

"Once upon a time," Shem Shem Tsien begins. He is circling them, almost casual, a fastidious cannibal considering whom to eat next. "Once upon a time, not so very long ago, there was a boy born in the nation of Addeh Sikkim, in the royal palace, who wanted nothing more than to lead his people into a new world of prosperity and hope. He was suited to the task: clever and able and well-favoured." The Opium Khan looks nostalgic.

"I locked him in a steel box and burned him alive. I used the ash to dye my mourning cloth, and I took his kingdom for my own. I needed it, you see, to understand divinity." Joe Spork steps slightly to one side, keeping Shem Shem Tsien in front of him. The Opium Khan nods approvingly, and moves on. Behind him, the Ruskinites bob, in unison with their master.

"I tested God quite scientifically. It was the commencement, after all, of the true scientific age. I assumed His role in every particular. I abused His servants—of every creed. I racked His people. I healed the sick and raised the dead. I reached out and found a magician, a foreign woman who could show me the universe as God sees it. And when, in the fullness of my own life, I began to wane, I realised that I must submit to the last test of godhood. I must return from death myself. Only then would I be able to meet God as an equal. Only then could I become Him."

Bastion growls in his bag. Polly Cradle watches Shem Shem Tsien as he moves past her, sword and pistol held lightly in his hands.

"She was right," he murmurs, indicating Edie's corpse. "You are so very like her. Not physically. But you have that same infuriating, utterly unmerited confidence in your ability to match me." He moves on, going back to his story.

"I caused myself to be recorded. Written down. Transcribed. I became, in the modern parlance, information. Do you see? I carved the pattern of my life into the world, in words and images. I measured the actual activity of my brain. And I stored it. I had a ready stock of test subjects in the orphans of the Wistithiel experiment. While I was still alive, I refined my apparatus by using it on them. I played them fragments of my life and taught them—with electric shocks and so on—to emulate me perfectly. Each of my Ruskinites is an aspect of my self . . ." He gestures, and the Ruskinites around him echo him, fluid motions indicating one another.

"Of course, I never allowed the whole to be shown to anyone. And to be honest with you, the Ruskinites are imperfect. They were neither entirely erased nor willing to learn. One had to employ crude, Pavlovian teaching methods. Pleasure and pain."

"Vaughn Parry was different."

He considers Cecily and Bob Foalbury now, reaches out with the tip of the sword towards them.

"Vaughn was an empty corpse walking. He had nothing inside him at all. He was a natural miracle: a body pretending to be a living man. And in that corpse, a desperate hunger to be a real boy . . . he studied so hard. He learned and learned and practised and practised and eventually he knew it all. He moved like me. He felt what I feel. He was surgically altered to look like me.

"And then he sat, day upon day upon night upon night, wired to my machines, and matched the pattern of his living brain's impulses to my own. Until, little by little, I returned. Do you not see the genius of it? No? You object, perhaps that there is a soul, a part distinct which I do not possess? But consider: if there is, that part fled when my body died, but my mind persists. In which case, I am the first man ever to possess not one soul, but two."

The attack comes as he says the final word, but his breath is completely even. He flourishes the sword around and back, light glinting on the blade, and as he does so his other hand stabs out towards Polly Cradle, pulling the trigger, and he screams a feral howl of triumph and delight.

But Polly Cradle is no longer there. Joe has caught her up, was moving even before Shem Shem Tsien was, knew instinctively the denouement of the Opium Khan's speech. *Because that's what bastards do.*

It begins in his chest as a heart-attack tightness, then unravels immediately in all directions like an electric shock. When it reaches his fingertips and toes it bounces, and his eyes fly open very wide. He can see now, quite clearly. The strange monochrome of his vision has receded, given way to sharp, vibrant colours. He's pretty sure he's glowing from within like Jack O'Lantern. The bounce reaches his stomach and there's a weird instant of calm before he can put a name to what is happening, and when he does it seems insufficient to the thing itself.

Rage.

It's not like a red mist or a thunderstorm, it's like a weight lifted from his shoulders and a clear light falling across the world.

Oh, I see. It's like that, is it?

Then screw you, too.

A man who tortures in white cells; who hates and has no appreciation of the beauty of what he destroys; a man who takes what is not his over and over and over again, who would casually shatter the strange, beautiful library of Edie Banister's brain: for the first time in Joe's entire life, here is someone he can hit as hard as he knows how, without fear of going too far. There is no such place. He can hear Polly Cradle and her brother saying something like "go" which is more probably "no," but in Polly at least he can hear the rawness which is also in him, and her soul's approval even as her mind urges caution.

Joe feels his face wrinkle up in a boar's-head snarl, and charges straight at Shem Shem Tsien. He hears a furious warble which resonates in his chest, sees the dog, Bastion; he scoops up this unlikely ally in a single motion and carries on. The dog's growl becomes a song of war.

Come, horologist. The old, dead man offends me. Let us be about him.

Ruskinites converge, black linen dolls with grasping hands and empty hoods. Halloween ghosts. Man or machine? Joe dumps Bastion on the first one and the dog latches onto the man's cowl and gets to work, does something appalling which will leave scars, Joe knows it will because he can hear screaming. He had no idea Ruskinites could scream, until now. His anger takes note: *pain works.*

Joe fields the second monk and lifts him bodily from the ground. The Opium Khan is firing his gun and the Ruskinite takes the hits, one, two, three. Six. Don't guns have six bullets? This one has more. An automatic can have fourteen, Joe dimly remembers, but it doesn't matter anyway; the distance is short. He throws the Ruskinite directly at Shem Shem Tsien and finds his arms occupied with more of them, but they're so light, so clumsy. He bites one of them horribly, grabs another with his hands and forces his arm in a wrong direction, hears something snap and crack. *HAH!*

Someone is next to him, a stout, grey-haired figure with a crowbar: Bob Foalbury, former Chief Petty Officer, in defence of his wife. "Bollocks!" Bob is yelling. "Bollocks, bollocks, bollocks!" and with each shout he slams his crowbar, to good effect—but he is slowing, old muscles betraying him. Joe grabs the crowbar—no, it's a length of Victorian iron pipe, even better—and yells to him: "Get Cecily! Get her out!" And Bob says "Aye aye," which almost makes Joe smile despite everything, and off he goes. Joe turns to find the next enemy, slaps him open-handed and spins him around, then slams an elbow down and across in the opposite direction. He follows with the pipe, hears a clang as he smashes a metal head.

He recalls his epiphany in the white room. Survival rests on an absolute lack of compunction. Martial artists achieve this through repetition: the decision to harm is taken in advance, the motion practised. The average person hesitates in order to judge what is necessary. Humanity requires the calculation: what to do, how far to escalate? Joe Spork is not escalating so much as he is erupting, straight up, from a deep well of anger at the world's injustices, at his mother's chill and his father's ease, at Frankie's abandonment of Daniel, at Daniel's weak response. Joe need not hold back. He is fighting machines and monsters, and beyond that, he is not fighting. He is fixing something broken. The world having Shem Shem Tsien in it is a flaw, like rust in the cogs. He feels no compunction at all.

They hit him. Often, they hit him quite hard. He knows it's happening, but pain is a register of inconvenience, and he has a great deal he wants to express to these people through the medium of crippling blows and wrenched limbs, and a little thing like knocking him over isn't going to stop him. Injury is different, and he guards against it— but there's a magic in forward momentum and molten rage: anyone wanting to injure him must come within reach. From the ground, he grabs a man leaning over him by the soft flesh under the arm, and heaves. The man screams, hauls back, and Joe Spork rides the movement upwards, regains his feet, reverses the position; softness underfoot. Shem Shem Tsien draws a line across Joe's arm with the sword, and he feels ice and then blood running freely. He yells, and the Opium Khan grins, steps forward again, blade teasing, tapping Joe's shoulders. Joe bellows, and tries to catch hold of him, plucks at his sleeve as Shem Shem Tsien steps lightly past him. The gun is in Shem's other hand, but he shows no inclination to use it. He closes down Joe's defences, whispers in his ear almost like a lover. Joe can smell brimstone on him, and realises he is breathing the shot which killed Edie. Hellfire, indeed. The Opium Khan's breath is minty, and his fingers are like Daniel's vise.

"You delight me, Mr. Spork. Never in my wildest dreams did I imagine I should have the privilege of killing Frankie Fossoyeur's grandson in person. It's too good of you." The gun comes to rest under Joe's ear.

And then a storm wind hurls them both across the room. Glass cases burst and papers whirl in a blizzard as Edie Banister's last piece of exploding Tupperware goes off belatedly and fills the room with smoke and flame.

Joe spins around and around, imagining Shem Shem Tsien doing the same, then finds a wall and moves along it, looking for . . . he doesn't know. He staggers to his feet, brushing himself down, preparing to go another round, knowing this time that he will not win. *What does it take to beat him? How, how, how?* Joe grinds his teeth. He will find out. He will.

Polly Cradle appears directly in front of him with Bastion, and it takes him a second to realise that she is real: an angel in faded jeans, ushering him out. In the corridor is Mercer.

"Move," Mercer yells roughly. Then, into what appears to be not a cellphone but an actual satellite handset, "Bethany! It's Mercer Cradle. The word is: 'Passchendaele'. We're crashing the shop, do you understand? We've been caught—you may be under direct threat. Burn the boxes, drop the shutters and turn the key. I say again, 'Passchendaele'."

Crashing the shop. Noblewhite Cradle's last gasp, in the face of utter destruction: records gone, guilt erased, favours called in. Money takes flight to the Caymans, to Belize and the canton of Thun and the Bahamas. House of Cradle flees on predetermined routes. The company is born again abroad. The U.K. is considered scorched earth.

"Mercer," Joe Spork says, "I'm sorry."

"Get a move on!"

"Yes," says another voice, "you had better do that."

Shem Shem Tsien stands in the smoke. He has lost his gun, but he still has a sword, and he is flanked by two of the remaining Ruskinites.

Joe growls, feeling the heat in his chest again, the urge to tear something with his fingers, and then Bob Foalbury steps smartly past him and with comical precision presses a stud in the wallpaper.

A vast, clanking iron curtain falls into place between them, and then another, and water pours from the ceiling. Somewhere, an alarm klaxon sounds, like an old-fashioned air-raid siren. From behind the screen comes a howl of thwarted fury.

"Cop that, you murdering sod," Bob Foalbury says, with feeling. And then, to Joe, "Fire and theft system, Baptiste Frères of Marseilles circa 1921." He turns sharply, beats on the metal grille. "Come into my house? Threaten my wife? Call me an old man? Well, I beat you, didn't I? *My name is Bob Foalbury! With an F, you bastards!*"

Cecily puts her hand on his arm, and he folds down onto her, relieved and afraid and tired.

"No time," Mercer says.

Joe Spork follows the Cradles back to the street and into yet another anonymous car. His exhaustion feels like a great, dark lake on which he floats and which will shortly drown him. And yet, at the same time, as he slips gratefully into the back seat for a few minutes, for an hour, for however long until his next staging place, he hears a part of himself—aloud or not, he does not know—asking a question.

Why am I always the one running away?

In the semi-darkness of public street lights and twilight gloom, the safe house in Sunbury looks to Joe Spork like a giant, rejected, saliva-covered mint. It makes him feel slightly sick. On the other hand, it is anonymous, which ultimately must be the point. A safe house: a house which is safe. Bartered on the spur from a startled estate agent, and paid in cash. *This day, this money, no discussion, no visitors. Are we clear? Oh, yes, sir, and thank you very much.*

Joe finds that his anger has drained away and, with its departure, his sense of hope. He does not honestly believe anywhere is safe.

He will be on the run for ever. Or—more likely—he will die.

The giant mint has a small door-knocker in the shape of an animal's head. It's probably supposed to be a lion, but it looks more like a sheep. Mercer fusses with the key and lets the little gang of refugees inside.

"Harticle's was prettier," Mercer says moodily. Polly nods.

"Yes, it was," she says. "But this is what we have."

She turns to Joe, looks him over. She's being careful. It's nice when someone who cares about you is careful. It means that they care. He's tired again, so tired he wonders if he can ever sleep enough. He wonders if he will dream of electric shocks. If he will keep her awake. If she will still want to share the bed if he cries in his sleep.

Mercer slips past them up the stairs. "I've got a change of clothes. You should shower, Joe, I don't mean to be unkind, but you smell bad enough that people will notice and you don't want to be noticed."

Story of my life. Don't make a fuss. You don't want to be noticed. Pay on time, work to order, play by the rules. Don't misbehave. Do as you're told, and you'll be all right.

Except I did, and I'm not.

Bastion slouches, jellied by grief, and whines very softly. Joe rocks him. The woven-gold bee, the one Ted Sholt gave Joe in Wistithiel, crawls out of Polly's handbag and flies slowly around the room as if in mourning. After a moment, it alights on a plastic shelf.

"I'm sorry," Mercer says a little briskly, reappearing with a pair of jeans and a shirt. "We did everything we could, but we just couldn't find you. We tried everything, Joe. We did. I promise." He nods to himself. "Anyway. What you need now is a way out of the country, a place to go, and all that bloody quickly. We can do that much, at least. You'll also need a false identity for travel, and then another one to live in, and finally an emergency one or maybe two. You've got to disappear."

Joe shrugs. Mercer hesitates, then: "You're very wanted. Very. Do you understand?"

Joe finds himself unsurprised. "What have I done? Did I blow up parliament?" He's not bitter. He's always felt there was no point in taking things personally. It's just a slack, empty curiosity. He has nowhere left to fall.

"No," Mercer says quietly. He slides a tabloid newspaper across the table. The front page is about the bees, a map showing their route around the world, the conflicts marked as little fires. Mercer sighs, and opens the paper. On pages four and five—just after Belinda from Carlisle in nothing but a pair of denim shorts—he finds SPORK: BLOOD WILL TELL! and LIKE FATHER, LIKE SON. Garish crime-scene photographs of places Joe has never seen, bodies draped. Old pictures, and new ones. A history of violence.

"This can't be right!"

"I'm sorry, Joe, it is. The houseboat's gone. The Watsons . . . It must have been the day after you borrowed the whaler. There was nothing you could have done. It's not your fault."

Joe feels the weight of it settle on his shoulders all the same. "What happened?"

"Someone set a fire. Abbie woke up just in time, she got the kids out, they're fine. Griff . . . he's in hospital. Smoke inhalation. He tried to save what they had. The police say you did it. Abbie called them to demand a full investigation and that little shit Patchkind told her this sort of thing was bound to happen if she *made time with terrorists*."

"Terrorists? What the fuck does that mean?"

"That's you, Joe, I'm sorry."

"I'm a terrorist now?"

"You are a suspect in a terror investigation. Yes."

"But I haven't done anything wrong!"

It is a cry of agony, emerging from somewhere in his gut, and his voice climbs, stretches, and breaks on the last word into something animal, kicked and bewildered.

"They are fucking with you, Joe," Polly Cradle says evenly into the silence which follows. "They are talking to you in the language of fucking. The message is: do as you're told. Do what we say, when we say it, tell us what we want to know even if you don't know it. The message is: don't piss us about, sonny, or you'll go the David Kelly road. The de Menezes road. Or whatever that poor bugger was called they topped at the G20 for walking with his hands in his pockets. This is the system coming down with all its might. The message is: this is what happens when you don't behave yourself." Her eyes are cold and flat, and there's something prowling in their depths.

Mercer draws breath and carries on. "In the course of your terroristic activities, you were discovered by several people who are now missing or dead."

"Who?"

"Billy, first of all. Then Joyce."

"Well, she'll say that's not true. They weren't going to be married. And she's not dead, so that's just ridiculous." But they are both looking at him, and he realises he still has somehow not understood something fundamental.

Mercer carries on, inexorable. "And a girl named Therese Chandler, of Wistithiel, in Cornwall, who was found dead in her home early this morning. Apparently you met her in a pub."

"Therese? *Tess?* She's dead?"

"Yes, Joe. Joyce as well."

"Joyce wasn't even with Billy any more!"

"I know. This isn't about that."

"They killed her to get to me?"

"Or because they thought she might know something, however tiny. Yes. And now that I've met the enemy, I should think just for fun, wouldn't you? I'm pretty sure he did for Billy in person. That seems about his style."

Yes. It does. But it also seems impossible, even now, with the smell of Edie's death still in his nostrils: blood and gunsmoke. "This is all wrong. It's against the law. All that stuff."

And somehow Mercer is angry, because he nearly shouts. "Yes, Joe! It is against the law! It always is! And yet it happens. Or did you think they only did this to taxi drivers from Karachi? They do it when they feel like it, when it's expedient, when the situation demands it. And no one cares because it never happens to them!" Polly puts a restraining hand on her brother's arm. "Sorry."

In the paper, pictures of Tess and Joyce, alive. Descriptions of how they died. Descriptions so lurid you can't help but wonder, unless you really know someone well, whether they might have done it, after all.

Almost everyone who trusts him that much is here, now.

Joe Spork stares at the dead faces, and the headline.

Every man's hand is against him now.

Joe Spork stares into nothing and waits for his heart to break, or his mind. He waits for the impact of this appalling, impossible lie to cause everything he is to crumble and collapse. He looks up and sees Polly watching, and Mercer, and knows they are waiting too. *Sorry*, he thinks. *I'm done. I don't have anything left.* He waits to hear his own mouth make nonsense sounds, for his body to curl up into a ball and just stay there, until they come for him.

Instead, a completely other thing happens which catches him quite by surprise. He comes to the end of himself and finds, at the last, a piece of solid ground and a hard wall to set his back against.

Sometime between the moment when his father's heart went *ba* but not *boom* and the dropping of Mathew's silver-chased casket into the earth, Joe Spork buried the part of himself which knew how to hustle, cheat, and rob in a coffin of its own, and in some indefinable way accepted that his was to be a life of inconsequence and hohummery. He studied with Daniel in an effort to turn back the clock to some previous point when Mathew was not just still alive but not yet criminal; he sought, in fact, to become the man his father might have been under other circumstances.

He stares into his own reflection in the double-glazed window, and tries to remember the man he could have been. *Crown Prince of Crime. Worse than his dad ever was, and that's God's honest truth. Mad bastard, he is. Not afraid of nothing.*

That person has never existed, and yet he has always been possible. He has never gone away. Now, finally, is the moment to make him real. And yet it seems to Joe a very long journey to that place in himself, a long, hard uphill struggle against years of accumulated obstacles and self-made fences.

He begins with the man he is now: Joe Spork, who did not murder his friend, but is accused of it, and of things more desperate and vile for reasons which are not his fault; who shares his bed with Polly Cradle, and means to make that matter.

He rolls his shoulders, sets his jaw, and goes on.

He is the man who was taken by monsters, and tortured, and is not dead.

He is the man who knows that innocence is not a shield, and that keeping your head down does not mean you will be safe.

He is the man who was set up by an old woman in the name of love and a better world, and who watched her die to save him.

He is the man who will look after her dog.

He is the man who charged a loaded gun and a sword with nothing more than his anger.

Oh, yes, and his father was trouble, too. And his grandmother before that.

A slow, satisfied grin moves across his face. Mad Dog Joe. White Knuckle Joe. Run-Amok Joe.

Crazy Joe.

All right, then. He looks at his reflection again. He judges the work good, but not finished: the new Joe should not slouch.

He breathes in and sticks out his chest, looks again. No, too much. Less is more. Solidity, not hot air. Strength, not bluster.

He straightens his back, flexes his arms, but the power is carried in the core, not the fists. The gangster doesn't bluff, doesn't threaten. He simply is, and you know the score.

The city belongs to me. The world. It is mine. Other men rule because I have more important things to do.

Good. Now, the hat. The gangster is perpetually wearing a hat. Even when he is not, he carries himself as if he is. The light falls across his face just so; one eye is in darkness, glinting. Piratical. A wolf eye on the edge of the firelight, a pirate captain in a storm. *Defiance.*

The coat, like armour. It needs to hang wide, open, to emphasise his scale. It casts its own shadow, hides him yet again. His hands are by his sides, so he might be armed . . . No, scratch that. One way or another, he is armed. Is it a baseball bat? Very American. Where would he get such a thing? A length of pipe. A gun. A boathook. Good. And in his pocket, some further surprise. Not a gun. Not a knife. Something more alarming. A Molotov cocktail, perhaps, or a grenade. He has heard that Russian mobsters use grenades. It seems like massive overkill. Ah. Yes. But that's the point, isn't it? Overkill. Bring a sledge-hammer to a knife fight. Bring a tank to play chicken. It's not about subtle or measured. Shem Shem Tsien is subtle, a crooked spider in the dark, a liar, a thief of hope, a killer of Watsons and Joyces. Mur-derer of old women and sorrower of dogs. *I am not a subtle or a mea-sured man. I am Crazy Joe Spork, and I will bring you down if I must topple the house around us.*

Yes.

From the window surface stares back the man he must be from now on: one-eyed wanderer; battlefield ghost; stranger; titan; mob-ster; angel of destruction.

A man who might be able to win, after all.

"Your escape route goes through Ireland," Mercer is saying. "Ferry, then a flight to Iceland, on to Canada. Canada's great for disappear-ing. It's very big and there's nothing in it. If you leave in the next few hours we can get you out before the bees arrive. I don't know if that will help, but it's worth a try."

Joe Spork doesn't seem to hear. Mercer moves around him, waves. "Do I have your attention, Joe?"

"Station Y," Joe says. Mercer raises his eyebrows. Joe nods. "Okay. Do that in a minute. Does anyone have the box from my mother?"

Mercer frowns.

"Yes," Polly says.

"May I have it, please?"

She rummages in her bag, produces it. The key is taped to the bot-tom, in the fashion of nuns rather than gangsters. He opens it.

Old pictures, Polaroids, wrapped with an elastic band from the Post Office—of course. Smiling lockpickers, the very first Old Cam-paigners of Mathew Spork's inner circle. Parties with women in baby-doll dresses and men in velvet suits. A candid picture of Harriet which Joe hastily pushes to the back, so lustful and alarmingly ripe does she appear.

And then, very much out of place, three more pictures in their own little group, with a smaller elastic band around them and a piece of paper with the single word "Josh" on it just to make the point, and Joe Spork finds he can read them as if they were postcards:

Uncle Tam and Mathew, looking very grave, shaking hands on a deal in the Marketman's fashion, a double clasp. *Your Uncle has something for you.*

Mercer and, yes, Polly, clasped in the arms of their parents on the steps of Cradle's. *These are the people you can trust.*

And Joe himself, in a sheepskin jacket, perched on Mathew's knee and punching the sky, Mathew's face for once quite open and joyous, gunman's hands on his son's narrow shoulders. That one's almost too simple, too primal to put into words. Even *I love you* doesn't really do it justice.

He can feel Mathew's breath on his hair. His father used to inhale him from time to time, simple, honest, mammalian.

"Ireland, Joe," Mercer says.

Joe looks over at him, genuinely surprised. "Oh, I'm not running."

"What? Of course you are."

"No."

"Joe, you can't fight this. It's too big."

"He's going to kill the world, Mercer. And he's already killed me. The old Joe is done. I won't be doing a lot of business now, will I? Even if the bank doesn't foreclose, which they will."

"It will blow over. Someone else will no doubt stop him. There are people who do those things."

"The Legacy Board. Rodney Titwhistle. Yes. He's on top of it, all right."

"For God's sake, Joe! You're a clockworker. That's what you wanted. That's who I've been trying to help!"

"And he says 'Thank you.' From the bottom of his heart. But he's gone, Mercer. Now it's me." He glances over at Polly Cradle.

"Tell him!" Mercer demands, but Polly just smiles back at Joe and slowly claps her hands, eyes shining.

"Oh, for God's sake," Mercer shouts. "You're not serious!"

"Yes," Joe says. "I began to get it when I was in there. I don't know when. Maybe after the first month."

Mercer hesitates. "Joe, you weren't in there a month. It wasn't even a full week. I know it must have seemed like longer, but you escaped after five days."

Joe Spork shakes his head, and his smile is very fey indeed.

"No, Mercer," he says gently. "It just felt like that to you, because you were on the outside."

There is a ghastly silence. Mercer starts to object, to correct him, and then the upside-down truth of this sinks into him and he crumples.

"I'm so sorry, Joe," he murmurs. "I'm sorry I couldn't help. I'm sorry. I did my best, and it wasn't . . . it wasn't anything like enough."

"You were superb," Joe Spork tells him gently. "They tried to tell me you'd given up. Both of you."

They bristle, and he smiles. "Look: this is just how it is now. My whole life I've been telling myself to be calm, to be reasonable, to be respectable. To toe the line. But here I am, all the same, because they cheated. They changed the game so that I couldn't win by being an honest man. But the thing is, I wasn't very good at being an honest man. I had to put so much of me away to do it. But being a crook, now . . . I've got the skills for that. I can be an amazing crook. I can be the greatest crook who ever lived. I can do that, and still do the right thing. I'm not bonkers, at all. I'm *free*."

Polly Cradle cocks her head, and considers.

"What right thing?" she asks.

Bastion growls softly.

Joe gestures at the newspaper.

"They're coming after me. They're killing people and it's only a matter of time before they get"—he looks around, and finds himself gazing at Polly, looks away—"one of you. I'm not running any more. It's time to give them something to think about."

He folds his arms.

Mercer opens his mouth to argue, and Bastion Banister chooses this moment to open *his* mouth and snap at the circling bee. To his own evident surprise, he captures it, and there's a curious little glonking noise as he swallows it whole. Mercer cringes slightly, as if expecting the dog to explode.

Nothing happens.

"All right," Polly Cradle says, and then, *pro forma*, "Bastion, you're a very naughty boy."

"Yes," Mercer says acidly. "The dog has consumed a possibly lethal technological device of immense sophistication, deprived us of our only piece of tangible evidence and possibly doomed us all to some sort of arcane scientific retaliative strike. By all means, chide him severely with your voice. That will solve everyone's problems."

There is silence, and then Joe Spork starts to sputter, and Polly

Cradle snorts, and then Joe actually laughs: a small snigger which grows into a loud, open laugh, and finally a great shout of mirth, and Polly is laughing right alongside him, with relief and delight and in honour of the expression of profound affront on her brother's face. Finally, even Mercer joins in.

When the fit is over, they regard one another with glad eyes.

"Mercer," Polly says, "we are now going to hug. As a group. The experience will be very un-English. It will be good for you. Do not speak, at all, especially not in an attempt to diffuse the emotional intensity of the situation."

They hug, somewhat awkwardly, but with great feeling.

"Well," Mercer says, after a moment, "that was certainly—"

"I will hit you with a shovel," Polly Cradle murmurs.

The clasp goes on a second longer, and then they step back.

"All right, then," Joe Spork says. "Let's get started."

"This is actually not something I've done before," Joe says a few moments later to the man in the pink shirt, "but I felt almost sure I would have natural talent."

The man nods hurriedly, but very gently, because he's worried about the Sabatier cleaver resting just under his chin. Joe liberated this gruesome item from the kitchen in the giant mint, and his face brightened significantly as he appreciated its weight and general nastiness. The owner of the house is apparently some sort of closet gourmet, because Polly was able to arm herself with a brace of short, fat-bladed items used for shucking oysters which, while small, possess a similar measure of menace and utility.

Joe smiles benignly, which in the circumstances makes him appear completely deranged. "Do you read the newspapers? No, don't nod again, that's not a good idea. Make a sort of squeak if you can . . . yes, there we are. One for yes, two for no . . . Good. So you are aware that I am an escaped mental patient, a sociopath, and an accused terrorist?"

The man squeaks.

"Great. So we're clear on the absolute and incontrovertible awfulness of your situation and how very dangerous I am? Oh, by the way, this is Polly. Polly, say hello to Mr . . . well, perhaps we won't ask his name, in case it makes him nervous. Say hello, anyway." Polly Cradle smoulders.

"Now, where was I? Oh, yes. This car. It is absolutely lovely. I can almost promise you it will not be damaged. I say 'almost' because there's a slight possibility that any car in which I travel will be shot at and blown up. It's a negligible risk from my point of view in that I would be past caring, but I can see that you might take exception. Anyway, it's a lovely car and I'll do my best. You don't mind, do you?"

An emphatic double-squeak: *mi casa, su casa.*

"Thank you. Now, can you tell me, will it get us to Portsmouth on that much petrol, do you think? No? Well, I suppose I can rob a garage. Now, can we be reasonably sure that you'll wait an hour or so before calling the police? Because otherwise I'll have to ask you to accompany us. How is the boot, by the way? Comfy? Oh, you're leaving? Yes, I think that might be best . . ."

Joe Spork opens the door. The man departs. Joe turns to Polly to say something about how they're obviously not going to Portsmouth, and finds an oyster knife balanced on his cheek, just under his eye.

"Can we be very clear," Polly Cradle murmurs, "that I am not your booby sidekick or your Bond girl? That I am an independent supervillain in my own right?"

Joe swallows. "Yes, we can," he says carefully.

"There will therefore be no more 'Say hello, Polly'?"

"There will not."

The knife disappears immediately, and she slides over to him, plants her lips on his. He feels her tongue, wide and muscular, in his mouth. Her hand puts his firmly on her arse.

"Start the engine," she says. "I find car-theft sexy."

"This was technically a car-jacking," Joe says.

"Do you want extra points for that?"

"Yes, please."

"Then don't say 'please.'"

From St. Albans they head north.

A brief conversation with Cecily Foalbury via public phone at a petrol station yielded the information that the "Station Y" of Ted Sholt's final, desperate confidence was better known as Bletchley Park. Cecily was somewhat scathing about this. "For God's sake, it's common knowledge, Joe. I took you there myself. They broke the Enigma code, won the war. Invented the digital computer. No?"

And yes, of course, Joe remembers Bletchley, with its mysterious Nissen huts in various stages of decay, surrounded by suspect little hills which were clearly anything but, and the sprawling red-brick house which had been home to the greatest mathematicians an embattled Britain could lay hands on. He'd been almost equally impressed by the model-train club which occupied part of the house and helped to pay the rent, and by the mothballed Harrier jump jet on the lawn. A decayed British institution, abandoned by its secrets and left to run to seed. You could hide almost anything at Bletchley. Who would ever ask?

Joe has swapped the car's number plates with those of another of the same make, and Polly disabled the satellite tracker, so the stolen vehicle has effectively vanished unless someone looks at the engine block. There's a strange feeling of freedom on the open road, however illusory.

"What's at Bletchley?" Polly asks, as Milton Keynes draws closer ahead of them.

He grins at her. "A train," he says, and sees her answering smile.

After the motorway, the road to Bletchley is flat and dull. It winds between bits of contoured landscape and modern box houses; the strange, tame outskirts of Milton Keynes, created whole and inviolate by the planners and somehow never quite human in its execution. Bletchley Park is on the outskirts, served by a spur road which opens onto what may once have been a machine-gun emplacement. Joe parks the car very neatly in a space. Even though it shouldn't be there, the English curator-type will usually ignore something which isn't in the way.

The dawn is coming, and with it comes a measure of risk. Joe hesitates, briefly worried that some late watchman or early modeller will catch him in the act, then remembers that he doesn't really care about that. He clambers onto the roof of the ticket office and peers around in the twilight.

Ted Sholt's instructions are not clear, were never exactly lucid. Joe lays them over the terrain like a pencil sketch, and adds another layer of his own, his Night Market instinct for concealment and deception. *If I were hiding an unlicensed boxing ring . . .* And sure enough, there it is, a long, low barrow which is too straight and too unexpected to be a natural rise, but too big to be easily recognised as artificial. And yes, it does indeed give onto a curve in the old railway, a suspicious valley with long grass at the bottom which he has no doubt will reveal a short stretch of track. He points. Polly nods, but when he makes for the mound directly she shakes her head.

"Over here," she murmurs, and draws him to the small, shattered remnant of a hut away to one side. A sign reads "Officers' Water Closet: upper ranks only." Inside, she produces a torch from her bag—which also contains, somewhat to his surprise, Edie Banister's dog—and illuminates a hatch in the floor which leads down into a passageway beneath ground level. She grins, and Joe nods, acknowledging her score.

Hand over hand, they climb down into the earth.

The passage smells of musty concrete and damp. At the end of it there is a door, very solid and serious. Hermetic, Joe suspects. He could have blown it, with the right gear—and where would he get that? The question of proper gangstering tools is next on the agenda, and right speedily.

But he doesn't need to blow this one, and that's for the best, given what may be behind it. The combination lock is old and rather pretty, rich brass dials engraved with Roman numerals. Done by hand, he thinks. *Open the door with Lizzie's birthday,* Sholt said, and yes, indeed: XXI-IV-XXVI does the trick, the arrival in this world of Her Britannic Majesty Queen Elizabeth II.

When he opens the door there is a rush of air inwards. Beyond it there's another door, forming a kind of dust trap, and hanging on the wall is a row of wind-up lanterns. He lifts one down, turns the handle a few times. Then he steps through the inner door.

The room beyond is comparatively narrow—it's more of a tunnel—but it's enormous. It slants gently down into the earth; the near end, the one leading out into the world, is at ground level. And there, in front of him, is what he came for. Endless scrolling patterns ripple along lines of sheer power. The boiler is taller than he is and long as a bus. The sections fade away into the distance—ten of them? Twelve? Each is as perfectly made as the last, and each one is subtly different. The name is cut into the black iron cowcatcher at the front: *Lovelace*.

The exterior looks like metal, but it could be something else—resin, ceramic . . . Joe runs his hand over it. The surface is cool and a little damp, because there's a layer of protective oil. He smells coal and a cosy, storage-space scent of leather and wood. As he moves the beam of the lantern up and around, he begins to get a sense of the thing, its scale. Trains are familiar things, clattering drones which rush by or wander through the countryside; passenger trains have windows through which one can see harried parents or commuters squeezed like chattels. Goods trains, these days, are rare. You have to watch for them on local lines or sidings, or sit in Polly Cradle's bedroom and feel them go by. Joe Spork glances at Polly. She is walking along behind him, silent, one hand tracing a single finger along the skin of the *Lovelace*. He can see a tiny rim of dust and rubble building up where she's touching the carriage. She's smiling as if he's given her diamonds.

The next door has the goose-foot symbol on it. The dog Bastion barks suddenly, and yearns towards it from his bag. Polly shrugs.

"This one, then," she says.

They open the door and climb aboard. There's a faint hiss as the door unseals, and a whisper of motion as a ventilation system starts working. At least, Joe hopes it's a ventilation system and not, for example, a deadly gas attack. He sniffs, then feels like an idiot, but since he doesn't fall over and die he assumes this is not poison, and steps forward.

Inside, the lantern picks out two workbenches. One of them is cluttered and covered in a now-familiar scrawl, rows of mathematical notations and scraps of metal and other substances more obscure. The other is perfectly neat, almost prim. A vise, a selection of tools . . . Daniel.

Yes, boy. This one was mine. We sat back to back and worked, and I listened to her frustration and her triumph and I never told her how much I wanted her back, because I knew she had no room for me any more. For Mathew. For you. She was just desperate to make things right.

Joe reaches out and touches the bench. It is a caress, a gesture of fellowship.

Then he hears a voice, and turning, sees a woman made of light.

"Hello," the woman says. She walks forward. Her body is an out-line, like a shadow in reverse. Looking around, Joe realises that she is composed of bright beams from a hundred tiny lenses around the compartment, reflecting off a column of moisture in the air. Her face is indistinct. Just barely, he can see her profile when she turns to one side, and the outline of her mouth when she speaks. Her voice is a recording, much better than the ones in Daniel's record collection—and with that realisation he names her, of course. *Frankie Fossoyeur.*

He studies her features, or tries to, feels fleeting recognition as the image turns and moves, though whether it is from old memories of Frankie or her reflection in Daniel and Mathew he does not know.

The whole numinous vision is . . . well. Not otherworldly. It's quite simple, just brilliantly executed. A three-dimensional magic-lantern show. Holograms without lasers. Exactly what you'd expect from the kind of genius who builds a truth machine in the shape of a beehive.

Frankie cocks her head to one side. "I'm afraid I don't know who you are. I hope Edie is there, somewhere. Or Daniel. Or both of you, perhaps. Maybe you are in love. That would be tidy . . . *Mais non.* I am cruel. I am sorry, both of you.

"So sorry . . ." She waves her hand, brushing all this away.

"You realise that this is just a recording. A clever one. But no doubt by now this sort of thing is commonplace and I look hopelessly old-fashioned . . . *Bien.* And perhaps the entire conversation is out of date, and everything is well. But in case it is not, and since you're here, I'm going to ask you to save the world for me. I hope that isn't too much trouble." She laughs, and then coughs. The cough is the bad kind, the kind which doesn't get better. "*Nom de chien . . .*"

The ghost leans on something off camera, and sighs. The invisible face is slightly at an angle to them, the projection out of sync with the real world. It gives Joe the curious sense that she is looking at someone behind him. "This is where you say 'Yes'," Frankie adds. "And then I'll tell you what you need to know."

Joe glances at Polly Cradle. She takes his hand and nods.

"Yes," they say together. There's a faint click somewhere. B-side, perhaps.

Frankie—thirty years ago and more—cocks her head. "*Bien.*

There are two things I must say, because I do not know what is happening," the ghost of Frankie Fossoyeur says. "There is a prescription and a proscription. As Daniel would say, the stricture of the machine is hope, but in fact it possesses many virtues, many aspects, and one of them is the opposite of hope.

"The prescription is very simple. If it has not started, you must begin the process. Switch on the machine. The bees will fly. They will gather truth and sort it from lies, as they were rumoured to do when I was a child. Lies shall wither and a net improvement of nine per cent in the human condition will occur over time. Edie knows how to make it so.

"Understand that it will not be without pain. The world will reject the truth. It always has and it will again. There will be violence. But in the end, we will not be destroyed by it. There are enough good people that the foolish and the wicked will not drag us down. There will be a better world.

"The proscription is more serious. Very serious. It is like the one for nuclear material: do not push two subcritical pieces of uranium together at great speed. Only it is *much* more important!

"The wave that is the human soul is fragile. At Wistithiel I saw how fragile, and that was the barest beginning. Do you understand? If the Apprehension Engine is incorrectly calibrated, it exposes the mind to too much knowledge, and the mind in turn determines the world. In perfect perception of the underlying universe we find the end of uncertainty, of choice. Without choice, no consciousness. Without an uncertain future, no future at all. After a certain point, it is possible that this process would become self-perpetuating. What is possible would cease and be replaced by . . . immutable history. Ice instead of water. Life would become Newtonian. Clockwork.

"This is what Shem Shem Tsien desires from me. From the machine. He wishes a great, appalling determination. He will know the universe into a kind of extinction. His union with God will not be complete until he has ended what God began. Somehow, this catastrophe is what he most desires.

"He will, unless prevented, destroy everything, not just now, but for ever. Our universe will drift in the void, a solid, changeless block.

"If he is involved, in any way, you cannot trust him. No one can. If he has the Apprehension Engine, then what he intends is atrocious. You must stop him. You must."

And the recording stops. The numinous ghost of Frankie Fossoyeur hangs in the air in front of them, pointing off to the side.

Joe leans one way, and then the other, gauging the angles. Then he lies down on his face and peers at the panelling, the floor, and then stands and taps gently at the polished ceiling. He takes a moment to reflect that this is the single largest and most beautiful mobile artwork he has ever seen. Ruskinite, he realises, from the days before Shem Shem Tsien. He could hate the man just for that, for the unmaking of the Order of John the Maker. If only there weren't so many other things to hate him for.

There. Under his fingertips: a faint line. He follows it, up and down. A seal. Which implies a compartment. But how to open it? If Daniel made it, then it would be elegant. If Frankie designed it, it might be mathematical . . . no. No, she intended this for an ordinary mind. Ordinary, but familiar. So, how . . . oh. Of course. From his pocket he takes the car keys, moves them gently across the blank face of the panel. Yes, there—the keys twitch towards the wood, as if in a high wind. A magnet, this time on the inside, so that any metal will suffice to move the catch. There's no pattern, though. How is he to know what movement will release the panel? He suspects a false step may have consequences greater than merely lost time. Frankie had learned caution by this point, of that much he is quite sure. He wonders if a decades-old booby trap will still work, and whether, if he doesn't disarm it soon, it will blow him up just for being there. How long does he have? When will his grandmother's ghost decide he is not her inheritor, but an enemy?

He drags his mind back to the job in hand.

No pattern. The line of the join? Like a number one? No. Meaningless. The square of the panel? It seems . . . too easy, and again, it means nothing. There is no way to be sure. Frankie was obsessed with certainty, for good or ill. With knowledge. And yet here, there is no pattern. A blank. No pattern where there should be a pattern.

He draws back, considering context, interrogating the puzzle.

What is the panel concealing?

A negation. Nothing where there was something, a very binary notion . . . Not a one, but a zero.

And there's your answer.

All right, a zero. To be drawn in which direction? How does an ambidextrous French supergenius write her numbers?

Any way she likes.

"Which direction?" he mutters.

Polly Cradle kneels down beside him, kisses him on the forehead, like a blessing. She draws a circle with her finger, and he realises she has understood the same thing at the same time. Reassurance. Confirmation. He takes a moment to appreciate her presence, her amazing brain, sees it for a moment as a wonderful mechanical angel in her head.

"Clockwise," she says. "Of course."

Clockwise. A last message to Daniel. *Do this, and all will be as it should be. Somehow.*

Oh, Frankie.

He moves the keys in a circle, starting at twelve o'clock and moving around to the right. A moment later, the panel slides open. He peers in, and sees the small, solid knot of explosive. Had he moved the keys the wrong way . . . Well, he's very pleased that he didn't. He reaches in, and then abruptly he is holding a few pages of handwritten notes in his hands. He flicks through them, puts them away.

"What's that?" Polly asks.

"The off switch," Joe replies, and when she looks at him sternly, "Well, all right. Not a switch. A list of what to break in the right order so that the world doesn't come to an end. A sabotage list."

Bastion, from his place in Polly Cradle's bag, snuffles through his tiny nose, and growls.

I am ready, horologist. Let us proceed.

Joe Spork looks at the dog.

"Simple as that, ey?"

On the way out, they close the doors and leave things exactly as they found them. At the railway station, Joe steals another car.

"Where now?" Polly asks.

Joe reaches into his pocket and passes her the Polaroid photo of Mathew and Tam. "Gentleman's outfitter," he says.

It takes longer to get to Uncle Tam's place than Joe was expecting, because so many people are leaving London. The radio talk shows are twittering with concerned believers and contemptuous realists. Experts have been found and trotted out: catastrophe mathematicians, lawyers and comedians are all contributing to the mix. You couldn't call it a panic, not yet. More a sort of jitter, like the rumour of a storm.

The house is at the end of a narrow road.

Knock, knock.

"Who's there?"

"It's me, Tam."

With a recently pinched Mercedes and a girlfriend who looks like some sort of crime all by herself.

Tam shouts back through the door. "No, no, this is where you say 'Oh, is it five in the bloody morning? I'm so sorry, I must be out of my fucking mind!' "

"Soot and sorrow, Tam. It's Joe Spork."

Uncle Tam—leaner and grizzlier, but verifiably the original—flings open the door and stares at him, meerkat eyes bright in a craggy face.

"Shit. I s'pose it was inevitable . . . Did I or did I not teach you, young Lochinvar—who is on the run and a plague to all men's houses—that folk of the Market do not have names? We don't say 'I am,' we say 'I am called,' and the reason for that is not so that fairies can't take our teeth when we sleep with our mouths open on Midsummer's Night, it is for perfectly simple deniability, so that old Tam does not have to fall back on 'I am an old fart, officer, and too senile to recognise a wanted felon when I see one.' Hullo," he says, looking at Polly Cradle, "all right, I've changed my mind, you can come in. What's my name?"

"I never heard it," she replies smartly.

"You was raised proper," Tam says approvingly, "not like Lochinvar. Always a troubled boy."

"We came here in a stolen car, and he's going to get me a bouncier one when we leave so we can screw like mink on the A303," Polly informs him brightly.

Tam glares at her, then groans. "Christ," he says, "I'm old." He leaves the door open as he sinks despairingly back inside.

They follow him. Tam's place is a bungalow, and he drags one foot. Joe, thinking of the great cat burglar of days gone by, feels a bit mournful.

The house is cramped and not very warm. It ought to have a kind of moth-eaten grandeur, but it doesn't. It's just lonely. There are books along the walls, old science fiction novels muddled with copies of the *European Timetable* and random magazines Tam hasn't thrown away. One shelf is taken up entirely with ledgers of old shipping companies.

"I am a wanted man, Tam. And she's a wanted woman, too, I suppose."

Tam doesn't answer Joe directly. He glances at Polly.

"I swear to God," he mutters, "he does this to upset me. Oy," he adds, turning to Joe, "if you don't tell me I can't know and I can't be done for not calling the rozzers, now can I? I am assuming all this is woeful bravado from a boy with a proper job who wants to impress an old mate of his dad's. You giant rollicking *twerp*. What do you want, Lochinvar? You and your girl with the naughty fect?"

"I need something, Tam. It's not anything big."

Tam glowers. "You're just like him. He used to say that just before he said something like 'Tam, old friend, it seems to me the Countess of Collywobble has too many diamonds and we have too few, so get your crampons, we're off to scale the north face of Mount Collywobble Hall!' and then before I knew it I was standing in front of the beak asking for clemency and pleading bloody stupid in mitigation. What are you looking for?"

"Whatever he left with you."

Tam frowns. "Are you sure? Times have changed, Joe. No room for Mathew's sort of living now."

"I'm sure."

Tam measures him, and nods. "Had to ask," he says, "before I gave this over. Mathew left it for you. Said you'd never need it, left it anyway. He believed in planning ahead, when it suited him." He scribbles on a piece of paper: three digits, then a letter and another three numbers. "It's round the corner," Tam says. "McMadden Storage. Looks all modern now, but nothing's really changed. First number tells you which door to use. The letter's for which floor, and the last one tells you which container it is. It's all locked up, of course."

"Where's the key?" Polly Cradle asks.

Tam grins. "Oh, well . . ."

Joe Spork grins back, a wolf's lolling tongue peeping out from under a sheep costume. "If you need a key, you've got no use for what's in the box."

Polly persuades Joe not to crash the car through the fence, which is his first, heady option, so he cuts the wire instead, right under a security camera. She waits for the alarm to go off, and nothing happens.

"Most of them don't have one," Joe murmurs, "and the ones which do, well, it's property crime, isn't it, not residential. Police'll show up in the morning. Guard's not about to come and see what's happening if he can help it, is he? Even if the cameras work, which that one likely doesn't because it's not plugged into anything. Most of the world works that way. It just assumes you're too chicken to find out."

"I think it's wireless," Polly Cradle says carefully. "I remember the catalogue."

"Oh." He looks at the little lens. It abruptly seems very alert. "Well, best we hurry, then." He grins, unrepentant, and she laughs.

A few moments later, in the shadow of the corrugated iron wall, he uses the same bolt-cutters on the padlock of door 334. He shoulders through, then shuts the door and turns on the lights.

"Wow," Joe Spork says after a moment.

This is almost certainly the most orange place in England. It may be the most orange place in the world. Row upon row of numbered orange boxes, and beyond them, orange doors set into orange walls. It is not a soft, sunset orange or a painter's orange, but a bright, plastic, waxed-fruit orange which knows no compromise. It's the kind of orange which would allow you to find your container in a blizzard or after an avalanche.

Polly Cradle assumes he will also cut the lock on container C193, but he doesn't. Instead, he just lifts the door up and out, and it comes off quite smoothly. He uses the padlock as a hinge.

Inside, there's a man.

He's sitting with his back to them in a big leather armchair. He wears a hat and a pair of gloves. By his left hand is a carpet bag, and by his right, a trombone case. He doesn't move.

Joe Spork edges forward, and breathes out. It's just a dressmaker's dummy. Very ha ha, he thinks. Very Mathew. A small shock, just to keep you on your toes, test your mettle. Or maybe just for fun. Mind you, Mathew himself might have shot it, and that would have ruined a perfectly decent hat. Exactly the kind of hat Joe was thinking of a few hours ago. A hat to ravish dancehall girls in, to shade a fellow's face while he runs moonshine. He moves closer.

The zip on the carpet bag is thick and dry. It sticks. He tugs at it, back, then forward, then back. Yes. The bag opens.

Shirts. A wad of money, perhaps a thousand pounds, in useless old-style ten-pound notes. A small pouch containing what can only be diamonds. Today's value in the straight world: a couple of hundred thousand. Walking-around money. A toothbrush, because Mathew hated to be without, and a couple of tins of preserved fruit. A bottle of Scotch, a packet of tobacco. And . . . oh. Another set of Polaroids, rather ribald: a rubicund fellow in a wealth of female company on the sofa at one of Mathew's parties. Not a lot of clothing to speak of, and a number of things going on which one newspaper or another might consider a bit naughty. *The Hon Don takes his pleasure, 1 of 6* in Mathew's hand on the back. A very solid bit of blackmail, ho ho, and surely this is what the somewhat dishonourable Donald was expecting when Joe bearded him the other day.

He looks around and sees what he's looking for, taped loosely to the trombone case: a dirty postcard from Brighton circa 1975 showing a cheeky disco girl with her dress falling down.

Joe glances at the card, praying to God the text on the back is not long, not tortured, most of all that it will not apologise or accuse, or tell him he has sisters in five counties and a brother in Scotland. Or that there's a corpse field under the warehouse.

Joe, it says, in large, friendly letters. *Oil the slide and watch the safety, it's loose. Love, Dad.*

Here, in this room, is evidence of care from Mathew Spork for his one begotten son, a gesture of love and an appeal for absolution. Not just a memento or an escape kit. A Gangster's Parachute. Just in case the straight life doesn't work out.

Without hesitation, Joe strips the dummy and changes his clothes. The suit is a little loose around the shoulders, but other than that, it's a good fit. His father's guess at his full growth, and the tailor's. Polly Cradle watches in silence as he puts on the hat.

He turns to the trombone case.

It isn't a trombone case, of course. It looks a bit like one, but— Arthur Sullivan notwithstanding—no one in Joe's situation actually believes their problems can be solved with a trombone. Unless he is greatly mistaken, the case contains something louder and less musical.

It is also extremely illegal, but Joe is rather a long way past the point where he cares about that. He opens the case. The not-trombone is resting in pieces in black velvet compartments. Various tools and expendables are included in the kit, so that he can maintain and furnish his not-trombone at home. There's even a score, telling you how to play music on it, and what ingredients are necessary for the creation of further vital supplies. And on the inside of the lid is the maker's mark: the Auto-Ordnance Corporation of New York.

Papa Spork's beloved Thompson sub-machine gun.

He realises, suddenly, how very long he has been waiting for this moment.

He grins, and carefully slots the pieces into place, then stands in the semi-dark. He lifts the tommy gun in across his chest, and smiles a smile of wide, boyish joy.

"'At last, my hand is whole again,'" says Crazy Joe Spork.

XVI

Drinks at the Pablum Club;
Jorge, Arvin, and the *Tricoteuses*;
dangerous to mess around with.

The Pablum Club is not actually in St. James's. It's off to one side, and it isn't nearly as ancient as the doorman's spectacles would suggest. Founded as a place where gentlemen who retained fire in the gut could escape from the fossilised remnants at the Athenaeum and the O&C, it has all the external trappings, all the leather chairs and expensive brandies, but the patrons generally discuss their mistresses rather than their handicaps, and an iron rule of secrecy applies to all conversations great or small, on pain of disenfranchisement. If the modern establishment has a special fortress, a medal for long service at the old boys' wheel, it is the Pablum.

The Hon Don is a major stakeholder, so Joe orders himself an obscenely ancient and expensive malt whisky and a Patrón Gold tequila (with actual gold in it) for Polly Cradle. Then he puts his two-tone brogues up on the mahogany coffee table and lets his head fall onto the backrest of his thronelike chair. After a moment, the fellows' butler arrives to ask him not to and to inquire as to whether the lady would not prefer the Ladies' Bar. Polly Cradle smiles and says she wouldn't, and the fellows' butler replies that he is almost sure she would, and Polly Cradle very gently tells him that really, she wouldn't, whereupon the fellows' butler appeals to Joe and Joe tells him to get the Hon Don *toot suite,* and shows him his gun.

The fellows' butler runs like hell, but does not—because gentlemen with fire in the gut are prone to this sort of outburst—call the police. Polly Cradle lets Bastion out of his bag, and he selects a damasked sofa and, despite being small, occupies it entirely. Joe smiles a smile of malign anticipation, and waits.

Part of him—he's coming to think of his hesitations as Old Joe—feels strongly that his presence here is premature. He should plan, he should husband his resources. He should, in fact, be sensible. To this injunction the inner gangster responds with a deep and flatulent raspberry. If life gives you lemons, you make lemonade. If it gives you compromising pictures of venal bankers with a wide and varied social acquaintance in the halls of power, then you blackmail while the sun shines.

"I need the Hon Don," he'd told Polly Cradle on the way back to London, "and I need the Night Market. Whatever I'm doing, I'm going to need them. I can feel it." She made love to him, as promised, between junctions fifteen and seven. He closes his eyes for a moment in heady recollection.

A notedly traditionalist bishop goes to sit on the damasked sofa, leaps up as the episcopal fundament is assailed by Bastion's one remaining tooth, and then nearly expires of sheer horror at the pink marble eyes and the halitotic sneer.

The Hon Don arrives a moment later with their drinks.

"Hello, Hon Don!" Joe carols.

"Hello, Hésus, my old friend," the Hon Don says loudly, and nods to the shaking bishop. "'Lo, Your Eminence, have you met Hésus, sounds like your sort of fellow, doesn't he, with a name like that, but of course it's very common *in Spain*, where he's from." This with a warning glance at Joe and Polly. "Yes, indeed, Count Hésus of Santa Mirabella—and I do believe I've not met the countess, you must be she, how charming, utterly," and at this point he's put down the drinks and is close enough to snarl "What the *fuck* are you doing here, you little shithead?" as he goes to embrace his guest.

Joe Spork smiles a beatific smile, and produces a colour photocopy of the incriminating Polaroid snaps. "I bring closure, Don. I bring joy to all mankind. My family's estates may lie in ruins, but I have my father's heritance. I know you'll be relieved to hear it's all intact and in a safe place. There was something he always wanted you to have, but death took him"—he smiles at the bishop, who has found a dogless and uncomfortable-looking lounger in the corner, and waves—"I should say 'the Lord God, merciful and mighty, took him off to his just reward,' hello, Your Eminence, most pleased to make your acquaintance, I am Hésus de la Castillia di Manchego di Rioja di Santa Mirabella, and this is my lady wife, Poli-Amora, greetings from the Most August Court of Spain! Yes, greetings, to you and your family, may they have many children within wedlock and rock the vault of Heaven with their procreations!" But when he turns back to the Hon Don *sotto voce* there is suddenly an absolute cold in his face, a shadow of days and nights in the tiny room at Happy Acres, "So you're all mine, you old goat, or your life will be miserable unto the last hour, you hear me? Because your first problem will be explaining what you were doing with two girls from the chorus at The Pink Parrot and that will be as nothing—*as nothing*—to the fuss which will kick off when they learn whose living room you were in and who dobbed you in, namely me, namely Britain's most wanted, and they will dig through every aspect of your life and fuck it up as they have done mine, and they will find nothing about me (which will only make them more suspicious) and doubtless a few dozen things which you would prefer were not revealed, and after that, if I am not dead, I will come into your house like a cleansing flame and I will smite you as you have never been smote before, *sing hallelujah!*"

He flings his hands high into the air and smiles at the bishop, who nods genially back and hides behind the *Financial Times*. The Hon Don glowers.

"What do you want?"

"Addresses, Donald. Names and places. I wish to know of the lives and loves of a fat man and a thin one, mandarins from the shady bit of our glorious civil service. I shall also require the use of one of your more secluded—no, let's stretch a point and say soundproofed—properties. I believe you have a couple on the edge of Hampstead Heath which would be ideal. We shall speak of it *in camera*. But have we established the principle?"

"Yes," the Hon Don mutters through gritted teeth, "we have."

Fifteen minutes later, Joshua Joseph Spork is on his hands and knees in a tide of local papers, cutting out the small ads for a hidden message: the perfect image of paranoid schizophrenia. The scissors are a nice touch, culled from an embroidery set and blunted at the ends. A selection of pencils of various colours is scattered across the floor of the Hon Don's office at the Pablum Club. The Hon Don is elsewhere, no doubt soothing his fevered brow with a brace of exotic dancers. Polly Cradle leans, Bacall-style, on the bar, and listens to her lover mutter.

"No, right, that's the *Advertiser*. Fine. So 'Come home Fred, all is forgiven,' fine. That's the *Crawley Sentinel*, and underneath . . . ha! Yes. Then . . . *Yaxley Times*, all right: 'Be mine, Abigail, be mine!' which is a bit desperate and I think . . . oh, bloody hell, it's real, fine . . ." and so it goes, a litany of clippings clipped and cast aside. A moment later, Joe grins. "Find the lady!"

Polly extends her hand, then stops. "What do I do?"

"Nothing! It's done. But help me: I was never very good at this. It's like a crossword . . . Here: 'For Sale: three matched mountain bikes. Divorce compels forced march to bank.' That's the date. 3 March. Right? Then here: 'Sing-a-long-a-*Sound-Of-Music*, Toxley Arms, Dover Street. Tickets in advance only.' So, Dover Street. But which Dover Street, because there are a few, and what number or what have you . . . oh." Joe looks disappointed. The third clipping holds no answers, obviously. Polly Cradle peers.

"Could it be the Toxley bit?"

He stares. "Yes! I'm back to front. Toxley Arms is the entrance. A pub. A pub in . . ." He scans the third clipping again. "Belfast? That can't be right."

"The ship, maybe?"

"Yes! On the Thames. The pub closest to HMS *Belfast*. There's a way down into the Beat. Yes. Exactly." He grins again. "Get out your best frock, Mistress Cradle, and your fine dancing shoes. I'm taking you to the Night Market."

The Market looks different and the same; today it's in a great Henry VIII–era water cistern pumped dry for refitting and filled with wooden scaffolding, hung with glowsticks in baroque lanterns and wind-up electrical lamps, the smell of water offset by great censers streaming fresh flower scent (stolen, a sign proudly proclaims, from a chemical company in Harchester which specialises in olfactory ambience, more available on request). People glance at them, then look again: *oh, fugi-*

tives. But the older ones, and the quicker, look a little longer and see Joshua Joseph Spork with a bad woman on his arm and a gangster's hat, and know that something is afoot, so that the whisper runs from stall to stall along the winding central aisle: *Is that Mathew's boy? My God, he's huge! And done something to upset Lily Law, but it's not what they say, that much I do know . . .*

A man named Achim gives them a glass of wine each and cheers. Others hurry to look the other way—no desire to learn anything which might be relevant to an ongoing inquiry. In any other place Joe would fear betrayal, but the Market is sacrosanct: it can only continue if it remains secret, and the penalties for betrayal are stark. Starker now, probably, than they were. Now that Jorge runs the place in Mathew's stead—or, as Jorge would be the first to acknowledge, in Joe's.

In what must be a maintenance room overlooking the cistern— a pumping station or an overflow—Jorge has established an office and is doing business, and you can be sure the whisper has reached him before they do, but Jorge is all about volume.

"Holy fucking crap, Joe Spork! Fuck! You are one most wanted fucker, you know that? There's a reward out on me just being in a room with you. Jesus! Vadim, this is totally cut-your-own-throat-after-reading, okay? This asshole was never here."

Jorge has no second name, no surname and no patronymic. He's just Jorge, the messy kid with the thick arms who shared his cake and scurried along at the back of the crowd. Jorge, chief among those who have kept the Market alive after the death of its king. He trailed Mathew like a puppy, worshipped him. Joe's father picked up followers and acolytes the way other men breathe, and Jorge carries that loyalty ridiculously forward to Mathew's son. He was small then, for his age. He's small now, vertically speaking, but he makes up for it with sheer volume and a Russian appetite. His breath, forcibly expelled in all directions, smells of salt fish and vodka. Joe is quite certain that Jorge plays up to his heritage, to people's expectations. Who, after all, living in London for his entire life, still sounds like a sailor from Krasnoyarsk? Only Jorge.

Vadim, across the desk from him, is an expensively dressed character in gold-rimmed glasses, with a look of deep self-regard which might just be mistaken for poetry, or pain. His eyes rest on Polly Cradle's cleavage, then skitter away when she favours him with a broad, challenging grin.

"Listen, Vadim," Jorge says, throwing short arms in the air, "I *got* to talk to this guy. Debt of honour, okay? So, look, being honest: you are the worst erotic photographer on the face of the planet. Seriously, it's better you point the camera away from the girls and make photos of the patio. These pictures . . ." He holds up a sheaf of eight-by-six-inch prints and flicks through them. "This one is like medical exam. This one is botany, maybe agriculture. Joe, Jesus, did you see this? What does this look like to you?"

"It's . . . well, I'm fairly sure that's an aubergine."

"Thank the merciful Lamb, old friend, it *is* an aubergine. But also, you see how there's fuck all else in the picture?"

"I do see that, Jorge, yes."

"And yet this is a photograph of Vadim's girlfriend Svetlana, who is—and I do not exaggerate here, okay?—she is the girl I most wish to see naked after Carrie Fisher in *Return of the Jedi*. In this picture she is entirely fucking naked. If it was not a close-up you would catch fire and explode looking at it. Would you like to see the wide shot?"

"All right."

"So would we all, Joseph, but this unfortunately is impossible, because that asshole there did not take a wide shot. Go, Vadim, please. I got to cry on my friend's shoulder, okay?"

Joe Spork waits until Vadim has removed himself, clutching the contraband aubergine porn, and then his face drops into its new, sharper lines. "Business," he says.

"You serious? Like real business? Not fucking slot machines?"

"Real business."

"You going to kick me out, Joe? Run the Market all of a sudden?" Jorge is joking. Kidding around. His wide face is clear of malice or alarm. Joe Spork wonders where the guns are, and the men.

"No, Jorge. The Market's all yours. I'm getting back into the game, for sure. But I don't want your chair. Too much hard work for an honest villain like me."

Relief flickers across Jorge's features. His shoulders relax a little, now that he's no longer carrying the weight of sudden violence. "Honest villain! Yes! My God, Joe, I tell you, we should have more honest villains in this world!"

"I'm glad you say that, Jorge, because I need some help."

Jorge looks grave. "The way I hear it, Cradle's is gone, you're on the run. Maybe you're too broke for business. I can get you away. Danish ambassador got little local problem, killed his wife's lover with lawn-mower. But no favours, Joseph, not big ones. Not even for you."

For answer, Joe removes from his pocket one of Mathew's larger diamonds, and sets it on the table.

Jorge brightens. "Okay, Mr. Spork does business. It's a great day! You tell me what you need."

"Phones. Untraceable credit. Can your Danish ambassador get us identities to use today, right now?"

"Sure. I put money into accounts for you, you pay in stones. Family rate. Good for ever unless you are loud. You buy a Ferrari and crash it in Pall Mall, we got serious problem." Jorge starts to laugh, then sees the speculation on Joe's face as he wonders whether this might actually happen. "Oh, sheee-it. You look just like Mathew. Don't do that, it freaks the crap out from me. Okay, what else?"

"Tell the Market I'm putting a job together."

"Big job?"

"Biggest ever. No kidding, Jorge. Bigger than anything, ever. I need them, Jorge. And they need me. The Old Campaigners, even. All of them."

"I don't think they think they need you, Joe. I think maybe they think you can go to Hell."

"Not for this job. I'm the only one who can do it."

"What kind of job?"

"Security."

"Getting around it?"

"Being it. Stopping an assassination."

"Whose?"

"The universe."

Jorge stares at him, then down at the diamond, then at Polly Cradle. She nods.

"The fucking universe is getting killed now?"

"Maybe."

"Not just the world, which by the way would be completely enough."

"The world to start with. Everyone on it."

Jorge lets his head roll back and stares up at the ceiling as if exhausted. "This is bee-related, maybe?"

"Very much so."

"Bee-related is not good. Word is out that anyone messing with bee situation will see the inside of some invisible shithole prison for terrorists. And you—you are very wanted, Joe. You're maybe the bad guy. It happens that nice people go batshit sometimes. I have to think maybe I shouldn't help you even this much, even for honour and family and shit. Even for very nice diamond."

"You know the Ruskinites?"

"The asshole-monk-bastard-sadist-fuck Ruskinites?"

"Yes."

"I know them to scrape off my fucking shoe."

Joe grins. "They're on the other side. They want me dead."

Jorge nods. "Okay, then you're maybe not entirely the bad guy." He jiggles his head left and right, a man ducking punches. "Not the bad guy. But you're playing in the fucking big leagues, even if there's no end of the world, for sure. Dangerous shit."

"Kings and princes, Jorge," Joe says sonorously, in his best Mathew impression. In spite of himself, Jorge smiles.

"For sure, Joe. Kings and princes, I remember. But . . . seriously? The fucking universe?"

"Seems so."

Jorge sighs. "Fuck me, Joe. You don't come here for twenty years, now you want to save creation?"

"I am a Spork. We don't do things small."

"Yes. I guess you are." Jorge rolls his huge head around his neck, and they can hear his neck clunk through the layers of flesh. "Fuck, Joe," he says again, in a rather pensive way. And then, by way of agreement: "Fuck."

In the daylight world, the Hon Don has left an envelope at the desk of the Pablum, along with stern instructions that the Prince is not to be allowed into the building. He has backed this order with some curiously aristocratic sort of slander such that the doorman's eyes are both stern and admiring as he hands over the envelope. It contains some typed pages, a handwritten note with two addresses, and a set of house keys labelled as belonging to a third.

Momentum, Joe considers, is the vital thing. He has to keep moving, gathering momentum. Even a very small object, travelling at the right sort of speed, can deliver a considerable wallop.

He glances over at Polly Cradle. "You don't have to do this one."

She tuts. "On the contrary. This is the one *you* don't have to do."

He stares at her. Polly raises one eyebrow and continues. "I would go so far as to say that you can't. God knows what will break loose in you. I like you crazy, Spork. I don't want you catatonic."

"But—"

"I will do this one, Joe. You will stand in the back and watch. Besides. It's time you saw me at work." She frowns. "Although . . . for this, I think I will want some additional muscle. No," she adds, as he immediately opens his mouth to volunteer, "not that kind of muscle. Suasion."

"Suasion?"

"I am an investigator, Joe Spork. Suasion is one of the things I do. Now: watch."

He does.

Polly Cradle plays Jorge's untraceable mobile telephone like a tin whistle. She is charming and plausible and ever so slightly needy. He remembers Mathew saying you can burgle a nice house with a ladder at noon so long as there's a pretty girl in a ball dress holding it steady. Old ladies will approve your gallantry and coppers will stop to give you a hand. Polly has a sunny, hopeful manner and a gentle appeal which makes people want to help her out. She sets organisational structures against themselves, deftly squeezing between switchboards and departments into the gaps, and coming back with all their secrets.

Via the bored receptionist at Lambeth Palace, she gets access to an old cleric in Salisbury who handles accommodation for protected witnesses in canon law cases. The cleric has recently been asked to find a safe place for a woman of late middle age who is sought by unfriendly eyes. Polly absolutely refuses any information about that, scolding him politely for even mentioning it, and he basks in her discretion. A moment later she is talking to his assistant about some completely other matter, but somehow comes away with the name of a layman newly returned from Afghanistan and seeking to atone for his sins who has lately been charged with the protection of an old lady. A brief call to an old friend in the London Authority yields the man's home phone number, where his wife is delighted to learn that her husband has won a substantial award for his service and concerned that he must be contacted immediately because he's in Royston on business and can't be reached.

This in turn yields a soldier's pub called the Cross Keys which has rooms, and which is just across the road from where Harriet Spork is safely ensconced in a temporary apartment the Church has rented for her, guarded by lay brothers Sergeant Boyle and Corporal Jones, late of Her Majesty's Special Air Service and now retired. Since they are Harriet's protection and not her warders, and since while Polly may be formidable she is clearly not in Sergeant Boyle's weight class, gaining entry is only a question of knocking.

"Mrs. Harriet Spork," Polly Cradle says.

"Sister," Harriet objects vaguely.

"I am Mary Angelica Cradle. We once made biscuits together. With Smarties."

"Oh. Yes, dear. Of course."

"I wish to confess to you, in the interests of full disclosure, that I ate about two-thirds of the Smarties during the cooking process."

"Yes," Harriet says again, with a slight smile. "I believe I knew that."

"Also, I am engaged in a very satisfactory emotional and sexual relationship with your magnificent son. This relationship is not sanctioned by the ostensible rules of the Christian Communion, but falls into the category of committed partnerships tacitly approved as a modern prelude to possible marriage and procreation."

Joe Spork tries not to swallow his tongue. One of the laymen slaps him cheerfully on the back. "You're in serious trouble with that one, boy."

Harriet nods. "I understand."

"I mention all this because I wish to invite you to participate in a significantly illegal plan I have recently devised to save your son's life and extract some measure of justice from those who have caused him and others considerable pain. I also believe that it will contribute to the process of saving the human race from a conclusion which is not only appalling but probably also blasphemous, or at the very least reduce the risk to society from a man of notable wickedness."

"Oh," Harriet Spork says.

"If you wish to take part, you must come with me now and do exactly as I say. I will not conceal from you that there is some risk. Say hello to your son."

"Hello, Joshua."

"Hello, Mum."

"I'll get my coat," says Harriet Spork.

"Good," Polly Cradle says. "That's one."

Abbie Watson sits on an uncomfortable bench outside the Hospital of St. Peter and St. George in Stoker Street. The wife of an anarchist who "makes time with terrorists" looks fragile and alone. She barely glances up as someone sits next to her.

"Mrs. Watson," the other woman says.

"Go away."

"Very shortly. I haven't much time. I am about to kidnap and interrogate one of the men ultimately responsible for your husband's injuries. I will then give that information to my lover, Joe Spork, who will use it to thwart the machinations of the individual who hopes to gain by their actions. It is likely that that person will expire in the course of this thwarting. If he doesn't, he will go to prison for ever. Also, those within the government who have sanctioned and even endorsed his behaviour will be held to some species of account."

Abbie Watson looks up. The woman is small and dark and very pretty, but there is a steel in her which Abbie has encountered only rarely. Behind her, somewhat abashed, is an emaciated-looking nun. Harriet Spork smiles nervously.

"I should also tell you," the woman goes on, "that unless you object, Griff will be moved to the care of a Swiss specialist later today. Dr. von Bergen is flying from Zürich with his team. Griff will be the recipient of an experimental treatment in which tissue and organs are seeded on a polymer matrix using a neutral stem-cell line. I understand the speed of this process is now so rapid that you can almost see them growing. Dr. von Bergen anticipates that Griff will recover quite happily, given time and care, both of which he will have in abundance. There is almost no risk involved, especially given what I understand are the somewhat limited alternatives. You may therefore wish to avoid any involvement in my activities. I would entirely understand."

Abbie Watson scowls. "Like Hell," she says.

Polly Cradle nods. "Then that's two."

"I thought you'd never bloody get here!" Cecily cries before Polly can even speak. "And then I thought you'd decided I was too old! Where is the bugger? Shut up, Foalbury, I'm going, and that's all there is to it. Oh, Harriet, hello, thank goodness, now I feel less like a crone among babes and more like a grandmother out with her brood. Speaking of broods, where's the boy? Never mind, never mind, let's get to the part where we smite the unrighteous. I've brought my most alarming teeth!"

And indeed, she has, a steel set made in 1919 for an American prospector who liked to chew rocks and taste the precious ores.

"Three," Polly Cradle says, and then explains what they are going to do. Joe Spork, listening in the back of the minibus Polly made him steal for the occasion, feels there is altogether too much cackling.

They follow the bus's excellent (female) satellite-navigation system to the address Polly has chosen from the two on the Hon Don's list, and take the lift to the right floor. With Joe waiting at the end of the corridor and Harriet, Abbie, and Cecily arranged behind her, Polly rings the bell.

When the doorbell rang, Arvin Cummerbund was in the walk-in shower of his apartment in Paddington. It is a modern apartment; off-white walls and sharp-edged furniture, a glass dining table in one corner of the open-plan space and an expensive cream leather sofa in the other. Arvin Cummerbund is very keen on the sofa, because it has a clever arrangement of rails which allows the back to be moved around for convenience. He has never actually used this facility, but he feels that its presence enriches his life.

Arvin, in the shower, considered himself, and found that he looked like a glistening Aztec pyramid made in flesh, step after step after step of glorious pink fat. Luxuriantly, he soaped. His hands lifted and loofahed, burnishing the edifice. He slipped his fingers under each precious layer, into the crease, around, and onto the top, beginning the process again. He examined himself, and found that he shone wetly in the mellow bathroom light. His strong, conical legs and knotted knees carried the remarkable burden of his body without strain. Arvin knew himself to be light on his feet. In a couple more decades, he would have to forsake some part of this majesty, lest his heart and joints begin to complain. In any case, his skin would stretch and droop, lose the resilient elasticity which made him so remarkably erotic.

He had it from Rodney Titwhistle that morning—a collegial bit of trivia over the morning reports—that sumo wrestlers, in the course of their training, must wash one another. Specifically, the younger, less lauded must assist the others in their ablutions. Arvin could not imagine wanting help. This daily ceremony was his chance to appreciate himself in fullest glory. Each roped handful was a memory of some vast, sumptuous, indulgent feast; every pound was earned in delight, represented physical excesses and lust. He treasured the stories beneath his skin almost as much as he enjoyed having this fabulous body. Arvin Cummerbund was more than fat, and far more than *obese,* which was a nay-sayers' term, a sad little epithet born of puritans and fear-mongering, and probably of jealousy. He was *gigantic,* and as he stood in his special wash-box, with its concrete floor and mirrored walls, and the many jets of water scoured and exfoliated him, he fancied he resembled Poseidon himself. He made a mental note to secure a trident and a fishy costume. Magnificent Arvin the water god.

Alas, all things must pass. He stepped out of the shower and considered his lotions. For Arvin, the business of getting ready to go out could take an entire day. But the rewards were equal to the effort: women—in all shapes and sizes, of all ages and from all corners of the Earth and all walks of life—once they had overcome the initial fashionable reluctance to be encompassed by a man of his measure, found in themselves a powerful fascination with his body, a need to throw themselves across him and wallow in him. His current girlfriend, Helena (by any standard utterly beautiful, also Argentinian by birth and monstrously wealthy), had declared via the electronic mail her intention to feed him caviar with her fingers and ride him like a polo pony. It was an idea which Arvin Cummerbund felt had distinct promise.

And then the doorbell rang. Helena was early, but eagerness, Arvin Cummerbund thought to himself, was a trait he could only accept gracefully. Still, she would have to learn patience as well. The business of preparing Arvin for the fight was long and splendid. Perhaps he would permit her to assist. The notion of her, dressed no doubt in some long evening gown, climbing nimbly around Mount Cummerbund, diligently and even worshipfully applying unguents, possessed a degree of appeal.

He hitched a bath towel—custom-made—around his middle, and

stepped lightly to his front door. He inhaled, so as to be at his most enormous, and flung it wide.

"My booty shake brings all the girls to the yard!" sang Arvin Cummerbund, striking a heroic pose.

None of the women on his step was Helena, and one of the Not-Helenas was staring at him and smiling with what appeared to be steel teeth. There were four of them, or rather, a group of three and a ringmaster or divine huntress who stood apart, whom he recognised unhappily from surveillance photographs as Mary Angelica "Polly" Cradle.

"I find that . . . profoundly disturbing, if true," she said.

Arvin Cummerbund hoped very much that his towel was well-secured, because he was conscious of shrinkage. The three women with her were, to a graduate of a good university, alarmingly familiar. The Graeae. The fates. The maiden must be (*oh, Jesus!*) Abbie Watson, with what appeared to be her husband's boating hook in one hand; the mother was Harriet Spork, gangster's moll and flagellant nun now apparently resuming her career in thuggery, and the crone—*the teeth! My God, the teeth!*—had to be Cecily Foalbury of Harticle's. His eye settled hopefully on Polly Cradle. She was small, and very intent, and . . . resolved. Discreetly, as if not wanting to make too much of a fuss about it, she was carrying a large pistol. It was an old one, very well-kept, and it seemed to have seen recent deployment. Arvin Cummerbund thought of the two dead men in Edie Banister's flat, and of the other piece of news Rodney had imparted to him, of Edie's death.

Not the Graeae. Worse: "*Tricoteuses!*" some part of his mind gargled in alarm. "The guillotine hags! Knitting of corpses' hair. Flee, Arvin! Flee!"

However, a Cummerbund does not flee at his own gate. He stands. Most especially when there is the additional issue of a Webley Mk VI whose target is one's own enormous belly, an easy mark at some remove, but at close quarters almost literally impossible to miss, even with the rather iffy Webley.

All of which is recent and regrettable history. Looking now at these three very determined women, and at the mistress of hounds with her enormous certainty, Arvin Cummerbund feels very cold, and very small. He glances southward, to his towel.

"Oh," Arvin Cummerbund says damply.

"Mr. Cummerbund," Polly Cradle murmurs. "Would you be so kind as to come with us?"

Somewhere back in the flat, there's a satellite-linked panic button which he carries in his pocket at all times. It actually has a lanyard so that he can wear it in the shower, but it gets in the way of the soap situation and is—being designed not by Apple or Sony but by the MOD—extremely ugly. It is therefore notably out of reach, even if he has remembered to replace the battery recently. He glances back at the boathook, seeing the name WATSON in large painted letters along the haft, and he chills—even further—as he tracks the message inherent in that. Abbie Watson glowers.

Arvin Cummerbund sighs, and allows them to lead him away.

"The error you have made," Polly Cradle says in the house by Hampstead Heath, "lies, if you will forgive me, in your assessment of yourself in relation to your enemies—of whom, incidentally, your attack upon Joshua Joseph Spork makes me one. You believe, because it suits you to do so as emissaries of a great and powerful conspiracy in service to commerce and personal gain, that you and your charming friend Mr. Titwhistle have what I will call the 'moral low ground.'"

Mercer Cradle sits at a kidney desk on the other side of the room, watching his sister work and leafing through a copious file. The *tricoteuses* occupy a nasty little semicircle close by, also watching. Cecily Foalbury has the largest chair, a wooden rocker, profoundly inappropriate for an interrogation, which she appears to enjoy. She is drinking tea and slurping it around her metal teeth. Leaning against a bookshelf at the back of the room is a tall, bulky figure in a long coat. He is in shadow, but Arvin Cummerbund recognises Britain's Most Wanted by the line of his jaw. That said, there is something . . . *collected* . . . about him. He's come of age somehow.

Arvin's own chair is an expensive one from Liberty, in chintz. It's very comfortable. He has also been allowed to retain his towel and even given a blanket for warmth. He fusses with it.

Polly Cradle waits until she has his full attention, and continues.

"You think there are no depths to which you will not stoop. From this perception you draw a sense of invulnerability. You believe that you are—if I may put it crudely—the *bad guys*. You cherish the notion that you serve a great necessity, and thus your evil deeds, from which you derive a certain frisson, are legitimised. Nonetheless, though regrettably necessary they are unquestionably evil, and in some small way, so are you. You bear this burden for the nation and the world, sacrificing your own nobility in the cause of higher salvation. I'm terribly impressed.

"This construction would make us," she indicates the room in general, "the *good guys*. Misguided, but morally clean. As a consequence of our goodness, you feel safe in this very quiet, very secluded room."

She smiles, then tuts as the dog Arvin Cummerbund earlier observed tugs at something in a carpet bag under the table, a rubbery sort of item. Harriet Spork picks the bag up off the floor and starts absently to unpack it. A rubber apron. A length of surgical hose. Arvin Cummerbund feels a sort of rushing feeling in his stomach. Polly Cradle nods a thank-you and goes on.

"The thing is, Arvin—you don't mind if I call you Arvin, do you?—the thing is that you and Rodney are really quite nice people. You don't break the law if you can help it, or misuse your personal power. You don't bear grudges. You're probably expecting me to say I don't hold a grudge, either, because good people don't, but actually I rather do. You sent my lover to be tortured. I do take that personally, Arvin. May I say also, *inter alia*, that torturing someone by proxy is even more contemptible than doing it oneself?"

From the bag: a box (half full) of surgical gloves. Gauze. Lint. Tape. Distilled water. Spirit. A pair of those odd little bent scissors which look like the ones used for cutting grapes, but which are intended for a more medical purpose. Cecily Foalbury leans over and scrabbles for a piece of plastic tubing, and measures it against her arm, then bites through it and measures again. Better.

Harriet Spork sighs. Something is missing from the pile. What is it? Has the dog got it? A quite obvious, commonplace something, a trivial item, no one in their right mind would leave home without one . . . where is it? Abbie Watson comes to her rescue.

"Bastion! Drop!"

There it is, dratted dog. *Tourniquet*. Abbie Watson sets it on the table, and looks at Arvin Cummerbund without compassion.

"My husband," she says distantly, "is going into surgery right about now."

Which gives rise to the first genuine silence Arvin has heard in years. Even Cecily Foalbury stops drinking her tea.

"Yes," Polly Cradle murmurs after a moment. "Even so, I must regretfully inform you that you and your friend Rodney are not bad men at all, not in that sense. You are driven by a perceived necessity. You are *good*. The corollary of which is that we are very much the other thing. You are fallen into the hands of villains. I would advise you to consider the implications of that for a moment." She does not point to the items on the table. Arvin looks at them anyway. "Mr. Cummerbund," Polly Cradle goes on gently, "you are under the delusion that your safety is assured by common decency, but it is not. We are wicked and we are angry. There is no decency in this room. You have connived in the assassination of Edie Banister. You have taken Harriet's son and put him to the question. You have done harm to this woman's mate. And you have deprived me of my lover.

"I do not know, at this point, whether Joshua Joseph Spork is the man of my life. He could be. I have given it considerable thought. The jury is still out. The issue between you and me is that you wish to deprive me of the opportunity to find out. Joe Spork is not yours to give or to withhold from me, Mr. Cummerbund. He is *mine*, until I decide otherwise. You have caused him grief, sullied his name, and you have hurt him. If anyone is going to make him weep, or lie about him, or even do bad things to him, it is *me*.

"We are more angry than you can understand. And you are here, with us, in the land of do-as-you-please. It's like wonderland, Mr. Cummerbund. Only much less good."

She smiles sharply.

"A friend of mine would have said," she adds, "that we are *aglæc-wif*. Monstrous hags. Or you could say we are 'women of consequence.' What happens to you here, in this room, can reflect that as little or as much as you wish."

And then they sit there without speaking, listening to the muffled sound of traffic, and the wind in the trees, and Cecily Foalbury working a piece of bourbon biscuit out of her heirloom dentures. The dog Bastion pads across the room to Joe Spork and burbles mournfully until he is lifted up and held.

Abbie Watson sorts through the sinister apparatus on the table as if wondering where she will begin. Arvin Cummerbund dimly remembers that she is a qualified nurse. He wonders who is watching her children, and whether she wanted to bring them along. Even Mercer Cradle looks a little windy about what will happen next, and this is truly alarming because, as far as Arvin Cummerbund has been able to ascertain, Mercer is absolutely devoid of compunction of any kind where those who interfere with his family's happiness are concerned.

A shadow falls across Arvin; a shadow which fills him with a measure of guilt. He inhales slightly, and winces at the odour of dog breath. Bastion snuffles at him curiously, and then yawns, displaying tooth stumps and slime.

"Mercer," Polly Cradle says, "if you wouldn't mind."

Mercer gets to his feet and goes outside, returning with a heavy glass jar or demijohn filled with reddish ooze.

"Excellent," Polly Cradle says. "Now that Mr. Titwhistle is here, you need have no scruples about speaking behind his back." She indicates the ooze. "Although I fear it's rather difficult to say in which direction he is facing."

Arvin Cummerbund stares at the jar. It cannot possibly be Rodney Titwhistle. These people would not do something so vile. He is almost certain of it. Yet Polly Cradle's analysis was compelling. As are the instruments on the table before him.

The silence is very thick as he thinks about that.

"No," Joe Spork says abruptly. "This isn't me. It isn't us."

Polly Cradle looks over at him.

"This—" He gestures at the room. "This is them. Not us."

Polly Cradle nods. "Okay."

Joe puts down the dog and looks Arvin in the eye.

"Arvin," Joe Spork says, "the jar is full of giblets. I think that's a grape. We're not going to bleed you to death or put you through a woodchipper."

"Nor am I going to eat you," Cecily Foalbury interjects, somewhat unreassuringly.

"Quite," Joe Spork continues, "although Abbie has put in a very strong bid that I should beat the shit out of you with a plank with salt on it for what happened to Griff."

"And I said I'd buy the plank," adds Sister Harriet primly.

"But Arvin, listen, seriously. You have to know that what's going on is a disaster. I mean, a bloody nightmare. Look what you've got. The Ruskinites are monsters. They scare professional crooks, which sounds oh-so-clever until you remember that you're supposed to be on the side of the angels. You've got torture camps in the shires; you've got imprisonment without trial. *Vaughn Parry* works for you! And don't tell me the end justifies the means because it doesn't. We never reach the end. All we ever get is means. That's what we live with.

"Unless Edie Banister was right and Shem Shem Tsien wants to bring the world to an end, in which case, see point one."

Arvin Cummerbund breathes deeply, in, out, in, out, and contemplates his soul. It occurs to him that Rodney Titwhistle's search for truth, for knowing, is a curious thing when a man may hear truth spoken and recognise it, by any human measure, quite without doubt.

"Could I have some of that tea?" he asks.

"I'll make some fresh," Harriet Spork says. "Start talking."

Well. It would not be entirely inappropriate, in this situation, to bargain for his release with unimportant information. More than that, however, Arvin Cummerbund is finding it increasingly difficult to suppress a nagging unease that these people know more about what is actually going on than he does. Rodney has been taking the lead on the Angelmaker situation. Rodney is very astute and very ruthless. But if he has a failing, it is that he is so astute, and so ruthless, that he occasionally misses things which are muddled and human. So Arvin Cummerbund says:

"What do you want to know?"

"Who killed Billy Friend?" Polly Cradle says.

Arvin had sort of forgotten about irritating, brash Billy in the interim, what with the business of trying to reclaim Britain's supremacy in the world and collaborating with an insane cultist. Curious, now that he thinks about it, that those two should go together.

"That was Sheamus," he says, "or maybe one of the . . . Automata." He sighs. "It was stupid, sending him. We just weren't thinking properly. We thought he'd be more careful. More circumspect, because this is his focus. But it went the other way. He's genuinely obsessed, you see, with truth and God and all that. Or I suppose you could be generous and say he believes. I think he had a moment of passion. Your friend was . . . shattered." He remembers the panic when he heard, and Rodney Titwhistle's calm acceptance: *Our amanuensis has murdered, and that is bad, but we are protecting the nation. These things must be seen in their proper context.*

Joe peers at Arvin Cummerbund and wonders. "Sheamus," the fat man keeps saying. Not "Shem Shem Tsien." "Do you know what

Sheamus plans to do with the Apprehension Engine, now that he has the calibration drum?"

Arvin Cummerbund shakes his head. "He doesn't have it. He's very upset about that. He says he can't switch the machine off unless he finds it."

Joe Spork glances at Polly Cradle. She meets his eyes: *Yes, Joe. Follow that.* Joe raises one index finger: point of information. "He does. The escape con worked and I bubbled. I told him outright where to find it." He searches Arvin Cummerbund's wide face. "But he hasn't passed that information on to you."

"No."

"I believe I know why. Do you know who—what—he is?"

"A monk. Obviously. A believer."

"No. Or, not exactly." And to Arvin Cummerbund's growing alarm, Joe outlines the history of Sheamus, Shem Shem Tsien and Vaughn Parry so far as he knows it, from Edie's time to the fake escape from Happy Acres, and the more he speaks, the more sallow and sick Arvin Cummerbund appears.

"I told Parry," Joe says. "I worked it out, in that place. At the last minute, actually. I told him and then I realised he . . . wasn't my friend. Because there was a moment when I thought the most wanted murderer in the country was my friend, or wanted to think so, because I was alone."

He laughs.

Cummerbunds do not mist up. They are not in touch with their feminine sides. They do not emote. Nor do they yield to the sudden fear that they've been stitched up like a kipper and induced to conspire against the existence of mankind. They do not change allegiances or defect. On certain occasions, however, it may be as well to consider one's position *vis-à-vis* the established lines of battle.

Joe Spork opens his hands, palms up. Big hands. Thug's hands, perhaps. Craftsman's hands. Not liar's hands. "So there you have it," he says.

Arvin swallows. "That's . . . not ideal."

"No."

"No, I mean it's very bad. They have a . . . an apparatus, at Sharrow House. We supplied the necessary materials and so on. It is supposed to control the bees. Bring them into line."

"Put the genie back in the bottle."

"Exactly. And give us access to the power source, possibly control the . . . truth aspect . . . of the whole thing. Not to mention keep a lid on our authorship of what has been a rather strained international incident. It's rather hard to argue that the Russians can't control their post-Soviet nuclear deterrent well enough if we . . . well. You see."

"Yes."

"But now," Arvin Cummerbund admits, "I think maybe that isn't quite what it will do. If Sheamus is Parry. If Parry is Shem Shem Tsien. If he has the calibration drum. If he has other plans, then . . . well, it's . . . it's not an area where other plans are a good idea."

A moment later, it is apparent that Arvin Cummerbund has turned his coat entirely. The prospect of the Opium Khan in charge of the Apprehension Engine is so ghastly that it frees his better nature from the grip of professional habit, in a transformation which Polly suspects is the fast version of what Edie Banister went through months before. Very shortly, Arvin is enthusiastically offering his testimony on the various crimes of the Legacy Board, somewhat disappointed to find that the Spork party is not considering a suit for damages in the foreseeable future. He is able to command via the telephone blueprints for Sharrow House itself, delivered by courier to the Pablum Club, and declares himself willing to get hold of anything else which might be of service. Arvin explains that a Cummerbund, having made up his mind to do something, does it whole.

In earnest of which, appallingly, he abases himself before Abbie Watson and offers swathes of his own skin in replacement for Griff's. Only the swift intervention of Polly Cradle prevents him from displaying a section of stomach he believes is particularly well-moisturised for her consideration, and Abbie, wide-eyed, assures him that this grisly act of contrition is unnecessary. Dr. von Bergen has pronounced all things good and Griff has no need of donor dermis.

From the name "Sharrow House" and the address in a rather rich bit of south-west London, Joe Spork had concluded that the headquarters of the Ruskinites must be a cool, grey-white neoclassical effort with the air of a Dickensian legal firm and a brass plaque. In his mind, he had conceded—indeed, had looked forward to—a significant police presence, some reinforced glass, and all manner of interior security precautions like unto a foreign embassy in a hostile land. In other words, a building fundamentally intended as a dwelling which had been substantially adapted for use as a lair or secret base. Keyword: adapted—and in that adaptation, he had envisaged finding weaknesses. Gaps between the skirting board and the wall where a person of low moral fibre might reasonably pry open a board. Even holding the plans which Arvin Cummerbund provided and seeing that he was dealing with something rather different, Joe had cherished a dream of incompetence in his enemy's precautions. He had with some confidence anticipated being able to gain entry via an unregarded loft space, to bribe a disaffected copper or blackmail an official, or, *in extremis,* simply blow the bloody doors off and make hay. Somewhere in the gamut of crime, from sneakthievery to bullion heisting, he had reckoned to find a technique of entry against which the Opium Khan and his minions had failed to guard. This is very much not that sort of house.

Sharrow House is—and has always been—a castle, or a keep.

On the open upper deck of a London tourist bus making a loop around London's grand gardens, Joe Spork wears a Gore-Tex coat with a waterproof rain-cape, and across his back is a rucksack in the pattern of the Danish flag. He has fended off a gregarious Dutch couple intent on sharing their bag of sunflower seeds and pine kernels (the husband addressed him with a generous bellow of "Would you like to eat my nuts?") and leaned on Polly's shoulder through the interminable lecture on King Edward and Mrs. Simpson. They have seen Hampton Court and Kew, and now the bus, in the grey rain and orange-purple twilight, is crawling past Sharrow House.

"On our left," the woman with the yellow umbrella says, "we see the Sharrow estate. Normally we like to go in there and feed the ducks and admire the remarkable blend of architectural styles"—this last as if announcing a death—"which is the result of the various changes in ownership of Sharrow House over the centuries. As you may know, Sharrow is one of London's defensive structures, dating from the time of Henry VIII. During the Cromwellian period, it was besieged twice, but never captured." Murmurs of approval from the bus. That's the sort of behaviour one looks for in a castle—unless, of course, one wants to break into it.

Through Joe's field glasses, Sharrow House is high and strange, with a single very tall spire in the centre, an abrupt Romantic fancy leaping from a sixteenth-century hall. On the plans, this looks like a bullseye. From here it has the feel of a spear, or a warning sign.

All around the main house, the later additions spread out, Victorian red brick and white stucco, even something a little Frank Lloyd Wright on one side of the roof, a floating wood-and-glass observatory—but all of them are sealed and solid, and Joe recognises the ethos of the Ruskinites, the real ones. Sharrow House has the same integrity and integration of design he saw in the *Lovelace*, the same strength. It has real defence in depth, too—a surrounding wall, guard posts, even a proper moat: a slick, greenish expanse clear two hundred feet wide, with a single narrow causeway leading to the main gate. Towards the back, there's an ancient fortified box—consequence of a brief incarnation as an ack-ack command post during the Blitz— and a short stretch of rail leading to a blank wall; what used to be the castle's ammunition dump. The lecture burbles on. "The House is presently the headquarters of a monastic order who specialise in church architecture and the care of orphans and the mentally ill, but these days those functions take place in purpose-built facilities elsewhere."

Joe keeps his face carefully blank, recalling the white room. Yes. *Purpose-built* indeed. He watches a pair of shrouded figures shuffle across the grass, their steps slow and just a little wrong. Polly Cradle's hand tightens on his shoulder, and he realises he has hissed, not a music-hall hiss, but an expulsion of air through clenched teeth. Everyone looks at him.

"Sorry," he says, as Danish as he knows how, "I have windiness."

The guide smiles flatly and gets back to her script. "Unlike so many of Henry's buildings it was never used to house inconvenient wives or desired mistresses, but it remains one of the capital's most interesting undiscovered buildings. I do advise you to come back some time when it isn't closed and take the tour."

"Why is it closed?" the dapper little man in the second row of the bus says, from beneath one of those rather surgical-looking plastic macs.

"Cleaning," the umbrella woman says briefly.

"Cleaning?"

"Yes. You'd think we could just go in anyway, wouldn't you, but apparently . . . Health and Safety." Even the Japanese party at the back are familiar with this so-British obsession. Everyone laughs.

As Joe watches, a woman, likely a housekeeper, leans from a window to throw something tubular and offal-ish into the moat; oily ripples abruptly transform into boiling, frothing spume.

Joe Spork takes the binoculars from his face and stares at Polly Cradle.

"Yes," she says, "I saw it, too."

"Piranhas? In London?"

"So it would appear."

"You are absolutely fucking kidding me," says Joshua Joseph Spork.

Polly Cradle dials a number on her phone. "Yes, hello, it's Linda here at Sharrow House? Yes, we're ready now, could you—thank you."

A moment later, a London taxi chugs towards the gates. Joe looks on with a slightly guilty frown. Before the cab is even on the causeway, it is surrounded by black-clad monks and soldiers, and the driver is on his knees in the gravel, and then flat on his face.

"Oh," says the umbrella lady hurriedly. "Well, there we are: British armed forces are using the maintenance work for training. A round of applause, please."

Everyone claps. The taxi driver lies in the dirt.

Joe winces. "We're not getting in that way."

A conversation with Arvin Cummerbund does not produce any better news: Arvin is painfully eager to continue his atonement, but has never been inside Sharrow House. The Legacy Board has a hands-off relationship with its religious subcontractor; a *laissez-faire,* light-touch management ethos. In other words, Arvin now acknowledges, Rodney Titwhistle and his political masters prefer not to know what the Ruskinites do. Sharrow House is like a giant blind spot in the vision of British officialdom, and the Legacy Board is specifically charged with making sure it does not become obnoxiously obvious—or, if it ever should, that it be absolutely clear that any crimes were committed without the knowledge of the government: a sad lack of oversight, but not actual complicity. *Lessons will be learned*, of course.

In an old brewery basement under the Thames, declared unsafe in 1975 by a surveyor on Mathew's payroll and hence forever vacant, Joe Spork sits on a three-legged stool and stares at the blueprints as if by sheer intensity he can force them to reveal what he needs. He inhales copier solvent and warm paper, and scowls, shifting his legs.

At his feet is the Thompson gun in its trombone case. He does not look at it, but the heavy metal haunts him. He can see himself firing it, riding the percussive blasts, but he cannot see what good it will do. He cannot shoot down the Opium Khan's gates. He cannot kill the Apprehension Engine, or erase the calibration drum, from three miles away. Before he can do anything, he needs to get inside.

Joe kicks back and stands in the semi-darkness, swinging his arms in a circle like a sportsman working out a cramp. Casting around, he finds the tube the blueprints came in, a plastic thing like a length of pipe, and, rolling them back into it, slings it over his shoulder. The lamp above the table makes a circle of light and warmth. Reluctantly, he turns his face away from it, and walks into the darkness of the Tosher's Beat.

Joe Spork loves the Beat. He loves the toshers themselves, weird, dry-suited moonmen that they are. He loves the whole place for its cosy closeness and its quiet, for the soaring majesty of the cisterns and vaults. And most of the time he does not think about what it is: a vast, subterranean webwork mostly below the water table, bits of which flood from floor to ceiling in winter and spring. The toshers wear those suits for a reason.

He crawls on his stomach along a dry clay pipe, and tries to ignore the high tide mark seven inches above his head. He can smell it all around: water which has been and gone, and water which is in the adjoining pipes, water welling up through the floor. He tries to forget, as well, that he will have to do this journey again in reverse, including the tight corner five minutes back which nearly snagged him for ever. He just pushes on towards Sharrow House, glancing from time to time at the compass which was in the side pocket of Mathew's gangster kit.

This is the last easy way into Sharrow House: up through the floors and the pipes, catch Shem Shem Tsien in his bath and blow his machine to slag before anyone even knows what's happening. Home in time for tea and medals and a speedy exit to a non-extradition-treaty nation with nice views.

He isn't doing this entirely blind: the toshers have marked the pipe as traversable: long yellow streaks of enamel paint along the entryway to indicate that you can do it and it will take you somewhere but it's not a great deal of fun. Green paint is better, blue better still. Red paint means no-go.

The pipe opens out into a shallow basin with a low roof. It's like being on the inside of a sandwich. All around the walls are other pipes, some large, some small, emptying into this same room. He's about to cross into the next section when he hears a shout. He turns, and sees three toshers waving. He waves back, Night Market style.

"It's no-go," the nearest one says as they reach him. "We're changing the tag now."

"What's happened?" Joe asks.

The tosher scowls. He's big and grey and has the face for it, his nose wrinkling like a bulldog's. "Some muckety muck has happened," he says, "gone and put bloody electric fences and all that in the bloody tunnel. Infrared cameras and the like. My mate's in the hospital with taser burns and a wonky ticker. They say he's lucky to be alive, the amount of juice it put through him. Sodding embassy or something, I should think. They're always trouble."

Joe nods. "Is there another way in?"

The man stares at him. "I know you."

"I doubt it, I'm not—"

"You're that Spork, you are. Crazy Joe." He turns, calls over his shoulder. "Oy, lads, it's Crazy Joe!" He looks back. "Come on, then, what'd you really do? Pinch the Queen's knickers, was it? Rob the Bank of England?"

"Nothing like that—"

"Bet it was. I knew your dad, back in the day. Well, you're a right 'un, I can see that. Anyone can see that. You a killer? Bollocks, is what it is. He's took the bullion from the vault, I reckon," he opines to the man behind him.

The other man nods. "Likely."

"So this house, you want in?" The first tosher gestures vaguely up and back.

"Yes, very much."

"Well, not from down here. It's all the same, all the way round. The Tosh Herself is hopping mad, I will say."

Joe ponders this for a moment, and looks around at the nexus of pipes in which they stand.

"You know," he says, carefully, "that Sharrow House has a moat?"

"A *moat*?"

"Seriously."

"Well, la-di-dah."

"And it occurs to me that Herself might want to do something about that. 'Block the Beat, the Beat blocks you,' isn't that what they say?"

"They do."

"Well, suppose somehow the pipes got all messed up and the supply for the pipe were to rupture . . . or maybe some high-pressure mains were diverted at just the right moment . . ."

"Oh," the tosher says, "I see. Yes. Do you think that would be upsetting for the muckety muck?"

"I do."

"That amount of water could pack quite a wallop, you know. Dangerous to mess around with. You could get the moat sort of spreading itself all over the place."

Everyone's grinning now.

"That would be," one of the other toshers says neutrally, "really distracting. If some bloke were thinking of robbing the place."

"That's true," the first man agrees. "Is there a particular moment, Mr. Spork, when you might think, with your unique understanding of the criminal mind, that such a heinous act might be perpetrated?"

"I wouldn't want to speculate," Joe says. "But roughly, if I had to guess, 2 a.m. the day after tomorrow, and then run like hell."

XVII

Back on track;

the Old Campaigners;

the Chairman declines to assist a wanted felon.

Back in the brewery basement, Joe stares down a long, wide gallery at a row of mannequins wearing army-surplus and thrift-shop clothes, posed in a variety of aggressive stances. Bald, blind enemies. Behind and beside them, boxes, boards and water barrels protect the brick. Mathew gave his stolen space over to practice; this was where he brought his boys before a caper to sharpen up, and the dim yellow electric bulbs they installed—running, of course, on pilfered current—are still hanging from the ceiling.

By now, if he is honest, he had assumed he would have a plan: a bold, deranged plan, both cunning and explosive, which would outwit and outgun the Opium Khan's soldiers and get them into Sharrow House. He had daydreamed himself coming up through the drains with an army, descending from the tower with the Fifth Floor Men, stepping from behind a curtain to reveal that he had bribed the butler.

Instead, he has nothing. A blueprint which exposes only strength; a promise of assistance with something which isn't really a big problem; a gun, a girl, and a lawyer.

In the semi-dark, he grins. That last part, at least, is completely authentic gangstery.

He opens the trombone case and looks at the gun. Shiny, oiled metal gleams up at him. He waits for revelation, but doesn't feel it. The gun is, after all, just a gun; an outdated, inaccurate piece of battlefield weaponry beloved of bootleggers in the United States during Prohibition time. And to be honest, it's more a prop than a piece of ordnance. There are—there were even in Mathew's day—better guns; lighter, faster, deadlier guns.

He unpacks it, lets his hands assemble the pieces. Click, twist, clunk. Rudimentary. Obvious. Not crude, just simple. In fact, it's an elegant thing, in its way. He pantomimes: *You'll never take me alive, copper!*

Less funny than it might be.

More carefully, he lifts the gun to his shoulder, selects the single-shot option and aims down the gallery. He breathes out, relaxes the tension in his body and then prepares to receive the impacts which will follow. Looking along the barrel, he keeps both eyes open, captures a mannequin in the V of the rear sight. He aims for the body, having no delusions of competence. He lets himself feel the moment. Young Joe, after all, wanted this more than anything else, in the world, ever, and somehow was never permitted.

He pulls the trigger.

The noise is stunning. A jet of flame spears out from the muzzle and the butt slams against his body. The shot whines away into the dark. Gritting his teeth, he fires five more times, having some notion that six is a marksman's number, and walks down to look at the damage.

There is none. The mannequins are unscathed. Behind them, his bullets have splintered boards and chipped stone.

He stares at the gun in his hands, and wonders if he will cry. Instead, he walks back to his stool and sits, smelling pointless gun smoke.

He has no idea what to do. This was supposed to lift him up. Instead, it has smashed him, at this late date and with the fate of the world apparently hanging in the balance.

So he sits, and stares at nothing.

"Need some help?" Polly Cradle asks.

She has come in very quietly, and now she touches Joe lightly on one shoulder. Her finger turns him towards her, and a soft kiss brushes his lips. In his gut, a flicker of angry bear: *I will keep this woman safe. I will bite anyone who is unkind to her.*

The bear, at least, has no doubts.

She grins at him, as if hearing the inner growl, and squirms onto his lap.

"So, come on. What are you doing?"

"Looking for Mathew," he confesses.

She nods. "But he's not here?"

"No."

"Why Mathew?"

"Because this is his kind of thing."

She stares at him, and then, very precisely, blows a raspberry into his face. "Rubbish!"

"What?"

"I said, rubbish. Utter nincompoopery. What . . . gah!" Words fail her. "Joe. You don't need to look for Mathew. You're you. His son. But, mostly, you. And *you are good at this!* Look at the last few weeks and tell me I'm wrong."

He is about to do so, but she points one finger sharply at his eye. *Independent supervillain in my own right.* Yes. That surely includes collegial respect.

"Good," Polly Cradle says. "Now. Show me the gun."

When he does, she laughs.

"You fire it the way you *want* to fire it, Joe," Polly Cradle says, when she can speak again, "not the way you think you *should.* Bollocks to should. Say it with me."

"Bollocks to should," Joe intones dutifully, and she makes him say it over and over with her, until the sense of transgression lifts him up again. Being the new unafraid Joe is wonderful, but it's also like a slippery log: he can walk along it for a while, but in the pauses he loses his footing and falls off. Momentum is important, and practice. And it's easier in opposition, too, in the face of someone who can be delighted or appalled. He finds himself feeding off the audience.

Polly grins at him, feral, from the shadows to one side. Motions to the gun: *go ahead.*

Joe sets himself, plants his feet wide, switches the Thompson to full-auto mode, feels the coat on his shoulders and the excitement of the child he was. This is the gun. *That* gun. *Dad's* gun! The strictly forbidden un-toy, the tool of a gangster's trade.

A mad grin tugs at his mouth; not the mild nostalgia of his first effort but a kind of deranged glee. He lets it show his teeth, then pulls the trigger as if launching an ocean liner.

The gun howls and jerks, sending ripples of shock through his arms and chest. He wrestles it, fights to hold it down, keeps his finger clamped on the trigger. You don't see a gangster squeezing off rounds like a miser. Hell, no. You see him hosing the enemy with hot lead, doing property damage, making a point. A gangster is not a sniper. He is profligate, needless, heedless. He is mad as a shaved cat.

He ends up almost leaning on the gun as if it were a small, wiry demon trying to get out of a box. He fires off the whole drum, and realises he is laughing outright, a deranged, terrified or terrifying cackle. Finally, the roar stops, the beast is still, and the damage is prodigious. He stares down the range, through wisps of smoke and dust.

The mannequins are in pieces. Chunks and strands of them are strewn all over, splattered into the wall behind. The wall itself is peppered and speckled with impacts, the boards and barrels stacked against it to absorb the ricochets are so much kindling. There are little fires and charred holes everywhere. He picks his way through the devastation, stares at what he has made. And once again, he understands.

"Wow," Polly murmurs.

Joe Spork grabs her up and kisses her soundly, triumphant. "You're a genius."

"I am?"

"Yes. You are. Because I get it. I get it now. This is what it's all about. The stricture of the gun."

She smiles. "Tell me."

He grins. "Imagine this: suppose you had some other gun and I had that thing. Right? And on the count of three, we're both going to start firing. Really, you ought to win. You'll be faster and more accurate, and you can duck and weave, you'll take me apart. Right? How do you feel about it?"

"I don't fancy it."

"Exactly. Because a man carrying a tommy gun plants his feet and lets loose and no one knows—literally no one—what will happen next. This is a gambler's weapon. A gangster's gun. It's not about perfection or skill or even surviving. It's about brass and swagger. It's big and loud and ridiculous and it says: *Give it your best! Because one of us is going down and I don't know or even really care which it is!*" He grins again.

"You're back on track, then," Polly murmurs happily, and sees him nod, and then nod again more slowly, his eyes opening very wide. Criminal epiphany.

"Oh, yes," he says fervently. "Yes, I am. Back on track, indeed."

"Mercer!" Joe Spork yells at the top of the stairs. "Your sister is a genius!"

"What?" Mercer peers at him, then blanches slightly. "No, she isn't, you must be mistaken." And when this makes no impact on the effervescing Joe, "Oh, shit. This is what old Jonah told me would happen. He said one day I'd be running along behind you like the last Marx brother trying to catch the vase. I told him you were sensible."

"I was. Look where it got me. So now I'm not."

"Joe, what—"

"No time. I need to prepare. So do you. Tell Jorge I need them all tonight."

"Need what?"

"He'll know."

"I don't!"

"I've got a plan."

"What sort of plan?"

"You're going to hate it."

"Oh, good."

"Let's see about the army first, and then we can argue."

"Army? What army?"

Joe grins and dashes out.

"What army? You don't have an army! Apart from"—he gestures at the dog lying flatulently on the sofa—"the world's smallest airborne toxic event over there! Joe? Joe!"

Polly Cradle emerges from the Tosher's Beat with her eyes fixed on one of the Sharrow House maps. "Oh," she says, after a moment. "Oh! Oh, my." Long nails scratch lightly at the glossy paper, tracing the line of the old railway which leads to one wall of the grounds. "Oh, my . . ." Her breath catches in her chest.

"What?" her brother asks.

"He's back on track."

Jorge's message goes out to one person at a time—the Night Market has no website, no bulletin board—but for every felon, receiver, forger or fixer he tells, five more find out, and then ten. Invitations go to the big players and rumours to the small, but in the Market a rumour might as well be embossed in gold. All this chatter comes, inevitably, to the notice of law enforcement, but Jorge is well-used to signal leakage and disperses lies and fables to nurtured snitches. A police task force is dispatched to Manchester on a snark hunt, another to Bray. Analysts are awash in Spork sightings by lunch, cursing by tea. All the while, the intended recipients of the message are hearing it louder and louder: Joe Spork is putting together something big.

Big Douggie, boxer and purveyor of doughnuts, did prison for the Post Office job in '75, and got out just in time for Mathew's death and the changing world. He's washing towels when the phone call comes, wishing he could find a way to stop them smelling like day-old fish stock.

Joe Spork's putting a job together.

What, Joe the Clockmaker?

Yeah, but not any more. They say it's the biggest ever. I heard Mathew planned it before he died.

Of course, Douggie says yes.

Dizzy Spencer runs the Carnaby-Royce School of Motoring, teaching older ladies who have never learned how to navigate the Congestion Charging zone. She does a roaring trade with recently arrived Saudi royals. In Mathew's time—when she wasn't under the sofa with the Honourable Donald—she was the best getaway driver between Shoreditch and Henley. She's bored out of her mind and ready to pop.

Joe Spork's putting a job together.

Dizzy doesn't hesitate for one second.

Caroline Cable—Aunt Caro—designs locks for the company no one's heard of which makes the locks you actually can't crack with a tensioner and a number three pick. The simplest one is the best: there's no keyhole, just a drawer you put the key into and a handle. Key goes inside, you shut the drawer and turn the handle, the key fits the lock and the door opens. If the key doesn't fit, no dice. No way to access the mechanism when the drawer's closed, no way to turn the handle when the drawer's open. Thank you and good night.

Poacher turned gamekeeper, and she hates every penny of it.

Joe Spork—

"Hell, yes," Caro Cable says.

Paul McCain, of the Grantchester McCains, missed the high days and wishes he hadn't. His dad ran with the great ones: Mathew Spork and Tam Coppice and the others. They nicked a dinosaur from the Natural History Museum once, bespoke, for a certain Indian gent who had a space for it in his house in Goa.

Honestly. Nicked a dinosaur. They don't do crimes like that these days.

Paul says yes, and feels as if he's won the lottery.

Word spreads, and London's crooks are not immune to sentiment. The fun's gone out of the life; it's a little professional, a bit grey. People have accountants now, and tax consultants, and Lily Law has them too and you don't want to be investigated by that lot, not even a little.

But here's the thing: Joe Spork is putting a job together.

And that has to mean fireworks.

And then there are the others: the ones who went pro and made good, who don't like surprises or displays. Dave Tregale, who can shift money around the globe, into the white economy and out of the black and back again; Lars the Swede, once Joe's teacher in basic personal defence, who can have you removed from circulation in seven languages; Alice Rebeck, of unknown origins, now a retriever of lost journalists from foreign lands, and—so it is whispered—vanisher at need of over-curious investigators. Half a dozen others, names to be mentioned with circumspection, if at all.

These, too, receive the invitation from Jorge, from Tam, from a new law firm titling itself Edelweiss Feldbett, or by signs and portents unknowable.

Joe Spork is putting a job together.

These are not people who are used to receiving instructions any more, not men or women who take kindly to midnight pre-emption. They do not enjoy fireworks. Still less are they comfortable with one another's company, here, in—of all places—the grand hall of the Pablum Club (to the Hon Don's most strenuous *sotto voce* discontent). But where, after all, would you be less likely to look for a gathering of serious crooks, than in a very exclusive members' club in St. James's?

The hour comes, and a little after, and this great, gathered mass of criminality grows restless. Sure, they've renewed some old acquaintances and seen some people they always thought there might be some chemistry with, back in the day, and met some new people there might be some with now (ho ho!) and of course it's always nice to hear what everyone else is up to, even in the most guarded terms, and work out where there might be an opportunity, perhaps even the possibility of collaboration. But still and all (murmur black suits and serious faces, pinstriped ladies and elegant dames) time is money, after all. And Big Douggie and Caro and Tony Wu, sitting at the edges and in the shadows, feel out of place and very straight-laced, and wish they were somewhere else.

And then a man comes in by the east door. He comes in quietly, as if they weren't all waiting for him. He grins and shakes hands and waves, and lets the rumour make him bigger. He flings wide his arms and embraces a respectable geezer whose bank specialises in discretion.

"Liam!" the fellow says. "As I live and breathe! Liam Doyle, of all the things, they said you were dead!"

"Not me," cries the oldster, much delighted, "I haven't gone on yet, and bollocks to those as wish I would! There's cash yet in the old cow!"

"I'm sure there is!" replies the other. "I'm sure indeed. Can you still dance, though, Liam? You danced the foxtrot with Caro once, in the Primrose Hill house."

"Blow me!" replies Liam Doyle. "I'm sure I did! I would have danced anything in those days! Well, I've no idea. I haven't danced in . . . oh, well . . ." And his voice trails away.

But before it can become maudlin, Liam's friend says "I bet you've still got it!" And Liam says it's true, he has, of course! Of course he has. And then it's "Hullo, Simon, I know that's you, my God, is this your wife? How superb, I swear, she looks like a queen, and I'm not talking about our bloody queen, God bless, I'm talking Titania! Yes, I am! May I kiss the bride?" And he does, planting a smacker on the gentle, homely face and grinning as if he's won a prize. "And Big Douggie! I see you there! Come off the bench, man! You remember Douggie, don't you, Simon?" And Simon does, in fact they had a brawl back in the day, and bloody Hell, if Douggie wasn't the toughest bastard ever threw a punch, *I swear to you, Douggie, I still dream about it, seeing that fist on its way!*

"Well," says Douggie, "I don't mix it up, now. I teach the young ones. But, well, every now and again I show them a thing or two, for laughs. I think they go easy on me, mind . . ." And he grins, gaptoothed, and everyone thinks *Not if they bloody want to get out of the ring alive, they don't.* "How about you, Simon?"

"Oh, well," says Simon, a bit sad, "I've moved on a bit. I still follow the boxing, or . . . I used to . . ."

And once again the whisper of regret. So many things we used to do. So many laws we used to break and laugh at. And now we creep around and make more money and what are we, if not crooks?

Well, rich, of course, and happier for it.

Happier, absolutely.

Around and around it goes. Joe has the touch, the memory for every face, and there's a fire in him, a rich desperate longing for days everyone had forgotten about, and the strength in his arm to make you believe. Behind him goes the whisper: that's Joe Spork. He's putting a job together, and he's going to ask us to help.

It must be some job.

He will ask, won't he?

Sure he will.

And finally, when the nerves and the nostalgia are about ready to boil over, Joe climbs up on the back of an extremely expensive Italian leather sofa in his workman's boots, and he says:

"I expect you're wondering why I asked you all here this evening!"

They are. Of course they are.

"I may have misled you a bit, in a way. I think I told Jorge I was planning a big job. Well, I'm not." He grins, a naughty-boy grin, Mathew's face staring over a mustard polo neck and a tan bullhide coat, superimposed on the weathered, blockish features of his son. "I'm not planning a big job. I'm planning ten. Or a hundred. However many it takes to make the point. I'm talking about the brass ring. I'm talking about robbing every bank in London and half of Hatton Garden, hitting the payroll and the Mint and everything in between.

"Now I know, because I've seen you, that you don't do those things any more. I know, at least, that that's what you think. And I also know, because I've seen you, that when you see the Bond Street caper, with those lads lifting a hundred grand a pop and busted by the end of the week, or the Heathrow diamonds, or the Millennium Dome, you look at those sorry jobs and you think to yourselves: I could have done that twice as fast and taken twice as much and I'd be sitting in bloody Duke's Bar when the Lily came and nothing to say I was ever anywhere else. Because those jobs were grand, but they had no exit, and they were brassy, but they had no class. And you've got class."

The Old Campaigners grin at one another. Sure enough, they have class. They know the importance of balls, for sure, but also of smarts and timing, and above all, of getting away with it. Robbing is easy. Robbing clean is hard—but that's what separates the men from the boys, isn't it?

"I remember, don't I, how it's done? I remember when the Boldbrook delivery was taken by person or persons unknown, and the police were swarming the Crespind Club because they'd had a tip-off the place was a brothel. Which it unquestionably was. But when they got there it was all awash with bigwigs in their drawers, so when the same fellow called in a robbery at Boldbrook—ten minutes before it happened—they told him to stick it in his ear, and then of course when Boldbrook himself called they told him the same thing. And no one ever told a bloody word of how it was done, not the cracksman nor the lookout nor not a one of them, because they were men of the life. Women of the life. (I won't name names, but I could. We all know who they were. And not a one of us has ever told, have they?)

"But I look at you, and I see one more thing. I see talent going to waste. I see skills like no one ever had before or since. I see the long con and the short, I see high-score planners and forgers and dippers and smugglers and high-wall men and strong arms and gunhands and lead-footed getaway drivers and what have you done for us lately? You've let crime get white-collar and dull. You're rich and you're dying of respectability. I see you, Boy Reynolds. I see you with your arm in a sling! Crashed a souped-up Mercedes into a sand dune at one hundred and eleven miles an hour between Paris and Dakar.

"Because you are bored. You are so bored you could die of it.

"You're all respectable and safe. And not one of you is having any fun.

"Well, I'm in deep shit. I touched something I wasn't supposed to. I know things I mayn't. I'm at war with Brother Sheamus of the Ruskinites and Mr. Rodney Titwhistle of the Legacy Board, and what they will do to me if they get me doesn't bear discussion. I'm on the run from the law, and these days that's a short course. They've had me once: not again. No more white rooms and torture for this lad. Not again.

"They'll have SO19 out there, anyway, so no matter. God help any poor bugger caught outside in a fedora this month!" Joe grins again, and this time it's the wolf grin, the wartime grin, the Englishman's inner barbarian, which every one of them keeps close at hand for the dark days.

A flash of Argyle socks as Joe shifts his weight and opens his arms to them again.

"And I'll tell you, people. I'm having more fun than I have ever had in my entire, safe, taxpaying life!

"What's it all about? I'll tell you. There's a wicked sort who wants something he can't have. He can't have it because if he gets it he'll likely kill us all. He's a lunatic and a bad egg. He's not a crook, he's a devil, and that's all there is to it. I mean to put a stop to him. I mean to stop him dead. And if I don't, well, it'll be down to you lot anyway, because he's bought the government or some such thing, and is sheltered in their breast. If I don't do the job, my lords, ladies, and assorted crooks, we shall all go down six feet. Think of him as a mad bugger who wants to test a nuclear bomb in Trafalgar Square. He doesn't, but it's as good as. But here, you leave that to me. I'll take care of the Opium Khan. All I want you to do . . . is steal every blighted thing that isn't nailed down and preferably most of what is!

"I am going to raise unholy Hell. The Tosher's Beat is going to ring again to the sound of escaping felons. The rooftops will buzz to the sound of our circular saws, and all across the mighty city of London things of enormous value will be liberated from vaults of veritable impenetrability. We will remind everyone on Earth that London's crooks are the best there have ever been.

"And in the process, we will save the world.

"And if that doesn't sound like fun, you rotten lot, you have forgotten the meaning of the word! So all those in favour . . ." he makes calming motions with both hands, as if holding them back. "All those in favour can signify by acclamation. My name is Joshua Joseph Spork. But you can call me: Crazy Joe! So let's hear you say it. If you raise the roof of this place, we're on, and we're away.

"Now, then: what's my name?"

There's a roar of laughter and applause, and a lot of glasses raised.

From the back, a woman's voice says: "Crazy Joe!" and then a man's from the far corner: "Crazy Joe!" And then Big Douggie growls it out and Tony Wu, and even Dizzy Spencer, and then the great, too-cool, too-professional black-suited multitude are chanting it in a gathering wave of noise which breaks over Joe Spork and seems to set him alight, and he roars like a great ape and swears to God he will embrace every one of them, all at once, and it seems he will really try, and then his arms are full of a small, sassy, dark-haired beauty with outrageous toes, and as he raises her into the air for a passionate, demonstrative kiss, no one remembers or cares that Polly Cradle was the first to call out his name, or that her brother was the second.

Later, when the Pablum's function room is all but empty, a man in a black suit is left standing with Mercer Cradle, who brings him to Joe Spork in a quiet corner. He's tall and pale and very grave. Joe Spork takes his hand.

"Mr. Spork," the man says, "my name is Simon Alleyn."

"Very pleased to meet you. Thank you for coming."

The Master of the Honoured & Enduring Brotherhood of Waiting Men nods and says nothing. It's very effective. Tool of the trade, no doubt.

"I've got myself into a big fight, Mr. Alleyn. I was wondering if you'd like to join me."

"So I understand. It's not really our kind of thing. Not even for Brother Friend, I'm afraid."

"No."

"No, we let the police handle that sort of thing."

"I'm sure. But there's something you might want to know, all the same."

"Go on, then."

"Billy Friend was murdered by Vaughn Parry."

Simon Alleyn doesn't blink. His face doesn't change at all. And yet Joe Spork is aware of having his fullest attention.

"Should I understand, then, Mr. Spork, that Vaughn Parry has somewhat to do with all this?"

"In a way, he is at the heart of it."

"In a way?"

"You could argue that he is . . . no longer who he was. That he has become someone worse."

"Worse."

"Very much worse."

"And you know where he is?"

"Yes."

Simon Alleyn studies the empty air in front of him for a moment. Then he nods. "The Waiting Men have business with Brother Vaughn. Whoever he is now."

And then, later still, in a quiet moment, in an empty room.

"Hello?" the voice on the other end of the phone says cautiously.

"Hello," Joe says. "You know who this is?"

"Well, I know who it can't be. There was a chap I once sent socks to, and you sound like him—but that fellow's been accused of all manner of frightful things. The government thinks he's a regular walking Armageddon. Amending the Human Rights Act and passing all sorts of rather iffy laws. I don't approve, to be honest. I think the law's the law and it says what it says for a reason. Do you know, they sent a rather indifferent policeman up here to ask me if I knew anything?"

"I'm sorry about that."

"Lord, it *is* you. How extraordinary."

"Yes, I suppose so. I hope I didn't cause you any trouble."

"No, no. It was rather exciting. I told him you breathed fire and ate raw meat. He seemed to think he knew that already."

"Oh. Yes."

"So what on Earth are you doing on my phone? I would have thought you had Sabine women to abduct and suchlike."

"How's the golf coming along?"

"God, what a question. Do you know, I think I hate golf? It was never my favourite thing, but somehow now I suspect it will kill me, in the end. That and the membership. I feel I can say this to you because you've got larger things to worry about than telling the board of governors I've gone off the game. And of course no one in their right mind will believe anything you say."

"That is quite true."

"But with the best will in the world, I doubt you really want to know about golf. It doesn't strike me as your biggest worry, just about now."

"Well, no. To be honest, I wondered if you'd do something for me."

"Highly unlikely. You're a sinner."

"I quite understand."

"Not an offer I can't refuse, or anything? No horse's head coming my way?"

"I always felt sorry for the horse. It didn't have anything to do with him, did it?"

"No. But I think I hate horses more than golf. My grandchildren are at that stage. It's actually more time-consuming than a marriage, having a horse, and suddenly I have four to take care of, because there's no question of a ten-year-old really looking after a horse by herself."

"Oh. Well, anyway, this isn't that sort of offer. It's the other sort, where you can say 'no' if you want to. I'm actually expecting you to, but I have to ask."

"I suppose I had better hear what you want, just so I can refuse in fullest understanding."

"Well, I sent you a package."

"Oh, was that you? Marvellous gallery of fancy and lies, I thought."

"It's all true."

"So you say."

"Yes. But you read it, is the point."

"Oh, yes. Mind you, I suppose, given what's happening with the bees and so on, it's no more far-fetched than the official line."

"No."

"So what do you want me to do?"

"Well, I'm going to steal a plane, and I wondered if you wanted to fly it."

"Definitely not."

"Right."

"In fact, I'm going to come down there and refuse in person. Where shall I meet you?"

"I'll have someone pick you up."

"As long as you understand the answer is absolutely no."

"I do."

"I'll bring my flight suit, just to rub it in."

"Right."

"What kind of plane am I refusing to fly here?"

"A Lancaster, I thought."

"Good choice. If I was mad enough to do anything of the kind for you, I'd appreciate your sense of history. Save the world, eh?"

"I'm a madman. Everyone says so."

"Hah. Well, I don't think I could argue with that even if I was going to help you. You better have someone meet my train, I always get frightfully lost in London."

On the roof of the Pablum Club, Joe Spork lies on his back and stares into the endless sky. The felons and free spirits have gone home, and the plan—call it one plan, though in truth it's about a thousand plans, all jumbled together in a tangle of criminal behaviour so bewildering as to make even his eyes water—is in motion. Everyone else's bit, at least. His own remains to be begun, let alone accomplished. The clock is ticking, and he can hear it in his head, imagines the tiny wings of Frankie's bees on their way home. When the circle closes, he must be ready, or it won't matter how good his plan was. On the other hand, if it's not good enough, he'll never get to where he needs to be. And yet, as he looks up and up and up, he finds that he is not worried about that at all. The things he will do over the next twenty-four hours—attack, fight, live or die—are the right things. The best things he could be doing.

A moment later, he hears a step on the asphalt, and feels the warmth of Polly Cradle lying next to him. Soon they must get up, and travel, and do gangster's work. But these stolen moments are theirs alone.

XVIII

Lovelace;
Misrule;
showdown.

Eighteen hours later, in the cave beneath the hill, the *Ada Lovelace* broods and grumbles. Arc lights burn and shadows jump on the walls. Joe Spork's shoulders are covered in soot and grime, and his hair is matted. From time to time, he dips his whole head in a vat of water and lets the run-off cool him. It is too hot, too smoky, too choking, too metallic.

It's perfect.

The Ruskinites—Ted Sholt's Ruskinites—left clear instructions for waking the *Lovelace*. Joe is following a handwritten guide, step by step, the pages open on a barrelhead. He has opened the drive cavity, cleaned and oiled the gears and replaced them. He can smell the grease on his skin.

He works, and in between times, when something must cool or set, he sits with Frankie's list, her off-switch, and reads them again and again. His hands twitch and twist in the air. Eyes closed, he can feel the outline of the Apprehension Engine, knows Frankie's clever clips and catches, the route through the wires and coils from the bee-hive shell to the heart. He commits it to memory, and makes Polly Cradle test him. For each correct answer, he gets a kiss. For each wrong one, a frown.

On a length of discarded rail Joe pounds red-white metal, folds and flattens, replacing a control lever in the floor of the driver's cab. There can be no weaknesses, not today.

The technique is called *Mokume-gane*. He laughs, suddenly, loudly, and it echoes through the enclosed space. Of course. If one were to do this with gold and iron, and then immerse the result in nitric acid, the iron would dissolve. A truly subtle metalworker—a genius—might fold the metal in leaf-thin layers, an *origami* so carefully executed that the resulting mesh of gold would flex like cloth, would appear to have been woven.

He takes the washed steel rod and quenches it, then—obedient to the requirements of the instruction manual—fits it and cools it again in place. There is a brief, high sound, like a chime as it settles into the mechanism. He hesitates.

"Try."

The *Lovelace* growls again, and this time whines as well, and the engine—decoupled, for the moment, from its massive load—shifts slightly on the track.

All night and much of the day he has worked like that, and he is not tired. It is as if twenty years of sleep and certainty have stored themselves up in him for discharge in a time of need. The *Lovelace* is ready.

Polly Cradle catches him around the neck and drags him up into the driver's cab. On the floor of the engine she makes love to him, skin slick with transferred grime.

"*Aglæc-wif*," he murmurs afterwards, and she isn't sure whether he means her or the train. Together, they wait for the beginning: the night of misrule.

It is known, among coppers and criminals alike, that society can be policed only because it consents. When the burden of law or government is too great, or too oppressive, or when economic need or famine breaks the normal course of life, there simply are not—can never be—enough coppers to hold the line. Thus, if a man wishes to commit a crime which by its nature must excite the immediate response of every policeman within twenty miles, his first precaution should be to await a volcano or a popular revolution, so that these diligent officers have other things on their minds.

On the other hand, if criminals were ever sufficiently organised as to commit a hundred major crimes on one night, or better yet, a thousand, the vast majority of them must get away scot-free. In such circumstances, a particular institution not immediately recognised as vital to the survival of the state—not, in fact, Downing Street, or the House of Commons, or the Palace—would have to fight for attention, might even be sorely neglected for some hours, especially if its champions in Whitehall were themselves distracted.

Of course, criminals being by and large self-interested and mistrustful of one another, such an event is generally thought by the forces of law and order to be quite impossible.

The night is very quiet, and very cold. On the Chantry Road in London's financial heart, the tall, imperial buildings sleep. Even the modern additions, steel and glass statement-constructs seeking to overmatch a heritage of blood, art, and conquest by sheer size, are closed up and cold. Lights burn on the upper floors, traders and analysts letting commerce take precedence over family one more time in a desperate attempt to add to a Christmas bonus they won't have time to spend. On the street, a fox wanders to and fro, plucking at the bulging dustbins and yowling.

At midnight oh one, with a flash so bright that for a moment it is daytime in the dark, open-plan offices all around, the doors come off the Ravenscroft Savings & Commodities Bank. The explosion is so unnecessarily huge that the great steel shutters on the front of the building are also torn away, flying across the street and destroying a vintage Aston Martin. The fox is flung bodily into a sculpture garden, and makes his displeasure at this imposition widely known. Policemen hasten to the spot. Terrorism or robbery, it hardly matters: the action has a blunt defiance which must be answered.

But when they get there, there's no one robbing the place. It's just open.

Which is when the alarm goes up from Ridley Street and Hatton Garden and Shottmore Park, and then from Bond Street, from the Silver Vaults, from the Strand, from the secure depository at Uxbridge and the Christie's warehouse in Bethnal Green.

London is alive with crime.

Caro Cable is cracking a safe in the British Museum.

Dizzy Spencer has her foot over the accelerator outside the Tower of London. Because why the Hell not?

Across the capital, from Dartford Creek to Staines Bridge, alarm bells ring and klaxons sound; electronic sentinels wail for assistance and police call centres are swamped. The main emergency station shunts capacity to the Dundee office, which is protocol, but someone cuts the line ten minutes later in Oxfordshire, which bounces the whole catastrophe to the emergency satellite. No one's going to steal that!

But Big Douggie's daughter knows a boy whose brother is a cracker—a professional computer-systems intruder—who knows someone in Sweden who does this kind of work. The satellite is now carrying Dutch pornography, in vast quantity, to the delighted sailors of a Russian factory ship in mid-Atlantic.

In Pimlico, a very old man is caught three floors up stealing undergarments from the linen cupboard of a woman who once, long ago, was a noted music-hall entertainer. She declines to press charges, and invites him to join her for tea. The attending sergeant—overstretched and rushing to a break-in at the local Lloyds Bank—nonetheless takes time to record that the chief witness has a twinkle in her eye.

The fire service withdraw their operators from the police switchboard, and ten minutes later the ambulance crews do the same. They are entitled. In the chaos, normal catastrophe continues, and they can't be swamped by police business.

At every crime scene, the same white card, and rumours of a hatted, spatted figure in the background, like the ghost of Humphrey Bogart.

YOU HAVE BEEN
ROBBED
BY CRAZY JOE.

Across the capital, amid the broken glass, a sense of outrage blossoms: *He's taunting us! He is!* The natural censoriousness of England asserts itself. *He ought to be ashamed!*

Many of the banks being raided are the keepers of sensitive documents, business deals not entirely honest, controversial decisions involving the treatment of indigenous peoples or the environment, or choices about cutting costs by risking customer welfare, and these, instead of being decently discarded as worthless or used in perfectly respectable blackmail, the cheeky bastard takes pains to return through the good offices of national newspapers and quite inappropriate websites, who naturally peruse them in the course of handing them over and make trouble. The outrage grows: *It's cheeky! It's revolution!*

Crazy Joe must pay. To make such a mess, at this moment, with the bees incoming, spotted over the Channel. It's irresponsible, is what it is. Lives will be lost. Reputations will suffer.

London is awake, and afraid, and excited. Families cluster around television sets, late bars with wireless internet fill with news-hungry clients. Long-distance lorry drivers, bus drivers and cabmen in traffic jams frown and grumble and turn on talk radio, and mutter about the state of things.

It's a complete disgrace!

Shocking.

But, on the other hand, it's *crime*. Not terrorism. Not war. Not drug violence or acid throwing or honour killing or celebrities or multiple rape. Not riots. Not financial collapse. Not magic, dreadful machines in the sky or the end of the world. Good, wholesome, old-fashioned British crime.

And, you know. Knocking off five million in precious stones, or stealing that Picasso collection from the snob with the shiny suit, well.

You have to admit, it's got class.

In green taxi shelters and terminals and postal depots, and in newsrooms and studios, bare whispers of smiles. You can't be glad, of course. You can't admire this sort of thing. It's against the law.

But just the same.

It's almost like the old days come again, isn't it?

Rodney Titwhistle is dragged from a camp bed in his office to a ringing phone: *London's on fire, Rodney. It's bloody insane. Is this your mess? Rumour says it is. Well, I don't care, I'm taking the reserves. Yes, I bloody am, and you can bloody wake him if you think—* Right, well, he knows where to find me!

With Arvin AWOL—Rodney suspects a sexual binge, though he has, of course, begun discreet inquiries—he must handle this himself.

It's not unusual to have to fight one's corner in Whitehall. Some idiot always believes his crisis is more critical than yours, his secret darker. In Rodney Titwhistle's experience, it never is.

This business with the banks, though, has an unsettling side. Sheamus wants the calibration drum for something—is it possible he's just taking pot luck? A tombola approach to armed robbery and safety deposit boxes? After all, he *is* religious, and those people can be rather absolute about their goals. That would be embarrassing.

Asssuming Sholt was wrong. If Brother Ted had the right of it, well. It could be more serious. A lot more serious. But that's ludicrous. Rodney Titwhistle has it on good authority that Brother Sheamus will not use the Apprehension Engine to destroy the world. He has personal assurances from Sheamus himself. He has looked into the man's eyes.

Anyway, Sheamus doesn't have the drum. So he can't. If he had the drum, that would be different. If he were even now stealing it. But even then . . . who really destroys the world? More than sixty-five years since the atomic bomb was dropped on Japan, most of it spent with America and Soviet Russia at daggers drawn, and neither of them ever pushed the button on purpose. Pushed and unpushed it by accident a couple of times, to be fair. But not on purpose.

Although it's a brave new world out there, with all these non-state actors. A mad person might do it.

He doesn't stop to consider Joe Spork as the culprit. The boy's a nobody, after all.

With the world burning outside his window, Rodney Titwhistle glances at the red phone on his desk. Time to make the first call. Number 10, probably, or the Cabinet Office. He should have details first, but he can't wait. He'll have to wing it a little. He reaches out.

And then he hears what must be his least favourite voice in the entire world.

"My dear Rodney, hello, hello! I let myself in, I was sure you wouldn't mind, so many friends we have in common, of course. So many. You may remember me, I threatened to sue you, frightfully coarse of me, I do apologise . . . My name is Mercer Cradle, I must have said, formerly of the old established firm of Noblewhite Cradle, now of Edelweiss Feldbett of Switzerland, a rather new organisation but we do like to make our mark early, it's part of our institutional culture which I am even now, um, well, I suppose we shall have to

say 'culturing', which is sadly redundant, but there you are, what can
you do? And specifically, Rodney, what can *you* do? No, please, don't
touch the phone, these gentlemen might take exception, they are from
a grass-roots organisation of concerned citizens, one might almost
say a sort of informal police service, or more sinisterly a mob. Oh,
and this paper, Mr. Titwhistle—well, these papers, being as they are
plural—these are writs and warrants and all manner of unfortunate
things which I am regrettably obliged to serve upon your good self on
charge of complicity in torture and so much else, do please surrender
in good order and I think we'll sit the night out here, where it's warm
and there's sherry, and deal with the paperwork in the morning if
we're all still alive . . .

"Because," Mercer Cradle adds bleakly, "you may have killed us all
with your bloody ignorant prideful mess, you stupid prick, so sit there
and leave the rest to someone else or I really will have your bollocks
in a jar. *Rodney*."

On the second floor of a rather pretty vicarage in Camden Town,
Harriet Spork listens to the chorus of sirens outside her window,
and hears her dead, beloved husband's voice. The radio in her room
announces that the mysterious golden bees have been seen over the
Channel, they're an hour from London at most—but her son has all
that in hand. He's come good, hasn't he? Despite everything. It just
goes to show.

For the first time in years, Harriet sleeps quietly.

Arvin Cummerbund watches Stansted Airport fade behind him.
Against his massive shoulder, the beautiful Helena slumbers, dream-
ing of Arvin and of her native Argentina. Below him, in the city he
has called home for his entire life but will not remotely miss, he can
see that Joe Spork is doing what Sporks do.

Arvin grins, and lets himself breathe in, and out, and in, and out,
and very soon the first-class cabin is filled with snoring as of a hiber-
nating walrus, if walruses hibernated, which Arvin Cummerbund
would be the first to aver that they do not.

When the Captain announces nervously that they're taking a slight detour today to avoid the incoming bees, he barely shifts in his seat.

In Milton Keynes, while London basks in scandalised delight, the ground is shaking. The sleeping city turns in its warm covers and wonders muzzily whether there's been an earthquake somewhere far away. A few late drinkers turn sharply, pull their coats about them— the wind is bitter—and hurry home.

Bletchley Park shudders from its neo-Gothic battlements to the empty, decaying Nissen huts. The doors of the long barrow are open. Wooden sleepers twist and groan.

A great black shape rolls up and out, massive body uncoiling. For a few moments it lumbers, then gathers speed. Across the long, straight stretches of the London line it becomes a vast shadow, impossibly huge and quick, belching smoke and roaring.

Behind it, the rails are scraped clean by sheer traction, gleaming silver.

Titan passing.

Sarah Ryce is the regional controller of routing for the London & Shires Freight Rail System (night shift). She works in a temperature-controlled office. She goes to work by car, because there isn't a passenger train which serves the only house she can afford. She can't really afford the car, either.

The man who stops to help her when she realises that her front-right tyre has been slashed is extremely polite and rather dishy in a dishevelled, older-generation sort of way. He's so nice that she absolutely doesn't feel threatened when he explains that she should call him Tam, and that he works for Britain's most wronged, most wanted man. He wants her to do something very simple, and will pay her more money than she has ever seen in one place at one time to help him save the world. It's probably because he is fixing her tyre, and in a position so absolutely compromised and vulnerable that it's clear he does not propose to do her harm. It might be because he's a bit like her older brother Peter, who died last year of cancer. Or it might be the feeling she has, that everyone has, that something is happening which is really important.

So Sarah Ryce says yes, and at one a.m. she presses a sequence of buttons she's never pressed before in that order, and watches the board light up with stopped locomotives dragging iron pilings from Hove to Carmarthen by way of Clapham Junction, and a bright green line shines in the darkness, its route clear all the way to central London and onward to the green reaches of Richmond and Barnes.

A few moments later, something passes her station going at what must be over a hundred and fifty miles an hour, and the old, rusted track protests, but holds. Sarah Ryce grins, secretly: whatever she's done, it's something big.

Green fields full of cows and sheep; occasional empty churches and shuttered pubs; the wide stretches of road alongside the railway line; the engine passes them by and is gone, trailing hot-metal stink, sulphurous coal smoke.

Past warehouses and school buildings, the backs of shops and restaurants and petrol stations, on and on and on into London. Brick houses shake, glasses jump from sideboards. Car alarms wail and windows crack. Polly Cradle's empty bed, in its basement, comes right off its springs and crashes to the floor.

In the darkness of the night of misrule, the *Ada Lovelace* drives like a spear towards Sharrow House.

Titan passing.

Ruskinites patrol the grounds of Shem Shem Tsien's fortress. There are machines and there are men, and there is very little to choose between them. The men are blank-faced in their linens, cold-eyed fragments of the Opium Khan walking and breathing, volitional only as sharks are. They feed, they fight, they sleep, and do it all again. They serve. They are part of something bigger.

And they hear something. They can feel it in their soles, in the gathering static in the air. Something big—no, *huge*.

In the grounds of Sharrow House, they gather, and wait. They are not afraid. They lack a sense of self; their identity is collective. Each is aware, peripherally, of his incompleteness, of the debt he owes to the template. They move like a swarm. They are a composite of horrors; endless hours of the life of Shem Shem Tsien embroidered with a pattern of torture and death, of theology and rage and hate.

They weave around one another, agitation growing. The sound is either much louder or much, much closer. The ground is thrumming. Other Ruskinites begin to emerge from Sharrow House in a seething mob, anticipating violence. Though each is driven by a different slice through the shape of Shem Shem Tsien's mind, one thing they have in common is their progenitor's love of murder.

And then, at this appointed hour, Queen Tosh expresses her irritation: with a great boiling detonation, the castle moat explodes.

Green water turns white and bows upward. It boils, collapses into bubbles, and then rushes up, on up and outwards like a mushroom cloud, then splatters down in blobs the size of packing crates. Individual Ruskinites are flattened to the ground, broken or dead. Ugly, triangle-toothed fish, stunned and semi-liquidised, fall like rain. For a moment, everything is mist and spume. Then the froth of pressure stops and the geyser vanishes, and the remaining water burbles away into the drains.

The Ruskinite swarm stares down into the empty ditch. Unexpected. Unexpected things are bad. Unwelcome. But there is nothing to strike out at, so they stare at the missing moat, and out towards whatever is coming, and wait.

Joe Spork, with twenty seconds to impact and both hands on the control yoke of the train, watches the wall around Sharrow House loom closer and closer, and knows that for the first time in his adult life he is not backing away from a showdown. In a heartbeat, half a heartbeat, this train will test itself against that wall. The skill of the Ruskinites of days gone—Ted Sholt's Ruskinites, not these present bastards—will be set against the immutable physics of collision. The cowcatcher will hold, or it will not. If the giant steam cylinder on the front of the train does not survive the impact intact, the explosion will be vast—but its vastness will be utterly irrelevant to a man standing on top of it. Any sort of bang will surely kill him.

In his chest, a golden cauldron of sheer excitement, like whisky in the soul. He grins at Polly Cradle, sees an answering smile of anticipation and sheer delight.

Hell, yeah.

The wall is huge in front of them, seems to be curving over to embrace the *Lovelace* like a gloved fist—

Impact.

Silence made from thunder.

A moment of absolute stillness, the smallest humanly perceptible division of time.

Joe is slammed against the driver's restraints, thinks he must surely be shaken apart. He can see the ground, then the sky. The train will flip, and then explode. He cannot possibly survive. He finds he has no regrets, or perhaps he has no time to summon them.

But the *Lovelace*'s maker knew his purpose: what he was tasked to build was not just a mobile laboratory or a code-station. It was a vessel of war, to withstand war's appalling forces and torsions. The train would not function without its driver, and so the driver must be shielded.

The *Lovelace* cuts through the wall, spraying concrete, brick, stone and mortar. The carriages shunt together, slotting into one another so that their combined kinetic energy is passed along the spine of the train to the front in a great heave. The black iron is thick and solid, the stress of the impact rebounds through interlocking buffers and supports is dispersed as heat and deafening noise. Rivets pop and wood panels crack. The engine shrieks. The great pressure tank sobs and moans.

But it holds.

Of course, it holds. This is what it was made for.

Just like me.

Joe is moving before the train is fully stationary. He surges from the driver's cab and down onto the burning grass, knowing somewhere inside himself that these first seconds will count, that the first battles will sway the outcome. Whoever flinches will fight uphill from then on, will lose momentum. He snarls and crouches low. A shadow skitters towards him on heron's feet, bobbing and weaving. The thing takes an iron pipe full in the chest and flies backwards, and Joe lets loose a yell of heady rage. *That for Edie! And that for Ted! And that one for Billy*

and Joyce, and one for Tess and however many others along the way. And for me. Oh, yes. For me. He stalks through the fog, bludgeoning and crushing, teeth bared. When he feels them begin to gather around him, he steps back towards the wrecked train and a curtain of burning-rubber stink. Metal hands and swords flicker after him.

He's already gone, silent on his big feet.

Behind him, from the *Lovelace*, the small but righteous army of Crazy Joe emerges into the beachhead: a collection of thugs and muggers, glad beyond anything they had expected at the chance of a day's heroism; retired boxers and questionable bodyguards, occasional assassins and professional leg-breakers, hearts uplifted at the prospect of a good fight, the right kind of fight, just this once. This one time, to pay for all. Behind them come Fifth Floor Men and safebreakers, for ease of access; and behind them the Waiting Men—a dozen mournful faces with broad shoulders from carrying coffins, retired soldiers who came by their Acquaintanceship the hard way. Not just an army. A wrecking crew.

The engine howls and grumbles. The fire in her gut is still burning, the steam still building. There's nowhere for it to go. The safety valves are blocked, the catches bent and hammered shut. One by one, fail-safes click on, and off again, each one meticulously sabotaged by a capable hand.

In the fog, Polly Cradle can hear her lover laughing at his enemy. She can see the shadow of his coat and hat, flicking, taunting, drawing them in. She can feel the steps of his dance, the rhythm of his humour.

She hopes he is fast enough. That he isn't having too much fun to remember the plan.

She raises her hands, gestures. From his place in the bag over her shoulder, the dog Bastion whiffles.

The wrecking crew slips away from the fight.

Joe Spork laughs in the smoke, laughs through the bandit's handkerchief over his nose and mouth. A long metal shaft slashes towards him. He lets it pass by, then tugs on it, then scampers away. He has them now, close behind him. He takes a second, gets his bearings. Yes. Yes. So, and so, and so. *Snickersnack*, as one might say.

Little by little, he draws his foes back towards the train, and the groaning engine. He wonders, briefly, if he will carry this through. There are men here. Real people, for all that they are unmade and mad. They may die. Then he thinks of Polly, and her brother, and of the whole, wide, impossible world beyond, which will stop if this night goes badly. And he thinks: these are my torturers.

So fuck 'em.

He laughs again, very loud, and hears them coming after him. He clangs his feet on the engine steps, then slides on his knees across the metal floor and ducks down and out the other side, off towards Polly Cradle and the others. He counts strides: onetwothreefour-fivesix . . . twenty . . . thirty . . .

He hears the clank of metal on metal, of men and machines by the engine housing. They are looking for him. The *Lovelace* moans again. Too hot. Too full. Too much.

Joe Spork wrenches his body around into a sliding turn, skids into a ditch between two low walls, and points his father's gun at the body of the engine, the great steam tank with its pent-up rage. He pulls the trigger.

Bangbangbang. And then: *bang*.

The night is white and orange, and the world is made of noise.

If he thought the crash was loud, now he knows the meaning of the word. Debris zings over him, whistling and whirring. A piece of wheel embeds itself in a statue. He lies on his back and laughs, and cannot hear himself. But here, at least, all the Ruskinites are gone. He picks himself up, and looks back at the site of the explosion.

A yawning black crater steams and smokes, strewn with bodies. None of them makes a sound.

He swallows guilt, and feels a tight burst of pride instead, a battle-field satisfaction, lets it rise in his chest.

Joe slings the tommy gun across his back, gathers his troops and gives orders. The wrecking crew strip the dead machines of their robes and everyone moves forward through the grounds, into the house.

Once upon a time, no doubt, this was a fine old manse, with marble floors and columns, and those big windows were the windows of the Empire Room, the Beaverbrook Suite and the Lady Hamilton Apartments.

Not any more. Now it's just a shell in which something else has taken up residence, like those eerie ocean worms which grow in the flesh of crabs and eventually devour them from within.

From the glass cupola of the tower on down, Sharrow House has been consumed, walls knocked through to make a space like a cathedral. Here and there, upright pillars of brick, strands of wallpaper hanging off, have been allowed to remain, bearing the weight of stark steel joists. Black cables lie like creepers along the walls across what remains of the ballroom. The hand-painted frescoes have been drilled through and the statues clubbed and cut and shunted to one side. Even with the residue of the *Lovelace*'s fiery end still in his mouth, Joe can taste the broad rubber flavour of hot electrician's tape, like a bar across the back of his tongue. In the middle of the floor, a gaping hole sinks down and down into the earth.

Of course. Everything must be as it was. The Opium Khan is living a fight from the last century, playing out his victory over Edie Banister and her lover and Abel Jasmine and Ted Sholt, over all of them. It isn't important that they're all dead. What's important is that he wins, and sees himself winning.

From out of the chasm comes a sound like breathing, and in the same moment that he becomes aware of it, Joe recognises from above, somewhere in the distance, the deep, alien drone of a hundred thousand wings.

The bees are coming.

The pathway to the pit is lined with pipe and electrical gear; Shem Shem Tsien's version of Frankie's machinery lacks her economy, her sense of humanity. Instead of hives and metaphor, this is brute industrial technology, fit for the launching of missiles and the incineration of nations. It is all instrumentality, without heart.

They follow the trail to the inmost chambers of Sharrow House, where a gaping maw has been cut or ripped into the old stone floor, and the cellars and crypts of the castle have been opened to the rooms above. The drop to the bottom is as far, easily, as the top of the spire

above them; a vertiginous two hundred feet. The way down is a makeshift staircase like a Bailey bridge, supported by a scaffold of girders
and ropes. The cabling wraps around it or hangs beside it in a curtain
of thick, choking vines.

Joe Spork peers. Down among the vines, he can see scarecrows.
Or—no. No, of course, not scarecrows. Not for Shem Shem Tsien.
No happy turnip-headed figures made from stuffed pyjamas and
straw. Real people. Maintenance men and security guards and lab
technicians, dead and hung out like so many rags. Newly dead; less
than a day. Perhaps he intends them as messengers to God: a calling
card before knocking on the door. Or possibly they were just in his
way. Or for no reason at all. The Opium Khan never needed reasons,
according to Edie Banister. He did what pleased him, and very often
that was bloody and vicious.

Joe feels his face stretch in a rictus of anger, draws it back and
holds onto it. He will need that. No sense sharing it up here.

The dog, Bastion, squirms out of Polly Cradle's grip and scurries away, blind eyes searching for his enemy. From the gloom come
flashes of electric light, like a thunderstorm in the depths of the sea.

Joe hefts his gun and leads the way down into the dark. The stair
spirals, and at every turn there's another body, gathering insects. The
scaffold shakes as they go down, too many feet and too much weight,
and Joe Spork reaches out to steady himself. Polly Cradle hauls his
hand back and glowers at him, furious.

"Idiot!" she growls. "Use your head! Use your eyes!"

She points at the guard rail. It glistens, sparkles. He peers. Cut
glass, and a smell like marzipan.

"What is it?"

"Cyanide, I expect. It ought to be, oughtn't it?"

One of the bruisers has already cut himself. He collapses, choking,
on the second landing. When his mate goes to help him, a trapdoor
gives way beneath them and they fall into an electrified net.

Joe Spork swears under his breath. He doesn't say "be careful,"
because no one in his crew is stupid. Hard, and angry now, but not
stupid.

The room at the bottom of the stair is a chasm, a blending of the
house with open space from the Tosher's Beat, cellars and tombs

and all. It's a giant whispering gallery, like being in the dome at St. Paul's—sounds echo from the walls, from the upper floors, and from the tower and the sky above. Here the sound of the approaching bees is like a constant grumble, the hiss of static from a radio between stations.

The Opium Khan is waiting for them on a great wrought-iron throne, surrounded by his machines. The beehive from Wistithiel sits in the middle of all of it, crudely sliced open and wired and invaded. Black gooseneck flexes run out to huge banks of computers, and back again to another, half-familiar edifice, like the one in the indoctrination room at Happy Acres, but so much bigger: the archive of the Recorded Man.

All around, the flare of lightning, actinic snaps and pops from the older, stranger work of Frankie Fossoyeur, and a few remaining corpses fizzing and jerking on old electrified frames.

As Joe Spork steps off the stair and onto the floor, Shem Shem Tsien smiles, and pushes a lever to his right, and the whole apparatus shudders and boils. The beehive shrieks.

"Hello, Mr. Spork," Shem Shem Tsien says.

"Vaughn."

"Oh, please, spare me that, at least . . . You're too late, by the way. It is done. The machine will show me Truth, and I will become as God."

"And everyone will die. Even you. You'll cease to be a person. You'll just be . . ." Oh. A copy. A pattern, endlessly repeating.

Shem Shem Tsien opens his hands. "You see? I am the future. And, in fact, that is truer than you can imagine. When the world has been made ready by the Apprehension Engine, I shall bless you all with my own mind. With the calibration drum, I can use the Engine as a transmitter. Like my Ruskinites, Mr. Spork, you shall all know every detail of me. And, gradually, you will become me. I will be everyone, and everything, for ever. My perception will be the only perception. My mind, the only mind. Your mind, Mr. Spork. You will be part of me.

"I will become God. It is too late to prevent this. It has always been, will always have been, too late."

After a moment, Joe Spork shrugs. "If I was too late, we wouldn't be talking."

Abruptly, he knows quite clearly and simply that this is true, and a moment later, he realises what that means: the Apprehension Engine is working. Stage one, Frankie called it. The thing she wanted. The safe zone. But that will change, very soon.

In a corner of his mind, the echo of confirmation.

He looks up, and sees a waterfall of bees, a tumbling, beautiful, appalling stream, and everything changes.

The Opium Khan snaps a command and men appear from the shadows, hard-bitten bastards to look at, and used to working together. Drug soldiers, maybe, or mercenaries. *Mercenaries.* As soon as Joe has the thought, he feels the rightness of it.

The bees descend, filling the air. They're all over London, he knows that, too, and there's a growing fear, an understanding that what is coming is very bad.

Shem Shem Tsien is laughing. Joe probes the edges of that name in his mind, but it seems there are limits to his comprehension; when he thinks of his enemy, he has no sense of who the Opium Khan truly is. A misunderstood question, then, insufficiently refined for the answer to be true or false. But soon that won't matter. Soon, the redefinition will attend the asking, and after that, questions will cease to exist at all.

Death by footnote.

Battle is joined, brutal and intense. Street fighting, without an elegant kick or a clever trick in sight. The noises of it are grim and desperate: grunts, tearing sounds, cries and impacts; slicings and shatterings. This close to the machine, both sides are nervous of guns. With their hands and feet and old-fashioned weapons of mayhem, the mercenaries fight. The bruisers fight back.

The bees descend into the chamber, a humming cloud of confusion and dismay, and abruptly the whole scene is glossed. Each man has a life, a history, apparent and real and immanently understood. At this moment, Joe Spork suspects, Frankie imagined that war would be forever impossible, just as the theorists of poison gas and the atomic bomb fondly cherished a notion of mankind which made such weapons unusable and which would understand the stricture of them, that war is wasteful and pointless.

The fight continues, if anything more bitter.

Amid a haze of golden bees zinging to and fro, the botched and butchered remnant of the Apprehension Engine is running, deepening, and every answer is more and more fractal, more complete. It

cannot be long now before everything is too late. Joe knows immediately exactly how long, can feel the measurement of time not in
seconds or minutes but with the perfect timekeeping of atoms. But in
minutes, yes, he's right: not more than five to the end.

Joe charges forward through the tumbling, struggling figures,
seeking Shem Shem Tsien. He slams his fist into a man's face, ducks
a counter, and laughs as he tips his foe over on his back and stamps
on him. Laughs, because he can see his victory reflected in the other's
movements before it happens. He wades through the fight, knowing
exactly where he is going, and where he needs to be. Briefly, he is
beset by too many, even for him, but then a man cries out in alarm
and horror and clutches at his leg, now missing a chunk of calf where
Bastion's narwhal tusk has torn into him. Joe ducks through the gap,
weaves, engages and retreats. The dog vanishes into the melee, and his
progress is audible in shrieks and curses.

Joe howls a berserker laugh, spreads his arms wide and springs forward to carry men down to the ground, rolls past them and onto his
feet. He feels fingers underfoot, stamps and hears a curse, slips away.
His path is a shifting ripple in the room, but he walks it with perfect
certainty and his hands are full of power. He lets himself understand
the pattern, knows his destination, can feel it drawing ever closer. And
then, in the very middle of the swirl, they are face to face.

The Opium Khan and his enemy, in perfect balance. They are the
fulcrum. What happens here will determine everything.

They know it to be true.

Shem Shem Tsien raises his hand: stop. Joe does the same.

And there is stillness, of a sort, over the moaning of the broken.

At the edges of the room, Ruskinites appear from the shadows,
robes torn and bathed in smoke. Shem Shem Tsien smirks. "It is genuinely satisfying, Joe Spork, to have you here. To have an enemy to
destroy while one ascends to godhead."

Joe does not reply. He waits.

The Ruskinites reach up and draw back their hoods, revealing
the faces of Simon Alleyn and the Waiting Men. The Opium Khan
stares at them for a moment, bewildered, and then his face cracks
into a broad smile. "You found the Waiting Men! You found them
and brought them along as a special surprise! Oh, Joe. It's too good.
Did you think that would bring poor Vaughn back to life? Scare me
with the terrible undertakers and up he pops, my old, buried soul? A

struggle for dominance inside my own head, a master stroke? You *did*! Let me just take a moment to savour it. It's splendid. And don't you worry, Brother Simon. I'll be with you directly.

"Do you know, Mr. Spork, I honestly think that under other circumstances, you and I—"

Joe Spork sighs. "Windbag," he says. He rolls his neck to loosen it, tosses his hat to the floor, then screams his fury and his hate, and leaps . . .

Except, he doesn't, because instantly he begins the motion, he knows infallibly what will happen if he follows through. He can feel the Apprehension Engine working inside his head, intimately and perfectly perceives action and consequence from every angle:

Joe leaps, huge hands grasping. Shem Shem Tsien receives him and they fall, together, rolling over and over. Joe bites off a piece of his enemy's ear. The Opium Khan breaks two of Joe's fingers. They tear one another apart; skill and savagery, evenly matched, so back and forth they go. On and on and on until, suddenly, nothing. The world stops. Finis.

Seeing him freeze, understanding in the same way the same causality, Shem Shem Tsien laughs and steps forward, raises his narrow sword, then stops:

The Opium Khan lunges. Joe twists to one side, the blade scoring a line along his hip. He brings up his gun and fires; a bullet bites the Opium Khan's arm. They close.

"I'm very sorry, Brother Vaughn. It's time."

Simon Alleyn has covered the distance between them so fast it seems that he must have flown. He rises up behind Vaughn Parry, strong limbs reaching. His left arm folds across Parry's throat, fingers reaching to catch the crook of his other elbow in a wrestler's lock. He pushes Parry's head forward from above, and slowly, slowly, the veterbrae separate, and the spinal cord snaps.

Vaughn Parry dies.

Shem Shem Tsien twists around, draws his gun and fires at Simon Alleyn. Alleyn cries out, falls, clutching his side. He may live. He may die. It's not decided. Not yet.

The Opium Khan turns back towards Joe Spork, pistol in hand, and Joe brings up the tommy gun and sets his feet.

"Go ahead," Joe says. "Let's see what happens."

Shem Shem Tsien stares.

And stares.

And does not know the answer.

For a moment, a look of panic flickers across the matinée-idol face. It is so swiftly suppressed that you could miss it. You could see it and never know it for what it was. Unless you were waiting for it.

"You like to be in the driving seat, don't you?" Joe Spork murmurs. "You don't like to gamble. You don't have faith, so you want to force God to talk to you. You can't control death, so you kill, because if you become death maybe you won't die. And just for insurance, you become a dead man, too . . ." He grins, wolfishly toothy. "This must be a real pisser. Staring down the barrel of this gun, knowing that even if you shoot me dead first time, I'll fire this thing, and there is absolutely no way of controlling whether it kills you or not. One of us will die, maybe both of us. But we can't know in advance."

"Stalemate," snaps the Opium Khan. "It hardly matters. Time is on my side."

Polly Cradle's laughter trills out, clear and unafraid. "Not by half, it's not," she says. She steps through the ranks of the Waiting Men to rest her hand on her lover's shoulder. "It's now, Joe. It's all right. Do what you have to do."

Joe Spork has fought and maybe killed already tonight. It is not impossible that the explosion of the *Lovelace* ended living men who might have been returned to themselves. He has, in combat, inflicted injuries which may prove to be fatal. All the same, he has never been a killer, not an executioner nor an assassin, not from a standing start. But on the other hand, here he is, and this is his life, and if he blinks or hesitates, the world ends. Staring across the gap which separates them, he sees that the Opium Khan already knows what he will say. He says it anyway, with a sense of growing certainty which comes not from outside, not from the Apprehension Engine or the bees, but from himself. With Polly beside him, this choice is easy. He fixes his eyes on Shem Shem Tsien.

"You took my home and murdered my friends. You tortured me to death, twice, and brought me back. You hounded my grandmother.

"You tried to kill Polly to spite me.

"You break things which are beautiful, because it pleases you."

The Opium Khan opens his mouth to say something in return.

The tommy gun blazes white fire.

Crazy Joe Spork, finger on the trigger, riding the thunder. His shoulders push down on the gangster's gun, his chest labours to hold it on target. He sweeps it back and forth across the space where Shem Shem Tsien was standing. He feels the sting of something against his cheek as he turns, feels something pluck at his coat, and realises these are bullets, and does not care. He fires until the magazine is empty, letting the gangster's gun have its head, seeking to erase his enemy from the world. When the gun clicks empty, he steps forward through a cloud of gun smoke of his own making to use the weapon's butt if he has to, to grab and tear. There's blood on his shirt, and his ear is torn and burned. He's been shot. Dull paths of pain are scored across his face, and one arm aches.

Shot, but not killed.

Through the smoke, he sees Shem Shem Tsien's mouth contort in a sneer of utter contempt—a sneer which cuts off sharply as Bastion Banister shuffles painfully forward to snarl a reply directly into his face. Joe can see—can feel, immanently—the Opium Khan's confusion. How can a pug nine inches high stand eye to eye with a god? Some ridiculous last-minute prank? A dog on stilts? A stratagem involving strings?

Shem Shem Tsien's head rests where it has fallen, a yard or more behind his body. The line of bullets from the tommy gun has cut through his neck like a sword.

Comprehension arrives, whether from the Apprehension Engine or from his fading vision, or from the feel of stone under his ravaged flesh and bone. Shem Shem Tsien's eyes open wide in inexpressible horror. His mouth opens, as if to speak.

And then it's done.

Joe Spork waits for a moment to be sure that his enemy has died, then walks past the Opium Khan's severed head towards the machine which will devour the world.

The beehive growls and stutters, black cables humming with power bursting from its smooth organic lines. The bees are in the air, but they are coiling and spiralling in a more and more perfect pattern, more and more like a grid. They look less and less like bees, and more like cogs turning, one over another. Joe wonders how long he has left.

It's nearly over. Two minutes. Maybe less.

Joe moves to the Apprehension Engine as if through a flow tide, pulled and buffeted, and then abruptly he has passed into the eye of the storm. The blanketing certainty is gone; the Engine's effect, this close to its heart, is muted. He contemplates briefly a future in which he fails, and is left alive as the only conscious creature on Earth. In the Universe, even.

He kneels, stares at the beehive. The frontpiece is gone. The shape of the casement has been changed. This is not the sequence as he learned it.

For a moment, he doesn't know what to do.

And then his hands move. The wordless part of him, ignorant of fear and peril and the destruction all around, sees the job and knows the shape of the machine. Shem Shem Tsien has ruined the art, oh, yes, and that's a weak and ugly thing to have done—but the schematic remains the same. Turn this. Now this. Now, very quickly, both of these switches.

A plate comes away, revealing the inner coils.

Joe glances over his shoulder at the room and sees fear. Hard men and women are weeping. He finds Polly, sees her face urging him on. *A minute left*, she's saying. *Joe, please*. So much left undone. No escape, no anything, just a stripping of the gears of the soul. A disintegration.

I love you.

Please.

Joe wrenches his head around, back to the machine. It feels like a betrayal. If Polly's going to die, if he fails, he should be looking at her when it happens.

So, having chosen to look away, he can't fail. The gangster digs his heels in. The craftsman rolls up his sleeves.

In the heart of the Engine, around the activation switch, there is a combination dial. The markings around the rim are not numbers, but letters:

O, P, E, J, A, H, U, S.

It was not in Frankie's list. Added at the last minute. Added by her, he recognises her style . . . Added, but why? What's the point?

What is the stricture?

Truth? Is there a word with those letters meaning truth? Is it Greek? French?

His hand hovers, withdraws. No.

When did she add it?

Late. Very late. While Sholt was Keeper. Mathew was grown up. Edie had left. And there, etched in the metal, the year: FF, 1974. And her goose-foot colophon. A last line of security, to preserve the machine. To keep it running. To hold to the truth in the face of those who would switch it off.

Why? What was she protecting? Herself? The world?

Behind him, people are falling to their knees—not in prayer, mostly, but exhaustion. They have screamed. Now they're just waiting. Seconds.

The machine is the maker. What was it all for? In the end, what was Frankie's heart?

He knows.

Edie.

Daniel.

Mathew.

And Mathew's son. Born that year. He wonders if she came to the hospital, peered, alone, through the glass.

He looks at the dial, and sees the letters of his name. And switches off the Apprehension Engine.

Overhead, the bees cease their wild swirling. The cloud becomes orderly, then sedate, and finally they drop to the ground and settle, returning to the hive in neat little lines. Around the world, if Frankie is to be trusted—and Joe no longer knows, mercifully: he has to trust—the same thing is happening.

He follows the procedure through to the end, sending the last signal, the one which will cause the other hives to burn and die, leaving only this last one.

He cuts the power and removes the calibration drum, then the book.

It is the first time he has held them both. They're very light and small to be so dangerous. He puts them in his pocket.

Finally, Joe hefts a discarded sledgehammer. In the rows upon rows of magnetic tape and cinematic film; in the books and records and photographs of his repugnant life, the Opium Khan persists. The potential for his resurrection lurks in every line and grain of it. This is the full and original copy of the Recorded Man. Even what was destroyed at Happy Acres will surely have been incomplete. Shem Shem Tsien would not permit the thing out of his hands, would not countenance the possible creation of a second true Khan.

And nor will Joe.

He hefts the hammer, and strikes.

It takes a very, very long time. Or perhaps just moments. His shoulders ache and his back screams at him. He batters the archive over and over, rips at it with his hands, bleeds from cuts and splinters. When he tires, he drives himself with images of the dead, of Polly's fear in the last moments. He uses everything to make himself go on.

At some point, there's nothing big enough left to smash, and Joe piles all the remains together and runs the main electric current through the stack, so that the tapes spit and sparkle and the celluloid burns. When the blaze has caught properly, he lifts the corpse of Shem Shem Tsien and throws it onto the flames.

XIX

After.

Joe Spork is the most arrested man the world has ever known. He stands in front of Sharrow House, face shining in the glow of searchlights and news cameras, and lays down his father's gun on the gravel. Lays it down very carefully, because it seems to him that every single member of CO19, every spare Marine and Special Air Serviceman, and even a few members of the Household Cavalry have turned out to shoot him dead.

Behind him, with great dignity, the small but righteous army of Crazy Joe does the same, and the hundreds and hundreds of rifles which are trained on all of them follow like a vast cloud of lethal geese, long metal necks swaying, beady eyes paying the closest attention.

There is, however, an issue of priority. Joe has broken so many laws that he represents something of a quandary. A knot of small bureaucratic men and women tussle in the midst of the arresting force. Issues of competence are thrashed out line by line with venomous politesse. All the while, the gooseguns do not waver. Joe supposes that is understandable.

And then, at the very back of this great tide of official disapproval, someone takes charge. Someone very grave, with a troubled, serious face and a sonorous voice which speaks of sepulchres and secret dooms.

"Good morning, ladies and gentlemen, good morning. May I have your attention? Thank you so much. My name is Rodney Arthur Cornelius Titwhistle, of the old and venerable family of Titwhistles of this city, and I am the Warden in Chief of the Legacy Board! Thank you, Detective Sergeant Patchkind, your services will not be required. Mr. Cummerbund, will you be so kind as to explain the matter to the very charming Basil? Thank you." And, indeed, a large man with a salmon tie does indeed bustle off the elfin Patchkind, who looks none too happy about it—but if it is the original Arvin Cummerbund, he has lost some considerable weight from his belly and transferred it to his shoulders.

"Now, where was I? Ah, yes, if I might just pass by, sir, good heavens, they grow them big where you come from, don't they? And where would that be? Shropshire, of course, of course, very A. E. Housman. If I might all the same pass by, very good.

"Joshua Joseph Spork. By the power vested in me by Her Majesty's Government, I hereby take you in charge for the crimes of Murder, Arson, Treason, Terrorism, Banditry, and Brigandage. I have always wanted to arrest someone for Brigandage, Mr. Spork, I feel it has a high tone, now if you will yield yourself up to this good fellow here . . . thank you. You will swing, sir, swing by your giblets from the mizzenmast of the ship of state, oh yes! Don't imagine some clever lawyer will get you out of this, Mr. Spork, though I understand that your lawyer is in fact the cleverest one available to mortal man, a positive paragon of the profession, a sort of earthbound god of advocacy. Bring him on, Mr. Spork, I shall shatter him with one prosecutorial fist! And you, missy," adds this terrifying personage to Polly Cradle, "you should be ashamed of yourself as well. A woman's place is in the home, girl, darning the socks of her family and scouring the pots and pans, not out skulduggering! Shame!"

"Don't push it," Polly Cradle mutters as Titwhistle claps her in irons. The Warden in Chief leans away from her in alarm. "Wildcat! Witch! Be along with you! Wait? Where is the ghastly dog? Tell me it's been incinerated! No? Blast. Well, he's under arrest, too. And the rest of you felonious scoundrels should also consider yourselves charged with conspiracy, fortunately I have brought a bus, yes, over there, you will wish to shackle yourselves with the leg irons provided . . ."

It takes a few minutes, but very shortly, Joe's entire company is aboard the black prison bus with tinted windows, and the men of the Legacy Board drive them away.

"Mercer," Polly Cradle says, as the bus ducks down into a garage and everyone hurriedly disembarks, to travel home by other means, "that was utterly ridiculous."

Mercer Cradle beams.

The day after, when the proper course of government has been resumed and—though dented by the spectacle—the institutions of law and order are once more working to their often impenetrable ends, a man in an old-fashioned flight suit stands in front of a Lancaster bomber. At a little after ten a.m., he hears the sound of an approaching engine and turns his head. A maroon Rolls-Royce, paint job somewhat marred by evidence of a recent gun battle and some species of explosion, comes to a halt a few yards off, and from it emerge a man and a woman. The pilot's pudgy face loses its look of wariness and breaks into a broad smile.

"What ho! You've been busy," the chairman of St. Andrews says.

"Yes," Joe Spork replies, "I suppose we have."

"I brought you a spare pair of socks. And some for the lady. Turns out I had a few extra in the cupboard. Thought after all that affray and arrest and such, you might need some."

The ugliest canary yellow Argyles in the world.

"Thank you. That's . . . that's very kind."

"And this is your girlfriend?"

"His lover," Polly Cradle says firmly, "with emphasis on the love part. I have decided."

"Oh, well," the chairman says. "Congratulations! And this is the cargo?"

"Yes, that's all of it."

"I can't help noticing that you seem to have a stuffed pug there."

Bastion opens one eye and growls. The chairman recoils rapidly. Polly grins. "He likes you," she says.

"Should I be concerned?"

"Very."

"And these are bits of . . . it . . . I suppose?"

"Yes," Joe says. "We didn't think it was safe to leave them behind."

"No. Absolutely not. Bloody idiots in government'll have chaps crawling all over them with magnifying lenses trying to do it all again, but better. Arseholes, the lot of them. Nice plane you've stolen, by the way, how did you find the time?"

"I subcontracted."

"Very good. Delegation. Excellent. Incidentally, you still seem to be rather wanted. I thought that would all go away. Not as if we didn't know the truth, there at the end, is it?" The chairman shudders.

"No. But as soon as that was gone, the damage control started. I'm . . . convenient."

"Well, your plummy friend has sorted a registration for us—nefarious little runt. Fond of long words, too. I rather liked him."

"My brother," Polly Cradle says.

"Poor you. You must be very proud. He's not with you?"

"He's meeting us out there."

"Of course. Well, where are we bound?"

Joe Spork passes him a piece of paper with a line of numbers.

The chairman quirks his eyebrows. Somehow, this is a little disappointing. "Beach holiday?"

"Actually, we're meeting some friends and going onward from there."

"Really? By boat, then."

"Submarine," Polly Cradle tells him. The chairman looks at Joe Spork, not quite believing, and sees confirmation in the brief, feral gleam in his eyes.

A slow smile spreads across the pudgy face. "Well," the chairman says, "that's more like it."

A few moments later, the Lancaster cuts a path eastwards, and fades from view.

Acknowledgements

Without my wife, Clare, this book would make a great deal less sense. Her grip on story and her finely-tuned drivel detector are assets no writer should be without—but I'm not sharing. Find your own.

My agent, Patrick Walsh, is a sort of portable, personable eye of the storm. Rumour has it he trains tigers in his spare time and can bend steel with only the power of his mind. I shouldn't be in the least surprised; with a team like that, anything's possible.

Edward Kastenmeier at Knopf and Jason Arthur at William Heinemann practiced the dark arts of the editor upon me, deployed the Blacksmith's Word to push me in the right direction and occasionally the Rosetta Stone to understand me. This book, or perhaps its author, required some kicking around—but the end product is the story I wanted to tell. There's no greater pleasure than being well-edited. (Yes, all right, that's a lie. But: aside from the obvious exceptions, there's no greater pleasure.)

Jason Booher's gorgeous U.S. cover designs arrived unexpectedly on a rather grim day in early 2011 and made me feel the whole thing was real and wonderful. Glenn O'Neill's effulgent U.K. jacket was unveiled a few months later, and it's honestly impossible to pick a winner.

John D. Sahr of the University of Washington was kind enough to advise me casually on matters relating to supercooled water and submarines. I promptly ignored the realities in the name of good storymaking. Thanks are due to John anyway, and to his legal advisor, Grape the Labrador Retriever.

Ginger & White provided tea, and a place to sit. Sometimes that's all you need.

I grew up in a house of stories, and some of those stories were tales of crooks and criminality. Some of them were of derring-do. All of

ACKNOWLEDGEMENTS

them were amazing. To everyone who sat at our table and took the time to spin a tale for a small, serious child: thank you.

My daughter, Clemency, was born during the edit, weighing approximately the same as the manuscript and considerably more demanding. Her tiny footprints are all over my life, and *Angelmaker*—in the case of pages 92, 307, and 513, quite literally. Thank you, little bear.

THE BLIND GIANT

Some say our devices will lead us to ruin: isolating us from our neighbors, warping communication, delivering an unregulated flood of information that will destroy our humanity. Some say they will be our salvation: enabling global communication and social engagement, putting all the world's facts at our fingertips, and erasing the barriers that divide us, bringing out the best qualities of humanity. In *The Blind Giant*, Nick Harkaway takes us on a lucid, insightful and personal tour of how we live our lives in our technology-obsessed culture. A self-described "missing link" between the pre-Internet generation and the "digital natives" who have grown up with technology, Nick is an enthusiastic guide to digital culture who weaves together examples from literature, psychology, neurology, sociology, history, and his own life while exploring the hazards and joys of the human-machine relationship. In the final analysis, whether we meaningfully engage with the machines we have created, or risk living in a world which is designed to serve computers and corporations rather than people, this book is a must-read for anyone concerned with our digital future.

Fiction

EDIE INVESTIGATES

"Edie Investigates" is an exhilarating espionage murder-mystery eShort. There has been a strange death in the quiet village of Shrewton: old Donny Caspian has lost his head. In the Copper Kettle tea rooms, Tom Rice, a junior nobody from the Treasury, puzzles over the details of the case. He has been sent by his superiors to oversee the investigation, but is he supposed to help or hinder? At the next table, octogenarian superspy Edie Banister nibbles a slice of cake and struggles not to become Miss Marple. But what is the connection between the two? Who killed Donny Caspian, and why? Taking in Rice's present and Edie's daring past, from duels on shipboard to death in back alleys, "Edie Investigates" is a superb short story from the incomparable Nick Harkaway.

Fiction

A hilarious, action-packed look at the apocalypse that combines a touching tale of friendship, a thrilling war story, and an all-out kung-fu infused mission to save the world. Gonzo Lubitch and his best friend have been inseparable since birth. They grew up together, they studied martial arts together, they rebelled in college together, and they fought in the Go-Away War together. Now, with the world in shambles and dark nightmarish clouds billowing over the wastelands, they have been tapped for an incredibly perilous mission. But they quickly realize that this assignment is not all it seems, and before it is over they will have encountered everything from mimes, ninjas, and pirates to one ultra-sinister mastermind whose only goal is world domination. Unlike anything else, *The Gone-Away World* is a remarkable literary debut that will be remembered and rediscovered for years to come.

Fiction

VINTAGE CONTEMPORARIES
Available wherever books are sold.
www.randomhouse.com